EASTERN
CONCEALMENT

ZONG PU

Translated by
Wen Lingxia

SINOIST

Published by
Sinoist Books (an imprint of ACA Publishing Ltd).
University House
11-13 Lower Grosvenor Place,
London SW1W 0EX, UK
Tel: +44 20 3289 3885
E-mail: info@alaincharlesasia.com
Web: www.alaincharlesasia.com

Beijing Office
Tel: +86(0)10 8472 1250

Author: Zong Pu
Translator: Wen Lingxia

Published by ACA Publishing Ltd in association with the People's Literature Publishing House

Original Chinese Text © 野葫芦引: 东藏记 *(Yě Hú Lú Yǐn: Dōng Cáng Jì)* 2016, by People's Literature Publishing House, Beijing, China

English Translation © 2019, by ACA Publishing Ltd, London, UK

Paperback ISBN: 978-1-910760-35-2
eBook ISBN: 978-1-83890-504-0

A catalogue record for *Eastern Concealment* is available from the National Bibliographic Service of the British Library.

EASTERN CONCEALMENT

ZONG PU

Translated by
WEN LINGXIA

SINOIST BOOKS

PREFACE

On the 50th anniversary of victory in the World Anti- Fascist War (World War Two), I would like to dedicate the *'Wild Gourd Overture'* series - *'Departure for the South', 'Eastern Concealment'* and *'Western Expedition'* which have been completed, and *'Return to the North'*, which is still in progress, to the men and women who sacrificed their lives on the battlefield, to my compatriots who were massacred by Japanese soldiers or died amid all kinds of disastrous suffering, and to all those who have given their lives for world peace. May they all rest in peace.

CHAPTER ONE

PART I

The sky in Kunming was an intense blue.

It was a kind of uninterrupted, pure blue free from flecks or even a wisp of cloud. The beauty and purity of this blue simply defied description. Even a tiny patch of such blue would be cause for amazement, but the blue Kunming sky was seamless, infinite, as if it extended into the stratoshpere. It was rich and radiant, grand and generous. Anyone who happened to raise their head would cry out in wonder at it: "Ah! How blue that sky is!"

The clouds in the sky were ever-changing, filling up the dome with their grotesque shapes. Sometimes they were thick and solid like clear-cut chunks from a giant piece of precious smooth jade. At other times they were mere traces of what they once were. The exceptional brightness of the sun's rays pierced through swaths of clouds, making the blueness of the sky appear even more intense.

'Clusters' is probably the best word to describe the clouds in Kunming. In an open area in the suburbs, enormous clusters of clouds circled around the skyline. They looked like giant buds, or rising helium balloons tugged by threads, then they would disperse into a giant sheer film of gauze, blurring the divide between earth and sky as if they had merged into one.

The clouds cantering around the dome were even more gorgeous. Here you might spot fold upon fold of mountains with streams trickling down from the boundary area between thick and thin cloud; there you might find a one-tree forest with old branches and roots intertwined with new twigs and branches. One looked like a violently blooming flower in a flowerpot. Another looked like a small sailboat ready for a voyage.

It seemed that these clouds were never able to settle on whether they wanted to gather together or just float around randomly, but when they decided to cluster in 'crowds' combining many small units, they arranged themselves into handsome patterns with perfect spacing. If they decided to go large, they would transform into magnificent mounds of fluffy cotton or snow, full of grandeur.

Sometimes they lost their form as if they had inflated and then burst into wisps dashed across the sky by some divine paintbrush. At other times, they might become as solid as wood or rock from which titanic pagodas were built, and collapsed at the blink of an eye.

As for shapes like dogs, sheep, people's clothes or decorative items like scarfs, they were just too regular to mention. Anyway, whether the clouds looked like clouds or greyhounds was all in the eye of the beholder.

The Yunnan plateau, standing 2,000 metres above sea level under such a fantastic blue dome, was in the west section of the bigger Yunnan-Guizhou plateau, which boasted more than a thousand flatlands of all sizes. All those flatlands shared the same character — they were surrounded by hills and mountains and had a lower central area with thick layers of fertile soil and excellent reservoirs of water. These flatlands were very people-friendly.

The Kunming flatland might be the champion among them all. Kunming city, which was in the centre of the flatland, had been the provincial capital since the Yuan dynasty (1271-1368 AD) and had nurtured much civil and military talent in its history with such natural beauty and advantagious resources.

The year 1938 witnessed many scholars departing from the north of China to Kunming, which initiated in Kunming a special period of history marked with a perfect blend of toughness and inspiration.

Minglun University was run jointly with two other prestigious universities in Changsha, Hunan province, when it first moved from Beiping to Changsha, and then the three moved together to Kunming. When the university settled in Kunming, it had no dormitories for students, no library, and it lacked lab equipment, but all the problems were tackled one by one.

For dormitories, they used boards to frame the walls and filled the framework with earth. When the earth was rammed tight, the walls were finished. For roofs? They used tinplate. When it rained, raindrops hitting the tinplate roofs sounded like someone hitting the piano with their index fingers. Such a combination of rammed earth walls and tinplate roofs were considered 'posh' back then.

Lab equipment? Easy peasy! The students and faculty made it with their own hands. For example, they used wire to make the cages to keep the lab mice, and bricks to build troughs for testing fluids.

Books for the library? The staff talked to the local universities and managed to borrow books from them. Later, when the books shipped from Changsha arrived, the library was quite worthy of its name, though it still looked rather shabby. With students filing in and out, it looked quite like a proper library, a place for study.

No one knew how long they would stay here, nor what would happen tomorrow. They just tried to spend each day in a meaningful way.

Meng Fuzhi finally resigned from his position as the dean of academic affairs, but Xiao Cheng refused to take up the position. Only when Fuzhi provided a compromise that Xiao Cheng would stay in the position for the time being, and if anyone qualified turned up, he would be let go, did Fuzhi literally earn his freedom.

Minglun University followed the tradition of having the university run by its academic staff. The council chosen by the committee of professors was the university authority responsible for all academic matters and student welfare. The president, the dean of studies, the dean of student affairs, and the secretary general were the four sitting committee members in the council. Other members of the council were from the committee of professors.

Not long after moving to Kunming, Fuzhi was elected as a council member. Xiao Cheng joked with Fuzhi after that assembly:

"You try hard to stay away from many positions, while many others are excluded from the positions they are after."

"That's how things work. Anyway, everyone is trying to do their best," answered Fuzhi.

Apart from the shortage of materials, the other big problem facing people in Kunming was air raids.

On 28 September 1938, the Japanese air force made its first air raid on Kunming, which defiled the immaculate blue sky and the magnificent clouds. From that day on, the lives of Kunming townsfolk regularly included 'running from air raids'. For the first few weeks, when the air raid siren sounded, people hurriedly dispersed out of the city to the outskirts, forgetting all about rules and manners. Several months later, people gradually got used to it and figured out their own ways of dispersing. If the air raid siren kept silent for more than a couple of days, people became alarmed at its silence. Some of the old folk even wondered whether the siren was malfunctioning, and they were even more ready to flee from the city.

It was already three months since the Mengs and the Tantais had moved to Kunming. Tantai Mian's power company was stationed in Xiao Shiba, Small Stone Flatland, in the outer suburbs. Since he also had to go to work at the Chongqing office, he shuttled frequently between Chongqing and Kunming. Thinking that he might be permanently stationed in Chongqing, he asked Tantai Wei to attend school in Chongqing. Although very reluctant to leave the Mengs, Tantai Wei said a pretty wet, teary goodbye to May and Kiddo, and left with his father for Chongqing.

The Meng family loved Kunming, a city famed as 'the City of Eternal Spring' for its pleasant climate, lush vegetation and flowers that bloomed all year long. The narrow streets, which were lined with small houses with courtyards, rose and fell rhythmically with the rise and fall of the landscape. One could always spot some flowers or trees in the gardens flourishing even without much tending. Some of these plants were very vigorous and curious, growing all the way up to the roofs as if they were looking up at the blue sky and the white clouds, and trying to touch them and blend in with them.

The Mengs wanted to blend in too, in such a world with its blue sky, white clouds, and the flowers blooming violently and vigorously. The place they stayed was an ancestral temple belonging to a local military bigshot. The main rooms of the ancestral temple served as the ancestral hall for the display of ancestor tablets and pictures, and for holding ceremonies, while several vacant side rooms served as places for participants in ceremonies to take a break. There was also an enormous garden. The Mengs moved in and took care of the hall to pay their rent. At the far end of the garden was a mini theatre. The university had rented the theatre for young bachelors. The stage and the seating areas, including seating for the balcony and the orchestra, had been separated into small rooms.

Bichu was satisfied with the living environment. She told the children how lucky they were to have access to a garden like this. At the entrance of the garden stood several camellias, blooming merrily and gregariously with crowns as big as teacups, ignoring the impending encroachment of winter and the suffering associated with the war.

There was a grove in front of the building. Several times they asked the gardener what type of trees they were, but the man was old and hard of hearing. He always repeated their question: "What do you mean? What?" Then one day, by pure chance, he was able to make out the question and shouted his answer: "They are wintersweet."

When the camellias faded, the wintersweet bloomed. The small flowers had translucent pale lemon-yellow petals so smooth that they looked like they were carved out of wax. A delicate and gentle sweetness filled the air and the heart. An image re-emerged in May's imagination — her father sitting under a tree in a wintersweet grove, with his eyes glued to his book.

The reality was somewhat different from that image, where the wintersweet grove was no longer a world of poems and dreams.

Wisps of white smoke rose from the open area in front of the rooms by the side of the grove. It was Bichu who was starting a coal stove with dry fir needles. She was now an expert at starting a stove with that material. She would first prepare the layers of fir needles, put the coal on top of the needles, and struck only one match, and then the stove would start. But the smoke from the burning fir needles was painfully choking. *'The newly brewed rice wine is mellow and fragrant. There's a good fire burning in the red stove.'* The two lines from the famed Tang dynasty poet Bai Juyi's *'Inviting a Friend for a Nightcap Before the Snow'* popped into Bichu's mind. Wouldn't they have had to light a stove first? mused Bichu.

"Close the door!" she shouted toward the room.

May and Kiddo were doing their homework in one of the rooms. May looked up from her work and said: "Ma, we are not afraid of the smoke."

"Of course you are!" snapped Bichu impatiently. "Close the door!"

May hurried to get up to close the door. Her mother's fuse had grown much shorter and her pitch much higher. She noticed how exhausted her mother always was and would try to give her a helping hand, but sometimes her attempts to help would simply make her mother angry.

Squatting, Bichu was fanning the stove with a big bulrush-leaf fan. With the white wisps of smoke disappearing, the coal in the stove began to glow. Sister Yao, their occasional helping hand, carried home two buckets of water with a shoulder pole, and emptied the buckets of water into a big clay water tank by the wall under the eave.

"Would you please wash the greens?" Bichu asked. Her head spun and her legs wobbled. She grabbed one leg of the table beside her to steady herself before she could stand up.

"I'm not going to make dinner. I have things to do at home," answered Sister Yao, showing no intention of compromising. But she put a kettle of water on the stove before she left.

Bichu had had several helping hands during the months they had been in Kunming. Some of them couldn't understand the Mengs' northern accent and wouldn't do much even when they were asked several times. Others enjoyed too much freedom and would disappear anytime during their work hours. This Sister Yao, a farm hand, was a relative of a nearby grocery store owner's wife. Her pet phrase was "I have things to do at home" and she always said that with perfect confidence, taking it as something for granted.

When she noticed that Bichu was at a loss about her announcement, she offered a solution: "Go to a diner to have rice noodles for dinner. They are delicious and convenient."

Yes, it was true that the streets were lined with diners and small restaurants of all kinds, and it was not expensive to dine out, either. The locals would often do this, too. When the Mengs had just arrived, they did the same thing and ate out at diners and restaurants frequently, but Bichu insisted that eating out should be temporary and didn't make it feel like home. Home-cooked meals would.

"Send your daughter for a take-away meal, so your husband won't need to go," Sister Yao offered one more suggestion, putting the lid back on the clay water tank.

"Alright, you just leave. We'll figure it out. Please come earlier tomorrow," smiled Bichu.

Sister Yao turned and left, disappearing into the wintersweet grove.

The door opened gently, with two heads popping round the edge, whispering: "Mum, we have finished our homework." Then Kiddo ran out and spotted a squirrel at the edge of the grove. He instantly chased after the animal.

May walked over to the stove and picked up the fan, trying to fan the stove.

"No more fanning," Bichu said. "The fire has started." Her head spun again, and she fell into the bamboo chair by her side.

"Mum, let me cook. I can do it," said May, offering her help. She was wearing a hand-me-down sweater from Earl, which was hanging loose around her tiny body. To show she was ready, she 'dried' her hands on the front of her sweater like her Sister Yao did.

"You'll have plenty of time to cook in the future, but this evening, we are eating out," Bichu told her.

Kiddo ran over to them. Upon hearing his mother, he yelped with excitement: "Eat out! Eat out!" May shared her little brother's happy excitement. Both of them loved going to the streets where they could find lots of fun stuff and goodies.

"When this kettle of water is boiled, your father will probably be home," said Bichu, thinking she might take a rest before Fuzhi came home. But then she spotted the unwanted green leaves on the ground and asked May to sweep them up immediately. May picked up a broom and Kiddo hurried to take the dustpan for her.

The crisp, clear sound of giggling wafted toward the house amid the sweetness of the wintersweet. Tantai Xuan ran all the way along the lane

8

leading through the grove, laughing, with several branches of wintersweet in her arms. She was wearing a mid-length silver-grey wool coat with scarlet patterns, and a lined *qipao*. Her short socks revealed a big section of her bare calves. Her outfit, though not as trendy as it would have been back in Beiping, was still capable of attracting lots of attention. Her cheeks were rosy with all the running. "Aunt Bichu, it's me!" she called merrily.

Xuan stayed with her eldest aunt, Suchu, in the Yan residence, while the rest of the Tantais stayed in Little Flatland out of town. After the Battle of Tai'erzhuang between the armies of the Republic of China and Japan in 1938, where the Chinese army had a major victory, Yan Liangzu had been promoted to army commander because of his army's courageous performance in the battle. Things became even smoother for the Yans.

The one walking slowly after Xuan was Meng Liji, Earl, holding only one branch of wintersweet as if she were holding a flag. The shortage of rooms at home and her unwillingness to share one with her two younger siblings made her decide to stay in the dormitory. Fuzhi and Bichu thought more contact with others might help cheer up this special daughter of theirs. Earl was wearing a dark blue wool coat, lined *qipao*, long socks and cotton-sole shoes. She was wrapped up and warm.

"Look at you two! I finally believe they don't have winter here. We are in the last month of the year, deep into the winter, but you don't even need to put on any winter coats. Those things you are wearing for spring and fall are warm enough," exclaimed Bichu.

She turned to Xuan: "Don't you feel cold, wearing so little?"

"Nope, not at all. I feel quite cool," answered Xuan, putting down her flowery branches and helping herself to a glass of water.

"We are now suffering this epidemic called 'fashion rheumatism in the legs'," said Earl with her typical dry humour. She turned to May: "Get me a vase. Hurry."

May was sweeping the leaf waste into the dustpan when she heard Earl's instruction. She straightened up, looked at the branches, and decided that, for the flowers' sake, she would comply with her sister's sour command without fighting back.

"I'll get it," she answered, bending down again, and took the dustpan to the back of the house, with Kiddo at her heels.

"I ran into dad in the new teaching building. He told me to tell you he won't be back for dinner. He says he has to visit someone with Professor Zhuang," said Earl.

"That works even better because we have no one to cook dinner tonight. Let's go and have rice noodles for dinner," said Bichu. She was feeling much

9

better after the short break. She took off her apron: "Why did you two pick flowers again? I told you this is not our garden."

"There are so many wintersweet trees. Don't worry, auntie. A few branches don't count for much in such a big grove of wintersweet," Xuan answered, and followed her aunt to the rooms, talking about what had happened at the Yan residence. Earl followed them into the rooms but kept herself busy finding clean laundry for the coming week.

May took an earthenware jar from the storage place under the eaves, put some water in it, and put all the branches in the jar one by one. This plain jar had held many gorgeous flowers. The lemon-coloured flowers on the twigs gave out a gentle kind of sweetness in the air, leaving enough space for one's imagination. The bundle in the jar looked like a well-trimmed tree standing on the wooden desk.

"May, you and Kiddo go and wash your hands," Bichu instructed.

May took Kiddo over, ladled some water and poured it onto his hands. "So cold!" Kiddo took a deep noisy breath, but he didn't cringe. When he was done, he took the ladle, stood on a short stool and poured water for May.

When Xuan came out of the room, she laughed and shouted at the two of them: "Come on! Dry your hands! It's not pleasant to have chilblains!"

May hurriedly dried Kiddo's hands first and then hers.

"Lots of students have got chilblains on both their hands and their feet. You can see ugly red swellings on their hands," Xuan continued, raising her smooth fair hands and staring at them.

"How long will you keep your hands in such an un-ugly condition?" jeered Earl, as she came out of the room, carrying a simple cloth bag, poking and inspecting the items inside.

"I'll try and keep them like this for the rest of my life," answered Xuan.

Earl responded with another sneer.

Bichu came out of the room and locked the door. They all went through the grove and out of the gate of the ancestral temple.

The footpath connecting the ancestral temple to the main street was paved with stone slabs which was the most popular paving material in Kunming city. For avenues and boulevards, the stone was cut more regularly and was paved in a more regular pattern; for side streets, it was done more casually. The Ancestral Temple street was a medium sized street. Going south, one could reach the busy city centre lined with all sorts of restaurants and bars; going north one would reach the city gate. There were several rice noodle diners along the street.

Bichu chose one at the top of a steep slope leading all the way down to the famous Green Lake Park. People called this diner the 'Steep Slope Rice

Noodles' where one could see everything tilting rhythmically when looking downhill.

Dusk had already settled in. The dim amber light from the low-wattage lightbulbs in the diner looked like something fluid. It was not busy with only a few customers. When the owner saw them, he cried out his welcome: "Welcome! Come and sit inside!"

The place was quite small with only three square tables. It was hard to tell which part was inside and which was outside. The tables were coated with grease but not as dirty as they looked.

Bichu ordered herself a bowl of rice noodles with quick-boiled sliced pork served in soup, and she asked for more soup, and also one egg each for everybody. Earl ordered fine mung bean noodles with tofu pudding on top. The other three all ordered rice cookies stewed in gravy, and two without hot red chillies.

"One bowl of rice noodles, one bowl of fine mung bean noodles with tofu pudding on top, and …" he repeated the orders loudly as if he were sending the orders to the chef, but it turned out when he walked over to the stove and cooked that he was the chef.

He moved the pot up and down to evenly heat the contents, and the fire in the stove danced up and down with his movements. Then he dipped his dipper into a row of bowls with seasonings inside on the table by the stove, and mixed them all together into the pot. He could only make one order at a time. It didn't take him much time to make, though. Only Bichu's order took some time since to quick-boil the sliced pork required complicated timing to make it tender and tasty.

Earl's fine mung bean noodles was served first. The layer of snow-white tofu topping sprinkled with chopped fresh green leeks and the tender poached egg were so inviting. Earl looked at Bichu. When her mother told her "to begin without waiting for the others", she started without bothering to wait for the rest of them.

"A ghost story is quite popular in our dormitory," Xuan told Bichu. "I don't buy such stuff, but you kids," she opined, pausing to take hold of May's hands to cover her ears, and continued: "Cover your ears."

"Then you may well drop it," Bichu said.

"Well, it's not that horrifying actually," but it was hard for Xuan to drop any topic she had started. "It is said that the new teaching building is built on the site of an unmarked graveyard for commoners…"

Noticing that May and Kiddo hadn't covered their ears, but were listening attentively to her, she had second thoughts, and quickly made up an excuse to stop: "Well, just as I said, there's nothing much to it."

"That's not what I heard!" Earl was curious.

Then the store owner-chef set four dishes on the table, and put the two without red chillies in front of May and Kiddo. The rice cookies looked transparent after being boiled in a special gravy, giving off an alluring spicy smell. Bichu's rice noodles looked rather plain in contrast to the rice cookies.

"Let's eat first and talk later," said Bichu.

Kiddo couldn't wait for another second because he was starving. But he immediately spat out his first bite, pushed his bowl away, opened his mouth wide, and panted hard and quick.

"What's wrong? Kiddo, what's wrong?" Bichu asked with great concern. Seeing Kiddo looking as if he was choking, she instructed: "Spit it all out, now!"

May ran round the table and patted Kiddo on the back.

"It's hot, hot!" Kiddo finally found his tongue.

Xuan drummed on her bowl with her chopsticks to get the owner's attention and complained in standard Yunnan dialect: "Why did you put in the red chillies? We told you no chillies for those two! Little kids can't eat red chillies."

The owner apologised and explained: "I didn't put any chillies in. No chillies at all. It's very likely my dipper is stained with chillies. I'll make another one."

"That won't be necessary," Bichu answered in Yunnan dialect, but with her northern tone. "Just bring him a bowl of soup to wash away the taste of chillies."

Then the scarlet gravy was washed away in the soup but, nonetheless, Kiddo enjoyed the light-coloured rice cookies.

"How's the rice from the canteen now? Do you still find gravel in it?" asked Bichu.

"Gravel is standard ration. We once found broken glass," answered Earl, implying that she suffered much more on campus than those who stayed at home.

"But we have many fresh vegetables. It's a pity that the workers don't clean them well," Xuan said. "Every time I take some salted vegetables mixed with sliced pork back to school, everyone grabs some of it."

She glanced at Bichu, and then continued: "Their cook is a very nice guy and he always makes whatever I ask him to make for me. It's quite convenient."

Earl had finished her rice noodles. She gave May a sudden pat on the head and asked: "I have an English class this evening in the new teaching building. I'd like you to go with me, will you?"

May raised her eyes from her bowl, somewhat overwhelmed by such an unexpectedly kind offer from her elder sister: "I will! I've finished all my homework." Both turned to look at Bichu for approval.

"You should have someone go with you for the evening class. Are you coming back home this evening?"

"Sure I am. I won't let May come back home alone. Don't worry."

When they went out of the diner, the sun had completely set behind the hills, and it was dark outside. Xuan offered to walk Bichu back home first, but she declined.

"I have Kiddo with me. Are you heading for the Yan residence? Watch your step at night. And besides, put on your long socks tomorrow," said Bichu.

Xuan, Earl and May followed the slope and walked downhill together. The stone slabs in the pavement shimmered in the remaining glow of dusk. The branches of a tree with dense leaves stretched over the fence. The three all felt how mysterious the slope looked in the dim light as if it were dipping into the earth. Several people overtook them from behind with big strides. The dimming light from the lantern carried by one of them as they disappeared into the distant darkness made the end of the slope seem even farther away.

It didn't take them long to get to the Green Lake Park when the three reached the foot of the slope. The Green Lake Park, the Cuihu Park, built back in the 17th century, was the 'jade' and pride of the Kunming people. The lake was divided into two halves by a dyke lined with weeping willows.

Xuan said good night to the two sisters and went in another direction. They didn't take the dyke until Xuan was lost from sight. Both tucked their coats tighter around them as the wind from the lake blew. "Cold?" Earl asked and held May close to her. That was rare for Earl. May didn't answer but nudged closer to her sister.

"I have always wondered why our family isn't as close to Aunt Suchu's family as Aunt Jiangchu's family is?" May asked.

Earl was taken by surprise: "You shouldn't worry about such things." She paused and then continued: "The two families are very different now. I think dad is not willing to take favours from others as he believes that a scholar like him should have an iron backbone and his principles."

May didn't say anything, but her gut feeling was to tell her that her father was worthy of much respect.

"You are so slow. Let's run!" Earl was afraid that she might be late for her class.

"Agreed!" May answered. The two readied themselves for a run by squatting a little bit and off they went.

They didn't run very fast, but the movement quickened the blood circulation in the veins of the two youthful bodies. The willows retreated as they ran along, their branches blurred into two swinging veils extending far behind the two runners. The glitter from the water in the lake danced through the veils, kissing and touching the road, the bridge, the pavilion and the two happy figures.

"Faster! Faster!" As they ran past some students, they clapped their hands and cheered the two on.

"Just ignore them!" Earl told May, who was ready to say 'thank you' and had to swallow the words.

"Let's go faster!" Earl urged. They ran up the hill, took a turn and entered the South Yard, which was the girl students' dormitory.

The girls' dormitory was built out of a big temple which had layers of yards of different sizes with many empty rooms. Having been deserted for years, it had lost all its statues of deities. When Minglun moved to Kunming, it rented the deserted temple, did some maintenance to meet the enormous shortage of facilities, and transformed it into the girls' dormitory.

Earl led May across the front yard. The paper windows in the rooms caught so many young silhouettes. The yard was teeming with mixed ripples of reading and laughter.

They walked through a tight door and entered a rectangular yard with two rows of rooms on each side, which were connected to form a giant, pleasantly tidy room. Two screens made of printed cloth functioned as walls to form a room for four. They walked to the one which belonged to Earl. There was only one person in the 'room', with her face buried in her arms on the table. It looked like she might be sobbing.

"Wu Jiaxin, what's going on? Are you OK?" Earl gave the girl a pat, putting down her package, and went to fetch her English book. Wu Jiaxin didn't answer.

"I have to rush now. I'm late for my English class. I'll talk to you later," said Earl, dragging May with her.

"What's wrong with her?" May asked with concern.

"I don't know. I don't want to know. I don't want to know anything, but you want to know everything. Run!"

They took the west gate of the temple and arrived at Fengzhu street. There was a night farmer's market that day and the whole street was lined with farmers' baskets full of fresh green vegetables. It was hard to believe it was deep into the winter at the sight of those fresh shades of green.

Several grocery stores in a row had rows of glass jars on display. The biggest ones were for pickles, a local delicacy loved by all the girls. Slivers of sun-dried beef jerky were laid out on linen bags on the floor. Another snack favoured by the students was called 'modern milk muffins', which was invented by a merchant's wife when she accidentally spilt a glass of milk into the dough when she was making traditional Yunnan-style muffins. The milk added a special, modern flavour to the muffins, hence the name. The sales boy from the muffin store cried rhythmically and tantalisingly: "mod—ern—muff—ins". At the other end of the street, the sticky-rice porridge vendor was crying "rice—por—ridge" in a regular tone combination of "*mi—so—fa —do*", as if the two of them were in a choir. All of the stores, stalls, and vendors' wares were illuminated with all sorts of lighting from traditional lanterns to carbide lamps and oil lamps. The boisterousness was tinged with a misty and mysterious aura by such a combination of dim lights.

The street was teeming with people, shoving and shouting in confusion, like a chaotic dream. Earl and May had to slow down in the throng of people. It was lucky the street was not very long, and it took them only several minutes to pass before they entered a pitch-dark alley with no lighting at all, which was the chief reason why Earl had asked May to accompany her. This dark section reminded Earl of the tale of the campus built on an unmarked graveyard for commoners.

Now as they crossed the road outside the town, they reached the gate of the new teaching building. Behind the gate was a straight avenue lined with neat rows of houses looming in the darkness. All the young people they met on campus were coming and going in a hurry. What were they busy doing?

Earl rushed into one of the classrooms, dragging May behind her. Nine or ten students had arrived. The light bulbs threw out arcs of dim yellow light against the blackness outside, not much brighter than the light from oil lamps.

Earl signalled May with her eyes to take a seat at the back of the class while she joined her classmates at the front. The two had barely settled down in their places when their American professor John Snow Sheldon arrived, who preferred to go by his Chinese name, Xia Zhengsi.

Xia Zhengsi, a true lover of Chinese culture, was an expert on Shakespeare who also had an erudite knowledge of English poetry. This was already his 10th year at Minglun. When Minglun decided to move to the south, Professor Xia was advised by many to go back to his native country, but he was determined to move with the university from Changsha to Kunming. He gladly settled down in one of the small rooms under the stage in the theatre in the ancestral temple. He used to teach only literature classes, but this English class he was teaching now was for the sophomores. It was an optional course for non-English majors. When the class ran out of teachers, he offered himself. Every time after the textbook study, he would read a poem. His students enjoyed the last part very much.

Everyone had a wooden chair with a writing board attached to the chair. So did Professor Xia. With his tall body seated in the chair, it creaked and squeaked. The noises alarmed May, who stood up from her chair to check whether he was OK.

"So, who is this?" asked Professor Xia when he noticed May. "You may come to join us in the front." Earl should have answered this question at that point, but she clammed up. May didn't know what to do under such circumstances, and her heart shook with anger at her sister's silence. Luckily, Professor Xia let May off the hook when he decided it was time to start his class.

Francis Bacon's essay 'Of Studies', was printed with ink on very coarse paper. Each student had a copy. Professor Xia asked those at the front of the class to pass a copy to May, who stood up immediately to say thank you, an action which caused a couple of students to turn back to look at May. May was so embarrassed that she regretted having come along with her sister who, as always, didn't care about anyone except herself.

The class was taught in English. As they read the lines "They perfect nature, and are perfected by experience: for natural abilities are like natural plants, that need pruning, by study", the word "plants" reminded Professor Xia of the plants in Kunming, where none of the plants seemed to need much pruning, since nature had provided sufficient means, such as climate and water, which were vital for the growth of plants. He told the class that once he had left his dirty laundry soaking in water for several days, and a huge mushroom grew out of the laundry.

"See? How lazy and lousy I am!" When he reached that conclusion, all the students laughed.

May couldn't figure out what they were laughing about, so she tried to keep herself entertained sitting alone at the back of the class by studying the backs of people's heads. Most of the girl students cut their hair short in shoulder-length bobs, but not too short. A few were wearing braids with a middle parting. Their braids hung over their chest. From behind, May felt sorry that they didn't look like they had a decent amount of hair. Most of the male students had a tangled mass of hair on the top of their heads, like unyielding wild grass defiantly growing with whatever was pressing on it. One or two did comb their hair properly, which made it look smooth and shiny. She studied each head carefully and found out that she knew one of the owners of these heads! It was Zhang Xinlei, Thunderhand, whose head was topped with his standard glossy hair.

"He has come to Kunming, too! But why had her sister never mentioned that?" thought May. "It would be like paradise if he could've brought some ice-cream for us from Hong Kong."

Then came the poetry section. The selection that day was 'We Are Seven' by William Wordsworth. The speaker in the poem met a young girl who insisted that she had six other siblings and altogether they were seven, though two were dead and lying in the graveyard. Although May could only understand one line 'we are seven', she was attracted by the rhythmic cadence of the poem and listened with all her heart.

"Da—dada, da—dada, da—da—da," Professor Xia beat the rhythm by clapping his hands, his head and body swinging with the rhythm.

Years later, May could still remember clearly in the dim yellow light that lesson which she didn't register for, but which had registered itself in her heart.

When the class was over, Earl stood at the door of the classroom in the front, waiting for May. Thunderhand walked over to May: "Meng Lingji! You're so grown up! Do you still recognise me?"

"Yes, of course. You haven't grown up at all."

"But I have grown much older."

They started walking along the main road on the new campus. A giant pearl-yellow disk of moon was rising from behind the hills in the distance.

"I have missed so many classes, and I need to get as many credits as I can," said Thunderhand, trying hard to begin a conversation. "I was lucky to get registered in time."

"We all thought you wouldn't come to Kunming," Earl answered, more out of politeness than because she was interested.

Several girls caught up with them from behind, laughing. One of them chided: "Hey, Meng, how could you guys be so slow?"

Another reminded her: "There are two Mengs", and patted May on the shoulder.

Earl gave no response to either. May didn't know how to respond and had to watch them go away in silence.

Thunderhand pointed at a path forking off the main road and said: "This way leads to my dormitory. The building looks like a shipwreck and I feel quite heroic living in it, though."

"Heroic? Are you planning to sacrifice yourself?" Earl retorted coldly.

"No, no. I am not qualified - such a life is quite interesting. I made a paper wall around my bed, though it won't withstand a poke."

"We use cloth curtains."

"Some of us try to go with cloth curtains, too. But most of us still go with paper."

When they reached the gate, Earl told Thunderhand he could go back to his dormitory if he wanted to, but he asked whether he could walk with them a while longer. Earl didn't say anything. Noticing few people visible in the street, the three picked up their pace. When they were approaching the girls' dormitory, Earl suddenly asked May: "Is it alright if I ask Thunderhand to walk you home? I'm thinking I might not go back home."

What? Two betrayals in one night?

May was mad and she showed it: "You promised you would take me home! You promised mum you would!"

"I want to check on Wu Jiaxin."

Oh, yes, was Wu Jiaxin still crying? Thinking about this, May's anger receded. She paused for a while and said: "Then it's up to you."

Earl paused for a while, too, before she realised that Thunderhand should be the one to check on Jiaxin since he was Jiaxin's cousin. She turned to him and asked: "Aren't you going to see her? She has been crying a lot and is surely on the way to becoming a crying star."

"Maybe tomorrow. I still have assignments to cover tonight. Ladies, hope to see you both tomorrow," said Thunderhand. He bowed, turned and left. May noticed that he definitely wanted to disappear before Earl came up with any other proposals.

Instead of the Green Lake Park, the two sisters decided to take Wenlin street, which brought them to the wintersweet grove much more quickly. The winding footpath was bathed in the sweet fragrance of the tiny flowers, leading them home.

"Why is Jiaxin crying?" May couldn't hold back her curiosity any longer.

"She is alone in Kunming and she misses her home and her family," answered Earl. She started again abruptly after a period of her standard silence: "Also, she likes someone. I don't know who he is. To like someone makes a person suffer, doesn't it?"

"That can't be," May couldn't figure out what her sister was implying, but she didn't want to dig into the question any further, either. She was happy with what she had right now. She skipped along, jumping from time to time to touch the blooming branches over her head. She was happy to know that at the end of the path stood their home, sweet home.

PART II

The sun rose behind the new school buildings from the east. Its morning glory like a flower blooming, awakened another day of earnest efforts to stand on one's own feet. In the reign of night, the buildings were vague without solid forms, but in the rising sun, the outlines of the same buildings became clear. Rows of rammed-earth adobe walls with tinplate rooftops lined up neatly against one another. At the feet of the walls grew plants of various kinds, growing untended here and there around the walls, making the walls themselves look less shabby. The sun's rays made the parts of the roofs less coated with dirt quite shiny. The students were very proud of this shiny effect, claiming those were their 'golden palaces'.

The real Golden Palace was a copper building in the eastern outskirts of Kunming city, a hybrid consisting of a pavilion and a tower, which could reflect the sunshine miles away. The shine from the new school buildings, the shine from knowledge, might be reflected much farther than that.

PE (physical education) teachers ran out of rows of dorms, followed by several students. The university encouraged students to get up early to do some morning exercises, but this had never been popular among students, who regarded getting up early as a torture since they tended to be more like night owls. They would manage to put in some shoddy appearances at the very beginning of a term before they disappeared completely for the rest of that term.

"One two three — four!" The PE teachers shouted.

"One two three — four!" the followers echoed. How could so few people make such a resonant chorus?

Students popped out of their dorms, some with their basins in hand to take water from the well to wash their faces. Some were topless, taking morning showers with the cold water from the well. Some looked arrogantly at the running team, books in hand. But there were also those who stood there, staring blankly at the sky. Maybe, they were thinking about the fate of the nation, or pondering how to make full use of their beautiful youth?

When the buildings cast shadows on the ground, all the doors of the classrooms opened. A moment later, the library, the only building built with bricks and wood, opened, too.

No one noticed when Fuzhi arrived at the library. He was in an old blue cotton gown with a thin-padded robe with a silk cover underneath. His printed cloth wrapper was by his side. To carry books in that cloth wrapper was a new habit he had developed since their arrival in Yunnan.

Each time he came to the new campus, he would pay a visit to the library first, although this library could barely be called a proper library in contrast with the enormous one back on the campus of Minglun in Beiping. None of the bookshelves on the walls were painted. The scars on the wooden boards looked like staring eyes. Newspapers and magazines were neatly presented on the shelf, such as *Central Daily News, Yunnan Daily, Saodang Bao (The Smashing Newspaper), Life Herald, Today's Comment, Philosophical Review, New Trends, Guowen Yuekan (Chinese Monthly), Weekly Review, Thoughts and Times, Journal of Yunnan University,* and *Yenching Journal of Chinese Studies.*

"Good morning, Professor Meng! You are so early," said the librarian working at the check-out counter as he greeted Fuzhi, busy wiping the dustless tables and chairs. There was much less dust in Kunming than in Beiping, so few were the books. Behind the check-out counter were dozens of book shelves. Some books were just piled against the wall. It took almost a year for these books to arrive in Kunming from Changsha. They had not been unpacked yet.

Fuzhi nodded his greeting, and took a newspaper close to him. There was an article in the paper analysing the effects of air raids. It claimed that although the air raids for the last several months hadn't caused any major casualties, they made life very inconvenient. There were even more robberies during air raid alerts. It reminded readers that in the coming year, the air raids might increase in both frequency and intensity.

More and more students came to the library. There was a queue in front of the counter already. When students noticed Fuzhi sitting nearby, some greeted him respectfully, some hurried away, some simply ignored him.

Fuzhi just sat there peacefully, reading his paper. That peacefulness radiated throughout the whole room.

Some people were talking loudly outside the library, discussing the topic of last night's current affairs meeting. Obviously, the speakers were activists from some sort of societies.

One said: "Why did Wang Jingwei[1] leave for Vietnam last month? What is he after?"

Another answered: "He is a coward when confronted with the Japanese. He just sold out his country for personal glory."

The third one insisted that Wang Jingwei was certainly a traitor and a turncoat. The fourth one reminded the third one of the need to understand a traitor's intentions before coming up with any solid rebuttal of his claims. Several suggested they wait for Professor Zhuang's opinion.

Fuzhi was moved by such a heated discussion and thought about Zhuang Youchen's proposal to hold a current affairs forum. Youchen, who used to focus all his attention on his microcosms, helped with the transfer in Tianjin when Minglun moved from Beiping to Changsha, and had much more interest in the outside world now.

When he went out of the library, a student smiled at him: "Good morning, Professor Meng. Are you giving classes? Professor Zhuang conducts a fortnightly analysis of the war. It's very interesting."

"Good," said Fuzhi. "How many times have you attended it?"

"Twice," answered the student. He suddenly raised his arm, pointing to the distance, and cried out: "The alert signal!"

Everyone looked in the direction of Wuhuashan (Wuhua mountain) to find that a red balloon had risen to the top of the flag pole on the mountain top. If it were not for air raids, it would have looked quite beautiful against the blue sky.

"It is so early today!" remarked several students, having a hard time believing it since it took time for the enemy fighter planes to cover the long distance from their base to Kunming, and they would always arrive around noon.

"I'm going to my class," Fuzhi nodded goodbye to the students.

The university followed the practice that classes would be cancelled only when the air raid sirens sounded, then students would be dispersed. When the first red balloon alert was shown, classes would keep going. Sometimes, the window between the alert signal and the first round of sirens varied from 20 minutes to two hours; at other times, there was no follow-up at all to the alert signal. This practice guaranteed that the minimum amount of time was wasted in case air raids never materialised.

Fuzhi entered his classroom, stopped by the teacher's desk, took his time to unpack his wrapper cloth, and took out his syllabus and teaching materials for his 'General Chinese History' course. He was holding two courses this term. One was his usual 'General Chinese History' and the new one was 'Dynastic History'.

The sound of the siren sliced through the peaceful morning air like a butcher's cleaver on a carcass.

"How fast the siren was sounded today!" someone muttered.

The siren wailed in a regular tone: it started low, rising all the way to the top of the scale, then dropped back to a low tone as if it were running out of steam, paused for a second, and then repeated the same pattern.

Fuzhi signalled the dismissal of the class by raising his hand a little, and took his time to wrap up all his materials back into his cloth wrapper. The students filed out of the classroom in an orderly fashion. When they first had the air raid alerts, people panicked. The term 'running for shelter' became literally true when people ran at full speed. As time went by and people got used to it, things slowed down and running for shelter came to be more like an outing to the outskirts for the townsfolk.

A student approached the teacher's desk and spoke up quite hesitantly: "Uncle Fuzhi."

Fuzhi raised his head to see Bichu's nephew Yan Yingshu standing in front of him. Yingshu was not very tall, but strong and sturdy with his broad shoulders and thick back. He had joined the history department the previous year and done quite well in his studies. Being fully aware of Fuzhi's reluctance to show any connection with the Yan family in public, he didn't greet Fuzhi when he was in the classroom. Even now his tone of address was more of a mumble.

"Any problem?" Fuzhi asked kindly.

"This Sunday is my mother's birthday," answered Yingshu. This was not his biological mother but Suchu, his legal mother. "My father has asked me to give you an invitation. Would you like to come?"

"Xuan already told me yesterday."

"We'll send a car to pick you up. It's not close. The children don't need to walk such a long distance."

"Such a distance is much shorter than when they run for shelter from the air raids. Don't send a car. We'll be there," said Fuzhi as he made ready to leave the classroom.

"Which way are you going?" Yingshu seemed inclined to try and stay with Fuzhi.

"I'm going home. You go round the back of the hill and be careful."

He sounded like he himself didn't need to be careful at all. Yingshu bowed to Fuzhi before leaving for the back of the hill.

Fuzhi tried to walk on the innermost side of the road because he was going the other way.

"Fuzhi." Someone called in the crowd. "Are you heading home?" It was Zhuang Youchen who was walking fast toward Fuzhi in the crowd.

Fuzhi stopped: "You are walking too fast for a run-for-shelter."

"Of course, I am, but I'm not running for shelter," laughed Youchen. He wore a dark overcoat, his walking stick in his hand as usual. His eyes shone with crystal-clear innocence, but his face was heavily wrinkled, probably due to so many reports about current affairs. He pointed at his lab behind several rows of buildings: "My rendezvous."

Fuzhi knew Youchen would guard the lab from fire and theft each time the siren sounded. His concern for the lab far outweighed his fear of the bombs. He preferred staying in the lab to running for shelter, claiming at least he would know how the bomb landed and destroyed the equipment.

President Qin and his friends had all been trying to persuade him to drop such a mad guard duty, but all their efforts were in vain when Youchen switched on his 'in one ear and out the other' mode. Youchen knew Fuzhi's practice, which he considered to be no less mad than his, of going back home and sitting in the wintersweet grove to wait out the raids. Fuzhi even conceived several articles while he was waiting.

"I have a bomb shelter to dive into in an emergency," said Fuzhi as a reminder to Youchen of the difference between them.

"I have my tinplate roof," answered Youchen cheerfully.

Both laughed and went their separate ways.

The city folk had been dispersing since the appearance of the red balloon. It was a sad scene to see the streets left empty as if waiting to be taken over.

When Fuzhi reached the Ancestral Temple street, he ran into a young girl supporting an old woman carrying a large parcel, hurrying out of town, panting. The young girl whined: "I told you so! You really don't need to carry that package! It's so heavy!"

"I don't need to carry that package? Then if we are lucky enough to be spared from the bombs, we will starve ourselves to death," chided the older one.

When they went past Fuzhi, a small purse dropped out of the large package. It was one of those purses for small valuables made of cloth with fine embroidery by the Dai nationality, an ethnic minority that was quite populous in Yunnan province. Fuzhi wanted to point out to them that they had dropped their purse, but they were in such a hurry that they were already disappearing from sight. So he picked up the purse and ran after them. When he handed them the purse, the two pairs of eyes, one crystal clear, one senile and turbid, stared at him.

"What a good man! A very good man!" the old woman muttered behind Fuzhi's back, and laboured on.

When Fuzhi arrived at the wintersweet grove, he slowed down, breathing in the refreshing fragrance. Seeing that the front door was locked, he knew that Bichu and the kids had gone to the bomb shelter. He went in the direction of the city wall.

The section of the city wall near their home was quite high, shaped like a miniature cliff, under which there used to be a small cave occupied by wild animals such as foxes. After consulting Grandpa Shen, the gatekeeper of the ancestral temple, the two neighbours invited Fuzhi to join them to build a bomb shelter out of the cave. Above the shelter was just a loose layer of dirt, not strong enough for a bomb shelter. Earl and Xuan both joked that it could only shelter those inside from grenades rather than air raids. But hiding there gave those inside a sense of security, which meant more than any solid physical form of security.

When Fuzhi walked close enough to the city wall, he spotted several cracks along the wall behind the tall grass. He decided next time he would take his family to disperse to the outskirts and advise the neighbours not to stay in the shelter either.

The wailing of the air-raid siren suddenly changed into a series of fast waves of screams, ripping through the air in horrifying shrieks. That was the emergency siren — the enemy fighter planes were coming! The red balloon on top of Wuhuashan had been taken down. It was too obvious a target.

Fuzhi went into the bomb shelter. He wanted to stay with his family. A wooden fence was set up several steps away from the entrance. Behind the fence sat a packed crowd of people.

Were we doomed to a life of running away and hiding out?

"Dad! Dad's here!" a child's tender voice broke the silent darkness.

"Shhhhhh! No crying out!" Luo the Grocer complained in a whisper, worried that the fighter pilots might hear.

Bichu and the three kids squeezed together even tighter to make room for Fuzhi. Two rows of brick benches had been set up against the two walls in the narrow cave, so people could sit shoulder to shoulder, and knee to knee. Fuzhi finally managed to squeeze himself past their knees and reached his spot between May and Luo the Grocer.

"Professor Meng," Luo the Grocer whispered. "Do you think the enemy planes are coming?"

"We have already had the emergency alert, so the planes must be over Kunming right now," answered Fuzhi.

Everything fell silent again as they cocked their ears to listen attentively for the noise of aero engines. Silence rippled through the dark cave.

They waited in silence for quite a long while, way beyond Kiddo's tolerance. He whispered in May's ear: "Can you tell me a story?"

"Shhhhh! No talking!" Luo the Grocer admonished Kiddo.

"Meow..." a cat cried. What a beautiful cry!

Rats were rampant in Kunming, which made cats very valuable pets. It looked as if Luo the Grocer's wife had brought their cat with them.

The child of another neighbour copied Luo the Grocer and hushed the cat: "Shhhhh! No meows!" At such a warning, the cat protested even more loudly.

Luo the Grocer bellowed: "Listen up! If you don't stop now, I'll kill you!"

Amid the cat calls and human bellows, a rumbling, roaring noise assaulted their ears. Everyone, including the cat, fell into absolute silence.

The enemy fighter planes were coming.

Just a moment ago, they were trying to spot the roaring of the engines, now they needed to focus on the bombs being dropped. Who was to know whether they would still be breathing in the next second? The roaring of the engines didn't last long before they disappeared completely in the far distance.

"Meow..." the cat cried out loud again. Everyone heaved a heavy sigh of relief, thinking they had survived the day.

They knew they hadn't when the roar of engines shattered the silence again, closer and closer as if they were hovering overhead. What a game of catch and release! The cat caught the mouse, released it, and caught it again when the mouse thought it had survived.

The cat cried louder in accordance with the loudness of the roaring engines. It didn't sound beautiful as it had just now, it sounded more like the emergency alert. Another neighbour obviously had a cow: "What should we do with it? Your cat!"

Earl's voice came from deep in the corner: "Let it cry! The enemy can't go underground! They won't be waiting at the entrance! The fighter planes are still far away."

Some time later, the roar of the engines sounded more and more indistinct, then finally died away.

It took another meal time before the siren sounded again. This time the sound of the sirens became a flat continuous long blast, signaling the lifting of the alert.

"It has been lifted! It has been lifted!" It took people several more seconds to realise the good news. They stood up from their brick benches one by one.

Luo the Grocer gave a happy, loud rendition of a limerick about air-raid sirens:

"At the alert signal, Put on your clothes.
When the sirens wail, Cry your hearts out.
At the emergency sirens, Register yourself in hell.
At the all-clear signal, Laugh your hearts out."

Many joined in his happiness and walked out of the bomb shelter. The sky was clear blue like before with the same wonderful clouds. The fragrance from the wintersweet grove filled the air like it always did.

Later people learned that the fighter planes were targeting other places, not Kunming.

That Sunday was Madam Lü Suchu's 45th birthday. She was the wife of Yan Liangzu, the army commander of the Yunnan clique. Since the three sisters were all in Kunming, it was the ideal time for a big get-together.

May and Kiddo were particularly happy since they hadn't attended any special occasions for such a long time, while their mother, Bichu, was stressed out over what the children would wear for the occasion. May was the biggest problem since she had just hit a growth spurt and had grown out of all her clothes in less than a year. Each day she wore an old hand-me-down coat from her elder sister. A couple of mean students would chant like those peddlers who collected old clothes at the sight of May in that coat: "Clothes! Old clothes for pennies!" May didn't mind hand-me-downs or people making fun of her, and didn't mention it to her mother either. Bichu was determined not to let May wear that coat to her sister Suchu's birthday dinner.

But what could she do now without dozens of delicate georgette dresses to choose for the girls, or Amah Zhao's skills with buttons and lace, or that large, oval-shaped mirror, embedded in the hardwood frame of the vanity unit, and carved with elaborate clouds and airy patterns? All she could do now was to rack her brains. Besides May, both Earl and she needed something proper to wear.

After debating with herself for several days, she set her eyes upon a woollen throw printed with small light-blue and pink flowers, which made the linen quite charming. Bichu told her it was a very fine piece of fabric with which to make a coat, but she didn't have the tailor's skills to transform the throw into a coat. When she told Fuzhi how incompetent she was, Fuzhi laughed: "I think May's coat will do. Or you could ask her to use the throw as a cape. She might set a new trend."

Bichu didn't say anything for a long while. Later, she said: "Maybe it won't be cold that day and then none of us will need coats. Well, it's not a big deal," she sighed.

When the day came, the weather obviously didn't want to pamper Bichu. It was dark and gloomy in the morning. Bichu had already left her outfit worries behind when someone came to her rescue. Qian Mingjing's wife, Zheng Huifen, who liked to call on Bichu, dropped by with a bag of clothes, saying her elder sister Zheng Huiyuan had sent her two coats and one was too small for her but just right for May.

"Did you happen to know that we are going to visit the Yans today?" asked Bichu.

"Are you? I didn't know. Are you going now?"

"We are going this afternoon. Do come in and take a seat. It's my eldest sister Suchu's birthday. I have been worrying that May doesn't have a proper outfit for the occasion."

The checked coat had three shades of blue in small grids: dark, royal and light. A big white button was attached at the collar. Bichu asked May to try it on. Bingo! It was perfect.

"See? Just like the old saying — 'the blessed don't need to busy themselves,'" said Huifen with a soft sigh.

"What's the matter?" Bichu asked, noticing how troubled Huifen was. Huifen wanted to say something but she forced herself to hold back. Bichu smiled: "You don't need to hold anything from me. With your sister Huiyuan not here, I'm the one you should share your worries with. I probably can't solve your problem, but talking about it can help relieve the pressure."

Huifen then said: "People think I live such an easy life, but I am actually quite bored with such a life. I'm thinking maybe it's time for me to find something to do. A job."

Bichu said, genuinely very happily: "I think you should find something to do. I'm telling you if I didn't have my family to take care of, I would definitely go to work."

"You are a different story. Look at you. Your life is so busy. It's brimming. My life — well, you need to get ready for the visit. I'll come back another day to talk."

Bichu watched Huiyuan going through the wintersweet grove, turning over in her mind that maybe Huiyuan needed a child. But to have a child would be such a challenge in such a tough time.

The sky, filled with a dense blanket of cloud, was even gloomier in the afternoon. Later it began to snow, but the snowflakes never made their way to the ground. They melted in mid-air, giving the impression that the upper half of the sky was snowing and the lower half was raining. It was wet everywhere.

Having dressed the children, Bichu changed her clothes. She put on her thin beige wool gown with a veiled scarlet pattern. When Earl asked why she wasn't wearing any jewellery, Bichu explained that the colour and pattern of the gown required something red to go with it, but she didn't have any red jewellery. May said green would be a good match, which attracted a glare from her sister, signaling her to shut up.

"Mum, someone from Aunt Suchu's family may think less of you if you don't wear any jewellery," opined Earl. They all knew who that 'someone' referred to. Even Earl would think twice now when it came to social activities, thought Bichu. She was moved, so she let her two daughters help her put on her favourite emerald jewellery. The earrings were like two solid sparkling drops of water, and the brooch made of the same material glimmered with the same glamour. But Bichu's face looked gaunter against the shiny jewellery.

"Shoes! Your shoes!" cried Kiddo. "I'll carry them in my backpack and we'll change when we arrive!"

They were all in a buoyant mood. No one seemed to notice how uncooperative the weather was.

"Aunt Bichu!" someone called from outside the door. Yan Yingshu came in. "I'm here to pick you up."

Yingshu had come here once when the Mengs had just moved to the ancestral temple with Suchu. When he found that the house was as shabby as the first time he had visited, he forgot to hide his concern and muttered: "The house needs proper maintenance…" Earl turned her head away coldly at his muttering. Bichu didn't want Earl to come up with anything unfriendly, so she hurried them all to get into the car.

The car drove slowly along the road paved with stone. From the Ancestral Temple street to the west bank of the Green Lake, it took almost 15 minutes.

The architectural sytle of the Yan residence, located on a slope facing a lake, was hard to define. It was like a sort of hybrid of western and Chinese styles, but if you looked harder, then it was neither. Two stone lions sat each side of the front gate, behind which was the narrow front garden planted with lots of trees and flowers. The second gate was by the left side, quite different from the second gate in a northern residence, which was always in the centre leading to the main rooms in the garden. The three sides of the garden were occupied by two-storey buildings with wide corridors upstairs and downstairs.

When Fuzhi and his company got out of the car, two servants came out of the gatekeeper's room, carrying two umbrellas for the guests. A burst of laughter emanated from one of the rooms and out came Yan Liangzu and Lü Suchu at the second gate, taking the steps from the corridor to the garden.

Yan Liangzu was from Dali city, Yunnan province, inhabited by the Bai nationality, and was one of the brave, legendary generals in the major local forces of the Yunnan clique. The Yan family, who were of Yi ethnic origin, used to be farmers on a small farm. Since Liangzu's father died when Liangzu was still young, the whole family had fallen on hard times before Liangzu grew up and managed to get things back on track through his hard work.

Liangzu was stout, a characteristic shared by his son, Yingshu. He had a big head like a leopard, big round eyes, and a bushy beard. All these characteristics were slightly reminiscent of Meng Zhangfei, a renowned protagonist in the famous 14th-century historical novel *Romance of the Three Kingdoms*, a blend of history, legends and myths during the Three Kingdoms period (reckoned by historians to have started in AD 184 or 220 and ended in 280).

Liangzu led his army into the Battle of Tai'erzhuang and rendered outstanding service with his proper command and leonine bravery, but he made a fatal mistake when he was intercepting the enemy in southeast Hubei province during the Battle of Wuhan, or the Defence of Wuhan, which lasted from 11 June to 27 October 1938. Since then, he and his troops had been pulled back to Kunming for rest and recuperation, and to await further instructions. Liangzu was always ready to go back into battle at any minute.

Liangzu's heroism and gallantry had impressed Grandpa Lü during his stay in Beiping when he was young. His insights into the political situation back then were much appreciated by the old man. At that time, the Lü family was preoccupied with finding a match for their eldest daughter Suchu and was disappointed not to have found anyone despite several attempts. When Liangzu proposed, the old man didn't hesitate to accept the proposal. When Suchu was consulted whether she was willing to accept such an arrangement, she just said she would count on her parents to make the decision for her. All the outsiders assumed Suchu's decision was out of pure filial piety to her parents against all the slogans crying out for women's freedom in marriage, but her family knew too well that she didn't care much about the difference between arranged or free marriage. She just accepted whatever was given to her.

Suchu wore a Chinese-red silk brocaded gown, and a gold bracelet inlaid with jade on each wrist. On her left wrist she also wore a bracelet made of pale-mauve emerald, the best and rarest of its kind. She had a dull face, and a dull voice, too: "Sister Bichu, we haven't seen each other for such a long time."

The two sisters went into the reception hall with their arms linked.

The reception hall, also a combination of western and Chinese styles, was equipped with matching hardwood furniture and sofas. In front of the marble screen stood Huishu, who went up to greet her aunt when she saw them coming in. She stood by May's side when she had finished her greetings.

"May is almost as tall as my Huishu now! You've grown really fast!" said Liangzu. The host and the guest didn't take their seats but kept talking about the different heights of the kids for a while.

Huishu was 14 then, in full bloom. All girls at such an age look beautiful. A more careful look revealed that her delicate appearance was tinged with a sort of dullness from her mother but, luckily, she had her father's big eyes, which didn't radiate intelligence or refinement, but were dark and gentle all the way down to their bottom. She looked elegant and reserved, mature for her age.

As the youngest child, and the only child of her mother, the legal hostess of the residence, she could have been spoiled, but she wasn't. Instead, she was prudent. Anyone who knew the Yan family would have drawn the same conclusion without much investigation that Huishu's prudence was rooted in the family's complicated situation.

When it began to rain harder in the lower half of the sky, an assistant came and reported that Mr and Mrs Tantai had arrived. Everyone in the reception hall came out to stand in the corridor for the Tantai couple.

"I'm on a business trip, so I took the opportunity to celebrate Sister Suchu's birthday," said Tantai Mian. Since falling from a horse and breaking his leg, his injured leg was a couple of inches shorter than the other when fully recovered. Since then he had to walk with a walking stick.

"Look at Mian! Always prevaricating! Why don't you just tell the truth that we took a flight from Chongqing just for Sister Suchu's birthday?" laughed Jiangchu. Jiangchu wore a lilac woollen gown with a veiled pattern and a blouse of the same material. Bichu guessed this might be the hottest trend in Chongqing. Her diamond earrings and the matching diamond ring sparkled when she moved.

Liangzu turned to his two brothers-in-law: "We are at war with such a powerful enemy and I, as a soldier, who should be fighting at the front, am now staying at home, hosting a birthday party. I'm ashamed of myself."

Both Mian and Fuzhi disagreed: "Brother Liangzu has served his country heroically. Everyone knows that. Rest and recuperation are a must for your troops if they are going to be better prepared for the next battle. You've no reason to feel ashamed."

Having exchanged pleasantries, they took their seats. Liangzu introduced the other relatives from his side to Mian and Fuzhi. The guests presented all felt that a very important person was missing, then Suchu spoke to Liangzu: "Shall we ask her to come out now?" Liangzu nodded at Suchu and then asked Yingshu to do it.

Those with no knowledge of the Yan family might have thought Yingshu had been sent to fetch an elderly member of the Yan family, such as Liangzu's mother, or someone from her generation, but when Yingshu came back to the hall a moment later, he came with a middle-aged woman.

She headed directly toward Suchu. When she was in front of Suchu, she put the cushion she was carrying on the floor and knelt on it, saying "Hezhu wishes my lady a happy birthday."

It looked like Suchu was well prepared for such a greeting since she grabbed the cushion by her side, tossed it onto the floor, and knelt to return the greeting. The guests all knew this was Liangzu's concubine, Hezhu (literally meaning 'lotus pearl'), who he had brought with him from his hometown. Awed by this woman's legendary razor sharpness, all the guests stood up when Hezhu appeared.

Hezhu was Han Chinese by birth but was adopted by a family from the Yi ethnic minority when she was very young. What she was wearing defied any specific style. It was not like the traditional Yi minority dress, nor the Han majority dress, not modern, not classic. She might well be described as a mixture of Yi and Han, a blend of modern and classical. She was wearing a short black coat woven with gold and silver piping and a row of plate buttons in the front, and a dark-green skirt embroidered with flowers. The pair of string pearls on her ears sparkled with blinding glamour when she moved. On her left hand, she had three rings, one gold, one diamond and one tourmaline.

For anyone interested in precious stones, Hezhu was very generous in sharing her knowledge about the cutting and inlaying of diamonds, and the special position of tourmaline among all precious stones. What was odd, though, was that one didn't have any clear impression about the face of the owner of those luxurious items. It was like a portrait with so much paint on it that all the colours had blurred the contours of her face. It was exactly such blurriness that permeated things in the Yan family.

Hezhu got up and walked across to Jiangchu and Bichu: "Miss Jiangchu and Miss Bichu have been here in Kunming more than half a year, yet I haven't paid you any visits. How damned I am!"

All were taken aback by the word.

"My lady is not in perfect shape, so she leaves all the trivial stuff in my care. The birthday wine today falls short of specifications. Please forgive my lack of decorum." No one was sure what kind of specifications she was referring to, and everyone fell silent for lack of an appropriate response.

Jiangchu said: "Xuan has been staying with her aunt, and thank you for taking care of her during her stay. We are moving to Chongqing, but Xuan will stay for her college. I'm afraid we will have to ask more favours from you."

Hezhu answered: "Don't mention it. They don't count as favours. The servants will always be of service."

Liangzu invited everyone to sit down. Hezhu took the seat on the far right, a seat reserved for someone of inferior position sitting at the same table. She busied herself with observing Xuan's cashmere coat, then she beckoned May to her side to check on May's coat while ordering Yingshu to run some errands with her eyes fixed on Bichu's emerald jewellery.

A while later, the servants came to serve tea. All the teacups were blue and white porcelain with matching covers of the same material.

"According to local custom, we serve three rounds of tea for our close kin and distinguished guests. Here comes the first round — puffed rice tea. Enjoy!" Liangzu's resonant voice added more grandeur to the tea ceremony.

All the guests lifted the cover to see a thin layer of puffed rice floating in the cup. The tea tasted mildly sweet. The kids chewed the puffed rice and all agreed it tasted quite delicious.

"How's the war going? Since Wuhan has been occupied, what's your evaluation of the situation and what will happen next?" Fuzhi asked Liangzu politely.

Liangzu brooded for a while before answering: "The enemy might target Nanchang which would free up some of its forces to stir up trouble in North China. But we don't know for sure what they are plotting. We are not their consultants anyway. They planned to end the war in three months but, as we can see, it has been going on for 18 months. We can wear them down if we have to, according to Generalissimo Chiang Kai-shek. If we only consider the present situation, it looks like we're losing; but in the long run, we are winning."

32

"The Burma road was finished last month. This will surely increase Kunming's economic and strategic importance," Mian said, thoughtfully.

"You mean the Yunnan clique will play a more vital role?" Fuzhi had known Mian for a very long time and the two were quite close as brothers-in-law having married daughters of the Lü family. He figured out what Mian was implying. For Generalissimo Chiang Kai-shek, the Yunnan clique hardly counted as a 'royal bloodline'.

Liangzu burst into hearty laughter: "A place like Yunnan can never do without an army — and we do listen to the central government." He suddenly broke off his laugher in thoughtful silence before speaking again: "I lost a battle in Hubei province. Have you heard about it?"

Mian answered: "We were told the news but with few details."

Liangzu said: "We did fail to intercept the enemy, but we tried our best and fought to the last drop of our blood. The enemy had ten times as many men as us. When we were besieged and cornered at the top of the mountain, after running out of both ammunition and food, we beat back seven rounds of attacks from the enemy using rocks and logs! Rolling stones and logs are nothing new for you historians, I suppose?" He turned to Fuzhi with a forthright laugh.

Fuzhi, aware of the many guests present, decided not to explore the topic: "Last year, shortly after our arrival in Kunming, we were in time to witness your army of 580,000 going into battle. Tens of thousands of city folk lined the streets to bid you farewell. Some were shouting slogans in tears like 'Long live China' and 'Victory for the Yunnan clique'. Their confidence made all those who heard the slogans believe that China couldn't lose the war. For a military commander, winning or losing a battle is a common occurrence. You don't need to cling to a couple of minor losses."

The servants came in again to serve the second round of tea. This time the tea cups were made of red porcelain with matching covers. The tea was *tuocha*, a very famous local tea pressed into the shape of a bowl, candied Chinese dates and ginger slices. The kids didn't enjoy the taste this time and began to goof around.

They went to the area behind the screen and found a row of bamboo pipes of all sizes and colours. Some were painted, some had different patterns carved on the raw outer layer. Huishu told them these were water pipes for tobacco.

When Xuan heard the word 'pipes', she went over and picked one up to have a close look at it. She said with a smile: "It is said that the men from the Yunnan clique were all brave and valiant warriors and were famous for their pipes, too. Maybe the Japanese devils thought these pipes were some kind of secret weapon."

"They were not talking about these water pipes. They meant opium pipes used for opium not for tobacco, although opium is also a native specialty in Yunnan. It's just an exaggerated joke to say everyone was carrying a pipe," explained Liangzu, on hearing Xuan.

All the guests felt awkward about how to respond since they all knew opium was allowed in the Yan residence. Liangzu used to smoke opium but quit several years ago. The one who couldn't quit was Suchu, who insisted that opium was the only thing that could bring her the most wonderful experience in her life. She just wouldn't quit. Hezhu only helped with the burning process for Liangzu, sometimes she even helped Suchu, but she herself never tried any.

"There is a reason for calling opium a weapon." Fuzhi didn't continue but paused, then smiled: "But such a weapon is pointed in the wrong direction. The real secret weapon is the unyielding perseverance of the Chinese nation which drives its people to forge forward, fight against the ruthless foreign invaders and strive on. These are the key elements of Chinese history. To quote from the interpretations of *Yi Jing* (*The Book of Changes*): 'Heaven rewards the industrious, the virtuous bear onerous duties, and we Chinese never pause in the pursuit of progress.' These lines are an interpretation of the first hexagram named *qian* (乾), meaning 'force', and the 2nd hexagram named *kun* (坤), meaning 'field', which also mirror the ideals of our forefathers. They wished that true gentlemen would keep forging ahead like the heavens, and sustain and contain everything like the earth."

All the listeners felt a surge of emotion. Liangzu said he would like to invite Fuzhi to give a lecture like this to his officers. Fuzhi happily agreed.

Then the servants came to serve the third round of tea, which was more like a dessert — it was a sweet stew made of rock sugar, dried lotus-seed and dried lily bulbs. It was served in golden bowls with matching spoons.

Seeing that all the three rounds of tea had been served, Hezhu stood up and excused herself, saying she was wanted in the kitchen.

The rest continued to chat before Jiangchu rose: "Sister, we'd like to see your rooms." And the three sisters stood up, excused themselves and headed out of the hall. Xuan and Earl fixed their gaze on the three ladies who all had very similar figures. Soon they discovered how similar their mothers Jiangchu and Bichu were, and how unlike her two younger sisters Suchu was. It was not because of differences in their facial features, but rather due to Suchu's lack of vitality. She moved the way a puppet would with someone behind the scenes pulling the strings. What was pulling the strings which controlled Suchu then?

Suchu lived upstairs in the east compound, while Huishu and Xuan stayed in the rooms downstairs. Yingshu stayed in the downstairs rooms in the west compound. All the other rooms belonged to Liangzu. Hezhu lived in a compound located in a separate garden, a place of mystery.

When they reached Suchu's rooms upstairs, Jiangchu and Bichu found the door was locked. As Suchu took out the key, Jiangchu exclaimed: "Really? You lock your own rooms in your own home?"

Suchu didn't respond.

The three sisters entered the room. What first caught Jiangchu and Bichu's attention were the opium pipes and lamps laid out on the low couch.

Jiangchu launched her attack on her elder sister before they were seated: "Big sister, why are you still using it? Fuzhi just said opium is a weapon against ourselves. Why should we kill ourselves with such a weapon? We should use it on the enemy! It has been a rare opportunity for the three of us to have spent more than half a year together in Kunming, but now Mian and I must move to Chongqing. Xuan is not willing to move there so we must leave her in your care. I will ask her to be more helpful to you."

Bichu said: "What matters most is your health. We know how tough your life has been all these years and we don't blame you for taking up opium. Today is your 45th birthday, how about you making a birthday wish to quit the drug? Father is now so far away, alone in Beiping. We have no idea what he might be doing today, but we know he has never been told about your addiction. Let's just count dad in, and the four of us make a deal: you quit opium!"

Suchu dropped her head, busying herself pushing her bracelets up and down her wrist for a very long while before speaking up: "I don't smoke much."

"It's not about the amount! It's about the addiction!" Jiangchu snapped. "Each time we see you, we ask you to quit. Why won't you just listen? If you don't care about yourself, you should at least think about Huishu! Think about the talk and gossip behind her back. Think about her future!"

Suchu managed a dry smile: "Everyone has his or her own fate. It is her fate that she was born in such a peculiar family... It's not that I won't quit. What's the point of quitting?"

Jiangchu and Bichu had never heard such hopeless words from Suchu before, and they held each other's gaze. Before they could say anything more, some croaking noises came out of a small screened cabinet against the wall under the window.

"Sounds like a toad," Jiangchu said as she walked over.

Suchu hastily told Jiangchu: "Don't touch. Just have a look."

Bichu leaned over out of curiosity. Both took a step back at the sight of the toad, and stared at Suchu for an explanation.

Sitting in the screened cabinet was a giant toad with hideous patterns on its skin, eyes jutting out, panting, croaking.

"It belongs to Hezhu. She keeps all kinds of pets," Suchu explained.

"It's up to her what pets she fancies keeping, but why did she put that one in your room?" yelped Jiangchu, almost losing control of herself.

Bichu's eyes became wet. Taking Suchu in her arms, she said: "Sister, you can't let her get her way all the time!"

Suchu waved at them in a panic to lower their voices and whispered: "She keeps several and she puts them into one's room on birthdays for three days to absorb the qi (anima, energy or life force). Even Liangzu and Yingshu must do the same, only Huishu has the privilege of being spared — Liangzu made sure of it. He likes Huishu very much." A trace of relief flashed across her face: "It's better this year. I had snakes a couple of years back."

Jiangchu turned to Bichu: "Let's talk to Mian and Fuzhi and ask them to talk to Liangzu. A concubine needs to be reminded more frequently of her position. How dare she cross the line like this?"

Suchu waved her hands frantically: "No! No! Please don't! After so many years, I know how to handle my life." She paused, and then continued: "And I know it is not easy either, for Liangzu, though I don't know his business. But I can feel it. He's going through tough times. I can't bring more trouble on this house."

Bichu said thoughtfully: "It's indeed not proper for us to interfere with our big sister's family affairs. Besides, Huishu will play her part when she grows up. It's best if father sends a letter, and we can take the opportunity to talk about how much father misses his eldest daughter to let Hezhu know that the whole Lü family are all behind our big sister."

"Father hasn't written us a letter for such a long time", thought the three sisters, but none mentioned it. Since Bichu's departure from Beiping, she had only received one letter from her father and that letter took several months to reach her. "It's so far away from father," sighed Bichu. For no reason at all, she suddenly remembered what her father once told her before she left: "A long road lies far ahead, but which way is closer?" Her heart sank.

They heard footsteps coming up the stairs. The kids came up, talking and laughing. Suchu took a piece of printed cloth to cover up the cabinet. Kiddo, who was leading the bunch, charged into the room and asked Jiangchu: "Aunt Jiangchu, when is cousin Wei coming to Kunming? We all miss him."

May raised her hand behind Kiddo, showing that she shared the same feeling.

Jiangchu answered: "Wei misses you, too, and wants to come to school in Kunming. But Chongqing has very good middle schools and it's more convenient for him to stay close to us."

Huishu stood in front of the cabinet and kept silent. But it didn't take her long to break that silence in an unusually loud voice: "Aunt Jiangchu and Aunt Bichu, please let cousin Wei come to school here just like cousin Xuan does. We can put him up in Yingshu's room. I'm sure they will enjoy each other's company. That won't be a problem. The climate in Kunming is perfect, not like in Chongqing. I was there last year, and it was as hot as hell. And Kiddo wanted to go on the swings, but it was raining, and the swings were wet and slippery. It might have been dangerous to go in such weather..." She talked like a runaway train, rambling here and there on any topics that crossed her mind. It didn't take much effort for Jiangchu and Bichu to figure out that her intention was to cover up the croaking noises of the toad, and the two sisters immediately joined in to converse loudly.

Luckily, they were soon relieved from such stress when the servants came to announce outside the door: "Madam, dinner is served!" Everyone in the room, except May and Kiddo, heaved a sigh of relief at the announcement. They went out of the room in single file.

The rain was stopping. Behind the dark gloomy clouds on the horizon, a flimsy sliver of light could be seen.

Dinner was held in the small yard next to the reception hall. Three tables had already been set. Liangzu, Mian, Fuzhi and some other relatives of the Yans were sitting at the table, waiting for the womenfolk to join them.

With the three sisters' appearance, Hezhu popped out from nowhere and began to arrange the seating as the mistress of a house would do on such occasions. Suchu, whose birthday it was, sat quietly beside Liangzu in the seats for the host and hostess at the middle table.

In the centre of each table was a giant tray of assorted hors d'oeuvres: sundried beef jerky, sliced Xuanwei ham (a famous dry-cured ham from Qujing prefecture in Yunnan province), spiced pork slices, thin-sliced pork with garlic sauce, dried cheese flans and cheese pies made of goat's milk, and braised assorted wild mushrooms which were famed local specialties such as king boletuses and chanterelle. All these items were carefully arranged to form the Chinese character shou (寿), meaning longevity.

When everyone was properly seated, Liangzu raised his cup: "We usually don't celebrate birthdays since birthdays come every year and we would be so rushed to celebrate them all! But this year it is special because the three sisters and their families are all in Kunming, and 45 counts as a special birthday for Suchu to celebrate, too, so Hezhu came up with the idea of inviting you all over to celebrate this special occasion together."

His words didn't exactly express what he had wanted to convey because Jiangchu stood up once he had finished: "It is indeed a very special occasion for us to be able to celebrate our big sister's birthday together. Our elder sister is the most capable of the three of us, way more capable than Bichu and me. Mian and I wish our sister more happiness and well-being!"

Bichu stood up when Jiangchu finished: "I couldn't agree more with my sister Jiangchu. Our elder sister is indeed the best of us three. The two of us are far, far behind her. But if we are talking about care and love for one another, then we are the same. Fuzhi and I wish our sister a peaceful and happy life! Now the whole nation from the leadership to the masses are fighting the Japanese invaders, it would be best if sister Suchu could do her share, too."

Liangzu was so amused seeing his two sisters-in-law taking turns to back up their elder sister. He exclaimed: "You two are indeed full-blooded sisters of Suchu! It would be perfect if father were here with us in Kunming!" He pronounced the word 'father' very clearly. "I have invited him to visit many times to appreciate the wintersweet flowers."

Then Xuan and the other youngsters came to the main table to convey their birthday wishes to Suchu. Between the talking and laughter, some hot dishes were served.

"This is Macrolepiota albuminosa stewed in brown sauce, a species of agaric fungus. Our chef's special." Hezhu pointed at the dish as she made the introduction. Her rings sparkled.

Liangzu's adjutant came in and whispered to him. Liangzu rose from the table and left with his man. When they were in the reception hall, the adjutant handed Liangzu a letter: "It's from Beiping." The envelope was already worn out. On one corner the words 'obituary notice' were written in black ink. Liangzu hastily opened the letter:

To Miss Suchu, Miss Jiangchu and Miss Bichu,
And Mr Yan, Mr Tantai and Mr Meng,

Mr Lü Qingfei passed away on the morning of
7th July 1938. The coffin has been temporarily
put in the main compound, pending burial. I,
Lianxiu, have failed your trust, and bear full responsibility.

It was signed with Lianxiu's name at the end and dated the night of 7th July 1938. Liangzu decided to break the terrible news to the three sisters the next day. He turned to go back to the dinner table, but found Hezhu standing behind him, so he asked: "Shall I tell them tomorrow?"

"Tomorrow? They'll all be gone tomorrow! It would save a lot of trouble to tell them in one sentence today."

"At least not until the dinner is over."

"You're fussing about it like a woman!" Hezhu snatched the obituary notice from Liangzu, went directly to Suchu, handed it to her and said: "From Beiping."

Suchu immediately rose from her seat upon seeing the two words "obituary notice", and steadied herself by holding the table with both her hands: "Dad..."

Jiangchu's tears rolled off her cheeks before she finished the letter. She complained resentfully: "Why didn't she mention the cause of death?"

Bichu felt the piece of paper was crushing her, dragging her all the way from the top of a cliff into an abyss, her heart tumbling and plummeting. Her body felt as light as a feather. She did her best to keep a calm appearance and she made it — she didn't shed a single tear until they left the Yan residence.

PART III

It must be hard for a northerner to imagine what the fields look like in winter here in Kunming. It looked like winter had forgotten its reign over this piece of land, leaving the other three seasons competing for their share, mingling and interfering with one another. The colour green was evenly smeared along the winding river by the village. Here and there, occasional patches of amber could be spotted on treetops. Even the bare ground looked so moist, flourishing with the fertility beneath.

One small stubborn cloud, patched on the crystal cobalt blue sky, not clearly defined, more like a lone sail in the blue ocean, was silently tagging along with the Mengs as they made their way out of the minor city gate in the east. The road paved with flag stones shrank, getting narrower and narrower. They had crossed a river and skirted around two villages, but they kept walking. Farther and farther. They wanted to go a little farther.

The remains of the morning dew gleamed on the bushes.

Earl and May took turns to carry a basket with a carrying pole with their father, who had proposed tfo carry the basket with one hand. That proposal was voted down by all the others. In the basket were a boiled chicken, a boiled chunk of pork, four steam buns, four pearl pears (Yunnan produce which used to be a tribute to the emperors in different dynasties), a bottle of wine, some cups and chopsticks. They were hunting for a suitable spot to hold a memorial ceremony for Grandpa Lü.

Bichu fell ill the day they came back from the birthday dinner at the Yan residence. It began with a fever, then she lost her appetite, and was bedbound for a couple of days before she was able to get out of bed and move about again. Although it was not beyond her expectation that her departure from her father in Beiping was doomed to be a farewell in life separated by death, she was grieving over the fact that she was absent at her father's last moment of life. How horrible was that for a daughter to cope with? Such grief, when complicated by other intense emotions like regret and guilt, made the burden of grief harder to bear.

"What had happened to dad?" Bichu had repeated the same question to Fuzhi dozens of times. "If dad passed away because of some illness, it wouldn't be hard to explain, but why didn't Aunt Lianxiu mention it in that letter? Why hadn't dad appeared in my dreams?"

Fuzhi thought he might have guessed the cause of the old man's death, knowing the old man already deemed that his life was more a burden, or a nuisance like a wart, to many. It was quite likely that he had removed this wart from the world by himself. But, of course, Fuzhi wouldn't have shared such an assumption with Bichu.

The offerings were prepared by May with some help from Sister Yao, who oversaw the cooking of the chicken, while May cooked the chunk of pork. She was meticulous about the hairs on the pork rind, trying to pluck them all out. She had to make it very clean since it was an offering to her grandpa.

When Earl came back from school and saw what May was trying to do, she immediately pointed out that May was wasting her time and energy since: "What difference do a few hairs make? All those things will be left behind in the wild after the ceremony."

May raised her head from the pork, looked at Earl, then turned back to her plucking.

Bichu struggled out of bed and made the steam buns.

Earl suggested they include the four pearl pears.

The three sisters had planned to hold the memorial ceremony together, but because of conflicting schedules, they agreed to go their separate ways. Xuan, who had wanted to join the Mengs, returned to Xiao Shiba with her parents who were leaving for Chongqing.

The five members of the Meng family walked into the fields. The narrow dirt track led them onto another one paved with flag stones. Then a fork in the path led them into a grove, where they spotted a mound coated with lush greenery.

Fuzhi asked Bichu: "Will this place do?"

Bichu nodded.

They cleaned up the space in front of the mound, and laid out the offerings. Five cups of wine and five pairs of chopsticks were laid out.

Kiddo asked: "Mum, I want to fetch a bowl of water for grandpa." Earl and May followed him until they found a creek bubbling happily not far away. Kiddo filled up the bowl with water and the three returned to the mound. The five of them stood silently, mourning.

Bichu took out a bundle of joss sticks, held them while Fuzhi lit them, and fanned them a little to keep them alight.The flame left a circular trace before it died out in the air. The couple stood in front with the three children behind them. They kneeled and were ready to do their kowtows.

Bichu held up one cup and said: "Dad, you are now gone. It was hardly a month after we left Beiping. Were you ill? What happened? None of your three daughters were with you. What irresponsible daughters we are!" She set down her cup and clasped onto the ground, choked with tears. The three kids, with floods of tears, tried to go and comfort their mother, but Fuzhi stopped them. A good cry might be exactly what Bichu needed if she was going to recover from her grief.

Fuzhi picked up another cup and said to himself: "Father, you devoted your life to this country and its people. Your strong sense of righteousness must have been such a hard nail in an occupied city like Beiping. We don't know what happened, but I do know you will always serve as an example to your offspring. Your spirit remains!" He spread the wine onto the ground, took up the front of his long gown, kneeled, and kowtowed three times.

Earl and the other two did the same. Kiddo added the bowl of water, weeping: "Give me back my country! Grandpa, you taught me this! Give me back my country!" The words reminded him of the seal his grandfather taught him to make and the characters the old man taught him to carve on the soap bars. His voice lingered amid the lush vegetation, echoing like an oath.

The red dots at the top of the joss sticks inched all the way down. When the last dim light was gone, they died completely. All five of them stood for a while longer and then Fuzhi gestured it was time to pack up and leave.

Bichu was no longer weeping. She asked: "Shall we take these things back?"

"I think we should," Fuzhi answered. "It's the same as paying tribute to the gods. If they are there, they have dined."

"We shouldn't waste such good stuff," May added. For sure, that's something her grandpa would have agreed with her about. After packing everything up, they headed back, taking the paved footpath and the dirt footpath in the field, and reached the villages near the city. That patch of cloud was still lingering in the blue sky.

"What a lovely day," Bichu said suddenly. "Since we have gone so far, why don't we stay a while longer? There might be an air raid alert."

"But it's already so late that..." Fuzhi didn't have time to finish his sentence before he spotted three bright red balloons rising from the top of Wuhuashan. He quickly modified what he was trying to say: "That we might take a rest here."

He soon found Bichu's face was as white as a sheet. She didn't look like she still had any strength to walk further. They hurried into the nearby grove and found a spot to sit down. Bichu sat down, resting against Earl. May and Kiddo ran about to explore the place.

"Don't go far!" Bichu called after them.

In less time than it takes to have a meal, the first air raid siren sounded. More people came into the grove. They had all taken the minor city gate in the east to get out of town. A couple of food vendors were mixed in with the crowd, one of which was selling jellied peas served with assorted seasoning. It was a delicious blended taste — hot, spicy and with a sweet after-taste. The kids loved it. Kiddo couldn't help casting several glances at the vendor but May tugged him away. Both knew how hard life was for the family and they tried their best not to ask for anything extra to eat or to wear.

"Miss May, Kiddo, you are here!" Someone called. It turned out that Li Lian and his family had come to the grove for shelter, too. It was Jin Shizhen who had just spotted May and Kiddo. Shizhen was stiff, as usual, but not gaunt like Bichu was. Her children, Zhiwei and Zhiquan, were also casting their eyes on the jellied-pea vendor.

May went up to greet them, and Shizhen took the opportunity to comment: "May, how tall you have grown! You are a big girl now."

Zhiquan cried out loud: "Let's ask sister May to play." The four kids ran all the way to the river lying west of the grove. It was somewhat too close to the city.

The two couples exchanged greetings. When Li Lian learned that the Mengs had just came back from a memorial ceremony for their late Grandpa Lü, he made three deep bows in the direction of the north. Fuzhi and Bichu bowed back to thank Li Lian, but Shizhen didn't bow as she should have. Instead, she rather harshly shared her opinion: "I don't think old Mr Lü died of natural causes."

That completely ignited the bomb of suspicion ticking in Bichu's mind. That was the final straw. She asked, her voice trembling: "What do you think might have happened?"

Shizhen didn't answer as if she were in a trance.

"Was he… did the Japanese…?" Bichu muttered to herself as fresh tears welled up in her eyes.

"No, I wouldn't think like that," Fuzhi butted in. "Father is gone, and we should stop brooding over this and let him rest in peace."

Earl also said: "Mum, there's no point in speculating!"

Bichu sighed: "How will Aunt Lianxiu carry on?"

"Is there anyone who doesn't have a lot on their plate nowadays?" said Earl.

Li Lian mentioned the student loans. Most students were forced to leave their hometowns and stay in unfamiliar places. With many still hitting their growth spurt, what they ate in the canteen was barely enough to keep them from starving. Besides that, the cost of living was set to soar since the old local Yunnan currency had already been declared invalid, which meant the new local Yunnan currency wouldn't hold much longer. The inflation of the legal currency issued by the central government made the situation even worse. It didn't take a genius to foresee a further drop in the quality of the food provided by the canteen. Some students began to find part-time jobs to earn extra money to feed themselves. More would join soon.

Li Lian concluded: "It's a good thing for the students to have some exposure to life's realities when they are young and staying on campus. A pharmacy is looking for an accountant. It's just to keep their records, so I don't think it would be too hard to learn. Several students have talked to me and all wanted to go desperately. They put me in such a tough position."

Earl suddenly walked over to them: "Dad, I want to find something to do."

"Do you?" Fuzhi was taken by surprise since Earl never used to show any signs of concern for the family. Now even she wanted to help. "No, you don't. You are only a sophomore, and we are not that desperate, either. We can manage."

Seeing what was going on, Li Lian suggested: "It would be best if Meng Liji could go. After all, biology and pharmacy are related."

"No, she can't," Fuzhi disagreed. "There are others more in need of the position. Earl can't take it." When he turned to Earl, his eyes became stern. Having received the message in her father's eyes, Earl reluctantly walked back to her mother.

Shizhen was talking, half to herself, half to Bichu: "It's such a strange place. Most of the holy spirits I used to see are gone. What I see now are only those colourful clouds and rain, oh rain like chains of beads. I feel I am like a stray kite that has lost its thread, wondering here and there. Otherwise I should have been aware of Grandpa Lü, shouldn't I?"

She paused thoughtfully and then began again in a whisper: "Some women here keep poisonous animals, like deadly snakes, scorpions, centipedes, and all sorts of stuff, as pets. It takes a lot of training. When one is well trained, one can poison someone by simply pointing at them!"

Earl asked quite curiously: "How's your religion related with such a practice?"

Shizhen replied sulkily: "Look at you! We are not related to such evil and monstrous practices. Not at all! You keep your nose out!"

If anyone talked to her like that, Earl would normally be sure to give them a piece of her mind, but since Shizhen was definitely not an ordinary person, Earl didn't take offence. She had no intention of apologising for her question without due consideration, either.

Deep in the grove, the owners of the portable snack stands were quite busy. Some people were already enjoying their snacks in a merry and noisy way, bowls in hand, sitting, standing, squatting, making themselves as comfortable as possible. The smell of good food filled the air.

Bichu, worrying where May and Kiddo had gone, asked Earl feebly: "Earl, would you go and check up on what May and Kiddo are doing? Ask them to come back." As Earl took a first step, Bichu stopped her: "If they are staying in a secure place, leave them where they are. No need for the family to huddle together."

Shizhen laughed loudly: "You are not going to put the father and the son in the same boat, are you? Don't worry. The planes won't come today."

She had hardly finished her comment when the emergency siren wailed. The grove fell into sudden silence with so many people vanishing in a split second. Where had they disappeared to?

"You just stay here. Don't walk around," Bichu stopped Earl gently.

Fuzhi went over to them and told Bichu he had seen the kids picking up pebbles along the slope of the river bank. It was a very safe spot. Besides, Li Lian was with them. Bichu nodded with relief.

Li Lian sat down by Zhiquan's side on the river bank. The kids were so familiar with the air raid sirens that they carried on their business — piling up pebbles into mounds, pushing them over and building them again. May was not playing the game. She was staring at the blue sky, lost in the realms of her imagination.

Before long, enemy fighter planes rumbled into view. Eighteen planes flying in three triangles could be seen silhouetted against the blue sky, appearing to move quite slowly. That small patch of cloud was still there. The planes pierced through it and headed over the grove.

Zhiquan cried out loud, pointing skyward: "Japanese planes!"

Kiddo gathered a handful of pebbles and was ready to throw them. "These are the shells from my machine gun!" May stepped forward and stopped him.

The planes had reached the grove. They were so close that the rumbling engines deafened people's ears and made their hearts tremble. Dead silence fell upon the grove against the roar of the fighter planes.

"Lie down! Hit the ground!" someone yelled. Instinctively, May pressed Kiddo onto the ground and she herself hit the ground too, thinking if anything should happen, she would be there to cover Kiddo.

The sky was the same blue with that leisurely patch of cloud. "Even if we all die, the sky and the clouds will still be beautiful like this," thought May.

One fighter plane dived toward the ground, as all fighter planes did in those days to shorten the distance and take better aim at the target. Right at that split second, May panicked. It felt like a huge hand had reached inside her and emptied her inside out. She wanted to run to her mother, but she was too stunned to move a muscle.

Several black dots emerged out of the blue, one slightly higher than the previous one, plummeting.

"Bombs!" When May realised what those dots were and tried to roll over to cover up Kiddo, she blacked out at the deafening sound of explosions.

It turned out that three bombs had landed neatly on the opposite bank of the river; shell splinters showered in a wide arc over the river bank where May and the other kids were hiding, sparing their lives under the projectile, but shovelling red dirt all over May and Kiddo. They passed out when they were hit by the violent shock waves of the explosions.

Zhiqin and Zhiwei were farther away from the spot where the bombs landed, but they also blacked out. Both burst into loud wails when they came back. Tears of terror crammed their cheeks caked in red dirt, smudging their faces and blurring their eyes. Li Lian hurriedly pulled them into his arms.

Suddenly another fighter plane dived in, firing at the defenceless Chinese with machine guns. The noise from the guns was sharp and loud, rattling the ear drums against the dead silence of the air. Li Lian stood rooted to the spot, covering his kids, staring upward at the fighter planes. Once the enemy planes had disappeared into the sky, he came to his senses and ran to check on May and Kiddo.

Kiddo came back first because he had a much thinner layer of earth on him. Apart from the fact that his limbs felt like jelly, he was OK. As he began to regain consciousness, he looked around for May, who was lying several feet away, most of her body buried under loose earth. He crawled over to her and began to dig with his hands, crying out loud: "May! Sister May! Wake up! Wake up!" But May's eyes remained shut tight.

"Am I going to have to hold a memorial ceremony for my dear sister May?" thought Kiddo. The thought almost froze his heart. No, he wouldn't cry!

Li Lian and the other kids came to help with the digging. Thankfully, May came to once the earth was almost removed. She didn't remember where she was since the sky was still blue, and the patch of cloud was still loitering in the sky. Grandpa, the siren, the fighter planes, the bombs, those fragmented memories flashed through her head. She then realised she had already lived her life once.

Fuzhi and the rest of the family rushed over to them. When Zhiwei and Zhiquan saw Shizhen, both stopped crying. May and Kiddo leaned closely against Bichu, feeling so secure.

Kiddo whispered in Bichu's ear: "Mum, I feel as if so many years have passed."

"And I have lived my life once, Mum," whispered May to herself.

Shizhen told them in a tense voice that several people had died in the explosions, and what a horrid scene it was. Her face had lost its usual colour.

Grieving wails came from the outer edge of the grove. It must have been the living bearing the pain of parting with the deceased.

Someone wailed: "Xiaochun, you were only 12! You were only 12!"

Xiaochun, which means early spring, was a common name for girls in Yunnan. This stranger of a girl the same age as May had been erased from this world.

The fighter planes came back, wheeling and howling overhead.

Beautiful blue sky, how could you allow the enemy fighter planes to fly rampant? Fertile fields, how could you silently put up with the tearing of the bombs dropped by the enemy?

Kiddo struggled to get back on his feet and asked his father: "Dad, where are our planes? Why don't we see them coming?"

"Our planes? A poor and undeveloped country like ours doesn't have planes!" Fuzhi sighed sorrowfully. Seeing Kiddo caked in red earth standing straight at attention like a boy scout and staring at him, Fuzhi had a lump in his throat. As young as Kiddo was, he was concerned about the country's air force. It wrenched Fuzhi's heart: "It's safe to say our country has no national defence at all. The people are so stricken with poverty, while the government is so corrupt — you are too young to understand such things."

47

The fighter planes wheeled several times more before they left. Just then a loud boom came from somewhere near the minor city gate in the east. People listened attentively, holding their breath. Several flashes of fire lept from the ground. They looked almost white under the sunshine.

"The minor city gate is on fire!" People exchanged their suspicions in muffled whispers.

One shouted out: "My home! It's my home! Those bastards just bombed my home!" He stumbled toward the opposite bank of the river but was dragged back.

"Wait! Wait a while longer!" someone advised. Many of these people in the grove lived near the minor east city gate. Several more rushed toward the city, saying they needed to help put out the fire.

Li Lian yelled: "We have fire fighters! We won't help!" But nobody listened to him. People left the grove one by one.

Fuzhi and Li Lian looked at each other, pained by their helplessness.

"I saw that Japanese soldier firing his machine gun. What a smug face! That little girl — they are my sworn enemy!" Li Lian growled with indignation.

Fuzhi turned over the word 'sworn enemy' in his mind and sighed. When would the world be free of war of any kind?

The enemy planes didn't come back, leaving behind dead bodies, broken limbs, ruins and ruined lives, and rubble and resentment. A while later, the alert was lifted.

The Mengs and Lis wended their way back to the city. When they passed the minor city gate in the east, they found the fires had been put out and people were sifting among the ruins. Several people were just sitting in front of the crumbled houses, staring at the debris. A tree, hit by the waves of explosions and almost uprooted, stood stubbornly, with something hanging on its bare branches. A closer look revealed it was a limb. The adults approaching the sight all covered the kids' eyes with their hands and hurried to the other side of the street, hoping to distance themselves from the horrid sight.

May saw it. She felt light-headed as if she had been hit on the head by something heavy and hard. Not wanting to add to her family's troubles, she tried her best to keep control of herself and followed her parents. No one noticed she was boiling inside: *Poor thing! That must have been someone who lived here and refused to go out of the city to take shelter. Now they have become a ghost. What does a ghost look like? They'd better go to fight the cruel, ruthless Japanese. Some of those who went out of the city to take shelter were killed, too. How many have died and become new ghosts? Oh please, don't haunt our home!*

It didn't occur to any one of the Mengs that they might no longer have a home to go back to.

Once they were back in the city, the Lis went south while the Mengs went north. And when the Mengs reached the Ancestral Temple street, they immediately noticed the difference. The doors of the neighbouring grocery store were all boarded up, with a prominent sign saying 'closed'; dark clouds of smoke curled above the garden inside the tall walls of the ancestral temple. People were coming and going from the gate.

Luo the Grocer spotted Fuzhi and the rest of the family as he was coming out of the gate: "Ah how lucky you are to have taken shelter outside the city! Our air-raid shelter collapsed. I just checked it out."

"Is anyone hurt"? asked Fuzhi immediately.

"No, no. No one's hurt," replied Luo the Grocer, waving his hands, his face mixed with anxiety and relief. "We were out of town visiting our relatives and somehow were spared!" He paused and hesitated, obviously struggling with himself, but at last he decided to say it: "Your place has been destroyed."

On hearing the news, the family didn't say anything, but hurried inside the gate. They ran into their neighbours carrying someone on a stretcher. Their hearts sank. Luo the Grocer said no one was hurt. A closer look revealed that it was Old Shen, the gate keeper who had been knocked unconscious by the shock wave rather than being hit by a bomb.

"Are you taking him to hospital?" Fuzhi asked.

"We have to try," one of them answered.

Fuzhi turned to Bichu to ask her to give them some money but found Bichu had already taken out a 100-yuan note and was profering it to him. Fuzhi handed the money to one of his neighbours, who said: "How kind you are, professor Meng! Hurry! Take a look at your place."

The Meng family went through the wintersweet grove. A bomb had hit the side of the grove near the bomb shelter. They couldn't see the shell crater from where they were standing, but they could see the scorched trees still smouldering with smoke. Under the curls of black smoke, the wintersweet trees were still blooming.

Catching sight of the smoke-blackened ruins where their home once stood, their hearts felt as if even the weight of a feather would be too much pain for them to bear after this. A shell crater big enough to hold a car stood guard in front of the house which had been reduced to rubble. Luckily the bomb was not that big and half of a room survived the blow and was still standing. May and Kiddo's calligraphy work was still visible on the broken adobe wall. The two had been copying the epic title *Jiucheng*

Palace by the famed Northern Song dynasty calligrapher, Ouyang Xun (557–641).

They were rooted to the spot, dumbstruck, unable to weep, as if time had frozen over in front of the crater.

"You need to sit down," Fuzhi said after a long miserable while, pulling a stool from the rubble for Bichu.

"It's lucky that all our family is together!" A faint smile touched Bichu's pale face. Yes! How lucky it was for the five of them to still be together at such a horrible moment!

After sitting for a while, Bichu began to issue instructions to sort things out. *We are all intact! We still have our heads on our shoulders, and we have our hands!*

"My manuscript!" Fuzhi yelped.

Bichu calmed him down with a peaceful, sad look in her eyes: "Don't worry," she said. "The box is under the bed."

They had planned to take the box with them, but the heavy load of the offerings made them activate plan B, which was to find a safe place for the box. Earl and May plunged into the debris. When they pulled out the bed, they were so relieved to see the box lying intact under it. Fuzhi opened the box to make sure his manuscript was safe, completely unaware of the fact that catastrophe had been averted. He sighed deeply with relief: "Now, now the whole family is together!"

They kept on digging and managed to extricate from the rubble a table, some chairs, boxes and baskets, and lined them up by the crater. All the bowls and cups were shattered. They had nothing to drink out of, although they were thirsty.

Then a handsome man emerged from the wintersweet grove. He was wearing a light beige wool sweater and dark-grey suit trousers, both of which made him a popular lady-killer on any campus in Beiping. It was Xiao Cheng.

"When we came back, we were told the shelter you built in the city gate had collapsed. Several people went to check it out and were relieved to discover that you were not there and no one was hurt." Xiao Cheng sighed gently: "I'm sorry your house was not spared."

"Don't be. I'm glad the enemy fighter planes' aim was so bad that the bomb landed in front of the house. If it had landed diretly on the house, we would have lost everything."

"Well, Fuzhi should be the one to blame since he is so popular that even the bomb wanted a popular spot," joked Xiao Cheng, turning to Bichu and trying to make light of it.

Sensing his kind intentions, Bichu managed a wry smile. Earl was touched. How could Uncle Xiao be so kind and considerate, comforting each suffering soul?

"We have already cleared out a room in the theatre. Mrs Meng, why don't you go over there and take a break? We'll be handling the moving," suggested Xiao Cheng. "I'm going to find a porter."

While they were talking, more people came. Some of them were from the faculty, and others were staff from the general affairs office. They claimed it was unlikely they might find any helping hands on the street and it would be better if they did it themselves. Then they all began to help, some carrying things by themselves, some lifting with a partner. Two even managed to find a carrying pole and carried two trunks with it. Everyone began to head for the theatre.

Fuzhi asked May to take her mother to go and have a rest, but May said: "Let sister Earl go, please. I want to help with the moving." She had been shuttling in and out of the ruins by the broken adobe wall, with Kiddo right on her heels. The red earth that had coated her during the explosion had not yet been cleaned off, and now it was tinged with dark smoke. May was covered all over with patches of red, amber and black, making her look quite spectacular. Kiddo, on the other hand, had transformed into a busybody with a muddy face coated in dirt and smoke. All those smaller items like the inkwell bought at Guihui were unearthed by two pairs of bare hands.

Earl accompanied Bichu to the theatre, carrying a net basket with her. The rest kept digging for a while and then decided they would leave whatever was buried deep under the debris for the next day.

Fuzhi was so grateful for all the help that he was unable to find words of thanks. One staff member told him: "Think nothing of it, Professor Meng. New bombs might drop on any of our houses. Who knows where they might land? I might need help to…" He swallowed the rest of the sentence with a lump in his throat. He had meant to say he might need help to bury his body if he was killed by an explosion.

They all left for the theatre, with this and that in their hands.

As May and Kiddo went through the wintersweet grove, they heard the sound of horse hoofs.

"Cavalry! No, it's unlikely to be cavalry," said May.

The two stopped under a tree, truning back to look in the direction of the Ancestral Temple street. Seconds later, a small black horse, a local breed, galloped inside the gate. On the horse was a clean, handsome young lad with a pair of sparkling eyes and a face so calm that he looked as if he had just walked out of his reading room. It was Zhuang Wuyin.

"Brother Wuyin!" Both greeted him excitedly.

Wuyin dismounted from his horse, tethered it to a nearby wintersweet tree, and took May and Kiddo by the hand. The three stood there silently for a long time.

"As soon as I was told about it, I rode here," Wuyin began, finally, his eyes full of concern and sadness. "Are you terrified? Aren't you tired?"

May and Kiddo dropped their heads but didn't respond.

"Listen," Wuyin said resolutely. "You two come with me and stay with us. I have been sent by my parents to pick you two up."

"No," May shook her head defiantly. "We are staying with our mum and dad."

"Brother Wuyin, we need to guard the wintersweet grove, too," added Kiddo.

"Meng Heji, you are very imaginative!" exclaimed Wuyin, patting Kiddo. "We'll talk about it later."

The three of them headed for the theatre together. At the entrance, they saw the glass was shattered and two window frames had fallen onto the ground. Except for that, no major damage was done.

The Meng family stayed in the attic, which had remained unoccupied because of the inconvenience of having to negotiate the very tight stairwell. It was fully occupied now with different people going up and down. The three of them saw Earl coming downstairs with a basin and a towel.

"I saw you from the window. Mum asked you to wash your faces first," said Earl, nodding at Wuyin.

"Brother Wuyin rode here," reported Kiddo.

"Can you read when you ride a horse?" asked Earl.

"No, I can't," answered Wuyin, but he turned to May and continued: "I would fall because the horse is fast. I can read when I ride a bike because I have 100% control over my bike. But when I ride a horse, I only have 80% control — probably even less than that."

The two kids had access to a basin of water in a public area, and soon the water became muddy. Earl asked them to wash one more time, but they both hesitated. They didn't want others to think they were using too much water which had to be paid for so that someone would bring it from a well.

"How can you two be so considerate? Are we going to make a Sherlock Holmes out of you?" teased Wuyin. "I'll go and get some water."

"Do you actually know where the well is?" sneered Earl.

"If I want to," Wuyin answered from some way away.

They were both reluctant to wash again not only due to the water shortage but also because the water was icy cold, yet both listened to Earl because it was such a privilege that their big sister was here to supervise them. Besides, Wuyin had gone to fetch some water. So they didn't need to worry anymore about the water shortage. This time, when the water in the basin was much cleaner, Earl gave them permission to go upstairs.

President Qin and his wife Xie Lifang were in the room. Xie Fangli, several years older than Bichu, had a very delicate face with a mixed look of gentleness and solemnity. The latter was very likely borrowed from her husband, Qin Xunheng.

Bichu picked up a dry towel to rub Kiddo's hands in order not to trigger chilblains while Xie Fangli taught May how to dry her own hands: "Your three kids are quite hale and hearty. They look tough enough to survive." The number 'two' almost rolled off her tongue, but she changed it to 'three' just in time. With a gentle sigh, she continued: "But life here is nothing like that in Square Teakettle or Round Rice-Steamer."

"They never complain. They know there's no point in complaining," said Bichu. Having dried Kiddo's face and hands, she asked Kiddo to run off and began to whisper to Fangli.

Kiddo went to Fuzhi's side and listened to him talking.

Qin Xunheng said: "Since the first air raid in Kunming on 28 September last year, today's is the worst. We have been letting our guard down these days. Today has proved that we should always stick to the plan to disperse to the countryside. I have already rented several places to the west of the city for the science institutes. Families such as Youchen's have already settled down in Xili village. I'm glad it's working well. Where should we put the art institutes?"

Fuzhi said: "One of Yan Liangzu's adjutants is willing to let his house at the far end of Dragon Tail village in the western suburbs, saying it is a suitable place for the institutes, but I haven't checked it out yet."

Qin Xunheng was overjoyed at Fuzhi's news: "Terrific! I'll send someone to liaise with Commander Yan and ask him to have a look at the house. Besides the institutes, the families should be relocated as soon as possible. Womenfolk like Mrs Meng don't have the strength to run for shelter."

"Should we look for a place to stay near Dragon Tail village, too?" Fuzhi glanced at his thin, pale wife, Bichu, and then at the box with his manuscript in, and sighed: "How come we still need to hide when we have travelled thousands of miles from Beiping to Kunming? To quote from Cao Cao, one of the greatest generals at the end of the Han dynasty, our generation should be 'a leader in peacetime and a hero in troubled times'. I don't know if I'm a leader in peacetime or not, but I know I'm a big eater and a layabout."

Xunheng laughed: "A big eater is a good worker, too."

53

Kiddo, who was leaning against Fuzhi and taking in every word, cut into the conversation: "If we have workers who can build planes, then we'll have our own planes."

Seeing Kiddo's dark flickering eyes looking so intensely at them, Xunheng, with no children of his own, was moved. He stroked Kiddo's head fondly and said: "I wish we could have more kids like Kiddo who could think so much. Kiddo, the aviation department in our university is aimed at cultivating capable people to build planes."

Fuzhi said: "Kiddo has loved planes since he was very little."

Kiddo answered thoughtfully: "I don't like killer planes, though."

"Zhuang Wuyin has come back with water." Earl and May were standing by the window and saw Wuyin carrying two big buckets of water with a carrying pole on his shoulder and heading steadily toward the public water area. The two sisters then explained how Wuyin had offered to carry water because May and Kiddo were concerned about using up their ration.

Xie Fangli smiled approvingly: "If only more people would think like you two."

Soon, Wuyin came upstairs. After greeting all the adults present, he walked up to Bichu and stayed beside her.

"Do you carry your own water in Xili village?" asked Xie Fangli.

"Not always. We hire someone to do the carrying, but if he doesn't turn up, I do it."

The adults carried on chatting and then the Qins took their leave. Only then did Wuyin ask Bichu whether May and Kiddo could go and stay with them in Xili village for a couple of days. He explained it was what his parents and his little sister Wucai wanted. He hurriedly added: "It's what I want, too."

Bichu caught Fuzhi's eye, who turned to May and Kiddo: "It's up to you two."

May answered immediately: "We have already discussed this with Brother Wuyin and we want to stay with our mum and dad. We don't want to be away even for a moment." Standing so close to Bichu, May had the impulse to hug her mother but she checked that impulse since she was no longer a little girl. She was almost as tall as her mother.

"Thank you, Wuyin," Bichu said gently. "I would be happy if they'd like to go but, as you can see, they don't want to leave home. I guess I can't push them."

Despite Wuyin's disappointment, he didn't show a trace of it. He had once discussed with Wei why he felt so peaceful and happy in May's presence. Neither of them had been able to figure out how May was able to exert such a calming and comforting influence.

The topic of staying with the Zhuangs was dropped there and then. The three kids went on talking about school. Wuyin shared his analysis that both their primary and secondary schools might have to relocate, and all the students would end up living on campus.

"It must be lots of fun for so many fellow students to live together!" May and Kiddo shared the same anticipation.

"It must be quite inconvenient if you have to spend all your time together in and out of the classroom," said Wuyin, voicing a different concern.

Xiao Cheng came to tell them dinner was ready. The bachelors among the staff outsourced their meals and shared different well organised roles in management of things such as purchase of cooking materials and supervising the kitchen. The kitchen had been told earlier to make dinner for the Mengs and it was ready. They all went downstairs. The kids had lots of thick, white kidney-bean stew cooked in thin rice gruel. The beans were almost as big as Kiddo's little fingers.

After dinner, Earl, May and Kiddo went to see Wuyin off. In front of the ancestral temple gate, Wuyin sprang up onto his horse and circled around once before riding northward, leaving the clatter of the horse's hoofs echoing in the air. It would have taken him less time if he had gone out of town first and then headed west. When the horse turned to the west, Wuyin turned to look at them and smiled. Wuyin seldom smiled, but that smile looked so charming, as if he were saying: "We are not afraid! We'll survive!". That smile and the figure on horseback were indelibly etched in May's memory like a close-up. They never faded away.

Darkness was gathering as the night closed in. Looking out of the cramped window in the attic, one could still spot several traces of the setting sun glowing against the sky on the horizon.

Earl said there was not enough room for the family: "I don't have a place at all." When Wu Jiaxin came to visit her later in the evening, the two went back to the girls' dormitory together.

Fuzhi put one gasoline can on top of the other, mumbling to himself while he did it: "This will serve as my work desk." He dragged over one more and set it up vertically: "And this will be my chair."

May was cleaning the glass lamp cover while Kiddo oversaw the stand. May kept puffing at the cover, and then wiped it while it was moist. Very soon the lamp cover was clean and transparent like crystal, blending so well into the air. Once they had lit the shiny, polished lamp for their father, they felt the whole day of panic, exhaustion, labour, hatred and humiliation was much mitigated.

"Of all our three kids I worry most about Earl," sighed Bichu softly, sitting in bed looking at Fuzhi.

Fuzhi shared her concern and sighed, too: "But our worries don't matter, do they?"

They gazed into each other's eyes, drawing consolation from each other.

Fuzhi put some paper on his 'work desk' and sat down in his 'chair', his back straight, as if he were still back in his office at Square Teakettle, with the giant pair of couplets, 'Not Me, Not You' and 'See Heaven, See Truth', hanging on the wall behind him. Seeing there was still ink in the inkwell, he dipped his writing brush in it, and wrote down on the paper: 'China's path to freedom'.

The noise of footsteps from the staircase interrupted Fuzhi's train of thought. Someone was saying: "Mind your step, Mrs Yan. Mrs Meng is upstairs."

Fuzhi rose from his 'chair' upon hearing the title 'Mrs Yan'. May and Kiddo were already at the door. Suchu came in.

Suchu first told Fuzhi: "Liangzu went to the capital when he heard the news and couldn't make it back in time, so he sent me to see how you are coping with things. Huishu wanted to come, too, but I asked her to stay to save causing you any trouble."

She then took a few steps to reach Bichu's bed. They addressed each other as 'elder sister' and 'younger sister', and both burst into tears. Fuzhi took the kids to the far corner of the room to make space for the two of them.

"Elder sister," Bichu began. "We are alright. It's just me. I have been feeling rather weak lately. We owe dad our lives today. If we hadn't made the trip to hold the ceremony for him, we might all have been buried in the city walls."

"Liangzu said the target of the air raid today was the southeastern suburbs. Up to a hundred houses were razed to the ground. It is the most serious and damaging air raid so far. We were thinking there might not be any air raid since it was already late, so we all stayed in the residence. It was unbelievable that it actually happened. Huishu was at home, too. When the planes droned above us, Hezhu kept chanting her incantations," narrated Suchu. She was not judgemental.

The two sisters then discussed Bichu's health. Suchu said: "We are moving out of the residence to stay in a house near Anning county, about 30 kilometres away from the city of Kunming. Just me and Hezhu. The others need to stay close to their work or their schooling."

Bichu wondered whether Hezhu would be taking her poisonous pets with her.

Seeing Bichu silent, Suchu continued: "You and your family should move to Dragon Tail village. Although it's only a simple country house, it's quite spacious."

"That's what I wanted to talk to you about, sister," Bichu said. "Fuzhi wanted to ask you a favour. Would you please talk to the owner of the house about renting it to the arts institute? They are in search of a place to relocate. Would you do that for him?"

Suchu answered thoughtfully: "But where are you going to stay if the house is given to the institute?"

"We are going to look for a place to rent from the villagers in Dragon Head village. We'll make sure it's nearby and it'll be convenient for Fuzhi to go to work."

Seeing that Bichu was already coming up with a plan, Suchu, who was never judgemental, then said: "I see no reason why the owner would disagree. That house is not occupied, after all." She took out a small embroidered purse: "You might need to buy some things after such a disaster…"

"You know Fuzhi, sister," Bichu didn't wait for Suchu to finish and pressed her hand on the purse to stop Suchu. "We can't take it."

Seeing how determined Bichu was, Suchu sighed, but didn't insist.

"I do need a favour from you, sister," Bichu said, taking a broad waistband from the inner side of the bed which had all the valuables Bichu had brought for the family from Beiping. She fumbled inside, took out a pair of gold bracelets, and handed one to Suchu: "I'm a total stranger in this place. Could you sell it for me? It will help with the family expenses."

Suchu took the bracelet silently, put it into her purse, and got ready to leave.

Cool silver moonlight streamed over the bombed city on the plateau, soothing all the souls, living and dead. Most people were fast asleep. Bichu, reclining on her pillow against the headboard, was exhausted, but somehow sleep eluded her. She gazed at the moonlight outside the window, and saw Fuzhi who was still writing at his 'desk'. She was lost in thought.

The lamp in front of Fuzhi kept burning.

THE INDESTRUCTIBLE WINTERSWEET GROVE

HOW BRIGHT THE MOONLIGHT IS, seeping into every corner of the wintersweet grove. The pungent smell of burnt earth and blood was almost lost in the refreshing sweet smell of the trees in the stream of moonlight. It was as if nothing horrible had happened.

I am looking northward through my north-facing window. In the distant sky I can see a loitering cloud, intangible like a sheer piece of gauze. Dad, are you there looking down on us? What has happened to you? How could you have missed seeing me in my dreams?

It is pathetic for human beings to have the ability to remember. If people lived in, and cared for, only the present without remembering the past, they might be happier. Then today's bombardment could be left behind. It is also lucky that people can remember. How could we forget the bombardment? We left Beiping for Yunnan, traversing half the country, yet we still have nowhere to settle! If we hadn't held a memorial ceremony for you, we would have been buried under the red earth. Dad, I know your departure was your way of saving us, and I also know that is what you yourself wanted. I am not crying, dad, I've just got some dust in my eyes.

Elder sister just came by and wanted to give us some money to help us out, but I refused her offer. Tomorrow, sister Jiangchu will send money to us, for sure, but I won't take that either. I am confident that sister Jiangchu understands me and won't feel it is anything unusual, but I remember Liangzu once mentioned that my family is pretentious. His original words were: "The books these professors have read are tougher than artillery shells!" Are they? If these professors could transform themselves into artillery shells, that would be wonderful. But no professor has such magic power.

We have already lost Wuhan, which also made the situation in Hunan and Guangxi provinces rather gloomy. What a tough mission it is if we are going to have to fight the invaders and reclaim the lost land inch by inch under these circumstances? The war won't end in one or two years, and that is why I insist on sticking to the principle of self-reliance, which you taught us. It is also a principle cherished by all the ages.

We Chinese never pause in the pursuit of progress. All the matters in the world, as big as running a country, and as small as running a household, rely on one's own efforts. All the households have their own principles and even one as tiny as mine has its own rules which defy any misrepresentation. That is why I have to turn down my two sisters' offers.

Since Fuzhi handed in his notice and retired from his position as the dean of studies, he has a lot more time on his hands and has been focusing on his writing. That's what I was hoping for since I have no career of my own, and thus can't contribute anything to society. Fuzhi should do more to make up for my failings.

When he writes, his writing brush moves with dizzying speed as he commits each character stroke to paper. Watching that makes me feel dizzy and exhausted. I always ask him to slow down since no one is chasing him, but his answer is always the same: "I need to write down my ideas as fast as I can before they elude me. Besides, how much time is the enemy likely to leave us?"

Judging from what President Qin and Professor Xiao Cheng have said, they still expect Fuzhi to shoulder some of the university's administrative responsibilities. For Fuzhi, education is such an onerous but noble task that he simply can't walk away from it if he is needed. But I do worry about him. One's energy is limited, and he can't afford any distractions at his age.

During our short stay in Yunnan, things have changed a lot. Things happen so fast, and the same applies to my energy. I always feel weak and feeble. I guess as I age, my health must have deteriorated, too. I don't know how long I can hold on. It is not unlikely that one day I might drop dead and then join you, dad, in the other world. When that day comes, I can count on elder sister and sister Jiangchu to take care of my three children, but who will take care of Fuzhi? The kids could survive without me, just like all kids who grow up and leave their parents. But not Fuzhi, who wouldn't survive long without me. So, I just can't afford to die! But I am so tired that I feel my body is wilting.

Dad, don't worry. When we relocate and settle down in the countryside, we won't need to disperse when the air raid sirens sound. That will make things easier and give me more time for the household chores. The only problem is that I haven't worked out a plan to take care of Fuzhi, who needs to work, and the kids, who need to go to school, at the same time. Besides, I don't think we'll be lucky enough to find another place with a grove of wintersweetness.

Elder sister and Hezhu are moving out of town to stay in Anning county. I guess all she'll do there is play mahjong to kill time. Elder sister and I are both awkward in social gatherings. She is like a donkey pulling a pole, circling around the mill with blinkers on, going in the direction it's required to go. Not like sister Jiangchu who enjoys herself to the full when she plays mahjong and comments on the jewellery of the wives at the mahjong table at the same time. Networking with the wives of high-ranking officials and officers is part of her regular life. She might even enjoy life more because she'll have more such opportunities in Chongqing.

However tough life is, it's all extrinsic, and one needs to rely on oneself to figure out how to cope. But Earl is the one that truly worries me for I don't have the slightest idea what path she's taking.

Her eccentricity is common knowledge among all our friends and relatives. She has grown up in the same environment as her two other younger siblings, with the same education and genes, but who knows why she is so different from the other two? Recently I was relieved to notice that she had become closer to the family and was more caring, too. That relief was shattered by the fragmented conversation I overheard yesterday.

I was trimming the vegetables before cooking them when Earl came back with Jiaxin. The two paused in the grove and whispered. I heard Earl telling Jiaxin: "Don't tell my mum", and I wondered what they were trying to keep from me. But it didn't take a genius to conclude that they were sharing a secret. Jiaxin's secret was about her boyfriend while Earl's was more about her family. On the one hand, I was relieved to know Earl is still not involved with any boy. If she was, it would terrify me! On the other hand, it is unsettling to know her secret has something to do with the family. How strange it is that Earl's secret has something to do with the family!

How people's personalities differ! I remember when Earl was 12, I made red birthday eggs for Kiddo's first birthday. Earl was holding three eggs in her hands, saying the paper-cut printing on the egg shells were very beautiful. Upon hearing that, May ran to her and asked Earl if she could spare one, but Earl didn't have the slightest intention of sharing. When I asked her to do so since there were plenty in the kitchen, she didn't say a word but squashed all three. Now, May is 12, like Earl years ago, but she is already in charge of sweeping the floor and doing the dishes, and worrying about not wasting any food.

May and Kiddo are hitting their growth spurt, which worries me, too. Malnutrition is so harmful to youngsters who are growing fast, but I only need to watch over their bodies. For Earl, I need to watch over her heart. How can I do that? How much energy do I have to guide her through the maze in her heart, which grows ever more bewildering with the changing world outside?

I am afraid I will drain myself of energy, and I don't want Fuzhi to be distracted by my worries. Dad, would you please guide me and help me out?

The bright moonlight slants through the branches and boughs of the trees, where I dry my laundry. I hang the wet laundry on the branches, stretching them out one by one; before they dry, I repeat the stretching process. Since our departure from Beiping, I have never ironed the laundry, not that I have an iron, but all our clothes are tidy and smooth because of the stretching.

The beautiful moonlight polished what remained of winter on the plateau with a tinge of clear coldness. Dad, do you still remember I once learned to play the xiao, the vertical bamboo flute? The flute I played belonged to my great grandmother. It was an old, thick one with its natural mahogany colour tarnished by time. For a beginner like me, it was quite easy to blow.

I took the flute and sat down in the thatched pavilion. You said: "The flute is the best match for the moonlight since flutes originate from nature and are connected with nature. Wang Bao, the famed writer who was also an expert musician in the Western Han dynasty, wrote in his masterpiece 'Ode to the Flute' that 'it absorbs the essence of nature', by which he meant the body of the flute, and that 'its sound soft and gentle, solid and delicate', 'the melodious tune sounds like a loving father teaching his son, and the whispering tune sounds like a loving son taking care of his father'".

But now, dad, I am no longer under your protection, and am deprived of any possibility of keeping you company and taking care of you.

How quiet the grove is!

Fuzhi once gave me a pair of flutes made in Yuping county, Guizhou province, a place with a reputation for making flutes for more than 400 years. They are also finely made, but they are thinner than great grandmother's flute. The bamboo bodies are golden, carved with the poem from the eminent Tang dynasty poet Du Mu, entitled: 'A Message to Han Chuo, Magistrate of Yangzhou City':

Remote green mountains harbour hidden streams;
Southern grasslands unbowed by the passage of autumn.
Twenty-four bridges bathed in moonlight,
Where are you giving flute-playing lessons?

Dad, do you still remember? 'Twenty-four bridges bathed in moonlight'! What a pity I left them behind in Beiping. But now the whole country has been downtrodden under the enemy's iron boots, its people are struggling on the brink of starvation, and the flute wails plaintively. When can we set off on our journey home?

Fuzhi also says flutes come from nature and that their sound is a fitting accompaniment to moonlight. I played only a few times in the garden at Square Teakettle. Dad, you never asked me why I stopped playing. I assumed you realised that my life was occupied with more beautiful and meaningful things then. I taught Earl, May and Kiddo a lullaby:

'Tall and straight, a black bamboo,
I save it for my darling baby,
To fashion it into a charming flute.
Put your lips to the mouthpiece, then blow.
The flute plays popular new tunes.'

I keep telling my children they need to keep playing popular new tunes to keep up with the changing times. Popular new tunes don't mean swimming with the stream, but finding a new, better self. Through all sorts of hardships such as leaving our home, taking refuge in a strange land, air raids, and disease, we will triumph over tragedy and transform into a new self.

No air raids can destroy the wintersweet grove, which has attracted so much of my admiration, and which has witnessed our own self-admiration, too.

We are Chinese!

The moon had risen high in the sky while Fuzhi continued writing industriously at his 'desk'.

Dad, I know you are watching us from that cloud...

CHAPTER TWO

PART I

The enemy bombardments had driven many townsfolk out of town to settle in the countryside. The Meng family had been reluctant to do the same since Earl needed to go to school and Fuzhi needed to go to work. Among all the schools, Kunjing school was the first one to act and move the school from the city to Copper Head village 10km away from the city right after the Spring Festival. The school chose to establish itself in two well preserved temples built on a medium-sized mountain. The Yongfeng temple halfway up the hill was the campus for the middle school, while the Yongquan temple near the top was for the primary school and served as the girl students' dormitory. Those who donated money to build the two temples would never have guessed at the new use their temples would be put to. But this should also count as a very charitable and pious deed to relinquish the temples as places of worship, in the same way as they gave money and offerings to the temples, shouldn't it?

Zhang Yongqiu, the headmistress of Kunjing school, had a doctorate from the Université de Paris, a willing spinster who devoted all her time to her career and had no time to spare for marriage. She was a strict disciplinarian in imposing order among the students in the school and classrooms, and was a fervent advocate of boarding schools, convinced that a boarding school helped better realise balanced well-rounded development for primary and middle school students. It was a novel idea for parents in Kunming. They complained jokingly that although Dr Zhang had graduated in France, she followed the English way of running her school. Now parents had no other option than to accept Dr Zhang's 'boarding school' idea. She had very specific requirements for the bedding and other daily items, too. Although it was wartime, she still insisted that all students use white quilt covers made of cotton and that all toiletries had to conform to certain sizes as well. She made an exception for the children of those teachers from other provinces who were living in austerity.

Bichu's habit was to follow reasonable rules rather than to make exceptions. She spent hours, several nights in a row, on needlework to prepare the required white quilt covers and other items of clothing. The two kids needed four wash basins, and Bichu managed to get four but only one was new, completely smooth inside and out. Bichu decided to give it to May for she was older, and she was a girl. But May protested: "It's a nice basin and Kiddo should have it."

Kiddo refused: "Little sister should have it. I'm afraid I might break it."

"You are so young but now you are going to stay and live in a school away from home. You deserve a new one."

"No, I insist you have the new one."

Bichu was almost moved to tears seeing them both trying to persuade each other to have the new one. She forced a tearful smile: "It's just a new basin. When we win the war, all of us will use new basins. May, just take it."

May thought for a while and then accepted her mother's advice.

Bichu and May tried to wrap the quilt in yellowish tarpaulin and tie it up in a roll with string. They tried several times until the package was rolled into a tight, neat shape. The two basins were placed upside down on top of the roll and fastened to the roll with string.

Yan Huishu came to pick up May and Kiddo in her family's car. She was taking a duffel bag, an imported item via the Yunnan-Burma road, and another bag for her toiletries. Having gently and quietly conveyed her greetings, she just waited silently. There was no public transportation to Copper Head village. If one didn't have a car, one had to hire a porter to carry the luggage and walk with him. When Suchu told Bichu she would send a car to take the two kids to school, Bichu accepted the offer. Anyway, it was a favour from her own sister, not anyone else.

Once the car reached the village, it couldn't go any further, so they had to climb up the mountain on foot. A footpath alongside a stream with white pebbles in its bed led all the way up into the woods thick with tall trees. Along the footpath were crumbling stone steps, each step as high as half a metre.

The driver carried Huishu's luggage on his shoulder, the servant carried Huishu's other bag in one hand and May's with the other, together with May.

They kept walking until they saw a fork in the path leading to the buildings in the woods.

"We have arrived! We have arrived!" shouted Kiddo.

"Not yet. This is Yongfeng temple," answered the servant. "The Yongquan temple is further up."

Several high school students appeared from the fork in the path, some carrying their luggage, others empty-handed since they had already settled in. Another one popped out of the woods by the path.

"Brother Wuyin!" cried Kiddo.

It was indeed Zhuang Wuyin, who matched their pace and took May's luggage.

"This is my cousin Yan Huishu," said May, by way of introduction.

Huishu's eyes shone. She said with a gentle smile: "I know Zhuang Wuyin, but we have never talked to each other before." She said those words in *putonghua* (the common Chinese language – Mandarin). Realising her switch of dialect, she added: "My *putonghua* is not good."

Wuyin knew Huishu, but didn't answer her. Instead, he glanced over at Huishu several times and shook his head: "No, no!"

"What?" asked May.

"No, Yan Huishu and Meng Lingji are not alike at all."

They all laughed. Kiddo couldn't agree more with Wuyin's conclusion since Kiddo thought the best-looking woman was his mother, closely followed by May. It would have been tough for him to admit that Huishu and May might look alike.

They soon reached the temple gate. On the gate were two words: "Yongquan temple".

Most of the statues in the temple had been relocated. Only the four heavenly kings and Wei Tuo, Skanta, the devoted guardian of Buddhist monasteries, which were set in the main shrine in the front hall, remained in place for the villagers when they came to pay homage.

"Wei Tuo is more like a police officer. The thunderbolt in his hand is for bad guys only," said Wuyin. "Look, he has a gentle appearance."

Well, the four heavenly kings were definitely not gentle. All were tall and ferocious except for the one carrying a *pipa*, a Chinese lute, who looked like a pale-faced scholar, although they were gods in charge of good weather for the crops and worked for the well-being of the people.

They all escorted Kiddo to the Depository of Buddhist Texts and handed him over to the dormitory supervisor before the rest headed for the girls' dormitory — the Arhat hall. Wuyin refused to go into the girl's dormitory, excused himself and went back to Yongfeng temple.

The girls' dorm had two giant beds. The one by the wall had places for 10, while the one behind the door had space for eight because the door took up some space. When Huishu and May arrived, most of the places were taken. The two by the door were still available.

The servant asked: "Where should I put the luggage?"

Many people were walking around the room. A middle-aged woman greeted Huishu: "Miss Yan, you are here. Our young miss has been here for quite a while." Her status seemed to be lower than a governess but higher than a housemaid.

"Our young miss" referred to the daughter of one of the wealthiest families in Yunnan, the Ying family. She attended the same class as Huishu. It was rather baffling that such a miss would have a manly given name like Dashi. The effect was very much like a girl being named Achilles.

Dashi was sitting at the innermost spot by the wall. Her bed was already made. The spot next to her was still not occupied.

"Yan Huishu, come here and take this spot," Dashi asked Huishu. She had actually occupied the spot in case anyone she didn't like wanted to have that spot next to her.

"Alright," answered Huishu, and walked toward the inside. "I'll take the one next to you."

The servant put down the luggage and had begun to untie it when the middle-aged woman walked over to him, saying: "You don't need to do this. Let me take care of that. Madam Yan seems to be quite at ease without even sending a female helper with her."

May settled down on one of the places beside the door. When she untied the string, the two basins fell on the floor, making a rather loud noise. A dent was immediately visible on the new one. May touched the dent, regretting that she hadn't thought to take more care.

"Hey! Hah!" Dashi laughed. "Meng Lingji! Even if that basin was broken, it wouldn't be worth as much sentimentality as you are showing now!"

May looked at Dashi without understanding what she meant. Dashi was a true belle. Why hadn't May noticed that before? Her magnolia-white skin was as smooth as jade, and her brows, her eyes, her nose and her mouth were perfectly formed to evoke an arresting charm blended with wild vitality.

"You are a daughter of Professor Meng. I know that," said Dashi, speaking in a way that made it clear she was impressed by Professor Meng's profound knowledge. Kunming people all respected knowledge very much. "Leave your luggage there. Ah Hong will take care of it for you."

"Don't worry. I can manage. But thank you all the same," said May, sounding so grown up that all the other girls laughed.

Dashi sprang to her feet and began to walk along the big bed, stepping on the others' quilts. They pretended they hadn't noticed and carried on whatever they were doing.

"Li Chunfang, go and fetch a basin of water and put it in the corridor," said Dashi, starting to issue orders. "Zhao Yupin, you go to the classroom and check if anyone is there." The two girls obediently went on their errands. When she was done with her orders, Dashi lept agilely from her side of the big bed onto the one behind the door, where May's place was, and walked toward May.

"Please, don't walk on my bed!" said May, who was busy struggling with the uneven floor under the bed as she tried to put her basins on the floor properly. When she noticed what Dashi was doing, she stood up and asked firmly again: "Please don't walk on my bed!"

Several girls turned to look at May with astonishment. Huishu hurried to May's side and gave her a gentle shove, looking at Dashi with mixed feelings of fear and apology. Dashi was taken by surprise by May's words at first, and then she said nothing and jumped back to her side of the bed.

What a peculiar night it was! May was a little bit concerned at first, but when she pulled her quilt up to cover herself, she fell asleep in no time. The wind rustled the pine trees and the rustling rocked the youngsters to sleep. She dreamed that the four heavenly kings passed her in single file, holding their holy instruments: the sword, dancing; the pipa (a four-stringed Chinese musical instrument), humming; the umbrella, opening and closing; and the serpent, slithering along its all-seeing master King Shun. They looked quite nice and gentle, not as ferocious as their statues did. May even asked them a question: "When can we beat the Japanese invaders and drive them out of China?" But none of the four responded. They all kept playing their instruments.

May's dream was interrupted by a a girl screaming "mum" in her dream. It was Zhao Yupin, who was from Shanghai, and whose mother had died from being unable to adapt to the local climate and food not long after their arrival in Kunming.

Several more girls were woken up by the scream and screamed with her. Some called mum or dad, some called out grandma or grandpa, some yelled "down with the Japanese imperialists", "beat the Japanese back to Japan", and "no air raids", and so on. Waves of sobs then ensued. The two dormitory supervisors hurried in, each carrying a kerosene lamp, and showered the girls with questions: "What's happening? What's going on?"

They felt and checked the girls with the light from the lantern, which also exposed their panic-ridden expressions.

Dashi, lying against the innermost wall, didn't cry at first, but when she started, she burst into loud sobs. And soon she was drenched with her tears. The elder of the two supervisors wondered what Dashi could be crying for, but she asked her younger colleague to take Dashi to the office to calm her down, and turned to the rest of the girls, scolding them loudly: "We have rules to follow in this dormitory. To cry in the middle of the night? What kind of chaos are you trying to bring about?"

The whole dormitory collapsed at her words. May felt the surge of sadness in the fresh tears that kept welling up in her eyes. Yan Huishu was the only one who didn't shed tears. She was sitting in her space, wrapping herself tightly with her quilt, watching the others somewhat nervously. When the junior supervisor left with Dashi and closed the door, she slipped off her bed and poked May: "How could you cry with the others?" With those words, she sat down on May's bed and held her hand. May gradually calmed down, as did the other girls.

The elder supervisor then began: "My good girls! I know this is your first night at this dormitory in the mountains. You will get used to it in no time." She tucked some of them in, stroked the heads of others, and didn't leave until she was sure no one was making any noise.

Back then, people said it was a prank by mischievous spirits. Only years later did May and Huishu realise it was a case of mass hysteria which is easily triggered among teenage girls. Many medical textbooks have records of such incidents now.

The following day in class, most of the teachers talked about the significance of relocating the school and expressed their wish that the students work harder. The Chinese teacher for May's class was Mr Yan Bulai. His given name Bulai (不来) literally meant 'not coming'. He used to be a student in the Chinese department, but he had to suspend his studies for a year to make a living by teaching. As a result of being neglectful of his appearance, his clothes looked like they were hanging off him. His hair was long and riotously unkempt. But when he began his class, he beamed with his unique charm which was always the precursor to a spontaneous speech of some sort.

That day, he didn't talk about the significance of relocating the school, like his colleagues did. Instead, he wrote down a line on the blackboard: "Never forget the shame of hiding from the enemy." When he had finished writing, he stared at the line for a while before beginning the text he had chosen for the class, which was printed on brownish paper. It was Liang Qichao[1]'s famous essay 'Young China', which discussed the significance of raising the young to be the backbone to lead the country through ups and downs, and how the young should try their best. During that class, even the naughtiest kids remained seated bolt upright.

When lunch time came, the girls went to Yongquan temple. The front hall had been transformed into a canteen. More than a dozen long tables were lined up in a row from the front of the deities reaching almost to the hall gate. The seats along the long table were arranged according to grades and classes. Students sat on both sides of the enormously long table with six people in each group sharing three dishes and one soup. In front of each group were a big bowl of rice, braised greens, stir-fried tofu pulp, and stir-fried shredded pork with mustard greens, a unique local speciality favoured by all girl students.

When May sat down, she found that the line sitting opposite her was from the ninth grade and that Dashi was sitting right opposite her. Dashi was handing a piece of fine paper to the person on her right to clean her chopsticks and bowls for her, and handing one bowl to the person on her left to fill up with rice for her. When everything was set, she took out a jar, put some of the contents into May's rice bowl, and some into her own, closed the jar, and put it back. May was touched by such a friendly gesture and gave Dashi a smile of appreciation. Dashi whispered to her: "Stir-fried mushrooms and ham sauce."

May didn't understand why Dashi whispered, but she was busy enjoying her rice with these two delicious dishes as the simple rice tasted much better with the dishes. She had no idea that Headmistress Zhang had stopped behind her or how long she had been watching her: "Meng Lingji, what are you having?"

May didn't know how to answer. Headmistress Zhang reminded her gently: "You may not know that homemade dishes are not allowed here at our school. All the students should eat the same food, so no one is different from the others. Now, do you understand?"

May stood up immediately, dropped her head, and replied that she did. Headmistress Zhang stroked her head affectionately, asked her to sit down for her meal and darted a stern look at Dashi before carrying on doing her rounds.

Everyone heaved a sigh of relief. Dashi had buried her homemade dishes under her rice before Headmistress Zhang came near, and now she began to enjoy her meal slowly, whispering to the person next to her: "I knew she wouldn't dare to say the dishes are mine. She may well have a try, though!"

May had no idea what Dashi was talking about, and she forced herself to empty her bowl since the school didn't allow anyone to leave anything in one's bowl.

Later May talked this over with Huishu, who told her that Dashi, of course, knew of the rule about no homemade dishes, but Dashi never thought any rules applied to her. Once she was caught passing notes in class. When the teacher asked, a classmate of hers said it was Dashi who had started it. Dashi then held such a grudge against that girl that she bullied the poor girl with all kinds of taunts, jeers and cutting remarks for the rest of the term. "That's why she thought you wouldn't dare to tell on her."

"It wasn't because I didn't dare. I just thought I shouldn't," May answered thoughtfully. "I thought she meant well when she shared her dishes with me."

"It's not hard to distinguish between 'dare not' and 'should not'," Huishu replied with the same thoughtfulness. "But many people can't tell the two apart. I guess it's easier for them not to, though."

"It is indeed quite easy to dump one's responsibility onto others because of cowardice," said May.

The two girls looked at each other like two musing philosophers.

After a month or so, most of the students had got used to life in the mountains. Life became much more settled without the harassment from enemy fighter planes, air-raid sirens, or the need to hide from air raids. The girl students had two round trips downhill and uphill each day along the babbling creek, parting the twigs and branches blocking the path with their hands. Those stone steps had become so easy for them to navigate as time went by. The familiarity of the buildings in the two temples encouraged them to explore further downhill.

Several families lived along the road between Yongfeng temple and Copper Head village. They used to put up stalls to sell candles, joss sticks and snacks to the devotees visiting the temples. After the school's relocation, they included several items on the list favoured by youngsters. One was papaya jelly drink, a cold drink made from the pulp by rubbing papaya seeds and served in brown-sugar syrup. The cool sweetness would tickle a young stomach all the way down to its young heart. Another snack was fried pea crackers. Dried whole peas were first fried in oil, then mixed into a paste made with flour, shaped in a ladle and then deep fried in oil. The cap-shaped crackers were inviting to the taste buds and challenging for strong teeth. All these snacks were quite cheap, and May would sometimes even spare a small amount of her allowance to buy some to share with Kiddo and Huishu. But Huishu always declined May's offer. Compared with other girls her age, she had very good control of her desire for food.

That afternoon, May and Zhao Yuping went for a walk after the earlier dismissal. It was at the end of spring when the azalea were in full bloom enveloping the whole mountain in a riot of red, white, pink and purple colour, transforming it into an enormous flowerbed. The lush trees tinged the sky with a green canopy. The teachers always warned the students to keep away from the grass for fear of snakes, but since no one had encountered any snakes over the last few months, they had all let down their guard. When the azalea were in full bloom, almost all the students loved to amble in all directions to get closer to the beauty of the flowers. Through the twigs and branches, one could spot the clear blue sky decorated with random patches of white clouds, matching the strident colours below.

The path lined with azalea took May and Yuping to the neighbouring Three House village. They didn't have money on them, nor did they intend to buy anything from the villagers. They were simply drawn by the flowers. Somehow the path led them to the back of a house. Behind a pile of firewood was a patch of red. Standing among the blooming flowers was a low adobe shed made of the local red earth. The red colour was rather conspicuous against the bright blue sky. An odd aroma in the air reached the two girls. A large black block of wood stood silently in the courtyard. A second look told them it was a coffin.

"Girls, what are you up to?" said a voice emanating from the shed. The two girls then spotted a man wrapped in red lying in the shed.

He was burning something over a shabby lamp. When it was done, he shoved it to the bottom of a bamboo pipe and then smoked the top of the pipe without any delay. He didn't speak up again until he had taken several puffs: "If you want to buy things, go to the front. Don't wander around."

May and Yuping turned around immediately to see a tiny thin woman standing by the pile of firewood, looking at them. She was so thin that she looked like all the water in her body had been squeezed out. She was carrying a rather big baby in the basket on her back. The baby's head was bobbing this way and that in the basket.

"Students, girl students! Don't say anything to anyone." Her tone was gentle. She then fumbled in the basket and took out two pea crackers from under the baby's body. When she handed over the crackers, she threw in a forced smile. A bitter smile.

"No, no. We won't take them," said the two girls, escaping from the place as if they had done something wrong.

When they were a short distance away, they heard the woman shouting: "Qinghuan, where the hell are you?"

The two didn't dare to look back but kept running up the hill, passing patch after patch of azalea bushes, until they reached the creek. It suddenly dawned on May that the man lying in the azalea bushes was smoking opium! She told Yuping about it since she had seen those pipes at her aunt Suchu's.

73

"Opium is a terrible thing," said Yuping. She paused for a moment and then said again: "Rumour has it that Yan Huishu's mother keeps venomous insects as pets. I don't believe such nonsense!"

"Who told you that?" May was furious. "My aunt Suchu is a very simple person. If she kept venomous insects as pets, then nobody in the world is beyond reproach! It is…" she paused, an image of Hezhu coming to mind. She imagined Hezhu pointing her finger in a given direction and a white flash of dark smoke shooting out in that direction. She was well aware this was not something she should comment on, so she held her tongue.

A person carrying a load of firewood walked down the hill. People called those who cut wood for firewood 'woodsmen' but this one was indeed a young woman aged 16 or 17. Her skin was a dark olive colour, a common complexion for local women who laboured in the fields. It was said that such a colour was the product of being in close proximity to the sun. When she reached a big rock, she stopped to rest, putting the firewood against the rock on a wooden stand she was carrying with her. When she found May and Yuping staring at her, she grinned at them, showing her snow-white teeth.

May's gut feeling told her this girl might be 'Qinghuan'. May smiled back: "Are you gathering firewood for your family?"

"I have been supplying firewood to the school for a couple of days. I'm taking some for my family today," answered the young woman.

Yuping asked her whether she lived in Three House village. She said she was from Dragon Head village and she was helping her aunt here. She thought for a while and then added: "My aunt is dead."

May and Yuping immediately thought about the coffin in the backyard. Without exchanging their concerns, both took off up the hill. They wanted to go back to school as soon as possible. At a turn in the creek, they found Mr Yan standing by the creek, facing the water, lost in thought. They didn't want to disturb him and tried to sneak away.

"Meng Lingji, I saw you two talking to the young woman carrying firewood," said Mr Yan, still facing the water, as if he were talking to himself. "When she passed me here, I reminded her to take a break."

"Her aunt has died," said May.

Mr Yan sighed: "The men in Yunnan are always lying in bed; the women in Yunnan only lie down when they are dead."

May and Yuping looked at each other, both amazed that this teacher knew so much. Then they mentioned the man in red smoking opium in the adobe shed.

"Opium is forbidden. I'm glad those who still smoke it are now afraid of being spotted." Mr Yan turned around to face them. "It would be unfair to conclude that all the men in Yunnan are good for nothing. Before we settled down in Kunming, the Yunnan division took part in the Battle of Tai'erzhuan where tens of thousands Yunnan soldiers lost their lives. Many wives of these martyred soldiers committed suicide when their husbands died. Now 200,000 Yunnan men are at the front."

The two girls looked at the hazels and azalea with admiration, aware of the fact that the earth under their feet was red.

A little bit later an accident happened in Kunjing school that shattered the peaceful atmosphere of the school.

When the azalea bloomed, the broad beans in the farmers' fields at the bottom of the hill matured, too. The stores in Three House village began to sell salty boiled broad beans at one cent per cup. The girls enjoyed beans wrapped in paper all the way back to Yongquan temple. From the stores, one could see the green patches of broad bean fields at the foot of the mountain. On Saturdays when students were dismissed from school and on their way back home, they could see the plump bean pods ready to burst out of their confinement rustling in the winds, as if whispering "eat me, eat me".

For the evening independent study hours, gas lamps were used for lighting. When the lamps were filled with gas, the whole classroom was lit up, shedding bright light on rows of small heads with black hair buried in their assignments. Though the walls were shoddy, and the window panes were made of paper rather than glass, the students inside were working with an orderly and industrious attitude. The teacher in charge of May's class once mentioned the school was trying to cultivate useful graduates, not near-sightedness. Unfortunately, the gas lamps never lasted long enough due to the lack of fuel. When the lights all dimmed, most students packed up their work and started to walk around. May preferred to read a novel in the dim light. Bichu had warned her many times and even asked Huishu to remind her, but May was still not ready to quit such a delight.

That evening, when the lighting dimmed as usual, May took out *Dream of the Red Chamber* that she had been reading recently. Last time, she had stopped at the place where Daiyu, the heroine, was predicting her death chanting a poem she had written, and she was ready to begin where she had left off.

"Meng Lingji!" May hadn't noticed that Yin Dashi had taken the seat next to her. The dim light didn't dim the glorious beauty radiating from her rosy lips, white teeth and clear, bright eyes brimming with vitality.

"Meng Lingji!" she continued. "I have something fun to share with you. Put down your book!"

"Tell me," said May, closing her book.

"Let's go down the hill and steal some broad beans! We'll cook them by the field. That'll be great fun!"

"Who are 'we'?"

"You and me, and Li Chunfang from my class, plus someone from the high-school section. Bring Zhao Yuping from your class, too." Dashi paused for a moment and then declared: "Yan Huishu isn't going."

As they were talking about Huishu, she came in. Someone muttered: "What a strange thing! Everyone is coming to our class."

Huishu told May: "It's up to you. I'm not going. I don't think you should, either."

"Yan Huishu, don't spoil the fun!" Dashi growled. She turned to May again: "There's a full moon and the whole mountain is lit up. The grass smells so sweet. I once went hunting in the night with my father. It was soooo much fun!"

"Let's go hunting for beans!" said May, in high spirits. She smiled apologetically at Huishu: "Cousin Huishu, come with us. We'll be back in no time." She felt the sweet moon-lit night was calling on her and she couldn't stay inside.

"If you want to go, go on then," said Huishu calmly, and left.

"Yan Huishu is getting more and more serious," Dashi pouted behind Huishu's back, but her tone was friendly. "She is not as lovely as you are."

"She knows much more than I do," answered May, tidying up her desk.

Headmistress Zhang had gone to Chongqing on business; the senior dormitory supervisor had asked for leave to attend to some family business and was off campus that night; the junior dormitory supervisor only did a routine check before she went back to her room to enjoy her sleep, assuming that all the girl students had got used to the boarding life since half a term had gone by and no more close supervision was needed.

During her last routine check, when she went into May's dorm, she found several girls still sitting on their beds, looking rather excited. She asked: "Why are you still up? Go to bed now!"

"Yes!" all the girls answered, except for Dashi, who remained in a sitting position against the wall, completely oblivious of the order.

The junior supervisor walked over to Dashi and talked to her in an ingratiating tone: "You should go to bed early so you can get up early in the morning without dozing off during the day."

Dashi didn't answer her. "Alright, alright. In case you need me, just call me," said the junior supervisor and left, looking rather embarrassed.

All the lights went out. The moonlight splashed its watery pearlescent glow onto the temple. A group of girls led by Dashi opened the gate without any noise and tiptoed out of the temple. When they passed the Four Heavenly Kings, they felt like familiar old friends. If these statues could have moved, they surely would have joined them in their exploration. Dashi even made faces at the one holding the *pipa*.

What a beautiful moon-lit night! The uneven empty ground in front of the temple was rippled with puddles of moonlight. Anyone who walked on them became a fairy floating in the air with fairy dust. The moon, full and high, looked clear and bright in the crystal sky free of any freckles. A couple of trees with clear-cut silhouettes looked like they were embedded in glass. Between the top of the inky woods and the sky floated a ribbon of light, blurring the boundary between the earth and the sky. This was the moon-lit night that was so characteristic of Yunnan. This was the moon-lit night that belonged to Kunming. This was the moon-lit night that could only be seen on the plateau. The moon was so big. It was so bright. Fuzhi once mentioned that the expression 'bright moon' was only really accurate when used in reference to Kunming, where the moon was truly bright.

May raised her head to look up at the moon. A thought popped into her mind: how was the moon over Square Teakettle? Was it round and full like this one?

"Meng Lingji!" cried Zhao Yuping, urging May to hurry and catch up.

All the girls ran jubilantly downhill, whispering and laughing all the way, followed by the moon, leaving behind the shadows of the trees and hills. Patch upon patch of azalea looked hazy at the edges as if they were immersed in water floating in mid air.

May blurted out: "Why should we bother to steal the beans? It would be perfect to enjoy the moonlight here."

"Hey, you! You can't swallow your words and change your mind! We agreed to steal the beans and we are going to steal the beans. Now you want to watch the moon!" Dashi grumbled.

She was possessed by a strong desire to hunt and she wouldn't be satisfied until her desire was quenched. If she had a gun in her hand right now, she would have shot at the beans: one bullet for each pod.

As they went through a grove, they could see the bean fields. After two more bends in the path, they were in the field. All the plants were laden with plump pods, carpeting the field with thick lush greenery, stroked by the gentle moonlight.

They all stood on the footpath in the field to have a look, and then Dashi jumped into the field while the others were still looking. She plucked several pods off their stalks. After peeling the shell off, she tossed several beans into her mouth and spat them out after several chews.

"You are supposed to be a lady. How could you eat the raw beans like a starving beggar?" high-school student Wang Dian teased her. Wang Dian chose a wider section of the footpath, gathered some dry twigs, took out a big enamel-coated cup, and then asked Li Chunfang to fetch some water with it.

"Come down here! Come down, all of you!" Dashi waved at May and Yuping. "Come and pick the beans first. I'm afraid none of you have ever done this before."

May stepped into the field. The soft moist earth sank beneath her feet. The stalks by her side gave off a smell like green grass. She looked up at the moon and tossed one pod toward it. In her imagination, it was a pod-boat, which would never reach the moon, of course.

A moment later, when Li Chunfang came back with the water, she joined the other three with the picking. Very soon, the four had gathered several handful of pods. The whole time, Wang Dian remained on the footpath, refusing to step into the field, busying herself with peeling and looking after the cooking.

A dark shadow appeared, approaching in the distance. Fear began to grip the girls, who went closer to one another. Zhao Yuping screamed: "Wolf! It's a wolf!"

The dark shadow trotted toward the small bonfire and wagged its tail at Wang Dian. It turned out to be a stray dog!

"I told you we have never heard of wolves around here," said Wang Dian, heaving a sigh of relief. The dog walked around the small crowd and the bonfire. After finding nothing to eat, it turned round and went back the way it had come.

"What a silly dog!" Dashi said.

"It must be wondering what these human beings are doing," May laughed out, turning over the idea in her head.

At these words, Zhao Yuping first burst out laughing, then the rest of the group joined her.

Peals of laughter rippled across the field bathed in silver moonlight. They laughed at the dog, at the swinging bean stalks, at the beans being cooked in the cup, and at themselves skipping their sleep to steal beans in the field!

Laughter, like collective hysteria, is contagious among girls. Even Wang Dian stopped being so serious, laughing with them, reminding them from time to time: "Hush! Keep it down!"

Very soon they had had enough laughter and beans. They all sat on the footpath and enjoyed the beans, which were coated with moonlight, seasoned with the fresh smell of plants, and laden with the joy of the girls, bobbing up and down in the cup.

If they had decided to go back to school there and then and put an end to their wild bean feast, it would have been like many other incidents of naughtiness, resulting in a lecture from their class teacher and nothing more.

But they didn't. They remained seated, looking here and there.

"My scarf!" Dashi yelped. "My scarf has gone! It must be hanging on a stalk. Has anyone seen it?"

Unsurprisingly, they all spotted the white scarf fluttering over a bean stalk in the distance. Such a nylon scarf, imported via the Yunnan-Vietnam road which was still not officially operating then, was considered a luxury item back then.

"Zhao Yuping, go and fetch it for me!" Upon Dashi's command, Zhao Yuping took several big strides into the field without any hesitation and recovered the scarf in no time.

"Ai-ya!" Zhao Yuping uttered a short cry as she fell among some stalks.

"Snake! Snake!" May spotted some shiny scales wriggling away from Yuping.

With no time for fear, she jumped into the field and supported Yuping to prevent her from falling. Dashi and the other girls closed in and helped May to get Yuping back onto the footpath.

Girls back then all wore the *qipao* like adult women did, so it was quite easy to examine the wound on Yuping's leg with such a loose dress. A small bite on the calf was bleeding.

Wang Dian's advice was to use a piece of cloth as a tourniquet on Yuping's leg to slow down the blood circulation in case the snake was poisonous.

Dashi snatched the scarf from Yuping and gave it to Wang Dian: "Hurry up! Tie it on her leg!"

Looking at the scarf, Wang Dian hesitated. May shouted at her: "What's more important? The scarf or her life?"

Wang Dian shot May an angry glance but hurried to tie the scarf around the part of Yuping's leg where the snakebite was. One corner of the scarf was soon tinged red.

"Come on! Does anyone know what we should do?" The girls panicked. After some discussion, they agreed that Dashi and Li Chunfang should go to the junior supervisor for help, and Wang Dian and May should stay with Yuping to protect her.

May ripped a piece of cloth from the lower edge of her blue cotton *qipao*, hesitating whether she should bandage the snakebite with it or not.

Dashi and Chunfang ran toward the school. May took Yuping's hand. Yuping said: "I'm so scared."

"Don't be!" May comforted her. "It'll be alright. It can't be poisonous."

May herself was scared. She was scared that the snake which bit Yuping might be poisonous and that it might shoot out again to bite May, too. "Really. We have never heard of any poisonous snakes around here."

Wang Dian asked Yuping: "Can you still walk? We'd better help you get back to school slowly. Who knows how long it will take for help to arrive here."

They helped Yuping and all moved slowly up the hill. When they reached the bridge in front of Yongfeng temple, they saw people coming down the hill. In front was Li Chunfang, followed by the junior supervisor, a male nurse and a school worker carrying a simple stretcher.

The male nurse was also the substitute school doctor. Although he was not a formal doctor, he was quite experienced. He examined the snakebite and the colour of the blood with his lamp and declared it was not a poisonous snake. Everyone heaved a big sigh of relief at his words.

"Where is Yin Dashi?" May asked. She should be here with Yuping!

"I asked her to go back to bed," answered the junior supervisor. "She won't be much help anyway."

When they were back at school, they sent Yuping to the school infirmary and settled her down there. The assistant doctor suggested someone keep Yuping company because she needed to take medicine during the night. Since Wang Dian had left, the junior supervisor then looked at May and Li Chufang.

Both said they were willing to stay with Yuping. On hearing their promises, the junior supervisor nodded with satisfaction and prepared to leave.

May suddenly blurted out: "You should ask Yin Dashi to stay overnight. Yuping got the snakebite because Dashi asked her to fetch her scarf." When she found her opinion was ignored by the junior supervisor, she rushed off to her dormitory.

Most of the people in the dormitory were asleep. When May went in, some were woken up, staring at May with big round eyes. Dashi was already lying down in her space, but Huishu was sitting, probably knowing it was not the end of the story.

May trotted up to Dashi's spot and said, resolutely: "Yin Dashi! Get up!"

Dashi meant to ask about Yuping, but she changed her mind when she noticed how aggressive May was. Instead, she adopted a confrontational tone: "It's none of your business whether I get up or not."

"It is my business! Get up, now! Go and stay with Zhao Yuping! She got the snakebite because you wanted her to retrieve your scarf. How could you sleep here as if nothing had happened? Get up!"

Dashi sneered: "Are you a teacher? Are you the headmistress? Are you the chairman or the general? Who do you think you are to shout at me like this? I dare you to keep shouting at me like this! I dare you! I will have you expelled!"

Her loud voice woke up many more. Huishu jumped off her space and nervously took May by the hand: "You can't do this! You can't do this!"

But May kept arguing until the junior supervisor arrived. She immediately ordered Huishu to take May out of the dorm and busied herself with calming down Dashi.

"It's not fair! It's not fair!" May felt so wronged that her tears kept streaming down the front of her dress.

"Don't act like a child," said Huishu. "It's not worth making her so angry. We need to continue our study here and it's best if we study well. I told you not to go with them to steal beans."

When she noticed that May kept silent, she continued: "Life isn't fair. My mum once told me 'fairness' is only meant for intellectuals."

May detected cowardice in her cousin and remained silent. She kept weeping for several more minutes and then bolted up from the chair, drying her tears with the back of her hands and heading to the infirmary.

Huishu shook her head behind May and went back into the dorm.

At the infirmary, May found Zhao Yuping sleeping peacefully in her bed. Even Li Chunfang, with her head resting on her arms against the back of the chair, was asleep. A sliver of moonlight spilled into the room from the window, painting the floor silvery white.

Seating herself on a small stool, May mulled over Huishu's words that "fairness is only meant for intellectuals". How true it was that so many things were still beyond her comprehension. Since they were beyond her comprehension, she could surely discard them. She rested her head in her arms by the bedside and fell asleep.

May woke up suddenly during the night. She got up and checked the clock on the table to see whether it was time for Yuping's medicine.

The person sitting in the chair was not Li Chunfang, but someone else. Who could it be? She was surprised to find it was Yin Dashi.

Dashi stared at May, and May stared back at her.

Zhao Yuping woke up and whispered: "Meng Lingji, I'm feeling much better."

"Yin Dashi is here, too," said May.

The following day, the news that Yin Dashi had got herself into huge trouble travelled to every nook and cranny on campus. Who had been bitten by a snake didn't seem to matter that much.

During the afternoon independent study time, the five were asked to report to the student affairs office. The director told them off and ordered them to pay for the beans.

The director wrapped up his speech by saying: "How could you girls behave like naughty boys? If anything like this happens again, you'll be severely punished! The headmistress has already made this very clear!"

He turned to Dashi as he said the last sentence.

When Dashi was in primary school, she had been given ten lashes on her hand by Headmistress Zhang herself for having hurt a student's head and refusing to apologise for her misdeed. Later Headmistress Zhang went to the Yins and explained why Dashi had received physical punishment. Her parents were quite reasonable in not blaming the headmistress and, on the contrary, they were appreciative of her strong sense of discipline, which was quite a rare quality.

Dashi, of course, remembered that incident. She muttered something like "the crow has croaked", implying the headmistress was like a crow. Everyone ignored her.

Around dusk, Zhuang Wuyin went up the hill to see May and Kiddo. May was doing her laundry in the brook flowing through the pool outside the temple, while Kiddo kept watch by her side.

Both were overjoyed to find Wuyin standing in front of the bush by the rock when they looked up.

"Hey! Wait a minute, I'm almost done," said May.

She was once teased by her classmates for addressing Wuyin as 'Brother Wuyin', claiming 'brother' was too cloying a title, so now only Kiddo addressed Wuyin as 'Brother Wuyin', as he was accustomed to do.

"Brother Wuyin!" he cried, running toward Wuyin until he reached his side.

"Have you heard about the accident? I'm afraid you haven't got the whole picture," said May.

"I only heard about your nocturnal bean theft, but not the cause or effects."

May told Wuyin what had happened that night in minute detail while she rinsed her laundry. Wuyin and Kiddo listened attentively, uttering exclamations from time to time.

When May was done telling the story, Wuyin said: "That's exactly what you would do."

"Really? I thought you might say it was not like me to behave like that," said May.

"Why would you think that? It was just what you would do. You know, you have always had a heroine's qualities."

May thought that comment was rather funny, but she kept the thought to herself and refrained from laughing.

When she had finished her laundry, the three sat together in a row on the rock at the edge of the cliff, watching the sunset.

The sun was slowly sinking between the blue sky and green trees. The clouds near the yellow fireball had dissolved into a glamorous mixture of iridescent colours so that it seemed as if all the colours in the world had gathered at that one spot.

The sky was still bright and clear except for a couple of white clouds roaming in the eastern corner. One was the shape of an enormous shepherd dog and the other looked like an old man with a very long nose.

Once the fiery red orb of light had sunk beneath the horizon, the last chalky mauve of the sunset melted away as stygian darkness smothered the sky. The clouds and the trees all assumed a different air, so peaceful and remote.

"I wonder whether the sun has set in Beiping now," said Wuyin thoughtfully.

"The moon last night was beautiful. I also wondered whether the one in Beiping was so full and round," said May.

"It is said that the thin air is the reason why the moon in Kunming is especially big and bright and stays full longer than the moon in other places."

"As I recall, the moon in Beiping was big and bright, too," said Kiddo with the same kind of thoughtfulness. "The moon shone over the..."

"Fireflies!"

The three shouted out the word in unison. Those sparkling fireflies twinkled over the brook and in their dreams.

"Our gate is brown and yours is red. Sometimes I dream I have gone back home, but neither of the gates would open for me," said May.

"I hate those Japanese!" said Wuyin.

> "Oh stinky Japanese,
> Eat the stinky cheese.
> Break their knees,
> And spill their peas!"

Kiddo chanted aloud a limerick in standard Beiping dialect, their first dialect that they had almost forgotten.

"When we stayed in town, Cousin Wei always asked us to play 'fight the Japanese,'" said May.

"I still remember the pair of couplets on each side of your front gate," said Wuyin.

"I remember them, too," said May. "On the count of three, let's start at the same time and see who remembers them best."

"Listen to different opinions while maintaining your own, pay attention to detail while looking out for the big picture; remain down-to-earth while nurturing ambition, leave your comfort zone and be ready to face challenges."

The two of them recited the couplet loudly at the same time, while Kiddo laughed and clapped his hands in amusement.

"Meng Heji, here's a question for you," said Wuyin, turning to Kiddo. "Do you remember the couplet on our small red gate?"

Kiddo closed his eyes and thought hard for a while.

May, trying hard not to burst into laughter, gave him a poke and told him: "Stop trying! He was tricking you. There's no couplet on their red gate."

"My parents wanted to put up a couplet, indeed, but it was too late. Anyway, let's get down to business. The head teacher in our grade asked to see me today…"

Just then Huishu and several other students came out of the temple gate.

When Huishu saw them, she came close and sat by May's side. Wuyin then stopped what he was saying.

They exchanged some small talk and then Huishu told Wuyin: "Several people have asked me more than once which one is Zhuang Wuyin, because they have all heard that you speak English to the English teacher and that the algebra teacher even asks for your help to solve some maths problems."

"Doesn't our algebra teacher know his maths problems? What nonsense. It's true, sometimes we discuss problems together, but my algebra teacher has taught me everything I know."

"Brother Wuyin is terrific!" said Kiddo, who had always been a great fan of Wuyin and he again showed his loyalty to his role model. Both girls' eyes sparkled with admiration.

"Good heavens! I can't stand you guys anymore," Wuyin frowned.

"Oh yes, when Yin Dashi's family came to deliver some things to her, my mother asked them to bring some refreshments for me, too. They are from the famous bakery Jiqingxiang. Wait for me while I go and get them." Huishu stood up, smoothed her lemon short-sleeve sweater, and then ran into the temple with light steps.

"The head teacher in our grade asked to see me today to suggest that I should skip the last year of high school and take the college entrance examination during the coming summer vacation."

"Are you going to college soon?" College seemed so far away for May.

"Yes. We all need to grow up. Even Kiddo needs to grow up."

They all sat there in silence.

Several birds landed in a tree nearby and twittered as if greeting each other and reminding each other that it was getting late and they should head for home.

"I need to go now," said Wuyin, standing up.

"But the refreshments!" May reminded Wuyin. "Cousin Huishu wanted to share them with us all."

Wuyin waved his hand to signify no and then walked down the hill with big strides, disappearing into the trees.

The moon, big and round, had risen.

PART II

K unming was still under the shadow of air raids.
Running for shelter from air raids was a regular part of the daily life of Kunming folks, just like eating and sleeping, which took a set amount of time each day. On days when the raids were very frequent, people would rise early, prepare their meals for the whole day, and go out of the city without waiting for the first alarms to go off. They would stay out of town until dusk fell. There were certain periods when the air raids were much less frequent, but the first thought that came into people's heads when they opened their eyes in the morning was always the same question — whether there might be alarms that day. If the enemy fighter planes failed to appear for several days in a row, people would gossip uneasily when they met in the market.

"Do you know why there haven't been any more air raids by the Japanese devils? The enemy fighter planes have been shot down!"

"How many?"

"A dozen."

"What I heard was that it was more than two dozen!"

Once they had exchanged such messages, which could never be proved, they would go on their way, laughing.

The real reason might have been that the Japanese air force had been nursing its strength for a full-scale air raid launched about a week after Dashi's broad-bean-theft incident, having spared the Kunming city folks and spoiled them with several days of peaceful life.

When the air raid siren was on, all the students and staff began to walk toward the suburbs. Most of them were already well trained and experienced runners, judging from the foldable stools they took with them to provide solid seats so they could resume their classes in the suburbs. Two classrooms were soon formed on both slopes of a hill. On one slope Professor Meng Fuzhi from the history department was talking about the Song dynasty (960-1279 AD), while on the other Professor Liang Mingshi from the maths department was talking about number theory.

Meng Fuzhi had already covered the causes of poverty and weakness in the Song dynasty and the famous men and women with lofty ideals in that period of history. Now he was on the development of intellectual ideas, taking Zhou Dunyi's *Diagram of the Supreme Ultimate Explained*[1] as an example. His history class always paid special attention to the development of intellectual ideas in different periods of history.

Liang Mingshi was talking about the first great contributor to number theory — Pierre de Fermat, who shared most of his inspiration about mathematics in letters he wrote to his friends. Number theory was more like a hobby for him. Liang Mingshi himself was a legend, too. When he graduated from his high school in a small town, he was hired to teach mathematics in the same high school. Several years later, he was enrolled, as expected, in the Mathematics Institute at Princeton University. After gaining his degree, he came back to China. He had achieved much in number theory since his return. What he believed was that where there are numbers, there is beauty. He couldn't raise his left hand because of polio that he suffered from as a child, but he had no problem writing with his right hand. The small blackboard set up on a pile of earth was already covered with numbers and symbols.

"Now I'd like to say something about the method of infinite descent — Fermat once mentioned the following theorem in a letter to one of his friends: every prime number in a form '4n + 1' is the square of two, and the form of this sum is unique..." Abstruse words like these tickled the eardrums of the students from the history department.

"According3 to *Diagram of the Supreme Ultimate Explained*, 'only those people imbued with these fine qualities become the most spiritual beings. Human physical form thus is generated and human spirit (神 *shen*) develops knowledge. The stimulation and mutual interaction of the five moral attributes (性 *xing*) – namely, benevolence (仁 *ren*), righteousness (义 *yi*), propriety (礼 *li*), wisdom (知 *zhi*) and trust (信 *xin*) - yield the distinction between good (善 *shan*) and bad (恶 *e*), and thus all human affairs proceed from that.'" Mystical words of philosophy tickled the eardrums of the students from the mathematics department.

The students from the two departments laughed in unison when they heard their professors' sonorous voices mingled with each other.

The emergency siren sounded but the classes continued. No one moved. Then the roar of engines from the enemy fighter planes rumbled overhead but still no one moved. At last, the fighter planes emerged in the air in two dark menacing squares, looming over the students and teachers. The two professors' voices were drowned by the deafening roar of aero engines. Both stopped their classes and signalled their students to look for proper cover.

"Look! Our fighter planes! Our fighter planes are in the air!" The students shouted in excitement. Two Chinese fighter planes were visible in the air, courageously facing the threat of the massed enemy aircraft. On the ground, Chinese antiaircraft guns opened fire. The enemy fighter planes, ignoring such a weak threat, maintained their course and launched an orderly attack, diving and then dropping their bombs on their predetermined targets. The earth shook and vibrated with each explosion.

"The new teaching buildings are on fire!" Several students cried out at the same time at the sight of the dark plumes of smoke rising from the buildings, which had obviously been hit by bombs.

"Youchen! Youchen is in the laboratory!" Fuzhi's heart missed a beat with that sudden realisation. He wished he could run back now to check on Youchen.

"I wonder whether all the people in the buildings have escaped the explosion," muttered Liang Mingshi. They had no other option but to wait.

Youchen had agreed to stop guarding the laboratory during the air raids and join the others to go and hide, but he just couldn't bear thinking about leaving behind the two newly purchased expensive instruments — a spectroscope and a wall-mounted ammeter. Besides, none of the enemy planes had arrived after several alarms, which further confirmed his assertion that hiding out was a genuine waste of time, which he'd rather spend reading and thinking in such rare quietness. Anyway, guarding the laboratory was really just a side issue.

He was reading a newly arrived physics journal published by Cambridge University Press in the spring of 1938. Most of the instruments had been packed into cabinets, only the spectroscope and the ammeter were placed at the foot of a wall. The ammeter should have been hung on the wall, as its name indicated, but Youchen was worried that it might be accidentally damaged and asked for it to be disassembled and for the components to be put into a special case every time they finished an experiment. The key part of the spectroscope was its diffraction grating, a part half the size of a regular book, which diffracted light and separated colours to reveal the source light's 'true colours'. Youchen reminded his students on several occasions: "It is very hard to see through nature to the properties of matter and energy. It requires generation upon generation of accumulated knowledge and exploration for us to get one step closer to the truth." Those instruments were concrete accumulations. The diffraction grating was small and easy to carry but Youchen was concerned about the possibility of unexpected damage. Besides, there were still other instruments which needed to be taken care of. This was another reason he decided to stay behind and continue his guard duty.

It was very quiet all around. He unbuttoned his gown and buried his nose in his reading, deaf to the rumbling noises in the distance. He didn't realise that the enemy fighter planes had arrived until the roaring noises hovered overhead.

A red flash of light came on the heels of an enormous explosion which shook the building and Youchen felt like the ground had been punched by a gigantic fist. He saw rows of houses collapsing and the tinplate roofs falling with metallic clanking sounds.

"That was close!" he thought. Instinctively, he took out the diffraction grating, put it under his gown against his chest and covered the ammeter with the cotton-padded quilt kept for those on night watch before heading for the door. The aircraft was flying so low that he felt it had targeted him. He could see the pilot grinning at him. Then there was another enormous explosion and he blacked out.

When Youchen came to, he found he was still standing on the same spot, intact. He didn't fall over because he couldn't with the lower half of his body buried in the earth from the explosion. He was still holding the diffraction grating which was also intact. Although the alarm hadn't been lifted yet, people were returning to the campus to assist in the rescue effort.

When they found Professor Zhuang Youchen, he was standing still like a statue in the debris, with tears running down his dust-coated cheeks like two tiny streams. Professor Zhuang was crying! People thought they might have been tears of terror but then they realised they were tears of happiness and relief because the diffraction grating was still intact.

"G... g..." he muttered, unable to complete even a single word.

The lower part of his body was trapped tight in the earth. He felt the crushing weight from all directions. The earth had been compacted by the pressure and was hard to remove, quite unlike the layer of earth on May from the explosion by the river when they were hiding from the bombing.

Afraid of hurting Youchen, people had to remove the earth around him slowly, alternately using shovels and their hands.

Meng Fuzhi and Liang Mingshi came with big, fast strides. Fuzhi called Youchen by name in his ear. Youchen opened his eyes, took out the diffraction grating and gave it to Fuzhi, mumbling something like "there, there".

"Jiang Fang is hurt! Professor Jiang Fang was hurt in the explosion!" someone cried out loud, running all the way from the school gate. On hearing the cries, Fuzhi put the diffraction grating in Mingshi's hands and ran toward the gate. Mingshi cried out behind Fuzhi, holding the diffraction grating: "Whether we live or perish, we are together!"

A few people gathered around the school gate. Jiang Fang was lying down on the ground, his head leaning against a wall with his eyes closed. His face was stained with blood, so was his gown. Fuzhi took several quick steps to hurry to Jiang Fang's side.

"Jiang Fang! Jiang Fang! Tell me where it hurts!" Fuzhi asked.

Jiang Fang didn't answer. Blood trickled down his cheeks.

"Get him to the hospital! Now!" yelled Fuzhi. He turned to a student and sent him to fetch the only school car at the president's office. He took out his big handkerchief and bandaged Jiang Fang's head clumsily. It was just moments before the handkerchief bandage was soaked in blood. Jiang Fang remained unconscious.

"No more delay!" said Fuzhi. At his words, several students who had gathered around him hurried to put Jiang Fang on one of their backs.

"Where should we go, Professor Meng?" one asked.

The closest clinic was on Justice road, so they all ran toward the city. Before they reached the main west city gate, Jiang Fang came to.

"What has happened? Who is carrying me?" he asked.

"You have come to!" Fuzhi was elated but he walked even faster.

The students answered Jiang Fang's questions: "Professor Jiang, you have been hurt in an explosion. We are now taking you to hospital."

When Jiang Fang saw Fuzhi running alongside, he got his answer: "It's you, Meng Fuzhi! Guys, put me down now! I'm not going to die. How can I be killed by a bomb? I'm not going to die!"

Sensing the strength in Jiang Fang's voice, Fuzhi signalled the students to put Jiang Fang down, while he was busy panting.

Jiang Fang squinted through the blood stains at Fuzhi: "You don't need to run alongside."

The car had arrived. Two students helped Jiang Fang to get in and took him to the hospital. Fuzhi went back to Youchen.

The earth burying Youchen had almost been removed. He was steadying himself by holding the arms of a chair in front of him since his feet were still planted in the earth. President Qin was standing by his side and trying to persuade him to sit down: "It would be better if you sit down."

President Qin had hardly finished his sentence when Youchen lost his strength and balance, and fell to the ground at his feet with a thump, literally. Several people hurried to hold him up. By combined efforts of supporting and pulling, Youchen's feet were released from the earth. They had to cut loose the lower rim of his gown stuck in the earth. When Youchen was settled on a stretcher which had been stationed properly on the site for a long time, he kept muttering "I... I..." He wanted to tell those around him that he was not hurt, but he couldn't finish his sentence.

Mingshi, holding the diffraction grating tight, couldn't resist teasing Youchen: "See how much more developed we are? For us who teach maths, we don't need gadgets of yours like this." But then he hurriedly added: "Don't worry about it. I have promised I'll live or perish with it!"

From the suppressed murmurs one could figure out how lucky Youchen had been. When the roof collapsed, he had just stepped out of the building; the wall that collapsed on him was made of adobe rather than hard bricks. Youchen was then carried away on the stretcher.

Fuzhi told President Qin Xunheng what had happened to Jiang Fang, thinking Jiang might have had a few injuries. Not too much to worry about, though. Qin Xunheng nodded. He asked the director of the general affairs office to set aside a room in the library to store the equipment from the physics laboratory. Liang Mingshi solemnly put down the diffraction grating in the room.

As people cleared away the debris and carefully took out the laboratory equipment, it turned out that the laboratory had not been hit by the bomb, but rather had collapsed due to the quake caused by the explosion of a nearby bomb. Seeing the dying flames on the rows of houses, people heaved a sigh of relief.

"We found two bodies. They're probably dead," said someone who had come to report from the fire site. President Qin and Fuzhi hurried to the site to see two half-burnt bodies lying on the lawn. Their faces, which might have been young and handsome, were not burnt, though they were obscured, mainly because they had tried to escape from the windows when the bomb had landed. Some students confirmed the identity of the two victims. They were students from the chemistry department who had walked with their group from Changsha to Kunming. Like millions of youngsters, they were full of passion, brains and ambition, ready to dedicate themselves to their people and their motherland. Alas! They had never expected to be reduced to ghosts in a split second, wandering in a strange land, longing for their homes thousands of miles away!

Clouds of white smoke from the burnt-out buildings hung over these people. Were they trying to stifle everything? Everyone - Qin Xunheng, Meng Fuzhi, Liang Mingshi and others - stood in solemn silence, letting the smoke engulf them.

Besides the two casualties, three were seriously injured and a dozen were wounded in the main school district. It was good news that Youchen was not injured at all, and Jiang Fang's wound was not serious. When the enemy fighter planes launched their attacks, Jiang Fang was near the school gate, trying to go through the rows of houses to hide out during the air raid in the grove behind the hill, like everyone else. He was distracted by the dirt road in front of the school gate. The khaki road, lined with fresh red earth, which formed a beautiful decoration like embroidery, looked so fascinating that he wondered where the road led and forgot completely that he had been running from the air raid. He stared at the road, lost in thought, until the enemy fighter planes appeared. Suddenly, thousands of pieces of bricks and tiles, a deadly shower, rained down on him. After a small thump on his head, he felt the shock and then lost consciousness. Fortunately, it wasn't a serious wound and only needed a couple of stitches in the clinic.

When he talked to Fuzhi later about his encounter, the latter mused: "Although the way ahead is long, I shall search high and low."

Jiang Fang responded quite seriously: "Indeed."

Depression had haunted the city for a while after the big air raid. But a little bit later, the same air raid alarm brought a happy encounter for one person, namely, Tantai Xuan.

That day when the alarm went off, Tantai Xuan went with several classmates heading for the hiding place behind the hill. They ran into Earl and Wu Jiaxin on their way up the hill. Xuan declared she wouldn't stay with Earl, Meng Liji, since Earl always made people around her depressed with her gloomy pessimism; Earl returned the favour by refusing to stay with Xuan, blaming her for her casual attitude toward things as if nothing mattered, which was more depressing. In the end, Earl and her friends went over to the other side of the hill, while Xuan and her friends stayed on the near side of the hill.

Xuan's hiding place was very close to the new school buildings. Not many planes came that day, so not many bombs were dropped. One bomb landed only metres away from their spot. They should have been killed with a bomb exploding so close by but the bomb didn't go off and the earth it displaced was quite limited. Xuan and her friends ended up intact and clean. After the bombardment, when Xuan sprang up from the ground, she was as gorgeous as when she had left in the morning. Her friends were in a similar condition, too.

"Oh my god! We are so lucky! I don't know who we are indebted to for that," Xuan said.

"Of course, we owe our good luck to Tantai Xuan!" a male student answered. "The plane was so close to the ground that the pilot must have spotted you."

"So he dropped the bomb?" teased Xuan.

"Seriously, it would be marvellous if we had had an antiaircraft machine gun. I would certainly have shot the Japanese invaders down and beaten them all!"

That afternoon, Xuan first went to the theatre for a movie with her classmates. It was an imported movie. The interpreter was interpreting on the stage. His interpretation in Yunnan dialect added a local flavour to the movie as if the story in the movie had once happened here in Yunnan.

Later in the evening, they held a gathering at Guansheng Yuan, the trendiest place in Kunming for a drink and some relaxation. Its huge French windows and white gauze drapery along with a cup of hot coffee or hot chocolate were almost enough to make one forget there was a war going on. In the evenings when night fell, each table would enjoy a red glass cup containing mini candles of all colours. The iridescent candle light, echoing the dim light of the place, created a gentle ambience. It cost more than having a bowl of rice noodles or a cup of tea in a teahouse, but the price was still acceptable. Xuan and her friends loved the place and had become regular patrons. She always took some western-style desserts and snacks back to the Yan residence for Suchu and Hezhu. Xuan and Yingshu, Yan Liangzu's son, had done many things together since Xuan had moved to the Yan residence to share the same roof as Yingshu, and Yingshu would join her at such gatherings from time to time, too. So, the participants of the gathering that evening included not only those who had narrowly escaped death, but also Yingshu.

Eight people were sitting around a table where snacks like shelled peanuts and pumpkin seeds were already laid out. What caught people's eye was a plateful of cakes decorated with beautiful cream. Each one had a drink in front of them. One person raised their drink and said: "As the old saying goes, those who survive a disaster will have more blessings in the future. We are all blessed survivors. It would be so nice if more on the campus could share the same good luck as ours."

Another continued: "We are survivors today, but who knows what will become of us tomorrow."

Xuan said: "Tomorrow? Tomorrow I want 95 out of 100 for my English test, and 90 for Yan Yingshu for his European history."

She pointed at someone at the table and said: "And 80 for your statistics."

The latter protested: "Why should I have such a low score?"

"Because you are preoccupied with something else, although I don't know what it is," answered Xuan.

One started humming *'The Exile Trilogy'*, a group of patriotic songs universally popular among Chinese: *"We left Mount Changbaishan and the Black Dragon river in tears, and we trudged along the Yellow river and Yangtze river in exile! In exile! Like fugitives! Like fugitives!"* The singer's voice was sad and sweet.

"We ran all the way to Kunming, and still we need to carry on running! I will fight with a real weapon when I graduate!" one claimed.

"We need to build our own planes," suggested the one from the aeronautics department. "Without learning advanced technology, we are doomed to be beaten."

Their conversation was interrupted by footsteps as several foreigners entered. It used to be a regular thing to see foreigners in Kunming because of the Yunnan-Vietnam railway. Now that the Yunnan-Burma road was open to traffic, more foreigners were coming to Kunming. A well-built young man with blonde hair in the group eyed Xuan's group and then froze in front of the gate with a look of shocked surprise on his face.

"Are we in for a duel? That man is quite rude to stare at you like that!" whispered someone in Xuan's group in a cavalier manner. Xuan was studying the piece of cake in front of her and was ready to take a big bite. When she raised her head at her friend's whisper, her eyes met the eyes of the blonde young man.

"Paul McAllen!" she let out a cry of happiness. Putting her fork down, she stood up.

"Tantai Xuan! I knew it was you!" Paul cried back, as excited as she was. He picked up his pace and planted himself in front of Xuan in seconds, ready to give Xuan a hug, but was stopped in his tracks when Xuan said, laughing: "We are in China. We need to switch to Chinese."

"Hah! Running into an old friend in a strange land!" commented one of Xuan's friends. "Do you know that guy, Yan Yingshu?"

Yingshu shook his head.

Xuan introduced Paul to her friends: "This is Paul McAllen." She then turned to the man in question: "And what are you doing now?"

"Vice-consul of the US Consulate in Kunming. I came to Kunming one month ago but spent four weeks in Chongqing first. My plan was to start looking for you next week because I thought it might take me at least a week to find you."

"This is exactly a case of 'Wearing out iron shoes seeking in vain, then finding what you've been looking for with the least pain'," said Xuan.

"Iron shoes?" Paul was confused.

Xuan then explained what the saying meant to Paul in English. All his fellow Americans pricked up their ears to listen to her explanation. When she finished, they were all amazed at the rich imagination of the Chinese people.

The Americans occupied another table because they wanted to have some alcoholic drinks. Paul spent some time with Xuan first, sitting by her side.

One year after his return to the US from Beiping, he was sent back to China. Xuan and her friends talked about the latest bombardment and the casualties and wounds of the students and the professors. All agreed that with the damage done to one of the two Chinese fighter planes, it would be even tougher to retaliate.

Paul said he had experienced many air raids in Chongqing and night bombardments, too. Many tunnels had been built to serve as air raid shelters in such a hilly city like Chongqing. But he refused to go down any of the tunnels, which were more terrifying than the air raids for him. Anyway, he concluded that China needed its own air force. Some American pilots had already seen the key to the problem. One senior pilot was working as a private coach helping to train pilots for the Chinese air force.

Although Paul's tone was friendly, the students still felt hurt at the realisation that the building of the Chinese air force depended on favours from the US. Yingshu asked Paul about the American government's position. Paul said his government's policy on this issue was, of course, based on US interests, but most American citizens were sympathetic toward China. Some Americans were indifferent about world affairs and ignorant about the war in Asia. But those who knew about the war between China and Japan all thought how irrational the Japanese government was since it was so obvious which side was the invader and which was the invaded.

The song 'Home, Sweet Home' could be heard coming from the table of Americans. The Chinese students at this table began to sing along. Only Yingshu and two others were local, all the rest were far from their hometowns. The cosiness of home for them all was reduced to just a haunting memory. When they sang, their eyes became wet with sadness invading their hearts.

Outside the French windows, the moon shone brightly. Looking through the gauze curtains, one could see only a world full of moonlight with few pedestrians visible on the street.

A couple of waiters rushed to different tables, informing all the customers they had to close for the moment because the first air raid alarm had already been sounded.

"Air raid alarm? At night?" This was a first for Kunming! All the lights went out, and people stood up. Some even blew out the mini candles on their tables.

"We still have time. The enemy fighter planes haven't arrived yet," someone said. At these words, two candles were lit again. Xuan's friends began to scramble to pay for the bill, and Xuan paid for the rest of the part they couldn't cover. Paul wanted to accompany Xuan back, and Xuan asked Yingshu to take a ride with her. Yingshu hesitated for a second before agreeing.

The street was shrouded in stifling silence. Three red beacons had been put up on top of Wuhuashan. The light bulbs inside the beacons blazed, turning the beacons into three giant drops of blood. Most of the cityfolk chose to hide in their homes, putting their fate in the hands of destiny. Paul drove slowly and quietly.

Xuan sighed: "I wonder what my parents and my brother are doing right now. Does Chongqing have frequent night attacks?"

Before Paul could answer, the emergency siren shattered the serene moonlight into a million shards.

The lights in the three red beacons went out. Paul asked Yingshu: "Where should we go? Back to your home or out of the city?"

Yingshu turned to Xuan. When Suchu and his mother Hezhu had moved to Anning county, Xuan had stayed in her dormitory much more often than at the Yan residence.

Xuan said: "How about we pay a visit to the Grand-View Pavilion? The moon is so nice tonight."

Paul didn't know the location, so Yingshu gave him directions. They went out of the city by the minor west city gate and drove along the Zhuantang road. A couple of wooden boats were anchored along the narrow river.

"Do you still remember how we took Wei Feng out of Beiping the summer before last?" Paul asked. "And tonight, again we are getting out of the city to hide out during the air raid."

Xuan said: "I'm not hiding from the air raid. What we are doing is a night trip. I haven't heard anything from Wei Feng since then. It's possible that

Uncle Fuzhi and Aunt Bichu have heard from him, but they haven't told me anything anyway."

They soon arrived at Grand-View Pavilion. When they got out of the car and walked to the back of the pavilion, they were amazed at the expanse of blue rippling with silver specks of moonlight presented in front of them. The lake was the finest of mirrors, not showing exactly what was above, but converting it into a blazing, glazed image. All three of them marvelled at the sight.

Paul cried: "This is the Dianchi lake!" And he saluted Yingshu for his local knowledge of such a wonder.

Yingshu was very happy and said that it was the first time he had seen such a beautiful view of the lake.

"There's another amazing thing nearby," Xuan added.

She was referring to the pair of couplets on the pavilion which had 90 characters on each scroll and were known as the longest couplets in the world.

The scrolls with the couplets were right behind them, inscribed on each side of the entrance to the pavilion. The weathered paint had peeled off in various places and the inscriptions were illegible in the moonlight.

Xuan assured the two gentlemen: "No worries. I can recite them for you."

She picked up a bough from the ground, using it as an improvised pointer, and began to recite, pointing at the characters as she went:

"The 500-li Dianchi is rushing into sight and so exhilarated am
I to unbutton my coat and headdress, enjoying the vast expanse
of water! Look around: Jinmashan (Mount Jinma) like a
galloping horse in the east, Bijishan (Mount Biji) resembling a
flying phoenix in the west, Hongshan (Mount Hong) rolling up
and down like a dragon in the north and Mount Crane
shrouded in the transient white clouds in the south. I would
have felt much regret if I hadn't seen the fragrant rice paddies
and long sandy beaches all around, lotus flowers in full bloom
in summer, and hanging willow branches green with new
sprouts in spring."[2]

Once she had finished reciting the couplet on the first scroll, Xuan was ready to move on to the second one when

Paul stopped her: "Please explain that part for me first. My mind is going to explode with so much new information."

So, Xuan gave a brief account of the first scroll and then explained in detail the historical allusions in the second scroll appearing in the verses:

"Terraced warships teemed with Han soldiers, iron monuments built in memory of the Tang's victories, territories settled by the first Song emperor with a jade axe and the whole land conquered by the Yuan tribesmen coming on an expedition on sheepskin rafts".

Yingshu listened attentively, admiring Xuan for her thorough understanding of these allusions while feeling ashamed of himself. As a student from the history department, he only had a very general knowledge about these facts. Xuan continued, as if reading Yingshu's mind: "I visited this place once with my Uncle Fuzhi and his family. He spent half an hour explaining the couplet to all of us kids. The Yuan tribesmen and their sheepskin rafts left a very deep impression on me. When Kublai Khan, the fifth Khan of the Mongol empire and the founding emperor of the Yuan dynasty, was blocked on his expedition by Jinsha Jiang (Gold Sand river), he ordered his men to make rafts by blowing up the hides of goats and buffaloes to make rafts to cross the river. He then beat the Dali kingdom and unified Yunnan province. Uncle Fuzhi said Kublai Khan's route is still of military significance. That's the only thing I can remember now. Maybe I'm wrong because I have a poor sense of geography. Anyway, the route through Southwest China is strategically important. If we lose the provinces in Southwest China, Shanghai or Nanjing would be doomed, too. He then asked us kids to remember this couplet. You two guess. Who remembered it first?"

"You did?" guessed Yingshu.

"Nope! You are wrong. It was May," said Xuan. "May is my younger cousin," she explained to Paul.

"I have met her before," answered Paul. "When I went to see you off before you left Beiping, three kids popped their heads into your room, and May was in the middle."

"You have a memory like an elephant!" said Xuan.

Before the three adorable heads popped up, there was something else. But Paul failed to recollect that fragment of his memory.

Sitting on the stone steps facing Dianchi lake, the three almost forgot about the air raid. Some people passed them, and one said curiously: "A foreigner? Looks like foreigners need to hide from the air raids, too!"

Paul laughed and answered: "Foreigners are human beings, too. We are

98

not bomb-proof." He turned to Xuan again: "That reminds me of my meeting with Mrs Zhuang and her daughter Zhuang Wucai at the home of the British Consul. I asked her for Professor Meng's address, so I could track you down."

The mother and daughter were there to accept the toys of the eight-year-old daughter of an English engineer who had participated in the construction of the Yunnan-Burma road. The family had spent half a year in Kunming. Unfortunately, their young daughter had died of meningitis the previous month. The grieving parents had decided to give all of their daughter's toy collection to Wucai before they left for England.

"There are many dolls in her collection. Some are in a sitting position, some standing. All look gorgeous. I thought this collection would be perfect for you, but the couple insisted that their daughter's collection go to a foreigner's child in Kunming."

"Wucai is half a foreigner. That almost counts. But I am no longer a child. I don't know when I can see those little old friends of mine again," sighed Xuan.

Paul's heart fluttered at the soft sigh. The moonlight had erected a gossamer over Xuan, dimming her features. Paul laughed suddenly: "Every time I look at you, I always feel you share so many similarities with my western culture. But now you look completely Chinese — an adorable Chinese."

"If we dig into history, my family name, Tantai, evolved from our minority ancestors," Xuan said. "My grandfather was from Sichuan province, a section of Southwest China which is populated by many minorities, hence the nickname 'the land of barbarians', and you, an American, are indeed a barbarian," said Xuan, giggling uncontrollably.

"My grandparents are both Irish. My parents are missionaries. They stayed in Kunming for some time, near Wenlin street. When my mother was pregnant with me, they decided to go back to America. They talked about Dianchi lake to me and I felt a kind of closeness to the lake. Your home lake," Paul explained seriously, feeling another kind of closeness to the girl next to him by the lakeside. Xuan turned to look at Paul.

There were many coincidences and mysteries which defied reasonable explanation, just like the gut feeling she used to have that Paul might be related to China in one way or another. But it had never occurred to her before that his parents had once been based in Kunming. She fell silent for a while before saying: "So, Kunming might count as your hometown."

"Now I do feel that way. But before I met you this evening, it had never occurred to me at all." Paul mused: "We have been preoccupied by the things on our plates now and planning for the future instead of looking backward."

A small boat approached them and moored at the stone steps. The woman rowing the boat raised her voice and asked: "Do you want to take a boat tour around the lake?"

Xuan sprang to her feet: "Fine, fine!" and got ready to step into the boat. Paul gave her his arm.

At the sight of the two, Yingshu fell into a sulk for being turned into a third wheel between Paul and Xuan. He said: "Cousin Xuan, please hold on for a moment. We came here to hide from the air raid, not for a tour. Now it seems that the enemy fighter planes aren't coming, let's go back." Once he had finished speaking, he stood up, dusted himself off and left.

Xuan had to take back her foot. Knowing what a serious guy Yingshu was, she decided not to push him. She then said again: "Fine, fine!" and took Paul's arm to keep her balance.

"Do you want to take the boat or not?" asked the woman, trying to confirm what Xuan actually meant by "fine".

"We are not taking the boat tour. It's too late, and we should go back home," answered Xuan.

"Where the two of you stay, that's home," said the woman. When she found Xuan didn't respond, she continued: "Well, I'm heading home, too."

Xuan was quiet on the outside, but she was boiling on the inside at the woman's words. Looking at Paul, she felt he might not have understood what the woman meant. The two watched the woman turn the boat around by pushing the step with her oar and then drift off into the vast expanse of misty, rolling water.

The two picked up their pace and caught up with Yingshu. On the way back, no one talked. Few pedestrians were on the street. When they arrived at the minor west city gate, they were told that the alarm had been lifted.

PART III

Yan Yingshu declined Paul's offer to drive him back home when Xuan got out and trotted back home alone. The light at the second gate leading to the main courtyard was off. Yingshu guessed it might have been because of the air raid alarm. He asked the guards on night patrol in the courtyard: "Is he home?" One answered the commander didn't go and hide, and had been at home since the afternoon. Yingshu wanted to go and see his father but ended up returning to his own room when he reached the foot of the staircase leading to his father's section. Although he didn't talk much to his father, he was very proud of the fact that his father was leading an army to fight the Japanese invaders, and he thought about his father a lot. On the wall in front of his desk hung a giant picture of his father in uniform, and a small picture of Suchu and his mother Hezhu. Both women wore *qipaos* and looked very much like two sisters. He listlessly cleaned his face with the water in the basin and lay down in bed, his mind tossing and turning restlessly.

Look at Xuan! She was old friends with a foreigner! Why didn't Aunt Jiangchu do something? It was a good thing that she didn't come so often during our mothers' absence, or Huishu would have been under her bad influence. Huishu probably was closer to her than to me! What was the point of thinking about this mess? Dad had been resting for several months since returning from Hubei province. It was kind that they said he was allowing his troops to recuperate, but I knew it was because he had lost the battle. What would they do to him? Everyone knew victory and failure were

101

common for a general. What mattered most was to drive the Japanese invaders out of the country! Well, we definitely can't drive them out tonight! I will just go to sleep!

Yingshu was woken up by a commotion from the courtyard.

"The ladies have returned!" said the guards, by way of greeting. People were rushing out of the darkness from everywhere. The lights in the corridors were turned on, which were dimmer than the moonlight. Yingshu sat up to see Hezhu coming into his room.

"Mum, you're back! Why did you come into town at such a late hour?"

Hezhu put her hands around her son and forced a smile: "We heard the alarm when we were outside the city, so we waited for a while. And here we are."

"What are you home for?"

"Your father sent for us, saying something has happened — it must be something bad."

"Could it be that he'll leave again?"

"It doesn't look like it."

Suddenly the stairs creaked as if someone was tumbling downstairs.

"Looks like he is already drunk — you have to go to school tomorrow. Just go back to sleep. Leave this to me," instructed Hezhu, and went out of Yingshu's room.

"Set up the mahjong table!" bellowed Liangzu in the garden. The lights in the reception hall were turned on immediately. A blanket was laid out on that old-fashioned, square, eight-seater table; a set of mahjong tiles were laid out on the table. Although the masters and servants in the Yan residence were quite accustomed to wild drinking and gambling, no one had a clue what all the midnight commotion was about. Was it just for a midnight mahjong game? Yingshu, though confounded, got dressed and went out of his room. When he turned on the light in his room, he immediately heard Yan Liangzu shouting: "Yan Yingshu! Get out of your room, now!"

Yingshu hurried out of his room and went into the reception hall. Yan Liangzu's short white cotton gown and trousers were crumpled like old cleaning rags, but his face looked calm. Suchu was in her regular indanthrene blue cotton *qipao*. Her bun was a little bit out of place since she hadn't had time to go back to her room to tidy herself up. She sat down obediently at Liangzu's bellowing.

"Dad, dearest Mum," greeted Yingshu. It was odd to realise that any mother labelled 'dearest' was probably not.

Liangzu ordered Yingshu and his adjutant to sit down at the table while he shuffled the tiles in an exaggerated manner.

"Dad, what has happened?" Yingshu delivered his question in a delicately controlled tone.

"Just play!" Liangzu commanded sternly, and then snarled at the guards: "Bring me some booze!"

The other three at the table began to take their tiles. Two rounds of games were finished with watchful trembling as if daggers were hanging over their heads. Hezhu reappeared in her regular outfit which was a mixture of Han majority and Yi minority style without wearing most of her jewellery like she did at Suchu's birthday dinner. But she kept the diamond ring on her ring finger.

Liangzu's adjutant rose at the sight of Hezhu and gave his seat to her. The four played more rounds in silence when Liangzu shuffled all his tiles toward the centre of the table and shouted: "I don't want to play anymore!"

No one dared to respond.

A moment later, Hezhu began: "What's bothering you? Spit it out now and give us a clue. Yingshu has to go to school tomorrow."

"Alright! Listen up!" Liangzu forced out each word. "I have been informed today that I have been removed from the position as army commander by the central government."

"What?" asked Hezhu.

"I have been removed from my position because I lost a battle. Some have even suggested that I be sentenced to death. It is only thanks to Mr Yin, who asked several senior officers to plead for mercy for me, that I have been spared."

"Oh!" All the colour drained out of Suchu's face. She stood up, but then immediately sat down again.

Hezhu, turning her ring unconsciously, the diamond sparkling from time to time, said: "It's a blessing that you don't need to go to war. Our hearts won't be on tenterhooks."

"I won't go to war? I can't fight? I don't care about being demoted, but now? They have removed me from my position! I'm a soldier! Do you know what this means to me if I can't lead my army to fight against the Japanese invaders during such a crisis when my country is being invaded and my countrymen are being butchered?"

"Dad!" Yingshu called his father.

Liangzu didn't stop: "It is crucial to map out strategies miles away from the battlefield. That's what a commander should do. But all battles need men to fight, blood to be shed, and lives to be sacrificed! Victories are traded with my men's blood. So are failures! Do you have any idea how hard we fought at Tai'erzhuang? In the end, I was stationed on the battlefield, shooting with my pistol at the officers or soldiers who dared to fall back! You all know what an expert marksman I am!" He punched the table with his iron fist, bouncing some tiles up and down.

"Commander," Suchu started rather timidly. "Don't hurt yourself. We have time." How she wanted to pat him on the shoulder or give him a tender rock! He had been suffering so much, enduring all this with such a heavy responsibility on his shoulders and pain in his heart. But she wasn't accustomed to show him love or tenderness. She turned to look at Hezhu instead, wishing Hezhu could offer him some comfort.

Hezhu stood up and left the hall but came back in no time with both her hands hidden behind her back. She walked up to Liangzu, took a few steps back in front of him, and swung her arms from her back over her head to the front with her hand waving left and right. She was holding a snake!

"Mum, I don't want to see such a thing right now," protested Yingshu, realising that his mother was ready for some bogus witchcraft which he loathed. The snake held its head high in Hezhu's hand, fluttering its fangs.

"Hah! A drink of snake bile!" Liangzu's attention shifted to the snake.

Hezhu took out a dagger. Aiming at its heart, she slit the snake to the tail and took out a gallbladder the size of a dove's egg.

"It clears heartburn and improves eyesight!" said Liangzu. "And it regulates energy in the liver and relieves internal inflammation."

Hezhu pricked the gallbladder with a toothpick and squeezed the bile into a wine cup, tinting the crystal-clear fluid emerald green. She raised the cup with a smile, muttering some incantations over the dead snake. Holding the cup in her outstretched arms, she walked around the table once and presented the cup to Liangzu: "Commander, please." Then she sat down. Several guards had rushed over to clean up the floor by sprinkling water on the spot and covering it with sawdust and pine needles.

According to gossip, such tricks of Hezhu's were intended to tame Liangzu, but Liangzu didn't fall for such tricks in the sure knowledge that they were only Hezhu's tricks to solidify her position in the Yan residence. For years she had been coming up with new ways of holding his attention, but Liangzu never took them seriously. The sight of the green drink strangely calmed him down. Looking up, his eyes settled on Suchu and his son, and his heart felt relieved to some extent: "I still have them by my side!" he said to himself. Taking up the cup, he heaved a long sigh: "Show your tile!"

The game continued and Liangzu's mind raced: "How did I lose the battle?" He had thought about the battle over and over again. Many factors had contributed to the failure such as the excessive amount of untrained, new recruits, the lack of communication among different units, poorly organised military depots, and insufficient logistics. These were precious lessons learned at the expense of the blood and lives of the officers and soldiers of the Yunnan division. But under his proper command, even the raw recruits could have been utilised to maximise the advantages and minimise the disadvantages. The thing that was really hard to overcome was that he could only direct his men, not his superior commanding officer. His division's mission was to defend the interior lines. He insisted that his division was ready to take the opportunity to go on the offensive rather than remaining passively defensive. He pushed his point of view several times and even went to see the theatre commander in person to ask to be allowed to attack. But the theatre commander told him: "We have been ordered to stay on the defensive by the supreme commander, so we're going to stay on the defensive. If we take the offensive and lose the battle, who will take responsibility for disobeying the supreme commander? Even if we win, which would be the best-case scenario, who would take responsibility for the loss of men? Besides, the supreme headquarters must be in a position to have an overall understanding of the war and to make their decisions based on such observations, which none of us may comprehend. Stay where you are, or you will suffer if you exceed your authority."

"Hah! I will suffer if I exceed my authority!" muttered Liangzu, discarding a tile at random. All four at the table played rather absent-mindedly, and no one had a winning hand so far.

"I will suffer if I exceed my authority!" Those words lingered in Liangzu's mind. "That can also count as a virtue! If Fuzhi were here, he would come up with a convincing explanation. But the truth is that I don't even get the chance to suffer now!" He felt as if he was back on the battlefield, standing on the last hill, ordering his men to roll rocks and tree trunks downhill at the enemy, who were bowled over when hit. Even as an ordinary man, I had the responsibility to defend my country. And I was not just a man. I was a soldier!

The image of a soldier rose in his mind. He dimly felt his removal from his position might be connected to his secretary Qin Yuan, a capable officer and a man of integrity, a communist party member. Liangzu's trust in him might have brought about the loss of trust in him by his superior officers.

"Is that the reason? Is it?" Liangzu asked himself, reluctant to pursue this question further.

He suddenly rose from his seat. Having paced around the room twice, ignoring the sawdust and twigs on the ground, he stopped: "I want to make this clear. Huishu is not home and remember to tell her this," he pointed at Suchu. "I, Yan Liangzu, will no longer be a hero though I have been one for decades. Win or lose, my determination to defend my country and fight against the Japanese invaders stays the same, right here as it has always been!" he declared, punching his chest with his fist, as he cast his eyes up to the sky and sighed deeply.

Both Suchu and Hezhu stood up. Yingshu walked to his father's side, trying to come up with something to comfort him, but ended up in silence.

Liangzu turned to Yingshu: "I think you should quit history. What's the use of studying history? History is all made up!"

Yingshu answered: "History might be made up, but there's still truth in it. Uncle Fuzhi has written a book on this subject."

"I'm sure the history Meng Fuzhi writes is true because even death wouldn't be able to stop him telling the truth!" He turned around at these words and went upstairs to his room, his footsteps strong and steady.

Hezhu, taking the cup of bile drink, tagged along, telling Yingshu as she walked: "Go back to your room and get some sleep. You've got to go to school."

Suchu followed Hezhu and hesitated at the foot of the stairs.

"Suchu, you come upstairs, too," Liangzu called, pausing at the top of the stairs.

Suchu was taken by surprise at Liangzu's call. She gathered her thoughts and prepared to go upstairs. But before she started, she heard Hezhu: "Milady hasn't had a chance to clean up since we came back. Let her go and get some rest."

Liangzu didn't say anything. What Suchu cared about was Liangzu's safety and health. She could let go of anything except that, so she just went back to her room as Hezhu wished.

Liangzu was already lying in bed when Hehzu came into the room. The small table in front of the window was in a mess from his drinking all afternoon. At such a sight, Hezhu would surely have scolded the guards for such a mess in the past but that day she began to clean it herself.

When she was done cleaning, she sat by the bedside: "Now you don't have many things to attend to, how about staying with us in Anning for a while? You haven't spent much time there."

"I'm thinking of going back to Dali to sort things out in my mind and see what I can do."

"Let's go back to Dali!" said Hezhu merrily, holding Liangzu by the hand. Dali was their birthplace which would surely awaken many memories.

When Liangzu was a teenager, he used to go to work for the villagers with his widowed mother at the village where Hezhu's family lived. One day when Liangzu passed the giant eucalyptus tree outside the border of the village, he spotted a thin figure crying by the tree.

"Hey! Why are you crying?" asked Liangzu, sitting beside the girl. But someone called from the village and she dried her tears with the back of her hand and ran away.

After meeting each other at the same spot several more times, they got to know each other. Liangzu learned that Hezhu's family were scorpion breeders and were quite well off. That explained why she had more silver headwear and other decorative items than an average village girl of her age. Still, she cried a lot. She said she was sad because she was not her parents' child. People in the village told her she was adopted. Her foster parents found her in the wild.

"How do you know you were not born by your parents?"

"My mum and dad have always been kind to me and never shown any disdain toward me, but look, I am really adopted," she showed him her little toe sticking out of her straw sandals. "See? The nail on this little toe is divided in the middle. I am the only person with such a toenail in my family."

Liangzu checked his own toes and found that none of them had a divided nail like that. He knew about the legend dating back to the beginning of the Ming dynasty regarding Zhu Yuanzhang, the founding emperor, who enforced a massive displacement of the population from the heavily populated province of Shanxi to the fallow lands in northern and central China. People who were forced to leave their homeland forever decided to cut one of their small toenails as proof of their connection when reunited in the future. A cleft toenail was said to be the hallmark of the Han majority. At that moment, he developed a strong desire to protect this poor girl who was uncertain of her origins.

As years went by, they grew to be more and more intimate. Hezhu could be seen frequently at the shabby home of Liangzu and his mother. She was sweet in word and swift in deed, and busied herself helping with all sorts of things. It was strange that Liangzu's mother disliked Hezhu so much, claiming she had been sent by a demon behind Hezhu's back.

Liangzu once reminded his mother: "Look at these shabby walls, mum. Do you think we have the right to be choosy? We don't even have a decent place to live in. This doesn't even count as a house. It's just a shack with something you can barely call a roof." The widow's motherly instinct told her that Hezhu and her poisonous insects might harm her son, but it turned out that Hezhu not only saved Liangzu once but twice.

Back then, Yunnan province, being poor, remote and backward, was rife with bandits and robbers. Even some officials were robbed and kidnapped on their way to assuming office in Yunnan and never arrived at their offices at all. So all the local chieftains of different villages organised their own armed forces.

Liangzu joined the watchmen of the village. His valour and resourcefulness earned him due respect and he became the head of about a hundred men. Being young and direct, he provoked jealousy. A chief from a minor tribe in the village framed him, saying that he was spying for the bandits. By the time he had led his men to fight off an attack by bandits and they were resting on the outskirts of the village, the chief was already plotting to murder him at the feast to celebrate their victory.

Luckily, the chief's mother needed a scorpion for her medication and asked for a home delivery. When Hezhu passed the reception hall, she overheard the chief saying: "If we don't get rid of Yan Liangzu now, who will he listen to when he grows up? Can we stand by and let him become the chieftain? We have to kill him with that jar of spirit, today!"

Hezhu was shocked at the words. She glanced around and found the jars of spirit prepared to celebrate the victory of Liangzu and his men. A small and delicate jar was put on top of a big one, which was the one containing the poisonous spirit brewed by her family. It contained the venom of 21 different poisonous creatures, but it had a charming name – 'Dream of Spring wine'. Hezhu stayed calm and collected. When she was done with her delivery, she ran all the way to the Yans and told Liangzu's mother the colour of the poisonous spirit and advised her the best way was not to drink at all at the feast. With that piece of information, Liangzu survived the murder attempt.

Since people were determined to plot against him, Liangzu was destined to have a hard time. Once, during a quarrel with the chief, Liangzu wounded him by slashing his cheek with a knife, which infuriated the chief who fired two shots at him. Liangzu was lucky to emerge unscathed, but the chief didn't want to let Liangzu off the hook since he was the one in charge. Liangzu had no alternative but to escape with his men into the depths of the forest and spent several days in the wilderness living like bandits. Speaking of his origins in later life, he would joke that he rose from being an outlaw in the woods.

Several days after Liangzu's escape into the forest, Kunming sent armed forces to suppress the bandits in the area, and Liangzu's men were among their targets. He had no intention of fighting government troops or sending his men to a meaningless death, so he dismissed his men and asked them to go back to their villages while he tried to hide out in the mountains. While he was hiding, he slipped and fell when he was walking along a high cliff. His good luck saved him again because he landed on a cluster of wild bamboo instead of at the foot of the cliff. Once he had calmed down and made some calculations, he decided he was trapped. How could he get up?

"Brother Liangzu?" a girl's voice was coming from the cluster of bamboo. It was Hezhu!

"What are you doing here? Did you fall from the top? Because I did," Liangzu was amazed to see Hezhu in such circumstances.

"I'm hunting insects," said Hezhu, showing him the jar in her hand as if they had run into each other on the street. "Gee! I wouldn't fall!"

Hezhu came down with a rope tied to a big tree by the cliff.

"Have you got enough?"

"Yes, I have."

Hezhu went up the cliff first. Having double-checked the end tied to the tree, she then asked Liangzu to climb up the rope. When Liangzu was back at the top of the cliff, he held Hezhu by the hand and asked: "How can I return the favour?"

Hezhu's face, which had indistinct features, was painted red and green, probably a mixture of dirt and plants, or the juice from some bugs. She didn't answer his question.

But Liangzu's mother was against their marriage out of her stubborn conviction that Liangzu was capable of marrying much better for his intelligence and capability. At her deathbed, she forced Liangzu to take an oath never to take Hezhu as his wife.

Whether as a wife or a concubine, Hezhu was tied to Liangzu. Their feelings were complicated with their love for their shared hometown, their life-and-death struggle, and their memories of shared youth. These feelings were never present with Liangzu's other concubines. Even Liangzu's wife, Suchu, was just an outsider.

The moon began to sink in the west, surrendering to the coming dawn. The row of shadows from the flowers along the corridor became slanted, fading. A confidential message was delivered by Yin Dashi's family to warn Liangzu to stay put, refrain from any personal influence, and wait for the official notice.

PART IV

Life was comparatively tranquil on the hill behind Copper Head village. Life in the temples was simple, but it was full of vigour with the loud readings, vigorous singing and youthful laughter and talk. Even the four heavenly kings looked less ferocious under such an influence and were very likely to greet the children "hello" together one day.

Like other teenagers, May was growing up, physically, psychologically and intellectually. She loved her school, her teachers, her classmates, the hill, the temple, and the deity statues in the temple. She just didn't love one thing — the memorial session.

The first period on Monday mornings in all the schools in China back then was designated as a memorial session dedicated to the late Dr Sun Yat-sen, the first president and founding father of the Republic of China. The memorial activities included raising the national flag, singing the national anthem, reciting the last testament of Dr Sun Yat-sen, and speeches from the headmistress and other people in positions of responsibility. All the students were lined up in long neat rows according to their grades and classes, beginning from the main hall and extending all the way to the steps leading to the garden. For the whole period, students were required to stand to attention. What May disliked most was standing to attention. In fact, it was not that she hated it but that she couldn't stand for such a long time in such a position. Her head became dizzy, her legs shook like jelly and she really wished she had something to lean on. She was ashamed of being so weak and she would always try her best to stand until the end.

During that memorial session when they began to recite the last testament of Dr Sun Yat-sen, May felt queasy:

> "For forty years I have devoted myself to the cause of the
> national revolution with but one end in view, the elevation of
> China to a position of freedom and equality among nations.
> My experiences during the past 40 years have firmly convinced
> me that to attain this goal we must bring about a thorough
> awakening of our own people and ally ourselves in a common
> struggle with those peoples of the world who treat us on the
> basis of equality."[1]

She tried her best not to faint, at least not during the recital of Dr Sun Yat-sen's last testament!

Then Headmistress Zhang Yongqiu gave a speech about building a playground for the school. Since Kunjing school was relocated to the countryside, they hadn't had a decent playground due to the lack of enough area for a playground on the hillside. Physical Education had been reduced to lining up for some exercises in the yard in front of the main hall or the place paved with bricks in front of the temple gate. They later set up two basketball stands to make a basketball court. But with two flag pole pedestals standing in the centre of the court, it was not possible to play any matches. So, students could only practice their shooting.

Headmistress Zhang had launched a fund-raising project among influential figures in the military, government and business in Kunming to build a playground along the slope near Yongfeng temple. The plan was opposed by some, claiming it violated the principle of frugality during wartime. But Headmistress Zhang responded that it was in line with her principle of perfection. For her, all-round educational development involved cultivating students in three principal aspects: moral, intellectual and physical. The younger generation had to be physically strong before they could take on the responsibility of fighting the enemy and rebuilding the country. Besides, the students would also provide the labour to build the playground. An appropriate amount of manual work would benefit their growth. With help from various sources, construction of the playground got under way. The employed villagers had removed a corner of the hill. Headmistress Zhang's speech during that week's memorial session was to motivate the students to remove one basketful of earth each every day from the construction site to the ravine behind Yongfeng temple, including everyone from herself to the middle schoolers and all the way down the age ladder to the fifth and sixth graders. They were given the freedom to choose how to remove the fixed amount of earth.

Headmistress Zhang's resonant voice sounded fainter and fainter for May. Her head spun. Cold sweat oozed up. She could barely stand up, so she leaned against Zhao Yuping who was standing in front of her.

"Are you OK? What's wrong?" Zhao Yuping whispered to May, concerned.

May's face was as white as a sheet. Her eyes were closed tight. Zhao Yuping felt more and more of May's weight against her back.

Yan Bulai went up to them and asked: "Meng Lingji, are you ill?" and asked several students to take May back to her dormitory for some rest.

It was not uncommon for students to faint due to anaemia. Lying down for a while helped them to recover. After lying in bed for a bit, May felt much better, as expected. Headmistress Zhang had finished her speech and reminded those who were in poor health that they didn't need to work.

"I want to," May said to herself.

The same afternoon saw the beginning of the earth-moving activity. For high schoolers, they chose to use a pole to carry on their shoulders one basket at each end of the pole; for middle schoolers, they carried one basket between two of them with a pole. May's class was divided into pairs by their teacher Yan Bulai. The most suitable pairing was a girl and a boy, but teenagers were quite sensitive to boy-girl relationships and a boy and a girl pair would attract monkey noises from their classmates. So, Yan Bulai didn't go with the most suitable arrangement, but with the sensible option of dividing girl and boy students. May was paired up with Zhao Yuping, which made both very happy. Mr Yan told them both several times not to push themselves and carry too much.

The loose earth dug from the hill was red. The deeper the layer of earth, the brighter the colour, as if the earth's intestines had been taken out. Even one load of earth would leave a red colour on the students, who would help dust each other off, laughing and joking. Some students didn't enjoy such work, saying student labour was just a way for the school to save money. They had paid their tuition fees, why should they do extra work? Whether they enjoyed it or not, they had no option but to finish their work. When the sun set in the west, one could see a row of baskets filled with red earth slowly threading their way through the green trees.

When May and Yuping took a basketful of earth away from the construction site, they saw Headmistress Zhang with Dashi tagging along behind, who stuck out her tongue and made a face at May and Yuping. Headmistress Zhang's regular shirt and pencil skirt had been replaced by a blue blouse and a pair of trousers in Chinese style. She went directly to where the baskets were kept, took one and began to shovel earth into it.

"Headmistress!"

"Headmistress Zhang!"

A couple of students shovelling earth called out to her, offering to fill the basket.

Looking around, she said: "We are working at a good pace. It looks like we will be able to have our first sports meeting earlier than we thought." Upon finishing these words, she and Dashi readied themselves to carry the basket. She pulled the rope around the carrying pole toward her end.

Once they had taken several steps, Dashi said: "It's quite light on my end," and tried to pull the rope toward her end of the pole.

"Please don't," said Headmistress Zhang. "You are still not old enough to take so much weight."

They picked up their pace and caught up with the pairs ahead of them. One of the pairs, Wang Dian, the high schooler who had joined in the broad bean hunt the night Yuping was bitten by a snake, was complaining: "What our school is doing now is quite unheard of. How can they treat girls like this? They are young ladies! How can they ask young ladies to do outdoor work like carrying earth? It's a job for servants!" When she turned around to see Headmistress Zhang and Dashi, she hurriedly greeted them: "Headmistress Zhang, you are here working, too!" Instinctively, she put down her basket and tried to take Dashi's carrying pole. Headmistress Zhang waved her hand to stop Wang Dian from taking Dashi's basket and ordered "You all hurry along", and she continued walking with Dashi.

May and Yuping had caught up with them. Only very recently had May learnt that Wang Dian, a distant relative of Dashi, was mainly here to take care of Dashi and her younger brother, Xiaolong, Little Dragon. Having let the headmistress and Dashi pass, Wang Dian took her time to tie the rope around the basket again. As May and Yuping waited for Wang Dian to move on and get out of the way, several more pairs had lined up behind them.

A mischievous one crowed: "Good dogs never get in the way." Wang Dian didn't take offence at all. Somehow, Lü Xiangge popped up in May's mind. How was she now? They stood for a moment until Wang Dian moved on, as did the rest of the queue that had built up.

When the students reached the back of Yongfeng temple, they dumped the earth into the ravine which was almost full of red earth. A man in a torn vest was trying hard to level the loose earth dumped into the ravine, his long hair and the lower part of the torn vest flapping wildly in the air. It was Yan Bulai.

"Mr Yan, are you the only one leveling the earth?" asked Zhang.

It looked as if Yan Bulai hadn't heard Headmistress Zhang at all as he kept shoveling away the lumps of earth. The ones who arrived after May and her classmates all emptied their baskets. Some went into the grove to play hide and seek, some stood enjoying the mountain scenery.

Yan Bulai stopped his shoveling abruptly and howled at the sky:

> "You may see someone roaming the mountains and valleys,
> Draped in mulberry leaves and girded with vines.[2]"

Lowering his head, he continued: "Only those who drink heavily and read Qu Yuan's 'Encountering Sorrow' closely can be categorised as respectable scholars!"

Knowing how wild this teacher of hers had always been, Zhang Yongqiu stood still with the students and continued to listen. But Yan Bulai stopped talking and started to sing loudly instead:

> "Give me a hoe,
> to get rid of the weeds.
> When the weeds are gone,
> The plants will grow."

After several more shovelfuls, he switched to singing *'Fighting the Enemy'*:
"Who does this land of charm and beauty belong to?
It has belonged to the 400 million of us for so long!"
He waved his hand and invited the students to join him. Some did, but not all of them were able to keep the right rhythm. He sighed: "Art education has fallen far, far behind!"

He suddenly turned around to face the students but found Zhang Yongqiu standing behind him, then he asked loudly: "Am I right, headmistress?"

Zhang Yongqiu smiled: "It would be great if Mr Yan could conduct some lectures for the students to teach them to sing and share your insights into poetry."

"Thank you for allocating me the time!" He then pointed at May and her companions: "You all remember to come."

With the combined efforts of two high-school students sent by Zhang Yongqiu, Yan Bulai quickly finished levelling the earth. Then they all returned to their dormitories. May walked with Yuping and Dashi. When they went through the newly levelled playground, the three felt very happy looking at the red extending in all directions. Dashi suggested they have a race. Dashi was the fastest runner of the three, but May didn't quit and tried her best to catch up with Dashi. After a couple of dozen metres, May felt dizzy, but continued to push herself. She failed to notice a lump of rock in her way since she was distracted by her dizziness. She tripped on the rock and fell heavily on all fours. Zhao Yuping ran up behind her and cried out: "Meng Lingji has tripped over!"

May promptly turned over and sat up: "I'm alright! I'm alright!" Then she tried to stand up but fell onto the ground because of the sharp pain from her left kneecap.

Dashi ran back. Standing beside them both, she teased: "Look at the two of you! One was bitten by a snake, and the other is now suffering from a heavy fall. You're taking it in turn to experience tragedies!"

May inspected her blood-stained kneecap embedded with dirt and grit.

After waiting while May remained sitting on the ground, Dashi then asked, as if it had just occurred to her: "Can you still walk?" She walked up and joined Yuping to try and help May stand up. May limped all the way back to Yongquan temple with one of them on either side to help her walk.

They went to the school infirmary first. At the sight of them, the assistant doctor blurted out: "You three, again!" He kept frowning as he cleaned up the wound by rinsing it with hydrogen peroxide solution. Only then did he see how deep the wound was — with an exposed piece of pink flesh. He then dressed and bandaged the wound. When he had finished, May's left knee cap had a big bulge on it like you would see on a wounded soldier.

Huishu arrived at the infirmary. She had been back home for the weekend and didn't return to school until Monday afternoon. Taciturn as she was by nature, she had become even more reserved and quiet the last couple of days. She was rather surprised to see Dashi with May: "Go back to the dormitory. I'll take it from here."

Dashi answered: "It's already finished. Let's go back together."

Huishu and Yuping helped May on each side. May had to hobble along without being able to bend her left knee. She started giggling first at such a funny way of walking. Her giggling set off Yuping and Dashi, who joined her. Huishu didn't laugh. She kept her composure and walked quietly by May's side.

The second they entered the dormitory, Kiddo rushed in like a tornado. He had grown much taller. The senior dorm supervisor teased Kiddo that he was as beautiful as a doll because of his fair skin and delicate features. All the girls in the dormitory liked him and addressed him as Kiddo, which he would always protest vehemently about and correct them: "My name is Meng Heji!"

He stared at May's knee, ignoring all the greetings and teasing.

"Zhao Yuping, go and fetch her meal!" Dashi began to order people about. When she saw Wang Dian standing nearby, she said: "Wang Dian, you go and fetch some hot water for her to wash her feet!"

Huishu stopped her hurriedly: "There's no need for you to do that. Go and have your meal. Meng Heji and I will stay here and take care of May."

Upon these words, Kiddo took May's basin to go and get some water. He first went to the sink where they washed their hands and faces with cold water, but then he changed his mind and headed to the infirmary. The door was open. He saw a thermos bottle on the table. Assuming that all the items in the infirmary were intended for patients, he poured out the hot water in the thermos bottle into the basin and prepared to take it back to May.

"Meng Heji is stealing water!" yelled Kiddo's classmate Yin Xiaolong, Little Dragon, Dashi's younger brother, popping out of nowhere.

Kiddo hated the word "steal" and he hated it even more when he was trying to get warm water to clean the bloodstained feet of his beloved little sister: "I'm not stealing water! This is from the infirmary and it's going to be used to clean up the wound!"

"When I say you are stealing water, you are stealing water!" shouted Little Dragon, mischievously and aggressively. He was always challenging others and looking for trouble. A fight began.

Little Dragon cried: "You are a dirty pig who steals hot water!"

"You are a worthless old Yunnan bank note!"

That sent Little Dragon into a fury. He leaped forward and punched Kiddo on the left shoulder. Kiddo steadied himself, keeping a watchful eye on the basin of hot water.

"Yin Xiaolong, listen up! Today I don't have time to fight with you. Tomorrow we'll have a duel!"

Little Dragon was overjoyed at such a proposal: "That's great! We'll meet at the gate tomorrow afternoon when school is over."

"Deal!" Kiddo didn't want to stay one second longer because he was afraid the hot water might get cold soon. He hurried off.

Putting her feet into the lukewarm water, May felt so comfortable that she gave Kiddo an appreciative smile. Would she still have smiled so sweetly at her younger brother if she had known about his promise to fight for the sake of this basin of lukewarm water?

Last time when Zhao Yuping was bitten by a snake, people were terrified that the snake might have been poisonous. But it turned out that the snake was not poisonous, and the wound healed fast. With the previous experience, this time people didn't worry much since May's wound didn't look as serious as a poisonous snakebite, and they all thought May would recover in no time. Unfortunately, May had a high fever after midnight. She felt pain in every muscle of her body from head to toe, and felt as if her body was as heavy as lead. Lying in her bed, she simply couldn't find a comfortable position to lie still, but she didn't want to wake up others who were close to her. She forced herself to lie still even in her dizziness.

The next morning, a couple of students passing May's spot noticed something was wrong with her: "Meng Lingji's face is so red!" Huishu hurriedly put her hand on May's forehead, which was flushed and burning hot. She rushed to ask for the assistant doctor.

When the assistant doctor arrived, he noticed she had a high fever and that her wounded knee was red and swollen. He mentioned several times that the wound was inflamed, and he suggested that May be sent home so that her family could take care of her.

Then the two dormitory supervisors and Mr Yan arrived. After some discussion, they decided to send May home since the weather was overcast and unsuitable for enemy aircraft to bomb the city, and it would be easier to get proper medical treatment in town. After rushing up and down the hill a couple of times, they managed to find a horse and cart. They parked the cart at the foot of the mountain. May was placed in a chair and carried downhill by two cooks from the canteen.

All the way, May was leaning her head against the back of the chair. The cool wind sobered her mind. Seeing the many people by her side, she wanted to smile, but her tears beat back her smile, rolling uncontrollably down her cheeks.

Huishu comforted her: "You'll recover in no time. I'll keep you company until you get home."

May gathered all her strength and shook her head: "No, you don't need to. I can take care of myself."

The teachers talked for some time and agreed that the junior dormitory supervisor would take May home.

Kiddo had been standing on the edge of the crowd. They all thought he would fight to accompany his sister home, but he just stood still there, although his black eyes were brimming with care and concern.

"Kiddo, are you alright?" May asked him, trying to dry her tears with a corner of her blouse.

"I'm alright, little sister. I'll see you again in two days," Kiddo answered, his tone sure and resolute.

May wanted to say more to Kiddo and asked him to take good care of himself during her absence, but she had run out of strength. A sudden chill came over her and she began to shudder involuntarily.

"Malaria?" Mr Yan asked himself. He hurried up the two cooks carrying the chair to take May downhill to the horse and cart, and then asked Kiddo to go back to his class. The small group accompanying May descended the hill without further delay.

When they went past Yongfeng temple, it was during a break, and many students came up to see what was going on. Yin Dashi, although she was just wearing an ordinary light-blue cotton *qipao*, stood out among her classmates because of her white crotchet knitwear blouse.

She took hold of May's hand and said: "No more shuddering, please. No more shuddering." She paused for a while and then continued: "It is all my fault for coming up with the idea of racing."

Everyone nearby was amazed at Dashi's words and actions.

May answered firmly: "It was my fault. I was careless and tripped over the rock."

Huishu followed May all the way to the foot of the mountain. She helped put a padded quilt in the cart, and helped May to lie down. Out of nowhere, she asked: "Why hasn't Zhuang Wuyin come?"

How true, thought May. Why was brother Wuyin nowhere to be seen? May thought for a while and then realised: "He is preparing for his college entrance examination, so he has stopped coming to school. He's going to skip the last year of high school."

Huishu bowed her head and said nothing.

When the junior dormitory supervisor sat down by May's side, the horse began to trot along the narrow dirt path. May had no strength left to enjoy the scenery as she used to. She passed out when the chill was over.

The cart had squeaked about halfway to its destination when it began to rain. The driver covered May up with his waterproof tarpaulin. The younger dorm supervisor had moved to sit beside the driver, holding an umbrella for the two of them. Both of their shoulders were wet on the outside since the umbrella was not big enough to shelter them both from the rain.

"We need to go faster! Faster, please," she urged the driver.

It was impossible for a cart in such a condition to go faster. Luckily, it didn't rain hard. It soon stopped raining. When they reached town, it was already noon. They went directly to the Ancestral Temple street. The junior dorm supervisor found Bichu alone in the attic at home.

Upon hearing the news, Bichu rushed down from the attic all the way to the cart. She scooped May into her arms. Seeing May breathing, though still in deep slumber because of her high temperature, she released the breath she had been holding in. She decided to send May to the nearby Zedian hospital in the same cart. The junior dorm supervisor left for the school once she had been told what was happening with May.

Bichu packed some clothes for May and left a note for Fuzhi. Sitting in the cart, she wiped May's face with a wet handkerchief. May slowly came to. She felt she had risen from the bottom of a deep valley. Her mother was by her side! That was the most secure and cosy place in the world!

"Mum!" May cooed, her flushed face radiant with feverish heat and passion.

"My poor, poor May!" said Bichu, rocking May in her arms. "I'm taking you to the hospital now. Everything will be alright — everything will be alright!"

Amid her mother's calming murmuring, May started to regain consciousness, feeling as if her body was floating on a tranquil lake. She was woken up abruptly by a booming voice: "You need to deposit 600 yuan first."

May sobered up. She was lying on a bench in the hospital. She looked around and saw her mother at the registration, talking to the registrar sitting behind the window. The booming voice behind the window had just blurted out those words which woke May from her coma. She wanted to answer to those words: "Mum, I can't stay here. We don't have that sort of money. I can't stay!"

Bichu turned to May and waved at her. Then she turned back to talk to the registrar again.

"Here's all the cash I have. I'm only short of about 40 yuan. Please take my daughter in. I'll cover the shortfall later. Please!" She had taken out all the cash the family had. It was 559.87 yuan. Things were so different now from how they were last year. These days she wasn't sure whether she could scrape together 50 yuan in cash.

The person behind the window tossed the cash out and shut the small window in Bichu's face. Bichu was dumbfounded for a few seconds before she decided to look for the president of the hospital.

A man in a white coat passed by. He looked at Bichu and asked: "Are you Mrs Meng?" When Bichu confirmed to him that was the case, he explained that he was Dr Huang, a surgeon at the hospital. He had once asked a friend of his a favour to get some calligraphy done by Professor Meng. Having heard what Bichu had been through, he sighed: "I can't believe that families like yours can't afford treatment in a proper hospital!"

He put May on a stretcher and sent her into a diagnostic room for a check-up. The result came very soon. May had caught acute lymphangitis when bacteria had entered the lymphatic channels through the infected wound on her knee. The huge number of bacteria caused the chills. May was accepted without paying the required deposit.

May was the only patient in the two-bed ward, a privilege arranged by Dr Huang after he had a word with the head of the surgical department. The local people had profound respect for the universities which chose to relocate to Kunming and were very generous in providing help to those who worked in the universities.

Bichu told herself many times: "How nice the Yunnan people are! How nice the Kunming people are!"

When May was settled in her bed, a nurse came to give her a shot of penicillin, a very expensive medicine back then. Seeing May sleeping peacefully, Bichu decided to go back to Ancestral Temple street to raise the money for the deposit. It was not in her nature to be in debt to anyone. After wandering up and down for some time, she remembered she hadn't had her lunch yet. So she bought three pieces of barbequed rice-flour cake from a street stall. Such cake was made from rice flour moulded into different shapes for different methods of cooking. The pie-shaped ones could be enjoyed simply by heating them up on a charcoal fire on a small open stove with dressings brushed on. Bichu felt embarrassed about eating anything as she walked along the street, so she just held on to the packed cakes and kept walking toward home.

Fuzhi was waiting for Bichu at the gate: "I was just going through the motions of 'Leaning against the door and looking for my wife and daughter to appear'. How's May?"

"It's acute lymphangitis. The doctor has given her some treatment. Don't worry about her. The thing is that we don't have enough cash for the deposit."

"The university just handed out 100 yuan. It's our subsidy," said Fuzhi.

Bichu sighed softly with relief at Fuzhi's words. May was lucky, she thought. The two of them sat down on each side of the dining table and began to enjoy the rice cakes for their lunch.

Some time later, Bichu started again: "Now we have the money to cover May's hospital treatment, but we don't have any for the household expenses. I asked my elder sister to sell a gold bracelet and we have managed for some time. How about selling the other one of the pair? I don't know when she will come back to town from Anning county."

"When I was having a meeting with President Qin this morning, I heard about what happened to Liangzu," Fuzhi's tone was rather hesitant.

"What has happened to Liangzu?" said Bichu, somewhat alarmed. She put down her cake.

Fuzhi said: "Carry on eating. I heard that he has been removed from his position as division commander."

"Ah!" Bichu heaved a long sigh of relief. "I thought he might have been wounded or something worse than that."

"He is not allowed to go into battle. I think that hurts him even more than getting wounded."

"But why has he been removed from his position?"

"Probably because he lost the last battle. But I don't think that is the main reason. Do you recall Liangzu got on quite well along with dad?"

"It's because of his point of view?"

"Probably."

The two fell into an anxious silence. May's illness concerned only one household, but Liangzu's removal from his position, which might even appear as a personal gain to some degree, implied some discordant notes in the symphony of unified efforts to fight against the invaders. Would those notes grow loud enough that one day they would determine the fate of the nation?

May enjoyed some privileged treatment in the hospital and was recovering fast. Many relatives and her classmates went to visit her. On Sunday, Bichu took Kiddo. May immediately noticed Kiddo's left eye had a blue circle around the edge of it.

"What happened?" May asked at once.

"I fell over," Kiddo replied vaguely, covering his face.

"How could you have hurt your eye if you just fell over?"

"I don't believe him, either. It looks like he has been hit. But he won't say anything," Bichu said. Having settled the things she had brought for May, she went to see the doctor.

Kiddo looked around and then whispered to May: "I just want to tell you only. I had a fight with Ying Xiaolong, Little Dragon. I won. Remember? Grandpa taught us martial arts."

"Why did you do it? It's never right to fight with anyone."

"He started it and he wanted it. It was because of a basin of hot water." Kiddo then told May the story.

May didn't say a word for a long while: "I was wondering where you had got the hot water! Are you hurt anywhere else? How's Little Dragon?"

"He has got a blue right eye. We drew two lines on the ground outside the entrance gate and agreed that whoever was forced outside the lines would lose the fight."

"Did he make a scene when he lost?"

"Many people were watching. But he didn't try to make a scene, anyway. He stuck to the rules."

"Then both of you played fair and square!" May smiled.

"Mum is coming. Don't say a word about this," said Kiddo, wagging his finger.

When Bichu went into the ward, she was concerned. Later, Suchu and Huishu came. They both looked worried. Suchu and Bichu whispered to each other.

Suchu told Bichu it had been announced that Liangzu had been removed from his position and confined to Yunnan province. She told Bichu that Liangzu's adjutant could help Bichu sell the gold bracelet because the whole family was moving to Anning county, including Huishu, who would come back to town to take her exams.

Bichu told Suchu that May had been suffering from severe anaemia as well as light tuberculosis. Both required long-term nursing. Huishu sat silently in her chair, crumpling the handkerchief in her hands. She had brought May a Chinese translation of French writer Hector Malot's *Sans Famille*, and four mangoes from Dashi.

When Suchu and Huishu left, Fuzhi and Earl arrived. When it was almost noon, the red beacon of the air raid warning was visible. The Meng family enjoyed their small gathering in the small ward and decided not to go out of town to hide out during the air raid. May pleaded with them to leave her behind.

Bichu said: "They won't drop bombs on hospitals. They have those big red crosses on top of the buildings."

Earl retorted coldly: "No one is sure about that."

The beacon was removed when it was clear that no enemy fighter planes were coming.

"We have to move to the countryside," said Bichu. She had made up her mind.

CHAPTER THREE

PART I

The Meng family finally moved to Dragon Tail village in the beginning of the summer of 1939. Most of the faculty from the science department stayed in the western suburbs, while the faculty from the humanities stayed in the eastern suburbs. Jiang Fang, Li Lian and Qian Mingjing had already moved to Dragon Tail village.

Dragon Tail village boasted a mountain and a river. The mountain, which was called Baotaishan (Mount Baotai), meaning precious temple, was not big, but covered with all kinds of trees. The Mang river, a tributary of the Dragon river roaring not far away, was not deep, but had crystal clear water. It seemed that the place had many associations with 'dragons'. A thornless shrubby vine plant from the rose family called the Lady Banks' rose (Rosa Banksiae) – a climbing rose native to Yunnan province - grew everywhere, clambering from the village to the mountain and the riverside. Some grew vigorously to a height of five or six metres, protecting the farm houses in the village. When it bloomed, its tiny flowers clustered together in thick layers like piled-up snow, giving out a faint sweet smell like violets or fragrant osmanthus. The Meng family's memories of Dragon Tail village were intertwined with the faint smell of Lady Banks' roses.

The village had only one street lined with shops and stores like the streets located in out-of-the-way corners in Kunming. Most of the houses were built in a similar style in alleys off the street. A proper house had two storeys with a main room in the middle flanked by a room in each wing for each storey. The main room downstairs had no front and back walls and served as the living room for the family, while the rooms in the wings downstairs served different purposes. One was the kitchen and the other was a pigsty. The Mengs' new place was the room in the wing on the second floor above the pigsty.

This room was even smaller than the attic in the theatre at the ancestral temple. The thin floorboards creaked with every footstep. The gaps between the floorboards were spacious enough to reveal the activities of the pigs below. Their hallmark odour and rhythmic grunting echoed around the upstairs space. The smell almost drove Bichu nuts at first. She tried to clean the furniture and her clothes again and again but failed to get rid of the smell. When she finally came to smell like a pigsty, she came to terms with the smell.

The thing that took a long while for the Mengs to get used to was the outhouse. It was built in a small yard for storing firewood. Among the piles of firewood was a pit the size of a shell crater. On the narrower part some boards had been positioned for people to stand on when they answered the call of nature. The rest of the crater was not covered up. Filth and maggots confronted those who were courageous enough to visit. The most terrifying thing was that the farmer kept pigs in the pit. When people came, the pigs grunted more loudly and expected to be fed from above the boards. The pigs liked to bully strangers and tried to bite them. That explained why cityfolk who moved from Kunming to these villages used to take a club to guard themselves agaisnt the pigs when they needed to use the pit.

The owner of the house was named Zhao, and was the second child of his parents, hence his name Zhao Er ('er' 二 meaning 'second' in Chinese). The Zhaos were considered to be well-off in the village. Besides pigs, they also had chickens, a cat, a dog and a horse. The horse was kept in a stable in the firewood yard. The owner, who was kind-hearted and generous, had promised much freedom to the household animals. For example, the pit pigs and the kitchen pigs could switch places any time they wished. The dog, with two white spots over its eyes, belonged to those silly four-eyed type, and enjoyed its privilege, too. Its doghouse was a kennel made of hay by the gate. As for the cat, it gained everyone's respect in the family. The fact that few cats in Kunming were able to survive the war against rats made the surviving cats rather expensive. The short table in the wall-less living room served as the dining room for the house owner's family and the cat. During meal times, the six family members spanning three generations would take their places on three sides of the table, while the cat would sit on the fourth side with its bowl. When the landlady served rice for her family, she would serve rice for the cat; when she served soup, she would serve the cat with soup.

Moreover, she would press the rice with the soup spoon when she poured soup into the cat's bowl to make sure there were no big chunks of rice which might choke the cat.

The horse, as a big animal, had its privacy. Although it was not that big, it was a workhorse capable of ploughing the field or pulling a cart. When it finished its work at dusk every day, standing in its stable, it would enjoy its porridge served in a basin in its unhurried and graceful manner. May and Kiddo, leaning against the rails, would watch it having its meal. It would raise its head from time to time to look at the two kids with its gentle and friendly eyes as if to say 'hello'.

Considering the distance between the campus in the city and the relocated faculty, classes for teachers were grouped together in a couple of days. Fuzhi's classes were from Monday through Wednesday, so he could spend the other four days writing his book at home. Living in the countryside saved him lots of time running from air raids and thus gave him more time to do his research. He had to walk to town to teach and come back without any means of transportation. At first it took him about three hours to walk to the school in town; later he managed to make it in two hours. Bichu made a shoulder bag out of the blue wrapping cloth he favoured. He could also carry it on his back like a sling bag. With an umbrella in his hand, he looked so much like those candidates who travelled across the country to the capital to take the grand exam in the old days.

Bichu described her weekly existence at that time as topsy-turvy because Fuzhi would leave for town on Monday and wouldn't come home until Wednesday while the kids were at school on weekdays. On the days she was alone, even the grunts from the pigs sounded nice to Bichu. At weekends when the children came home and all five of them were crammed into the tiny wing room, she was overwhelmed by a feeling of cosiness and comfort.

Even Earl was happy at such homecoming gatherings. On Sunday afternoons, May and Kiddo would walk back to their school. It was lucky for the two since Dragon Tail village was close to Copper Head village where their school had been relocated. Earl sometimes joined May and Kiddo and left on Sundays; at other times she would leave on Mondays with her father. May was still weak since her discharge from hospital, but she insisted on going to school.

Early one Monday morning, Bichu saw Fuzhi off at the village. Seeing him striding along the Mang river with light and agile steps, she noticed that he was stooping a little.

"It would be much better if we could move back to town," thought Bichu. "No more such hard commuting on foot." When Fuzhi disappeared from sight at a bend in the road, Bichu had a good look at the tree-lined roads along the river before heading home. The kids had all left for school the day before. Most of the Zhao family hadn't got up yet, only the landlady was up, leaning against the window, combing her hair. It was quiet in the yard.

Qian Mingjing and his wife lived at the opposite side of the alley, but the two households shared the same well located in the Qians' yard. The Mengs had hired help to carry water from the well. The daily supply of four buckets of water wasn't sufficient on Mondays when Bichu had so much to wash and clean. She often took one bucket of water home on Monday mornings when she was back from seeing Fuzhi off. Since Mingjing's neighbours shared the well, the gate to his courtyard was not locked, which Mingjing couldn't bear. But such a house with an independent yard and free of any livestock was a rare find in the village, so Mingjing decided to put up with this drawback.

When Bichu returned, she didn't go upstairs. Instead, she picked up the bucket and went directly to the Qians' yard. She quietly pushed open the unlocked door to the yard. A pail tied to a long rope was placed beside the well for drawing water. She stood by the well, took a deep breath, and lowered the pail down slowly. She wiggled the rope and managed to fill half of the pail.

The sound of a woman chuckling came from the room. "It's not right to have a public well in one's private courtyard," thought Bichu. When she tried to lift the pail, she felt nauseous and she lost her grip on the rope. The pail fell deep into the well.

"Huifen!" Bichu cried, thinking about asking Huifen to ask for Mingjing's help. There was no response. The courtyard fell into absolute silence. Did I make a mistake? "Huifen!" Bichu called again, but she clammed up immediately, remembering that Huifen had gone to town the day before yesterday because her elder sister Huiyuan had come to see her from Chongqing. Bichu even asked why Huiyuan wouldn't come to live with her sister in the countryside for a couple of days. Huifen must have returned yesterday, thought Bichu. Thinking of this, she didn't want to delve any deeper and went home.

She met Zhao Er going out of their yard heading for the stable. On hearing about Bichu losing the pail in the well and having no water to take back, Zhao Er said: "This happens a lot." After a moment, he came back with two buckets of water on a carrying-pole and told Bichu he had retrieved the pail. Sitting on a small stool in the wall-less living room, Bichu began to do her laundry.

The landlord's other family members came into the living room, too. The landlady began to rinse the rice to cook breakfast. The locals had a special way of cooking rice. They would first cook the rice with water, then ladle out the half-cooked rice into a sieve to drain it and then put the drained rice into a rice steamer to continue cooking. The water in which the rice had been cooked was tasty, but was often used for the pigs or simply poured away. The rice steamer had a pointed lid in the shape of a straw hat. Kiddo once asked if he could touch it.

When cooking the rice, the landlady busied herself chopping fresh red chillies. The bright colour perfectly complemented their pungent smell, which was no bother for the landlady, while Bichu kept sneezing in the far corner of the room, with tears streaming down her face and a runny nose.

"You don't look like someone who is accustomed to doing chores like this. Look at your fair skin, soft hands and thin figure. They are not built for such chores. Ah you Shanghainese! Do they have chillies in Shanghai?" asked the landlady. For the villagers, all strangers were from Shanghai.

"I'll get used to it," said Bichu, walking out of the room. She stayed under the eaves for a while and sat down again to do her laundry.

The landlady ladled the rice out into the rice steamer. The sweet smell of cooked rice counteracted the pungent smell of the chillies. She squatted by Bichu's laundry basin for a while before suggesting: "How about hiring a helping hand? You just need to feed her. As for the pay, it's up to you. What do you think?"

Fuzhi once proposed that they hire a helping hand, but Bichu wanted to do everything herself because she was worried how they could manage the extra expense when Fuzhi's pay barely made ends meet. But now, her health was going from bad to worse. She couldn't risk exhausting herself. She answered listlessly: "How about if she came several days a week if she lives nearby?"

"She does live nearby. She lives in the same street. To be honest, she's my niece. When my sister died, she was badly treated by her stepmother, so she often lives with her aunt on her father's side. Then after her aunt's death, the girlfriend of her aunt's husband tried everything to drive her away. This girl seems jinxed to her family but does no harm to strangers."

"Where is she now?" asked Bichu with deep sympathy.

"She has gone to help the caravans with their trade. She'll be back in about a month."

"Do girls work in the caravans, too?"

"Why not? Girls do all sorts of jobs. Only the caravans are done mainly by men. Almost all other jobs are done by women."

The four-eyed dog at the gate barked twice before turning around and lying down again. Zheng Huifen stood in the yard, chuckling.

"I have walked all the way back from the city! Am I early?" Huifen walked happily toward Bichu, with a cotton cloth bag in her hand.

"I ran into Professor Meng," she said. "He asked me to tell you to take your medicine on time because he forgot to tell you before he left for work. So, I came directly to you to deliver this important message without going home first."

"You came from town?"

"Yes, I sure did. I haven't been home yet. What a pile of laundry! Let me give you a hand!" With these words, Huifen pulled over another small stool and sat down by the basin.

"You don't need to do this, really," Bichu told Huifen in Yunnan dialect. Both laughed at Bichu's natural improvisation.

"I've already soaped it all. Let it soak for a while. Come on! Let's go upstairs." Bichu took out a cup of water with a ladle from a water bucket and rinsed her hands.

"You are too economical with water! We have plenty," teased Huifen on seeing Bichu rinse her hands so sparingly with water.

"I know. But it's a big deal to fetch water from the well." She almost told Huifen about dropping the pail into the well, but then thought better of it.

When the two sat down, Huifen took out of her cloth bag a box of water colours, a box of oil paint and a row of paint brushes of different sizes, and showed them all to Bichu: "My sister complained that I spend all my time and energy taking care of Qian Mingjing, which is not becoming for someone from a family like mine. She said I shouldn't neglect my painting even though I don't have a proper job. I'm going to paint several pictures to give you as wall paper."

"Which wall do you think is good enough for your paintings?" laughed Bichu. "But speaking of Huiyuan, how's that thing going?"

That thing referred to Huiyuan's divorce. During 10 years of marriage, she had been fighting for her divorce for nine and a half years. She had acquired an enviable reputation in music circles as Mrs Liu, but few people had heard of Mr Liu. Now a solid piece of information revealed that he was unwilling to leave behind his huge properties in Shanghai. With the distance between the two, things got even trickier.

Huifen said: "I'm not so concerned about her. It has been going on like this for so many years. I'm more concerned about myself. How do sisters of a family share such a similar fate? Look at you and your other two sisters. All have married well. Look at me and my sister. We are both filing for divorce."

Bichu was quite surprised at Huifen's words: "How have things got into such a mess?"

"I have been thinking about getting divorced since the beginning of this year. But only yesterday did I bring it up with my sister." Huifen's tone was not disappointed or depressed. Rather, she was in high spirits.

"If I go back to taking my painting more seriously, life might be much better for me." She picked up a piece of pickled turnip when she saw the bowl on the table.

Bichu took a jar out of the small cabinet. The red and white pickled turnip slices looked so inviting.

"I just learned from our landlady how to make pickles. The kids finished a big jarful. This is all that's left."

"It's so funny that pickles are a delicacy now," said Huifen.

Huifen spared some time to talk between her attacks on the pickled turnips: "I won't bring it up with him right now. I think I'll wait a bit longer, although he has been with another woman for almost a year. I was told that she sells jade pieces in the western part of Yunnan province. Her family is quite well-off by local standards. I forget the name of the village, but the family is very close to the local chieftain. She has been giving financial support to my husband. I'm just embarrassed that I might be using some of her things. Who knows where she has found that stuff."

Bichu remembered the giggling she overheard earlier that morning and was rather hesitant whether she should tell Huifen or not. As Huifen's good friend, she should have done. But it was so against her nature to poke her nose into other people's personal lives. Besides, it was wrong to drive a wedge between a husband and wife, especially when their relationship looked like it was wrecked. Turning over those thoughts in her mind, she took her Chinese medicine pills and sat down to comb her hair.

She let down her bun of hair and combed it carefully. The reflection of her emaciated face in the mirror looked even more withered against her bushy hair.

"You still have so much hair," Huifen commented.

"It has been thinning out fast. It's a lot of trouble to comb and wash such long hair!" Bichu said without thinking much about it. Looking into the mirror, she froze: "How about you cut my hair short?"

Huifen froze, too, at Bichu's proposal: "Wouldn't you regret it? Although it is indeed a lot of trouble to maintain such thick long hair."

"I mean it. Short hair doesn't need pomade, either." Bichu looked left and right at herself in the mirror for some time before making up her mind: "I'd like you to cut my hair for me!" She stood up and handed a big pair of scissors to Huifen, who didn't dare to take them at first.

"Wouldn't it be better if you talk to Professor Meng first?" said Huifen.

"We have talked about it. He thought it would be better to save me the trouble of combing it. Wait a moment. Let me comb my hair through," said Bichu, putting down the scissors and picking up her comb. She combed her hair slowly.

Her mother used to comb her hair for her when she was young. She wore a long braid back then. Her mother had a set of nine different-sized combs with their backs delicately inlaid with mother-of-pearl. Whenever Jiangchu and Bichu combed their hair in their mother's bedroom, the two sisters would use all nine of them from the smallest to the biggest. That set of combs had been lying underground with their mother for almost 30 years. Bichu let out her breath in one long sigh, put down the comb and waved at Huifen to begin.

Huifen divided the dark cascade of lush hair into four strands. Holding one strand in her left hand, and the scissors in her right, she measured how much she should cut before asking: "I'm going to cut it. Are you sure?"

"Go ahead. Don't hesitate," Bichu said with a smile, closing her eyes.

Seconds later, four long strands of hair were coiled on the floor. Huifen carefully trimmed the locks of hair over Bichu's ears. Bichu's reflection in the mirror looked much younger with short hair.

"Very nice! It suits you!" Huifen was very happy with her work. "You seem like someone with a very open mind for trying new things."

Bichu responded with a soft sigh. She braided the four strands of hair into four braids and wrapped them up in an old piece of cloth before putting the package at the bottom of a case. The two friends gave each other an understanding smile like people who had just achieved something great.

"Let's go and have a walk along the river," Huifen suggested.

Knowing Huifen's reluctance to return home, Bichu walked downstairs with her. On seeing the basin of soapy dirty laundry, an idea occurred to her. The water in the Mang river was clear and clean. Why hadn't she thought about doing her laundry in the river before? When Bichu told Huifen of her idea, Huifen held Bichu by the shoulder as if they had just invented the light bulb.

The landlady, who was ready to go out to work in the field, overheard their conversation: "Are you two going to the river? Be careful. Don't fall into it!" she warned. She went back into the house and came out again with her washing paddle for Bichu. Bichu was very grateful for such a useful tool. She and Huifen found a basket and carried the wet laundry in it all the way to the riverbank.

The Mang river was three to four metres wide with deep water in the middle but quite shallow waters by the banks. Fish could be seen in the water. Weeping willows were planted along the banks. Some huge rocks along the banks were deeply embedded into the riverbed.

Bichu and Huifen found a rock that was fairly easy for them to climb up and down, and then squatted down to do the laundry. Seeing the pieces of clothing swimming this way and that, getting cleaner and cleaner, both felt refreshed.

Bichu wrang out several pieces, battered several more with the washing paddle, and exclaimed: "How wonderful nature is to provide us with such a river to do our laundry!"

Huifen answered: "It also provides us with those Japanese invaders who provide us with such an opportunity to do our laundry this way."

Soon, they both got their feet wet. Huifen decided to take her shoes off, while Bichu refused. Then they agreed to go their separate ways. Huifen stood with one bare foot on the rock, and the other in the water, and switched feet from time to time. The lower edge of her blue cotton *qipao* was drooping with the weight of water.

Bichu smiled: "You conjure up such a beautiful image of 'doing the laundry by the river'!"

Huifen said: "Oh yes! Professor Xiao told me when I was in town yesterday about your relative, Wei Feng, who is married to a granddaughter of the Yue family. She left Beiping and headed northwest." She used geographical concepts rather than politically charged terms.

Bichu was amazed at the news: "I haven't heard from Wei Feng and Xueyan for a very long time. Why didn't Professor Xiao tell us before?"

"It doesn't take too much imagination to figure out that Professor Xiao probably learnt this from my sister. The truth is that my sister said she met the Wei couple at a friend of hers after her concert in Guiyang, Guizhou province."

Bichu put down the washing paddle and stared at Huifen: "Did you say she didn't hear of Wei Feng but she actually saw the couple?"

"True, true! The couple is now staying with a friend in Huaxi district, Guiyang city. Besides helping with the cooking and laundry, they also help their friends grow vegetables in the garden."

"There's no human being who is not capable of adapting to their environment. But it must be extremely tough for someone like Xueyan who grew up in clover."

"My sister said the same thing. I thought Wei Feng was a relative from Professor Meng's side, so I didn't think it was a big deal and didn't tell you immediately."

"His relatives are also mine, well, our family's. It is very big news!"

They wrang out the rinsed laundry and put it all into the basket. More big news broke out along the opposite bank of the river. A man and a woman walked into Bichu's sight. The man was looking at the ground while the woman was looking up, talking to the man. The two looked very intimate. The man was none other than Qian Mingjing.

"It looks like the two haven't finished their talk yet from early this morning," thought Bichu, hoping they wouldn't look her way and that it would be better if they just passed her and Huifen to save them all from embarrassment. But the rock Huifen was standing on moved a little bit and she stood up to grab hold of Bichu to keep her balance. Her eyes were pinned on the opposite riverbank.

When the pair walked closer, she cried suddenly: "Good morning, Qian Mingjing!"

Qian Mingjing froze upon hearing Huifen as if someone had cast a spell on him. The woman hurried several steps away from Qian and smiled: "I'm coming to see Mrs Qian. I have just got hold of several jade bracelets with very good quality and very low prices. I was thinking of asking Mrs Qian a favour to see whether some of her acquaintances might be interested in buying some."

"You have come to the wrong person," Huifen smiled back. "I don't know anyone working at the university who would be interested in buying jewellery nowadays. If you want my advice: don't be a greedy war profiteer profiting from the national crisis!"

As if to underscore what 'national crisis' meant, a couple of dozen fighter planes appeared in the distance. They could tell from the rumbling noise that these planes were just circling over Kunming.

The four held their breath, wondering how many bombs would land on the city. But a moment later, the planes flew away and disappeared into the same blue sky. The pain and bitterness of life resumed after this momentary pause.

Bichu began: "Professor Qian, you carry on with whatever it is you were doing. I'll look after Huifen."

Qian Mingjing answered calmly: "I'm seeing the guest off. She is heading to Salt Falls."

He motioned to the woman and the two walked in the direction of Dragon river. Salt Falls was a small village located at the fork of two small rivers. The woman was carrying a small case which most likely contained some jade artefacts.

Huifen snatched a pebble and threw it in the direction where the two disappeared. The pebble barely made its way into the grass by the riverbank opposite. She sneered: "My view of the world has been greatly updated!"

Bichu asked her to put on her shoes so as not to catch a cold and said they should go back home since the laundry was done.

"I don't have a home to go back to."

Huifen covered her face in her hands and stayed in that pose for a while before she stood up to pack with Bichu. When they had hung up all the clothes, Bichu asked Huifen to take a break upstairs while she went to cook lunch in the wall-less living room downstairs. She made a pot of ratatouille with the leftovers from the previous night and brought it upstairs. Huifen was sitting on the bed, sobbing.

Bichu's heart ached. The two daughters from the Zheng family were once the belles of Shanghai city. Who could have foreseen such horrible marriages for both? Things were better for Huiyuan because she was loved and was in love, but Huifen had given up everything for her marriage, including her painting career. All her efforts turned out to be in vain. But who could have foreseen such a future?

When she set the bowls and chopsticks on the table, she was seized by nausea again and fell into the chair by her side, coughing. Huifen sprang up from the bed and dried her tears when she saw what was going on. The two comforted and encouraged each other. After taking several bites, both felt much better. It was amazing that food was such a powerful remedy.

"How true it is that people won't survive without substance," Huifen was half talking to herself and half to Bichu. "This ratatouille is delicious."

"I made braised beef yesterday. I put the leftovers into the pot."

Kunming folk knew the right way to cook beef. There were beef restaurants in the streets which only sold cooked beef. The most popular way was to stew the big chunks of beef in a cauldron until the beef was soft and tender. When you had finished your bowl, the restaurant keeper's wife would always come up to provide you with an extra bowl of the soup from the stew. Bichu would make a beef stew every week as a treat for the kids while she always waited for whatever was left over.

"What exactly is bothering you? You must diagnose the problem before you can treat it properly. What you are taking is only common tonics. Is it working?"

"It's related to my period. The bleeding never actually stops. It started during our stay in Guihui. Later, it got better for a while, but then came back again. The bleeding lasts for the whole cycle, although it's not that heavy. That's why I always feel weak and dizzy. Another thing is my cough. It's new and I don't know the reason for it."

Huifen said: "When May was hospitalised, why didn't you have a check-up?"

"I felt alright back then — and I was quite busy." Bichu paused. "Mrs Li once said she had some people working in a hospital and asked me to go and have a check-up with her."

"Mrs Li? I'm not sure if I trust her," Huifen said. She suddenly remembered her encounter with Mrs Li, Jin Shizhen, at the fair the previous week. Her heart missed a beat. How could she not trust Jin Shizhen? Shizhen had already foreseen what would happen.

That day, she and Mingjing went to the fair for the week's grocery shopping. When they were bargaining with the stall owner at a stall, Mrs Li pulled Huifen away from Mingjing and whispered to her that she had seen pink and green hovering over Mingjing. She was sure Mingjing was having an affair. Huifen teased Mrs Li whether Mingjing had met the legendary Lady White, the gentle, loving and beautiful snake fairy? Mrs Li told her gravely that Lady White was a rare find, and unlikely to be encountered by chance. She told Huifen of Mingjing's obsession that his own desires might wreck their marriage. It wouldn't take long to find out.

Ordinary fortune tellers tended to veil their predictions while Shizhen was always direct in her interpretation of whatever she foresaw. Such directness annoyed many. Huifen was quite suspicious about such predictions. Maybe Shizhen had just heard some rumours and used her imagination to cook up such a story. After all, it was not news that Huifen and Mingjing's marriage had been bumpy.

Huifen had no intention of relaying Shizhen's prediction to Bichu, but since Shizhen had been mentioned, she told Bichu what Shizhen had told her at the fair. The latter said: "It's just another case of those mind games. If you believe it, it is true. You can't solve your problem in one or two days, so for now the most important task for you is to stay healthy. Now go and take your nap!"

Lying in bed in the Mengs' outer room, Huifen tried hard to block out her thoughts and fall into oblivion to make up for the sleep she had lost due to having woken up so early that morning, but things seldom turn out the way one anticipates.

The more she tried not to remember, the more she remembered. Her mind flashed back to the time when she first met Mingjing. After her graduation from St John's University in Shanghai, she went to learn painting at the Shanghai Art School. She met Mingjing at an art exhibition. His graceful bearing made a deep impression on her. Back then, he was already employed by Minglun University and had published several papers about his research findings on oracle bone scripts. Such nerdy academic achievements didn't match his image of a handsome dapper gentleman with fine breeding. Besides, he had already made a name for himself as a poet.

That day, they watched the exhibits together. When they moved to two small gouache paintings, one dim and shrouded with mist and rain, the other filled with the force of a strong, pervasive wind, Mingjing planted himself in front of the two paintings for a long time, claiming they were rich in profound poetic flavour. The two paintings were her work, although she hadn't signed her name on them. Later, after they got married, Huifen asked Mingjing several times whether he had managed to discover beforehand that those two paintings were her work, and he had always denied such a supposition.

When they got married, they settled down in the west garden on campus. It was a traditional Chinese-style courtyard decorated with his oracle-bone-script calligraphy and her paintings. Most of her paintings were landscapes of the western suburbs of Beiping, such as the remains of the Old Summer Palace which looked like a giant ship anchored in the mist, and the red maple leaves of Fragrant Hills against the backdrop of evergreen pine groves. After all the years she had learnt about painting, it was the first time she had noticed how gorgeous the colour red was when set against such a green background. Ah! And the bubbling creeks in the Cherry Valley! She should have invited Huiyuan to sing along with the rhythm of the water. She was intoxicated by the happiness oozing out of her family and reflected by those beautiful things around her, until one day she found the letter which shattered her sweet dreams.

It was rather an ordinary story often found in popular romantic novels. Qian Mingjing had an affair with one of his female students. He didn't deny the affair and expressed sincere regret for all his actions. Huifen took in his regret and forgave him. She didn't make it public and even tried to cover it up. Outsiders still envied their happy marriage, but the two of them were aware of the bumpy ride they were taking.

About half a year before the Marco Polo bridge incident in July 1937, Mingjing had another affair with the wife of a high-ranking government official. He paid frequent visits to her since her husband stayed most of the time in Nanjing. The affair ended inconclusively when Huifen and Mingjing hurriedly departed to the South. Huifen warned Mingjing not to try her patience a third time, and Mingjing guaranteed that he wouldn't dare to chance a third encounter.

When they settled down in Guihui, their life entered a peaceful phase. Huifen also tried her best to take care of the house and her husband.

Mingjing developed a new hobby of collecting antiques amid such a transient lifestyle filled with hardships. He made a good profit from a set of hardwood furniture inlaid with mother of pearl when he sold it in Kunming. The profit covered their daily expenses for a while.

Inspired by this success, he soon directed his interest toward jade and other precious stones and made friends with several experts in the field. The woman who dealt with jade was one of them, whom Huifen later found out was the head of a small village.

Mingjing was gifted in many ways. He had made great achievements as a scholar and a poet. What amazed everyone was his talent in business for which he had an acute skill for buying and selling. When they relocated to the countryside, Mingjing, like his colleagues, worked for three days in a row every week. When he came back home, he always brought back some jade artefacts and spent lots of time from dawn till dusk pouring over those items.

Once he brought back a pure white incense burner the size of an inkbottle with delicate carvings all over. He told Huifen: "This is made of the legendary quality white jade. Would you like to burn some incense in it when you worship Guanyin, the Goddess of Mercy?"

Huifen teased him: "You know I don't worship Guanyin or anything. Probably you know someone who does? That's why you pay so much attention to such items, isn't it?"

Surprisingly, Mingjing's face sank at Huifen's joke, and he immediately put away the white jade incense burner. Little by little, Huifen came to the realisation that behind all those jade items, there was a woman who was a faithful believer in the Goddess of Mercy.

Huifen once did a humble comparative study between herself and the other women Mingjing had fallen for. Honestly, she didn't find herself inferior in any way to any of them. Maybe all the affairs could be traced back to Mingjing's unsettled nature. He did have plenty of opportunities to make things happen, though. Let it be. It was time to put an end to all of this.

Someone knocked at the door.

Bichu opened the door to see Mingjing standing outside, smiling unconcernedly. "Mrs Meng, how've you been these days? Thank you for taking the trouble to look after Huifen." Bichu invited him to come in for tea. When she had finished the standard procedures of greeting, she gave an encouraging and understanding nudge to Huifen who covered her head in the quilt and went downstairs.

Mingjing stooped a little and whispered to Huifen: "I'm not going to keep you in the dark anymore since you have already seen what's going on.

Whatever you want to know, and you want to do, let's go back home first. We can't make a scene here at the Mengs'." Pigs in the downstairs pigsty grunted and paced back and forth, backing up Mingjing's observation that it was indeed not the right place to talk.

Huifen sat up on the quilt and answered coldly: "What's there to talk about? It looks quite simple to me. Let's get a divorce."

"A divorce is not so simple," Mingjing answered with an ingratiating smile, picking up Huifen's shoes. "It's simple if we just have a fight. But we must go back home first. My dear lady, please come back home with me!" He gave Huifen a deep bow and tried to help Huifen with her shoes.

How much Huifen wanted to give the man bending in front of her a hard kick, but she was afraid she might make a noise. It was rather embarrassing for her to have a fist fight with her husband at someone else's place. At that thought, she grabbed her shoes and put them on herself, then turned to make the bed. Mingjing picked up her bag without delay. The two walked downstairs together. For anyone who didn't know the backstory, they still looked like a happily married couple.

Bichu was mending some clothes in the living room downstairs. When she saw them off at the gate, she wondered whether Mingjing would again take advantage of Huifen's tender nature and kindness. Mingjing was not a bad guy by nature, but how could Huifen suffer more from such a lecherous personality?

Once the two were back in their home, Mingjing asked Huifen at once: "Are you willing to break up our family in such a cruel wartime?"

Without giving any response, Huifen sank into the rocking chair, her eyes glancing from the curtains made of homespun cloth falling from the ceiling almost to the floor in the bedroom to the home office occupied by four walls of books. A whole layer on a shelf was taken up by jade items of all sizes and shapes.

She sighed: "It's not easy to file for divorce at such a time, but it's easy to rearrange our lives right now. You move out of the bedroom to sleep in the home office and cook your own meals. We'll stay out of each other's way."

Thump! Mingjing dropped to his knees at Huifen's words, which startled her. "I just want to ask one favour from you. Professor Jiang has asked me to sort out my publications these last few years. The academic committee of my department is going to review my application for promotion to professor. I just want to ask you to hang on until my promotion is settled."

"What sort of professor will you be promoted to? A professor of Ming dynasty furniture or Song dynasty chinaware? A professor of Yunnan jade artefacts or Burmese precious stones?" taunted Huifen.

Mingjing rose and went to take out a neatly bound manuscript written on handmade paper and a couple of journals which had published his papers on oracle scripts. He asked her: "Those women only know about my good appearance. They know nothing about my research. Only you do!"

"Only you do!" The words pounded in her heart. She covered up her face with her hands, her tears trickling down along her arms.

At dusk, Li Lian came back from town with the news that Minglun University's office in Kunming had been bombed. A courtyard had been destroyed, and a senior worker had been killed on site. The main building was intact. He then told Bichu: "Professor Meng is very well. He had his class today in the graveyard; later in the afternoon, he went on writing his book at the attic in the theatre."

A few days later, May and Kiddo were let out of school for the summer vacation. Earl said she wanted to find a job, so she intended to stay in town and go home every couple of days during the summer vacation. May's mild fever returned. The doctor prescribed liver extract injections, a kind of blood tonic, every two days, and recommended she take antituberculosis drugs, too. A physician who stayed in Salt Falls transformed his house into a temporary clinic to give injections and such things. The distance between Salt Falls and Dragon Tail village was about 3 to 4 kilometres. After several trips with Bichu, May claimed she knew the way very well and could manage to go for the injections by herself. Bichu didn't approve of this and asked Huifen to accompany May on two trips. But the day May needed the injection, Huifen was in town. Bichu then had to agree to let May go alone.

May listened to her mother in the living room, her straw hat in her hands: "When you walk, pay attention to the road. Don't look this way and that. If the enemy fighter planes come, when they get near, you must hide out in the grass and bushes. If the one giving you the injection is not the doctor but his wife, remember you need to address her as 'doctor', too. You need to bear all these things in mind. Do you understand?"

May said yes and put on her straw hat. It was rather an old hat, but it looked much better when May sewed a ribbon onto it. Kiddo saw her off at the gate. He gave the ribbon a tug. He had wanted to go with May, but when he was told it was too much for him to walk so far, he agreed to stay at home to read 'Journey to the West', one of the four great Chinese classical novels.

May started out alone. She took her time and loitered along the Mang river, ran into a couple of peddlers, and spotted several dogs running past with their tongues hanging out. About half an hour later, she arrived at Salt Falls village located on a hillside rising at the narrow strip between the Dragon river and the Mang river. At the foot of the hillside was a deep pool spring. The white water from upstream tumbled down into the plunge pool against several rocky outcrops, sending out white plumes of water vapour all over the pool. It dawned on May suddenly why it was called 'Salt Falls'.

The local people loved to rinse their laundry in torrents. The downstream section below the pool was much slower. It was said that the pool was connected to the Dragon river since anything lost in the pool would find its way into the Dragon river some time later. When water drops fell back into the pool, they melted into ripples flowing along its course.

"Girl, who are you looking for?" asked a woman carrying a baby on her back.

"The doctor," answered May.

"The doctor has foreign visitors over." She sounded as if she attached more significance to foreigners from farther away than to strangers from other provinces. "Two foreigners. One is a man in his 50s or 60s, the other is a woman. Some say she is his daughter, others say she is his wife. You are from Dragon Tail village. You have many strangers from other provinces."

The baby's head bobbed this way and that. May smiled at it and walked up the hillside.

The gate to the doctor's house was behind half of a wall, which appeared to function as a screen wall. When May entered, she found a middle-aged foreign woman in a bright dress who was busy carrying bricks from the west wing of the house to the garden. She smiled and nodded at May when she saw her. Her hair was hanging loose, covering almost half her face.

May went to the east wing where the doctor and his family lived. It was messy as usual. The doctor's wife was feeding two kids. The younger one was in her arms, while the elder one was standing in front of her against her knees.

"Oh, here you are! Just a moment."

May put down her medicine on the table. When the doctor's wife had finished feeding the two kids and settled them both down properly, she took inside the box of needles being heated on the open stove and muttered to herself: "Is it already done?" While mumbling, she fumbled and tried to take out one needle with a pair of tweezers, but the needle slipped into the wastepaper basket.

"That's quite alright," she said calmly. She pulled the plunger and began to extract the medicine out of the vial.

"If the needle dropped onto the floor, then I have to sterilise it again for you. Have you got it?" asked the doctor's wife. "We are moving to the western part of the city for cheaper rent. See what's going on?" she pouted her lips and pointed at the garden with her chin.

May found the foreign woman was still carrying bricks and asked: "Are they new neighbours?"

"Yes, they are. We don't like the new neighbours, but the landlord does. He likes higher rents, too. It's not because they are foreign. They are Jews!"

"What's wrong with being a Jew? They are people, too." That was what May had been taught.

"People say Jews have been driven out everywhere. Now they have reached Salt Falls. They bring bad luck."

"Those who drive Jews out are not nice."

"How do you know anything, little girl?" She finished administering the injection. One of her children began to cry, and she hurried to placate it.

May walked out of the room right up to the foreign woman and greeted her with a friendly: "Good morning."

The woman raised her head and tossed her long hair back, revealing a hideous scar covering the left corner of her forehead all the way down to her left cheek. The poor stitches twisted the muscles out of shape. A scary look. May looked away as if she hadn't seen it. The woman smiled, put down her bricks and returned May's greeting with the same friendliness.

She pointed at her scar: "Sorry about this." She turned to talk toward the back room in a language May couldn't understand. A tall old Jewish man appeared at the door. When he spoke, May's jaw dropped — he spoke idiomatic Shandong dialect!

"How do you do, young miss? Please allow me to introduce myself. My family name is Milmann, but we go with 'Mi', which means rice. This is my wife, Mrs Mi."

At his words, Mrs Mi extended her hand out of habit to give May a handshake, but she took it back noticing how muddy they were. She shook her hand and her head to indicate that she couldn't shake hands with May right then. "We are trying to build a flowerbed in the yard to plant wild flowers," explained Mr Mi.

May introduced herself and her family with slow and clear Chinese. Mr Mi listened attentively. When May had finished, he asked: "You are one of the daughters of the Meng family? I know many famous people have settled in Dragon Tail village. I'll be sure to go and visit them later." When he said the Chinese character '人' for people, he pronounced it as 'yen' in standard Shandong dialect instead of 'ren' in standard mandarin Chinese. May wanted very much to ask him why he spoke Shandong dialect, but she held her tongue. The couple invited her to stay for a while inside, but May declined the invitation, saying she had to head home immediately. When she was ready to leave the garden, the third member of the Mi family popped up.

It was a dog, a big dog, very dark brown with a very long nose. When it saw Mr Mi, it panted happily, wagging its tail and trotting. It approached May and was ready to lick her hand.

"No, no," May held up her hands. The big dog misunderstood the gesture as a signal to play and stood up on its hind legs. It was taller than May! The warm breath from its nose caused May to recoil a few steps.

"Liu! Down," Mr Mi ordered. It lay down immediately at May's feet, looking up at her.

"This is Liu," Mr Mi said. "I think he has made friends with you."

May bent down and patted the dog on the head. Its fur was as smooth as silk. "Liu," May cooed. The dog rested its head on its front paws, its eyes brimming with happiness.

"He is our child," said Mrs Mi, speaking Chinese with a funny accent. She pointed at Mr Mi and said: "Shandong dialect. East of Mount Tai." She pointed at herself: "Shanxi dialect? West of Mount Tai?" All three of them laughed.

Mr Mi walked May to the half wall and asked: "Miss, have you heard of a nationality called the Jews?"

"Yes, I have," May answered with deliberation.

"I'm Jewish. I'm from Germany," he said solemnly.

"Welcome to Salt Falls," said May sincerely, looking up into Mr Mi's eyes, who wanted to hug this tiny girl so much. But in the end, he just shook hands gratefully with the owner of the tiny hands.

May felt a little tired and she walked slowly downhill. Feeling as if she were being followed, she turned around to find Liu. He wagged his tail gently at her. His docile facial expression seemed to be asking May: "Can I walk with you for a while?" May stroked him and the two walked on side by side. The road led them to a turn on the other side of the village. A wild river tumbled into sight. It was the Dragon river with a grander aura from that of the Mang river. Downstream a giant white rock surrounded by luxuriant vegetation looked like a ship moored in the river. As a less frequented spot, it looked even more bleak under the clear summer sky.

Liu suddenly stopped, drew one step back and pounced toward the grass. He caught a bird flying out of the bush. Without a moment's delay, he was ready to gobble down his prey. May told him: "You are so barbaric, Liu!" Liu's attention was solely on his prey. He busied himself with his food. May didn't want to watch and ran all the way downhill back home.

In front of the garden, May saw her father was back from town. She ran to him and took his umbrella.

"Dad, you are so early today."

"Rice day. I got the rice," explained Fuzhi.

May looked behind him and saw a porter carrying two loads with his carrying pole. The rice was part of Fuzhi's salary. No one could tell how long the rice had been stored in the granary. It had become red with mould. But it was still rice.

Bichu was picking leafy vegetables in the living room. Fuzhi's heart ached upon seeing her gaunt face as if her whole body had been desiccated.

A line of a poem from the famed Qing dynasty poet Jiang Shizhao came to mind: "You have seldom had proper jewellery or enjoyed material comfort". In his mind, he immediately changed the line to read: "When will you have proper jewellery and enjoy material comfort?" When? Nobody could answer that question.

His eyes settled on the rice in front of him. May had already picked out several fat worms: "Dad, I saw two Jews today in Salt Falls. Their family name is 'Mi'."

"I did hear that a German family has just moved in here. They used to be the German consul in Qingdao, Shandong province," said Fuzhi.

"Mr Mi speaks Shandong dialect," said May, confirming Fuzhi's supposition. "They have a huge dog named 'Liu'. Sounds like willow. It's not a suitable name for such a big dog, is it?"

Fuzhi thought for a moment: "It might be the German pronunciation of the word 'lion'. 'Leo', I guess. When the Nazi regime took over Germany, it implemented an anti-Semitic policy in 1933 and revoked Jewish people's citizenship in 1935. It is so tragic when people like us are not allowed to go back to our home or others to go back to their homeland, but we still have a home and a country. But the Jews? They have lost both their home and their homeland. They have nowhere to go. Some countries have even expelled their Jewish citizens and refused to give refuge to Jews. China is different. Such a mighty land as China takes in people of all nationalities."

"We are lucky that we can still have a life in our own country," said Bichu, picking up a handful of rice, which escaped through her fingers. "And this is real rice, not chaff."

Fuzhi took a handful of rice, too, with rice worms wriggling in it. "I feed my wife and my children with such rice!" He spoke loudly to himself, making up his mind to buy one kilo of good rice for Bichu to cook porridge with next time they went to the village fair.

PART II

Outside the main street of Dragon Tail village on the Mang river was a pine grove with a spacious clearing. The bushy canopies of pine trees had formed a natural roof under which a village fair was held regularly every five days. Villagers from different villages nearby would come with all sorts of containers: baskets, buckets and bags. Some came to sell, some came to buy, others came for fun. Among the grain, rice and beans had the richest varieties; one could buy pork, beef, poultry, mutton, eggs and even horse meat; vegetables and fruit, fresh and dried, were also available. One could also buy neatly packed firewood, pine needle bundles to start a stove, and hard coke. As for articles for everyday use, from needles and thread to combs and mirrors, one could discover what an amazing abundance of produce such a small-scale country fair could provide. The cost of living had been rising, but inflation wasn't completely rampant, so people's enthusiasm for consumption was still maintained. Sometimes, enemy fighter planes might appear in the sky, but people at the fair simply raised their heads to look at the planes and then resumed whatever bargain they were trying to make. "Let's see how you invaders can stop us from living our lives!" some muttered to themselves.

A couple of families of university professors had already been seen at the fair. Some were buying bundles of needles, hard coke and firewood. The hard coke was piled up neatly like pieces of art rather than like cooking fuel. Speaking of art pieces, there were three stalls with some rocks, old basins and bowls, and crudely made jade items laid on the ground. In front of the three stalls of art stood a young couple, the Qians.

Qian Mingjing picked out a ring-shaped pendant the size of a coin and said he wanted to buy it for Huifen, who coldly reminded him: "If you want to buy new items besides what we have agreed, we have to talk it over first." Upon her words, Mingjing put it back, looking embarrassed.

It was Mingjing's idea that the two should come to the fair to show others that they were still on good terms. He was confident that Huifen would accept such a suggestion to cover up for him because of his knowledge about Huifen's nature. He was also grateful for this action on Huifen's behalf and he tried to make her happy while he could show others the picture of a loving couple engaged in a discussion over a jade ring-shaped pendant. Since he was ready to be rebuffed, he didn't take any offence when Huifen did rebuff him.

Not very far away from the Qian couple stood Li Lian and his family in front of two baskets of green leafy vegetables. When the Li family were out, they followed a set pattern with Jin Shizhen taking the two kids in each of her hands walking in front while Li Lian tagged along reluctantly behind. The vegetables were Indian mustard greens with big, fat and fresh leaves rarely seen in northern China. Shizhen squatted down to pick some up. As Li Lian surveyed all kinds of stalls, he spotted several butterflies fluttering on the outer rim of the grove.

Huifen walked close to Shizhen and whispered something into her ear. Shizhen stood up and stared at Mingjing, who fidgeted and engaged in some small talk: "All the villagers have heard of Mrs Li's speciality. Have you already taken in many who came to ask for your help?"

Shizhen dismissed Mingjing's question with a simple wave of her hand. She drew Huifen to one side and whispered back in Huifen's ear: "The pink and green haze hovering over his head has gone. I guess he has brought his heart back. Congratulations to you! A philandering heart is not a rare thing among men. Don't take it too seriously. Look at mine," she cast a glance over at Li Lian. "Can you imagine? He is also high maintenance!"

Shizhen's idiomatic Beiping dialect almost melted Huifen's heart. Whether Mingjing had brought back his heart or not was no longer of concern to her.

Li Lian and Mingjing had moved away from the stalls since they didn't want to get in other people's way while they talked. The butterflies had fluttered away.

Seeing Li Lian gazing at the butterflies, Mingjing commented, unaware of Li Lian's heart aching for his dead daughter: "The butterflies in Yunnan are very beautiful, but I would never agree that they are lovely. I don't know why they always remind me of the time when those beautiful things are hideous caterpillars. When the Tang dynasty poet Li Shangyin wrote in his famed poem 'A Beautiful Zither' that 'In Master Zhuang Zhou's dream / A beautiful butterfly he had become', I always wanted to ask why Zhuangzi dreamed of becoming a butterfly instead of something else. Has anyone researched this already?"

Li Lian answered: "Children like butterflies only because they look beautiful. Children wouldn't care otherwise." Mingjing didn't understand the relevance of this answer to his question.

The two exchanged looks and then switched the topic to the performance assessment held by the university. Two professor positions were available, and they were assigned to the Chinese and history departments. Both Li Lian and Mingjing had applied for the jobs.

Li Lian asked Mingjing how many applicants the Chinese department had. Mingjing answered: "Three. And I am the youngest, but I am the most popular teacher among the three, and I have the most academic turnout."

"That's so true. Our department has three applicants, too, but I am the oldest and the senior of the three. My academic performance is not bad, but speaking of popularity, I seem not to be one of the students' favourite teachers. For the past several years, I have refrained from mentioning anything mysterious in my class. That should be regarded as an attitude of 'righting the wrongs once recognised'. I don't think I can make the cut, so I don't fret," said Li Lian.

"It is said that a very interesting paper recently published by Professor Meng which has a critical review of the Ming dynasty founding emperor Zhu Yuanzhang was actually written by you," said Mingjing.

"How could that be? I just read the literature and we did talk the topic over on one occasion. Maybe my words inspired him. But that's all! Then Professor Meng insisted on including my name, though I declined."

"What's the review all about? Did he talk about Zhu Yuanzhang's systematic murder of those who rendered him great service in founding his empire?" asked Mingjing.

"No. He reviewed Zhu Yuanzhang's choice of his heir. He concluded that if Zhu Yuanzhang had chosen Zhu Di as his heir, the Song dynasty might have escaped a war, which would have benefited the people. But he chose Zhu Yunwen, who was young, raised in the palace and lacked any sort of experience. Besides, Zhu Yunwen had no intention of murdering his uncle Zhu Di to succeed him. Though Zhu Di was the second son, he was still the son. There was even a case during the Song dynasty that when the emperor died, his younger brother succeeded him. And Zhu Di had been accumulating his strength when he served as the governor of Beiping. When Zhu Yuanzhang decided to pass the empire to Zhu Yunwen, war was inevitable."

"But, what's Professor Meng's point?" asked Mingjing.

Li Lian thought for a moment before answering: "He might have wanted to draw a lesson from history that an accurate assessment of the situation may help make the best of the situation. It would be best if people could be spared the sufferings of war. But he wasn't talking about a war caused by foreign invaders. It is one of the series of Professor Meng's papers, covering several different topics which all relate to the Song dynasty."

Mingjing was somewhat jealous about how much Li Lian knew about Professor Meng's research while he was so ignorant. He used to be on close terms with Professor Meng, but since his bickering with Huifen, he was embarrassed to visit the Mengs as he used to, hence the lack of information. He decided to change the topic: "Have you read Professor Jiang Fang's paper about mythology published recently?"

"I was told that he has come up with some new interpretations. You seem to be a prolific writer of poetry. Do you have any collected works? I'd like to read one," said Li Lian. He had always wondered how a sociable person like Qian Mingjing who would butter his bread on both sides and manage to succeed one way or another, could write poetry. He had always wanted to read some.

"Yes, I do!" Mingjing was delighted to be asked. "I have collected my works in one handmade book. A publishing house is quite likely to publish it. I'm going to publish a treatise about my research findings on oracle bone inscriptions with a potential sponsor. I want to ask Professor Meng to write an introduction to my book."

"Why don't you ask Bai Liwen? He is the guru in oracle bone inscriptions," said Li Lian, bemused by Mingjing's plan.

The Bai Liwen that Li Lian was refering to was an expert in the field of palaeography. Li Lian knew how familiar Mingjing was with Bai Liwen, but Mingjing also knew how peculiar Bai was. He also knew he might end up being taunted and jeered at in that introduction by Bai Liwen. That was why he didn't want to ask Bai.

Zhiquan, Li Lian's youngest son, came up to them and leaned against Li Lian's knees, bending the playing cards in his hand while picking his running nose rhythmically. Li Lian asked Zhiquan to blow his nose and cleaned it up for the little kid. He said, rather hesitantly: "Now most of us are struggling with life. It looks like you are the only one who can keep up some semblance of decency. You must be taking to it like a duck to water since the opening of the Yunnan-Burma road." His tone was full of envy. Sincere envy. He stroked Zhiquan's head gently, looking at the cards in his hands. The cards were the kid's only toy.

Mingjing reacted rather absentmindedly to such a comment. All his 'business' activities were categorised by him as 'connoisseurship'. Thinking of jade and of the one dealing with jade artefacts who might sponsor the publication of his treatise, his head and heart lightened up. How annoying this snotty kid was! He wanted to look for Huifen when he heard the clattering of horse hoofs. He looked toward the Mang river to find a man slowly riding a horse along the river followed by another horse carrying two wooden kerosene crates. When the man and the horse arrived at the fair, he dismounted.

The man was dressed in tight black top and trousers, which made him look like a swordsman from one of those literary works about martial arts. Although he had a pistol hanging from his waist band, he had a gentle face. When he approached Qian Mingjing and Li Lian, he asked politely: "Excuse me. Do you happen to know which way leads to Professor Bai Liwen?" When he sensed the doubt from the two, he hurried to explain: "I have been sent by my chieftain to present gifts to Professor Bai." Patting the stuff on the horse's back, he added the village over which his chieftain reigned.

Having quickly appraised the man, Qian Mingjing decided he wouldn't be a threat to Professor Bai, so he gave the man directions, who then thanked him and rode off.

Shizhen and Huifen had finished talking and went back to the two men, asking who they were talking to. Some villagers had been pointing at the man's back, saying he was the man from the chieftain of Wali miles away. Non-locals only had a vague impression that chieftains were more or less like the rulers of a region. Without any interest in pursuing the matter further, they all decided to go back home

As if to prove Shizhen's words, Mingjing had been staying at home without going anywhere for several days in a row. In only two weeks, he finished five essays on Tang dynasty poetry and wrote several poems he was very proud of. When he showed his essays and poems to Huifen, the latter simply refused to have a look. He kept begging and pestering her until she agreed. Once she started reading even the first few lines, she couldn't stop and finished all the essays. She began, trying to sound indifferent: "Your interpretation of Wang Wei sounds quite..." she didn't finish her sentence because a poem caught her eye. It was entitled 'Moonlit Village'. The last two lines read: "*Only one flickering lamp cast its warmth onto my lonely shadow*". Huifen looked up at Mingjing.

"Huifen, I know what you are thinking!" Mingjing said. "Mingjing is lonely? What a prank! How can he be lonely when he has different women around him? Am I right?"

"No, you are wrong. I think you are indeed lonely because you only love one person – you," said Huifen, putting down the manuscripts and continuing to mend a sock.

Mingjing was surprised at her remarks, but he soon regained his composure and laughed: "This is exactly where a wife knows her husband. My manuscript has another function. Can you guess what it is?"

"Not interested."

"I'm going out and will be back before dusk. I won't let you have only one lamp to keep you company." His tone sounded somewhat ironic. But Huifen didn't care. Who was not lonely? Whose heart was not cold, longing for warmth from someone? Whose heart was not thirsty for the nurture of love? She missed a stitch, and the needle pricked her finger. She grabbed a piece of paper to staunch the bleeding to prevent any blood stains on the sock.

Taking the manuscript, Mingjing left on his mission to probe for inside information about his promotion to professor. His destinations were Jiang Fang and Bai Liwen. He wanted to give Li Lian his collection of poems on the way, too. All the poems were written on course papyrus paper and hand-bound by Huifen.

Li Lian's place was located right at the foot of Baotai mountain. His pigsty and chicken coop were built against the hillside, saving one wall. Finding that the gate made of plain whitewood had been left ajar, he decided to go in without knocking. A rhythmic chanting reached his ears blended with the smell of candles, joss sticks and pickles that reached his nose. Mingjing realised Mrs Li was hosting a cult meeting. Hesitantly, he opened the door to see Mrs Li and four other women sitting in the yard, eyes cast down, chanting their sutras. According to Mrs Li, they read the sutras of Tantric Buddhism, but Mingjing was rather pessimistic about whether Tantric Buddhism would accept Mrs Li and her friends as its followers. With Li Lian reading in the room and their landlady making pickles, it seemed they were all satisfied since everyone was doing their own thing.

"Lian," Mingjing called.

Li Lian raised his head from his book and hurried out to greet Mingjing. He cast a bitter look at what was going on in the yard and then said: "Come on! Let's sit outside."

Mingjing handed over his collection of poems: "I'm looking forward to your reaction. I'm not staying. You are going to cook dinner, aren't you?"

Li Lian answered: "Since Zhiqin left, cooking has become my chore! To be honest, my wife is quite capable. It's just her…" He swallowed the rest of the sentence and forced a bitter smile instead.

Mingjing's next visit was to Jiang Fang. Turning over all the other applicants in his mind on his way, he was more confident about himself. The room Jiang Fang had rented was a tight room upstairs with a window overlooking Baotai mountain. The small collection of books had been carefully categorised and put in order. Jiang Fang was busy working at his desk piled up on wooden kerosene crates. Loose pages and open books had taken over the whole 'table'. Mingjing entered the room, bowed and sat on the opposite side of the table. He handed over a pack of Camel cigarettes to Jiang Fang.

Jiang Fang's eyes shone at the pack. He took it and exclaimed: "How could you even manage to get such stuff?" He hurried to find a match, struck it hastily to light up one cigarette, and took a deep breath.

Jiang Fang was very thin. His face was covered by deep, wide wrinkles. His eyebrows were long enough to cover his eyes. Right then, he was working on a paper on 'Nine Songs', a set of Chinese poems written around 300 BC, which was part of his treatise 'History of Ancient Chinese Literature'.

Gazing at the papers on the table, Mingjing said sincerely: "Academics have always disagreed about the author of 'Nine Songs', but I think Professor Jiang's interpretation is the most convincing."

Jiang Fang was indulging himself so much in the pleasure induced by such a quality cigarette he hadn't had an opportunity to touch for so long, that he seemingly ignored Mingjing's compliment. A moment later, he put out the cigarette and put the rest of it on an earthenware plate before he began to talk. That way, he wouldn't waste even one breath of the cigarette.

"Any news?" Jiang Fang asked. Without waiting for Mingjing's answer, he continued: "When Nanchang city in Jiangxi province was taken, according to the reports, our army launched a counterattack and retook the airport and the railway station. What has happened exactly? The reports in the paper are so sketchy nowadays. We need to study the newspaper, not just to read it."

Mingjing readily responded: "Reading between the lines of newspaper reports has been a tradition for Chinese." He handed Jiang Fang his papers. "I dabbled on these topics during the summer vacation. I'd like your opinion. I don't know whether they're meaningful."

Jiang Fang took the manuscript and began to read. He liked smart guys like Qian Mingjing, thinking Mingjing was brilliant and industrious, which was a rather rare combination. But he also thought Mingjing shouldn't involve himself in so many things. Anyway, how could he manage to get the Camels without such active involvement?

"Your research on Song Yu is very convincing. And our department has decided to recommend you for the professorship. Professor Meng has already approved it. You still need another recommendation which has to be an expert in the study of oracle bone scripts. Professor Bai is no doubt the authority in this field. Hopefully he won't raise any objections at the discussions of the department committee."

This Professor Bai was a legendary figure. A capable and sociable man like Mingjing fretted in front of Professor Bai. "I have to visit Professor Bai, come hell or high water," thought Mingjing. But what he said to Jiang Fang was: "Whatever he might say, I have these papers to back me up."

"I guess he won't object," Jiang Fang turned to the earthenware plate and picked up the butt end. "It's not easy to study ancient scripts due to the lack of data and materials."

"I haven't touched one bone since my arrival in Yunnan. Luckily, I have written these papers," said Mingjing. After exchanging more pleasantries, he rose and excused himself.

When Professor Jiang raised his eyes to 'see' Mingjing off, he suddenly sprang up from his chair and shouted: "Splendid! Splendid!"

Mingjing thought Jiang Fang was referring to his papers. The great elation led him to catch his breath. Then it turned out Jiang Fang had been moved by the bushy green colour of Baotai mountain. He took two strides to stand in front of the window, pointing at the mountain outside: "Splendid! So splendidly green!"

The sunshine lit up the bushy dark green of the mountain embedded with several lines of bright red earth. The green offset against the red looked greener. Mingjing, who had reached the staircase, responded: "Many of the place names around here have something to do with dragons. I guess there might be some dragon stories."

"Yes, there are!" answered Jiang Fang almost triumphantly like a child. "I have already heard stories about dragons and have shared them with some people. When the stories reach me again, I find they have already grown into a much more elaborate version. Haven't you heard about it yet?"

Mingjing laughed: "I'm certainly out of touch."

"The story goes like this. Once upon a time, a dragon neglected his duty to provide rain to the region he was in charge of. Then the supreme emperor punished him by transforming his body into the Dragon river, and his whiskers and paws into smaller rivers, creeks and streams. The water has been nurturing the land ever since. He was only able to leave earth and return to heaven 90,000 years later." Jiang Fang fixed his gaze on the mountain outside the window.

"The whole mountain of green is a giant screen painted with dragons, birds, flowers, myths and poetry for my shabby room!" Jiang Fang had already forgotten his beloved Camel cigarette and taken up his pen to resume writing.

Well aware of this combination of a scholar and a poet that characterised Professor Jiang, Mingjing tiptoed downstairs, trying not to interrupt Jiang Fang's thoughts. Just as he reached the typical wall-less living room downstairs, he heard Jiang Fang yelling upstairs: "Qian Mingjing!"

Mingjing turned to go back upstairs and popped his head around the door into the room: "Did you just call me?"

Jiang Fang nodded: "I went to Youchen's current affairs lecture in town the day before yesterday. This physics nerd shared with us an insightful analysis of the situation. Can you imagine that? He said Hitler won't stop at occupying Czechoslovakia. Europe will be at war."

Mingjing laughed: "Did he calculate this according to some law of physics?"

Jiang Fang surprised him with another question: "Do you admire people who commit suicide?"

Mingjing thought about Jiang Fang's question, not sure what he was getting at.

As usual, Jiang Fang didn't allow time for any hesitation and he answered: "Of course you should! It takes a lot of courage to put an end to a life which one has decided is no longer productive. Qu Yuan did it. But the one I admire more is Lord Byron who got himself killed on a battlefield, which is much more splendid than dying on one's deathbed. When the flame of life cracks at its peak, it is suddenly snuffed out, death in collision with fate! How splendid such a death is! Do you still remember the lines from his 'The Isles of Greece'?"

He began to recite it with his clear and idiomatic pronunciation in his sonorous voice. When he had finished one stanza, he paused, looked up and heaved a long sigh: "Mingjing, do you know why I sighed?"

Mingjing, with his head still sticking round the door to the room, answered: "I guess you want to go to the battlefield?"

Jiang Fang laughed out loud: "You guessed half right!" He waved his hand to dismiss Mingjing.

Once Mingjing was out of the house, Jiang Fang was already out of Mingjing's mind. What he then turned over in his mind was how he should convey his intentions to Professor Bai. He decided he had to direct their conversation and clarify what he wanted.

Bai Liwen's place was another sight. On one side wall of the wall-less living room hung several hams, with crates and sacks piled up at the foot of the wall. It didn't take Mingjing one second to guess where the hams came from. A casserole bowl was cooking over the stove, bubbling with the great aroma of ham and pork. Yunnan ham was at the top of Professor Bai's four favourite items. His footman, Old Jin, who was dozing by the stove, was startled when Mingjing cleared his throat to announce his presence. Old Jin rubbed his eyes and muttered: "It's you."

Professor Bai's father was a very rich landlord in Chengdu, the capital city of Sichuan province. Old Jin followed his young master to Beiping first and then departed with him to the south to escape from the war.

"Has Professor Bai got up?" asked Mingjing, though it was already four o'clock in the afternoon.

"I'll go and check," Old Jin answered, and went into the back room. "He's asking you to go in," said Old Jin in a flat tone. This was typical of Old Jin's attitude.

Mingjing walked into a room bigger than regular rooms piled up with books and various stuff. Someone once described Professor Bai's place as smelling like somewhere with dozens of dead mice. The truth was that the smell was more complicated than the alleged dead mice. On the wall and on some of the wooden crates hung Professor Bai's calligraphy done with swift stroke movements, though not necessarily elegant. Calligraphy used to be Mingjing's hobby, but since the war, he had lost interest in such elegant hobbies. The item that occupied most of the space in the room was a bed, where Bai Liwen was enjoying his opium. When he saw Mingjing come in, he raised himself up a little and handed over his pipe: "Do you want a puff?"

Mingjing kept bowing to decline the offer and then lowered himself down onto the rags at the foot of a wall.

"Good. You just sit over there," he said, and resumed smoking. Opium was Bai Liwen's second favourite item, a habit cultivated during his youth as the sole heir of a big rich family back in Sichuan province, and was strongly opposed by his colleagues at the university. He did quit smoking for a while in Beiping, but he resumed it again when they settled in Kunming. When criticised he always retorted in self-justification: "Don't blame me! You guys should blame the supreme quality of the opium in Yunnan!"

He finished his last puff and put down his pipe before sitting up, content and refreshed. When he was content and refreshed, he did his third favourite thing – to give anyone present a piece of his mind, disrespecting the time, the occasion, and the identity of those present. If he felt he wanted to begin, then he began. If he wanted to stop, then he stopped. Sometimes he might even stop in the middle of a sentence. His students were not spared from his strange habits, either. The university authorities simply succumbed to his peculiarities.

Since Qin Xunheng and Meng Fuzhi insisted that a university should cultivate open-mindedness and inclusiveness, they tried to attract all talented scholars. Bai Liwen, who was distinguished in the field of ancient scripts, had been treated with privilege. No one was certain where he acquired his profound knowledge since he had never enrolled in any prestigious universities as other professors at the university had. He often claimed that a diploma didn't mean much to him since his knowledge didn't only come from books, but also stemmed from talent and field work. He left Sichuan at a young age. Before he was employed by Minglun, he worked for an archaeological team. To borrow his own words, what he did was the kind of dirty work that tomb raiders did.

During an excavation, some tiles were unearthed, and all the rare scripts were deciphered by the palaeographer employed by the team. A naughty student played a prank on the palaeographer by showing the expert an ordinary tile he had picked up randomly in the field. The palaeographer deliberated over the tile for a long time and couldn't come up with an explanation. Bai Liwen appeared and snapped at the student: "How dare you pass off that fake as genuine!" The student was scared to admit to the truth. Other similar cases later further proved that Bai Liwen's expertise was out of the ordinary. Since his employment at Minglun, he had been prolific in his academic output, though his four favourite things had also gained him a lot of negative attention. Even Fuzhi had once mentioned that however eccentric one was, one should at least pay basic respect to the rules. Rumour had it that Bai Liwen got lucky and happened to see the student picking up the tile. But it had never been confirmed.

Qian Mingjing had made up his mind to start before Bai Liwen gave him "a piece of his mind", or he would never have the chance to open his mouth, let alone to tell Professor Bai what he wanted.

"Professor Bai, I came for…" his words were interrupted by a coughing fit from Bai Liwen.

When Bai Liwen was done with his coughing, he immediately snatched the chance and began: "I had a bad dream last night. I dreamed a group of Japanese bastard soldiers were shooting at us with their machine guns. Generalissimo Chiang Kai-shek was standing in front of me. He turned around and waved at us to run away. What is inside that bald head of his? Is there anything besides running and hiding? Now we have run all the way to the stable and pigsty, but we are still teaching and doing our research. Look at Meng Fuzhi! People like him are still aggressive and ambitious. I guess they have mobilised every nerve cell, haven't they? Despite the fact that Fuzhi has published so many dissertations, he won't change the course of history. How can you make a mountain with sand? Look at Jiang Fang then. He is just a laughing stock. He is as innocent as a child? What bullshit! He is just immature! And about you, Qian Mingjing! Your study on oracle bone scripts is just like studying ants from an aeroplane. What can you see from so high up in the air?"

Words like those were not news to Mingjing, who had already heard similar things said on different occasions. Nobody attacked by Bai Liwen took him seriously. But what he was going to say was a different story.

"War! Fighting! Resistance! Look at these grovelling lines we study! Can they be used as cannon fodder to fight against the enemy? They can't! What's the point of teaching such stuff to students, then?"

His colleagues had always disapproved of Bai's way of thinking. Meng Fuzhi, for example, mentioned in several lectures: "To protect our motherland is vital; it's equally important to maintain and carry forward Chinese culture. We cannot risk losing our spiritual homeland. We should expand and enrich it."

These words just went in one of Bai Liwen's ears and out the other. He still prattled on about whatever he wanted to. The truth was that he was passionate about his study of ancient scripts. If he were asked to give up his study, he would tell you it would never happen.

Bai Liwen's prattle was interrupted by a shrieking noise from the living room. He slipped off the bed: "Shoes! Where are my shoes?" His feet fumbled around the floor in panic. Mingjing joined him to look for his shoes. He shuffled outside without lifting the backs of his shoes.

"Where are we heading?" asked Mingjing.

"Hiding from the air raids!" retorted Bai.

Some mischievous fellow teased that running to hide-outs was Professor Bai's fourth hobby.

Bai Liwen bumped into Old Jin on his way out.

"It's the whistle from the kettle, sir. Do you remember we had a similar sound once? The whistle sounds quite strange," said Old Jin.

Bai Liwen collected his thoughts and tried to calm himself down. Upon seeing the kettle on the stove instead of the casserole bowl, he was relieved and enlightened. He wagged his head from left to right and took a deep breath: "Ummm! What a waste that the aroma has escaped." Then he shuffled back to his bed.

Once he was settled down again in his bed, Mingjing told him the purpose of his visit.

With his eyes shut tight, he wagged his head once more and said: "Why do you want to become a professor? What's the significance of being a professor? You should start your own business by taking advantage of the Yunnan-Burma road. Everyone will profit from such a road!"

Mingjing raised his voice: "I have heard people say Professor Bai is an avid fan of studying ancient scripts, but now you are suggesting that I start a business. Are you afraid that I might steal your thunder?"

Mingjing's reaction took Bai Liwen by surprise. With his eyes wide open, he sneered at Mingjing: "Are you kidding me? Do I look like someone who is afraid of losing my position? What's there to fight for in those four baskets of red mouldy rice? As for the intricate knowledge, even if you wanted to steal from me, you couldn't."

"No one is capable of stealing Professor Bai's expert knowledge! Fellows like me are just skirting round the edges of your field of study. I'm afraid we don't even know where the door is. Take the character for female '女' (nü) as an example. You think that '女' indicates a person who has been bound with ropes. Those who challenge you for such an interpretation must have been picking bones in an egg!"

These words bucked Bai Liwen up. He dipped his finger into his mouth and began to write other characters on the table, sharing more of his interpretation. Although his interpretations had been interrupted from time to time by his verbal abuse, Mingjing felt relieved that the discussion was finally focused on what he wanted to bring up. He kept offering his opinions on Bai's interpretations.

Bai was very pleased: "People all say you are smart. Indeed, you are smart!"

Mingjing was smart enough to strike while the iron was hot and asked Bai to write down his opinion about Mingjing's application to become a professor. Bai nodded his consent. Old Jin came in to clean the table before bringing up the casserole. Mingjing hurried to excuse himself.

Bai Liwen, with his eyes glued on the casserole, muttered: "Today we have jasmine rice, a Yunnan specialty. Have you tried it yet? It's a gift from the chieftain in Wali. He has been asking me to write an epitaph for his mother and sending gifts as advance payment. But his mother is still strong and healthy — I hope she lives to a ripe old age, so I can get more advance payments. Why don't you stay and have a bowl of this nice rice?"

What a rare offer! Professor Bai inviting someone to have a meal with him! Mingjing repeatedly declined the offer, saying to himself that it was just jasmine rice!

He hurried out of the yard, chaotic thoughts racing through his smart head: "Me? Start a business via the Yunnan-Burma road? What a joke! As versatile as I am, I'm focusing on ancient scripts and poetry. There's no way I could give them up! Besides, I'm not going to give up that professorship, even if it's akin to a cold iron bench!"

Walking out of the lane, and not willing to go home right away, he decided to take a walk along the Mang river, ruminating over Bai Liwen's words: "To start a business via the Yunnan-Burma road! But, that old chap's words might also reflect some people's view about me. People don't realise that it's just a game for me to change and exercise my mind. Such a tiny distraction doesn't stop me from being better than those who stay focused." He had such a competitive mindset which constantly led him to compare people with each other, and himself to other people. Subconsciously, his tendency toward having affairs might be rooted in his obsession of comparing the women involved with one another.

The sparkling water flowed by peacefully. The afterglow of the sun danced over the water as if the war had left this small remote village in Yunnan behind. A flock of crows cried as they fluttered across the river, leaving quietness in their wake.

At a bend in the river stood a neat screen of trees, from which emerged three people. One, Mingjing recognised, was a senior staff member working for the art institute called Old Wei: "Hey, Qian! Look who is coming!"

Mingjing looked and yelled: "Ah? Wow!"

PART III

The two people walking in Mingjing's direction, a man and woman, both dark and lean like beanpoles, bore the stains of travel fatigue. They stopped at Mingjing's exclamation. They smiled and extended their hands for a handshake in a natural, polite and unaffected manner.

It was Wei Feng and Ling Xueyan! The beautiful pair Mingjing saw at the wedding were long since gone. Even those who had relocated to Kunming hadn't suffered such dramatic changes.

"You! It's you two!" Mingjing held Wei Feng's hand with both of his, while his eyes settled on Xueyan, amazed at how much she had changed.

Wei Feng began: "We have come from Guiyang on a long-distance bus. Since our arrival yesterday morning, we have already run twice to hide from air raids. We didn't wait for the alarm to be lifted and have been walking for about three hours."

"We have been doing well," added Xueyan.

"You are going to the Mengs, aren't you? This way," said Mingjing.

Old Wei said: "The two are now staying in the theatre at the ancestral temple. I ran into them in the Ancestral Temple street, so we came together."

"Thank you for showing us the way. Otherwise we would have arrived much later," said Xueyan.

They talked as they walked toward the Mengs' place. Wei Feng said they had first arrived in his hometown of Fuyang city in northwest Anhui province, then they had gone to Chongqing and Guiyang, where they had stayed for several months until they realised that two years had passed.

"It took us some time to scrape together the money to travel that far. Otherwise, we would have got here a long time ago." That was Wei Feng's version of the story.

When they passed an entrance to a lane, Mingjing pointed at a gate: "The second gate." And then he left with the senior staff member.

As the Wei couple approached the gate, the tinkling sound of laughter reached their ears. It was May! Then they heard a child's voice calling "Mum". It was Kiddo! The two looked at each other, tidied up their shabby clothes, and walked into the garden.

The two families were having dinner in the downstairs living room. Zhao Er and his family were sitting around the bigger short table, together with the cat, while the Mengs, except for Earl, were crowded around a small table under the staircase. May was laughing at something Zhao Er had just said. Kiddo was ready to share what he had learned from reading 'Journey to the West', but he tried to catch Bichu's attention first. They all noticed the two strangers enter.

Zhao Er rose from his seat and asked: "Who are you looking for?"

May sprang up from her seat, flew off the steps leading to the garden, and plunged into the female stranger's arms: "Sister Xueyan! It's sister Xueyan!"

May's words sparked great consternation among everyone seated at the tables. Greetings and inquiries were complicated by the Zhao family's hospitality: "Have you had your dinner? Come and join us!" When they declined, the Zhao family quickly finished up their dinner to free up the bigger table for the Mengs.

Holding Bichu's hand tight, Xueyan forced a smile, her face streaming with tears: "Seeing Aunt Bichu is just like seeing my mother. All the pain and suffering I have endured seem to rush out to seek comfort."

"Eat first. We'll talk later." Bichu and Fuzhi were so happy to see the two of them, but then their hearts ached upon seeing how bony they had both become. It immediately dawned on Bichu that Xueyan must know what had happened to her father, but she held her tongue. She would ask later.

"Would you like to wash your faces?" May and Kiddo hurried to take out a basin and pour hot water into it. Zhao Er's wife even took a thermos flask from their room upstairs.

Bichu quickly asked everyone to sit down again at the tables while she busied herself making pancakes and scrambled eggs. May and Kiddo, sitting by the smaller table, continued to eat the mouldy red rice without even a single glance at the delicious dishes over on the bigger table.

"Aunt Bichu," Xueyan asked, "We'll have the red rice, too."

Fuzhi laughed: "We don't have the right to choose. Even I have to listen to your aunt."

Everyone settled down to talk.

Wei Feng and Xueyan started to describe their latest long trip. It was quite crowded on the bus. The bumpy and winding mountain roads added to their discomfort. It was way behind schedule due to frequent breakdowns. When enemy fighter planes appeared, it had to hide under trees, which slowed down their journey, too. Once, the bus was out of action for two days in the middle of nowhere. People were starving, but they collected all their food to feed the driver in case something went wrong with him and no one could drive the bus.

Wei Feng sighed when he came to this part: "What we went through was nothing compared with what our country has been going through."

Bichu asked: "How did Xueyan survive such hardship, considering what a comfortable childhood she had?"

Xueyan answered: "Human beings are quite resilient creatures. Nothing is unbearable — I just cross the bridge when I get there. What we have been through would take at least three days to tell you." When she smiled, her teeth shone like pearls as they used to.

Zhao Er came to tell them that the attic over the gate, which was used for storing some old pieces of furniture, had a piece made of wooden boards that could function as a double bed. They were so grateful for such a kind offer.

When they had all finished their meal, May began to do the dishes while Kiddo offered to help. The adults went upstairs. Upon seeing the simple but clean room, Wei Feng and Xueyan sighed together: "How we envy you such a cosy shelter in time of war."

Bichu held Fuzhi's gaze and then asked Xueyan when she had left Beiping.

Xueyan said: "I went to the countryside in Hebei province last October."

"So, do you know how my father died?" Bichu's voice trembled.

Xueyan stood up from her chair: "You have already heard the news?"

Fuzhi said: "We only got an obituary notice from Aunt Lianxiu who didn't explain how Grandpa Lü died."

"I have been turning over in my mind how I should deliver the news to you when I met you," hesitated Xueyan.

"Tell us the truth." Fuzhi held Bichu's shoulders.

Calmly and clearly, Xueyan announced: "Grandpa Lü committed suicide."

They all rose to their feet on hearing these words.

Fuzhi repeated unconsciously: "Suicide!" That was what he had surmised.

Tears came so fast to Bichu's eyes that a pool of tears formed on the table in front of her.

Xueyan then explained that when Grandpa Lü had refused to take the position in the puppet municipal government, the enemy had tried to force him to accept. He ran out of options and took his life to register his protest.

"When my father came back from Grandpa Lü's funeral, he grieved that such a noble spirit as Grandpa Lü had given up his life for the sake of righteousness and would no longer be available to the younger generations to come," added Xueyan, her tears gushing again.

Bichu asked rather abruptly: "Where is the coffin? Is it being stored in the residence?"

Xueyan answered rather hesitantly: "The Japanese were concerned that he might have feigned death and insisted on checking it. Once it was confirmed, they arranged a cremation."

"Cremation!" Bichu stopped crying. She sneered: "Well, that's quite thorough and clean!"

They all fell silent until the silence was shattered for a long while by Xueyan's stifled cry of agony: "Aunt Bichu, Uncle Fuzhi, my father is already among the walking dead in hell — he has accepted the offer from the Japanese to preside over the Art and Literature Union of Northern China."

Fuzhi and Bichu were stunned at the news. Xueyan covered her face with her hands. Seeing Xueyan's skinny arms protruding from the loose sleeves of her blue *qipao* made of rough homespun cotton cloth and her tidy hair which was lustreless like dry grass, made Bichu's heart ache. She helped Xueyan to sit down again: "My dear girl! My dear girl!" Wei Feng took Xueyan's hand.

Fuzhi took several paces and then said, in an unusually loud voice: "Jingyao is weak by nature. We should have insisted he leave with us!"

He paused, and then turned around: "Now that the older generation is history, let's talk about the present."

But Bichu wanted to know about one more person of the older generation. She asked Xueyan about Lianxiu. Xueyan told her what she knew about Lianxiu and added that Lü Xiangge had left with her when she left Beiping.

Bichu was surprised: "You took Xiangge with you? Where is she now? Has she been making trouble?"

"A troublemaker needs trouble to make," opined Wei Feng. "It's a long and winding tale. We can only give you a brief account."

May and Kiddo ran upstairs at that moment. Bichu sent them to go and sleep in their parents' bedroom. The four adults were ready to stay up all night to catch up on each other's news.

Wei Feng escaped from Beiping in July 1937. He first worked as a copy clerk for the guerrillas active around Hebei province. When autumn came, he joined a team of college students dedicated to the resistance against the Japanese and headed for Yan'an. Their patriotism and revolutionary ambitions made them feel even the sky in Yan'an was bluer, the water sweeter, and all the strangers walking on the street were closer like family members.

After staying in a hostel for a while, most of his travelling companions had been given something to do. Some continued their studies and others went to work. Wei Feng was the only one who had not been assigned a task. His friends talked this over with Wei Feng and all agreed that the fact that Wei Feng was already a teaching assistant in a university majoring in science and had experience as an underground party member would surely make him suitable for something.

More time passed, the party came to talk the matter over and decided he should go and teach at the Anti-Japanese Military and Political College.

The person who came to talk to Wei Feng advised him: "You are not only going to teach students, you should also learn from those worker-peasant soldiers." Without any doubt, Wei Feng promised he would.

He was quite busy once he got started. He was used to teaching maths for middle schoolers, but his students included teenagers and those in their 40s. Several young soldiers who had survived the Long March were very smart and quick to learn, though they hadn't had much education before.

Wei Feng compiled several textbooks for students of different abilities. He was very satisfied with what he was doing and never thought that his talent was wasted as some might have thought. If he couldn't fire a gun at the enemy or go to work in the fields, it would be perfect if he could support the war effort indirectly. He took his teaching so seriously that it almost became something sacred for him with his assumption that all these students would grow to be officers at all levels in the army to fight against the Japanese invaders! He was popular among students, who felt that he was good at making things easy to understand. He led a simple life, freeing his mind of complexity. The old days began to fade as time went by. Only Xueyan's image survived the devastating fading process.

Besides Wei Feng, there were also other young teachers from different places such as Beiping, Shanghai and Tianjin. Like kinsmen, these young souls would gather together and chat. People joked that they were members of the 'professors' club'.

One night the group had a walk along the Yan river. Their discussion of current affairs didn't last long since they didn't have much access to reading materials about what was going on. Someone from Shanghai shared several dates with the others, which triggered a new discussion about food. Everyone had something they missed terribly. Someone from Beiping missed the instant-boiled mutton and *douzhi*, a fermented drink made from ground mung beans, while what someone from Shanghai missed most was the giant smooth rice-balls made of sticky rice and stuffed with assorted fillings served in soup.

The talk rambled on until one person mentioned what their daily diet was: "We board with the ordinary masses. What about those who board with the junior and senior officials?"

One guy snapped at him: "If you are ordered to board with the ordinary masses, then keep your mind on the ordinary masses."

The first one retorted: "We are not students after all. We are teachers specialised in different fields. Aren't we entitled to a little bit of privilege?"

Old Ding from Shanghai said: "I don't care much about what we eat every day. But I do have different opinions about learning from the worker-peasant soldiers and regularly being introspective. I came here to share my knowledge. It never occurred to me that knowledge is not respected here."

Upon his words, they all fell silent. A moment later, a writer of literary theory spoke up: "Knowledge alone doesn't work. It has to be guided by correct views about life and the world. We have to learn from the worker-peasant soldiers to ensure we're on the correct path."

Old Ding laughed: "Do you know Vladimir Lenin once said the most important thing is to educate the peasants?"

Not seeing eye to eye with each other, the discussion was soon over and the group dispersed.

Unexpectedly, a couple of days after the walk, when the unit Old Ding was with held a struggle session, they invited members of the 'professors' club' to attend. The session was aimed at helping Old Ding to right his wrongs so that he wouldn't be so cocky just because he was educated, and so that he would embrace the fact that the only correct path to revolution and resistance against the Japanese was to accept re-education from the worker-peasant soldiers. The session went on. Then someone mentioned that a clique like the 'professors' club' was corrupting the revolution. The members of the club shuddered with terror at such an accusation, cold sweat dripping down their backs. Then the person presiding over the session asked Wei Feng to say something. Wei Feng muttered a few perfunctory words.

Several days after the struggle session, Old Ding came to Wei Feng and told him he was leaving Yan'an. He implied that Wei Feng should think about leaving, too. Following Old Ding's departure, more members of the 'professors' club' left. Wei Feng had several sleepless nights, sitting in bed, watching the moonlight outside the *yaodong*, a cave dwelling, waxing and waning in turn. He knew it was wrong to disrespect knowledge, but he also knew such disrespect would change sooner or later. What attracted him was the unifying ideology in this place. Besides the short-term goal of fighting the Japanese invaders, there was the long-term goal to build a socialist country where everyone was equal, which would not be realised by his physics studies. He wanted to wait and see what was going on.

After that, Wei Feng severed communication with the club members and sometimes joined his students to work in the fields, laughing and talking. He had built up a solid bond with them.

One day when he had finished his teaching and was helping a student with an algebra problem on a big rock under a tree, someone came and tapped him on the shoulder: "Are you comrade Wei Feng?"

Wei Feng stood up with delight to see Old Shen, who was his leader when they were in Beiping. Back in Beiping, Old Shen carried out his work under the cover of a registered university student, although he looked as if he was in his 30s. Wei Feng had had a lot of contact with Old Shen and managed to escape from Beiping with Old Shen's instructions after Wei Feng had finished his last liaison task.

Old Shen was pleased: "Though we did meet in person a couple of times, I was still afraid that you might not recognise me." He then told Wei Feng the name he now went under. It was the name of the person who had been put in charge of office administration in the latest announcement. They shook hands.

Old Shen said: "I know you are a reliable comrade." It seemed that Old Shen was well aware of what Wei Feng had been doing since he didn't ask the usual questions for a newcomer, such as whether he was accustomed to living here or not.

Wei Feng said: "If you have time to spare, I'd like to talk to you."

Old Shen said: "I'll ask for you when I have time."

They parted after talking more about the current situation.

About a week later, someone else in authority approached Wei Feng, informing him that the radio station needed a technician and wanted to transfer Wei Feng to the station since his field of study was physics. Wei Feng stated that he had studied optics but knew nothing about radios. The guy looked at Wei Feng rather suspiciously and said it would be a joke if someone who had graduated from the physics department of a prestigious university didn't know how to handle a radio. On second thoughts, Wei Feng felt it wouldn't be a big deal, so he agreed.

He moved from the cave dwelling to the top of the hill. Metaphorically, he was being promoted to a 'higher position'. Once he had settled in, he went to see the station manager. The radio was down for several days. It had taken a handful of people to repair it for two days in a row. They were all happy to see Wei Feng, who immediately occupied himself with the repair. In about an hour, he fixed it. It took him a while to figure out his new role. With the new methods he proposed, the radio station functioned normally, broadcasting the voice of Yan'an countrywide.

It reminded Wei Feng of the nervous excitement he had felt when he had received CPC announcements via his secret radio station and then delivered the message to all involved. But he didn't feel the same sense of excitement now he was responsible for maintaining the station to broadcast the party's message. He was prudent and never poked his nose into affairs which were not related to his work. He continued to teach in the college and kept his distance from everyone.

Many of those who came from all parts of the country to join the revolution were young. When those youngsters spent enough time together, love would blossom for some. Those who did well became happily married couples, those for whom things didn't go well suffered. Several young women fell for Wei Feng and paid frequent visits to his cave dwelling. It drove Wei Feng nuts. He used a paint brush to copy his marriage announcement published in the newspaper, put it in a wooden frame and hung it up on the wall. But the paper Xueyan didn't seem capable of fending off these suitors. Wei Feng sighed. At one point he was worried that Xueyan wouldn't be able to handle the tough life of a revolutionary and he left Xueyan behind when he escaped from Beiping. Now that he was feeling more settled, he thought it would be better for the two to stay together.

One evening, on his way back from college, he saw someone walking toward him. The man looked extremely tall since he was walking downhill. His hair was back-combed, revealing his broad forehead. He had an air of peace and solemnity.

As Wei Feng got close to him, he asked: "Student, what kind of work do you do?"

Wei Feng answered.

"Do you need me to introduce myself?" the man asked again.

"No, no. I know who you are," said Wei Feng.

"Then you introduce yourself to me. Which city are you from?"

Wei Feng gave a detailed answer. Upon hearing the name Minglun, the man's eyes shone with something almost like admiration. He asked immediately: "Have you heard of someone called Meng Fuzhi?"

166

Taken rather by surprise, Wei Feng said anyone who went to Minglun knew who Professor Meng was.

The man said: "I'd like to meet him to discuss something with him — 'Dream of the Red Chamber'. Ha ha ha!" he cackled. As he passed Wei Feng, he said: "Go and get your wife and ask her to come here. Why should two hearts be kept apart and suffer?"

Wei Feng didn't realise it was an instruction from the top and he hesitated. Not until the day Li Yuming appeared in his cave dwelling did he make up his mind to send someone to fetch Xueyan.

Li Yuming had been active in Beiping and Tianjin and his task was to transport various drugs and necessities. When the then groom and his best man met, the two looked at each other with mixed emotions welling up.

Yuming's first sentence was: "I have been to Chestnut street several times." Then he told Wei Feng about Grandpa Lü's suicide and Ling Jingyao's acceptance of the appointment from the puppet government.

Wei Feng said: "Grandpa Lü was admirable. Ling is reluctant to leave behind his life of comfort in Beiping, and this is an inevitable end for him. But my Xueyan! How will she survive all these things? No, I have to help her to leave Beiping!"

"I will go!" said Li Yuming galantly.

Hence the note "Xueyan, come" which finally made its way to Xueyan after months of traveling. When Xueyan had engraved these words on her heart, she burnt the note. Travelling with Li Yuming, she and Xiangge made their way as far as Anci district of Langfang city, Hebei province. Then they took a bus and later rode donkeys until they reached a small remote village.

Xueyan maintained her composure throughout. When interrogated, she answered without changing the tone of her voice or her expression. She didn't complain about the horrible food and beds. When they paused in a small town, Xiangge was struck down by a sudden illness and was bedbound for two days with no appetite. It was Xueyan who nursed Xiangge. She bought some flour at a high price on the black market to make a bowl of paste seasoned with salt and chopped chives, which was thicker and better than the kind of paste available for those in good health. She begged Xiangge to eat it all for her own sake. Xiangge felt better when she had finished it. She sobbed bitterly, claiming she had never suffered from anything like that back in her hometown before she went to Beiping. If she had known how painful it was going to be, she would have stayed in Beiping. Xueyan forced herself to keep her chin up and take care of things. She also asked Li Yuming to finish the paste left in the pot. Li Yuming thought that paste was the most delicious thing he had ever tasted.

Once they were back on the road again, they managed to hire a small shabby donkey. Xueyan asked Xiangge to ride the donkey while she and Yuming walked on foot. After a while, Yuming suggested Xiangge and Xueyan take turns to ride the donkey, but Xueyan declined. Xiangge sprang off the donkey and forced Xueyan onto the back of the animal, whispering: "Mrs Wei, you have a kind heart."

Looking at Xueyan's pale face which almost looked transparent, Yuming told himself: "You are my Virgin Mary."

Two days later, Xiangge fully recovered. Her flurry of numerous little attentions to Yuming resumed. She also took good care of Xueyan. As smart as Xiangge was, she always did things well if she wanted to. Her constant revelations of surprise and disappointment had been nagging her. Believing in the proverb that "Water flows downward while people should strive to move upward", it was baffling for her why Miss Ling, Mrs Wei, was willing to leave behind all her comforts and suffer such pain.

Xueyan was no saint, after all. Undergoing such pain was a real trial for her. What bothered her most were two things. The first were the bed bugs in those small private inns and the second were the outhouses which provided almost no clean place to put one's feet and no privacy. The two things would sometimes quickly bring her to tears, which she would dry immediately so as not to get chilblains.

It was not that she didn't care about such suffering, but her heart had been reassuring her that she could overcome all kinds of pain since she was on her way to meet her other half.

She was on her way to a reunion and to translate her ideal of doing her bit for the war into reality. She was no longer the daughter of Ling Jingyao. Rather, she was the wife of Wei Feng, a new identity which sympathised with the rustic style of country life.

It was hard for Xueyan to convey these thoughts to Xiangge. When she talked with Xiangge about the significance of the war of resistance, her words were treated like lectures by Xiangge, who would pout and laugh it off. She had a glorious smile. Gradually, Yuming was not sure whether life in the liberated areas was suitable for Xiangge. Under her veneer of vitality and smartness was something that had been long established. Such a mixture made her very different from the average youngster soon to be twenty.

Li Yuming accompanied the two women until they reached their destination — a small village located in a valley, which served as their depot. Before he left, Yuming told Xueyan the things she should pay special attention to. As for Xiangge, he suggested that if she couldn't make her way to Yan'an, she would be better off going to the rear area.

It snowed when Li Yuming bade farewell to the two of them. The earth and sky were veiled in a thick layer of white. Xueyan saw Yuming off at the end of the street, concerned that his journey alone was getting off to such a tough start. But Yuming couldn't wait for the snow to stop since he had lost so much time escorting Xueyan to keep his promise to Wei Feng and as a source of power for himself. Now he had to leave because he had tasks to take care of.

No one knew when the people who were supposed to travel with Xueyan and Xiangge would arrive. How could she handle all the odds and ends during the indefinite wait? But he had confidence in Xueyan because of her intelligence, her bravery and her kind heart.

Xueyan, in her short scarlet cotton coat that she had bought en route, stood in the snow with her eyes fixed on Yuming: "Thank you, Yuming! Take care of yourself and stay alert. I'm saying this on behalf of Wei Feng, too." She held out her hand with a smile.

Li Yuming took up this gentle delicate hand, stooped and gave it a gentle peck.

Xueyan was taken by surprise by such an action, but not offended. She understood the feeling of being gnawed by bitterness and the need for gentle support. She said: "I know from the bottom of my heart you are our friend. A true friend."

"You don't," said Yuming to himself. He smiled, took a step back from her, turned around, and strode out of the valley, leaving behind the lonely trail of his footsteps, which were erased in no time by the heavy snow.

Xueyan and Xiangge settled down in a farmer's house to wait for further instructions from Wei Feng. The farmer's family name was Wang, which literally meant 'king'. The old couple lived with their son, their daughter-in-law and their grandson named Shuanzhu, which meant 'to be tied', in the hope that the little boy would be tied to the family and live a long and healthy life. Their son was out doing some business during winter. His wife, a very short woman, who might have suffered on account of her short stature, would sit on the *kang*, a heatable brick bed popular in north China, to make soles for shoes with her fine and neat stiches. Xueyan admired such needlework and said it was a virtue to master the art of needlework.

Xiangge sneered at such a comment: "It's much easier to learn how to use a needle than to learn to use a pen. I haven't made soles for years. When we get to..." She paused because she didn't know where they were going... "I will make you and Mr Wei Feng each a pair of shoes."

Xueyan said: "I think I'm going to ask you to teach me how to make shoes."

When the daughter-in-law cooked, Xueyan always offered to help or to look after the child. Xiangge didn't want Xueyan to do such things, claiming: "We have paid them well. Have they ever seen so much money?"

When the daughter-in-law heard what Xiangge said, she gave Xiangge a sideways glance but didn't say anything.

Xueyan wanted to help because she had no books to read. She did have pens and paper, but she didn't dare to write down anything. Helping out was a welcome distraction for her and made her happy. She even tried to knit a vest for the kid with yarn, but unlike her smart head, her clumsy hands scrambled to finish her work. When Xueyan helped the kid put on his vest, all three adults in the Wang family were very happy.

Xiangge, unwilling to help, went out to visit different houses. You might well call her visits investigating and exploring the countryside. One day, the daughter-in-law whispered to Xueyan: "That girl who came with you said you are a young lady from a very rich landlord's family and she is just a poor maid at your service. This doesn't sound good." Back then, although landlords were not yet the targets of class struggle sessions, landlords were definitely viewed negatively.

Xueyan hurried to explain: "I was not born into a landlord's family. My father teaches. Besides, I have left my family behind and am no longer connected to them."

The woman kept nodding her head: "I know. I know. You are on your way to find your husband, but your parents didn't allow you to do so. Like Wang Baochuan in the play 'The Return of Xue Pinggui'. She swore to leave her family to marry Xue Pinggui against her father's will who flatly refused three times to allow his daughter of noble birth to marry a man from such a low station in life."

After the conversation, Xueyan gently reminded Xiangge she should go out less often and talk less. Xiangge restrained herself for the next couple of days and then further intensified her activities. Some men even came to the door to ask for Xiangge. The Wang family couldn't bear such disturbances and suggested to Xueyan that the two of them should go and talk to the head of the village and find another household to stay with. Xueyan pleaded until, finally, the family reluctantly agreed to let them stay.

Time flew by. Spring Festival was almost round the corner. One day Xueyan was sitting on the kang in her regular aimless manner. There was the sound of a man's voice. She thought it might be another man looking for Xiangge, but she saw the daughter-in-law fly toward the courtyard while the man pushed open the gate and came in. The daughter-in-law urged her son to call the man 'dad'. It turned out the son of the Wang couple had come back.

Lifting up the piece of printed cloth functioning as a curtain, Xueyan saw a man carrying a basket on his back handing a baby rattle to the kid, who took it, cocked his head at the man hesitantly in expectation, and then extended his short chubby arms for a hug. The man scooped up the child, calling out "dad" and "mum", and walked into the room with his wife amid the soft sounds of rattling. Xueyan watched, tears coursing down her cheeks, and muffled her impulse to cry out.

When Xiangge came back later and heard about the son's return, she immediately went to the main northern room. She could be heard talking and laughing. Soon she came back to the room she and Xueyan shared and told Xueyan the Wangs were overjoyed. They bought some liquor to celebrate and invited her to take some, too. She then added the son was quite good looking, too good for his wife. Xueyan laughed and teased Xiangge that she had figured that out fast.

The old couple's son was called Wang Yi (— *yi* meaning 'one') for the sake of convenience rather than for any profound reason. After his return, the garden underwent many changes. The crumbling wall was fixed; the hens clucked with vitality; even Xiangge stayed around without going out visiting, offering a helping hand to the junior Wang couple. Only Xueyan remained aloof, waiting. Each day was lengthened into a year in her expectation for someone from Wei Feng to come and fetch her.

Spring came to the valley unnoticed. The frozen river was decorated with little pools of water everywhere; the icicles along the slope trickled with drops of water as they thawed. Xueyan was secretly planning to leave for Xi'an first and then to try and reach Wei Feng there if no one appeared for her soon. She talked about her plan with Xiangge, who answered with a laugh: "What a coincidence! I'm thinking about leaving, but not with you. I'm leaving with Wang Yi. He's taking me with him!" She tossed her head smugly, eyes sparkling. Xueyan was stunned by her words at first, but then asked calmly about their route. Xiangge said she didn't know and didn't care because Wang Yi would take care of her.

Xueyan knew only too well that she had no right to supervise Xiangge, and she didn't want to ask any favours from Xiangge either, so she turned to Wang Yi to enquire about an appropriate route. Wang Yi told her she might head west all the way and climb over the mountains until she reached Shanxi province because this route was safe, although tough, to travel. He then confessed to Xueyan that Xiangge was leaving with him. They were going into town to buy and resell things to make money like he always did. They were not heading for Shanxi.

Wang Yi was a handsome northerner, well-built and with delicate features, who seemed to have inherited all the best traits from the different races that comprised his kinsmen. He looked smart, too. Xueyan overheard the couple quarrelling in the next room that night. The short wife wailed: "You must have been possessed! Don't you see she is a monster? She is going to devour me and our son and your parents!" Wang Yi answered rather calmly that Xiangge was just asking him to show her how to run a business and she shouldn't be jealous about Xiangge. The more Xueyan listened, the more concerned she became about what would happen to the family.

Since Xiangge had made it clear that she would go her own way, she had been extremely good to Xueyan, claiming she didn't know when they would meet again, and that she wouldn't want the Mengs to think ill of her. She was eager to help Xueyan, which moved Xueyan because it had been a long time since she had felt Xiangge's sincerity. Xueyan told Xiangge again and again: "Though you have Wang Yi traveling with you, you should still stay alert all the time and obey the rules when doing things. Remind him he has his family waiting for him. It would still be the best option if you head for the rear area to find Aunt Bichu."

Xiangge answered immediately: "I'll turn to them for sure! Nothing is better than that."

When Xueyan handed her 150 yuan, Xiangge took it with no intention of declining it or feigning politeness. She asked: "I don't think you still need your scarlet jacket. May I have it?"

Xueyan nodded. Seeing Xiangge sewing the money into the inside pocket of the scarlet coat with a contented smile hanging on the corner of her mouth, Xueyan felt the turmoil surging inside her. What if anything happened to her in a remote village like this in such a wild valley, how would anybody ever know what had happened?

Several more days passed. That day Xiangge came back from outside and told Xueyan: "The village head wants to see you. Maybe he has got some news."

Xueyan, taking a stick from the pile of firewood to use as a walking stick, hurried through the muddy puddles along the short street toward the village head's house. The village head was dumfounded: "No. I haven't sent anyone for you. It must be a misunderstanding."

Xueyan hurried back to ask Xiangge why. But before she reached the Wangs' gate, she could already see the short wife bawling and stamping her feet in front of the gate, with the old couple by her side, trying to comfort her. It turned out Wang Yi had left with Xiangge already.

Things always have their own schedules. After so many months of waiting, there was still no news for Xueyan. On the third day after Xiangge left with Wang Yi, the village head brought four students to meet Xueyan. They were the travel companions Li Yuming had mentioned to her. The two female students were from Tianjin and the other two male students were from northeast China.

"Heaven always has a door open!" thought Xueyan, who was overwhelmed by the signs of hope she had been awaiting for so long.

The village head said the enemy might come to loot the village now that the snow and ice had melted with the coming spring and that they should leave now while they still could. Before Xueyan left, she gave 100 yuan to the Wangs. The old couple were so grateful for her generosity, claiming this huge sum was enough to buy food for the family and coffins for the two of them. Xueyan told Wang Yi's wife she should send her son to school. The short wife said tearfully: "I'm not blaming you for what has happened. People should be held to account for their deeds."

Xueyan had a sore nose: "Who should they blame for everything that has happened?"

Xing, one of the students from northeast China, said he knew which way to go. It was indeed as Wang Yi had told Xueyan — to go westward all the way over the mountains in order to reach Shanxi province, which was under the control of the warlord Yan Xishan during the second world war. The depot there provided all sorts of services to those engaged in the war by various means and a bus station with long-distance buses taking passengers to different towns. With such a clear destination in mind, the five departed from the village in high spirits.

The mountain path wound ahead effortlessly, yet each footfall cost more strength for the five. The going became difficult and rocky with muddy puddles everywhere. When they stopped for the night, they were almost up to their eyes in mud.

One of the female student's feet was red and swollen with blisters. She sank down by the roadside and cried. Xueyan stopped by her side to comfort her.

Xing asked Xueyan: "I heard that you are the only daughter of the richest family in Beiping. It's amazing you can endure so much."

Xueyan smiled by way of response.

They didn't reach the top of the mountain until the second night. When they looked back the way they had come, they saw fires in the far distance, lighting up the horizon. They stared at the fires for some time when Xing cried: "It must be the Japanese army looting some places. Wait! Isn't that the location of the village?" They all gathered around but, except for staring, there was nothing they could do. One suggested they pick up their pace to reach the base earlier so they could join the war one day earlier.

Xueyan was scared. What would happen to the Wang family?

Later news came that the enemy raided seven villages that night. The Japanese soldiers looted, burned, massacred and stopped at nothing. The old Wang couple were killed. The short wife escaped in time with her son deep into the mountains with the survivors in the village, saving the last descendant bearing the Wang family name.

The five raced against the clock for about 10 days when they reached a fair which miraculously had several diners. The dim light from the diners was cosy enough for the travellers. Xing proposed that they should have some hot soup, so they walked into one of the diners. One of them picked up one of the bottles on the table. After one smell, he cried they must have reached Shanxi province, famed for its vinegar.

The rest picked up the bottle, too, smelling and observing.

Xueyan sat down at the table, too dizzy and weak to lift the bottle. She felt someone sit quite close to her. When she gathered her strength to turn her head to check, she couldn't believe what she saw. She rubbed her eyes, threw herself at the person and passed out.

It was Wei Feng. Her Wei Feng had come for her!

After Wei Feng was transferred to the radio station, his excellent performance was soon recognised. But somehow the station manager never let his guard down. He asked behind Wei Feng's back how could the son-in-law of a turncoat be serving at such a vital post. Very soon, Old Shen told Wei Feng northwest Shanxi province was trying to open up a new base, but they were in need of someone to do the publicity. Old Shen recommend Wei Feng in the belief that it was a good opportunity for Wei Feng to further train and improve himself.

It was quite alright for Wei Feng. Besides, Xueyan was coming from Shanxi province. He could go up to meet her midway.

A couple of days later, Old Shen talked to Wei Feng again, informing him the plan had changed. Since there were a lot of young people in the liberated area, it was felt that some of them might work better and achieve more in the areas under KMT rule. Wei Feng, who used to teach at Minglun University, fell into this category. It seemed the perfect cover for him to work under. Besides, he could use his cover to build up the strength of the CPC on campus.

He patted Wei Feng on the shoulder and said: "It is the best thing for you. I am happy it has worked out!" He even agreed that Wei Feng could go and meet Xueyan first before the two of them headed for Kunming together.

No one would have known how Wei Feng and Xueyan would have recognised each other in such dim light. When Xing figured out what was going on, he managed to find a room for Xueyan to have a proper rest. Xueyan woke up to see Wei Feng bending over, staring at her, one hand stroking her hair. Reason was telling them it was not a dream, but their hearts felt it was too good to be true. They clutched each other's hands so tightly as if they feared that if they loosened their grip by just a fraction, it would all vanish into thin air.

"Uncle Fuzhi, Aunt Bichu," Wei Feng looked at the Meng couple. "We are now together. So all the suffering we have both shared seems less serious."

The rooster crowed in the yard. The pigs were already up and about. Day was breaking.

THE ENDLESSLY FLOWING MANG RIVER

FENG, I AM WRITING TO YOU. This is the first time we have been apart for the last six months. You have gone with Professor Zhuang to escort students to a neighbouring county. Nine days have already passed since you left. It seems unbearably long. I myself even wonder how I survived those dozens upon dozens of days and nights waiting to be with you again six months ago.

The clear water of the Mang river flows at a pleasant speed. Have you noticed that the closer it flows to the city, the slower it becomes? By the river, we finally have a place we can call home. Standing in front of the gate, we can see the river between the green screen of trees. We walked all the way down the Mang river to find our beloved relatives; later we walked all the way up the river and found this place to settle down.

When you met Professor Zhuang and Della, you must have told them in detail about our new home. This room in the west wing, though small and shabby, provides us with shelter. Outside the window we can see rows of different-coloured flowers. It is the 'garden' of our neighbours Mr and Mrs Mi, who are nice, kind and funny. The Zhuangs wanted us to join them in the western suburbs because they have spare rooms, but we both love Salt Falls, which is within walking distance of Aunt Bichu.

You teased me that I am like a fairy who, by waving her magic wand, has brought about so many changes step by step to our love nest. I can tell you our home has changed more during your absence. The two dozen kerosene crates I gathered have been transformed into our bed, chairs, stools and a sofa! Can you imagine that? I cushioned the crate which has lost the two side boards with dried corn husks and covered the husks up with a piece of cloth. It's comfortable to sit in like a rocking chair. What a pity you can't squeeze yourself in. It'll be too tight like a splint for you. Our dining table, which is made of two crates, has a floral tablecloth with frills from Mrs Mi. In the middle stands a clay jar full of flowers I collected in the fields. When you come back home, I'm sure you will mutter again and again: "Our lovely nest! Our beautiful home!" Feng, what a pair of lucky birds we are that we can live in our motherland and have the freedom to decorate a tiny place in a world full of pain and suffering; many are not so lucky!

How much I wanted to share my new life with my parents! But where are my parents? The place in my heart that used to be reserved for my parents has been gouged out, leaving a gigantic pool of blood, tears and sorrow beyond repair. Sometimes you stroke my head and tell me if I miss them, I should go ahead and miss them. If I want to talk to them, go ahead and talk to them. No one can cut off the ties of blood. I know how tolerant and generous you are, but I can't forget the gnawing pain.

Xueyan, do you hate me? Have you heard my moaning?

Dad's words are still lingering in my ears. I can hear dad asking me.

My dear parents! My poor parents! I'm Xueyan, a free Xueyan, not a conquered subject!

If I were still in Beiping, I don't think I would go out to work. The seemingly comfy life was a sugar-coated jail. Now I want to work and am going to get a job. Feng, will you be proud of me? What I'm going to tell you now is the most important news. The day after you left, I paid a visit to Aunt Bichu. On the way I ran into Professor John Snow Sheldon. Do you still remember that he prefers to be known by his Chinese name, Xia Zhengsi? He was with Professor Xiao Cheng. They mentioned that the foreign language department is looking for a teaching assistant to help Professor Xia teach French, and who can also teach several English courses. Out of courtesy, he asked me whether I had learned French. I gathered my courage and said "yes". You know my father has always said that French is the most beautiful language. He sent me to learn French when I was still in primary school. When I graduated from high school, I spent two years in Paris. My French was greatly improved even though the school I went to was not very academically demanding. We switched to French and talked for about half an hour. Amazingly, all the words and grammar I needed for communication came back to me. I sailed through the conversation.

Professor Xia was very happy: "Do you like reading poetry?"

"I do, but it seems so far away to me now," I answered.

"How come? Poetry never leaves people." Then he recited a stanza from a poem in French:

> When I passed by the prairie,
> I saw, this evening, on the path,
> A flower trembling and withered,
> A pale briar flower.
> A green bud beside it
> Was balancing on the shrub;
> I saw a new flower bloom;
> The youngest was the most beautiful:
> Men are like this, always looking for something new.

He asked me who the poet was. I told him that was Alfred de Musset's 'La nuit d'août'. He happily reached out to shake hands with me: "You are competent for this position. I'm going to recommend you to the department."

Two days later, I finished a narrative about this village located in Salt Falls. Most of the ideas were from May, though. I don't know why French is so perfect for conveying all the emotions. I took it to Professor Xia in town, who took me to meet the dean. I'm not quite sure about his name. Maybe he is called Wang Dingyi. Professor Wang, a lean and serious character, said he had listened to Professor Xia on this issue, while the latter winked at me upon being mentioned. I was told that several people were after this position. I guess I might have been the least experienced and least academically qualified applicant. And I didn't have proper French training. But I am the one who is most likely to get the job!

I am going to be one of your colleagues. Though Minglun has a rule that no couple should teach at the same time in the same university, I am just working temporarily in the faculty. I guess that doesn't count, does it?

When Mrs Mi delivered the table cloth to us, she threw in a small cake she had baked. I'm saving it for you. The three of us talked for a while in the garden. They speak fluent English. Mr Mi speaks French but it's a pity I can't speak their mother tongue German. So, there was one more person involved in the conversation. You must have guessed. It was Leo, sitting on the ground, turning his eyes toward whoever was speaking. His ears are expressive. When he is happy, his ears fold backward; when he gets excited, his ears pop up. If one day Leo starts to talk, no one would be surprised.

We saw enemy fighter planes flying over this morning. The alarms must have been on in town. When the planes had passed, it was peaceful and quiet as usual here at Salt Falls, oblivious to the hustle and bustle of the outside world resounding far and wide. Perhaps the ability to fade into oblivion is only available to a lucky few.

I'm waiting for you to come back. The porridge I burn, the dishes I cook, salty or tasteless, are all delicious to you, aren't they? It takes talent to make green leafy vegetables tougher than old steak! You said that, didn't you?

I'm waiting for you to come back. I've just finished reading several pages from *Notre-Dame de Paris* lent to me by Professor Xia and a French textbook compiled by Jacques Reclus, aka Shao Kelü. I think I'm approaching what has been drifting so far away, or at least I'm going to stop it from drifting further away. It turns out that my negligence in studying psychology in college was rewarded by the opportunity to indulge myself in reading fiction and poetry. I told Professor Xia that my lack of systematic training in learning the French language might be a problem, but Professor Xia laughed it off: "I'll let you know and fire you when I find it out."

One more day has passed. You'll be back this afternoon. Guess what I did just now? I did the laundry. Oh, the pool of water at the entrance of the village! If we had had such a pond in the Wang village where Xiangge and I waited for our travelling companions, they would have been overjoyed! The water is clean and clear. Where the water is deep, it looks fathomless; the water near the shore is quite shallow and convenient for me to put a small stool in to sit on when I do my laundry. It's interesting to see how the river transforms into cascades, falling incessantly. The water keeps running as if it has an endless life. Looking at the sparkling splashes, I see life and vitality.

A married woman came to me and felt my laundry. She then came closer for a better look. When she finally spoke up, she sounded surprised: "All made of homespun cotton?" I answered yes. Clothes made of homespun cotton are quite comfortable to wear.

She thought for a while and then added that she understood. We were running for our lives; how could we be bothered to travel with such good quality stuff? I told her what really matters is that the whole family is together. Tears welled up in her eyes, splashing into the pool. She dried her tears with the back of her hand first and then her wet clothes. I panicked, worrying whether I had said something wrong.

Through the sobs, she told me: "It's not about you. My husband was killed in a battle in Hubei province."

Then I really didn't know what to say. I comforted her that his death was for the country, and for us. We are all being protected by our ordinary soldiers. Without them, the Japanese army would run rampant over the land. Then no one would survive.

She said: "My husband was a platoon leader. The whole platoon was killed. Some of them were from our village." She paused for a moment and continued: "How could there be such a race obsessed with killing and looting? The foreigners who share your garden are also refugees."

I didn't know how to answer her question. But I believe that force is never powerful enough to conquer another nation. If a nation is conquered by force, maybe it deserves such a fate.

The water flowing in the Mang river is a mixture of blood, sweat and tears which will never return.

The water splashed and danced, sending fine drops onto the bluestone by my side. It reminded me of a line from an ode to snow – 'drifts of snow are almost like sprinklings of salt' - although the best line of this poem is the next one - 'the falling snow is like willow catkins fluttering in the wind'.[1] The splashes of water looked quite like grains of salt, though. I finally figured out why the village was named 'Salt Falls Slope'. For me they looked like a small pile of snow, a pile of falling snow. Snow Falls Slope? Snow Falls Slope!

When I stood up, I tripped over the small stool and almost fell. The wife warned me I should be more careful because the pond is very deep. It is connected to the Mang river at the bottom. I thought we should make a railing for those who come to do their laundry - something to hold on to. But in wartime, wouldn't such a railing be a luxury? We should thank our good luck for such a pond of water. What else should we pray for?

You should be back any minute. If the Mang river is navigable, it would have saved you lots of time for the trip. Luckily, it is still not hot. Will you drop by Uncle Fuzhi's on your way back? I guess you won't, but you might if you have something to handle. But you won't stay long, will you? I am just back from checking out the slope by the pond at the gate. I didn't see a living soul. Where are you right now?

Among the piles of yellowish blueprints, I am writing my first teaching plan. I heard a noise at the garden gate and you come in. I have made up my mind that I'm not going to rise to greet you. I'm waiting for you to bend down and whisper in my ear: "My darling Xue, what are you writing?"

CHAPTER FOUR

PART I

One night in May 1940.

Nine months had already passed since the outbreak of war in Europe. Britain and France had declared war on Germany but had no intention of fighting. When Germany took over Eastern Europe, their ambitions turned to Northern Europe.

What the German army achieved greatly inspired the Japanese imperialists. The Japanese military was not satisfied with the strategic stalemate in the Chinese theatre. A bellicose Japanese fever permeated the air.

In the spring of 1940, 20 divisions of Japanese troops launched an attack on Zaoyang-Yichang (known as the battle of Zaoyi) in Hubei province, their biggest attack since the battle of Wuhan. The Chinese army resisted bravely. In the first battle of Zaoyang, Zhang Zizhong, the commander-in-chief on the right flank of the fifth war zone, made a heroic sacrifice. The capture of Yichang, only about 480km away from Chongqing, the gateway to Chongqing, also made it suitable as a base area for aerial bombardment of Chongqing. Yichang fell on 14 June. Then the Chinese army struggled to keep Jiangling, Dangyang, Yichang and Jingmen and succeeded in achieving a stalemate with the Japanese.

Meanwhile, the Japanese army implemented a blockade policy in north China, taking "railroads as pillars, roads as chains, and bunkers as locks." The goal was to crack down on the Eighth Route Army base. The fighting was fierce.

I'd like to cite some historical data and figures to give you, my dear readers, to better explain the situation than an empty verbal account.

From 18 May to 4 September, the Japanese air force conducted unprecedentedly heavy bombing of key cities such as Chongqing and Chengdu. They carried out 4,555 sorties and dropped 27,107 bombs, totalling 1,957 tons of ammunition. The Chinese air force shot down and destroyed only 403 Japanese aircraft. Civilian casualties were countless.

This was one night in May. One night in Kunming.

Kunming was not the main target of the Japanese air raid, but it also suffered from the dumping of steel warheads. The day and night filled with horror and exhaustion did not affect the imparting of knowledge or the cultivation of character. The bright moonlight and the gentle starlit night were reflected in the kindling thoughts.

Small groups of students ran into the new school gate. One said: "Hurry up!"

The other answered: "No hurry."

A tidy student with his hair combed neatly came out of the gate and teased the two of them: "What are you running for? Haven't you had enough running for one day?"

The third answered: "We are going to Professor Zhuang's current affairs lecture." Pointing at a small piece of paper on the wall by the gate, he asked: "Haven't you seen the notice?" It read: "Professor Zhuang's current affairs lectures: Round 18 — the European theatre. Classroom No. 4."

The one with carefully combed hair was Zhang Xinlei, Thunderhand, who was heading to the girls' dormitory located in Wenlin street to see Meng Liji (Earl) and his cousin Wu Jiaxin. When he had finished reading the notice, he turned around and headed for classroom No. 4 as did the other three. He soon discovered that the meeting place had been changed from the classroom to the smaller playground because of the huge number of people in attendance. On the ground, bright gas lamps were lit. The student in charge of the lamps would put them out immediately if the red balloon alert was put up.

The chairs and stools on the playground were all taken by the audience themselves, and some were sitting on bricks. Thunderhand spotted Earl and Jiaxin right away sitting in the back row. Tantai Xuan and several of her classmates from the foreign language department were standing on the edge of the crowd and seemed ready to withdraw at any minute.

Zhuang Youchen got up from his seat in the front row, took several steps to stand on the low table to use it as a podium and turned to face the audience. He was still in an old suit and tie. The crowd soon calmed down and listened to him.

"Today, we have the biggest audience since I opened up the lecture. I'm sorry we've had to move from the classroom to the playground." His clear voice reached far and wide.

"The presence of such a huge audience is not because my voice is so charming but because the changes in the world situation are so concerning. It has been almost a year since the outbreak of the war in the European theatre. The rampant German fascists haven't yet met any genuine resistance. They occupied Czechoslovakia without a fight. Even though the Polish people resisted for more than 20 days, they ended up being invaded. What a shame that the strong continental forces of Britain and France looked on and didn't offer any help in the naive expectation that Germany would be satisfied with the territory it had acquired. But have we seen any robbers and bandits stop and rest in peace with what they have got? Last month, Germany attacked Northern Europe and Denmark surrendered. What is worth mentioning is Norway's refusal to surrender. When Germany attacked Oslo, it thought that it could sail into Oslo without resistance. The German embassy had even sent out their personnel to welcome the German warships. Unexpectedly, the guns of the Norwegian navy violently opened fire and sank the German flagship. We cheer for Norway! Haakon II and his government were aware of the disparity in power and could not face a frontal attack by the enemy and have retreated to a northern town. Norwegian forces ambushed the pursuing German soldiers along the way. Haakon II refused to surrender to Germany and via radio broadcasts called on the military and civilians to fight against the invaders. When the Germans discovered the Norwegian government had relocated to a small village, they bombed the village to the ground. In fact, the Norwegian government had moved to the forest about 10 days previously. I once visited the rich dense forest there in the 1920s, and it seemed to me that a mountain monster might pop out at any time. I think that the spirit of Norway is inseparable from its mountains and fjords, and from Henrik Johan Ibsen, their beloved playwright, and Edvard Hagerup Grieg, their great composer.

"Today's highlight is that the British prime minister has changed. When Chamberlain stepped down, Churchill took office and formed a coalition government of the conservatives, the labour party and the liberal party. The following is a quotation from Churchill's speech in the House of Commons: 'I have nothing to offer but blood, toil, tears and sweat.'

"'You may ask: What is our policy? I want to tell you this: Our policy is to use all the capabilities and all the power that god has granted us to wage war on the sea, on land, and in the air; and to fight a fierce and sinister tyranny never before seen in the human history of sins and crimes. This is our policy. You may ask: What is our purpose? I can reply in one word: Victory - victory at all costs...'"

"Our war of resistance against Japan is not isolated!" added Youchen.

Someone in the audience cried out: "Victory for the war of resistance!" The rest of the audience echoed these words with the force of a landslide and the power of a tidal wave.

Zhuang Youchen continued to analyse the movement of the Japanese army. Some people whispered: "It's said that Professor Zhuang's profound knowledge about the war comes from an insider linked with the UK." Much of the news Youchen shared with the students was indeed news releases from the British consulate.

When he was listening to Youchen, Thunderhand looked around to find Professor Meng and a couple of other professors were present. Meng Liji was sitting by Zhuang Wuyin. "Oh yes, Wuyin is finishing his first year in college and I am graduating, and getting older, too," thought Thunderhand.

"The war of resistance has been going on for almost three years. I don't know how long it will continue," said Professor Zhuang, as he resumed talking. "What I know for sure is that we will fight for 30 years or 300 years until we drive away the Japanese devils, recover all our lost territory and build a great country!"

The student yelled out another slogan: "Victory over the Japanese! Return our homeland!" The slogan drifted away far into the darkness.

When Youchen had finished his lecture, Sun Lisheng, a student from the Chinese department who was presiding over the speech, invited Professor Meng to say a few words. Everyone applauded enthusiastically.

Fuzhi stood up and thanked Youchen. He said that understanding the world would lead to a better understanding of one's own affairs.

Then he said: "Professor Zhuang mentioned just now that even if it takes us 30 years or 300 years, we will fight on until we win the war. My dear students, you might think that after 30 more years, we will already be old, and that in 300 years, we will be long dead. So what does it matter? No, it matters because the Chinese nation will not age nor will it die! The justice and fair play of humanity will never age or die!"

"Our senior students will soon graduate and leave school. Every year during the graduation season, I feel a strong sense of success. I am proud of the fact that most of you have completed your studies and will grow to be pillars of your country. Your teachers feel such a sense of success because of your success. I want to thank you, but there are things I want to say to you which I will save for a later time."

All the senior students present felt Professor Meng's eyes were fixed on them. Someone asked: "When?"

Fuzhi smiled and waved his hand to indicate 'no comment'. Youchen stood up and said something to Fuzhi. Many students walked up to the professors and showered them with questions.

Wuyin stood by his father's side, waiting patiently. He had grown much taller, but his delicate eyebrows and beautiful eyes bore the same melancholy which, complicated with their limpidness, left people with the impression that he could see through everything. When he went to college, he had attracted lots of attention with his excellent academic performance, handsome appearance, unusually young age and his rare brand of gravitas. He didn't care much about such talk. When he saw Earl, he came to sit by her side, nodded his greeting to her and remained silent. He didn't ask about May.

If this was a competition for silence, Earl was confident she could beat Wuyin hands down. So she ignored him and later walked away with Jiaxin. When she spotted Xuan on the edge of the crowd, the two stopped to chat.

Seeing Thunderhand walking toward them, Xuan pointed at him and smiled: "Here comes another graduate. I always think we haven't learnt much, but then, woosh, we are graduating! Come on, let's go to Precious Pearl alley and have a chat." Since the three women from the Yan family were all staying in Anning county, Xuan had moved out of the Yan residence and rented a room from a family on Precious Pearl alley. It was common for better-off students at Minglun University to rent a place to live instead of living on campus. They walked toward Xuan's place. Jiaxin stayed by Thunderhand's side after greeting him with a timid "cousin".

Thunderhand and Jiaxin were third cousins several times removed. When they started college together, Jiaxin had developed a crush on Thunderhand. Later she left Beiping for Changsha with her elder brother Jiagu, who joined the field service upon graduation. She developed a kind of familial affection toward Thunderhand after her brother left, though she was surrounded by the love and care of her teachers and classmates. But she had been tortured by the fact that Thunderhand ignored her and cried so much that Earl had nicknamed her 'crying star'. Thunderhand didn't pay much attention to her because she was rather homely. He focused all his attention on Earl, who had such an extraordinary personality and such an influential family background. Earl was rather aloof and indifferent back in Beiping. But when they relocated to

Kunming, the tough life there didn't diminish her friends' respect for her. Besides, he gradually came to discover that Earl had distinguished relatives.

When they had almost reached the great west city gate, Earl suddenly declared that she didn't want to go to Precious Pearl alley and asked Xuan whether she would like to drop by Dragon Tail village the coming Saturday. Xuan said she wanted to visit Aunt Bichu, so she would go in several days. Since she was graduating, who knew where she could get a job and whether she would move to some faraway place. When Xuan and her friends turned and walked into the alley, she turned back and told Earl that Wei was fighting with his parents, struggling to find a way to attend college in Kunming and asked Earl whether she had heard about the story or not. Earl answered no.

Earl, Jiaxin and Thunderhand walked along the street. Thunderhand wanted to invite them to have rice noodles, but both girls declined. Then he proposed to spend some time in a teahouse, where they could enjoy limited varieties of snacks such as sesame candy bars, sticky candy, roasted sunflower seeds and peanuts. The girls agreed.

The dimly lit teahouse had several smoking pipes displayed on the steps leading to the gate. One type of pipe was long and slender, almost one metre long, with a tiny bowl on the top. The others were water pipes with thick stems made of bamboo. When the waiter greeted the three, his first reaction was to go and fetch the pipes, but then it dawned on him that students didn't smoke. He neatly set down the teacups and carried the giant teakettle to the table while recommending the shaved ice with fresh fruit juice. It was a popular new cold drink made of shaved ice with colourful fruit juice toppings. When the waiter saw there was no objection, he brought them three servings. Jiaxin and Earl began to enjoy the cool sweet drink with the small spoons provided.

Thunderhand seized the opportunity: "I want to discuss something with you."

Upon his words, Earl pushed away the drink and said: "Then excuse me. Carry on."

Thunderhand hastened to stop her: "I want to discuss something with YOU. How can you leave?"

That took Earl by surprise. She cast a glance at him and listened.

Thunderhand continued: "Earl, do you still remember what you told me in Hong Kong? You said everyone should contribute his or her share when the homeland is in danger instead of running away. I have taken those words to heart ever since."

It was nice to know one's words were remembered. Earl didn't realise someone like Thunderhand would pay so much attention to what she said.

"Is that what I said?" asked Earl.

"Yes, you did. Mrs Meng and your siblings were there, too," explained Thunderhand, hurriedly. "I'm graduating. My family want me to go to work in Hong Kong, but I want to stay on the mainland. I was told that the resource committee needs agents to handle economic intelligence. Agents might be sent to countries in Southeast Asia. What do you think?" asked Thunderhand. He turned to Jiaxin: "And what do you think?"

Jiaxin, with tears brimming in her eyes upon seeing Thunderhand focusing all his attention on Earl, didn't respond but fixed her eyes on the melting ice shavings.

Earl pondered: "I don't know what the resource committee does." After further thought, she casually added: "It sounds like it has something to do with what my aunt Jiangchu's husband does."

Thunderhand was overjoyed at the information and said, "I think so too... In short, this is a way that I can serve my country with what I have learned."

Earl felt there was no need to state her position, so she decided to change the topic and turned to ask Jiaxin: "I heard that the field work next week has been moved to this week?"

Jiaxin said: "I think so. Mr Zhou Bi has notified us about it. It's probably because Professor Xiao will be busy next week." She took a shelled peanut and slowly squeezed it between her fingers.

Thunderhand broke in: "Some goofy soul launched a campaign to identify the best-looking man at Minglun. Who do you guess has won the title? Professor Xiao!"

Jiaxin said she would have voted for him, too. Earl blushed. Nobody in the dim light noticed her blush, though.

"Meng Liji! Wu Jiaxin!" A few people greeted them and came over to the table. One of them was Sun Lisheng, who had just presided over Zhuang Youchen's lecture. His hair was a riot of spikes pointing in all directions. One has to admit it was the trendy style back then. Another one was a girl named He Man, also known as Helen, from the foreign language department. She was a transfer student, older and more experienced in getting along with people.

Sun Lisheng said: "Professor Zhuang's analysis of the international situation is very insightful, but it sounds like he doesn't have enough materials to back up his analysis on the domestic situation."

Thunderhand said: "For me, it all sounded quite fresh."

Helen said: "Churchill's speech is really moving. The changed situation in the European theatre might restrain the Japanese devils to some extent." She sat down and joined the group after some small discussion. Sun Lisheng went off to greet the incoming classmates, most of whom were leaders from different student associations.

At that time, various student associations and societies were springing up all over the place. Some were named in accordance with their leading political ideology, such as the Democratic Society and the Free Society. Helen was the leader of a society called 'Teachers of the Masses', meaning to learn from the broad masses of the people. Some were named by their academic or artistic preferences, such as the History and Literature Society and the New Poetry Society. All those societies and associations had regular wall newspapers to share their innovative ideas and opinions. Most maintained communication with relevant professors. Some societies also had different political tendencies which became more obvious as time went by.

Helen said: "Participating in these activities is very good for us to acquire knowledge and understand things. Wu Jiaxin has participated in several activities of my association. Isn't it a very interesting experience? Baffling things happening off campus are no longer baffling when we sit and discuss them together."

Jiaxin said: "I participated in the YMCA communions a couple of times and I felt they were very consoling. The activities of your association seem to be more scientific and more focused on society, though I don't know why I feel so."

Helen laughed and said: "It's good you have got some feelings. In the upcoming event, will Earl come and have a look? We will invite Professor Meng to give a speech."

Earl smiled but didn't say anything.

Helen then continued: "Tantai Xuan doesn't go to the dorms, though I see her often in the class for reading English novels. Who is the elder one of you two?" she asked Earl.

"If I were older than her, how could I be a junior and she a graduating senior?" A standard Earl answer.

Thunderhand said: "Look at you. How I envy you all! I cannot participate in anything now."

Around another table, several students were talking passionately about something. Helen went over to see what was going on. When she came back, she put down one cold yam each in front of Earl and Jiaxin.

Thunderhand sighed: "See? I don't even have a share of a cold yam!"

When the three went out of the teahouse and walked back to the girls' dormitory, they were all preoccupied with their own concerns. When they reached the dormitory, Thunderhand said: "I'm finally feeling somewhat confident."

Looking at Jiaxin, Earl said: "We haven't said anything."

Thunderhand said with grave sincerity: "You are not like mortals and you don't have to say anything. I'm the most common mortal, maybe a secular one, too. Since I don't have much to contribute, I don't have much to ask."

When Earl and Jiaxin were back in their own room, they talked more about the European theatre of war as well as Thunderhand.

Earl said: "In fact, everyone is mortal. If he had put it like that, it might have been a more interesting discussion."

Jiaxin asked: "Do you think he is interesting?"

"You can encourage him to develop into something interesting," said Earl casually as she readied herself to go to bed.

Jiaxin kept sitting in the chair a long time until the lights were turned off. She dried her tears several times before she finally fell asleep.

A couple of days later, Earl and Jiaxin went for the field course, which was scheduled in the first year. But neither Earl nor Jiaxin had taken this course, so they joined the freshmen now to make it up.

On this day, it was dark with drizzle. Some two dozen students were waiting to board the boat at the dock. Most of them wore straw hats to keep them dry from the rain. There were very few people who had big red umbrellas made of heavy oiled paper, but they guaranteed those who used them wouldn't get wet. Most female students wore blue work trousers, but there was still a handful wearing starched light-blue cotton *qipaos*. Several weeping willows were planted by the side of the dock. Rain slowly trickled down the branches and twigs. It seemed that the green colour of the willows was dripping off the trees. Several stands at the roots of the willows were selling flowers from white jade orchid trees. Most of the stands were taken care of by young girls. Some female students had bought some of these sweet flowers and hung them on the front of their work trousers or on the buttons of their *qipaos*. A few decided not to buy them after they were told what the price was. Then the girl on the stand would give them a timely discount by saying: "Affordable! Affordable!" The younger students snapped the willow branches to sprinkle the water on others, and on the white flowers, too.

"Why has Professor Xiao not come yet?" A few classmates tiptoed and looked in the direction of the city gate. Xiao Cheng's specialty was in biochemistry, but because he was the head of the department, he maintained his frequent connection to general courses and took students to collect specimens, which also enabled him to know more about the students. Zhou Bi, the one who taught this course of common botany, was still very young. When he was arranging the boats, he kept casting glances over at the city gate from time to time.

The city walls of Kunming were not high, thus the city gates built in them were correspondingly small. No one knew exactly when the minor west city gate was built, but it had a certain gravitas like all the other city gates did. More and more people were entering and exiting the city gate. Since the War of Resistance, Kunming people had been getting up earlier. It was said that when the schools had just moved in, local people were not accustomed to getting up early like the teachers and students from those schools. The city government sent policemen along the streets, yelling and knocking on doors and windows to urge the shops to open. At this moment that morning, farmers with vegetables and firewood were already entering the city with their loads. A man who used a petrol can to carry clean water home was following someone carrying a pail of manure. The steel petrol cans were quite a sight to behold back then.

"Professor Xiao is coming!" An eagle-eyed female student was the first to spot Xiao Cheng. Everyone turned to watch him walking toward them in the crowd, wearing a soft beige plainly woven silk gown, instead of a fieldwork outfit. He approached gradually, looking tired.

Everyone went up to greet him respectfully. Xiao Cheng returned their greetings with a smile and walked up the steps to speak to Zhou Bi. Not long afterward, the two men came back to the crowd. Zhou Bi clapped his hands and asked everyone to gather and listen to Professor Xiao.

Xiao Cheng said: "I am very happy to see all of you waiting to set off so early. I have been looking forward to this excursion as everyone else has. Our students must understand nature, which is not an easy achievement. Some of you may be wondering why I am speaking to you at the pier. Some of you might have guessed right. I have something else to attend to and I can't accompany you on this interesting lesson. I don't think it's necessary to reschedule the event. Mr Zhou will explain the main purpose of this lesson and give you instructions while you work. Here I'd like to share an entertaining story with you to make up for my not being able to accompany you. The highest point of Xishan (West mountain) is called Dragon Gate, where the cave, the deity statues inside the cave, even the passage leading to the cave, have all been hewn from the rock of the mountain. The stone artist behind these artistic works finally arrived at the last stage of his work. When he was going to wrap up his work by finishing the writing brush held by the God of Literature, which would mark the pinnacle of his

194

work, I guess, he was so cautious that he accidentally cut off the tip of the brush."

Xiao Cheng stopped for a moment: "So the God of Literature doesn't have a proper writing brush. The God of Literature has lost his writing brush! It was said that the artist picked up the broken stone that had fallen to the ground, from which he was supposed to have carved out the tip of the brush, jumped off the cliff into the lake, and killed himself."

A sigh mixed with pity, sympathy and admiration rippled among the students.

Xiao Cheng went on: "I like this legend very much and have always been moved by the artist's spirit of pursuing perfection. For those of us engaged in scientific work, we must also try our best to continue the pursuit of perfection, even though perfection may never be achieved. Our determination will manifest itself in our efforts during the process. I genuinely wish I could go to collect specimens with everyone and get to touch those fresh plants, but now I have to say: please excuse my absence."

Then Xiao Cheng stooped slightly and said something to the students near him. When he turned, he saw Earl and Wu Jiaxin standing under a willow tree. When he walked past them, he noticed that Wu Jiaxin was not very spirited. He told her to take care of herself and not to push herself too much. If she couldn't walk far, she could collect plants around Huating temple halfway up the mountain. Having not thought of what to say to Earl, who was staring at him, obviously waiting for him to say something to her, he just smiled at her and walked on.

Zhou Bi called on everyone to board the two boats. These boats were larger than those typically used to sail around Dianchi lake. Each was covered with a half canopy. Wu Jiaxin was asked to sit inside the canopy. Earl stood at the stern, staring at the wake behind the boats as they sailed on, lost in thought.

As the boats sailed past the Grand View pavilion, the building looked different in the rain. The pavilions seemed to be enveloped by a veil connected to the waves, fluctuating up and down with the rise and fall of the water. Local classmates were busy pointing out places of interest to others, such as the famous Jinhuapu street, which earned its name due to its vicinity to the Grand View pavilion, Backwater Meander, and the Embankment, and private villas named this and that manor. Zhou Bi reminded the students of the abundance of vegetation in this area. They didn't have time to observe it all this time, but they might come back another time.

It reminded Earl of the visit with her parents to this place last fall. Her father told her the giant white flower she found was called 'Mandrake' in

Sanskrit, or 'common thorn apple' or 'devil's trumpet'. Xuan asked why a flower had such a weird name. Fuzhi explained that in Sanskrit, 'Mandrake' meant a holy shrine. Why was this flower named after that? That was one of the problems for Earl and her kind to solve. Back then, Earl didn't think much about her father's words. Now it suddenly dawned on her that her father was expressing his earnest wish for her, just as Professor Xiao had implied in his legend of the writing brush of the God of Literature.

When the boats reached the centre of Dianchi lake, they were immediately surrounded by blue waves. Xishan looked like a giant lying in the distance, hence its nickname the Sleeping Beauty mountain. Feeling relieved, some began to sing, and some shouted their greetings to other boats. At one o'clock, they arrived at Gaoqiao wharf. Everyone left the boats to go ashore. A small path led them up the mountain.

The path was lined with shrubs and dotted with rich wild flowers blooming riotously. The tweeting and chirping of birds filled the air. The entire mountain seemed to welcome these young people. Zhou Bi was showered with questions about the names of all kinds of plants. He laughingly protested: "When will I be knowledgeable enough to answer all your questions?" But when he walked with Earl and Jiaxin, he did tell them the names of many plants.

When they had all climbed up the mountain, a grand temple loomed in front of them. This was Huating temple. Hardly did they have time to acknowledge the solemnity of the Buddhist constructions when they saw people outside the gate, sitting or lying down, some standing around, talking. Some were cooking things over an open fire. They all looked exhausted, although their clothes were not in very bad condition. Zhou Bi thought for a minute before saying: "Yes, they are refugees from the Yunnan-Vietnam railroad!" His guess was immediately confirmed.

To cut off supplies to China from the outside, the enemy heavily bombed the Yunnan-Vietnam railroad. People living alongside the railroad had to leave their homes to flee the bombardment. The Japanese also negotiated with France and on 20 July, the Japanese office in Hanoi took off the railroad tracks on the iron bridge in Lào Cai province to stop all supplies going to China. But that was another story.

When the refugees saw the students, some went up and asked eagerly: "Have you brought any rice? Can you sell some to us? The town has run out of rice."

Zhou Bi said something to comfort them; the students who had put on more layers of clothing took off their tops and gave them to the refugees. Although it was summer, it was chilly at night in the mountains.

Rolls of quilts were seen in the gallery behind the temple gate. When opened, these rolls became beds, which were a real privilege for the refugees. Disturbed by such a scene, neither the teacher nor the students had any interest in appreciating the magnificent architecture of the grand hall of the temple. They hurried to the back of the temple, found a clear space and sat down. Zhou Bi talked about the class requirements, how to identify plants, how to collect and make specimens, how to identify poisonous plants and protect themselves. He reminded them to pay special attention to avoid nettles. If the skin touched the fine hairs covering the leaves, one would surely regret it because it was as painful as a bee sting and would instantly become red and swollen. He then reminded them that as a famed giant plant kingdom, even a single mountain like Xishan boasted more than 2,000 species of plants. Some of them were toxic, but toxins could also be used to benefit human beings. They had to get to know them, differentiate between them, and explore the uses of various plants. Earl and Jiaxin didn't want to mingle with the freshmen, the 'kids', and headed all the way uphill. They soon arrived at Taihua temple.

With fewer refugees in evidence at Taihua temple, now the two could feel the unique peaceful and secluded ambiance of a quiet Buddhist temple and the surrounding bushes, trees and flowers. The old buildings in the temple were still impressive. A pair of couplets was carved on the stone arch at the Heavenly Kings Hall: 'A lake and a mountain come into view', and 'the pain and happiness of people to the heart'. On the main hall, there was a placard that read: 'Not revealed'. When the two saw it, they both wanted some revelation. The smoke from the burning of joss sticks lingered in the hall. A stranger was drawing divination sticks for a sign. An old monk was knocking his wooden fish. The sign-seeker, who looked like a homeless person from elsewhere, might have been asking about his future. He prayed first and then drew a bamboo lot from a bamboo holder, had a look at the lot, sneered, and walked out of the temple.

"Let's ask for one," Jiaxin suddenly proposed

"But you have to kowtow first," hesitated Earl. The old monk explained that a bow would do just as well. As long as one was sincere and honest, it would even be alright not to bow.

Jiaxin tried first. She felt that the divine spirit might not reveal big things such as when they could win the War of Resistance, so she'd better focus on personal things. She bowed respectfully and drew a lot during the knocks on the wooden fish and the monk's chanting. It said: "Let nature take its course. Don't push. Don't force." She fell silent after reading the lines.

The old monk saw Earl standing by and asked: "Would this lady like to ask for a sign, too?"

A wish was forming in Earl's heart and she did want to ask for a sign. She thought for a moment and went up to the table to draw a lot without bowing. What she got was the same as Jiaxin. "Do you have the same lots in the holder?" she confronted the old monk.

The old monk said: "You are so wrong! You two have drawn the same lots because you're asking about the same thing. They are good signs. Everything has its own course and that's the way it should be."

Jiaxin whispered to Earl: "You should try again and ask about something really important and see what you get." What she meant was the thing that had been bothering Earl, a knot. Earl once told her that it was her secret.

Earl stood solemnly and gave three deep bows before she took out a sign. She covered it with her hands for a moment, took a deep breath and then opened her hands to read. It said: "Don't ask your parents. Ask their friends. You come from whence you have come, and you are going to the place you are bound for." Earl whined: "What a verbose statement! Why must it repeat the same words so many times?"

Jiaxin took over the lot and said: "It's quite clear to me. See? You have been told who you should go and ask."

Earl nodded. She already knew who she should ask.

The two of them continued uphill. Some freshmen students had already gone ahead of them both, talking loudly all the way. One said that it would be best to make a poison that would put the Japanese soldiers into a coma. One asked why he didn't want to kill them and noted jeeringly what a sympathetic heart he must have. Another said maybe some of them would make up their minds to stay in Yunnan to study plants after this field trip.

Earl's heart flipped at the words, and she slowed down. She spotted several giant flowers in the grass. Thinking she was wearing long trousers to protect her legs, she stepped into the grass for the bright colourful flowers. Wrapping the flower stem with a piece of coarse paper, she got the flower. She got a sting on the back of her foot, and yelped "ouch".

"What's wrong? What's wrong?" Jiaxin rushed to help steady Earl, who shouted loudly: "Stop! Don't go any further!"

Earl managed to walk out of the grass by herself and found both of her feet were red and swollen.

Zhou Bi came for a quick check. He said Earl's feet had touched some nettles.

Earl said: "I am wearing socks. I don't usually wear socks but I saved them for the field trip."

Zhou Bi said: "The socks are not thick enough to stop the fine hairs from the nettles. I'm pretty sure there must be another plant which can handle those fine hairs." He looked around and identified some leaves. When he put those leaves on Earl's feet, her feet felt cool and the pain was greatly relieved.

Earl put the big flower into the old folder which temporarily functioned as her specimen clip and carefully smoothed it between the two layers of paper. She limped on for a while before sitting down on a roadside rock and letting Zhou Bi and Jiaxin go on ahead. The walking had become strenuous for her. She looked down at Dianchi lake with its blue waves slapping against the shore fringed by reeds. In the distance, the grey sails of the wooden boats added an air of dignity to the water. She scrutinised the specimens she had collected. The flowers were beautiful and varied, bearing the wonders of nature. She remembered the two divine lots: "Let nature take its course. Don't push. Don't force." And "You come from whence you have come, and you are going to the place you are bound for."

"Bah!" thought Earl. A handful of first-year students came along, and she got up and joined them.

PART II

The biology department had two laboratories in the new school building. One served as a classroom lab for students for activities like dissecting frogs and distinguishing between plants. The other one was for the teaching faculty, where all the basic biochemical experiments would take place in bottles and jars. The laboratory was in a nursery where the flowers would open at random with complete discernment of the seasons and constantly smeared the adobe walls with rich colours.

Xiao Cheng was scrubbing utensils in a poorly equipped clean room in the lab. Cleaning was a laboratory janitor's chore, even the lab assistant would not do it. Now it was different with the frequent absence of the janitor and the poor health of the lab assistant. Unwilling to exploit students as some teachers might, he cleaned the utensils by himself from time to time. Wearing an apron and rubber gloves, he was skilfully turning around his glass soldiers in the sink.

That day he had skipped the scheduled field trip for two reasons - one work-related and the other for personal reasons. In the morning, he attended the appointment committee for the appointments in the coming academic school year, and other related issues, too. In the afternoon, he went to see Zheng Huiyuan off on her trip back to the National Academy of Music located in Qingmuguan, a small ancient town 50km northwest of Chongqing city centre. It was the top music institution in China during the War of Resistance. Since Huiyuan had a ride, Xiao Cheng accompanied her all the way from Kunming to Qujing city 120km from Kunming. The next morning, he saw Huiyuan and her friend off. Once they had settled in, the moment the car started, Xiao Cheng saw the familiar handkerchief waving outside the car window. Standing by the roadside staring at the car and the handkerchief disappearing into the distance, he felt his heart was gone and lost, too.

When would they see each other again? Huiyuan went to Guiyang to hold a couple of concerts at the invitation of the commander of a clique in appreciation of the service of his men. When she arrived in Kunming, she had planned to give concerts, too. But then she couldn't squeeze them into her tight schedule, so she had to drop the idea. Besides, she preferred to sing only for Xiao Cheng. Once she sang him 14 songs in a row. That should count as a concert, too, but unique with the emotions and expectations brimming out of each song. Few had the luck to enjoy such a feast.

They went to the Catholic church on Pingzheng street several times during Huiyuan's short stay in Kumming. The church had an unused piano. When Huiyuan first visited Kunming, Xiao Cheng had managed to borrow it for her. Having not been tuned for a long time, it was not suitable for Huiyuan, but they were still willing to go and sit on the hard bench in the church. Even without any carved pillars or tinted glass windows, the church oozed with the same solemn atmosphere. The Virgin Mary holding the holy baby in her arms looked down from a simple wooden platform at the benches. It made the visitors feel so calm, peaceful and solemn. They could listen to their hearts in such silence.

The two hearts had been colliding with each other for a long time, compiling a song mixed with joy and pain. Their acquaintance started from a concert.

Xiao Cheng would never forget the first time he heard Huiyuan sing. Her voice sounded as if she were sailing from the sky. He looked for her on the ground when she fell and saw her sitting behind piles of flowers. He had no flowers to offer her but his heart. Unfortunately, at the time, Huiyuan was no longer unattached. Xiao Cheng hated the fact that he hadn't returned to China a year earlier. They could not shake off their feelings for each other, neither could they get rid of their embarrassing, tight corner. They received a mixture of sympathy and accusations. But they couldn't find a way out because two fused hearts could never be separated.

Xiao Cheng had a manual gramophone and very few records. What they valued most was Bach's 'The St Matthew Passion'. Those without any religious tendencies would also be shocked by this masterpiece. Huiyuan had been a soprano soloist in the German Requiem when she was in Shanghai. Her artistic interpretation of Arthur Brahms' songs was also highly praised. She was quite familiar with 'The St Matthew Passion' but had never officially sung the song herself in public. When listening to the gramophone with Xiao Cheng and it reached the emotional parts, she would stand up and sing along. Both would shed tears.

Sometimes, there was one more person who would join them to listen and shed a tear. That was Xia Zhengsi, the American professor and a fervent lover of classical music who spent most of his free time listening to music.

Legend had it that Professor Xia would stay awake in a world of music for three days without food or sleep. Even the air raid alerts wouldn't interrupt his listening to music. When the sky was shaken by the rumble of fighter planes, on the ground he would indulge himself in a world of symphony. He was not afraid of anything because he had his music. This music lover admired Zheng Huiyuan very much. He said that there were almost no good sopranos in China because they were too thin and thin people had no strength. However, Zheng Huiyuan was an exception.

They had seen some friends together over the years, such as the Mengs and the Zhuangs. Della had once arranged a mini-concert at the British consulate. Huiyuan didn't sing much, but they all had a pleasant chat.

What worried Huiyuan most was her younger sister Huifen's marriage. Her knowledge of her sister's weak character told her that Huifen might not be strong enough to go through a divorce. She didn't want to see Qian Mingjing, though. And that was why she didn't visit Huifen in the countryside. When she visited, she would ask Huifen to meet her in town.

Huiyuan was now gone. When would they see each other again? The question lingered in Xiao Cheng's heart.

His mind finally found its way back to the appointment meeting the previous morning. Student loans were also discussed at the meeting. In sharp contrast to the rising prices, the amount of loans was too steady and small. The university needed to negotiate with the Ministry of Education for a raise.

Due to difficult living conditions, students needed to work during their spare time to make ends meet. Some faculty members also took part-time jobs. It was agreed in the meeting that the university would not set limits on their part-time job activities, as Qian Mingjing had been doing.

Some pointed out that it didn't sound right when experts in the field of chemistry wanted to open a small factory to make soap to earn some money. After discussion, they all agreed that the university shouldn't interfere with such personal activities.

The committee then held a formal discussion about appointments for the next academic year. The discussion focused on three people. The first one was Wei Feng from the physics department. When the university was relocated from Beiping in 1937, teaching assistants and lecturers were not granted travel expenses, but most of them reported to the university in one year. Few had been away for as long as Wei Feng.

Someone asked where Wei Feng had been for the last three years. People all knew he had been to Yan'an, like many others. Some stayed, and others had left and come back to the university. It was not a proper issue to discuss openly, so many tried to change the topic. Zhuang Youchen insisted that since Wei Feng had returned, he was still one of the best teachers in the physics department as he had always been. Wei Feng's expert knowledge and performance were well accepted. In the end, his appointment was approved.

Wang Dingyi, the dean of the foreign language department, proposed dismissing a French teacher. She was the wife of an official at the French consulate and was not responsible for her job. They decided to end her contract in the second half of the year. She had been introduced by Xia Zhengsi, so he took the opportunity to propose hiring Ling Xueyan to the department. Probably he had been considering the replacement already. Wang Dingyi got his Ph.D. at Yale University, and he tended to look down on anyone who went to study abroad without getting a degree. But, unexpectedly, he said that Ling Xueyan hadn't exaggerated her study abroad which showed that she was an honest person.

At the meeting, someone mentioned the university's rule that couples should not be allowed to teach in the same university, but President Qin believed that exceptional times called for exceptional measures. Besides, as Wei Feng was in science while Ling Xueyan was involved with the arts, their jobs wouldn't impact each other. So, the appointment of Xueyan was approved.

At the meeting, the promotion of Qian Mingjing and Li Lian to professorship was also discussed. Some criticised Qian Mingjing's part-time activities. Jiang Fang said that since all had agreed that part-time activities were people's personal affair, how about those who smoked opium and played mahjong during their spare time? As long as the applicant met the academic requirements, they should be promoted.

Some other people backed Mingjing, saying Qian Mingjing was indeed versatile, and his part-time activities did not affect his teaching and research at all.

That reminded someone else that the most irresponsible teacher must be Bai Liwen. His students reported that he was absent for the whole of last week. This week when he was present, he didn't teach but engaged in abuse in the classroom. Was there anything the university could do to deal with him?

Jiang Fang said: "I have run out of options to deal with him. Fuzhi, would you please talk to him some time?"

Fuzhi didn't respond.

There was a classical Chinese expert who had returned to China from England and was employed a year ago, although he hadn't reported to take up his position yet. But the committee agreed to renew his contract. In the end, applications from Qian Mingjing and Li Lian for the professorship were approved. Everyone was dismissed.

Xiao Cheng left with Fuzhi and then asked him about Bai Liwen. Fuzhi said there had been a lot of talk critical of Bai and that Jiang Fang wanted to dismiss him. However, Bai's exceptional knowledge made it hard to dismiss him. Fuzhi paused a second as if to collect his thoughts: "An article of mine might have caused trouble."

Xiao Cheng held his step: "During dinner last night, I did hear people mention that the Chongqing administration was upset. Which article was that?"

Fuzhi said: "The one talking about the redundant staff in the Song dynasty. Overstaffing was one of the reasons for the fall of the Song dynasty. It didn't have a big population, but it had a comparatively huge contingent of officers and officials. There was no set number of positions. The land area for a county or a province was fixed, but the number of officials appointed to the place was on the rise. During the first four years under the reign of Emperor Zhenzong (998-1001 AD), the number of provincial governors increased to almost 80, and the officials subordinate to those governors amounted to thousands. It is not hard to imagine the enormous expense."

Xiao Cheng said: "That is a good lesson to learn from."

Fuzhi said: "That's what I meant when I wrote the essay. I mentioned some despicable means of pursuing a position. This might have annoyed some people."

"Compared to breaking the law, offending people is more troublesome," said Xiao Cheng.

Fuzhi forced a bitter smile: "That's right. I had no intention of offending anyone. What I tried to do was to propose a healthier system for the country, which has been corrupted by feudal thinking."

Xiao Cheng asked to read the essay, and Fuzhi promised to give him a journal containing the essay. "I will write one more about corruption in the Song dynasty. That was the other reason for the fall of the dynasty," added

Fuzhi. Then they went their separate ways without further pursuing the topic as each was preoccupied with their own business.

Xiao Cheng's heart tumbled back to Qujing, the old, remote, small town, which was surely imprinted on his heart now. There was a small pond on the edge of the town, full of red mud. Could that be called a pond with mud instead of water in it? A few tanned children were swimming in the pond. Huiyuan whispered in his ear that the water was too dirty and that the kids might catch trachoma. Xiao Cheng answered her with a soft sigh.

"Uncle Xiao," someone called him gently. He turned to see a student standing outside the window. Her black hair in a short bob made her face look clean and handsome, and her chin even pointier. The flower bed behind her framed her as if she was standing in a picture.

Xiao Cheng was stunned at such a beautiful sight, but he gathered his thoughts without being noticed and said: "Ah, Meng Liji, it's you. What's up?"

Earl had been standing outside the window for a while. She came into the room and asked: "Can I help with anything?"

"I'm almost done. Take a seat," Xiao Cheng began to wrap up. "Have you run into any difficulties with your study?"

Before Earl could answer, the air raid siren sounded.

Xiao Cheng asked: "Didn't you see the red balloon alert when you came?"

"I did."

"So how about looking for a hideout?" Xiao Cheng suggested, taking off his apron and gloves. He had planned to finish the cleaning before the siren sounded.

"I don't want to hide," said Earl gently. "Are you scared, Uncle Xiao?" She paused for a moment and then said, "I need to figure something out, and I'd like to ask Uncle Xiao to help me out."

Xiao Cheng looked at her as if to ask her what was the matter.

Earl said: "Two things, actually, but today I'd like to figure out one of the two first." Her tone sounded stubborn.

"Alright," Xiao Cheng sighed and sat down. After a long period of silence when Earl still didn't say anything, he asked, "What about the field trip that day? Did you have fun?"

Earl handed the specimen folder to Xiao Cheng. He opened it and exclaimed: "This is a kind of tropical flower, and it is a rare find even in Yunnan! We'll have to look up in a dictionary to find its name."

"We call it 'super poisonous flower'."

"Is it poisonous?"

"We don't know yet. We just gave it that name."

"Such a bright colour is a good match for poisonous plants," Xiao Cheng said thoughtfully.

"It is guarded by nettles," said Earl.

Xiao Cheng remembered the poisonous flowers by Nathaniel Hawthorne and the belle who shared the fate of poisonous flowers. He thought that he might call it 'The Flower of Rappaccini's Daughter'. Then he asked: "There is a short story called 'Rappaccini's Daughter'. Have you ever read it?"

"No," answered Earl. Students in twos or threes walked past the window. Someone called out: "Professor Xiao, hurry up." When the crowds were gone, silence returned, waiting for the air raids.

For a moment, Xiao Cheng just looked through specimens. After another long silence, Earl began: "Uncle Xiao, are you losing your patience? I have been gathering my courage."

"What do you want to ask me? Don't worry, all problems have keys to solve them," Xiao Cheng said gently. He grew a little bit uneasy at what Earl might ask him. The year before when he had promised to take Earl to school in Kunming and help her with her transfer, he had come to realise how peculiar this Meng girl was.

"When we were at Xishan, we did one more thing," Earl began. "I drew a divine lot in Taihua temple."

"Was the lot the best of the best?" asked Xiao Cheng, smiling. "If my memory hasn't betrayed me, I think you like Christianity."

"I do need a deity, a god, to guide me," pondered Earl. "I then asked the Buddhist deity in the temple and the sign asked me to ask someone else. The sign read: Don't ask your parents. Ask their friends. You have come from whence you have come, and you are going to the place you are bound for."

"Ask their friends?"

"Yes."

"So, you have come to ask me?"

"Yes," Earl stood up and raised her voice a bit. "My question is… am I my parents' daughter?"

"How can you not be their daughter?" Xiao Cheng stood up, too.

"I have an impression, a vague impression… that I, I might be adopted."

Xiao Cheng was shocked at such an 'impression' and was speechless.

"When I was seven, we had a servant we called Amah Li. Once when she blamed me, I hit her. She then yelled at me: 'Don't give yourself airs! You are just like us. No, you are no better than us. Your parents picked you up beside a pile of dirt.' I didn't go to ask my mum what Amah Li had meant, but Amah Li said the same thing on several other occasions. She hated me. And some people also mention that I don't bear much resemblance to May and Kiddo."

Xiao Cheng stared at a glass vial. Some time later, he raised his head, turned to look at Earl's beautiful young face and said: "Earl, I'm grateful for your trust in me regarding such an important issue. I hope you will believe what I'm going to tell you. You were born one year after your father had finished his study abroad and returned to China. Back then I was a student at Minglun and saw your mother in her loose blouse taking walks on campus. I was not qualified to be invited to attend your one-month birthday party, but I did know Professor Meng had a daughter. You may also ask your aunts. Or you may go to President Qin's wife, Mrs Qin, who has known you since even before your birth. I'm sure she'll tell you what I have just told you."

Earl, with her head bowed, heaved a sigh of relief. This was the answer she had been expecting because she had faith from the bottom of her heart that she was a Meng. But the shadow of doubt had such a drowning, negative power that it might have engulfed the positive truth. She was grateful to Xiao Cheng for dispelling such a shadow. She raised her head and cast a glance at Xiao Cheng. Her second question almost escaped from her throat at the sight of that kind and good-looking face.

The rumbling engines roared close. It sounded like the enemy fighter planes were hovering over the city. Both looked up at the roof to see whether it would fall in due to the vibration. The planes flew away without dropping any bombs. Earl had a mad wish that a bomb would drop on them and that she would die together with her Uncle Xiao.

Xiao Cheng opened the door to see several black dots disappearing into the sky. He told Earl: "The enemy might come back. You'd better go behind the hill to hide until the alert is lifted."

Earl thought, OK, now you are sending me away, so she said: "Thank you for telling me these things." She was ready to leave the room.

Xiao Cheng frowned: "Hold on a second, Earl. Do you believe what I told you or not?"

"Why wouldn't I? I do."

"You are the daughter of Meng Fuzhi and Lü Bichu! Honour them well and love them! Don't give another thought to the story made up by an ignorant servant. It's not worth letting that woman's words impact your life for so many years — that might be the trigger for your peculiarity." He swallowed the last sentence.

"I know," said Earl, absent-mindedly.

"You should strive for more glory for your country, your family and for yourself! Such glory has nothing to do with fame or wealth. It's more about the fulfilment of your own identity, your connection with the universe and the mutual understanding between you and the universe." He paused and thought for a while before he continued: "Can I tell your parents about this?"

Both felt the pressure from the piercing silence between them. Earl thought for a moment and then shook her head. She'd rather keep it a secret and not share it with her parents.

Her pointed chin quivered as if she was gathering the strength to say something. Xiao Cheng didn't wait for her to start: "I think I should tell your parents. You and your parents should have mutual understanding, too. If they don't know you, how can they understand you?"

At these words, Earl stooped a little as if to show she agreed. Then she excused herself. When she was out of the room, she picked up her pace and ran toward the back of the hill. Some people were already heading back to the campus. Ignoring all the greetings from her acquaintances, she ran to a tree, sank at the foot of it and had a good cry to sort out her tangled thoughts. Both her body and heart felt lighter when she eventually dried her waves of tears. It was Professor Xiao who had lifted the weight off her shoulders. She felt lucky that she had had the opportunity to share her tragic secret with him.

A small brook was babbling by the tree. She dipped her handkerchief into the water and wiped away the tear stains on her face. On the surface of the clear water, she thought she had seen Uncle Xiao's radiant face fluctuating, smiling at her.

Gratitude welled up in her heart. She wanted to thank her parents for having such a great friend. Would she go to ask Mrs Qin? Absolutely unnecessary! Uncle Xiao's words were a better endorsement than the testimony of tens of thousands of witnesses. My dear mother, you gave birth to me and raised me, and now you are worried about me! Earl was eager to cling to her mother like May often did, but she knew she would not even extend her arms to her mother if her mother was standing in front of her.

Earl was the last one back to the dormitory from the hide-out that day. Wu Jiaxin and other dorm mates all teased her, saying Meng Liji was genuinely serious about running from the air raids!

With the final examinations around the corner, students, whether they were industrious or not, all felt the pressure of their studies. Earl was particularly serious about the coming exams and carefully and thoroughly revised all her courses, which was indeed the purpose of exams. For several weeks in a row, she hadn't had the time to go back home, but she felt closer to her home and her parents, to her classmates, to biology and to Uncle Xiao. She wrapped up the junior year of her college life in a peaceful frame of mind.

During the first week of the summer vacation, there was a first-aid training course to teach people how to rescue the wounded in case of emergency during air raids. Both Earl and Jiaxin signed up for the class. One afternoon near dusk, at the playground of a local university, after listening to instructions, all the participants were then divided into groups to practice. Most of the students attending the class were junior or senior students. They were teamed up in accordance with the universities they came from. Earl, Jiaxin and Helen took turns to play the part of the wounded person and let other team members practice bandaging them. Earl's head was bandaged heavily with only her eyes spared.

Helen said: "Your eyes look so dark against the white bandage."

Earl answered: "Aren't they always dark?"

Helen didn't know how to respond. Jiaxin said: "Those who don't know Meng Liji might think she is rather mean, but she is, she is just..." Her tongue was stuck for words. She laughed.

Earl said: "Here is the word you are looking for. 'Weird'." She turned her eyes to see row upon row of 'the wounded' in bandages. Some people were walking around, giving instructions. Earl hoped that what all of them learned today would never have to be put to use.

Besides bandaging, they also learned how to make a make-shift stretcher and how to carry the wounded, which were indeed things that a scout should learn. Due to the shortage of equipment to practice with, Earl and Jiaxin waited on one side. Sitting on the steps, staring at the wild flowers blooming in the earth, the two were lost in their own worlds.

The sun sank over the horizon. In the twilight came a man with strong arms and steady steps. He stopped by the two girls. It turned out he was Yan Yingshu. "You two are here, too." When he spoke Mandarin, he always sounded as if he had caught a cold. Earl raised her head to look at him but remained silent.

Jiaxin said: "Here you are."

"I'm on a stretcher team made up of strong guys like me. But we don't have enough teaching aids to practice. There's much room for improvement regarding the organisation of the course. They should have contacted more departments and done more mobilisation," commented Yingshu. He had joined the Three Youth League (the Youth League of the Three People's Principles) the previous year with the aim of fighting against the Japanese and saving the country. The members of the group studied the 'Three People's Principles' together and read and played together. They were quite motivated.

A few of Yingshu's classmates came. After exchanging greetings, they began to sing. The lyrics were:

When the Great Way prevails,
The world is like a community.
The virtuous and the capable sit in office,
And people value honesty and strive for harmony.

People treat the old the way they treat their parents,
The young the way they treat their children.
The aged enjoy their last years in comfort,
The adults are properly employed and do their part,
The young are educated and grow healthily.
The widowed, the disabled, the ill, the orphaned,

Are all provided for.
Men have work to do,
Women have homes to care for.
Money is tossed onto the ground and despised
Instead of being hoarded in the pocket and cherished.

People despise indolence,
Yet they don't use labour for their own purposes.
So, people don't engage in plots or tricks,
And society is free of rebellion, robbery and theft.
So, when they leave their houses, they leave the door open.
That is what we call 'The Great Harmony'.

This was a very famous chapter entitled 'The Operation of Li (Etiquette)' from 'The Book of Li (Etiquette)' by Confucius. It depicted an ideal society, utopia, dating back to ancient times. Ideals are always beautiful, although the tone Yingshu and his classmates sang in sounded odd.

Helen waved at Earl and Jiaxin, indicating that it was their turn to practice. Yingshu followed. One of Yingshu's classmates said: "Some people are going camping in Haigeng park by Dianchi lake next month. It would be great if you three could come." The 'some people' he referred to was the Three Youth League.

Helen shook her head at Earl and Jiaxin, then answered as if she were the leader of the three: "We can't. We have a reading club next month." They were now on 'Popular Philosophy' by Ai Siqi, the pen name of Li Shengxuan.

Yingshu and his friends left for their stretcher practice while Earl and her friends continue to practice their bandaging. Now they were bandaging feet. Soon, all the white bandaged heads became white bandaged feet. The light was almost gone and it was getting dark, which made the white bandages seem even whiter.

Someone fetched a gas lamp and hung it on a big tree. He himself stood under the tree and gave a speech. He said the effective ways to deal with air raids were dispersal and first-aid. The first one aimed to prevent casualties, while the latter aimed to minimise casualties. He thanked everyone for their efforts in the War of Resistance and wished them all well with their practice, which was what mattered most.

"You've missed the real issue!" Helen yelled loudly. "The real issue is that we need our own air force to protect our air sovereignty!"

"Aye! Aye!" Jiaxin gave her support. This was an extremely simple truth. Even Kiddo had long figured it out. But knowledge of the truth couldn't change the facts!

When the training was over, Yingshu came to join Earl and her friends to walk back on campus. They started a heated debate on the way.

Yingshu said it was as obvious as lice on a bald head that China needed an air force, but the country was too poor to afford such a force which would surely make it stronger, though. No one was to blame for the status quo. The corrupt Qing dynasty and the civil war caused by the warlords had already exhausted the resources for national defence.

"I'm not blaming anyone," Helen answered calmly. "Dispersal and first-aid are important, but I think it is more important that we have the protection of our own air force."

Yingshu said: "The time wasted and the things neglected in the past all have to be made up by our generation."

Helen mused: "We share the same goal, but we have different perspectives and different paths."

They all fell silent until a male student said: "The song we just sang is about The Great Way, our utopia. I think there are many ways to realise that ideal."

"From different ways to the same way," said Earl.

When they went past the Green lake, Yingshu told Earl: "My mothers are enjoying themselves a lot in Anning county. Now it's already summer vacation, why don't you take the opportunity to take May and Kiddo to pay them a visit and stay for a couple of days?"

Earl remained silent. The dyke of the Green lake was already familiar to the students. The bridges and shadows in the water were a perfect blend of clarity and obscurity in the night light.

When Earl returned to her dormitory, she immediately spotted two people sitting in chairs against the wall in the doorway. They greeted her as if they had found their long-lost treasure. It was her parents! But she was somewhat reserved. When she called out "Mum, Dad", she stopped in her tracks. The three stood silently together for a moment, with lumps in their throats.

Earl whispered: "Mum, why have you come? You should be resting." Bichu was indeed exhausted after the long walk. She was still panting. With people coming and going in the doorway, they didn't say much to one another. When Earl promised to go back home when the school was officially off for summer, she didn't say any more and left, her head bowed.

PART III

G raduation day had finally arrived. It was an extraordinary day for Tantai Xuan.

At 7 o'clock in the morning, the university was going to hold a graduation ceremony. The sky was bright. Xuan felt that daybreak had come earlier than usual on that day. When she arrived at the playground, she overheard someone saying the same: "Daybreak was so early today." Someone else teased the first one: "That's probably because you were up all night."

The students were assigned to different places according to their departments. Everyone had mixed feelings. They were glad they had completed their studies, but they were also anxious about entering society. All these young faces were tinted with different shades of excitement to be embarking on a new section of life's journey. They greeted one another and talked loudly, assuming they wouldn't see each other again and keen to say more today. Xuan was standing among her classmates. She wore a starched cotton *qipao*, and a thin light-blue short-sleeved sweater, white shoes and white socks, which she had taken a few days to get used to. The clothes were simple and plain but were proper enough to emphasise the beautiful curves of her body. She was attractive, and many males students knew it.

The foreign language department was next to the economics department, where Thunderhand was. He asked where Xuan was going to find a job. Xuan answered: "I haven't made up my mind yet." Thunderhand said that he had a few options, but that he would probably go to Chongqing. A classmate of Thunderhand's whispered to him: "We didn't know you knew Miss Tantai!" Xuan didn't take any offense upon hearing the words.

The ceremony was presided over by Xiao Cheng, who delivered a very concise speech before he read out the graduation list. Hearing their own names, most of the graduates all answered in their hearts: "Here!" But some cried out "here". Their voices reverberated far and wide on the playground. When Xuan heard her name, she stood to attention, proud of herself going to serve in one of the posts to fight the Japanese invaders and to save her country.

When the list was read out, President Qin began to speak: "We are now in the fourth year of the War of Resistance, and the war in the European theatre has also been going for a year. The situation is severe since we cannot see when we can achieve victory. You are our third set of graduates during the War of Resistance. The first two have made many contributions to the cause of the war and saving our country. I believe that you will be the pride of your alma mater, and your alma mater will always be proud of you." President Qin's calming but candid voice struck a chord in every graduate's heart.

The ceremony was arranged early in the morning to avoid air raids, but today it was destined to be special. Just as President Qin finished his speech, a wave of whispers rippled from the crowd to the rostrum. "The red balloon!" "The red balloon is out!" At the top of Wuhuashan in the distance, a red balloon appeared.

Principal Qin lifted his glasses and said humorously: "It seems that the enemy planes also know that you are graduating today and want to present their congratulations to you."

By convention, the school wouldn't disperse until the whistle of the air raid siren sounded. After an exchange of opinions, the professors agreed to cancel several speeches and stand in silent tribute for the three graduates who had died in battle. Then came the final procedure where Professor Meng Fuzhi spoke on behalf of all the teaching faculty. Everyone pricked up their ears for the sincere wishes from their teachers.

"My dear students," Fuzhi began, as the air raid siren sounded.

Fuzhi looked at President Qin and Xiao Cheng, then he said decisively: "I'm not going to say any more today. Before you leave school, we can speak freely with each other. Now I'd like to wish everyone all the best in their work and a prosperous future."

Xiao Cheng stepped forward and said: "We have to adjourn the meeting. Your graduation ceremony has been wrapped up by the air raid siren. I think everyone will remember it for this reason. Now let's sing the university song!"

"Progress! Progress! We strive incessantly for progress! Progress! Progress! We strive incessantly for progress!" The high tone of the last two lines of the song represented the accumulation of all the strength and dreams of the young hearts radiating with thunderous energy and grandeur, counteracting the wailing of the siren. Xiao Cheng announced the end of the ceremony.

Everyone slowly left the playground and walked to the hillside behind the school building. Xuan walked with her classmates and saw Helen ahead of her, sharing the new book she had been reading with some people near her. Wei Feng, who had been standing not far off, came up to congratulate her.

Xuan joked: "Now I have graduated, I have lost my source of support."

Wei Feng taunted: "That would be news! Miss Xuan has no source of support!"

Xuan was meant to have grimaced at such a comment, but her face beamed instead. Wei Feng said nothing more but headed for Helen, joining the discussion about the book, and left with them. Xuan felt somewhat offended. After one second of hesitation, she decided she was not going to run from the air raid. She turned around and headed for her rented place. Several classmates of hers greeted her and asked: "Tantai Xuan, why are you heading into town?" Two even wanted to tag along, but Xuan waved her hand at them to indicate no. She wanted to stay alone.

The shops along the street hadn't opened for business yet. The wailing of the siren was mixed with yells from different families, urging their members to get up and go. In just moments, people left for the outskirts in groups. They didn't bother to close the shops. Turning to what Wei Feng had said and did to her, Xuan couldn't figure out why Wei Feng had behaved like that. He was so complicated. Did Xueyan really know him? She was simple and innocent while Wei Feng was so sophisticated. "But why should I worry about this?" She fanned herself with her handkerchief. "What I should worry about is Paul. How funny the Chinese surname he picked for himself. Mai — wheat!"

During the last year, there had been much progress in the relationship between Xuan and Paul. They were almost at the stage of a proposal. When Xuan had engaged in girl talk with her mother, she was already treating Paul as a candidate for marriage. Back then, the average Chinese family could not accept a foreigner, but Xuan's parents were more open-minded and did not have anything against interracial marriage. When they discovered that Paul's grandfather was quite rich, though his father was a poor priest, they thought it was acceptable. The pathways ahead of Xuan were tortuous. Who could see that far ahead?

Xuan's small nest at Precious Pearl lane was quite a sight. Her small room was upstairs. A wax-printed homespun cotton cloth hung all the way down from the roof, covering the two walls facing each other. A small bed was covered with a bed cover of the same colour. A couple of dolls were crammed in the corner, clustered around a doll standing on a short side table. She was blonde, wearing a short pale mauve dress, holding a chubby little hand out as if she were observing something. What a lovely doll!

When Xuan came in, she first tugged the little hand of the blonde doll and said to her: "I have graduated, but I haven't had my breakfast yet!" Then she made herself a cup of milk with milk powder and sat down at the window, sipping her milk, which was too hot to drink. She went out of the room to the porch and leaned against the railing, her eyes fixed on a pear tree. The branches were laden with pears, and the little fruits were just taking shape, swarming all over the twigs and branches. Without any reason, Wei Feng popped into her mind, "Why did he come to mind again! How annoying!" After a while, the air raid alert was lifted. The landlord's family commented on how little time it had taken to lift the alert. Did the enemy fighter planes turn in the wrong direction? They amused themselves with such a joke.

The courtyard door squeaked open and in walked a blonde young man sharing the same blonde hair and blue eyes as the doll. He walked across the yard and whistled at the room upstairs.

"Paul!" Xuan waved at the man downstairs. He came in with a bright smile and a bouquet of roses.

"Nine flowers for you and I wish you a brilliant future!" Paul presented Xuan with the flowers and told her the specific number. He knew 'nine' was considered the biggest number in Chinese culture. He gave her a kiss on the cheek. This was the etiquette they used back then.

Paul said: "I knew you wouldn't run from the air raid."

Xuan smiled by way of reply and asked Paul to sit in a chair. Then she said: "My fellow graduates are going to go through tremendous changes after graduation. Many have decided to leave Kunming. I don't know what kind of life they are going to have."

"Well, only Miss Tantai is staying put," Paul laughed, fascinated by Xuan sitting on the bed with the wax-printed bed cover, radiating with glamour.

Xuan had already accepted a job. She had had a couple of offers because of her fluent English. One was to work at the US consulate in Kunming. They all believed that she would be an excellent employee and had tried to persuade her to take the offer several times. But she had declined because she did not want to work in the same place as Paul. Two government departments in Chongqing had positions open, and her parents wanted her to take one of them. She didn't accept the offer because of her reluctance to leave Kunming. The position she decided to take was somewhat mundane. She was employed as translator at a department in the Yunnan provincial administration. People thought she was doing it for fun, but she was actually quite serious.

"Everyone needs to do his or her bit to fight in the War of Resistance. At least this is my principle. Besides," she added, "I'll get my revenge for what they did to me back in Beiping when they insulted me by damaging my dress with the tip of a bayonet!"

Xuan said: "I used to go west every day to school, and what I need to do is to go east to work every day instead."

"From Precious Pearl lane, the provincial government building is on the other side of the city. But from China, the US is on the other side of the earth. You are not going east or west, you'll go to the opposite side," said Paul.

He had hinted many times that he wished Xuan would go back to the US with him, but he had never had a proper occasion to raise this with Xuan. Today was the best occasion because Xuan had graduated. And this tiny glamorous nest was the right place. He decided he was going to quit hinting. As if guided by some sacred light, he strode out of the room and then strode back, planting himself in front of Xuan and asked solemnly in English: "Tantai Xuan, will you marry me?" He repeated the same sentence in Chinese.

Xuan had long expected that Paul would propose, and sometimes she even wondered why he had not. She was touched by these words of his she had been waiting to hear for so long. She thought for a moment and then said, solemnly: "Give me some time to think it through since going from this side of the earth to the opposite side is a very important issue. Do people there walk upside down?" They both laughed.

"I know you have to talk this over with your family," said Paul. "In fact, we Americans also respect the opinions of our parents."

"You have already asked your parents?"

"Yes, I have," said Paul. "They thought this must be God's arrangement that I found you, a dark-haired Chinese in Kunming." Paul took up Xuan's hand and asked: "Do you know when I had this idea?"

"By the Dianchi lake the night we ran from the air raids to the Grand View pavilion." At Xuan's words, Paul held Xuan in his arms and spun her once around the room, shouting: "Smart! You are so smart!"

Xuan wriggled free of him and put a finger to her lips to hush him. "Hey! Sit! Sit! Do you Americans actually know how to sit properly?"

"Yes, of course. We even know how to sit in meditation," Paul answered, sitting in the chair, dropping his arms like a well behaved child.

Xuan looked at him and then at the blonde doll and smiled sweetly.

They went on talking about their arrangements that day. Xuan said she had a gathering with her classmates in the afternoon and would attend Fuzhi's speech in the evening, while Paul had to work in the afternoon, so they decided to have lunch together.

Paul asked: "How about that important issue in your life? I'm still waiting for your answer."

"You won't have to wait long," Xuan assured him, patting Paul gently on the arm. "I need to go back home. I need to go to Chongqing." When they went past the landlord's kitchen downstairs, the landlady cast a peculiar look at Xuan. It happened every time Paul visited. This morning, Xuan had wanted to cry out loud at the landlady: "This is my fiancé!" But she ended up saying nothing. Giving the woman a polite smile, she walked out with Paul, arm in arm.

The beautiful clear sky dotted with fluffy white clouds loitering like stray hydrogen balloons suddenly changed its demeanour. Just as they walked out of the alley, it showered. "Your clothes are going to get wet. I should have driven the car!" Paul didn't drive often here in Kunming. He preferred walking.

The clouds drifted overhead, raining cats and dogs mixed with hailstones. They walked under the eaves of the shops along the street. As they walked into another small alley, they heard someone saying: "Come in and sit. It will rain more." It was the wife of a small shop owner. That reminded them both that they hadn't talked about where they would go for lunch.

This was a newly opened shop which looked quite clean, so they walked in and sat at a small table. The store owner's wife, beaming with hospitality, asked what they would like to order. Slips of paper with words like Yuxi rice noodles and Shiping tofu were casually stuck on the wall, serving as the menu. They ordered a dish of Shiping tofu, which was a long slice of tofu grilled over charcoal and then served with hot chili sauce. Xuan took a look at Paul and then at the tofu slice and burst out laughing again. Paul patted her on the head and teased her: "My little girl, you're so happy to see food. You must be starving!" He picked up the piece of tofu, took a bite and lept to his feet.

At such a sight, Xuan continued to laugh. Luckily, there were only the two of them in the diner, which they had to themselves. Besides, the owner's wife was quite open-minded. She didn't fuss. Instead, she minded her own business. At that moment, a young woman soaked in the rain came back from some grocery shopping. She whispered something to the store owner's wife and said a few words before she carried the vegetables to the back. As she went across the room and saw Xuan doubled up laughing, she paused temporarily in surprise but immediately went on toward the back of the building.

The rain finally stopped, revealing a blindingly bright blue sky. They didn't want to sit any longer in the diner, so they stood up and left. When Xuan looked back, she saw the woman saying to the store owner's wife: "Going to buy charcoal," and went in the other direction. Her wet clothes clung to her body, revealing her beautiful womanly curves. Xuan's heart missed a beat. Why did this figure look familiar? But she didn't have time to think it over as she was preoccupied, talking to Paul. They used both Chinese and English. Sometimes, they didn't even understand what they said to each other, but they were very happy like lovebirds chirping and tweeting. No one ever mentioned lunch again. On this day, they had been caught in a shower, met someone who gave them a sense of déjà vu and forgotten their lunch.

In the afternoon, the foreign language department held a simple tea party for the graduates. Wang Dingyi, the dean of the department, used to think highly of Xuan and advised her to stay on and teach. He told Xuan that she might be disappointed with work in the provincial government and that she might reconsider teaching. Xuan said with a smile that she didn't hold out high hopes. What she wanted was to try a new environment. The teacher and the student said a fond goodbye.

A couple of classmates had dinner together and everyone was a little depressed. Someone said that graduation was a big deal and that they should inform their parents, but they didn't know where they were or how to reach them. Someone else said: "Wherever they are, they'll always pray for you and give you their blessing. Whether the way ahead of us is blessed is hard to say." Having shared some information with one another about where they were going to be working, they said goodbye to one another.

The lecture that evening was still held on the playground. Professor Meng intended to do without a gas lamp since the moonlight was bright enough. Well before the scheduled time, many people, from students of all grades to the teaching faculty, such as Jiang Fang, Li Lian and Qian Mingjing, had arrived and were walking with one another on the playground. Xuan and her friends were clustered in front of the 'rostrum', sitting on their brick stools.

Professor Meng was sitting on a section of a tree trunk on the edge of the playground, looking at the crowd. The trunk was enormous and functioned as a rostrum. When everything had quietened down, he began: "I wanted to have a talk with the students from the history department but Professor Xiao said that I should share the talk with you all. I don't have any wise words, but since many of you here are far from your parents, you may be willing to listen to a few words from someone elderly like me. You are now facing a new starting point in life but also are involved in a sacred war where the entire nation is working together to fight the Japanese invaders. The situation you are going to dive into will inevitably be complicated and the life you are going to start will inevitably be hard. There will be many unexpected things in life, and no one can foresee what might be coming, but I think that four years of university life will help you to find your way."

"You might be familiar with the three large-scale migrations to the south due to foreign invasions in Chinese history. When the regime moved to the south, so did its culture. The first migration happened when the founding emperor of the Jin dynasty, Sima Rui (276-323 AD), crossed the Yangtze river and established today's Nanjing as its capital. Those notable families and great clans in the central plains (comprising the middle and lower reaches of the Yellow river) also moved southwards. The second one happened at the end of the Northern Song dynasty when Emperor Gaozong (1107-1187 AD) crossed the river and took today's Hangzhou city, Zhejiang province, as its capital. The third one happened at the end of the Ming dynasty. None of the people migrating to the south had the opportunity to return to their hometowns again. The war we are now in is not only confined to one country but has engulfed the whole world. We are fighting to eliminate fascist evils against humanity and we are fighting for justice for mankind. We have not only crossed the Yellow river and the Yangtze river, we have also reached the southwestern borders of China. It is amazing that the music and our singing never stop because of the hardships from such a tough life. As long as we have you, my young graduates, we can fight our way back home. This is my sincere belief, although it is an abstract belief. With our combined efforts, we can transform it into reality."

"Efforts can be defined in various ways and each person's ability varies, too. So does one's fate. One's ability can be said to be one's given gift. If such a given gift is not developed to its full potential, it is then almost wasted. One's efforts can bring full strength to one's given gift but cannot increase it. To make full use of your given gifts is your ultimate goal. In addition to our efforts, to achieve the goal, we must rely on the environment. This calls for a reasonable society. For everyone, the environment where you can do your best is a good one, and the environment that hinders you from doing so is an adverse one. When you go to work, you may encounter good times and you may also encounter adversity. In the good times, we must work hard to achieve the best results, and we must work harder in times of adversity with limited resources. At any time, we must do our utmost to do our duty, which has two aspects. To fulfil your duty as a member of the nation and stick to what your profession requires you to do. If you are a capable person in good times or bad, you should always try your utmost to do your duty."

"Recently, I have been thinking a lot about China's way out. To beat the strong enemy is the immediate mission. In the long run, China's only way out is modernisation. We have been bullied by the big powers because of our backward production and our economy. Compared with the great powers, we are like country bumpkins while the major powers are like city dwellers. We must change rural people into urban residents. To advance, we must achieve modernisation. This requires everyone to do his or her utmost to contribute your given gifts and contribute the knowledge and skills you have acquired to such a cause. Only in this way can we guarantee the victory of the War of Resistance and ensure the success of building a new nation in the future."

Fuzhi sometimes included questions in his speech, as if he was having a conversation with the students. He talked for about an hour and stopped to take questions.

Some hand-written notes were handed in. In the moonlight, one read "Professor Meng's modernisation is exciting, but how can we achieve it? I want to go to Yan'an. What do you think?" Another one read: "Can going to school really help the country?"

Meng Fuzhi said: "If our culture survives, so will the Chinese nation. In this sense, going to school is also an effort to save the nation. The War of Resistance requires a lot of practical work. If you do not want to continue your education, it is important, too, to take part in all forms of work to save the country. I think it's alright to go to Yan'an for the road to founding a new nation must be explored."

At this time, a student stood up and said: "Professor Meng, you encourage your students to go to Yan'an. Isn't it inappropriate?"

Another student said loudly: "That's the path to freedom!"

A third one with broad shoulders, Yan Yingshu, said: "If we want to win the war and establish a new country, the best guidance should be the Three People's Principles."

Some immediately agreed while some disagreed. Several students started talking at the same time. Fuzhi clapped his hands to quieten down the students and said: "It's great to see so much enthusiastic discussion. How about we invite a professor to share a few words?"

Jiang Fang stood up and began slowly: "I often hear you sing a song called 'The Great Harmony'. The lyrics are taken from the *Book of Etiquette*. Our ancestors have been yearning for an equal and prosperous society for more than 2,000 years. Yet, we haven't achieved it. Do you think there might be a new theory, a more scientific one, to guide us?"

Everyone knew he was referring to Marxism. He went on: "I totally agree with Professor Meng that the road to the War of Resistance is still very long. Maybe we all have to go to the front when the time comes. But you must learn and study hard as long as you are in school."

A vehement and grave silence fell on the playground as everyone contemplated what path to take. A female student's sob broke the silence. Fuzhi said gently: "Life is already such a burden to you all, but you have to remember what lies on your shoulders is the fate of the nation, which needs you to fight the Japanese devils and build a modern country. In other words, you are bearing the fate of the world and all mankind because you are fighting evil. Justice will win. Sinners against humanity will fail."

Looking around, Fuzhi ended his speech by saying: "Whichever path you take, I believe you will all be worthy of your motherland."

After the meeting, Xuan walked together with her classmates, turning over in her mind the fact that Uncle Fuzhi's speech tonight was a bit heavy, different from his regular humorous style. "What path am I going to take?" The path led her to the school gate where she saw Paul waiting for her on the street. She left her path problem behind and joined Paul in the shadows, away from the crowds. After a while, Fuzhi walked past, accompanied by several students and followed by Earl and Jiaxin. Jiaxin was drying her tears. Xuan and Paul didn't walk out of the shadows to the jeep parked nearby until everyone had disappeared from sight.

Fuzhi and the people accompanying him strolled in the moonlight. The students walked Fuzhi all the way to the theatre, discussing China's modernisation, its talent and other issues.

PART IV

Summer vacation officially took off.

Earl walked quietly with her father along the Mang river, answering his questions when asked. Although she never started anything with her father all the way, she felt so close to him. The relinquishment of her secret marked the thawing of the invisible barrier between her and her parents.

"Dad, let me carry your bag." Fuzhi had the same old stuff: his bag with the shoulder strap across his body made of blue printed cloth and his red umbrella made of tarpaulin.

"The books are quite heavy," said Fuzhi gently. "How about you carry my umbrella?"

Earl took the umbrella from him and carried it on her shoulder. Fuzhi smiled at Earl's childish manner. They walked past the dyke imbued with multiple shades of green, went on the only street in the village, took a turn into a lane and reached their courtyard, where all sorts of noises of vitality from the barking of the dog and the grunts of the pigs mixed with May and Kiddo's cheerful greetings welcomed the two back home: "Dad, big sister, you are home!"

May ran up and took hold of the bag, Kiddo the umbrella. The staircase creaked as Bichu came down to join them, steadying herself by holding the side of the wall made of wooden boards, radiant with joy. Earl walked over to her mother, who clasped her shoulders. Both had so much to say to each other, yet neither could find any words.

Fuzhi moved to the attic over the gate that night, offering his spot to Earl to share with her mother. Earl insisted on making the bed for her mother. Bichu asked: "Why didn't you ever mention it or just ask me?" Earl answered with her regular silence. Bichu sighed: "I'm to blame for being so negligent." Earl took her mother's hand and rubbed it against her cheek in silence. The topic was never mentioned again between mother and daughter.

Life over the pigsty was tough, but it didn't change the vitality and aggression running through the Meng family. It was even more harmonious with Earl growing so much closer to her family.

Since May's release from hospital, she hadn't fully recovered. She barely managed to go to school for one semester before she had to quit schooling completely. Without May's company, the boarding life on campus was too much for Kiddo to manage at such a young age, so he quit school, too, when May stopped going. They immersed themselves in their reading, copying characters and helping with the household chores.

All the four board walls were decorated with their works like a gallery. Half of May's copy of the epic title *Jiucheng Palace* by the famed Northern Song dynasty calligrapher Ouyang Xun was destroyed by the blast of a bomb that landed in front of their dwelling in the ancestral temple, so May decided to copy a new one. When she put her work up on the wall, she remembered the nightmare moment when she was buried under the layer of earth. She shuddered at the memory.

"I was like a homeless dog," she thought. "All those who have lost their motherland are like homeless dogs and pigs."

They did drawings, too. Kiddo was engrossed with drawing all kinds of planes while May indulged herself only in landscapes in water colours, but she dreamed the same dream as Kiddo. In their shared dreams, Kiddo's planes fought heroically against the enemy fighter planes.

A few days later, Fuzhi and Bichu announced another happy event to the children: they were going to move to Baotaishan (Baotai mountain) into a side courtyard attached to the place where the Institute of Liberal Arts had been relocated. Although the rooms were too worn and shabby for anyone to live in, they could almost be considered decent after being smartened up compared to life in a room over a pigsty.

The day before they moved, a stranger paid a visit. This guest, the chief steward for the grand chieftain of Wali, had appeared at Bai Liwen's before. He brought two boxes of gifts containing hams and milk fans (cheese made into the shape of a fan), and a pair of jade cups in bright lemon yellow with a smooth mirror-like surface. A letter was presented to Fuzhi from the guest. What the grand chieftain said in his letter was quite beyond Fuzhi's expectations.

The chieftain was inviting Fuzhi and his family, in a combined effort with the chieftains of smaller villages in the vicinity bordering Sichuan province, to stay for some time in their villages. Fuzhi didn't need to give classes or lectures. The chieftain claimed it was fortunate for them if a famed scholar like Fuzhi could influence those around him by his presence.

As Fuzhi was reading the letter, Bichu offered the man some tea; the latter hurriedly rose to his feet, full of gratitude.

Fuzhi sighed as he finished reading the letter. What a perfect place to hide in the depths of the mountains from the air raids, he thought. But he couldn't go.

He asked the guest to sit down again. After asking about the man's journey, Fuzhi continued: "Please convey my gratitude to your chieftain for thinking of me. It is very meaningful to serve our brothers of different ethnic minorities, but I am a full-time faculty member employed by Minglun University and I have my own work and duties to cover. I cannot leave without being given permission. My sincere wish is that more children from the villages will come to attend schools here and then go back to serve their hometowns when they graduate. Now that many schools have relocated inland, it is a good opportunity for them."

The man responded: "My chieftain has always admired knowledgeable scholars. We are all looking forward to having a scholar like you stay with us for a while. We don't have any extravagant hopes that you will stay long. But if you could stay for a year, it would be such a blessing for us all. Besides, you may take the time to have a proper rest."

One year? Fuzhi turned these words over in his mind. One year later, who could tell what the situation might be?

He said: "How about I write a letter of response to your chieftain?" Taking out his ink box and brush from a net basket, Fuzhi began to write a letter to the chieftain, explaining why he had to decline such a generous offer.

The two pigs in the downstairs pigsty had a fight. Noisy grunting filled the upstairs room. Kiddo tried to calm them down by talking to them between the floorboards: "Don't fight! We are moving tomorrow. You should behave yourselves and be polite!"

May ran upstairs with a shallow bamboo strainer in her hands to get some rice for cooking lunch. She reached out into the rice jar, picked out several wriggling rice worms and tossed them downstairs through the gap between the floorboards, commented with a smile: "You guys are rude. We have guests!"

225

The man, watching May and Kiddo attentively, said to Bichu: "What a blessed family with your young master and miss!"

Bichu smiled gently in response. Fuzhi handed the man the letter. The man took it and secured it in his pocket. What he did next took Fuzhi totally by surprise. The man knelt and kowtowed to Fuzhi, who moved sideways, saying "You don't need to do this".

The man said: "Although we haven't had the opportunity to read Professor Meng's books, we have always known we should respect the learned. I feel so sorry to see the hardships you are having to endure."

Fuzhi said with sincerity: "A bitter life and tough living environment don't do any harm. Compared with thousands of my compatriots or the roving refugees, we are living in paradise. As long as we are united in the war against Japan, we won't ask for more."

The man then excused himself, insisting on leaving behind the presents, claiming that if he returned with the presents, he would be punished. Knowing the man had a point, Fuzhi didn't insist, but he only kept the food while asking the man to take back the jade cups.

The man tightened his belt and strode downstairs. In a moment, the clatter of horse hoofs was heard, leading all the way out of the yard. The man was on his way back.

Fuzhi said to Bichu: "Dali used to be known as the Nanzhao kingdom for a period of time. Back then, it was quite strong militarily. In 748 AD, when the second king of the kingdom, Ge Luofeng, took Sichuan province, he captured a county magistrate called Zheng Hui and some skilled craftsmen as well. Later, Ge Luofeng appointed Zheng Hui as his prime minister. Legend later had it that the king of Nanzhao raided Sichuan province to capture a prime minister to help the king run his kingdom. How eager the king was to seek worthy talent! It must have been a moving scene for both the king and Zheng Hui. However tyrannical and powerful an enemy we are facing, we must save our culture! Our country will be doomed with the extermination of our own culture. But I really wish you could go there and have a proper rest. You need rest."

Bichu responded: "No, you need to drop that idea. How can we leave behind the university? I have been feeling much better. Haven't you noticed?" She busied herself with her chores while she talked. Her spontaneous cough betrayed her. She went downstairs with May to cook.

The following day, Zhao Er found two men to carry the Mengs' package to their new place. Mingjing and Huifen came to help with the move, too. All the Zhaos were clustered at the gate to see the Mengs off, Zhao Er's wife holding the children's hands, his old parents tottering around, the dog and the cat tagging along. All were reluctant to part.

Zhao Er's wife told Bichu: "Mrs Meng, my niece should have been back by now. I don't know what has kept her. I'll send her to you in a couple of days, so you can take a look at her."

Bichu hadn't hired anyone to help with the chores in order to reduce their expenses, but she hadn't been feeling well for some time. Besides, Fuzhi had suggested they needed an extra hand with the moving, so she accepted the offer: "Please send her to me at your convenience."

Everyone pitched in with the moving, carrying things in their hands or on their backs. Since the Mengs didn't have much to take away, they finished the move in one trip.

After having had pigs as neighbours for a whole year, the Mengs were so grateful now that they had an adobe house with three rooms which were built on firm ground instead of on floorboards. All were overjoyed when they found one room even had a narrow backroom, which was perfect for Earl, who was genuinely happy about it: "This is surely for me. See? Even the landlord of this house cares about me."

Bichu fished out lots of nice items for Earl to decorate her 'room' with, while Kiddo bustled in and out to help. May was tackling the cooking utensils on her own on the ground from pots and pans to bowls and spoons.

Earl wanted to put up her specimen on the wall, although it was nothing more than a piece of cardboard pinned with dried plants fixed in position. She hurt her hand when she was trying to drive the nails into the wall. May offered to help her: "I'll do it for you!" With their combined efforts, the cardboard was put up.

When the two sisters took several steps back to check whether the cardboard was in the right position, the rest of the Meng family suddenly saw that May was as tall as Earl! Kiddo cried out first: "Sister May is as tall as sister Earl!" And he ran to stand by them, straightening himself up as high as he could. He reached up to May's eyes.

Fuzhi and Bichu caught each other's eye and exchanged a smile. Yes! Their children had all grown up. They could walk. They could run. They could take care of themselves however hard the life ahead of them might become.

When it was almost noon, Wei Feng and Xueyan came. The two had got used to the life in Salt Falls. Both radiated with a kind of peacefulness. Xueyan was in a navy-blue *qipao* fringed with bright coloured printed cloth, the style set by Huifen. The *qipao* showed off the beautiful lady-like curves she was known for. Wei Feng was in a completely different style. He didn't wear gowns like other teachers. Instead he was in shirt and trousers with legs rolled up. He was carrying two baskets with a carrying pole. His handsome features and neat figure blended with his scholarly manner made him such an attractive porter. He and Xueyan had first gone to the fair for their grocery shopping and for some ingredients to make lunch at the Mengs'. They were shocked at the soaring price for rice which was three times higher than last time. Their money was short even for the most essential items they planned to buy, but they still managed to buy a big chunk of beef for making bouillon.

"This must have something to do with the blockade," commented Mingjing. From July 1st, the British government closed the Yunnan-Burma road, and later the same month, the French government shut down the Yunnan-Vietnam railroad. "Villains get helpers! What a funny world!"

Wei Feng said: "When Paris was taken, France looked like it had lost all its strength to parry any more blows. Great Britain and France are doomed to suffer the consequences of their appeasement policy toward Japan. The other day when I ran into Della, she told me the British citizens in Kunming are also wondering what Churchill will do now that he is in office."

The joy of moving to a new home was dampened by the shadow of war. But all of them had long got so used to living in darkness that they were able to generate a halo of light out of the shadows.

Everyone helped arrange the furniture, which involved all sorts of rearrangement of kerosene crates of all sizes. Fuzhi's work desk had the privilege of being set up first. It was made of the original four crates with a piece of unpainted wooden board serving as the surface. That 'table' was his world. He carefully wiped the inkwell he had bought at Guihui and then put it on the table with the brush holder. When he began to tidy up the loose papers and his books, he suddenly said: "At the university's weekly meeting last week, President Qin mentioned that the provincial government had decided to open the provincial granaries to ease the suffering of the poor. I guess we are very short of food? But I haven't heard Zhao Er complaining about a shortage of food."

Huifen, who was cleaning windows, said: "When I go to fetch water by the well, I have heard some talk of price rises. It is said that the price for firewood has risen, too. Everyone hates the Japanese devils so much. If they had any chance, they would surely jump on us and strangle us all to death."

Hearing Huifen talking, Mingjing immediately joined her: "It sounds quite poetic to listen to the gossip by the well. After more careful analysis, I think prices are rising too fast. Some profiteers must be taking the opportunity to make a killing!"

Wei Feng agreed: "I think so. The consequences of the blockade couldn't be reflected in such a short time. It must have something to do with profiteering. It might not even be profiteers. Those who are in charge of the release of the granaries have also been trying to profit from their posts. It is said that when the amount was released, it had already been reduced to only a third of the planned amount."

Fuzhi lost his cool: "How could this have happened? This is corruption! How could those officials pursue profit with those profiteers?"

Wei Feng said: "Their crimes are certain, though we don't know whether they will be busted or not."

While the men were engaged in conversation, Bichu was leading the kids to start the stove to make lunch. Xueyan was very skilful at these chores. Bichu smiled at Xueyan: "Xueyan, you have changed so much! Look how skilful you already are!"

Huifen went over to them and said: "I'm quite jealous of Xueyan's good luck in finding such a nice job at Minglun after having arrived in Kunming so recently. Why isn't anyone asking me to teach drawing? I don't understand!" Huifen and Xueyan didn't know each other in Beiping, but now they had become very close friends.

Xueyan smiled her gentle smile: "It's easier for English majors to find a good position. I am just lucky that not many people learn French and that Minglun needs someone to teach French. Here I am!"

"Our first lady speaks perfect English. That's why all the wives of high-ranking officials and officers pitch in to learn English," said Mingjing.

Bichu said: "That's very true. Xuan has been offered positions to teach English."

"I hear she has decided to go to work with the provincial government?" asked Wei Feng, wondering why Xuan would accept such an offer.

Mingjing said: "She should go to work at the US consulate." But his opinion was overwhelmingly opposed. Huifen shot an angry look at Mingjing. Xueyan wanted to say how one needed to support oneself, but she refrained from doing so because Bichu and Huifen didn't work. Besides, it involved Xuan. Not knowing what to say, she fell silent.

The summer weather in Kunming was very mild and refreshing. The womenfolk busied themselves with cooking and talking. From time to time, they would raise their heads to look at the transparent blue sky. They basked in the illumination of the blue sky and the green trees penetrating the thick shadow of war.

Wei Feng and Qian Mingjing walked into the yard and looked around. Wei Feng said: "We can build a small kitchen in the yard. What we need are a couple of logs. For the roof, we can use wooden planks covered with fur branches and twigs. It's never cold in Kunming, anyway."

Mingjing thought for a moment and said: "It won't take much trouble to build a kitchen, indeed. I can find the materials we need. It's better to use a few bricks."

"When did you two start studying construction?" teased Bichu. They all laughed. Huifen gave Mingjing her enthusiastic approval.

During lunch, two young teaching staff came. They had been to search for some books in the arts institute and dropped by when they were done. Bichu handed them chopsticks and bowls and invited them to join the meal. The two happily accepted the invitation, claiming: "We all know Mrs Meng is a good cook!" They all began to attack the dishes: a giant bowl of stew made of pork rind, a giant bowl of cooked snow thistle and another giant bowl of assorted beans. Soon nothing was left in the three bowls.

Looking at Bichu's short hair, Fuzhi said: "Now I finally understand the function of hair pins on the buns of those women in olden times."

Mingjing picked up on the topic: "That's why we have the two beautiful legendary idioms 'to cut one's long hair to buy food for one's guest' and 'to pawn the wife's gold hairpin to buy wine for the husband'."

Bichu said: "Now I don't have my long hair anymore, and I have no gold hairpin to pawn, so my poor guests, you all have to put up with bitter snow thistles for your lunch."

Xueyan whispered: "Aunt Bichu, you look younger with your hair short. No one needs to pawn hairpins. We still have bouillon." She stood up to get bouillon for everybody. The chunk of beef had been cut into small cubes and cooked with leafy greens. Everyone was amazed how delicious the bouillon tasted.

In the afternoon, the guests left one by one. When Wei Feng was rearranging his baskets before they left, he reviewed with Xueyan the items they had bought for the Mi couple. Fuzhi overheard them mentioning the Mi couple and asked how they were doing. Wei Feng answered: "Mrs Mi, although much younger than her husband, is in very poor heath due to her injury. Although they always have friends from town visiting them, they can't manage all their daily chores."

After once again asking Bichu to take a good rest, Xueyan and Wei Feng left, going downhill. They looked so much like those farmer couples on their way back from visiting their relatives.

After the move, Earl found a temporary job at the radio station in the city and stayed in town. Bichu fell ill again due to the heavy load of housework. Most of the chores were shifted to May, who had the privilege of ordering both Fuzhi and Kiddo around. Once, when Fuzhi and May tried to start the stove with pine needles, the dry pine needles, which seemed so efficient for starting fires in Bichu's hands, became so disobedient in Fuzhi and May's hands. The fire kept smouldering instead of lighting up. The father and daughter studied the problem for a while and realised that the needles needed air to burn. When they poked a stick under the needles, they caught fire. The rice May cooked was always half burnt, but they all felt it tasted delicious. May also did the laundry. Soap was rare back then in Kunming, so people used charcoal ash water as a replacement. This ash water was a strong detergent and worked very well for cleaning, but it was caustic for human skin. The chaps, big and small, on Bichu's hands were caused by the ash water. Bichu didn't allow May to use the ash water, but May would use some behind her mother's back in order to make the laundry cleaner.

The scenery on Baotaishan was a totally different story from that above the pigsty. A stone path zigzagged uphill from the foot of Baotaishan and twisted around a few rocks before reaching the Mengs' courtyard. Standing in front of the gate to the yard, one could see the Mang river flowing by, guarded by two rows of trees lining its banks. On the other side, one could discern mountain ranges extending far into the distance. At night, when there was a full moon, those ranges would be tinted different shades of grey. Various species of trees, tall and short, mingled with miscellaneous wild flowers, undefeated and unrelenting. As one species faded, another began to bloom. The not-so-brilliant colours always embellished the bushes with richness and mysterious depth, as if the colour had beamed through the trees until it reached the hillside. Meng Fuzhi often took walks around the mountain alone, absorbing inspiration from the Yunnan earth under his feet to generate many lively thoughts.

Because of the limited space over the pigsty, Fuzhi had not done any calligraphy for a long time. When they moved to the house in the mountains, he wrote down on a banner a poem by Shao Yong, a famous Song dynasty Chinese philosopher and historian:

> Thousands of flowers downhill are too common to observe,
> While one uphill is enough.
> The spring breeze lingers in the mountains,
> And the creek tints the sweet flags growing nearby green.

When Qian Mingjing came and saw the work, he said there was a kind of grace in Professor Meng's calligraphy which couldn't be found in others' work or be copied. He took it to be mounted and framed and then hung it on the wall opposite Fuzhi's work desk.

On another day, Qian Mingjing asked someone to carry a load of bricks to the Mengs and piled them at the foot of a wall in the yard for the new kitchen. When everything was arranged properly, he sat down with Fuzhi at the work desk and talked about poetry. At this time a strange couple visited. The two were not tall. The gentleman's face looked slightly yellowish. To borrow an expression used in old-fashioned novels, his face was the colour of gold-tinted paper. The grey coat he wore made him look unrestrained . The wife's face was dark and graceful. She wore a navy-blue *qipao*, and one could tell immediately that the material was very special.

Fuzhi was very happy to see them both and introduced them to Bichu and Mingjing. The man was called You Jiaren, who had just returned from the UK, and was about to teach at Minglun. Fuzhi couldn't recall the name of Mrs You, Yao Qiu'er. The couple smiled profusely and addressed Fuzhi and Bichu courteously as Professor Meng and Madam Meng. Mrs You even took May's hand and asked her all sorts of questions to show her friendliness. The couple spoke with a marked accent. A careful examination revealed it was a Tianjin accent. They added an English word in two or three Chinese sentences. Their pronunciation of those English words was particularly clear, which made it sound as if they were clenching their teeth. They spoke English with each other from time to time. The two of them had returned to China before the outbreak of war in Europe and stayed in Guilin, keeping in touch with Fuzhi all the while. Now Mr You was going to start teaching at Minglun.

You Jiaren then mentioned that the British sinology community was full of praise for Professor Meng and was very concerned about his life in such a time of war. Fuzhi sighed: "Now life is also very tough for them. The bombing in London is much more intense than that in Kunming."

Jiaren then asked about Fuzhi's books. Fuzhi answered: "I won't stop teaching and writing, although a lot of my time is spent like a vagrant, running and hiding from the air raids."

He then introduced Mingjing to Jiaren: "Faced with such a dire shortage of research materials, Mingjing has devoted himself to the study of oracle bone inscriptions. He has never lost his love of poetry, either. He writes poems, modern-style poems. What he has been doing can be described as extremely ancient and extremely new."

The couple both looked at Mingjing, then Yao Qiu'er smiled and said: "When Jiaren spoke English in England, the locals didn't think he was a foreigner. Once when he gave a speech, crowds of people arrived. Even the windows of the lecture hall were broken, the audience was so big."

You Jiaren said: "When my wife's articles were published in *The Times*, even people on the train would find time to read that page of the newspaper."

On hearing this, a fanciful thought struck Mingjing — he wanted to try this Mr You. Seeing Fuzhi had no intention of commenting, he then asked tentatively: "Since Mr You has just come back from Britain, it goes without saying that you must be very familiar with English literature. You must be even more familiar with Chinese literature as an expert in classical literature. When I read *On the 24 Styles of Poetry* by the late Tang dynasty poet and critic Sikong Tu, the chapter entitled 'Fresh and Elegant'..."

Jiaren didn't wait for Mingjing to finish his sentence and began to recite the chapter from the first line *"Under the graceful pine trees, flow the babbling creeks"* to the very end.

Mingjing nodded: "I don't quite understand the last lines *'Indescribably vague / Like the clear setting moon at daybreak / Or the refreshing wind deep into the autumn'*. This chapter is about the elegance and freshness in style, why do I sense bleakness in these lines? What do you think?"

You Jiaren readily offered several different interpretations of these lines by other scholars with clear logic and clarity. Yao Qiu'er's face oozed with pride.

Mingjing asked: "I have read those interpretations, too. I'd like to hear how you would interpret this."

After briefly being at a loss for words, Jiaren offered the opinion of a Qing dynasty scholar.

"So, when one reads too much, one can only think with someone else's head instead of one's own. Did Arthur Schopenhauer say that?" thought Mingjing to himself. Before he could ask more, Fuzhi broke in: "Professor Jiang, who presides over the Chinese department, has been longing to equip each teaching faculty with a solid background knowledge of foreign literature. Your arrival will give him the strength of leadership he is looking for."

Mingjing thought to himself: "He can't even offer his own opinions. How can he be counted as a leading force?" He talked a little bit more and then excused himself.

Fuzhi then invited the You couple to have more tea. You Jiaren said: "My wife Qiu'er didn't study for any degrees when we were in Great Britain, but she went to the Leeds Institute. It would be better if she could have a teaching position at the university, too."

Fuzhi did a quick calculation of the teaching faculty and found the English department was well staffed, while the French and German departments were short-handed, so he said: "You may ask to meet Professor Wang Dingyi and see what he has to say."

Yao Qiu'er said: "I just want to make my contribution to the war effort. A proper job would enable me to make a more direct contribution." Her voice was soft. When she spoke, she kept dabbing her cheeks with her handkerchief.

After asking in detail about the Chinese department, Jiaren put forward his plans to open new courses. Fuzhi approved of these ideas and asked Jiaren to talk to Professor Jiang. When the couple excused themselves, they heaped vehement praise on May and Kiddo.

Although living in a place that was out of reach and out of touch, the Mengs had a lot of visitors. Fuzhi's colleagues and old neighbours often visited. An uninvited guest later became a member of their family. It was a kitten found by May and Kiddo on the stone path leading to the house. It was tiny and only the size of an adult's fist, with its eyes not yet open. They wrapped it up in a handkerchief and brought it back home. Bichu said that it was probably taken from its mother by a larger animal and then somehow it was dropped. How lucky the little guy was. They fed it with rice gruel with a pipette used for administering eye drops. It survived and grew up. May named it 'Found'. 'Found' had three sections of colours in its tail, which was characteristic of Siamese cats. Its fur was silver-grey, shining with lustre as it grew. Everyone agreed it was a handsome cat.

Among the guests, the Zhuang family was the most exciting one. When they arrived that day, it was already afternoon. They took turns riding a horse, and it took them a long time to walk from the West village to the Mengs. All the Mengs came to the gate to welcome the Zhuangs. Mrs Zhuang was riding the horse when they arrived, while the other three tagged along, walking along the stone path lined with Lady Banks' roses growing riotously all over the hill. Wherever one stopped, one was standing in a picture framed by the flower. When the Zhuangs reached the gate, they all greeted one another affectionately.

Zhuang Wuyin looked rather serious as a college student. When May saw him, she was somewhat reserved for she didn't rush up to greet him like Kiddo did but stood behind her mother instead. Wuyin spotted her immediately even though she was hiding behind her mother. The two then just stared at each other silently. May cocked her head and burst into laughter first. Wuyin teased her: "You're too tall to laugh like that." Wucai was even taller. Her hair and eyes were dark, but the outline of her face was too clear like a Westerner, different from the delicate and gentle features seen on a regular oriental girl. Both she and her mother wore blue work trousers and checked shirts. They looked full of vigour.

They all entered the house after greeting one another. After taking a breather, they divided themselves into four groups: the two professors, the two ladies, the four youngsters and the little black horse. May knew the little black horse. This kind of Yunnan horse was small, with a smooth skin, and strong and smart movements. Wuyin tied it to a tree in front of the gate. It stood there docilely, its eyes tracking Wuyin. "It knows you," said Kiddo. May offered to fetch water for it to drink, but Wuyin suggested: "Let's take it to the riverside to drink." He fed the horse with the food he had brought with him. The little horse licked his hands affectionately.

In the evening, Wuyin and the other three took the horse to the river. They brought a bucket and drew water for the horse to drink. Both May and Kiddo wanted to ride the horse. Wuyin assured them: "This horse is very obedient." Then he vaulted into the saddle and rode around the embankment. He then let May have a try, but May couldn't ride a horse with the *qipao* she was in. She then realised why Wucai was wearing trousers. Embarrassed, she turned away from the horse and said: "I don't want to ride it."

Wuyin at first didn't understand May's change of heart. When he finally figured out it was the *qipao*, which restrained the thin figure blooming into a young lady, he said: "Let me lift you onto the horse."

May said: "Let Kiddo ride it." Taking Wucai by the hand, she ran away. Kiddo stood on a big rock and mounted the horse without difficulty. He sat with his back straight on it while Wuyin took the reins and walked the horse at a slow pace. May and Wucai clapped their hands and cheered for Kiddo, laughing. Back then, taking a picture was a luxury, and they did not have a camera. Otherwise, they would have recorded this perfect picture: a black horse and two handsome boys in the setting sun.

"Come and walk the horse," Wuyin asked May, who extended her hand to take the reins at his invitation. Wuyin at once noticed the chaps of different sizes on her delicate and thin palms with slender long fingers.

"What are those?" asked Wuyin.

May hurried to pull her hands back and hid them behind her, claiming: "Nothing."

"I know what they are. You must be doing the laundry with the ash water. My mother told me about it."

May didn't answer. She took hold of the reins neatly, gave the horse a pat, and walked forward. Wuyin wanted to go back home immediately to take two packages of soap to the Mengs', but he checked his impulse and said things might be better when the blockade was lifted. May walked the horse back and asked Kiddo to ride the horse while she walked. The younger brother sitting on horseback, the elder sister holding the reins under the shade of the weeping willows by the creek! Another even more perfect picture.

During dinner, they talked about the name of Dragon Tail village. Fuzhi said he had been told there was a dragon king temple on the upper reaches of the Dragon river. Professor Jiang Fang had collected some dragon tales around the area. He gave a brief account of Jiang Fang's collection, which intrigued them all. Wuyin proposed that they go the next day to explore the temple. Della said, smiling: "Why! Wuyin becomes another person when he's here." After some talk, they agreed that the adults would stay behind since Bichu was not strong enough to walk so far.

The next day, the four of them packed some steamed buns and some fodder for the horse and set off toward the Dragon King temple. Kiddo was the first one to ride the horse, and they all walked along the embankment. It was easier for May to ride the horse in her old pair of work trousers. She wore her old straw hat, too, the face under which looked bright and beautiful.

They sang loudly all the way, ran for a section and walked the next. Baotaishan was soon left far behind. When it was May's turn to ride the horse, she copied how Wucai mounted the horse by putting her foot into the stirrup and swinging the other leg over the horse. A handful of villagers passed them, one cried his greetings and asked them where they were heading. When they heard the destination was the Dragon King temple, they laughed heartily, claiming it was nothing but a house with two run-down rooms. Another one said teasingly: "Ride your horse well! When you grow up, you may then join the caravans!"

The group of four walked on for a while until Kiddo blurted out: "Why haven't we thought about organising caravans to help with the transportation? That might work!"

Wuyin was surprised by such a smart suggestion: "Wow! How smart Kiddo is!"

Wucai taunted him, saying: "You still think you are the only person who's smart?"

When they walked over Salt Falls, they saw the small waterfall shining in the sun. May pointed out to the other three where Wei Feng and Xueyan lived. At the col between the mountains, they took a turn and temporarily left the Dragon river. A few more turns, and suddenly a large river flowed in front of them. Above the loud noise of the torrent of water, they could detect people shouting and screaming. They walked further along the river and spotted a crowd of people by the bank. As they approached, they saw some people beating and kicking someone. When the person who was being beaten fell to the ground, someone picked up their hair and, sure enough, it was a woman.

"What are you doing?" May ran a few steps toward the crowd, yelling loudly. Wuyin tried to hold her back but failed. At this point, it was Wucai riding the horse. The assailants stopped what they were doing when they saw Wucai, who looked like a foreigner, and shouted: "Who are you? Mind your own business!"

May answered: "We are students. Who gave you the right to beat people? And... and..." She was at her wits' end to come up with something more convincing.

Two guys walked menacingly toward May and shouted: "She tried to poison us with her venomous insects and has been found guilty by our chieftain. Surely you are not her accomplice, are you?"

Seeing what was happening, Wuyin knew he had to do something. He stepped forward and said: "We won't interfere with your business." He signalled to May to ride on the horse but May ignored him.

"I don't know who your chieftain is, but you need to solve problems with reason, not violence." While they were arguing, they overheard one crying: "She has run away!" They all turned to see the woman dashing off the bank to the river bed, her long hair flowing behind her, adding a morsel of black to the picture of the river and mountains. She plunged into the river without making much noise or a splash, and disappeared beneath the water in seconds.

"She has killed herself!" someone shouted.

Those people said to May: "Now you have let that woman run away. You have to come back with us to see our chieftain."

May was worried about the woman: "Why aren't you saving her?"

"Saving her? Think about how you are going to save yourself!" They pressed toward May. Wuyin, Wucai and Kiddo all gathered around her.

Wucai asked Wuyin in English: "Who are these people? What should we do?"

An idea struck Wuyin. He began to speak English loudly, imitating a pastor who was preaching. The people froze, wondering what kind of spells Wuyin was casting.

At that moment, two horses ran from the direction of the Dragon King temple. One of the riders came over to check what was going on. It turned out they were the chief steward of the grand Wali chieftain and his servant. He recognised May and Kiddo at once. Dismounting from his horse, he said: "They are the young master and miss of the Meng family." Knowing who the man was, all the other people took a few steps back from Wuyin and his friends.

Wuyin explained what had happened and the armed man told his side of the story, too. The chief steward pinched his eyebrows: "It's a tough case since the chieftain of Pingjiang village has settled it. Anyway, the woman has killed herself by drowning, you may just go back and report the death to your chieftain." The other men didn't argue more in the presence of the chief steward and all took the other path toward the col.

The chief steward then turned to May and her friends: "If you hadn't run into me, you would all have suffered." Although Pingjiang village is a small village, their chieftain, a woman, is a hard nut."

Wuyin led the group of four in sincerely thanking the chief steward. When he knew they were heading for the Dragon King temple, he laughed: "It is nothing but a run-down place with a couple of rooms. I strongly suggest you quit that idea and head back home. I'm heading to Dragon Tail village, too, to deliver our chieftain's invitation to Professor Bai Liwen. From there I have to go to town. Excuse me, then!" He mounted his horse and rode away with his servant.

When the chief steward was some distance away, May couldn't hold herself back any longer and burst into tears. Kiddo and Wucai joined her. Not knowing what to say, Wuyin said something comforting to them and asked May to ride the horse. They slowly walked back home. The mountains and the water were no longer so bright, and the birds didn't tweet or chirp. May was crying with big sobs at the thought of how terrifying those people were to the woman that would rather throw herself into the rolling water which swallowed her up. She wept for the woman and wept for herself and her friends over their inability to save the woman. Thankfully, brother Wuyin had been quick-witted enough to buy the woman some time. Wuyin later told them what he had said was a speech by Einstein.

Both pairs of parents were curious about the kids' unusually early return. Having learned what had happened, they were a little scared. The two mothers cuddled their daughters tightly in their arms and whispered words of comfort. Even Kiddo clung to his mother's side. They were all worried about what had happened to the woman. How could they just kill someone without getting punished? But what could they do?

Bichu told Fuzhi: "The so-called female chieftain from Pingjiang village seems to be the jade dealer who has been seeing Mingjing. She must have had a grudge against the woman for setting venomous insects on people to poison them."

Fuzhi responded with a sigh: "Have we ever been free from wrongdoing? Those who are sure to suffer are always the ordinary people under such a foolish autocracy."

The following day, the Zhuangs went to visit Wei Feng and Xueyan at Salt Falls. They intended to head home from there. All the Mengs saw them off by the Mang river. Wuyin pointed at May's hands. May whispered to him: "They'll get better." She raised her eyes at him with a smile.

The two families bade farewell to each other. They returned the same way they had come, with Della riding the horse, while the other three walked by her side. The sound of hoofs was gradually carried away by the rolling water of the river.

A couple of days later, Zhao Er's wife took a young woman to see the Mengs, saying the woman was the helper she had mentioned before. At first glance, May called out 'Qinghuan' (which literally means 'blue ring'), the woman they had once met in Copper Head village carrying a load of firewood on her back. A smile revealed her white teeth. "We have met her before," May explained. "I saw her carrying firewood."

Qinghuan walked with a limp, and Zhao Er's wife explained that Qinghuan had fallen and hurt her leg when she was collecting firewood for her paternal uncle. Bichu immediately said she'd like to keep Qinghuan. When Zhao Er's wife was ready to leave, Qinghuan looked at her as if she was waiting for Zhao Er's wife to say something. Zhao Er's wife came back in a moment and said to Bichu: "I wanted to hold this back, and I asked Qinghuan to hold it back, too. But my heart won't let me rest in peace. Do you still remember I mentioned once that Qinghuan is like a jinx on her family? She worked for a caravan and cooked for the men. When they reached Pingjiang village, she was left behind according to the tradition that no woman could go beyond that point because of the toughness of the road ahead. She then found a position in the chieftain's house and did some manual labour. She somehow offended the chieftain. At the same time, two men from the caravan died, and the caravan accused Qinghuan, claiming the death was caused by the venomous insects she had put in the caravan. She escaped by jumping into the Dragon river after being imprisoned for more than a month. How could she know anything about such witchcraft? She doesn't even have anywhere to keep those poisonous insects!"

Qinghuan started timidly: "I might have been killed without those nice people that helped me that day."

Bichu raised her voice: "You stay with us. I don't buy such nonsense."

239

Zhao Er's wife said: "I can't betray my conscience. You are so kind to keep her."

So, Qinghuan stayed with the Mengs. Her leg healed after some time. She was diligent, though not very smart. The house was tidy and clean thanks to her hard work. Bichu felt much better on seeing such a change in the place. May later quietly told Bichu that Qinghuan was the woman who had jumped into the river the other day when they had tried to visit the Dragon King temple. She had survived. Bichu said: "What a lucky girl!" But they didn't seek to confirm this with Qinghuan, worrying that it might upset her to be reminded of such a terrible experience.

One day before the new term started, Bai Liwen visited. He shuffled along in his shoes and was carrying a cattail leaf fan. No one could figure out what the fan was for in such cool weather. He had a hearty chat with Fuzhi, covering a wide range of topics. Then he blurted out: "What are you writing now, bro?"

Fuzhi said: "I'm working on an essay against corrupt officials."

Bai Liwen said: "Yes, yes, we should condemn such people. This is not a free world at all. The price of tobacco has soared so high that no one will be able to afford to smoke." He stood up and began to pace back and forth. "I want to know your opinion about this, bro. The grand chieftain of Wali is inviting me to give lectures. He said you have turned down his invitation. I want to go. Their tobacco is of supreme quality."

Fuzhi said: "It depends on how you arrange your classes. Have you talked this over with Professor Jiang?"

"You know him. He treats people like donkeys. He won't let me go."

Fuzhi said: "Professor Jiang is a serious and earnest person. I advise you to talk it over with him first."

During the conversation, Bai Liwen suddenly cried out: "What's this? It smells so good! Have you made a stew?"

Fuzhi laughed and said: "Please stay for dinner." He then went out to tell Bichu. Before the meal, Bai Liwen went to the outhouse located outside the courtyard. There were a few bricks on the adobe wall of the outhouse. He examined carefully the lines on the bricks and groped with his hands over them until Kiddo went to look for him to tell him dinner was ready. Since the new term was about to begin, Bichu wanted to increase everyone's nutrition and had stewed a pot of meat. Bai Liwen attacked the pot and finished up more than half. He left with great satisfaction.

That summer vacation flowed away somehow like the water in the Mang river.

CHAPTER FIVE

PART I

It had been several weeks since the new term began, but Bai Liwen never showed up to class. Since one of the two students who had chosen his palaeography course always skipped the class, the other one who attended his class reported the teacher's absence to Professor Jiang Fang. When Jiang Fang went back to Dragon Tail village, he went to check on Bai Liwen first. But the landlord said Bai was long gone and that he had been picked up by the grand chieftain of Wali. Jiang Fang flew into a fury at the news and stormed all the way to the Mengs to confront Fuzhi: Did the university uphold any rules at all? How could an opium addict shoulder the sacred mission of teaching? When the storm of anger subsided, he sank into a chair and sulked. Having figured out what had happened, Fuzhi acknowledged that it had never occurred to him that Bai Liwen would leave without notice, which suggested that Bai wouldn't be back any time soon. So the main priority was to find a substitute for Bai's class.

The two readily agreed that the best candidate was Qian Mingjing. Jiang Fang then trotted all the way to the Qians. Mingjing was happy at the news which announced the disappearance of the strong opponent towering in the way of his promotion. He asked Jiang Fang to sit down and let Jiang bask in his hospitality by making him three cups of tea. The first cup was the Pu'er tea produced in southwestern Yunnan. The second was a tea grown on the snow-covered Jade Dragon mountain in Lijiang. The third one turned out to be a cup of jasmine tea produced in Beiping. How did he manage to get that? He then took out a pack of Camel cigarettes and lit one up for Jiang Fang.

"It is not a bad thing to have a new teacher for this course. Professor Bai's teaching methods are somewhat outdated although he is quite knowledgeable. If he was still dominating the class, I wouldn't have any opportunity to say things like that. So, it's not bad. It's not bad at all that he has left," Mingjing said. He then chuckled: "If these words reach Professor Bai, he will surely rebuke me and say how dare Qian Mingjing say things like that! For someone who has touched only a few dozen oracle bones, where did he find the confidence to say my teaching is outdated? How can one know about those ancient pieces thousands of years old if one is not outdated?"

Jiang Fang laughed at such a hilarious, vivid imitation of Bai Liwen. Mingjing then briefed Jiang Fang on his teaching plan for the course as if he had anticipated such a change and had prepared himself for this task.

Bai Liwen was a rare case. Most of the teaching faculty were very responsible. If a course had only one student, the teacher wouldn't goof off. That day when Fuzhi brought Bai Liwen's case to President Qin, both agreed that such behaviour meant Bai was no longer suitable to stay on. Fuzhi sighed: "He really knows his field of study well. If only he could quit smoking but that would be impossible."

They moved on to talk about other things. Qin said: "Things are quite complicated. Your essay on redundant staffing in the Song dynasty has attracted attention from the Chongqing administration. A key member of the government has said that Meng Fuzhi is getting more and more leftist. See? He's attacking the government."

Fuzhi said: "I'm a long way from being 'leftist'. I have always said the study of history involves two key aspects. On one hand, we need to find the truth in history; and on the other, we need to learn from history. Wouldn't it be a good thing if we could avoid repeating the same mistakes? I've just finished writing about the extortion of the boats transporting exotic flowers, plants and rocks by water in the Song dynasty for the royal family during the reign of Emperor Huizong, and the illegal practice of selling and buying government posts. I'm going to publish this essay, too."

"The truth behind this is obvious, but sometimes simple things can be complicated by people with different agendas." Qin Xunheng paused. "Some people have said that you encourage students to go to Yan'an. This may cause trouble for you, too."

Fuzhi smiled: "I also encourage people to stay. For me if they are engaged in fighting the Japanese, it is a just cause. Frankly speaking, those in Yan'an are also dissatisfied with me, saying I am a 'rightist'."

The two looked at each other in silence.

Such a dilemma faithfully mirrored the fact that the KMT and the CPC had never eliminated their differences even when they claimed to be sticking to the slogan of unity. With the arduous and protracted war of resistance against Japan, military friction between the two parties had become more frequent. In early 1941, the "South Anhui Incident"[1] took place, which witnessed the end of cooperation between the KMT and the CPC as a united anti-Japanese force. Those with insight were deeply concerned. How could such a disintegrated and tortured country afford a civil war?

Life in Kunming and Chongqing was increasingly difficult with daily necessities in short supply under the cruel air bombardment. By the summer of 1914, many schools could not pay their employees. Although many faculty members took up side occupations, their hearts remained on campus. Few quit teaching. Teachers immersed themselves in their teaching, as did students in their learning, regardless of the hardships. The air of Kunming was a bastion of free thinking because Kunming was not under the direct control of the Nationalist government, which made the acquisition of information from multiple sources possible. Besides, some of the best minds in China were active here in Kunming, which never ceased disseminating knowledge and pursuing truth. All these elements made Kunming a place many of the students in the rear area aspired to.

Tantai Wei finally obtained the consent of his parents and came to Kunming to attend college. He took a flight with a few US officials in the power field in a US aircraft. For more than three hours on the plane, he had been thinking about the future. The life of the teachers and students in Chongqing was very bitter, but it must have been even harder for the teachers and students in Kunming with the limited supply of vegetables and grain. Sometimes they went hungry due to the food shortage.

Of course, this was the least of Tantai Wei's concerns. From Xuan's letters, he was already aware of his cousins' situation. Yingshu and Huishu attended school regularly. Earl was graduating this year and was hoping to stay at the university to work as Xiao Cheng's teaching assistant. However, Professor Xiao did not agree but introduced her to the Provincial Botany Institute. Because of her illness, May had dropped out of school and was going to attend high school this year. Who knew how many novice ideas she would have fed into that smart head. Kiddo sent him a photo of a plane to show how much he welcomed the news that Wei was coming to attend college in Kunming.

"I'm going to Kunming in an actual airplane," thought Wei. "But it's a pity it's not a Chinese airplane."

After the bumpy ride, the plane landed at Kunming Wujiaba airport.

Yingshu came to pick him up and took him to the Yan residence, which was somewhat empty with only a few guards in evidence on their arrival. Yan Liangzu and the womenfolk of the family were still staying in Anning county.

Yingshu said: "There are only the two of us. Why don't you stay here?"

Wei answered: "I want to live on campus."

"You don't know how campus life is."

"It doesn't matter," answered Wei.

After the adjutants had prepared dinner, Xuan came. The sister and brother were together just a couple of days ago, but they were so happy to see each other, they greeted each other as if they hadn't met for a long while. Wei first planned to visit Aunt Bichu's family at Dragon Tail village. Since the Yans' car was going to Anning the next day, he decided to take a ride and visit Aunt Suchu first. Xuan couldn't accompany him to Anning for she had to work.

Anning county was true to its name. It remained tranquil even in wartime. Because of the hot springs in the county, wealthy and influential people had built simple, comfortable residences dating back many years previously. The Yans' house comprised two rows of single-storey rooms on the edge of a grove. When Yingshu and Wei arrived, two servant soldiers were cleaning the living room in the front row.

Wei asked: "Where is Aunt Suchu?"

Yingshu answered: "Probably praying," and he led Wei along the passage leading to a small room where they found Suchu sitting in a giant wooden chair, with a rosary in her hands, praying. Not wanting to disturb his aunt, Wei stood rooted to the spot, wondering what to do next. Then a gorgeously dressed middle-aged woman emerged from another room. Seeing Wei hesitating, she giggled: "This must be Master Wei! Please go and ask for Madam Suchu." She turned to Yingshu.

Wei immediately realised this must be Hezhu. He offered her his timely greetings and then said: "I'm not in a rush. I'll wait."

Yingshu went into the room and called: "Dear mother," which startled Suchu. When she turned round to find Wei, her face beamed with happiness, although she didn't say anything. Wei greeted his aunt and presented the gifts from his parents.

Hezhu ordered the servants to take care of the gifts and said: "Madam Jiangchu is so generous. Please convey my gratitude to her. We are now staying in such a remote place and can't afford proper entertainment. Besides, we have a friend staying with us…" It was rather hard for Wei to tell whether his presence was welcome or not from Hezhu's ambiguous words, but he just focused on his aunt Suchu.

Guffaws of laughter reached Wei from outside the window, and two girls ran out of the grove. Yan Huishu, who was in the lead, had already blossomed into a beautiful woman. As they went past the window, the one running after Huishu raised her head. Their eyes met in the middle. Both showed a trace of surprise.

"Yin Dashi!" Huishu called out, turning around. Upon hearing Huishu, Dashi whispered: "You have a guest." The two walked into the living room from the front. Huishu introduced Dashi to Wei. The two looked at each other with equal astonishment: "How could there be such a fine-looking person in this world!"

Huishu said: "Dashi is leaving..."

Dashi interrupted: "Who said I'm leaving? Are you trying to get rid of me?" She chuckled. Dashi came to visit Huishu often although the Ying household was much more comfortably equipped and was only about 500 metres away. Huishu seldom went to the Yings.

Huishu grinned at Dashi's words: "Even if I wanted to get rid of you, I couldn't force you to do something against your will."

Wei suddenly spoke up: "When May, I mean Meng Lingji, had a nasty fall, you were with her, weren't you?"

Dashi chuckled again: "See? Bad things travel much faster than good things! Right, you are the cousin of Meng Lingji and Yan Huishu. I know that." The four then sat down and continued talking.

A while later, Suchu finished saying her prayers and called Wei in. Dashi also got up and said, "I'll come back later."

At lunch time, Wei felt disappointed not to see Dashi and asked Huishu: "Where is that classmate of yours?"

Huishu said: "She has gone back home, but I'm sure she'll come back." Before she had finished speaking, Dashi returned with an adjutant at her heels carrying a giant gunny sack. Her fair face was flushed after the exertion of running.

"Can you guess what is inside? Crabs! I took them from our kitchen without being noticed," Dashi said.

As if to support what she had said, several crabs' legs poked out of the sack. For a place like Yunnan which didn't produce crabs, crabs were considered as delicacies. When Wei asked Dashi where they had got the crabs, Hezhu answered on Dashi's behalf: "Master Wei, Miss Dashi is so generous to share these crabs with us. How could she know where they come from?" She then ordered the servants to take the crabs to the kitchen and cook them.

The crabs were soon done and brought to the table. Hezhu said: "We should have some wine to go with the crabs. Let's try the fruit wine from Kaiyuan[2]."

Rich families in Beiping always had a set of utensils for enjoying crabs including scissors, hammers, drills and anvils, which eased the process. The Yans didn't have these utensils, so they all used their teeth and fingers. Dashi soon lost her patience after finishing only two front legs. Hezhu took out the meat and put it onto a plate for her. Huishu enjoyed herself, using her fingers to carefully get at the meat.

Wei said: "It never occurred to me that since our departure from Beiping, so many things which used to be normal would become luxuries. Chongqing people also like crabs but they eat them with chopped red chillies."

Hezhu asked: "How did you eat crabs back then?"

Wei said: "The most popular way was to dip them in a vinegar and ginger sauce, but different people had different preferences. Grandpa Lü didn't eat crab meat with anything."

Suchu, who had been silent all along, said: "Yes, father didn't."

Yingshu said: "It's a pity I never met Grandpa Lü." Hezhu sneered at Yingshu's words, which puzzled everyone at the table, and asked for vinegar and ginger to be served. But they all copied Grandpa Lü and enjoyed the meat without any seasoning.

"Huishu," Dashi said, pushing her plate away from her. She didn't like crabs. "Let's all go to my house. We can go mountain climbing."

Huishu couldn't help thinking about the broad bean theft accident and whispered to Dashi: "I'm glad you suggested climbing mountains, not trees."

Dashi cast a glance over at Wei. She straightened her face and left the table to sit on the sofa, blaming in her heart how talkative Huishu was to bring up things like that.

Wei kept talking with Yingshu about the university, ignoring Dashi. Yingshu was due to graduate the following year. He was worried whether he would find a job. "Oh, dear me!" Hezhu said affectionately to Yingshu. "You don't need to worry about a job. It will just take a few words. Miss Yin, won't you join us for more?" Seeing that no one was taking any notice of her, Dashi accepted the invitation and sat back at the table.

Yingshu, ignoring his mother, continued: "It's well known that professor Meng loves his students. He never refuses if a student asks to talk to him. In addition to attending his classes, talking to him is also very informative."

Wei asked: "What do you usually talk about?"

248

Yingshu said: "Literally anything, from the current situation and the state of society to study. But what we talk about most is history. Ah, I am not suited to conduct academic research."

After the meal, Yingshu took Wei for a walk in the hills behind the house. A winding path among the green trees brought them to a clearing. A man who looked like a soldier was practicing with his sword. The blade flashed against the green around him, which reminded Wei of the expression 'heroes of the greenwood'. The man saw people coming and stopped his practicing. It was Yan Liangzu. Wei walked up to greet him. Liangzu didn't recognise Wei at first, but then he quickly remembered Wei was the son of Suchu's second younger sister. He let out a long cry, tossed the sword to his adjutant and asked Wei: "Did you come from Chongqing? How is it?"

Wei knew he was asking about the political situation, but he didn't know how to describe it, so he said: "The bombardment is terrible. I heard that the US is assisting with a squadron of aircraft manned by volunteer pilots. They may be able to challenge the enemy's air superiority."

Liangzu said: "I heard this too. If I am ordered to fight the CPC, I don't mind enjoying the hot springs here like I'm doing now." He gave Wei a second look and said: "It is said that Grandpa Lü taught you some martial arts?" Upon his words, he was already in a combat position: "Let's do some practice. I never learned martial arts."

Although the invitation was unexpected, Wei didn't hesitate and sprang on Liangzu. Liangzu parried the attack. After several rounds of sparring, Liangzu clapped his hands as a signal to stop. He laughed heartily: "You are rusty from lack of practice, but I can still discern the Lü boxing moves."

Wei took the sword from the adjutant and examined it. The blade was fine and shiny. A shade of red emanated from the back of the sword. He said while examining it: "Grandpa himself had a gorgeous sword."

Liangzu said: "This one is rather ordinary, but it can kill."

Yingshu said: "Dad, it's time for your lunch. We have already had ours."

The three walked back, talking. Hezhu greeted them at the gate: "Almost everything is ready. The stir-fried eel slices need to be cooked when you return." She walked Liangzu to his bedroom and then went to the kitchen to oversee the cooking of the dish.

Yingshu took Wei to see their hot spring bathroom, which was a shabby room with one stone wall and three walls made of dark bricks.

Bubbles kept rising from the bottom of the pool and a layer of warm air was floating above it. Wei said: "The earth is so strange. I originally wanted to study geology."

Yingshu said: "I once wanted to see what was inside the earth, but assuming it must be very tiring to do that, I dropped the idea."

Wei stood by the pool for a while and put his hand in the water. The water was silky and warm. He scooped handfuls of the water over his arms, feeling refreshed. Suddenly he spotted a glistening in the water. "Snake!" he yelled. The snake squirmed into the stone wall. "There is a snake in the water!" said Wei.

Yingshu was not alarmed at all: "Snakes are quite common. It doesn't matter. Sometimes several appear together. They don't bother us, and we don't bother them."

Wei thought: "That might be because those snakes know you guys."

Later Huishu told Wei that the Yin family's bathroom had been lavishly redecorated, but at the sight of the snake, Wei didn't want to risk his luck.

On the following day, Dashi came to the Yans early in the morning. She wore a pair of blue and white plaid cotton trousers and a new straw hat. The hat had an asymmetrical brim, with one side narrower than the other which didn't look like a local product, at first glance. She was in high spirits and keen to go hiking. She invited the other three for lunch at her house later. When they were ready to leave, they heard a commotion from the back row of rooms. A house maid rushed out in panic, crying: "Madam Hezhu is having an attack!" Yingshu and Huishu ran inside. When Wei tried to follow, he was stopped by Dashi. She murmured to him: "You can't go inside. You are not a Yan." While he was hesitating whether he should go in or not, Yingshu ran out and called Wei to go in: "Mother Suchu is asking for you." Dashi was then left alone in the living room.

In the room located in the back room, an utterly confusing drama was in progress. Hezhu was lying on the floor, eyes straight, legs shaking with spasmodic contractions. She was a professional at this. Suchu was sitting in a chair, undisturbed and silent. After a while, Hezhu slowly gave her instructions:

"A relative. 33." Yingshu interpreted: "Mum wants a relative to feed her 33 spoons of water."

Wei was the best choice. Although reluctantly, Wei took the spoon from Yingshu and fed water to Hezhu, who gradually 'regained' consciousness. Yingshu and Huishu helped her to sit in a chair for a while and then she walked slowly back to her room, steadying herself by putting her hand against the wall. Her room was infested with poisonous insects all year round. Few would go in. Few dared.

Suchu waved her hand: "You all run along." The three went back to the living room to find Dashi long gone.

Huishu said: "She's not the type to be kept waiting. I need to go and check on her." When she returned, she told the two of them: "Apparently she has left for town." All three were disappointed at the news.

Wei quietly asked Huishu: "What is wrong with Aunt Hezhu?"

Huishu answered: "She calls it being 'possessed', which is nothing but trickery. But if she doesn't get what she wants, we'll all be in big trouble."

Wei sighed: "How has Aunt Suchu survived all these years?"

Huishu didn't answer. She paused for a while before asking: "Do you still remember Lü Guitang and his daughter Lü Xiangge who stayed at the Lü residence in Chestnut street? She visited several months ago and borrowed a big sum of money from Mother Hezhu."

"Ah! She has made her way to Kunming," Wei said half-heartedly, not remembering much about the father and the daughter because of Jiangchu's tough household management. Besides, the Lü residence in Chestnut street was a complicated compound with multiple layers of rooms for the masters and servants, so Wei didn't make much impression on the two with such limited contact with the servants.

In the afternoon that day, when Wei learned that he could hitch a ride back to town, he insisted on leaving, no matter how hard the Yans tried to prevent him. He went directly to the attic of the theatre. Fuzhi was writing something on his table made of kerosene crates.

"You've been to Anning?" He looked up from his writing to greet Wei. He stood up when Wei approached him, rubbing his hair happily. "What made you decide to choose biology?"

Wei laughed: "To be a successor of Cousin Earl! I'm also interested in history, but…"

"But history isn't useful, is it?" Fuzhi finished the sentence for Wei. "This is your bed. Take a seat." He pointed at a bunk with bed legs made of four kerosene crates. Wei sat down on the bunk bed. It felt so much more comfortable than the bed at the Yans.

A moment later, they heard someone going upstairs, calling "Fuzhi" as they mounted the steps. Pushing the door open, Xiao Cheng came in.

Fuzhi introduced Wei to him: "This is your new student."

"Professor Xiao," Wei greeted Xiao shyly and bowed respectfully to him.

Xiao Cheng had seen Wei in Guihui several years ago. He was so fond of Wei and saw that he had grown to become such a handsome young man: "Tantai Wei, I really want to rub your hair."

Wei said: "Uncle Fuzhi has done that." The three men burst into hearty laughter. Xiao was the director of the 'theatre canteen'. To cope with the skyrocketing prices, they grew their own vegetables on a plot of land by the

251

wintersweet grove. Someone was asking to join them gardening, so Xiao Cheng had come to ask Fuzhi if they could go to the allotment together. Fuzhi oversaw a very small patch because he didn't have all his meals here, but Xiao Cheng had an enormous one. Currently the autumn vegetables were growing vigorously, radiating with green life over the patch of land.

When the two had finished tending the allotment for the newcomer, they wanted to get some water to water the plants. Upon seeing what they were trying to do, Wei rushed to take the buckets and did three rounds in a row. Xiao Cheng and Fuzhi did one round each, too. The buckets of water used to douse the vegetables with glowed in the setting sun as the water slowly seeped into the soil. Wei bent down and watched attentively: "The vegetables are drinking!"

Xiao Cheng used a spade to loosen the soil around the roots of a plant: "This helps them to drink more." Wei hurried to find a twig to do the same. At the other end of the vegetable bed, Fuzhi was trimming the edges of the patch.

Next to the vegetable bed was a small patch of peanuts. When Wei leaned over and looked closely, he saw that both ends of the stems of the plant were in the soil and asked why.

Xiao Cheng explained: "This is an unusual characteristic of peanuts. When they flower, the stems grow first. After fertilisation, short stalks form a thread-like structure which grows down into the soil, and the tip develops into a mature peanut pod." He added, happily: "You are an inquisitive student!" Wei watered the peanuts carefully, smiling: "This is my first lesson."

Wei stayed at Dragon Tail village for two days. He was very sorry to see how hard life was, even with Qinghuan helping the Mengs, due to Bichu's poor health and May's lingering low fever. But the Mengs seemed to be at ease, just like Yan Hui, the favourite disciple of Confucius who didn't allow his joy to be killed by the hardships and distress of his poverty-stricken life which others couldn't bear.

May laughed heartily at his reference to Yan Hui: "We are not that poor as to have just bamboo bowls and gourds serving as drinking cups. We still have pots to cook our meals!" The moment they met, they had been talking. When the light fell, they lit a lamp and burnt a huge amount of lamp oil, enough to last all night long. What a pity that Earl was not home.

When Wei went back to Kunming city, the new term had already arrived. Having gone through the whole process of registration as a freshman, he declined the offer to be taken to his dormitory but carried his luggage there himself. What he saw first were rows of adobe houses. He entered one of the houses to see a big room like the steerage section on a passenger ship which was divided into different sections by students using old newspapers as partitions between beds. Some newspapers of the paper partitions were torn, fluttering like flags in the wind. It was quite a novel sight for Wei. He chose one of the unoccupied beds and put his luggage on it.

A student emerged from one of the paper-partitioned spots and fired questions at Wei: "Are you a freshman? Which department are you with? Where are you from? Would you like me to show you where we have classes?"

As Wei followed him toward the teaching buildings, a man came over to them and hit them with a question: "Which path should China take? The democratic path like Europe and the US, or the socialist path like the Soviet Union? I think each has its pros and cons." He then began to prattle on loudly about his opinions. The one who was showing Wei around voted for socialism, while another stranger joined and supported democracy. They argued for a while and then walked on. No one ever asked what anyone else's name was.

Wei walked to the school gate and found small posters on both sides of the walls near the gate, covering a wide range of topics from outlines for academic papers and comments on current affairs to assorted advertisements for private tuition and used books or clothing for sale. A line of colourful snack stands stood alongside the wall outside the campus. The air was filled with complex aromas.

Wei finally got to taste the much vaunted 'rice cooked with eight treasures' by Xuan at the university canteen. Wei, being unaccustomed to barnyard millet and gravel mixed in the rice, picked them all out and created a small pile on the table in no time. People sitting around criticised such girly behaviour. At this time, a real girl appeared. It turned out to be his sister, Xuan.

Xuan beamed: "What does our future biologist think?"

Wei answered: "I want to think, but I haven't got the time." He finished his meal in several bites and offered to show his sister his dormitory, but Xuan didn't want to go to the men's dormitory.

"Well, I will walk you back then," said Wei.

Xuan was upset: "Aren't you going to ask about Paul? It looks like this person doesn't exist for you at all."

Wei hurried to offer his apology and confessed that he had indeed forgotten about Paul. The two went out of the school gate, followed the red dirt road, crossed the gap in the city wall, and soon came to the bank of Green lake.

Wei asked: "Were you serious when you said you were going to marry Paul?"

Xuan said: "Of course I was. I am. What's wrong? When Paul is not in Kunming, his image becomes very vague. Once, in a dream, I desperately tried to recall what he looked like but wasn't able to. Don't you think this is weird?" Xuan's tone was slow and thoughtful. Seldom had Wei seen such a look on his sister's face.

He asked cautiously: "Is it due to the fact that he is a foreigner and we are not good at remembering foreign faces?"

Xuan shook her head with a smile lingering on her face.

Since part of the American air force group was training in Kunming, snacks like rice noodles and rice cookies served in gravy were no longer sufficient for these foreigners. Many western-style restaurants and cafés had opened in the Jinma-Biji area of the city centre, which sprawled all the way to the bank of Green lake. The Tantai sister and brother paused in Denghuapo street, facing a small café. The wisps of coffee aroma floated straight out of the shop. The name of the café 'Greensleeves Café', written under the eaves, was ablaze with two symmetrically placed lamps guarding each side of the signboard.

By then, Xuan's tender melancholy had already dissipated and been replaced by her usual delicate and delightful appearance. She pointed at the shop door and said: "Paul is waiting for us inside." They pushed the door open and walked into the dimly lit shop. Paul, standing, was talking to a brightly dressed woman. When he saw Xuan, he came up to meet her while the woman he was talking to went to the back of the shop.

For the past several days, Wei had met many friends and relatives who he had not seen for many years. Some had grown up, and others had not aged well, but only Paul retained the same handsome look with his blonde hair and blue eyes. He picked a table and asked Xuan to sit beside him while Wei sat opposite them, which somewhat offended him.

Very soon the brightly dressed woman brought coffee and snacks. Paul said: "This is the shop owner. She has another café near the American air force group."

Xuan raised her eyes to look at this woman who wore a shirt and trousers adorned with enormous red-and-white flowers. Her hair was wrapped up in a bun at the back of her head secured with a jade hairpin. When she had finished laying the table with cups and plates, she raised her head and exclaimed: "Miss Xuan! Master Wei!"

"Lü Xiangge!" Wei and Xuan yelled with one voice, which dumbfounded Paul.

"How did you end up here? How long have you been staying in Kunming?" asked Xuan.

Xiangge replied: "I arrived about a year ago, but I stayed in a nearby county for a couple of months before opening this shop in town."

"Why has Aunt Bichu never mentioned you?"

"I've been rather busy, so I haven't had the opportunity to visit Madam Bichu, although I have been planning to." Then more customers came in, and Xiangge hurried over to greet them.

It suddenly dawned on Xuan that the day Paul had proposed to her, the woman she had seen in the tofu diner must have been Xiangge! She then explained to Paul about the relationship between Xiangge and the Lü family. Paul blurted out: "This woman offered to bring tea for me at the Chestnut street residence, didn't she?"

Xuan taunted him: "You do remember."

"Miss Lü has always boasted of having several learned, upper-class aunts and uncles. Now I see what she means! She must be referring to your family and the Meng family," smiled Paul. "This is one of her promotion gimmicks, too."

Since parting with Ling Xueyan, Xiangge had joined Wang Yi to do some retail business. Later, when she ran into several students on their way to the rear area, she had dumped Wang Yi and travelled with the students all the way to Guilin. During an air raid, two of her student companions were killed. While Xiangge was sitting at the roadside, caked in dust with tears washing two fair trails down her cheeks, a tin dealer from Gejiu county, the capital city of Honghe prefecture with the largest tin deposits in the country, came over to her and offered to buy her two bowls of noodles from a roadside stall. She then agreed to follow the tin dealer and later became his mistress. She enjoyed one peaceful year of life until the tin dealer lost contact after he had left on a business trip months ago. How could one fish out any information about a lost contact in such a troubled time of war? Xiangge raided the place the man had rented for her. Taking away all the valuable items she could carry, she left for Kunming. At first, she did some chores at diners before leaving for a neighbouring county to get to know some people and build up her connections. Knowing that all the professors were struggling to make ends meet with their meagre incomes and had no spare money to lend her, she called in on the Yan residence in Anning county and borrowed the money to open the Greensleeves Café. With the increased foreign population and her sophisticated hospitality, combined with her touching sob stories about how she had travelled far and wide before reaching Kunming, the café thrived among the numerous small shops thanks to her innate beauty, her capability and her shrewdness.

Xiangge didn't have time to elaborate on her stories but highlighted how many difficulties she had run into when she opened the two cafés. Before leaving to attend to her customers, she asked Xuan and Wei to convey her greetings to their parents. The three then talked among themselves. Wei told Xuan and Paul about the air raids in Chongqing and the most tragic catastrophe on 5 June 1941 when more than a thousand civilians were trapped in the Jiaochangkou tunnel, suffocated and trampled to death during the air raid.

Paul said when the volunteer aviation group had completed its training, it could defend China's air sovereignty, but Wei told him: "I will enlist in the air force the first chance I get to defend our own air sovereignty."

Soft music was on. It was the famous traditional English folk song 'Greensleeves'. Friends and acquaintances of Paul and Xuan came to greet them. They all got talking together, forgetting such an insignificant woman as Lü Xiangge.

PART II

Wei saw Zhuang Wuyin, his best friend since middle school, a couple of days after the new term started. Wuyin had just come back for the new term several days later than the scheduled time since he had joined his father to teach in a teacher's school in Chengjiang county to help train physics teachers. The first thing he did when he came back was to find Tantai Wei. The two good friends greeted each other like they used to when they were back in middle school: "Hi! Zhuang Wuyin!" "Hi! Tantai Wei!" They sounded as if they had just seen each other the day before.

But the air raid siren wailed on the occasion of such a friendly meeting. They followed the crowds heading behind the hill of the university and ended up sitting on the head of a grave.

Wuyin said: "How did you survive the severe bombardments back in Chongqing?"

Wei answered: "Most people chose to go underground. But since our school's relocation to the countryside, our classes used to continue when the alarms were on."

Wuyin said: "Sometimes we took a blackboard with us and continued our class in this graveyard!"

Their talk switched from air raids to what they had been doing during each other's absence. Wuyin was amazed by the mysterious world of physics seething with infinite changes and puzzles. Through physics, he came to know more about his family, especially his father. He even grew closer to Della and his half-sister Wucai, although he couldn't figure out why.

Wei said he didn't know either why he had ended up with biology. He used to fancy geology and wanted to study electrical engineering like his father did, but those fields seemed too concrete. He wanted to study living beings because life for him was the most mysterious and strangest thing in the world.

Wuyin said: "Physics formulas are also living beings. One may try to use them and see how powerful they are." Before Wei could say anything, he changed the topic: "Have you seen May already?"

"Of course, I have. May is growing up and looks even more beautiful. So is Huishu." But he didn't mention the most beautiful one to Wuyin.

Wuyin mused: "I thought May would never grow up."

When Wei asked Wuyin about the societies on campus, Wuyin was totally ignorant of those organisations.

Suddenly, the emergency siren shrieked with fast waves of screams. Everyone stared quietly at the blue sky. Amid rumbling noises appeared a flight of enemy fighter planes over Kunming. The enormous bellies of the planes must have been loaded with bombs. The fighter planes dived one by one to release their bombs. The city centre was on fire! The blaze sprawled in the sunshine. Wei and Wuyin stood up to watch that daylight nightmare. Wei raised his arm and shouted: "Beautiful Kunming!" The student by his side hushed: "Down! Get down!" Upon his warning, the planes headed for the campus. Diving, dropping their bombs, and climbing, they performed their set series of actions with such ease one would think they had been endowed with absolute freedom.

Long after the planes were gone, the people lying down on the ground got up. Wei and Wuyin exchanged a bitter smile with each other. How fragile their study and their lives were when subjected to such bombing sorties! They found they had run out of strength for more talking.

When Wei and a couple of his classmates went to the city centre that evening, the fire on campus had been put out, but the fire from a couple of shops on Justice street was still raging. Rows of patched-up coffins lined the street. Some dead bodies had been left unattended. Wails permeated the crumbling walls. The city was under a shroud of bleak silence and phantom darkness because of the power outage caused by the bombing. Indignant resentment was burning inside everyone.

Two months passed in the blink of an eye. 'Running from air raids' was as regular as a compulsive course. People lived on healthily and happily as they used to. Wei loved his simple but rich life characterised by freedom and routine. For his teachers, he was an excellent student; for his classmates, he was the perfect companion; for the girls, he was as handsome as Wuyin. He made a box-shaped screen in front of his bed with the discarded paper May and Kiddo used for practicing their calligraphy. All those characters on the paper screen danced into any viewer's eyes. The roof of the dormitory was made of tin plate. When it rained, the pitter-patter of the rain drops sounded like music. The students called it 'the tin-plate symphony', rocking the young to sleep like a lullaby. It was rather a pity for Wei that the lullaby didn't last long.

That day when Wei came back to his dorm after his classes, he saw that the students staying in the row of rooms in front of his were moving their things out. Judging by what was being said by those standing round in a circle, Wei gathered that the roof needed replacing and that the students had to move out and crash for several nights in the classrooms. That night the accommodation officer came to Wei's room and explained why the roof needed to be replaced.

It turned out that due to a shortage of funds, the university had decided to sell the tin-plate roofs. It was a relief that the youngsters didn't care much about what the roof over their heads was made of. Someone added that no wonder the price of modern muffins had also risen. Another complained that the food from the canteen was going from bad to worse.

The officer said: "The school has run out of options. Our available funds are no match for the soaring prices. This is the classic situation that however clever a housewife is, she can't cook without ingredients. It was President Qin's idea to sell the tin-plate roofs. He planned to give an explanation to you all, but the buyer is in urgent need of the roof. That's why we need to act now."

Wei asked: "Why do they need tin plates?"

The officer said: "To make money by selling them to another buyer?"

"Why can't we make money by selling the tin plates ourselves?"

The officer laughed: "You are asking too many questions."

Then the moving dates were settled. When those in the front-row quarters moved back to their rooms from the classrooms, Wei and his roommates would move out to stay in the classrooms instead.

The following morning Wei found the front-row quarters were all roofless, leaving the four walls gaping like an open mouth gasping for air. Workers rushed in to carry out the replacement work before the air raid alarm was sounded. When the students came running back from hiding out from the air raids in the afternoon, thin planks of wood had already been fitted on the rafters. With some thatch, they made proper roofs against the mild rain and wind in Kunming, the only place where such shabby roofs would suffice.

The roofs of Wei's quarters were due to be removed the following day. There was a shower. Wei was lying in bed enjoying the pitter-patter sound of raindrops on the tin-plate roof that sounded so sad, which was unusual for Wei. Four students were playing poker, muttering sounds of joy and regret alternately. Someone else who was enjoying the tin-plate music asked them to quieten down. Wei didn't want to interfere since everything would be gone, the 'music' and the poker games. Everything would be gone. Gazing at the shiny tin plate, he slipped into sleep.

When he woke up, the rain had stopped. So had the poker game. Wei lept out of bed and headed for the library. His jaw dropped at the sight of a girl when he went out of the door. Holding a volleyball in her hands, she stood there quietly smiling at him. She was in a pair of light-and-dark-blue-checked trousers and a Chinese-red woollen sweater. It was none other than Yin Dashi.

"Why are you here?" asked Wei rather curiously.

"Am I not welcome?" said Dashi. "We had a game and we were allowed to go home when the game was over."

It was popular for the schools in Kunming to hold inter-school volleyball games back then. Dashi was on the school team and she played front centre. Wei invited her in, claiming that since she had already come in, she could have a look around. Dashi followed him into the room. She was surprised to find out the dormitory was rather different from her image of a regular male dormitory. At the sight of Wei's box screen, she giggled, which successfully attracted attention. Wei took her out in a hurry.

"So why are you here?" asked Wei.

"No particular reason," answered Dashi.

The two walked out of the school gate and along the red dirt road. It didn't rain for long, so the dirt road was wet without being muddy after the shower. The long shadows of the trees blended with the two figures in the setting sun. Dashi felt rather sorry that Tantai Wei was not in high spirits as she had expected. She had chosen to wear the same pair of work trousers she had worn the very first day they had met in case Tantai Wei couldn't remember her. It was unusual for Dashi to think about others like this.

Courteously, Wei tried to start a conversation: "How long have you been on the school team?"

"I have always been on the school team," answered Dashi. She began to tell him what fun volleyball was. Back then volleyball played in Kunming had nine players who didn't rotate as in traditional volleyball. Attacks, spikes and drops were mostly performed by the front centre player, who grabbed most of the limelight.

"At first, I always ignored the rules. My coach told me if I couldn't follow the rules, I shouldn't play."

"It sounds like sports are quite useful," said Wei.

"Do you do any sports?" asked Dashi.

"I played basketball a lot back in high school. I haven't got into it here, though." The two of them talked more about basketball and volleyball before they reached the north city gate at the end of the road.

Dashi wanted to go to the lotus pond, but Wei suggested they went into town. When they went past the Ancestral Temple street, Dashi pointed at the theatre and asked: "Many professors are said to live in the theatre. Does Meng Lingji's father stay there, too?"

Wei said: "You're right. I have a bunk bed there, too!"

The street somehow led them to the Green lake while they talked. Although it was already early winter, the weeping willows around the lake were as green as in spring time. Wild water birds were frolicking in the lake. They paused under a tree, gazing at the clouds in the distance and then at the water in front of them before Dashi blurted out a question: "Do you have a mother?"

Wei was puzzled by such a question: "Of course I have. Everyone does."

"I don't. Mine is a stepmother," answered Dashi, smilingly.

"A stepmother counts as a mother," comforted Wei.

Dashi darted a severe look at Wei and dropped her head without responding. While they loitered along the way, Dashi told Wei her mother had died three days after giving birth to her due to postpartum infections. "I killed my mother," said Dashi.

Wei patted the volleyball Dashi was carrying and said: "How can you think like that? You can't think like that."

"I have never shared such a thought with others before. Not even with my father," said Dashi.

Wei, not knowing what to say, patted the ball some more. They had walked into the vicinity of the Greensleeves Café. Dashi suddenly tossed the ball at Wei, who was taken off-guard and failed to catch it, which resulted in the ball rolling into the centre of the street. Wei ran over to pick it up. A woman, Lü Xiangge, trotted out of the café. She had already spotted Wei and Dashi walking in her direction behind the window. Seeing one of them tossing the ball and the other picking it up, she was overcome by her natural curiosity, wondering whether the two of them were playing a 'winning-the-bride-by-catching-the-ball' game. She walked out to greet Wei and showered him with numerous warm-hearted enquiries, inviting them for some refreshments. Running out of patience, Dashi told Wei she would come back another day, and walked off. Wei hurried to catch up with her, crying "Wait!" and threw the ball back to Dashi. He told Xiangge he had a lab class that evening and then left via the dyke. Lü Xiangge stared at his back for a while, grunted sneeringly, and went back into her café.

When Wei and his roommates were moving out of the quarters the next day amid chaos, leaving their belongings strewn on the ground, the air-raid sirens sounded before they had time to sort things out. They had to leave for their hide-outs. When they came back, many items were missing, including Wei's quality bedding packed by his mother Jiangchu. After a moment of deliberation, Wei decided to go to the theatre where a bunk bed made of kerosene crates awaited him. When they saw how crowded the classroom was, a handful of the students left to find other places to crash for several nights.

Wei pitched in to move the beds and other stuff with his roommates. When they had wrapped up for the day, dusk had already fallen. At the school gate, Wei met Yingshu who had come to ask Wei to stay with him at the Yan residence, but Wei told Yingshu he wanted to stay at the theatre and help tend the garden.

Yingshu sulked: "My dear mother won't understand. She'll think that I haven't shown you proper hospitality."

Wei said: "Aunt Suchu is busy with her Buddhist prayers and won't mind about such mundane stuff."

Yingshu tried to say something more but eventually decided to hold his tongue. He walked with Wei all the way to the theatre, claiming he wanted to say hello to Uncle Fuzhi, too. Fuzhi was out of town that day, so Wei went to the old man in charge of the building and fetched the key to open the room.

Standing by the window for a moment, Yingshu turned around and hesitated: "My mother has come back from the country."

On hearing Yingshu's words, Wei told himself "that's even more reason not to go to the Yan residence" while he tidied up the bunk bed. Seeing that Wei was not interested, Yingshu talked more about some trivial stuff and then left. After Wei had seen Yingshu off at the gate, he immediately went to see Professor Xiao, who was happy to see Wei and asked how the students were getting on with the move.

He sighed: "We are indeed running out of options. Someone proposed to sell President Qin's car since he walks instead of taking the car, but President Qin insists on keeping it even though he doesn't need it. A university does. His words make sense. Now you see how we manage our work and life." Xiao Cheng's room didn't have many books, but most of them were about biology or music. He asked Wei to help himself. Wei took out the book 'Annals of Biology: 1940'.

Xiao Cheng laughed at Wei's choice: "If I were you, I would surely take a book about music. This is called 'fiddling on the wrong side'!" The two went to the dining hall for dinner. This small dining group had about 20 members. Today it was Zhou Bi's turn to help with the cooking. He explained further to Wei how the kitchen functioned: "We are divided up and each take turns to do different jobs such as grocery shopping and helping in the kitchen." He turned to everyone: "The turnips for the turnip soup tonight are from our own garden. The turnips are the last of our garden vegetables."

Xiao Cheng glanced over at the pile of turnips in the corner of the room and said: "It's enough for two meals."

Wei said: "I was thinking of watering the plants." Someone answered that he had to wait until next spring to do that.

Since it was Sunday the following day, Wei got up rather late. He didn't leave to meet Xuan until noon. As he walked down the steep slope, he noticed a figure emerging at the foot of the slope. It was Yin Dashi again. Without worrying that she might not be remembered, she was wearing a long dark-green sweater over a celadon *qipao*. As her eyes met Wei's, they were brimming with joy. Wei's joy was tinged with some uneasiness: "She is so direct and brave."

Dashi began first: "I'm joining you to run from the air-raids."

"What if there are none?" asked Wei.

Both laughed at such a stupid notion that they were almost looking forward to an air raid, although there had been fewer air raids recently.

"How about if we run beforehand?" proposed Dashi.

"I'm actually on my way to meet my sister," said Wei.

"I thought you were waiting for me!"

Someone rushed toward them from the foot of the slope as the two of them were talking. The person cried: "Dashi, a guest has arrived. Madam is looking for you!"

Dashi dropped her smile: "It's not my guest!" She turned around and left, dragging Wei along with her.

Wei hurried to explain to Dashi: "I'm really on my way to meet my sister."

The other one said: "Tantai Wei, you are sensible."

Wei was surprised that she knew who he was: "How do you know my name?"

Dashi answered for the girl: "You will know hers now. Her name is Wang Dian and she is my parents' secret agent."

Wei nodded at the girl politely and said: "Nice to meet you!"

Seeing the two girls blocking the exit of the slope, he lied that he had forgotten something and had to go back to the theatre at the ancestral temple. Dashi then began to head out of town, claiming: "I'm running from the air raid by myself." Wang Dian chased after her and tried to make Dashi change her mind. The two went in the direction of the northern city gate.

When Wei was back up in the attic, he found he was haunted by Dashi's image. That realisation upset him most. He knew that Dashi's bossy personality was the product of the absence of a mother's love and her father's indulgence to compensate for such an absence. Her heart needed careful nurturing. He thought for a while and decided to go and see Xuan. Unexpectedly, he didn't find Xuan at her place. She must have been with Paul. Wei had a bowl of rice noodles for lunch and strolled back to the attic to write to his parents.

Hearing a creaking noise at the door, Wei stood up to open it. It was Dashi, again! Her face was grim with a mixture of anger and complaint. Wei's heart was in turmoil at the thought of how he should handle the situation.

Dashi asked: "Is professor Meng home? I'd like to ask him for his opinions about an issue of life."

Wei teased her: "Professor Meng is not home, but Tantai Wei is."

The two caught each other's eye before bursting into laughter.

Wei asked Dashi: "How did you know about the attic?"

Dashi said: "If I wanted to find it out, how could I fail? Wang Dian and I reached an agreement. She gave me one day of freedom and I promised her a term of freedom from getting myself into any trouble. She doesn't feel like watching over me, but she's on Dashi-watch duty and has to take orders from my parents."

The two sat down and engaged in casual conversation. They were happy.

Dashi said: "You are a good friend of mine now, I want you to meet my father and ask him to take us hunting."

Wei said: "I have never hunted anything and I'm against hunting."

Dashi asked: "Why? I love hunting. It feels so awesome. When I was little, I rode with my father. Now I ride my own horse. It gets me so excited chasing after prey."

Wei said musingly: "So, when you set a target, you are not aiming at construction but at destruction. Isn't it cruel to take a life?"

Dashi dropped her head and thought for a moment: "We only hunt animals like wolves and foxes... but I won't hunt anymore. When one bullet is fired, one wolf puppy might then lose its parent. I want them to have both their parents." Her voice slid into sobs. Her heart had been covered in hard armour, shielding her tenderness from others. Wei's heart was overflowing with sympathy. How he wished to stroke her silky dark hair! But he handed her a glass of water and his handkerchief instead. Howling with or without stomping, smashing things and cursing, was routine for Dashi. Never

had she cried the way she did this time: so elegant and profound, so satisfying and comforting.

She raised a pair of tearful eyes and said: "I will graduate from high school next year. My family wants me to go to college in the US, but I won't go."

Wei said: "Studying abroad is a good thing! If we have won the war against the Japanese invaders already by the time you graduate, you may go and attend college in Beiping. Ah Beiping! You have no idea what a wonderful city it is! From a geographical point of view, it is also a plain surrounded by mountains in all directions. From the perspective of the inhabitants, you see students and hear them reading everywhere — this atmosphere is unique to Beiping."

Dashi said: "I have heard that it is popular for schools in Beiping to choose their campus queen. Your sister was chosen and she is beautiful. I think your mother must be a belle, too."

He laughed: "Of course she is, and my father is also a good-looking man. He is a man of action whose actions always speak louder than his words."

Dashi sighed gently: "You are happy."

Wei said: "I want to introduce you to them and let them know you are my good friend."

Dashi dabbed her face which shone with a dazzling smile. A large teardrop dangling on her eyelashes reflected the smile on Wei's face, a young man's sincere and passionate smile. This was the moment which would be engraved on two hearts. They had different destinies, they had different lives, be it long or short, they would both remember each other's smile in their hearts until the last moment of their lives. Anyone who has encountered such a moment is blessed.

They gazed at each other over the kerosene crates.

"Tantai Wei!" cried Xiao Cheng at the door. "Are you still sleeping?" He pushed the door open to see a girl sitting in the room. "So, you have a visitor," said Xiao.

Wei stood up hurriedly and introduced Dashi to Xiao Cheng: "This is a schoolmate of May and Huishu —Yin Dashi. She is a good friend of mine."

Dashi, having guessed who the man was, stood up quietly and bowed at Xiao Cheng. Xiao Cheng smiled amiably at Dashi: "Then you must be a student from Kunjing middle school. Every time I go to the plant institute, I go through Copper Head village where the middle school has been relocated." After chatting some more, he turned to Wei: "I didn't come for anything special, just taking a walk." He turned and went downstairs.

Dashi picked up Wei's handkerchief and carefully folded it: "I'll wash it before I give it back to you next time." Wei saw her off at the gate of the ancestral temple, feeling a bit uneasy about the propriety of meeting Dashi in the attic.

Dashi said: "My algebra is terrible. I'll bring the exercises next week. Will you show me how to do them?"

Wei hesitated: "I'm going to Dragon Tail village next weekend."

Dashi said: "Then the week after next." The next second, she waved goodbye as she started down the steep slope, disappearing from Wei's sight.

The rice-noodle diner at the top of the slope jingled with the noises of cooks and crockery colliding with one another and the owner's shouted orders: "Two rice noodles with tofu topping, no red chili sauce! Three stewed rice cakes, no sauce!"

Wei planted himself at the gate for a while before he turned back and went up to the attic.

A couple of days later, Wei moved back to the dormitory. Seams were visible on the roof due to the hastily laid thatch. One dorm mate joked that they were lucky to have 'lines of sky' instead of a 'one-line sky', referring to a famous landform of a narrow passage between enormous rock formations, where the sky looked like a single line. The moonlight seeping through the seams cast geometric shapes onto the floor, woven into young people's wild dreams.

One day, as Wei was running from an air raid, he ran into Yingshu.

"Wang Dian has been visiting my mother quite frequently these days. I don't know what she is after," Yingshu told Wei.

"Is she going to poison someone with witchcraft?" teased Wei. But on seeing how fast the colour drained from Yingshu's face, turning it as white as a sheet, Wei hurried to explain: "I was just joking."

As the colour gradually returned to Yingshu's face, he said: "You must be careful. I'm worried about you. Anyway, I have something serious to ask you. Would you like to join our Three Youth League?"

Wei waved his hand: "I don't join any societies, like my father did when he was at college."

Yingshu said: "Every member of a political group can work together to realise the desire to resist the Japanese and save the nation."

Wei meditated: "That's rather hard to tell."

They sank into silence.

To their left and right, the voices of lecturing teachers, not wanting to waste a single minute of classtime on hiding from air raids, reached their ears.

Zhou Bi and Wu Jiaxin came to Wei and said: "The Teachers of the Masses is holding a reading club tonight and we are scheduled to share our reading responses. You are invited!" Wu Jiaxin came all the way from the plant institute located near the Black Dragon pond.

Wei asked: "Why isn't Meng Liji coming with you?"

"She has attended several times. Probably she doesn't want to come this time around," said Jiaxin. She was telling the truth because she could provide so few explanations for things involving Earl.

Wei said: "We seem to be in the process of gradual separation which requires frequent choices and decisions to be made. It's a big headache for me."

Jiaxin urged: "Then you should come. It's interesting to listen to others' opinions." Then the lifting of the alert sounded. Everyone dispersed in their chosen directions.

In the evening, Wei went to attend the gathering of the Teachers of the Masses. They began with some discussion about current affairs. Some talked about the KMT corruption, quoting the case of government officials hooking up with profiteers to profit by raising the price of rice. They read a booklet explaining historical materialism. It was a fresh experience for Wei.

After the meeting, some classmates were still reluctant to part with one another, so they proposed to go to a teahouse and play a few rounds of poker. Wei went with them and walked out of the school gate. When they arrived at the section of the city wall where the breach was, a rather out-of-the-way corner, two men who looked like students approached Wei and asked: "Are you Tantai Wei?" Wei answered yes and tried to figure out what they looked like in the darkness. One said: "Would you please come this way? We'd like to talk to you." Wei, his mind still lingering over the meeting, didn't pay much attention and followed the two of them. He didn't realise the abnormality of the situation until they had covered a long section of the road.

He stopped abruptly upon this sudden realisation: "What do you want to talk about?" The two responded with a low growl and punched Wei. The four fists knocked Wei flat on the ground. Luckily Wei had learned martial arts with his grandfather. Before the two assailants came at him for a second attack, Wei had somersaulted up and backed away.

Wei's fast move took the two of them by surprise. Before one of them launched another attack, he was stopped by his companion: "We have been instructed to inform you not to see Miss Yin again. Since you are a smart guy, we won't elaborate." With these words, the two marched off. Wei felt a burning pain in his shoulders. Surrounded by boundless darkness, he felt he had fallen into the world of a martial-arts novel. He stood on the spot for a while before he trudged back to his dormitory, deaf to the greetings from some of his classmates on the way.

In addition to the pains in his shoulders, his waist began to hurt. Lying in bed, Wei suffered more from his inner turmoil than the physical pain. "Why can't I see Dashi? Why did they attack me? How could life be so barbaric beyond the classrooms, labs and the playground? Will Dashi cry at the news? What will my parents think when they hear about it? What would Uncle Fuzhi and Professor Xiao do if they knew? Will they blame me? What have I done wrong?" He pulled the quilt over himself in an attempt to cover his head and his painful groans. A dorm mate came to ask what was wrong and whether he had a fever. Wei told him he was under the weather but there was nothing to worry about. Tossing and turning, Wei had a sleepless night.

The next day Wei struggled out of bed to go to class. He suddenly realised in the classroom that the two attackers had not hit him in the face because they didn't want to leave too obvious traces. After thinking things over several times, he decided not to tell anyone else about this incident. He could not tell his sister, Xuan, in particular, who surely would go to confront Dashi, which would not be fair to Dashi.

In the evening, he decided to go to bed early and get a good night's sleep. However hard he tried, he couldn't find a comfortable posture. Besides the pains, he felt he was being clutched by something like a talon. He opened his eyes to see Xuan standing in front of his bed. He wanted to sit up immediately, but the pain slowed him down: "When did you change your mind about visiting a male dormitory?"

"I'm worried you may not be able to walk. Does it hurt? One look would be enough to know you feel terrible," answered Xuan.

Wei put on his shoes slowly and retorted: "I attended my classes as usual. Let's get out of here first." He took Xuan to the lab and opened the door with the key he had.

"How did you know?" asked Wei.

"In the afternoon, Hezhu went to my office, saying she had visited Mrs Yin and was dropping by me on the way back. She told me that the Yin family would not allow Yin Dashi to see you again. The family is furious."

"We only met twice. Why are they reacting like this?"

"According to Hezhu, the attackers are from one of the families who are seeking marriage into the Yin family."

"So, they are going to take turns to attack me, those families?"

"I don't know which family attacked you. We will do something when we have the evidence."

The sister and brother talked for a while and decided to report the matter to Uncle Fuzhi and Professor Xiao Cheng first. Xuan asked Wei to move to the living room she had rented beside her bedroom at Precious Pearl alley until he had recovered from his injuries.

Wei laughed at her dramatic reaction: "It's not that serious!" Before they parted with each other, Wei asked about Paul.

Xuan answered: "He's gone to Chongqing again. That guy is quite busy."

The two professors talked over the issue and concluded that it would be better for the two young students involved if the story didn't spread since it might affect the relationship between influential local families and the university. Besides, Wei's priority was his studies, so it would be better for him not to see Dashi now. Wei agreed with the decision, but he told Xuan of his concern about what he would do if Dashi disobeyed her parents' orders and came to visit him.

Xuan came up with an idea: "You may tell her that you two are still young and should focus on your studies."

Wei thought to himself whether Dashi would buy such a flimsy excuse.

Xuan laughed: "It's hard to deny that Dashi is a belle. A wild belle is a rare find."

"She said you are a belle, too!"

"Me? I'm a proud belle," Xuan said.

Wei didn't anticipate that the problem would later take care of itself.

Two weeks later, on the Sunday that Dashi was due to come to Wei for help with her algebra, Wei received a letter: "I can't come to you for my algebra exercise. My father is taking me to Chongqing. He said it is a fun place. Maybe I'll come back in one month and then I'll give you your handkerchief back."

The letter had no addressee or return address and the handwriting looked wild. An ink stain on the paper reminded Wei of the enormous teardrop dangling on Dashi's eyelash last time they saw each other. Such a convenient separation didn't bring Wei relief. Instead, he felt his heart was being twisted by something inexplicable. When would he see Dashi again? Such a question would bubble up even when Wei was buried under his busy schedule of studies and social activities.

It was said that Yin Dashi went to Chongqing for her college. Rumour had it that she was forced to go, like a hostage or something.

PART III

One day in mid-December, it was clear and fine, another perfect day for running from air raids. The red balloon had been hoisted and the air raid siren wailed loudly. People headed out of town in twos and threes, and it didn't feel unlike any other day. Meng Fuzhi, who had been occupied with university affairs, had been away from home for about ten days. Now he was walking in the crowd, heading for the east city gate toward Dragon Tail village. He couldn't wait to tell Bichu and the kids about the Pearl Harbour incident.

There were no newspapers in the countryside. Without a radio or people visiting with news, those staying in the countryside remained ignorant of major events. He thought about the war. It was a good thing that the US was now engaged in fighting the Japanese, who gained a major enemy while we gained a friend. He was also concerned at the hardships confronting the university and Wei's recent accident. The article about redundant staffing in the Song dynasty was only one aspect of the corruption. He had finished several more articles this year, but there was much more to write about.

His thoughts shifted to the recent news about American General Claire Lee Chennault and his 14th Air Force (the American Volunteer Group also known as The Flying Tigers). It was reported that many fighter planes had arrived in Kunming and were ready to fight back against the Japanese air raids. The pilots were trained in Kunming and Rangoon. When would they be ready for battle? When could we manufacture our own fighter planes?

These questions were shared by millions of Chinese as Fuzhi returned home deep in contemplation.

Once one becomes familiar with one's route, one does not feel the distance. In the past two years, Fuzhi had walked a lot and he found that if he set a target, he could go faster. Now he was walking quickly behind a small black horse. The closer he got to Dragon Tail village, the lighter his heart grew. Before he knew it, he had already reached the pine grove outside the village. The line of various stands and the crowds of people filing to and fro told Fuzhi it was a fair day. Two kids, May and Kiddo, emerged from the crowd. They were carrying more than a dozen strings of dried pine needles with a carrying pole. May was carrying a basketful of green vegetables in her free hand. The strings of pine needles slid toward Kiddo, who was shorter than his sister. May urged: "Push it up toward me! Push it up toward me!"

Fuzhi strode up to them and tried to take over the strings.

"Dad!" The two were overjoyed upon seeing their father, but they stopped Fuzhi.

"We can manage this."

"Mum is sick again, but she feels better today."

As the three walked to the bank of the Mang river, they heard the rumbling of aero engines. They didn't sound like the familiar noises of the Japanese fighter planes, thought Fuzhi. They spotted a squadron of planes in the blue sky with their wings free of Japanese flags.

"They are our planes!" someone in the crowd shouted.

It turned out that these planes were intercepting the enemy fighter planes appearing on the horizon.

Our fighter planes fired at the nine heavily armed enemy bombers lined up in three rows! They were flexible, flying up and down, shooting bullets and shells at the enemy bombers. Lines of tracer fire were followed by flashes of light. A fireball of flames plummeted earthward, exploding in mid-air, scattering great plumes of fire in all directions. Another fireball dropped. They were the Japanese bombers! The rampaging, unstoppable Japanese planes had been shot down! The monstrous, devilish Japanese planes had been downed!

Everyone at the fair tossed away whatever they had in their hands and clapped hard, yelling: "Down! They have been shot down!" Cries of "down with Japanese imperialism" rose one after another. Kiddo pulled out the carrying pole made of bamboo and waved it as he ran around, shouting: "Come on! Come on!" as if he were rooting for his favourite team on a football field.

Fuzhi stood still on the bank like a stone statue. May looked up and asked, "Dad, are we going to fight back to Beiping now?"

Fuzhi heaved a heavy sigh: "It's not that easy!"

The enemy planes in the sky turned around and fled, with the Chinese planes on their tails, leaving behind some light explosions in the air. Fuzhi called Kiddo back and gathered up the strings of pine needles. The three went home together. Later it was said that three enemy planes had been shot down. The Kunming folk, who had got used to being bullied by the Japanese air raids, straightened up their backbones as if they were a couple of feet taller than before. To shoot down the enemy planes was what May and Kiddo had been dreaming of!

The paving stones on the path along Baotaishan were laid rather half-heartedly, leaving gaps between the flagstones, and the green grass grew happily between the gaps, sending out a false message that it was a smooth grassy path. Kiddo had sprained his ankles several times on this path because of the grassy gaps. May babbled to her father all the way home about what had happened at home. Qinghuan had been called back by her aunt; Mum had been bed-bound for several days in a row but, thankfully, Mrs Qian and cousin Xueyan came to their assistance during that period.

As they were approaching the house, the two children speeded up and literally flew through the door, shouting: "Mum, we have shot down the Japanese planes!" Bichu, who was sitting on a stool doing some laundry, stood up in surprise but almost blacked out as her head spun. Fuzhi strode toward her to get to her before she fell.

May and Kiddo ran over and snatched the laundry out of her hands and complained: "Mum, you have been naughty again. We have only been away for a while and yet now you are doing chores!"

Bichu smiled: "I'm feeling much better." But she had shifted all her weight onto Fuzhi's shoulder.

"Thank goodness that dad is home!" thought the two kids with relief.

The three of them helped Bichu into the room and sat her down on the bed, leaning her back against the headboard. Fuzhi noticed Bichu was in a cold sweat. His heart sank: "You were alright last week. How has it become so serious?"

Bichu gathered her strength and answered: "Nothing to worry about. It has always been bumpy like this. Sometimes it's better, other times it's not so good. I should have followed May's instructions, though."

The three bustled around her, stuffing pillows behind her back and tucking her in. 'Found', the cat, pitched into action, too, rubbing itself against their feet.

Bichu sighed with satisfaction: "I'm so blessed. I couldn't ask for more."

Fuzhi told Bichu how the Japanese army had launched a surprise attack at Pearl Harbour, which had prompted the US to declare war against Japan.

Bichu said joyfully: "It seems that hope is in sight."

May and Kiddo immediately brought a map to show Bichu. Fuzhi stopped them: "Let your mother rest. Kiddo, let's listen to May."

May asked Kiddo to do his assignment while she finished the laundry and then hung it out to dry. She was skilful at this task. She cleaned the room with the water from doing the laundry before going to cook in the kitchen. She noticed someone was coming through the wet laundry. It was Professor Jiang Fang. Jiang Fang's eyes glowed with excitement. The pipe in his mouth moved rhythmically as he shouted: "The day has finally arrived! I just watched the match from a vantage point on the mountain. Did you see it?"

Fuzhi answered while pouring a cup of water for Bichu: "We saw it on the embankment of the Mang river. People at the fair were so excited they kept shouting slogans. The changes in the global situation give us some hope. At least the air raids will be fewer when the Japanese are preoccupied."

When the two sat down, Jiang Fang said: "Look at your tables and chairs! They are immaculate! It's amazing that we have survived so many bombing raids for so long! As the external situation changes, the internal problems will gradually reveal themselves. I heard that a division of the Central Military Commission has pocketed a portion of the soldiers' pay, leaving the soldiers struggling with hardships. It is also said that fraudulent claims for soldiers' pay are not uncommon, either. These profiteers over the national crisis should be condemned to hell."

Fuzhi added: "The opening of the granary is also disappointing. Those who were in power bought the rice at the moderate price set for needy civilians but then sold it at the high black-market price. One single sale earns them tens of thousands of yuan. But how can the civilians survive?"

Jiang Fang said: "The people's hearts are not as close as they used to be. To quote from the Tang poet Gao Shi's poem entitled 'An Ode to Those Fighting on the Borders': At the frontier, half of the soldiers perish, fighting and shedding blood; in the rear, beautiful girls dance to melodies for the captains in the camps'. Although we are not facing such a serious situation, the prospect is not promising."

Fuzhi continued: "Corruption has been the bane of all dynasties. The commoners have long concluded that 'even an honest government official would pocket a fortune after one term in office'."

Jiang Fang said: "This was even more true for the Qing dynasty. Li Baojia's novel in the late Qing dynasty 'Officialdom Unmasked'[1] has recorded concrete evidence." With those words, he stood up and began to pace the room. He turned around after several steps: "It is said that Yan'an has a clean and honest system where common soldiers are equal to the officers. That shows they do have ideals."

Fuzhi said: "I think the history of the old China has reached its end. It's time for a new system. Yan'an has its problems, too, the most prominent of which is the lack of proper respect for knowledge. Such a lack is the root of disaster."

Jiang Fang didn't share the same concern: "Knowledge is important, but it is more important to stand in the same line with the masses."

The brittle sound of a teacup dropping onto the hard brick floor reached their ears from inside. Fuzhi hurried into the room to see Bichu forcing a smile on her pale face: "I can't even grip a cup." Fuzhi bent over to comfort her.

Jiang Fang sighed at the door: "My wife told me she is ill too in her letter which arrived the day before yesterday. She is in even poorer health than Mrs Meng. You all need to be strong to survive the war!"

Jiang's family was in Chengdu. They had been talking about coming to join him in Kunming, but they never made the trip.

Sometime later, Bichu dozed off and had a nap. Fuzhi cleaned up the broken cup and asked Jiang Fang to sit down again.

Jiang put down his pipe: "I think your article on the redundant staffing in the Song dynasty is too gentle. The root is the lingering remnants of the feudal system. You just mentioned that the old system has come to an end. Why didn't you include that in your writing?"

Fuzhi smiled a bitter smile: "That article has already made me a marked man. You have always known that I've never been a sharp person, but I always end up in trouble like this. The progressives accuse me of being backward, while the conservatives blame me for being too radical. Either way, I'm not popular."

Jiang Fang knocked his pipe against the floor to clean out the ash and said: "I only need to handle criticism from one end, which leaves me much more room and freedom than you have. I'm trying to live up to saying whatever I want to say. This is called 'give me liberty or give me death'!" He chortled at such a smart quotation. When he looked up, he spotted Fuzhi's calligraphy work of the poem of the Northern Song dynasty poet and philosopher Shao Yong (posthumously named Kangjie): "What a perfect state of mind! But who can achieve that in a troubled world like ours?"

Fuzhi pondered: "It won't be easy to keep a tiny portion of the natural beauty in the poem at heart."

Jiang Fang said: "Ideas will influence actions, but if one day we can achieve such mental freedom, will it be too selfish?"

Fuzhi smiled: "I'm sure you are longing for the day when you can enjoy your pure peace and freedom to roam in your world created by Qu Yuan's 'Nine Songs'."

Jiang Fang knocked his pipe again and said: "You have seen through me," and put his pipe back in his mouth. That reminded Fuzhi of the pack of shredded tobacco stored in the corner of the cabinet. He found it and handed it to Jiang Fang, explaining: "This is a gift from one of my relatives. But I don't smoke."

Jiang Fang took it and laughed: "May he give you more! The more, the better!"

A burst of laughter came from outside the door, and they

heard May calling: "Cousin Feng! Cousin Xueyan! And you, Leo!" Sure enough, an enormous dog's head popped up among the wet laundry hanging on the clothes line. You could see he was smiling. Xueyan followed Fuzhi into the room to see Bichu while Wei Feng and Jiang Fang walked into the courtyard to talk, and Leo sat down by May, watching her cooking.

May had grown to become a leader now. She was clear about what to do first, what to do last, and what to do at the same time, which was very much in line with operational research. When her hands were busy, her mind was on reciting *A Visit to an Ancient Battlefield* by Tang dynasty poet Li Hua, an assignment from her mother.

> The soldiers travelled thousands of miles across the country,
> Exposed in the wilderness year after year.
> In the morning, they searched for water and grass in the desert
> to water and graze their horses;
> At night they forded the frozen river.
>
> When could they head homeward?
> Which way would lead them homeward?
> Their lives were pinned between swords and knives,
> Who could they share their sorrow and sadness with?
>
> The drums were weak,
> And the soldiers were exhausted;
> The arrows had been shot
> And the bow strings were slack.
> The shiny blades had struck flesh and bones,

All the swords had been broken.
The two forces were approaching each other,
Both in despair.

Surrender? And face lifetime in captivity with barbarians.
Fight on? And have your bones smashed to pieces.

How terrible war was when it took away millions of lives! Could any war spare justice? We finally saw with our own eyes that Japanese planes were being shot down. This was justice! How could we pay a visit to the battlefield in the blue sky? As she was indulging herself in these thoughts, she felt a tug. It was Leo who was trying to direct her attention with his eyes to the stove.

"Oh, the water for the rice is boiling over!" May quickly lifted the lid and propped it up with a chopstick, saying: "Good boy, Leo! Thank you for reminding me." Leo extended a paw to shake hands with May.

"Not now, Leo! You see, you see, I'm busy!" explained May. Leo put his paw down, disappointed, got up, turned round and sat beside May. His obsession for watching people cooking was known to all. He would sit by either Mrs Mi or Xueyan, watching attentively by their side as if he were ready to lend a 'hand' at any minute.

By the gate to the courtyard, Jiang Fang was ready to leave after talking to Wei Feng for a while. As soon as he stepped out of the gate, Wei Feng spotted a big hole in the hem of his gown and said, hurriedly: "Hold on a second, Professor Jiang! There's a hole in your gown."

Jiang Fang stooped to have a look and laughed: "It might have happened several days ago. I would never have noticed it if you hadn't pointed it out to me."

When she heard what was being said, Xueyan took out a needle and thread, and crouched down by Jiang Fang's side to mend the hole. Leo immediately went to sit by her side. Leo was even taller than Xueyan. Xueyan gave Leo a smile, who seemed to smile back. The dog and the lady had become best friends with each other. Soon Xueyan had finished mending the hole. Jiang Fang cupped his hands in front of his chest to thank Xueyan for her help and then went down the hill. Wei Feng picked up the buckets to fetch water.

When Xueyan went back into the room again, she saw an old bit of clothing with holes in it and picked it up to mend it. Bichu felt much better after her nap. When she knew Leo was here, she called him in. Leo offered his paw to shake hands with Bichu. He gazed anxiously at Bichu as if to ask whether she was feeling better.

Xueyan said: "I can see Aunt Bichu is feeling much better."

Bichu answered: "I was feeling dizzy, but I feel much better after the nap."

Xueyan continued: "Mrs Mi doesn't feel well these days. She's pregnant."

Bichu was happy at the news: "What good news! They are going to have their own children!"

Xueyan sighed: "Who knows how long this child will have to roam around during such tough times. They are going to come and visit you."

When talking about this Jewish family, everyone was sympathetic. How strange it was that there were people in the world without a motherland! People who came into contact with the Jewish couple often felt proud because the sight of the poor couple would remind them that they had a motherland that was suffering and which they were fighting for.

When Xueyan was done mending clothes, she looked around and saw a flute in a jar. She picked it up and stroked it, claiming this was an heirloom. The other day when she heard May blowing on the flute, it sounded as if it were drifting to them from the distant mountains.

Kiddo, who had finished his assignment, took the flute and began to play an old piece entitled 'Su Wu the Shepherd'. Su Wu, a Chinese diplomat and statesman of the Han dynasty, was captured in a diplomatic mission and then detained for 19 years in a foreign country. He endured the long years of servitude herding sheep but remained loyal to his motherland before he managed to return. The tune Kiddo played, though not wonderful, was played with confidence and conviction.

Leo let out a low growl from his throat and ran to the door. A moment later Wei Feng came back, carrying two buckets of water, followed by two foreigners. Leo circled around the two of them as if they had been away for ages. It was the Mi couple. Mr Mi was wearing a tie and walking with a stick. Mrs Mi was in a long dress, with a book in her hand. Half of her hair was combed forward to cover her face, her regular hair style.

The room was too narrow, so only Mrs Mi entered. She said that she had heard long ago that Bichu was not well and wanted to pay her a visit but hadn't come until today because they were worried about disturbing Bichu's rest.

Bichu, leaning against the headboard, smiled: "It's nothing serious. When the dizziness is gone, it's fine. You must be tired walking all the way here from Salt Falls?" Xueyan interpreted Bichu's words into French.

Mrs Mi, covering her face with a book like she always did, asked: "Has Xueyan told you our good news? I'm pregnant. I was a mother once, but I lost that child. I know you, being a successful mother, will bring me luck and share your experience with me."

Bichu sighed softly. She didn't think of herself as a successful mother. The three women whispered, all their faces oozing with happiness.

Fuzhi invited Mr Mi to sit in the courtyard. They talked about the situation after Pearl Harbour and about living in such a small village in Yunnan. Fuzhi said he was concerned about the Mi couple's living conditions. Mr Mi, a true diplomat, was humorous and aimiable. He told Fuzhi he and his wife loved this village. The Dragon river and the Mang river often reminded them of the Rhine river where he grew up. Germany had always been his homeland, which he was ready to live and die for. In 1933, he was recalled from office and deported on false charges — maybe very true charges — that he was Jewish.

Fuzhi sighed: "The Jews are a great people. You have retained your own culture and traditions after thousands of years of exile and persecution. It has never been easy for you to survive. Hitler's aggression against other nations has proved that Nazi anti-semitism is inhuman."

After putting down the buckets, Wei Feng walked over to them to join the conversation: "It would be such a wonderful thing if the barriers between races could be eliminated. But, of course, Hitler's utterly inhuman holocaust is based on his political needs rather than racial barriers."

Mr Mi said: "Feng understands us. I always thought he was more than just an excellent physics teacher."

Wei Feng laughed: "I'm also an excellent neighbour!"

May walked up to them and added: "And an excellent cousin, too."

On hearing May's words, Mr Mi gave her a look of approval. The old and the young talked happily in the courtyard and in the room.

That morning, the Meng household was bathed in a festive atmosphere due to the rare, successful interception of the enemy planes and the conception of a new life.

New Year's Day 1942 came, followed by the Spring Festival. The air raids had decreased significantly in the past couple of months. It felt rather weird for Kunming townsfolk not to have to run for cover from air raids. There seemed to be a temporary lull in the war.

The families of Meng Fuzhi and Li Lian celebrated the Spring Festival together with the bachelors from the institute of liberal arts. The floor covered with pine twigs felt soft. The exquisite smell of pine trees filled the whole house. May and Zhiwei made many tiny red lanterns with the red paper someone had brought and hung them up on the wall. The few candles were lit, transforming the shabby room into an iridescent dreamland with the flickering candlelight reflecting the greenness from the pine twigs. This was a special festival full of hope for everyone during their eastern concealment.

Another spring came. Kunming's high elevation bestowed the city with the mildest climate in China, obscuring the differences between seasons. No season was marked without blooming flowers of this kind or that. The mild Kunming spring was nothing like the joyfully violent version of the season in the North. The spring in Kunming was quiet and gentle, with the demeanour of a plain beauty. On Baotaishan, a variety of colourful wild flowers bloomed one after another, wrapping the hillside with a giant printed floral Persian rug.

A performance to give thanks to the army was scheduled to be held in the clearing outside the liberal arts institute. All the villagers in the area were very excited at the news. It took the soldiers sent by the military two days to erect a temporary stage. May and Kiddo went to check on the progress each day. Those people were building, not destroying. The two had a solid and concrete sense of success upon seeing the development of the stage. Unlike May, who had gone to the theatre a couple of times before the war broke out, Kiddo had never been to a theatre. He had been bugging May with the same question whether there would be real people performing on the stage. On learning that the performance was to be 'Distinguished Gathering of Heroes', Bichu gave the kids a brief account of the story. They had read *The Romance of the Three Kingdoms*, so they had a profound knowledge of the major protagonists such as Zhuge Liang and Zhou Yu.

On the day of the performance, Kiddo asked several times when it would get dark. When it was finally dark, a couple of efficient gas lights hung in front of the stage shone blindingly, chasing the bright moonlight to hide somewhere else. All the soldiers, neatly dressed, and the villagers in their best clothes, were sitting in front of the stage long before the planned starting time. The Mengs didn't dress up like they used to back in Beiping for a visit to a theatre. The only standard they stuck to was to ensure everyone was warmly clad. A section had been assigned to the university faculty and their families. It was the first pleasant gathering for several years.

The curtain was sewn from several military blankets. Although they weren't hung properly, they opened smoothly. No one knew the name of the troupe, but all its performers were adept at the use of speech, song, dance and combat movements. Here came Zhuge Liang. There went Jiang Gan and Zhou Yu. The different roles' elaborate singing and colourful costumes brought to life an imaginative section of history. The same stage prompted differing thoughts from the audience.

Xueyan hadn't planned on coming because she was afraid that seeing the stage would remind her of her father, a true lover of drama and theatre, who couldn't let go of his beloved theatre when he was forced to accept the position from the puppet government. But the whole village, including the Mi couple, was so happy. How could she spoil the fun? So, here she was. The singing on stage took her back to the gatherings of fans at the Ling residence in Beiping, with the same clear and expressive singing. Yet the turbid waters of life had smeared its victims with mud and blood. How were her parents? Both must have grown much older. Was her father still absent-minded? Was her mother picky and calculating as usual? Was the comfy home empty in her absence? The performance on the stage was lively and merry, but Xueyan was busy drying her tears. Wei Feng noticed Xueyan's reaction and asked whether she would like to leave early to sit it out at Uncle Fuzhi's. Xueyan shook her head.

For Mrs Mi, the stage and performance reminded her of her career as an actress. She played various supporting roles in famous dramas back in Hamburg. Once she played a river maiden guarding the Rhine Gold and participated in the chorus to sing a few lines in Wagner's opera 'Der Ring des Nibelungen' which was on stage for four nights in a row. It was the pinnacle of her acting career which she could never forget. What a pity it was that her husband, David, had never seen her in her river maiden costume.

She held Mr Mi's hand in hers. Both felt the strength from each other's hand and felt comforted in such a strange string of colours and sounds. Both loved the German culture and considered it their own, even though they had been forcibly ripped away from such a culture. The thought of such pain pounded her head and her heart, transmitting itself all the way down to her abdomen, pounding something dear to her.

Mr Mi tightened his grip and asked her what was wrong. She pointed at her abdomen. The pain was too sharp for her to sit still. Beads of cold sweat stood on her forehead. Xueyan noticed the abnormal situation and asked Bichu to help Mrs Mi go back to the Mengs'. As soon as they entered the courtyard, a stream of blood gushed down between Mrs Mi's legs. She had had a miscarriage.

Bichu asked her to lie down in Earl's bed and hurried to gather some old clothes, cotton pads, and wads of toilet paper to put under her as a mat. A bloody bundle lay among the blood-soaked clothes. It was supposed to be a small bundle of life.

Bichu whispered to Xueyan: "If the bleeding won't stop, her life could be in danger. What should we do?"

Xueyan tried to remind her: "The medication Aunt Bichu has been taking…"

"Yes! Yes! I still have some Yunnan White Drug which is very good at stopping the bleeding!"

She went on hunting down the powdered medicine and let Mrs Mi wash down the medicine with water. Bichu and Xueyan then cooked thick rice water, heated up the water and tidied up. Mr Mi had been holding one of his wife's hands, reciting psalms from the Bible for her in Yiddish. Fuzhi and Wei Feng had been waiting at the door, arguing whether they should borrow the horse from Zhang Er to send for the closest doctor who lived about 10km away.

Wei Feng said with determination: "The sooner, the better. I'm leaving."

As he was going out of the yard, he ran into Mrs Li who had come as soon as she got the news. She cried: "When there is sickness, we need to worship the Holy Spirits! I will conduct the ceremony."

Fuzhi tried to discourage her: "You don't share the same religion. Don't offend them."

Mrs Li sulked: "I'm trying to save a life!" She began muttering her special prayers while pacing around the courtyard.

It was never really clear which one worked — Mrs Li's prayers or the Yunnan White Drug. Either way, Mrs Mi's bleeding stopped. When she opened her eyes, all of the people crowded around her heaved a sigh of relief. Wei Feng ran back soon, saying Zhao Er had left with the caravan and he had asked a herbalist living nearby to come and take a look. Once he realised Mrs Mi was getting better, he sent the herbalist back.

Mrs Li danced around in the moonlight for a while. Upon hearing that the patient was getting better, she felt satisfied with herself. Presenting herself in front of Wei Feng, she smiled and asked: "You two should have given us some good news. What's going on? Why is there no news at all?"

Wei Feng was too embarrassed to answer, so he prevaricated: "Thank you for asking, Mrs Li."

Mrs Li opined: "Life and death are just two sides of a piece of cloth. The Holy Spirit waves that piece of cloth and then determines who is doomed, and who is blessed." She turned to ask Fuzhi: "Don't you think so, Professor Meng?"

Fuzhi said: "It's admirable that you are so ready to offer your help. Now Mrs Mi is stable, would you like to go back and enjoy the rest of the performance?"

At this time, the rhythmic beating of gongs and drums reached them. She then strode off amid the rhythmic beats.

Seeing that his wife's situation had stabilised, Mr Mi put his hand under the quilt, tucked her in, and picked up the bloody package to bury it. Wei

Feng found a shovel and accompanied him out of the yard. The performance was progressing toward its climax, where Zhou Yu asked Zhuge Liang to pledge his word to borrow the east wind or to be punished in accordance with military discipline. The singing from the young actor playing the part of Zhou Yu was as clear as a clarion, and that of an old man playing Zhuge Liang was sonorous, both reaching far into the depths of the mountains and fields. The two headed to the other side of the hill where there was a small grove with thick trees and long grass. Seeing people coming, birds fluttered away. Mr Mi chose a spot near a stone, dug out a small grave to put the bloody package in, covered it with loose dirt, and patted the mound gently with the shovel. Here lay his child who didn't have the chance to mature into human form. Would he be able to have another child? He didn't know. He crossed himself again and again. Tears dropped onto his fingers, forming shiny crystal stains.

Everyone stayed over at the Mengs' that night. May and Kiddo were happy to have so many guests staying when they returned from the performance, ignorant of what had happened. Kiddo was on top of the world and somersaulted onto the bed — a move he had just learned from the actors. May was silent as if she had something on her mind. She gave her bed to Mr Mi while she went to her parents' room to sleep on the bench. Wei Feng and Xueyan sat by the step leading to the kitchen, sharing one blanket. They felt they were again back on the road heading for Dragon Tail village from Shanxi province. They reminisced over the shabby diner in the deserted village and the shaggy horse pulling the rickety carriage. What mattered most to the two of them, especially to Xueyan, was that they were together, complete, content and colourful. Wei Feng whispered Mrs Li's question in Xueyan's ear, who blushed and complained: "You are bad!" and tapped the back of Wei Feng's hand. She then added, rather concerned: "What if we do, how can we raise it?"

"How can we not raise it? It's more about what parents it's going to have. If we are going to win the war, how can we not raise it?" said Wei Feng.

Xueyan didn't say a word for a long time. The moon was high in the sky, splashing its light on to an ink painting in black and white. The temperature dropped more, and the two sat closer to each other.

"I often feel life is fragile and might end anytime. It deserves to be continued," said Xueyan with a shudder.

Wei Feng held her closer to him: "You are exhausted. Get some sleep now," he urged her, although he himself couldn't sleep.

Over the years, Wei Feng had changed a lot and was rather indifferent about many things, but the bloody package of life tonight shocked him, reminding him of his paradoxical life. He was becoming convinced that the cause he believed in was not lovely at all because it ripped and tore, which required a heart of steel dead to all feelings, which he lacked. He was not satisfied with life in Yan'an, but he was disappointed at this life in Kunming. The only consolation was his lovely wife, but it was not enough for a man. Maybe, just maybe, he should have a son.

He pulled the blanket over Xueyan to cover her better and gazed at the full moon, as shiny as a disk.

Early the next morning, Wei Feng asked two villagers to come and help carry Mrs Mi in a bamboo chair back to Salt Falls. When Wei Feng and Xueyan passed the splashing waterfall, they felt that the small waterfall was somehow magnificent. They did not say that out loud. They just caught each other's eye and read what was on the other's mind.

Word of Mrs Mi's miscarriage spread throughout the village. The womenfolk were very surprised to hear that Jewish women could also bear children! What a blessing! A well-meaning neighbour even sent a pack of herbal medicine for protecting the foetus. Mr Mi thanked them sincerely for the kind gesture. He spread his hands, shrugged a little bit, and forced a bitter smile: "But the foetus has gone."

"You'll have more! China is a blessed place!" A villager's wife told him so.

Mrs Mi recovered gradually after being bedbound for about two weeks. One day, a handful of foreigners from the city visited her. The bleak chanting of psalms from the Hebrew Bible could be heard. What they chanted most was 'The Two Paths' from Matthew:

> Blessed is the man who doesn't walk in the counsel of the
>   wicked, nor stand in the way of sinners, nor sit in the seat of
>   those who mock;
> But his delight is in Yahweh's law. On his law he meditates day
>   and night.
> He will be like a tree planted by streams of water, that brings
>   forth its fruit in its season, whose leaves also do not wither.
>   Whatever he does shall prosper.
> The wicked are not so but are like the chaff which the wind
>   drives away.
> Therefore, the wicked shall not stand in judgment, nor sinners
>   in the congregation of the righteous.
> For Yahweh knows the way of the righteous, but the way of the
>   wicked shall perish.

It was their faith shared and cherished by the kind-hearted for thousands of years.

Leo, who had been terrified by Mrs Mi's illness and been worried with his drooping tail, was getting energetic again. He followed the visitors, offering his front paw or standing up on his hind legs. When he was shut outside the door if some visitors didn't like him, he would cock his ears and listen attentively at what was going on behind the closed door. Mrs Mi baked a big cake to apologise for the trouble that day and to thank Mrs Meng for her experienced treatment. They said that the well-educated were nice to them, and the less educated villagers offered them lots of sympathy as well. The villagers got to know more about the Jewish couple, hence the popular stories about the Jews and their hardships among those mountain villages in Yunnan.

THE TRIALS AND TRIBULATIONS OF
WANDERING JEWS

EVERYONE HAS THEIR HOMETOWN, where there is always a piece of land that people can depend on. The expression 'to leave one's hometown' means more specifically to leave the land one is attached to and the well where one gets one's drinking water. What a disastrous and painful experience! All of you, roaming around the country, hiding from the war, have somewhere you came from and a piece of land and a well you are attached to. You have a shared goal – to fight your way back to your hometown!

But for us Jews, we don't have anywhere to go back to. Not even an inch of land on earth has been spared for us to attach our hearts to. We have been sentenced to extreme punishment by the country we defined as our 'motherland' and have been rejected by most other countries.

In such a vast world, where can we find our country which we can call 'home'?

I am the son of a wealthy businessman and have received a quality education. I once worked in several German embassies in foreign countries. The three years working as the Consul at the Qingdao consulate in Shandong province, marked the last section of my life as a normal human being.

In 1933, I was recalled to Germany. My first wife, Ingrid, and I had known each other since our childhood and fell in love and got married when we grew up. We were happy back then. We were even happier to go back to our motherland when I received the order. Unexpectedly, what awaited me in my hometown was imprisonment!

They arrested me, sent me to prison, released me and did the same thing over again without interrogation. Growing hatred for my race permeated the alleys and streets. Once when Ingrid went to a bakery for some bread, the shop owner pushed her out of the door and locked the shop up behind her. We didn't dare to speak to anyone.

When violence against us spread, we managed to escape. We stayed in Spain and later Italy for a couple of years. When our relatives in Latin America invited us to join them there, we went. But we were denied entry since our visas were not valid. We tried to go to other countries on the continent, but none were willing to take us.

I sincerely hope no one will have to experience what we have suffered. All the doors were shut in front of us. We felt like we were being hung upside down. I remember a Chinese expression 'to be hung upside down' which describes people's suffering. But what have we done to deserve such a penalty?

Ingrid was stricken by a sudden illness. Complicated by her despair, her situation went from bad to worse. So far, I still don't know what was the cause of her illness. When we were cornered by despair, we were told that Shanghai didn't require any entry visa. Going to China was the last straw of hope for Jews. But poor Ingrid didn't survive her illness. She died on the deck of the ship heading for Shanghai. The last words she managed to say were "go to China".

The crew tossed her body into the sea. I watched, deprived of the right to say anything. She sank to sleep under the waves. If I were not restrained by my religion, I might have jumped after her.

Then I returned to Europe where no country offered to shelter the Jews against Hitler. Luckily, I had two days of sojourn in Italy, during which I managed to get a ticket for a voyage to Shanghai.

Go to China!

This trip to China was so different from the last one. The country I used to represent now labels me as an outlaw. I had to run away from my own motherland to China.

Relatively speaking, life on the ship was peaceful. I got a temporary break. Seeing the boundless sky and the vast ocean each day, I felt as if my burden had been washed off into the ocean by the waves. Thank the Lord for granting me a two-week break without running about and with meals served at regular intervals. I almost wished I could stay like this, floating on the ocean forever, not only for the break but for the hope to live on.

However, such peacefulness could break people after they had endured painful torture. Their nerves simply snapped hysterically, regardless of their sex. They cried, they yelled, they ran wild on the deck. Many would join such a violent outbreak. I hope you never have the chance to hear such a thing! In such grief, all I could do was to pray and to pray more.

Among the passengers, I noticed a woman who was in her 30s with a slim figure. Half of her hair was combed down to cover half of her forehead. Later I found out it was to cover up a hideous scar from a knife.

You may have guessed who the woman was. Yes, she is my wife.

She didn't cry or yell. What she did was to gaze at the sea quietly.

Stories about each other were told. Including hers. She lost her husband during the night of a Nazi massacre. When she threw herself upon her husband's dead body, the murderous executioner sliced at her forehead. Blood gushed out. But she survived because the murderer thought it was not necessary to finish off a bleeding body.

She took her son and fled. But her beloved five-year-old boy was killed in a stampede at a chaotic station. He didn't have the time to call his mother for help.

Without her only motivation to run, life lost its meaning for her. She sat quietly in the filthy passage in the inn like a statue. People tried to tell her how precious her ticket was for it could take a Jew to a place where they could survive. Several kind strangers of her race forced her to board the ship. Since then, she had been sitting on the deck, motionless like a statue.

I spent a lot of time leaning against the rail, watching the sea, and her as well. She was a Jewish statue of suffering. The wind blew up her hair, revealing that red scar from time to time. I watched her for a long while before I made up my mind to approach her slowly: "Cry out, please."

She didn't answer.

I sat down by her side and whispered: "Look at me! I'm so old but our race needs to live on, my daughter…"

Two days later, she leaned on my shoulder and sobbed uncontollably.

He was old. He couldn't walk straight. But his straight back would always bring him back in the right direction. He looked refreshed. I had been surviving on water for days until he brought me some soup. I rediscovered how soup was supposed to taste. He brought up meals for me. I found a smile hidden among the wrinkles on his face while he watched me nibbling at my food. We Jews still had the right to smile!

We helped and supported each other to take walks on the deck. We didn't talk much, but we reached a silent agreement that we would live on! For his wife, for my husband and for my son! And for tens of thousands of Jewish compatriots! We would demonstrate to the murderers they couldn't extinguish our race!

We must live on!

When our ship passed through the Suez Canal, the Jews in Egypt boarded our ship to express their sympathy and support. Our ancestors started their migration from this land. We had been leading such a vagrant life for about a thousand years, sending sparks of life over this planet. We wouldn't die out!

Our Egyptian compatriots boarded our ship and joined our prayers. They left us with small gifts such as flashlights and lighters. I got a handkerchief printed with an Egyptian pyramid.

Where was our pyramid, the symbol of our culture?

Each time when our ship reached a port, our hearts would be in suspense, terrified at the thought that some anti-Semitic forces might bring trouble to us. Each time he would stand by my side, holding my hand and whispering in my ear: "Don't be afraid, my daughter."

Day by day, we came closer to Shanghai. He told me what China was like. I had limited knowledge of the country except for simple facts like a vast territory, a long history and a big population. That country was undergoing a great war to protect its land and its people. We felt like we were dying sparrows in a chill which had finally found a place to perch.

The representative from the Shanghai Jewish Joint Distribution Committee said in his welcome speech: "Welcome to Shanghai. From today on, you are no longer Germans, Austrians, Czechs or Romanians. From today on, you are Jews. All the Jews spreading all over the world have prepared your homes for you."

From today on, we were nobody but Jews. I felt I had been stripped clean and hung on a tree — I still had a tree to lean on.

We stayed in different rooms prepared for single men and women and met each other at the synagogue.

His mastery of multiple languages gained him some regular translation tasks to do from the commercial departments stationed in the international settlement. One day, an oil company asked him whether he was willing to go to work in the rear area where there were many opportunities for temporary work.

The next day, he came to my room with a flower and told me he had been turning this over and over again in his mind for days and nights, for months, actually. If we went our separate ways, his heart would never settle in peace.

In the end, all his considerations and worries were summed up into one question: "Are you willing to go with me?"

Of course, not to go as his daughter.

There was a big age gap between us but there was no gap between our hearts. My hideously scarred face drew frequent gazes full of appreciation from him. I almost had an illusion that my late husband was looking at me through such a gaze.

I, Felizia Shine, take David Milmann to be my lawful wedded husband.

I took the flower from his hand.

Not long after we arrived in Kunming, the guy in charge of the oil company went back to the US, leaving many articles of daily use and Leo — our friend — with us. This is my small family granted by the Lord. Looking at the clear blue Yunnan sky, listening to the bubbling water at Salt Falls, drinking from the rolling waters of the Dragon river, living on the crops and vegetables we plant in front of our house, we won't die!

We won't die!

Along the bank of the small Mang river, a Jewish couple was walking slowly, following their ancestors' wandering footsteps.

CHAPTER SIX

PART I

In times of war, many, besides the Jews, led a nomadic life. When China was bearing the cross of war, many Chinese were driven by gunfire and had to push their memories of home into the far distance. But that distant memory, heavy but rich, lingered on and on, never fading or washed away by the rolling river of time. These people were lucky to have a hometown to look back to and forward to. They were lucky to have the opportunity to pray they would fight their way back.

When the Meng family left Beiping, they stayed in Kunming for four years. Now it was already the third year since their relocation in the countryside outside the Kunming city centre. Since Pearl Harbour, the war had changed. For people in Kunming, the most obvious change was the reduction of Japanese air raids over the city. In response to the requirements of the allied forces, China dispatched its expeditionary force to Burma to join the British Army for joint operations. But the British military's delay of the operation complicated by its lack of cooperation resulted in the loss of some major cities such as Lashio. Some of the expeditionary force retreated to India and part of it tried to return to China. They were ambushed and attacked by the enemy along the route. The casualties increased when the army forged through the jungle teaming with poisonous snakes and mosquitos. Of the 100,000 men that departed for Burma, only 40,000 returned.

The Japanese forces intensified their efforts toward western Yunnan, which turned it into a strategically important spot. In May, the Japanese army occupied several key cities such as Wanding, Mangshi, Longling and Tengchong. The Kunming townsfolk, who were just enjoying a breather from the Japanese bombing, were threatened overnight by the occupation of Kunming! There were even rumours about another relocation of the university. However, life was more normal than when there were more frequent, intense aerial bombardments. Later most of the schools at all levels returned to the city one after another. Few professors from the university were able to react quickly enough to find housing back in town. So most of them stayed on comfortably in the countryside.

At the end of the semester, before the summer vacation arrived, the appointments for the next academic year had become a popular concern for the faculty. One day, Li Lian brought back a letter addressed to Meng Fuzhi from the department. Written on a large envelope was Fuzhi's name in dancing Chinese characters the size of chestnuts. A single look at the handwriting made it clear the letter was from Bai Liwen.

"Long time no news, and now there is a letter. My guess is that he is probably coming back," said Fuzhi. He had guessed right. Bai Liwen said he would like to come back to teach since he had enjoyed enough quality opium and Yunnan ham. Fuzhi was well aware how inappropriate it would be to reemploy Bai Liwen after his one-year unauthorized absence from his position and what Jiang Fang's stance would be. He was concerned what would happen to Bai's expertise in his field of study without employment. He decided he would listen to some more opinions before he made up his mind. But Bai Liwen popped up a few days after Fuzhi got his letter.

Bai Liwen looked casual as usual as if he was dropping by to visit a neighbour in the village. The shoes he wore looked like his usual slippers. When he entered, he bowed deeply at Fuzhi. This was a rare ritual from Bai Liwen. After addressing him as "Professor Meng", he sat down. Old Jin put down the luggage he was carrying with a pole, took out two hams and put them on the table.

Bai Liwen began: "You are looking down on me as if you think I'm bribing you! I'm thinking that you, Meng Fuzhi, a truly nice guy, deserve such a treat."

Fuzhi laughed: "I know what you are thinking. How've you been for the last year?"

Bai Liwen answered: "Great! Bravo! The mother of the Wali village chief passed away and I drafted the epitaph. Look how gorgeous the diction is! No one else can write better!" He took out a scroll from his satchel and showed Fuzhi his "masterpiece". Fuzhi spread out the scroll and scanned it, exclaiming to himself how amazing it was that Bai could have managed such a beautiful piece of writing just for flamboyant praise.

"The chief admires you," Bai continued. "He has read several of your journal articles and copied your book 'Introduction to Chinese History'. Of course, he asked someone to copy it for him. Anyway, he has his insight. Comparatively speaking, he doesn't give me such treatment." He stopped in mid-sentence.

Fuzhi then asked: "So, what's your plan, my friend?"

"Now I need to find a place to stay," Bai Liwen answered straightforwardly. He took off his shoes and dusted the dirt off the soles against the chair leg one by one. "And to find a job."

Fuzhi said: "To find a job is a long-term plan. Now that most people have gone back to the city, are you willing to stay in the countryside?"

"It's hard to find housing in town. Besides, it is not as free as living in the countryside."

Bichu came out and told Fuzhi he was needed in the kitchen. When Fuzhi came to the kitchen, she whispered to him: "Huifen's house is not occupied. They have moved most of their belongings and have left me the keys. Is it OK to give the place to Mr Bai?" Fuzhi nodded and then went out to tell Bai the news.

Bai Liwen rejoiced at the good news. As he took the keys, he took away one ham from the table, declaring: "You don't have a big family. One ham will do." He then excused himself and left.

As for looking for a house in the city, Qian Mingjing was certainly among the first successful ones. He earnestly asked Huifen to return to the city with him. Huifen was hesitant. Since a divorce was not possible, she was thinking the best way forward might be to make the most of their relationship. Besides, living in the city, it would be more convenient for her to visit her friends in painting circles, so she eventually accepted Mingjing's earnest invitation. Bichu and Fuzhi felt relieved and were quietly happy for the couple, assuming the family might survive the crisis.

Bai Liwen moved into Qian's house and resumed his carefree lifestyle which involved both his smoking in bed and hanging the smoked ham on the wall. Since there was almost no need to run away from air raids, he resumed his old hobby of calligraphy. When he wrote a character, he would write down the different forms of the character as it evolved throughout its history from the ancient times of oracle bone inscriptions through the Han dynasty and Song dynasty until modern times. Sometimes when he was in high spirits, the ink on the brush would feel the same and went splashing around. When he was done, both the paper and his characters danced wildly.

It took painstaking efforts to tidy the paper and put them up neatly on the wall. Each time when he finished the process, he would tell Old Jin cheerfully and confidently that every character bore the history of its evolution. Old Jin would keep nodding and muttering: "They are alive! They are alive!" A couple of days later, the white walls were stained, but Bai Liwen felt as comfy and at ease as a breeze.

When Zhao Er carried water uphill for the Mengs, he told them what Bai Liwen had been doing. Bichu was appalled by the situation: "What should we do when we have to give the house back to the Qians?"

Fuzhi said: "Don't worry. Mingjing won't come back."

"But Huifen might," Bichu hesitated. "Mrs Li has got some sewing work to do from the city, but she is not quick with her needlework, so she wants to make some food to sell and has invited Huifen and me to join her and give her a helping hand. Huifen thinks it might be fun."

"What do you think?" asked Fuzhi.

"I think it might be fun, too," answered Bichu.

The next day, Fuzhi went to the city to preside over the final examinations for the two courses he taught. He took the exam papers back to the attic at the ancestral theatre to grade. Though history was an antiquity which was always out of date, many students chose his courses, claiming his lessons were true to the facts with his unique insights. They could see through layers of fog with the light shed by Professor Meng's class. It was one thing to be enthusiastic about selecting his course but their test results didn't usually justify it. It was no exception for the students who chose this optional course this year.

In the afternoon, Qin Xunheng sent a note to Fuzhi, inviting him to dinner with them that evening. After finishing the grading, he went to Qin's house, which had rooms on two levels. The rooms in the front yard were the offices for Minglun University, and the Qin couple lived in the upstairs rooms in the back yard. When Fuzhi entered the back yard, Xie Fangli, Qin's wife, was ironing the clean laundry in the passage by the railing upstairs. Wearing ironed clothes was the only luxury Qin Xunheng allowed himself.

"Professor Meng, welcome! Please come upstairs," greeted Xie Fangli.

Xunheng, who was busy with documents, got up and walked a couple of steps to welcome Fuzhi. After inviting Fuzhi to sit down, he said: "The situation in west Yunnan is not promising. If not for the isolation of the Nujiang river and Gauri Gvong mountain, we would be in big trouble. Our army is very brave, but it has so many problems." He handed Fuzhi a document about the bombing of Baoshan and the casualties, injuries and losses.

Xunheng smiled bitterly: "The Ministry of Education has been suggesting we should get ready for another relocation, although it is a long-term plan."

Fuzhi said: "What's the point of another relocation? If Yunnan is lost, so is the future of China."

They then talked more about the war and the university.

Xie Fangli brought tea to them: "We have a thermal bottle with hot water and tea, but I know you won't make tea for our guest." Fuzhi stood up and thanked Fangli for the tea. Xunheng teased his wife: "Fangli has telescopic eyes which can see through walls." Then he turned to Fuzhi: "We do have an urgent matter. The Ministry of Education requires all colleges and universities to continue to offer a class on morality and to present a detailed report at the end of each term. We have held such a course for several terms in a row, but none of the teachers could stay for one more term. Someone suggested that I ask you to try the class. But I wanted to ask you first since the class might end up being a case of 'good intentions never working out'." He cast an enquiring look at Fuzhi.

Fuzhi didn't answer immediately. He thought for a while before saying: "I did a quick calculation. We have had four teachers for the course already. It's not that the teachers didn't teach well. It's more because of the students' assumption that this course is a tool for the central government to exercise restraint over their thinking. Whoever teaches the course, I think the result will be the same. Anyway, I may give it a try. Someone has to teach the course. It's no more than a competition to see who is better at keeping calm. However chaotic the students are, I will teach the way I plan to."

Xunheng smiled: "No one can beat you at keeping calm!"

Fuzhi added: "I don't think I can manage 'The Three People's Principles'."

Xunheng explained: "You may include different aspects and make it an interesting course like your other courses."

"I just hope I won't be jeered out of the classroom," responded Fuzhi. Then the morality class was settled. Fuzhi mentioned Bai Liwen's case and the two agreed that discipline was discipline, and no one should be exempt because the academic freedom the university promoted didn't mean that privilege took precedence over discipline.

It was getting dark and Xie Fangli urged Fuzhi to stay for dinner. Cooking was convenient since the office had a kitchen.

During the meal, Fangli talked about the ways professors' wives tried to make ends meet. Some wanted to make snacks and others won contracts to make silk banners (as gifts or awards). These wives were all well educated, but now they had to rely on their handicraft skills to help cover the daily expenses.

Fuzhi said: "When the talented poetess Zhuo Wenjun opened a wine shop to sell wine, she was helping one person out, the true love of her life, her husband, Sima Xiangru. Now all the activities from our respectful ladies are indirectly helping us with the nation's education during such a national crisis. Bichu and Mrs Li are also thinking of doing something."

"I'm sure a woman as capable as Mrs Meng has come up with some wonderful ideas," said Xie Fangli.

Fuzhi gave a soft sigh: "Her health is too poor. I have told her not to join."

Some days later, there was not much disagreement at the appointments committee. Everyone agreed with Jiang's proposal not to renew Bai Liwen's appointment. Jiang Fang said at the meeting: "I personally have no objection to Bai Liwen. We can still drink three cups in a row and share a journey into never-never land. But no one should disrespect students and classes. How can we face the students in class without a sense of responsibility and respect for discipline?"

Bai Liwen sighed repeatedly at the news: "No one really knows the value of these antique bends and curves! Do you really think that I was after your bowl of red rice wriggling with worms?"

Fuzhi paid Bai a visit when the notice was made official. Bai Liwen was doing his calligraphy when Fuzhi arrived. Dipping a giant brush into a broken bowl filled with ink, he finished one piece of work with his fluent dance-like brush movements. After staring at his work with genuine admiration, he enthused over and over again, completely unaware of Fuzhi's arrival. He didn't notice Fuzhi until he decided to hang his work up on the wall. Fuzhi held one upper corner of the paper to help him hang it up. It was a paragraph about the character '鱼' (fish) from *Shuowen Jiezi* (literally *'Explaining Graphs and Analysing Characters'*), an ancient Chinese dictionary compiled in the Han dynasty (206 BC–220 AD): "Fish, an aquatic animal. A pictographic character. The tail of a fish is like the tail of a swallow."

Fuzhi's heart missed a beat at the various forms of the lively and lovely character '鱼'. He blurted out: "Liwen, we have been colleagues for years and I know how special your expertise is. Now you know about the committee's decision, do you mind if I let you know what's on my mind?"

Bai Liwen stared silently at Fuzhi.

"I'm thinking maybe it's time for you to take a decision to quit opium. I know how painful it is for ordinary people to quit, but you are no ordinary person and I'm confident you can do it. If you quit taking the drug, then you won't ignore rules and discipline and there would be no problem renewing your appointment." Fuzhi's words were soaked with sincerity, but Bai Liwen

298

was still silent. Instead, he picked up his ragged brush and wrote down several lines on a new piece of paper:

Bends, curves and strokes,
An old odd fish.
Rosy clouds roll out of the petals,
What a fantastic scene to behold.
Here lies the truth,
There lies my freedom.

He paused and stared at the broken bowl as if conceiving the next lines. Fuzhi took his brush and wrote two more lines:

If I quit,
I'd be me no more.

The two looked at each other in silence. Fuzhi wrote down an address of a teacher's school in a city in Sichuan province and said: "This school has been asking me to recommend a teacher. The pay is very generous. If you like, you may go there to have a look and stay for a while." Bai Liwen didn't thank Fuzhi, but bowed to him, who bowed back and left.

Bai Liwen remained seated on the low couch for a long time. When Old Jin handed him the pipe, he shook his hand. A moment later, he paced around the room, howling: "Where is the thing? Where is my thing?" He again lay down on his bed and resumed the enjoyment of his 'freedom'. A couple of days later, he left Dragon Tail village and loafed around in Kunming for a while before disappearing completely, refusing to accept employment from a local university or to go to the city in Sichuan province recommended by Fuzhi.

Bai Liwen's departure attracted much less attention than the activities of the professors' wives such as Bichu, Huifen and Shizhen did, mostly because of the limited knowledge about his exceptional expertise in ancient scripts. Not far from Dragon Tail village several institutes such as the plant institute were relocated. Bichu and her team had chosen the spot to open a stand to sell some northern food like steamed buns. Their plan was to make one round of products in the morning to sell at noon. Bichu was responsible for the planning and they made the buns in Huifen's house. Huifen didn't enjoy her stay in town and was quite interested in helping them with the sales. Since Mingjing was not back, the whole house could be used for production. Besides, Shizhen was skilled in all the procedures of making buns from kneading and leavening to making the stuffing, rolling out the wrappings and the wrapping. Shizhen was passionate, claiming it was a virtuous deed both for her and for the others.

When the stand opened for business, Fuzhi was not home. Bichu rose earlier than usual, tucked the sound-asleep May and Kiddo in, told Qinghuan what to do and then left for Huifen's. Walking down the trail paved with flagstones, Bichu breathed in the chilly refreshing air. The Lady Banks roses and azaleas along the way brushed the edges of her clothes. She felt as if she were on a mission for something big. Then it dawned on her that her elder sisters Suchu and Jiangchu might think differently. Dad was different. He would back me up, saying his youngest daughter was so brave. When she arrived, she found Shizhen was already there. All the ingredients had been prepared the day before, so they began their operation with tacit understanding and neat organisation. In less than two hours, they had finished a steamer of flavoured *baozi*, steamed buns with minced meat and chopped spring onion stuffing, a steamer of steamed buns with sweet ground sesame stuffing, and *mantou* (steamed buns with no stuffing) and salty spicy steamrolls. Everyone who came to fetch water from the well was amazed by the lovely smells, which attracted many children nosing around.

Zhao Er used his cart to help carry the loads to a spot near the institutes and set up the stand under a big tree. The three ladies each picked a rock to sit on, joking with one another that no one would have thought the day would come when they would become peddlers. Huifen made her point that peddling was work and earning a living on it was also worthy. Her words didn't exactly match her deeds when she refused to take the money as people came to buy the buns. She was too embarrassed. Fortunately, Shizhen was also skilled at selling and she took charge of everything at the stand. Around 10 o'clock when the institutes took their morning recess, many came to the stand upon seeing the hot fresh food. Most of the items went during just one recess. Shizhen and Huifen took turns to push the empty cart back to the village. The buns they had left over were enough to provide lunch for the three families that day.

After a few days, people in the vicinity all knew that there was a 'ladies' stand' selling delicate and delicious buns, which were sold out almost every day. Although Bichu was tired, she didn't feel any discomfort. She laughed when she told Fuzhi that nothing in the world was difficult when one put one's mind to it. She paused and muttered: "If this counts as something difficult, it would be a real joke."

Fuzhi's heart ached at the words. He brushed a strand of hair stuck to her cheek behind her ear and said: "It's not that what you are doing is difficult.

What's more difficult and requires courage is to set aside the class stereotype and embarrassment, and feel comfortable and confident when doing it."

The opposition from Earl was beyond Bichu's expectation, though. At the very beginning when Bichu was just planning things, Earl didn't say anything. So, it took Bichu rather by surprise when she told her grimly when she came back home that Saturday: "Mum, I don't want you to sell anything at a stand. Especially not one near our institute."

Bichu, who was busy cooking in the kitchen, hurried to dry her hands and came to her: "What has happened? Has anyone said anything?"

Earl answered from her room: "Just banal stuff like life is not easy and the ladies are not easy. Nothing particular. I was telling you my opinion. You can barely manage your poor health. Now you pitch in like a kid into a fun game. How much can you make from such a stand?"

"It was Mrs Li who came up with the idea. Huifen and I are just helping. I don't know how much we can make. We have to wait and see once we have finished this round." Bichu felt somewhat offended at Earl's reaction. She entered Earl's room: "May just cleaned up your room, including your crucifix."

Earl chucked the book onto her bed and snapped: "May! May! It's always May! She's perfect! Is she behind this meaningless plan?"

Bichu didn't understand why Earl was so angry, but she still tried to explain patiently: "When your father is at home this evening, we'll talk it over again. Mrs Li needs more help than we do."

Earl retorted impatiently: "Mum, you just love to poke your nose into other people's business." She covered her face up with her book and refused to talk any more.

When Fuzhi arrived home in the evening, the couple discussed Earl's reaction. Knowing that their eldest daughter was not the affected kind, they agreed that her words did make some sense. During dinner, Fuzhi encouraged Earl to elaborate on her opinions, but Earl expressed indifference: "I don't care." And then she resumed her regular silence. May and Kiddo just buried their faces quietly in a plate of stir-fried rice noodles, trying their best not to irritate their elder sister and only exchanging looks from time to time with each other. The harmonious atmosphere at the Mengs' dinner table was interrupted by a sudden frost that night. Luckily, the frost didn't stay long and passed the next day.

The most embarrassing was Mrs Li, who was passionate about all sorts of work. When she was selling things, she often threw in a free interpretation of the customer's good and bad luck, which annoyed many. After Earl raised her opposition, the stand was moved out of the vicinity of the institutes, but the customers were still the same group of people from those offices. Once Mrs Li stopped Earl who was walking with a couple of colleagues. Earl taunted her: "So, is Mrs Li trying to sell me something?"

Shizhen waved her hand: "No! No!" Pointing at one of Earl's colleagues, she said his face was enveloped with an unholy aura and he'd better stay at home for three days. The man chortled and ignored Shizhen's advice, coming and going as usual. On the third day, he paid a special visit to the stand. Shizhen said: "I know you are complacent, thinking I was wrong. What you don't know is that I have been trying to soften the blow for you!"

Another time when a female staff member, a gorgeous girl in her printed floral cotton *qipao* with two long braids, passed the stand, Shizhen gawped at the girl. Before she could make any unwelcome prediction, Bichu whispered to Shizhen: "Mrs Li, we only sell buns and should stay out of other people's business." Shizhen ignored Bichu and followed the girl all the way down to the bank of the Dragon river. Seeing the girl going downhill, she turned back and whispered in Bichu's ear: "I saw something going down to the river. Now that girl is safe." Surprisingly, Earl didn't say anything about Shizhen and her deeds.

The three had overcome all the operational difficulties in making food. Huifen was a fast learner, claiming that learning to make buns was much easier than learning to paint. She also volunteered to bake some Shanghai snacks with a pan over the stove but never got it right. The sweet rice pudding Bichu made with sticky rice was quite popular.

A month passed and the three did make some profits. Bichu divided the money into four portions. She gave Mrs Li two and kept one each for her and Huifen because Mrs Li did most of the hard work and because her family was in greater need.

They also went to the village fair. Mixed up among rows of vendors, the stand and the three women loomed out of the steam from the food. The very first time, the villagers all came to look but were reproached by Zhao Er's wife: "What are you looking at? If you look, you have to buy! If you don't buy, get lost!"

Bichu hastened to say: "It's alright to look. You have to look before you know what it is." Huifen welcomed everyone in her fluent Yunnan dialect while Shizhen stuffed buns into kids' arms. It was an affectionate scene.

That day, Bichu and Shizhen went to the fair. The sales at the fair were far less than those near the institutes. It was almost noon, but they still had some buns left. Many vendors in the grove had left. Along the bank came a woman. She looked peaceful and elegant among the crowds. As she approached the bun stand, she called out with a sweet smile: "Aunt Bichu, Mrs Li, I'm here to help."

Shizhen said: "The school bag you are carrying has your teaching materials for your French class and books for a literature class. These greasy hands of ours can manage." Never a mean person, Shizhen spoke with good intentions. However, it sounded like sarcasm to Xueyan, who stopped on the spot, looking at Bichu.

Bichu said: "Xueyan should help, but you have walked such a long distance from the city. Now sit down and take a break before you help." She pulled up a stool for Xueyan to sit on. Xueyan didn't take the stool. Instead, she hung her bag on the branch of a tree and picked up a broom to sweep up the litter in front of the stand.

Bichu said: "We don't need three to take care of the sales, so Huifen didn't come today. You take a break first." Looking at Xueyan's almost transparent face, Bichu thought Xueyan had lost some weight and was even skinnier. People came to buy things while they talked. Soon, when not much was left, they decided to wrap things up for the day. The three pushed the cart along the 'main street', heading for Huifen's yard. Huifen met them at the gate, teasing: "I'm just absent for one day, and you have found my replacement." Bichu told Shizhen to take the rest of the food home while she talked to Huifen and Xueyan by the well.

"You are all amazing," said Xueyan, who was overcome by a sudden dizziness before she could finish her sentence. She first leaned against Bichu, but then passed out and fell to the ground. Bichu and Huifen were shocked. The two of them carried her in and laid her on a bed. At first, they unbuttoned her *qipao* and rubbed her chest, thinking Xueyan might be suffering from heat stroke, but it dawned on them both that heat stroke was rare in such a mild climate as Kunming. Huifen rushed off to fetch a doctor. Bichu held Xueyan's hand. How cold her hand was, and how weak her pulse felt. She kept calling her name: "Xueyan, Xueyan, can you hear me? Xueyan, wake up!" Tears streamed down her cheeks and onto Xueyan's face, which woke her up.

She opened her eyes and managed a faint smile: "What's wrong with me, Aunt Bichu?"

"Don't move! I'll fetch you some water." Bichu went to find a glass. Xueyan tried to sit up, but the moment she lifted her head, she plummeted back down onto the pillow.

"Don't move! Don't you move!" Bichu hurried to get a spoon. Huifen had already returned, dragging a herbalist behind her. When she saw Xueyan had come round, she then let out the breath she had been holding. The herbalist felt Xueyan's pulse, studied it for a while, stood up and bowed in the direction of the south in keeping with their professional tradition to salute the Holy Spirit in charge of medicine for an important diagnosis before saying solemnly to Bichu: "She is pregnant."

All three were overjoyed, albeit, to differing degrees. The herbalist prescribed two herbs which would be good to steady the embryo and instructed them not to tire the new mother out. He left once he had been paid.

"What is more sacred than a pregnant woman? It's great to nurture a life and to deliver it to the world! What's more, this is the extension of my life and the life of my beloved husband. I now have a child and my child will have their child. This way I won't die!" Thinking of this, Xueyan touched her belly and found nothing unusual.

Bichu smiled: "You can't feel it right now. Soon you will feel it all the time, anytime, and you just won't be able to get away from such a feeling anymore."

"Will it be scary? I am a bit afraid," said Xueyan, managing to sit up slowly.

Bichu said: "Different people have different reactions, but even morning sickness is nothing compared with the joy."

Huifen was happy for Xueyan, but such happiness brought a feeling of emptiness in her heart. She seemed to have run out of hope of becoming a mother. When he had belonged to her only, she didn't have a child; now he was gone, how could she have one? As her heart tossed and turned, she busied herself in the living room to make two milk drinks with condensed milk and brought them to Xueyan and Bichu. Xueyan took it gratefully and drank it slowly. Bichu took the glass and gave it back to Huifen: "You need to take care of yourself, too." Her tone was full of concern. When marriage became a brutal burden, it consumed more than any internal injury. Huifen shook her head gently.

Xueyan was eager to go home. Bichu and Huifen wanted to walk her back, but she declined their offers, claiming she was aware of her situation. Bichu and Huifen didn't return until they had walked her all the way to the embankment of the Mang river.

Xueyan walked slowly and carefully with each step. She now had two lives in her body. How amazing it was! But her situation would probably affect her teaching. Her popularity among her students was beyond everyone's expectation. Her smart teaching methods made up for her lack of systematic education. Besides textbooks, she wrote short stories in French and sketches for some classic works. Her students loved to listen to these stories. Their French improved quickly, especially their spoken French. They were fluent in conversation. Back then, foreign language teaching focused more on reading and writing, resulting in poor listening and speaking skills. Xueyan wanted to change that. She felt lost at the thought of teaching. If the child had arrived a couple of years later, her students would have graduated. But now she had to stop teaching for several months, at least. But this was what Feng wanted. This was his child. It belonged to him. She belonged to him. He would never agree it had arrived at the wrong time.

As her thoughts raced, she realised she had already reached Salt Falls. Like every other time before she entered the village, she stood in front of the waterfall, feeling the splashes of water on her skin and then walked uphill. Wei Feng was already waiting for her at the gate. He held her in his arms and the two crossed the threshold. Xueyan raised her head to look at Feng, her eyes dancing with love, and cooed: "Feng, now there are three of us coming home."

PART II

K unming was much livelier and busier than in previous years. The main street, Justice avenue, was teeming with pedestrians, Chinese and foreigners, most of the latter were from the American air force in uniforms with giant Chinese characters on their backs reading: 'These foreigners are here to help the Chinese. Military and civilians, please do no harm'. They often drove around in jeeps, saying "hello!" along the way. Some local passers-by would give them thumbs up and shout "Well done", some might just grunt "cocky". Near Xiaodong street, fancy shops selling clothing and jewellery, mixed with bars and restaurants, brought a dazzling look to the street. Among all the hubbub, the opening of a new cinema transformed the life of the Kunming city folk.

Kunming's old cinemas were quite shabby. When a foreign, which specifically meant 'American', movie was on, an interpreter would sit among the audience and yell out his interpretation. All the heroes were named John, and heroines Mary. If there was a person who just opened the door in the movie, he would interpret it as "he opened the door"; if people in the movie cried or laughed, he would interpret "he laughed" or "he cried".

Once some college students in the audience couldn't help offer more faithful and interesting interpretations, but they ended up being stopped and threatened not to stick their noses into other people's business by interpreters outside the cinema. The combination of exotic scenes from the movies and the lyrical local Yunnan dialect was a rare sight offered by the old Kunming.

The newly opened cinema, Sound of Yunnan, was different. Subtitles were a much more satisfactory replacement for the 'simultaneous interpretation'. It seemed to have good ties to Hollywood because it was always able to obtain the latest movies, offering Kunming people the opportunity to keep up with the latest trends. It had a matinee showing with a 50% discount off the regular price every Sunday morning. Movie fans, such as May, among the students, were frequent customers for these showings.

May had been absent from school for two years. At this time, she and Kiddo resumed schooling when their school moved back into town. They stayed in the attic at the theatre in the ancestral temple near the wintersweet grove during weekdays. The house they used to stay in, which was destroyed during an air raid, remained in ruins. Dead leaves over the years had filled half of the crater created by the bomb in front of the house. They stood on the edge of it when they returned to town, trying to bring something back. But all they encountered was surging layers of pain when they witnessed the destruction of their home by the enemy and how helpless they had been when they realised they couldn't fight but only escape and hide. The old gardener who tended the garden, Old Shen, had passed away, replaced by a deaf-mute. Pointing at his mouth and ears, he kept smiling at them. They failed to communicate to him that this pile of debris used to be their home.

They stayed in the attic at the theatre like they did after the bombing and before their move to the countryside. The low space was now getting too cramped for May and Kiddo. A piece of old batik cloth cut off a corner in the room, big enough to set up a single bed for May, who was relieved at the limited amount of cloth she needed for herself, while Kiddo took over Wei's bed on kerosene crates. Now, they all had shelter.

In her corner, May would play her *xiao*, a Chinese vertical end-blown flute, which she began to learn when she came back from the opera performance 'The Distinguished Gathering of Heroes' staged a long time ago. Though it might have been forgotten by many, it was etched indelibly on May's heart. Like the fireflies over the brook behind Square Teakettle, which illuminated her childhood, the blinding gas lamps hung in front of the curtains on the stage built for the performance was a catalyst for the growth in various forms of her fear of death, her struggle against disease and her other rich experiences of life. She was on the threshold of the full bloom of youth.

The intricate and expressive opera performances had faded for May. Her memory only focused on one person, and that was Zhou Yu, the image of Zhou Yu on the stage with the fluttering pheasant tail feather on his helmet and the colourful banners attached to his armour. His agile movements carried the charm of a beautiful young man full of vitality. As young as he was, he commanded thousands of troops and even cornered Zhuge Liang, the Prime Minister of the State of Shu Han, the legendary mastermind, to record a solemn pledge. May could have gone to her parents for all the questions involving the Three Kingdoms but, instead, she went on sneaky visits to the institute of liberal arts in search of records of Zhou Yu from various sources. Old Wei the librarian was puzzled by what May was doing and asked: "Miss Meng, are you going to write a research paper or what?"

May was puzzled, too, by the way Old Wei addressed her: "Why 'Miss Meng' now? Didn't you always address me as 'Meng Lingji'?"

Old Wei answered: "You have grown out of that." He helped May locate the chapter about Zhou Yu in the book entitled *History of the Three Kingdoms*, which May felt was rather boring to read except for the reference to the fact that Zhou Yu was a musician, hence the saying "if you play your tune wrong, Zhou Yu will cast a glance to remind you". With that knowledge, May played her flute more often in the yard, wishfully thinking Zhou Yu would travel from two thousand years ago to hear her play. She kept such an expectation all to herself, not revealing a little bit even to her mother. Seeing that May was keen on the flute, Bichu would sometimes give May some tips. Everyone in the family agreed that May was getting better with the flute day by day. Sometimes, she would deliberately play the tune wrong but, of course, Zhou Yu never showed up to cast her a glance. The sound of the flute from Baotaishan now echoed in the wintersweet grove, drawing down the light from the moon and the stars, touching the attic with a pale beam of light.

The new school May and Kiddo attended back in town was called China Experimental Middle School, which was attached to the Minglun University teachers' college. It was planning to cut down the primary and secondary education from 12 years to 10. May went to the senior high while Kiddo, no longer called 'Kiddo' but his formal given name 'Heji', went to junior high. When the professors dropped their children at school, they would joke: "We are delivering your experimental subjects."

As most of the schools could now hold regular classes without having to improvise graveyards as their classrooms, China Experimental Middle School took a romantic detour. It didn't have regular classrooms. Instead, they would commandeer an unoccupied classroom in the university or from another middle school and use it for one or two periods. Sometimes when the weather was fine, they would hang up a blackboard on the trunk of a giant tree and hold a class in the shade. It was an enormous bonus when there was a breeze. When it drizzled, they would carry those big red waxed paper umbrellas which looked like the mushrooms that suddenly shoot up when it rains. The eager young faces under the umbrellas were all attentive. The raindrops pattering on top of the umbrellas were the best accompaniment for the class.

Their teachers were anything but ordinary. Several university professors were employed to deal with these experimental subjects. May's teacher of geometry and algebra was Professor Liang Mingshi's student, but Professor Liang himself would sometimes cover several lessons, which greatly intrigued the whole class. People joked that if no mathematicians would grow out of this class, it would not do justice to Professor Liang's efforts. But Professor Liang didn't agree, claiming the fewer mathematicians or philosophers, the better, although for other fields of study, the more great minds, the better. When May forwarded Liang's words to her father, Fuzhi chuckled: "The more one is into maths or philosophy, the less one knows. Few can survive such a paradox."

During a brainstorming session to resolve a geometry problem, what May came up with amazed Liang Mingshi: "Aiya! Meng Lingji! You have such a wild brain!" Later he repeated the conclusion to Fuzhi: "Your May has a wild brain! I like it!"

Fuzhi smiled: "Fortunately, she listens and obeys life's rules."

Professor Liang's eyes widened and he mused for a moment: "It wouldn't be good if she did the opposite."

Yan Bulai, who used to teach May Chinese in Kunjing Middle School, was a graduate student now at the Liberal Arts Institute and specialised in studying the 'ci' form of poetry in the Song dynasty. He came to teach May's class as a part-time job. The class recited hundreds of ci-form poems, excluding the traditional poems during his teaching. Once when he recited a ci-form poem from the famed Song poet Yan Jidao entitled: '*Iridescent Sleeves in the Tune of Zhegutian*', he broke down in tears. His students didn't share the same emotional turbulence, though. It reminded them of no more than Zhou Yu or some movie star. All the experimental subjects, absorbing all kinds of rain and sunshine, grew with great vitality and a promising future.

May's best friend at school was Li Zhiwei, who was in May's class, too. Being neighbours, they always went to and from school together. Besides, the two friends shared the same experience shrouded by a layer of loose red earth when they came close to death during the explosion of a bomb on the riverbank. No one could easily forget that nightmare. Mrs Li, Zhiwei's mother, had lacked ardent religious passion for the last couple of years, and her mind had become dulled ever since. Zhiwei had to take over most of the family housework, which occupied most of her out-of-school time and thus affected her study tremendously. She seldom complained, though. At most she would say a few words to May on their way to school.

One day Zhiwei didn't turn up for school. The following day when she did, she told May her mother had been visited by some sort of holy spirit the day before and that she had to stay at home. She said she was glad those holy spirits had paid far fewer visits in these last few years, or she would have long since been consumed by it. May said maybe they should study what her mother's religion was since she overheard the adults labelling religion as some kind of inner sustenance and supplement to their spirit before they were consumed by it and it became a burden. Zhiwei said she had become a firm atheist since witnessing what effect a mixed-up religion had had on her mother. Instead of holiness and beauty, it had stirred up ignorance and blind obedience. As Zhiwei talked, she glanced left and right, afraid of offending any passing holy spirits. Proud of their fine insight, the two burst into laughter while they chatted.

The happiest thing for May was to listen to records. She and Kiddo, who preferred being addressed by his formal given name Heji, would go to Uncle Xiao Cheng's place to listen. Wuyin and Wei sometimes joined them, too. Xiao Cheng's mini collections had grown a little bit bigger than they were two years ago. Occasionally, Professor Xia Zhengsi would bring some records to share with them all. When May first listened to the prelude to *La Traviata*, she felt a ball of fire was expanding and about to burst out of her chest. The melodious voice enriched her spirit, making her feel as if she was wrapped in a fresh spring. What a peculiar experience! Through the songs, she felt she saw Zhou Yu again. If anyone had got hold of her association, they might have come up with a fancy idea for a voluminous research paper on how music crossed borders and directly appealed to the mind.

Schools are never paradises on earth but connected to the rest of the world. Many high school students had already participated in society and club activities on the university campus due to their teachers' influence. Some of their teachers were activists from different societies. Yan Bulai, for example, was a member of the Teachers of the Masses Society. Apart from being concerned with words and poetry, he was very concerned with society. One day at his Chinese class, he stormed into the classroom, rather annoyed, and yelled: "My dear students, can you guess what has happened? Before Hong Kong was taken over, a plane had been organised to evacuate the local culturati, but they didn't make it. They couldn't because the seats on that plane were saved for those Pekinese pet dogs! Can you imagine leaving the cultural talent under the iron hooves of the enemy to give the dogs a chance to live? Can we put up with such nonsense?" He pounded on the desk, his hair standing on end. You could tell with one glance that he was enraged. "Do you know who did such a hideous thing? Liu Kezhen did!" he added furiously.

May and her classmates were vaguely aware that Liu Kezhen was the Minister of Finance and came from one of the most influential clans in Chongqing. They hadn't cared much about what he did, but now his lot had given their dogs priority over the country's talent! What had they been thinking?

Yan Bulai gave more details, saying the person behind such a brainless action was the second daughter of Liu Kezhen. "The rich had hogged all the means of transportation out of Hong Kong and they could do whatever they liked. What a corrupt country we have!"

Several students asked in unison: "What will happen to those who have to stay? Will they die?"

"I do hope they won't!" Yan Bulai pounded on the desk again.

The same afternoon, many students took part in a joint demonstration organised by the schools in Kunming. Almost every student in May's class participated. They shouted slogans all the way: "Down with Liu Kezhen who transported his dogs by plane!" "Corruption is ruining the country!" "Do away with privilege!" The crowd engaged in conversation when they were not shouting slogans. Some said that although Liu Kezhen was monstrous, the Japanese were even more monstrous than him. Others retorted that Liu was ruining his own country and trampling on his compatriots, which made him all the more monstrous.

May looked up and saw the scudding patches of white clouds. The Meng family had always been kind to all kinds of creatures in the belief that life was precious. But when these dogs snatched away the opportunity to live from the country's talented people, they had fallen into the category of the corrupt. Her thoughts drifted to the beggars she saw on the street, Qinghuan who suffered all sorts of unfair treatment, and Yin Dashi. Would Yin Dashi let her dogs get on the plane if she were faced with a similar situation? May shook her head hard and tried to shake off such an idea before concluding: it was hard to say. When one's position offered one the freedom to do things, one was morally vulnerable. It took May years to understand that sentence, though.

"Down with Liu Kezhen who transported his dogs by plane!" "No corruption!" "No profiteering!" "Do away with privilege!" Yan Bulai trotted back and forth along the procession, his dark suntanned face darkening with the running. He said that profiteers always worked with the privileged who were in power. The plot to resell grain was such a case. The demonstrators started around the grand west city gate, taking the Green lake all the way to Justice avenue, attracting the city folks who paused whatever they were doing and stared. Some were amazed: "It's obvious that the students are no longer starving. What are they up to now?" Others adopted an attitude of mild approval: "The students are great. They still have their conscience!"

That was the first student demonstration in Kunming. As time went by, more and more such demonstrations were held in due course. People had mixed views about the demonstrations. Some understood better. Others opposed more.

It looked as though the demonstration had sailed through without meeting any interference. The participants had no idea that at the same time as they were engaged in their procession, President Qin, Professor Xiao Cheng and a president from a local university were sitting in the provincial government's reception room, engaged in a meeting with the head of the provincial government.

The atmosphere became more intense when an official from the provincial government insisted on sending armed police to maintain order, saying the force was already waiting for orders to proceed. That was the reason why Qin Xunheng and others rushed to the government offices when they were informed of the student demonstration. Nothing worried them more than the prospect of conflicts between the students and the government's armed forces. Qin explained that it was a way for the students to demonstrate their patriotism, although the target might not be the most appropriate, and that persuasion should be tried before any conflict took place.

The director of the office said sternly: "We can't encourage such behaviour. Students should focus on their studies."

Xiao Cheng responded: "The students' major task is, of course, to study, but it is also appropriate for them to care about national affairs."

A soldier cried "attention", announcing outside the meeting room the arrival of Governor Yin, who came in before the soldier's cry had died out. He was wearing a long gown made of the finest Tibetan grey serge and a short dark-blue vest with round floral patterns over the gown. The outfit made him look more like a scholar than a military commander. Besides, he always had great respect for professors such as Qin Xunheng.

He greeted those present one by one and listened to the discussion before offering his opinion: "This is not something trivial, but we should minimise its impact. Armed police internvention would only make things worse. How about letting the students finish their demonstration? They will calm down once they have made their point."

President Qin's heart, which had been hanging in mid-air, finally dropped back to his chest upon hearing those words. He readily supported the proposal. Then Governor Yin dismissed the armed police and talked more with his guests before excusing himself. President Qin left with Xiao Cheng in the same car. When they passed a sidestreet, they saw the demonstrating students walking along the main street, shouting their slogans and carrying banners with the same words. Qin Xunheng thought, such a demonstration would never have happened if you had not come up with the idea of transporting your dogs by plane! He sighed. As the procession moved on, the car drove onto the main street to take Xiao Cheng back to the theatre first. When the two bade goodbye to each other, they exchanged looks of concern in the knowledge that they were now heading into an eventful era.

As the procession reached the minor east city gate, it began to drizzle enough to soak through people's clothing. The lines began to fray around the edges. Seeing what they were heading into, the college student who was leading the procession asked everyone to sing along with him. Lyrics like "we have reached the critical moment of life and death", "the flags are fluttering, the horses are neighing. Men, old and young, are serving their country" vibrated in the damp air, reaching into their hearts and invigorating them all. The rain turned out to be a bonus for the demonstration. They walked on for a while and dispersed when the rain stopped, going this way and that, heading for the campus or home along the muddy streets.

Some female students stopped at the corner of Ancestral Temple street to buy roasted peanuts in a small store, which had become very popular among students in Kunming for its especially crispy roasted peanuts. May walked past the store without giving it a second glance. She was saving every penny for movies. Sometimes she would skip lunch to save enough money for a movie ticket, which meant Kiddo needed to do her a favour and keep it a secret. She became aware of someone approaching her. Before she could turn around, someone patted her on the shoulder and stuffed a pack of roasted peanuts into her hands.

"Cousin Wei!" May was delighted to see Wei. "I knew it must be you!" She took the pack of peanuts and began gorging herself on the big red-coated seeds.

"I knew you would love some!" said Wei. "Peanuts are amazing. Once a classmate pawned two old shirts to buy a pack of roasted peanuts to share with his friends on his birthday. Everyone had a couple of the crunchy seeds, which made a remarkable birthday celebration!"

"I'm not going to share any of these with you!" May cocked her head and secured the pack in one hand while sticking the other one into the paper bag. She picked up one seed between her thumb, index and middle fingers and squeezed the coat off before popping it into her mouth. They talked about the state of affairs over the peanuts en route to the theatre. Meng Heji, who was doing his homework over the kerosene crates, jumped with joy on seeing Wei, who didn't visit much when his 'spot' in the atttic was taken by Heji.

"Cousin Wei, I was thinking on the way back," May said, "would Yin Dashi do the same thing if she had a chance to transport her dogs in a plane?"

"No, she wouln't! She would never do that!" Wei answered with complete confidence. Even though May was vaguely aware that Wei and Dashi were seeing each other, she had never expected such a strong reaction from Wei. Neither had she realised how serious it was to offer any criticism of 'Dashi' from Wei's point of view.

The truth was Dashi had only written one letter to Wei since her departure for Chongqing, telling him how much fun she had been having without mentioning school at all. Wei tried to write back to her many times. Each time he picked up his pen, he lost his train of thought and had to put it down. How much he wanted to talk about his bewilderment! But he didn't have the right opportunity. Now being with May and Heji, he felt they were back in the giant garden at the Lü residence in Chestnut street. He wanted to talk about what had been weighing on his mind with his cousins. He didn't need to mention the details, which only concerned Dashi and him, although there were not many details. He wanted to tell them that Dashi was different, but then it occurred to him how hard it was for him to justify such a judgement. He ended up repeating himself with the same dogged confidence: "She wouldn't! She would never do anything like that!"

Two pairs of dazzling dark eyes were fixed on Wei.

"You are so sure about Yin Dashi!" May was amazed by Wei's confidence.

Wei forced a bitter smile: "I wish I knew her better."

Heji continued rather innocently: "But Yin Xiaolong, the Little Dragon, says his elder sister is evil. She always takes a stand against his mother."

Wei growled at Heji: "No more such nonsense!"

Heji froze. May cradled Heji's shoulder gently in her arm and whispered in his ear: "We are not going to talk about such things with Cousin Wei." She could feel something precious and admirable was lodged in Wei's heart.

"Kiddo, one day, you'll feel the same," added Wei, smiling apologetically at Heji. "Someone who was distant suddenly becomes so close to you."

"You mean close to your heart?" mused May.

"Yes. And I mean Dashi."

"My body, without phoenix wings, cannot fly side by side with you; but my heart, with a thread from the magic horn, is connected to your heart ," muttered May thoughtfully.

Wei turned the two lines over in his mind several times to let the meaning sink in. He had recited many poems, including long poems in English, but he didn't know much about this famed Tang poet Li Shangyin that May had just quoted from because of his parents' dislike of his poetry. Wei asked May to find the textbook compiled by Yan Bulai, and the three plunged into reading poems from the book, interrupted only by occasional pauses for interpretation.

Roaming in the realm of poetry, the three completely forgot about dinner until Heji complained he was starving. Since it was long past dinner time, they decided to eat out. The light had gone completely and Ancestral Temple street was enveloped in darkness. Jewelled clusters of lights in different sections of the city centre caused the buildings to glitter. The lights on top of Wuhuashan (Wuhua mountain) were turned on. The red balloon had been absent for a long time. Someone walking out of the darkness grabbed Heji by his hand. A voice arose: "Meng Heji, where are you all going?"

The three cousins halted to find a smartly dressed man wearing gold-framed glasses standing in front of them.

"Aiya! Zhang Xinlei! It is you! Thunderhand!" Heji cried out.

"Haven't you been working in Chongqing?" asked May.

"It's a long story," said Thunderhand. "Are you going out? Can I join you?" When he realised that the three hadn't had dinner yet, he suggested: "I'd like to invite you all to eat Western food."

Wei answered politely: "Thank you very much, but I'll take care of them."

Thunderhand sighed: "Look at you, Tantai Wei! You are already a college student! How impressive! Kunming is impressive, too! It has become much more prosperous with lots of famous restaurants and hotels flooding into the city. But why do the dormitories look even shabbier than ever?"

Wei said: "The tin roofs have been sold. Didn't you hear about it?"

"I've been there. With the thatched roofs, you guys really live in huts," said Thunderhand.

The four walked into a small Western-style restaurant. Thunderhand asked them to sit down to order while he went out. The three loved soup and ordered one each. Wei whispered to his cousins: "You guys go ahead and order your main courses. Don't worry. I have money for it." He then ordered himself a steak while May and Heji ordered grilled mixed meat with white cream sauce to share. Thunderhand ordered soup and coffee because he had already had dinner. He tried a couple of times to speak up but then hesitated and ended up saying nothing.

Seeing that, May asked him: "Why are you now in Chongqing?"

Thunderhand answered: "Have you heard of the resources committee? I work for it. I was going to be appointed to the Singapore office but before my departure, Southeast Asia fell into the hands of the Japanese. I was on a business trip here, so I thought I should drop by and pay you a visit. People in Chongqing know about the hardship the academic community in Kunming has been going through. The wives of the professors setting up stalls to help support their families has been much talked about and admired in Chongqing. Are Professor Meng and Madam Meng alright?"

"My big sister is working with the plant institute. I assume you two have been keeping in touch?" May asked, ignoring Thunderhand's question to her.

"She writes me a note for every three or four letters she gets from me. She is the definition of 'unequal communication'."

"Sometimes not getting letters doesn't mean that someone doesn't want to write," Wei drawled. "It's quite likely that the person doesn't know what to write."

"Very enlightening. But I'm content with a few lines because that testifies to the fact that we have always been in touch. See? I'm not picky."

When the soup arrived, they talked over the soup. In the bright light, May found that Thunderhand had put on weight, which made him look more impressive.

Thunderhand continued: "When Hong Kong was taken over, my family couldn't send me money. Luckily, I already had a job. I have met so many colourful people at work. You wouldn't understand, anyway."

When the transportation of dogs by plane was mentioned, Thunderhand said: "There was a demonstration in Chongqing, too. How shameful it is that the central government prioritised dogs over its own citizens! My elder uncle in Hong Kong has no plans to escape since he thinks there is no escape at all. He'll try to keep living there. Hopefully, he won't become one of the abjectly obedient citizens."

"I won't become an abjectly obedient citizen! I'd rather run away," said May while cutting the bread into small pieces and spreading butter carefully on them before nibbling at them. Heji copied her.

Seeing the three cousins, Thunderhand sighed again: "Usually the environment plays a decisive role on human behaviour. Somehow, you guys always leave me with the impression that you never let go of your noble decency wherever you are. That's beyond my comprehension."

316

Wei answered thoughtfully: "Although what we eat is 'eight-treasure' rice, we are living in a spiritually rich community which is far more powerful than its material means."

"I'm enlightened again," said Thunderhand. "However limited the colleges and universities are in terms of material support, the presence of these great minds has brought an atmosphere of culture to the city of Kunming."

Wei added: "Or something poetic, distinct from many other means."

When they were finished and ready to go, Thunderhand asked May whether it was a good idea for him to visit Earl at the plant institute.

"The soup was tasty. We haven't had such a decent soup for a long time," remarked May, again ignoring Thunderhand's question.

Wei rushed to pay the bill and was informed that Thunderhand had already settled it. The three thanked Thunderhand, who said: "You are all very welcome. I wish I could do more." The four walked out of the restaurant and walked May and Heji back to the theatre first before Thunderhand, who was staying at a friend's place, and Wei went their separate ways.

PART III

When Wei and his two cousins were having dinner with Thunderhand, Earl was on her way back to her home at Baotaishan. It took her almost an hour to cover the short distance between the plant institute and her home because of her constant preoccupied pauses. The road was lined with trees with gently swaying branches and twigs and flanked by a babbling brook. It was a narrow but even road, distinct from the wiggly one in Earl's mind teeming with caves, falls, slopes and drops. She had deferred the big thing she wanted to do for too long. It was now or never, but she felt as if she were fumbling in the caves, or lingering over the steps. What tremendous courage it was going to take her to do it! But if she didn't do it, she would spend the rest of her life regretting it. She had to go and get an answer. She finished the distance under her feet. The moment she stepped over the threshold of her home, she stepped over the threshold in her heart, too. She had arrived at a major inflection point in her life and she was going to do it tomorrow.

"How come you came back today?" said Bichu, happily surprised. Fuzhi came out of the bedroom to greet his daughter.

"I have to go into town tomorrow for a meeting about biological taxonomy," said Earl, putting down her bag to pour herself a glass of water. "So, I thought I'd come back to see you and stay overnight."

She walked around the room, stooping down a little to have a look at Fuzhi's manuscript and touching the bright red sweater Bichu was knitting. She looked happy. But Bichu felt something heavy was mixed with her joy.

She could never see through this daughter of hers. Maybe that will change if she gets married? Marriage is powerful enough to transform any abnormal soul into a normal one. Earl is not too young to get married at her age. Oh, time! How fleeting it is! Now she has grown up! Who does she like? She has always been preoccupied with something which, of course, she keeps close to her chest. Maybe Professor Xiao has got some clues? Earl trusts him. She even asked him to interpret the lot she drew in a temple instead of coming to me. But love? Who knows what's best for her.

Bichu's heart thumped as she turned over all these facts about Earl in her mind. She sighed.

"Mum," said Earl, as she walked over and squeezed into Bichu's chair. Although she had never stopped bickering with her family, she had acknowledged from the bottom of her heart that the strength she drew from her mother was fathomless. How could she be in any doubt that she might have been adopted for so many years? Now she would love Bichu as her mother even if she had been adopted. She wanted to stay with her parents before plunging into her quest.

"Earl, guess who this is for?" Bichu stopped knitting and tried the sweater on Earl, who naturally clammed up. She knew this must be her mother's reward for her hard work selling buns. They hadn't been able to afford anything new for such a long time.

Bichu tugged the finished lower part of the sweater and said with satisfaction: "Mmm, quite a good fit."

"The colour is a bit loud. I don't want it," said Earl.

"This pattern is not like those ordinary stitches and purls. It stitches up easily and is not so tight. Besides, girls can't always wear plain clothes."

Fuzhi added: "I like the colour. It's very joyful."

On hearing her father's words, Earl almost jumped for joy. Things looked so auspicious for her! They had 'Broken Stuffed Buns Wrapped in Pastry', a local delicacy that Bichu and her two friends had learned to make. The buns sold well in the morning, and the three of them took the few that were left over back home.

Earl said: "The plant institute is going to set up a research division in Dali, but no one is willing to go, claiming Dali will fall before Kunming if the Japanese get that far."

Fuzhi said: "If the Japanese reach Dali, then the war is well and truly lost."

Bichu said: "Then we have to wage guerrilla warfare in Diancangshan (Dancang mountain), even if it proves to be futile."

Mum sounds so much like grandpa and always reverts to guerrilla warfare, thought Earl.

Fuzhi and Bichu caught each other's gaze as if something had just dawned on them and asked, almost at the same time: "Are you going to Dali?"

Earl laughed: "I'm not going. I have so many things to do here. Besides, it's so far away from you." Bichu and Fuzhi were heartily relieved, though puzzled by Earl's words at the same time. But they didn't ask any more questions.

After dinner, Earl helped with the dishes and then the knitting. She tried a few lines. She even invited Found the cat to sit on her lap. When Found refused, she was not upset at all.

In her dream that night when she wandered, the same unsettling gravity attacked her again. Tomorrow was going to be the day of her life. Why did she pick tomorrow as the day? Because she was in town for a meeting? Half awake, she slipped back into the dream in which she was walking with a man beside a steep cliff which dropped into an abyss. The faces of the people around her were fuzzy and it was hard for her to distinguish friends from strangers. But he was neither a stranger nor an acquaintance. He gave his side of the path to her while he walked by the edge of the cliff. The next step, he stepped onto a branch of a tree over the cliff. Earl yelled in horror: "Watch out! You'll fall!" Then she was woken up by her yell. Dawn had already broken.

Early that morning when a crimson dot emerged at the top of the mountain in the east, Earl left home with Bichu. The two went in different directions at the foot of the mountain, but Earl walked back to Bichu when she got a few steps ahead.

"Have you forgotten anything?" asked Bichu.

"No, I haven't. I just want to have one more look at you, mum."

Bichu patted Earl's bag affectionately and said: "Take your time. Remember, don't push. Let fate take its course." Bichu never figured out why she said that to Earl that day.

Earl walked fast, leaving behind the crisscrossing footpaths along the road and the Mang river in no time. She passed two villages with gates fringed with clusters of golden corn cobs hanging on string side by side with scarlet chilies. Having taken all the rises and falls along the way in her stride, she felt at peace, which allowed her free access to her old memories.

She didn't know when she had first had such a wish to go to him and tell him everything. It might have been the moment when he walked out from behind the pine tree the week before her college entrance examination. The lightness in his step made him look like a being from a perfect world. Beiping was now thousands of miles away, but the moments and the feelings back there never got an inch away from her. When she followed him on the train trip from Guihui to Kunming, he had explained the scenery along the way and shared with her lots of knowledge about trains. He knew about almost everything except biology. Upon their arrival in Kunming, they took jinrikishas from the station to the university. When they found how bumpy and hilly the streets in Kunming were, they got off the jinrikishas, leaving their luggage there, and walked. The drivers were uneasy about their decision and repeatedly pleaded: "Please come back and sit!" They didn't sit in the back. They even helped push the jinrikishas when they went uphill. Lots of people, students and teachers, greeted him: "Professor Xiao, you have arrived!" Once he had helped her settle down in the girls' dormitory, he left. He strode slowly along the street paved with quartzite, the lower edge of his long gown flying as if he were walking into another perfect world. How much she wanted to run after him and tell him she wanted to follow him wherever he went. This line had been haunting her since then. Now it was time for her to tell him.

As Earl was approaching the city, she walked onto the newly-built road for vehicles. It was a simple road for transporting goods. One section of the road rose steeply like a cliff. The village at the foot of it was immersed in the morning mist mixed with the smoke from the villagers cooking breakfast. As more and more people gradually appeared along the road, she slowed down and arrived at the meeting on time. Others who had started early that morning from the suburbs were all late. It was a small and very special meeting. Zhou Bi and Wu Jiaxin were present.

Zhou Bi said: "We have invited Professor Xiao, but he declined the invitation, saying since he doesn't specialise in this field of study, it would be better for him to forgo the title of 'instructor' for nothing."

Each of the participants presented their own research. Earl also made a speech and showed her classified samples, including the bright-coloured poisonous flower. They all felt very satisfied. In the afternoon after the meeting, Wu Jiaxin asked Earl to join her for a visit back to the campus, but Earl said she had other things to attend to. She walked alone around the Green lake, turning over the question in her mind over and over again. She wanted to gather more strength now that she was on the threshold of carrying out the heroic deed. She knew her chances of getting a yes or no to her question were 50/50, but her principle of life urged her that she'd rather die knowing than live without knowing. Even if her chances were 1 in 100, she still wouldn't regret doing it, but she would if she didn't. After walking back and forth along the dyke over the lake three times, she paused under a tree and then strode toward the theatre. She didn't stop until she reached the box in the east which served as Xiao Cheng's room.

Earl knocked.

When she entered, Xiao Cheng was typing on his English typewriter. He looked up from the slightly curled-up paper set in the typewriter and asked: "You've come from the meeting? How was it?"

Earl sat down in the chair by the door, gave a very brief account of the meeting and then clammed up, twisting a strand on her bag. It was silent inside the room. Xiao Cheng stood up and walked over to an old chair by the table, thinking about asking Earl what was going on. Without his outfit, his braces emphasised his slender figure and charm.

Earl finally began: "Do you still remember I came to you with my puzzle about whether I was adopted during an air raid, and you offered me a sound answer? I have finally found inner peace and come to the conclusion that I love my parents deeply."

Xiao Cheng smiled: "That's the right thing! I remember you drew lots in a temple to consult the holy spirit."

"Yes, I did. I drew two lots."

Xiao Cheng, in anticipation of being put on the spot, frowned: "Do you need another interpretation from me?"

"No one else can," said Earl. "I don't want to push anyone to do anything. I just need an answer." Earl's facial expression was somewhat intense. "I haven't mentioned the second lot yet. Would you like to hear about it? 'Let nature take its course. Don't push. Don't force.' This is an oracle from Buddha. Am I pushing or forcing?"

Xiao Cheng suddenly saw the light. What could be more devastating than the stubborn fascination of a young soul? He had to put a stop to such a fascination! He responded promptly: "Earl, you don't need to ask me the question. I know what you are going to ask. Have we always been friends? Have I always been sincere and candid with you? Now, you need to listen to me."

Upon these words, Earl got up from her seat, her head bowed.

"The question you want to ask me is why I never got married, isn't it? I appreciate your concern for me. The fact that I'm single doesn't mean I'm not in love with anyone. I have been in love with one of the best women in the world. The fact that we have been in love with each other for several years is known to many. Despite the unusualness of our relationship, everyone respects our decision. You will do the same, won't you?"

Earl felt it was she who was now stepping onto the branch over the abyss. She bit her lower lip hard until it bled, but she ignored the blood:

"Who is she?" She knew well who his love was, but she wanted him to tell her.

"I know you know who she is," answered Xiao Cheng in a tone as if he had been hit by a sudden surge of sadness when he saw something was dying in front of him. He tried to gather his composure before he continued gently: "Earl, this is a fact no one can deny. We are not going to say anything more about your question. And I'm not going to mention your visit today to anyone. You haven't asked me anything."

Earl fell down the branch and into the abyss and was engulfed by darkness. She would never be able to crawl her way back out. She forced herself to stand still, bowed quietly to Professor Xiao and then left.

Xiao Cheng bowed back: "We are still friends, equal friends. You have to listen to me. At least this time. I assume that a girl of your age must have some suitors. You can't rush into any marriage right now. I'm sure your parents share my concern."

Earl bowed again, turned, and forced her way out of Xiao Cheng's room.

How could I have taken all this? How was I able to keep standing still? How could I have not forgotten my manners and bowed goodbye? How was I able to walk out and run downstairs? I couldn't help turning back when I reached the gate at the ancestral temple to find you standing by the window. I will never bug you again. Yes, I should let fate decide. I paused by the side of the street and made up my mind about the next step I was going to take — I would marry the first acquaintance who spoke to me when I walked out of the city gate. When I arrived at the mound outside the city gate, I saw nothing but a vast expanse of white extending all the way like the water in a lake. Several people passed by me, one of whom looked familiar and nodded at me, smiling, but he passed by without saying anything. The water was rising so high in front of me I thought I might walk into it. Someone coming in the opposite direction called suddenly: "Earl, it's you!" I stopped walking and looked hard. It was Thunderhand.

Thunderhand said: "I have been looking for you since early this morning. I went to the plant institute, then Dragon Tail village. I never expected I would run into you here."

I didn't know what to say. I couldn't say anything.

"What has happened? Where are you heading? I'll keep you company." He gingerly took the bag from my grip and turned around to walk in my direction. We walked into a graveyard and wandered among the graves.

"Earl, where are you going, indeed? What's here to explore?"

What was here to explore? I thought each grave looked so lovely. Each was worthy of intensive exploration.

We walked through the graveyard and found a small teahouse. Thunderhand wanted to sit down for a while. "I have been walking since I got up this morning!" said Thunderhand. His face looked rather fuzzy, but I knew it was Thunderhand.

"Are you going to ask me why I popped up in Kunming? I have been working in Chongqing."

"I was," I heard my voice.

"That's better! Now you're talking!" He began to drink water. Lots of water.

"I came to Kunming on a business trip. But I am also on a private mission, which is to meet you and ask you a big question. Today may not be the day to ask you that question, though. You look terrible."

"Go ahead," I heard myself say. Whatever he was going to ask of me, I would say yes.

"You are so nice!" Thunderhand was happy. "Since we don't have much time, I think I'll ask you anyway. This is a nice place to ask such a question, which might suit your taste. I think you can guess what I'm going to ask you. Will you marry me?"

"Yes," I said. He jumped up. It was obvious he had never expected it would go so smoothly.

"Really?"

"Really."

"When?"

"Any time."

He stared at me hard: "Earl, the way you behave is quite extraordinary! But you have never been ordinary." He looked at me as I was looking outside the teahouse.

"It's getting dark and late, isn't it?"

"Yes, it is." But instead of darkness, I saw the enormous white expanse of water surging towards me.

"Are you feeling alright?" I heard him asking something like that.

"Shall I walk you back to the theatre, so you can have some rest?"

"No!" I snapped. I heard my voice again. I didn't want to go to the theatre. Not even close to it. He jumped again at my words, knocking over his teacup. He took me out of the teahouse, holding my hand in silence.

We walked back to the graveyard. The lake was lost from view. Even in the dimming light, every grave was distinct. I wished one would open up and I could just walk into it, leaving him outside. He gripped my hand. Was he afraid that I might run away? We walked aimlessly among the graves. Finally, we were through it and standing at the side of the road.

"Are you sure you want to go with me tonight?" he asked. I nodded, resolutely. Still holding my hand in his, he walked me up the mound and into the city gate. When we went past the ancestral temple, I covered my face with my free hand. We walked all the way to the city centre. He didn't have any set destination in mind, just like me. Walking this way and that, we stopped in front of an inn.

"Listen, Earl. I think we'll have to crash here tonight. We can't walk all night. What do you think?" What did I think? For someone who was willing to walk alive into a grave, she wouldn't be afraid of going into an inn with a man.

It was dark inside the inn. He booked two rooms. As we went upstairs, he whispered to me: "The way those people looked at us at the counter made me feel like we are eloping." I didn't feel that way. I didn't feel any way. In the tight room, I sat down, feeling worn out.

"You are exhausted," he said. "We are getting married tomorrow."

"I have told you I don't mind."

"But you have to eat something. Rice noodles? Scrambled eggs with rice?"

"I don't want to eat."

He stroked my head: "I know something must have happened. You will tell me later, won't you?" He ordered something for himself and soon finished it. "See? I'm fit as usual and I can back you up. We are getting married tomorrow."

Standing in front of the bed, he scooped up my shoulders and gave me a peck on the cheek. "However peculiar you are, you always bring me good luck." I knew I wasn't going to say no to whatever he wanted to do with me at that moment. The determination to destroy myself was burning, raging inside me, whatever it took.

But he just kissed my hand and repeated: "We are getting married tomorrow. Tonight, we both need a good rest. Sleep tight and don't worry about a thing. You have me now!" He walked toward the door of the room, turned back, raised his glasses a little bit, smiled at me, and then left. I was touched. I hadn't lost my senses and wasn't insane after all. I wanted to thank him, but in the end, I said nothing.

When Earl woke up the next morning, she couldn't figure out where she was. Unexpectedly, she had slept soundly the previous night. She was worn out, body and soul.

Thunderhand came from the room next to hers and kissed her hand: "My fiancée, what should we do now? I think we should go back to Dragon Tail village to report to your parents and my parents-in-law."

"It's up to you," said Earl.

Thunderhand was overjoyed, although his joy was mixed with a certain degree of uneasiness. It had been too easy to satisfy his long-lasting yearning for her like this. Earl had always been peculiar. Maybe that's the right way for her to decide such a big thing like marriage? I will know what has happened to her sooner or later. I just hope she doesn't change her mind, Thunderhand thought to himself.

They took the north city gate and walked eastward along the red dirt road. The sky was dazzling blue, and the trees oozed with greenness. From time to time, some military vehicles passed by. It was a road less frequented by neighbouring villagers. As they walked along a narrow section, they reached a steep cliff. They kept walking as a convoy of military vehicles rumbled towards them. It felt like it took ages for the trucks to go past.

"Stay away from the trucks," reminded Thunderhand. As he turned to continue walking, one truck swerved off its course toward them. Instinctively, they tried to dodge it, but missed their footing. Without any branches growing out of the cliff to block their fall, they rolled over the edge of the cliff. Earl's fall was broken by a bush which scratched her face and hands. Blood stained her face. Nonetheless, she was OK. When she came to her senses, she found Thunderhand was missing. Where was he? She struggled to get back on her feet and spotted Thunderhand lying still at the bottom of the cliff by a boulder.

"Thunderhand!" she cried, crawling downhill on her hands and knees.

"Thunderhand!" Her cries were swallowed by the rumbling of the trucks.

The villagers living in the village at the foot of the cliff gathered round and some tried to rescue Thunderhand.

One said: "The boulder rolled over him. He might have sustained internal injuries."

Another said: "There's no pulse."

Earl scrambled to him. He was neat and clean, without any sign of bleeding.

"Thunderhand!" She plunged onto him and yelled. He didn't respond. He was dead.

"Who are you?" someone asked her.

"I'm his fiancée," answered Earl. Her vision was blocked by the surging white expanse of lake water. She forced out the last line before she blacked out: "Plant institute." The water rose and engulfed both her and Thunderhand.

The plant institute was informed promptly and several of Earl's colleagues came, including Wu Jiaxin and Zhou Bi. At the sight of

326

Thunderhand, Jiaxin burst out sobbing. The villagers asked the same question: "Who are you?"

Jiaxin answered between sobs: "I'm... I'm his cousin."

Earl had been put on a bed in a villager's home while Thunderhand was put outside the house. They were about to join each other for their journey in life, but now they were separated forever by death.

Jiaxin asked to stay with Thunderhand, while two other colleagues drove Earl back home in a buggy. Fuzhi was in town, teaching. When Bichu saw Earl's bloodstained face and the stupor she was in, she was rather calm. She cleaned Earl up with a wet towel, cooing gently at the same time: "Earl, my beloved daughter." Earl opened her eyes at the words and uttered one word "mum". Her voice, though weak, was clear. Bichu breathed a deep sigh of relief. Having tucked Earl in, she went to see Earl's colleagues off.

Earl stayed in bed for two days quietly and silently without having anything to drink or eat. Her friends felt sorry for her loss of her former college mate in the accident when the two were together. Two days later, Earl got out of bed. Bichu took her a bowl of egg-drop soup. Bichu had lost so much weight. Her eyes were red-rimmed due to loss of sleep. The dark circles under her eyes were darker than usual.

Earl forced herself to swallow the soup. When she had finished, she told Bichu slowly that she was going to attend Thunderhand's funeral. Bichu told Earl she needed rest. Earl insisted she had to go: "Why can't I go? I have to go." She put her hands against the wall to support herself. Bichu had to tell her that the funeral had already been held by the resource committee and that Thunderhand's body had been buried.

Earl was sure she had heard her mother, but the words seemed to fail to sink in. A long while later, she muttered to herself: "So, it's all done." After another long pause, she said: "Mum, I think I need to draft an announcement. This is what I should do."

"What is the announcement for?"

"Thunderhand and I were engaged."

Bichu was so surprised to hear that: "You were engaged?" She heaved a sigh without waiting for Earl's confirmation: "My poor child!"

"He was ordinary, but he was a nice person. We were on our way to tell you and dad about our engagement that day."

"Is it still necessary since he has passed away?"

"It is. I promised him I would marry him. This announcement will be a comfort for him," said Earl, in broken sentences. She succumbed to loud sobs as she fell onto her mother's shoulder. Tears rolled off Bichu's cheeks, too. Combing through Earl's hair with her fingers, she patted her on the back and whispered: "Have a good cry, my daughter! Mum's here!" Earl continued crying for a while, saying she still felt dizzy and then lay down in bed, sobbing.

Fuzhi had already been told about the accident when he was in town. When he came back and heard about Earl's engagement, he shared Bichu's surprise at such a decision. They were sure that Earl had suffered a blow of some kind, and that Thunderhand's sudden death must have complicated the matter. Life is full of uncertainties. The fact that Thunderhand was in another world didn't free the Mengs from their principle that a promise made was a promise kept.

Several days later, a short notice was seen in the major newspapers in Kunming: "Zhang Xinlei (Thunderhand) and Meng Liji (Earl) were engaged", with Thunderhand's name in a black-printed box, a Chinese tradition in the printing industry to indicate the passing of the bearer of the name. Everyone who read the papers sighed, feeling sorry for both.

Bichu told Earl several times: "If you don't want to talk about the things you are not willing to talk about, I understand that and will respect your decision. But if you can share with me even a few hints, your mum would be so relieved and appreciative, is that alright?" At first, on hearing Bichu's words, Earl started sobbing again; then she didn't respond to Bichu at all as if she were deaf.

That night, Bichu had difficulty sleeping again. After tossing and turning for a long while, she nudged Fuzhi with her elbow.

"I'm awake," Fuzhi told her.

"It's about Earl. I think what has happened might have something to do with Professor Xiao. Or at least he might know what's on Earl's mind." Seeing Fuzhi remain silent, she nudged his arm: "Earl didn't feel that much for Thunderhand, but she has strong feelings for Professor Xiao."

Bichu was interrupted by a thump when Found the cat landed on the floor from the paper-paned window. Both of their hearts weighed heavily. They fell into silence. Fuzhi broke the silence later: "This must be a dilemma for an honourable man like Xiao Cheng. We can't go and ask him. We don't need to. Luckily Earl hasn't done anything worse, but it was too unfortunate for Thunderhand."

"If he were alive, we would treat him well like our own son rather than as a son-in-law," said Bichu, drying her tears with a corner of the cover.

A new grave was built in the graveyard Earl and Thunderhand had wandered about in that day. Thunderhand, a fine human being, was lying in a shabby coffin, leaving his parents thousands of miles away immersed in endless remembrance. The Mengs, except for Earl, all attended the funeral

328

and showered the grave with wild flowers they had gathered from Baotaishan. Fuzhi and Bichu stood in silence, wishing that Thunderhand would rest in peace. May and Heji circled once around the grave, wishing that Thunderhand would come back, and that they could treat Thunderhand to a meal in a western-style restaurant when they grew up. Earl didn't come with her family.

Some time later, the plant institute again proposed to establish a branch in Dali. Earl immediately signed up for it.

In the winter of 1942, Earl left for Dali. Before her departure, she went to say goodbye to Thunderhand. She sat quietly by his grave for a long, long time until the white expanse of water surged up in her vision. But it didn't engulf her. It retreated. She was the one who should be lying now in the grave, not him. Now he was inside and she was outside. A world apart. A life apart. At the bottom of her heart arose one grave where she had buried the other person.

Bichu wanted to see Earl off, but it was such a challenging trip for her to walk to town from Dragon Tail village to Near-the-Sun tower where the coach would pick Earl and others up.

Wrapping her arms around her mother's shoulders, Earl whispered in Bichu's ear: "Mum, I have been such an unworthy daughter to you. Please don't come to see me off. It adds to my many layers of guilt." Then Earl left home.

She crashed for the night in the girls' dormitory with her colleagues since she refused to go to the theatre. It was a dark, wet rainy morning the next day. The gloomy sky looked almost like it was crumbling into the mushy ground. Fuzhi hurried to see Earl off at Near-the-Sun tower, with May and Heji tagging along. Xuan, Wei and Yingshu had arrived. Xueyan didn't feel well these days and asked Wei Feng to deliver a letter of apology to Xuan. Xuan, in a grey sweater over her bright aubergine padded *qipao*, was busy greeting everyone, energetically trying to engage everybody in conversation. She gave Earl a fountain pen because its small size made it easy to carry. It pained her heart to see Fuzhi's stooped back and the wrinkles of concern burrowed into his face. Uncle Fuzhi is getting old, thought Xuan.

"Wuyin has come," someone whispered. They all saw Wuyin approaching on a black horse. He stopped by the waiting line of people and dismounted from the horse. After greeting Fuzhi, he took out a delicate sample book from his backpack and gave it to Earl, who took it and saw a note attached to the book "For the Future botanist Meng Liji" and his signature. Yingshu commented on what a beautiful and suitable gift it was for Earl. He gave Earl a flashlight which was packed into Earl's luggage.

When the coach was leaving, the director of the branch in Dali, Professor Wu, came up to Fuzhi: "Professor Meng, please don't worry. We'll take care of Meng Liji."

Earl, who had been nestling against her father, took May's hand: "May, I never did much when I was at home. From now on, you'll shoulder even more responsibilities." May had never felt such intimacy with her sister. She wiped her tears with Earl's hand. Earl put the other hand on Heji's shoulder but didn't say anything. Sister and brother just stared at each other before Heji took her arm and cried.

Earl didn't cry. Hanging her head low, she said to Fuzhi: "Dad, I have to go now."

The coach started and scurried off into the distance, leaving behind puffs of black smoke.

The people who had come to see Earl and others off stared at the coach until it disappeared from sight. They lingered for a while and then went their separate ways for their classes. Wuyin walked up to May and was ready to say something but ended up saying nothing.

At the end of the year, Wu Jiaxin and Zhou Bi got married. They invited Professor Xiao to witness their wedding. Professor Xiao gave a speech, congratulating them and saying they were a match made in heaven. He wrapped up his speech in a rather strange way: "I was once asked to interpret a lot drawn from a temple, which said we should let fate decide rather than push fate, which means we shouldn't force ourselves to do the impossible. Just think about it. Sometimes, the fact that one might have done nothing is already creating pain for someone else. How sorry that must make one feel."

Jiaxin's heart missed a beat at Xiao Cheng's words. Her eyes became wet. She put on a smile and turned to talk to people. Others present at the wedding were rather puzzled by Professor Xiao's closing remarks.

Both Thunderhand, Jiaxin's cousin, and Earl, Jiaxin's best friend, were absent at her wedding.

PART IV

The death of Thunderhand, Earl's engagement to him, and her hasty
departure had more of an impact on Xuan than on most others, except
for the Mengs. She had a vague feeling that Earl must have fallen for
someone, but definitely not Thunderhand. At the sight of Wuyin, she asked
herself whether that person was Wuyin, but then she laughed at her own
groundless assumption. If Earl's personality was at the root of the twists and
turns in her life, then hers would ensure that life was smooth sailing for her.
If Earl was autumn tinted with dusty twilight, she was spring ablaze with
glory and the glamour of clouds at dawn. Didn't someone once say that
'anatomy is destiny'? That would sufficiently sum up what had happened to
Earl. Would it apply to her, too? She was not certain.

When Xuan began her work at the provincial government, she had a lot
of free time because of the light workload. Although staff there were often
late for work in the morning because they got up late, Xuan was never late
for work even though she was spoiled by her parents when she grew up. She
had never been spared the application of Grandpa Lü's family discipline
which deemed getting up late to be a sin. She walked to her office and was
never late.

Since there was not much to translate, Xuan was always free in the
afternoons. That was why she eventually accepted Professor Wang Dingyi's
offer to teach oral English to one class. A handful of wives of influential local
officials had also been asking her to coach them in English, so she made a
careful selection and agreed to tutor a couple of the ladies. Back then, it was

popular for officials' wives to want to be able to speak fluent English when accompanying their husbands at social gatherings. She had seen so many in such a position and was able to sail through. These ladies were generous and respectful to Xuan due to her prominent family background.

So Xuan had a regular life. She didn't feel bored, although she didn't feel as happy as she used to. She didn't think of herself as a scholar, or an office lady, or a weirdo, or a commoner. She felt she was an outsider. Her heart ached at such a conclusion. Did Earl feel the same way?

She was aware of the major factor behind all her worries. It was her relationship with Paul. The question Paul asked in the small room - "Will you marry me?" - was still ringing in her ears. Two years had passed, but she hadn't given him her answer yet. Would she keep him waiting until his name was written in a black-printed box? Paul was lovely and loved her, but why would there always be disharmony between them when they faced trifles? Was it because she was not American enough? Or Paul wasn't Chinese enough? But look at Professor Zhuang and his English wife Della. What a beautiful match and a happy marriage! Although they might have had their regrets, if so, only the two of them would know.

After Paul proposed to Xuan, she took a flight on one of those regular airliners between Kunming and Chongqing to seek her parents' opinion. They both thought that it would take time for the two to settle down. Tantai Mian's theory was that the key to a successful cross-cultural marriage was the unconditional admiration of one party for the other, just like Della's admiration for Zhuang Youchen. Xuan's self-awareness that she didn't have such a strong feeling like Della had toward her husband was the reason behind her delayed response. Sometimes when they were together, they were happy, and it was so easy to understand one another as if they were both made of crystal. At other times there were walls between them. Once Paul told Xuan that two of his friends loved talent-spotting on the street and would place bets on it - whoever spotted the first beautiful girl in five minutes won the game. Paul thought it was so funny while Xuan regarded it as too silly. The two had a heated argument. On reflection, how silly they were!

The American consulate in Kunming held all kinds of events, such as tea parties and concerts, to keep in contact with people from all walks of life. Xuan was a frequent guest and would help with the meet and greet. Her slender body and fluent spoken English added a lot of energy and glamour to the atmosphere. Paul said she was to a party like gourmet powder was to a delicate dish. Xuan didn't always enjoy herself on such occasions when she felt she was more an employee than gourmet powder.

At one event, two university professors were talking about a patient suffering from flea-borne typhus. One commented that he had never seen a flea before, and that they were rarely seen in recent times. When Paul figured out what they were talking about, he showed some sympathy toward the patient who was suffering from the consequences of such a tiny bite from a tiny flea and was rather paranoid at the possibility that the two of them might have brought fleas with them. He demanded a clean-up of the reception hall after the event. Xuan was disgusted by such a reaction and confronted Paul: "Don't you Americans have fleas?"

Paul shrugged and said they did have fleas in the trenches, but this was not a trench.

Xuan lost her temper: "This is all because of the war! Can't you see that?"

Paul didn't understand why she was so upset. The dazzling blue in his widened blue eyes looked like it was melting away, which reminded Xuan so much of her favourite doll.

That day, Xuan walked to work as usual. The soft green twigs from the weeping willows lining the dyke brushed the air and several birds frolicking around the lake didn't cheer her up the way they usually did. She dragged herself slowly to the foot of the long set of steps leading to the high-platformed office building of the provincial government. She was amazed how she had ended up working in such a bureaucratic organisation.

She was the first one to arrive at the office as usual. Sitting at her desk, she scanned the previous day's newspapers. Some time later, a couple of her colleagues arrived and began their day with their regular chitchat. One said the price of daily groceries had risen. When she said that, she glanced at Xuan and said Miss Tantai didn't need to worry about groceries. Xuan thought for a second and said the price of coffee had risen, too. Another reminded them that what had risen most was rents, but they didn't need to worry about rent because they lived in their own houses. Xuan corrected her, smilingly: "I don't have a house." She thought again and remembered her rent had risen by a third from the previous month.

Most of her office colleagues were from influential local families. Even they had started talking about rising prices, sighed Xuan. Besides the talk about prices, a special topic grabbed their attention — local millionaire Mr Zhu Yanqing was hosting a grand ball the following evening. The gossips had already managed to find out who was invited. It turned out that only three people at the office were invited: their director, Xuan and someone who was related to some VIP. Xuan didn't have any idea who this millionaire was, so she asked about him. The VIP's relative laughed at Xuan's ignorance: "Miss Tantai has been working here for more than a year, why haven't you heard of the list yet? All the department stores in Kunming belong to this Mr Zhu. It is said that he also has a substantial stake in a tin mine in Gejiu county, although no one knows how much he has."

Xuan wasn't paying much attention to the 'important' information and had her eyes glued on the old newspapers. Later the office director gave her two documents to translate. One was a Chinese article about mahjong with a detailed account of its origin, development and rules of playing the game. It was a smooth and neat piece of writing. The other one was a report in English by a foreign journalist about a small-scale act of 'pacification' by the government military force against a riot somewhere. He commented that the unrest arising from the domestic conflicts between the KMT and CPC against the background of the war of resistance against Japan was more and more concerning. It was a bit funny to put these two types of material together. Xuan didn't reveal her emotions and soon finished translating the English report into Chinese but her director came to remind her that he was waiting for the English translation of the mahjong. Xuan knew very well that he could wait for a couple of days when he said he was waiting. She stuffed both the finished work and the unfinished work into her drawer and was ready to wrap up that day's work. Someone came to invite her to a Beijing Opera performance featuring a famous performer from Chongqing that evening; someone else came to ask her for dinner at the New Elegance Restaurant because the new chef was superb; a third person wanted her to go to the theatre for a newly released melodrama. She wanted to see the movie, but she didn't want to accept any favours, so she declined all the invitations. That day's newspaper arrived. They all saved them for the next day.

When a millionaire holds a party, the intention is often to strengthen their connections with people from all walks of life. That goes some way to explaining why people from different circles were invited to attend the party held in Mr Zhu's villa near the Grand View tower. Many Americans were invited, including Paul. The next evening, Paul drove to Xuan's place to pick her up for the party. He vaulted up the stairs, whistling all the way. When he saw Xuan, he was amazed how glamorous she looked, claiming she was more gorgeous than a fairy. Xuan picked a lightly-padded emerald silk *qipao* and a black hollowed-out silk shawl. Emerald is a difficult colour to match but Xuan balanced the bright colour with black. The contrast of the two colours emphasised her fair complexion to the maximum.

Paul asked, with a smile lingering on his face: "You are very happy, and you are fully dressed up. What is the Chinese expression for such a state?"

Xuan told him it was 'shengzhuang' (盛装), which meant to dress up. They talked and laughed and went downstairs to drive to the Grand View tower.

The villa, built on a lake, was connected to the land by a bamboo footbridge. The two camellia bushes were blooming riotously in the garden. The grand reception hall was already half full of prominent figures from military, government and business circles. Among the guests were also officials from Chongqing, the war-time capital, Americans and female students from the universities. Paul and Xuan both encountered acquittances of theirs and exchanged greetings with them. Someone whispered that Harvey, the US military commander, had arrived, accompanied by several high-ranking officials from the provincial government. The host himself led them to their seats.

The host, who was in his 40s, looked gentle and refined. When he had seated Harvey and his companions properly, he walked around, greeting his guests. He paused to talk to Paul and his colleagues. Paul, being polite, introduced Xuan to Zhu Yanqing, whose eyes lit up at mention of her name. He said he had heard about Miss Tantai for so long, and finally he had the opportunity to meet her in person.

A servant came in and whispered in Mr Zhu's ear. He nodded. When the concert performance began, Zhu went to Harvey to invite him to get the party started by leading the first dance. Harvey looked around. When he spotted Xuan, he went over to invite her to join him for the dance. Xuan was very happy. They danced two rounds before the rest of the guests joined. That flickering emerald dress attracted so much attention. "That is Tantai Xuan", they murmured to one another. The commander was a skilful dancer, and Xuan was an elegant partner. When the music finished, Harvey took the next dance with another lady, while Xuan joined Paul, who was so proud of her. Xuan felt a gaze fixed upon her from a table outside the dancing pool during her dance. She spotted Yan Liangzu when she danced closer to the source of the gaze.

When the music stopped, Xuan went to Liangzu's table to greet him. Seeing his deeply-furrowed brow, Xuan bemoaned the fact that Uncle Liangzu looked even older than Uncle Fuzhi.

Liangzu smiled at Xuan: "See? I'm here, too. They all nagged at me to get out of the house." He then asked Xuan why she and her cousins hadn't visited them and told her Suchu was still staying in Anning county for her retreat. "Huishu was invited, but she refused to come." He asked Xuan to sit down and enjoy the delicate refreshments. They exchanged some pleasantries and Liangzu said: "I only have a few days of leisure before I take up the position to supervise water resources. You know me. I won't do it just to kill time. I'll pitch in as I always do."

Someone else sharing the table said: "Commander Yan's rigorous attitude is legendary." The rest readily agreed. Zhu Yanqing came over and said it was indeed wise to pay attention to water resources during wartime.

The music began again. Zhu Yanqing invited Xuan to dance. It was a foxtrot but he slowed down the pace, taking his time to chat with Xuan: "I heard that Miss Tantai is working at the provincial government. I assume you must be busy." The translation of the mahjong article came to mind. Xuan smiled at the thought.

Zhu Yanqing continued: "How long have you been in Kunming? Four or five years?" Xuan said she loved Kunming and so did her friends and relatives.

Zhu Yanqing said: "When so many educated people settle down here, we locals feels as if Kunming has been blessed with God's nectar!" Xuan gave another smile as her answer. When she was invited for several more dances by other guests, she lost track of Paul. Feeling she needed a break, she found a quiet corner and sat down to take a sip of tea. She turned around to find Paul talking to Lü Xiangge by the door leading to the platform out of the reception hall. Xiangge was wearing an apricot floral silk *qipao*, her hair tied in a bun and decorated with a hairpin. Xuan stared at the two of them for several minutes, holding the cup in her hands. It was Xiangge who first noticed Xuan's gaze. She pointed at Xuan and walked toward her with Paul.

Paul told Xuan: "The ball tonight has been arranged by Miss Lü."

Xiangge said humbly: "I'm so lucky to have been given such an opportunity on account of the ladies' kindness."

Someone came up to invite Xuan for the next dance. As Xuan got back into the rhythm of the music, she found Xiangge and Paul were dancing together, which rather upset her. Although reason told her it was nothing, her heart wouldn't listen to her head. All the pieces of music for the latter half of the ball sounded hideous.

Yan Liangzu didn't dance. He just sat by the table, enjoying his tea in a leisurely and yet solemn way. When she blinked, she found Xiangge talking to Liangzu in a rather intimate way. For a moment Xuan wondered if it was Xiangge's intention to connect with the Yan family. Her partner sensed her absentmindedness and muttered an apology for his poor skills. Soon, Yan Liangzu was ready to leave. Zhu Yanqing saw him off at the door to the reception hall. When Zhu came back to invite Xuan for another dance, Harvey had already beaten him to it. All the attention was drawn to the flashing emerald dress again.

When the ball was over, Paul told Xuan he was giving Xiangge a lift back to the city. Xuan had thought about going to sit with Paul for a while on the steps outside the Grand View tower to review what the boatwoman had once said to them during their last visit: "Where the two of you are together, that is home." In the gentle dimness of the night, maybe she could finally give him her answer. But now Xiangge had come between them. Xuan was silent all the way. She thought this might be what people called 'fate'.

For the next few weeks, Xuan was distant toward Paul when they were together. Paul mentioned several times how much he admired a young woman like Xiangge for so successfully managing those stores of hers. Xuan never gave her response. Once when the two were talking about how different the Chinese and American governments were, Paul said he had heard many rumours about the Chinese government and its unimaginable corruption. Xuan was well aware that what Paul was saying was true, but she challenged him intentionally: "Is there no corruption in your government? I don't think so."

Paul answered seriously: "Yes, there is corruption in America, but it's no match for what is happening here." But he hastened to add: "Governments are governments, but the Chinese people are noble, and one Chinese in particular is perfect. Can you guess who it is?"

Xuan rolled her eyes at him: "China is still suffering many social problems since the country hasn't eradicated the effects of feudal society. I'm well aware of that." She was sure she had heard this from Wei Feng, although she couldn't remember when.

Paul said: "A society without democracy is like a pool of dead water without any mechanism to clean its pollution."

Xuan said: "I think the worst part of human nature, the blind intensive pursuit of profit, is the bane of a society."

"There's nothing wrong with pursuit of profit," chided Paul.

"I was talking about blind intensive pursuit of profit! Get it?" Xuan raised her voice.

Paul clammed up. After a long pause, he began again: "Do you remember on the day when war broke out, you insisted on going to the ball? You have changed. A lot."

Xuan didn't disagree with that.

Speaking of pursuing profits, Lü Xiangge counted as an outstanding case. Besides her cafés, she also sold goods smuggled via the Yunnan-Burma road, which had become something normal for many. She was also involved in several opium trades, which she covered up skilfully. Paul tried his best to treat Xiangge fairly because he thought it was rather hard for someone like

Xiangge from such a low social background to achieve so much by her own hard work. In Xiangge's case, logically, Xuan didn't think she could offer a more reasonable explanation than Paul while, regarding the facts, she herself didn't know much about what Xiangge had been doing.

After the ball, Zhu Yanqing had a couple more invitations for Xuan, who agreed to attend only two small dinner parties. Zhu's intentions became more obvious. One day when Xuan had wrapped up the day's work and was walking out of the gate of the government building, someone patted her on the shoulder. She turned around to find Hezhu in her regular sparkling earrings, her hairpins, her hybrid dress of Han majority and Yi minority, and her face with indistinct features.

Hezhu said: "I haven't seen you for quite a long time, Miss Xuan. I know after the commander's accident, it is rather inconvenient for him to receive guests."

Xuan said she had met Uncle Liangzu some time ago and he seemed to be quite fit.

Hezhu said: "The commander and I have moved back to the city. I have so many things to attend to. Unlike milady, she can always enjoy her peace. What a rare occasion it is for me to run into you. Let's go and sit for a while at the New Elegance restaurant." Xuan said she had classes to teach in the afternoon but Hezhu said: "You still need to have lunch first!"

Without allowing Xuan another moment of hesitation, she dragged her to an upstairs reserved room in the New Elegance restaurant.

Xuan ordered a bowl of noodles while Hezhu insisted on ordering three more dishes. After enthusing profusely about the restaurant, she finally was ready to talk business: "Miss Xuan, I have been entrusted to discuss an important issue with you. The best option is indeed milady, or at least your Aunt Bichu, but you know milady doesn't care a jot about local things, while Aunt Bichu has been preoccupied with her own worries. I'm a very blunt person, so I beg your forgiveness if what I'm going to say is inappropriate."

Xuan had always prided herself on her ability to figure out what someone was after before they were halfway through their sentence, but this time she was dumbfounded at what Hezhu had to say. She opened her eyes wider to try and discern any clues from the bland face but found none. Then she answered courteously: "Aunt Hezhu, how can I help you?"

Hezhu smiled: "You know Mr Zhu Yanqing, and I'm entrusted by him. His wife passed away three years ago. Since then many ladies in Kunming city have been trying to marry him!"

That was why she had come! Xuan cried out without waiting for Hezhu to finish: "I see. You don't need to say more. Mr Zhu is destined to meet some perfect match with his prominent personality. I'm sorry, I don't think my path is destined to cross with his!" She stood up and prepared to leave.

Hezhu followed Xuan, trying to feed her more information: "Mr Zhu is not going to stay in Kunming. He's going to settle down in the US."

Xuan swallowed her rage and maintained her manners as she said goodbye to Hezhu. When she was back at her apartment, she furiously tossed all her dolls onto the floor. She was sad too, thinking she was getting so old that they had the idea of marrying me off to some old codger whose wife has died! Tantai Wei came to see her at that moment, and she told him what had happened. Wei was furious, too: "How rude this Hezhu is! Just ignore her. Anyway, what's happening between you and Paul?"

Xuan said: "I'm thinking about it, too. I can't put it off anymore. Yes or no, I need to give him an answer."

Wei mused: "Is it that difficult?"

"Of course," answered Xuan.

A while later, the landlord sent them lunch on a tray. Xuan wouldn't even have picked up her chopsticks if it weren't for Wei's sincere pleading. Holding her chopsticks, she said: "We haven't had a meal with our parents for a long while. I want to go back home during the winter vacation."

Wei said: "I'd like to go back with you, but I can't. Professor Xiao is offering a short-term course on the development of biology. I don't want to miss it. I have heard that many students from Chongqing and Guiyang have registered for the course already." The sister and brother then talked about visiting their Aunt Bichu. That was something they could do together right now.

A couple of days later, they received some airmail from their parents, saying Tantai Mian was going to work in the American unit for two years. Jiangchu changed her mind and decided to go with her husband. The two of them wanted to visit their children before they left. In the letter, they also asked about the relationship between Xuan and Paul and suggested the sooner Xuan made up her mind the better. They also asked Wei not to have a girlfriend during his college years. The letter was full of love and concern for Xuan and Wei, who were more eager than ever to see their parents in Kunming. A second letter arrived shortly afterwards saying they had had to cancel their visit to Kunming due to their tight schedule. When Xuan and Wei went to visit their Aunt Bichu, they knew she had got the letter from their parents, too. They all regretted the fact that they had had to wait for two years to meet again.

That day when Xuan stormed off, Hezhu thought to herself what a temper Xuan had. Maybe she was just shy and embarrassed? If so, her mission was not a failure, then. But if she had failed, Mr Zhu would surely look down on her! Zhu Yanqing didn't know Hezhu. The so-called trust was more of a roundabout connection. Although Hezhu was in charge of the Yan residence, her lack of confidence complicated her sense of vulnerability. She had assumed that if she could manage to do something for such a prominent figure as Zhu Yanqing, that would add a lot of weight to her authority in the Yan residence. She went down the slope until she reached the 'Greensleeves Café' and went directly to the backyard of the store.

"Xiangge," she called.

Xiangge was busy with her accounts in her bedroom. On hearing Hezhu's call, she hurried out and invited Hezhu to come in and take a seat. When she heard Hezhu's account of her mission, she laughed: "Miss Xuan is the toughest nut in the family. It's rather impetuous of you to go to her with such a tactless approach. Why did you mention emigrating to the US? People like her don't fancy such a thing at all! She has an American boyfriend right now!"

"Ai-yah! I spend all my time at home. How would I know such things? Are things settled between her and her American boyfriend?"

"I don't think so. I don't think it would be hard to break them up."

That greatly intrigued Hezhu. The two engaged in a whispered discussion. Xiangge heard some rustling noises from Hezhu and spotted a tiny black head poking out of her pocket. The black head wriggled its way up to Hezhu's shoulder and then fell on the table. It was a lizard.

"Are you carrying them with you?" Xiangge asked curiously.

"I have more," said Hezhu, reaching into her pocket to get out a small snake, which coiled quietly on the table with its docile head sticking straight up. The lizard had climbed back onto Hezhu's shoulder, its beady eyes the size of millet spinning in all directions. Hezhu said calmly: "I grew up with these venomous bugs. These are non-poisonous and good-natured ones. They won't bite. How different you are! Those young misses and ladies would scream their heads off at the sight of these things."

Xiangge couldn't contain her curiosity: "What does Huishu think of them? Is she scared?"

"She's got used to them and is not that scared. She hates this home. And, indeed, I know she just hates me. She'll leave and never return the first chance she gets."

"People say you know how to poison others with your bugs. Can you actually enchant someone and make them obey you?"

Hezhu straightened up her face and waved her hand: "Never speak about that again! If you do, you'll be in big trouble." But she knew too well that the so-called mysterious poisoning was nothing other than allowlng those venomous bugs to mingle and fight one another. The survivor was the most poisonous. Its venom was deadly to human beings, but it was complete baloney to think that someone who bred bugs could poison someone else by pointing their fingers at the victim. Bug breeding was still an industry, but people used bugs to make Chinese medicines. If they had other motives, no one would know. What Hezhu had been doing was just to show her uniqueness and to remind Liangzu about the Dream-of-Spring wine and his oath to her.

As for Xiangge, her specialty didn't lie in any of these poisonous bugs. Her specialty was her craftiness. Her plan was to marry a well-off man. If she was going to marry into a regular rich Chinese family, her past was a big obstacle. She had found herself several American boyfriends, who had no interest in her past but were focused on the present due to their different values. She had become quite close to Paul recently and had listed him as a candidate, too, because of his good looks, good nature and simplicity. She thought he was easy prey. "That would create a lovely drama if I could snatch Paul from Xuan," said Xiangge, looking at the non-poisonlous bugs. She thought about prey, and then her profession, which reminded her to ask Hezhu whether she'd like a cup of coffee.

"You know I don't like that foreign stuff," said Hezhu, brushing the lizard off her shoulder into her pocket. Picking up the small snake, she said: "I'll leave this one for you as a companion."

Xiangge took one step back and hastily declined such a generous offer. "I have prepared something for you," she said, and turned around to take out a package of Pond's skincare. One bottle of Pond's lotion, or cream, was a luxury. A whole set sent Hezhu directly to seventh heaven! She almost blurted out whether Xiangge was going to sell poisonous bugs and, if so, that she would be willing to be her supplier.

When Hezhu left, Xiangge went to the kitchen to prepare for the afternoon. With help from two waitresses, the café was filled with the aroma of freshly brewed coffee. The snacks and cakes were bought from Guanshengyuan bakery. At the turn inside the café was a newly erected screen painted with assorted brightly-coloured peonies, which added more elegance to the place. Together with the soft music, it was quite an attractive café. Customers streamed in.

Two college students who had dropped out to run a business along the Yunnan-Burma road came in and sat by a table near a window. Xiangge went over to greet these two acquaintances. The two whispered to her whether she wanted cosmetics like Pond's facial cream, Max Factor lipsticks, perfume and nail polish. If she was short of cash, they could wait and come back to collect the money when she had sold out. Xiangge sneered at such an offer, claiming she had such a small sum. Their goods were packed in four kerosene crates in a jeep outside the café. It didn't take them much time to move the crates from the jeep to the backyard and seal the transaction.

The two complained: "It's tricky to get through customs, but with an American army vehicle, you can sail through customs."

"Cosmetics are very popular, but you can try other stuff, too," said Xiangge.

The two said: "You think it would be easy for us? Besides the long, tiring journey, we have to endure all kinds of worries, fears and anxieties."

Xiangge laughed: "The roar of your engine brings you rolls of cash. It's so worthwhile for that negligible amount of suffering."

When she had seen the two off, she came back to the front again. The lights were already on, and more customers were streaming into the shop. Lots of lower-rank officers from the American army took their female companions for a cup of coffee and drinks as well. The limited choice of drinks were new items on the menu, which brought more customers, making the place even more crowded. That was why Xiangge had a plan to enlarge the café. She hustled and bustled, scrambling between the back and front of the café, balancing cups and glasses in her hands, greeting people, and using her brain to calculate her grandiose development plan.

Amid this hive of activity, she hatched an idea to kill two birds with one stone, which would perfectly integrate her expansion with wrecking a relationship.

Late into that night, sitting in her bed, she finished the conception of her integrated plan. First, she would describe her dream to open up a ballroom before she went on to ask Paul to lend her a big sum of money. If Paul agreed to help her, that would definitely upset Tantai Xuan. That was the first step. She had to plan her second and third steps carefully. She slipped into a dream and had a very good night's sleep.

Xuan hadn't seen Paul for several days in a row. Paul came to look for her but she was not home. So he left a note asking her whether she would join him for a gramophone concert at the consulate. She didn't give him an answer. She thought of him quite often but when it was time to put her thoughts into action to go and see him, she found she didn't have the heart already. Maybe their passion had been worn out by time, which only left the voice of reason between them.

That morning, on her way to work as she passed the Greensleeves Café, she decided to have one cup to cheer herself up.

It was dim inside the café as usual. No other customers were visible apart from some noise coming from behind the new screen. Xuan went over to see a man and woman whispering to each other quite intimately. It didn't take much time or effort on her part to recognise Paul and Xiangge. When Xiangge saw Xuan coming in, she deliberately leaned her head on Paul's shoulder and left it there for several seconds, which seemed to Xuan like centuries. Paul was alarmed by the quietness and immediately stood up to face Xuan, smiling his lovely smile: "Let's have coffee together. I was heading to the university and dropped by on the way."

"Me, too. What a coincidence," said Xuan calmly.

"Are you free this evening?" asked Paul while he put sugar and milk into her cup for her.

"I have to work until midnight," Xuan beamed.

Paul's big blue eyes opened wide: "Are you mad at me? I haven't done anything wrong."

Lü Xiangge came to their table, busying herself with 'Miss Xuan' this and 'Miss Xuan' that, and saying how the coffee today was a local specialty from Baoshan district, a real quality product.

They sat for a while and then Paul offered to walk Xuan to the provincial government building. On the way, neither talked much except that Paul explained again: "I haven't done anything wrong. I think it is very tough for Lü Xiangge to have achieved so much through her hard work. She asked me to lend her some money to help her to expand her café, and I agreed to help her."

Xuan felt a wall of ice was rising between them foot by foot like the steps under her feet leading to the tall building. Xuan talked to Paul calmly. When it was time for them to say goodbye at the gate, Paul asked what they were going to do for the weekend. Xuan smiled and shook her head.

Paul gazed at her, muttering: "This doesn't feel right."

Xuan's heart was pained by the tough decision she had just made. Their differences were deeply rooted in their cultures, which would be the roots of lifelong conflict.

Xuan and Paul broke up. They didn't even make it as far as getting engaged.

CHAPTER SEVEN

PART I

Behind the west city gate along the main street, there were three alleys running parallel with Precious Pearl alley. Qian Mingjing had set up his comfy home in Comfort alley while Wei Feng had found a spot in Wasted alley, but he and Xueyan still lived in Salt Falls. Mingjing had managed to rent a house for the Wei couple. Since You Jiaren hadn't found a place to live, and the Wei couple had no intention of moving back soon, he gave that one to the You couple. The address was No. 1 at Mean alley. Whether these names were coined by coincidence by later residents or were named that way when they were built, there was no means of verifying.

You Jiaren's classes were very popular among students when he started at Minglun. Although he was a professor of Chinese, he started an English course called 'Selected Readings of 18th-Century English Novels and Their Translations'. Together with his 'Classical Chinese Literature', he was crowned as 'the scholar bridging the gap between East and West'. Everyone present in his class was amazed by his rich allusions and fluency in memorising any of the works mentioned, classical or popular, Chinese or English.

Yao Qiu'er, too, had found her a position to teach English in a middle school through an introduction by Qian Mingjing. Her talent and knowledge enabled her to handle those middle schoolers with ease. During their breaks between classes, they travelled around Kunming, enjoying its natural beauty.

Months passed. No. 1 Mean alley had a small but cosy courtyard. The house, with two rooms on each floor, faced south. In the downstairs room lived a lecturer from the maths department, Shao Wei, and his wife, Liu

Wanfang, who was born and raised in Tianjin like Yao Qiu'er. As a lovely and innocent woman, Liu Wanfang was a good neighbour. The You couple lived in the upstairs rooms, which were simply furnished in line with Yao Qiu'er's habit with only a fat Oxford dictionary standing out in the simple environment. They hadn't shown their appreciation for Mingjing's help when they settled down, though. Instead, they felt rather sorry for Mingjing for his hard work to raise the family since Mrs Qian didn't want to lower herself to work.

That statement had profound implications. Literally, they were flattering Mrs Qian for her decency, but what they implied - reading between the lines - was the allusion to the marital discord between the Qian couple. How could someone as smart as Qian Mingjing fail to read between the lines? But Mingjing didn't care much. As time went by, as people got to know more about the You couple, they agreed that beneath the profound knowledge of You Jiaren lurked something inexplicable.

That afternoon, You Jiaren came back home from his teaching in high spirits. Yao Qiu'er, who was grading her students' assignments by the desk, raised her head, smiled charmingly at her husband, and asked: "What's the news?" It was a popular pet phrase for both.

You Jiaren took out a newspaper, pointing at the engagement notice of Earl and Thunderhand, and said: "The notice was published three days after the fiancé's death. In olden times, there were those who got married to the tablets of the deceased. Now we have witnessed an engagement with the deceased! How could Meng Fuzhi allow such a thing to happen?"

Yao Qiu'er blinked: "Maybe the two had materialised their marital oath already."

The two smiled at each other knowingly.

You Jiaren sat down to a cup of tea. He pointed at the book he had taken back: "Speaking of oaths, I do have some interesting news. I went to Xia Zhengsi to borrow some books from him, and we talked in English. He said he hadn't heard such fluent English for such a long time that it made him nostalgic. Then he shared with me many of his memories, one of which was a romance!"

Yao Qiu'er closed up the homework she was grading, immediately sat by Jiaren's side and urged: "So tell me now! Hurry!"

"Xia Zhengsi told me that when he was young, he lived by the Atlantic ocean where he fell in love. He proposed to the lady three times but eventually she changed her mind. It almost drove him so crazy that he wanted to throw himself into the sea."

Yao Qiu'er muttered: "What stopped him from doing so then?"

"As he was about to jump, he felt an invisible force grabbing his hair and, in the blink of an eye, he was sitting on the steps at the porch of his home. He then thought maybe he shouldn't kill himself. Although he didn't kill himself, he didn't live well because he often ran into his love, who changed lovers quite often. To escape such horrible torture, he left his hometown for China."

Yao Qiu'er stood up to cook dinner, complaining: "What a dull story it is with so few twists and turns!"

Sure enough, the new version of Xia Zhengsi's love story that later became known among his colleagues was much richer with the addition of a sentimental scene of him bidding farewell to his love before he went to the seaside and his profound inner struggles by the seaside. With the multiple in-and-outs of the story in Mean alley, it didn't bear the slightest resemblance to the original plot and characters.

Xueyan told Bichu and Huifen how such a sad story had been treated as a joke and how those people who heard the story enjoyed themselves. They agreed that it was a relief that they only talked about it behind Professor Xia's back.

The 'eternal bachelor' Xiao Cheng was also a constant target of observation from You Jiaren. He told people that any research on these classic bachelors would provide sufficient material to write a romantic novel. People used to include these bachelors in their small talk, but the small talk was sympathetic. Once the You couple joined the discussion, the talk inevitably descended into Mean alley style. People avoided the two when they realised how mean the couple were, which was somehow detected by the couple. They tried to refrain from such meanness but they couldn't let go of their addiction to wallowing in other people's misfortunes.

I guess when they did this, they must have felt they were much cleverer than other mortal beings. Their enjoyment came without the slightest concern for other people's feelings. If their target didn't get the message, they would strive to make sure they would. It was just like hunting where the predator must shoot its moving, living prey to quench the hunter's thirst for killing. Where would the fun be if such delightful gossip were kept between the two of them behind closed doors in Mean alley?

They were so lucky that their downstairs neighbour, Liu Wanfang, the wife of a teacher in the maths department, Shao Wei, had a great predilection for spreading gossip since her husband's world of numbers was a domain guarded by iron walls for her. Liu Wanfang envied the couple's marital harmony and admired their profound knowledge. Did she feel she had become more learned when she was retelling the secrets fabricated by Qiu'er?

After Earl's newspaper announcement and Xia Zhengsi's love story, the You couple was quiet for a while.

When the Chinese department invited You Jiaren to give a lecture, he didn't pick just any poem, novel, theory or translation. He went with 'Shakespeare and Tang Xianzu'. Although drama was not his line of study, he could sail through it with the knowledge he had. He first gave an outline of Shakespeare's most important plays, and then recited chunks of the original texts with rich cadence and emotion, heightening the dramatic effect. He also recited the famous lyrics from Tang Xianzu's best-known work *'The Peony Pavilion'*[1] without dropping a single word. It was a pity that he couldn't sing Kunqu opera. Otherwise, his lecture would have been even more intriguing with his singing of *'The Peony Pavilion'*.

It was a rich and lively lecture, but it didn't highlight any comparisons or point out any differences in the ideas or artistic presentations of the two playwrights as the title of his lecture indicated. He just put the two together, as he did with the title of the lecture. There were mixed reactions from the audience. Some were amazed while others were confused. When news of such contrasting reactions reached Jiang Fang, he commented that some foreign sinologists were like this, only able to bury their noses in reciting the lines without forming their own ideas. When the comment reached Mean alley, it immediately ignited the ire of the You couple.

Two reporters in Chongqing were detained for reporting what was prohibited by the government. Professor Jiang Fang published an article in a journal criticising this undemocratic practice and advocated the protection of human rights. Both his words and his opinions were sharp. The students all supported Professor Jiang, even though a few also said that Jiang was getting more and more 'leftist'. You Jiaren had always refrained from any political talk.

Some people said that he was too lofty while others thought he was selfish for not wanting to get into any trouble. But this time when he heard his colleagues talking about the event, he dived into attacks against Jiang Fang's article, ignoring the detained reporters: "Human rights is a very popular topic nowadays. Now it's not hard to understand why Jiang Fang is said to be an opportunist. But it is not I who said that!"

Some days passed but the two reporters still hadn't been released. A couple of societies made vague noises in support of the two of them. Professor Jiang presented his opinion vehemently: "What is the use of a man's mouth if not to talk? If one is not allowed to talk, is one still a man?"

These words were first quoted on wall posters beside the university gate, and then quoted by several avant-garde newspapers.

When You Jiaren read the paper, he told Li Lian: "I think Jiang Fang has been talking big. He pretends he has progressive ideas to polish someone's apples."

Li Lian, candid and righteous, asked: "Why should he pretend and whose apples is he polishing?"

You Jiaren was speechless at Li Lian's questions. Meng Fuzhi used to appreciate You Jiaren's expert knowledge, but he lowered his opinion of You Jiaren when he heard these words. Someone told Jiang Fang about You's comments, but his generous mind simply ignored them. He wasn't in the habit of arguing with anyone over trivial matters.

When they were free, the You couple loved to spend their time at the Greensleeves Café, enjoying the weeping willows and the ripples outside the window. They had written some poems inspired by the willows and the café, the publication of which in the supplement pages of some newspapers gained lots of favourable comments and admiration for their versatility. Lü Xiangge would join in the conversation at their table sometimes. The knowledge that Xiangge was related to Mrs Meng and had left Beiping with Xueyan intrigued the couple.

"There were only the two of you when you left Beiping? How brave you were!" Yao Qiu'er said.

"Wei Feng sent his former classmate in college called Li Yuming to meet us. Then we rode on small donkeys and stayed in inns along the way. It took us so many days to get out of Hebei province," said Xiangge.

"I heard people say they had been to Yan'an?" asked You Jiaren.

"Li Yuming turned us over to others. I couldn't wait for so long, so I left first. I guess they must have been to Yan'an," answered Xiangge.

"Li Yuming sounds like a human trafficker!"

Looking around, Xiangge lowered her voice and laughed: "No, he's not like that. But I did see he likes Miss Xueyan very much."

The You couple was fascinated by such a revelation and tried to get more juicy details from Xiangge. But Xiangge, though good at fabricating, was confined by her poor imagination and barely provided an outline of the 'story'. Still, a rich romance came into being from such a shabby outline by the You couple.

Rumours spread fast like the plague, even among the educated. Ling Xueyan traveling thousands of miles in search of her husband was received and studied like a ballad. The most romantic section was when the best man fulfilled the duties for the bridegroom, which 'represented' the emotional struggle between Xueyan and Li Yuming. If the You couple's talent had been devoted to writing, they could have made popular writers. What a pity it was that they were determined to harm the lives of those around them to satisfy their salacious delight in gossiping since it wouldn't have been complete for the two of them if gossip once created was not well delivered, and even worse if it was not well received.

Xueyan and Wei Feng would stay at Wasted alley for two or three days when they were in town. Yao Qiu'er and Liu Wanfang both liked to call on her. Xueyan's quiet nature meant she didn't like gossiping about anyone. When people came to her with gossip, she just listened. At the sight of the two vividly engaged in their gossiping, Xueyan felt she was doing the two a favour.

When Yao Qiu'er told other female colleagues and the wives of the faculty about Xueyan's ballad, some contradicted her on the spot for such nonsense and some reminded her how inappropriate such an action was while others listened and then the story stopped circulating. Yao Qiu'er was very frustrated to see such a wall acting as a barrier for the spreading of her masterpiece. It was a relief that she still had Liu Wanfang, who paid an extraordinary amount of attention to Xueyan and sighed with dismay upon hearing Yao Qiu'er's 'Xueyan Ballad' as Wanfang claimed it was beyond her understanding how Xueyan would be so willing to leave her celebrated family to marry someone poor like Wei Feng. Although Liu Wanfang herself was the target of the You couple's taunts and gossip, her lack of comprehension to read between the lines because of the subtle words of the Yous damped the effect and nurtured her passion to pass on the gossip. When she visited Huifen one day, she sincerely recommended the 'ballad'.

Huifen was furious: "What nonsense! This is too harsh for Xueyan! You mustn't tell her!"

Wanfang answered rather kind-heartedly: "If you say this is nonsense, then someone must have made it up. Is it proper to keep her in the dark?"

Huifen grudgingly agreed that rumours would spread without any clarification because they were rumours, but they would spread even faster with clarification. What a tricky dilemma! Huifen had been quite busy helping a friend's exhibition recently. She decided she would go and talk to Bichu the moment she could leave for a while. She just hoped she had enough time to attend to all the details of the exhibition now that she had to worry about such annoying tittle-tattle. She was raging inside and cursed in her Shanghai dialect: "It's just lousy tittle-tattle!"

It was quite popular for colleagues in the same university to hold family parties. That afternoon, the Yous held a recitation party where all who attended could read aloud a passage from a favourite novel or a stanza from a poem. It was said to be a tradition borrowed from Europe or America. Xia Zhengsi read from 'The Brothers Karamazov' by Fyodor Dostoyevsky, while You Jiaren read a passage from 'A Tale of Two Cities' by Charles Dickens. The atmosphere changed according to the materials being read, but it remained attentive and lively. Xueyan read several lines in French from 'Les Fleurs du Mal' ('The Flowers of Evil') by French poet Charles Baudelaire. Her pronunciation was natural and relaxed, her voice sweet and soft. A gentle ray of sunshine rested on her old white loose silk blouse, bringing out the radiant beauty of her delicate face. When she was done, Xia Zhengsi teased her: "When you read 'The Flowers of Evil' it sounds more like 'The Flowers of Good'. You should have picked 'La Nuit d'Août' or 'La Nuit de Mai'".

Xueyan smiled. "I like Alfred De Musset, too, but this poem has puzzled me ever since I first read it. It still does."

After several more readings, someone noticed that Mrs You was absent. Qiu'er and Wanfang were busy making *ersi*, a popular local Yunnan snack made of sliced rice cake and served with different toppings. Xueyan went over to help but stopped when Qiu'er whispered: "It's not the first time two men both loved the same woman passionately, just like in 'A Tale of Two Cities'. As I told you before..." she chuckled: "Just like what has happened between Mrs Wei and their old friend Li Yuming." They lowered their voices and prattled on. Completely aware that this was just pure gossip, Liu Wanfang listened with intense enjoyment. When Xueyan heard the two mentioning "Mrs Wei" and "Li Yuming", she listened quietly until the turmoil inside her was ready to burst out. She could listen no more!

Striding into the yard, she confronted Yao Qiu'er: "Mrs You, how could you say that?"

Yao Qiu'er dried her hands with a cloth, turned around to face Xueyan with a smile: "What? Nothing! We were just chatting!"

Xueyan said: "I heard you talking about me!"

Liu Wanfang put her arm around Xueyan's waist: "Mrs Wei, we were not talking about you."

Xueyan knew the two wouldn't admit what they had talked about and that she shouldn't make a scene. Before the dizziness in her head and the sickness in her stomach seized her, she hurried out of the Yous'.

When Yao Qiu'er walked into the room, someone suggested asking Xueyan to read a stanza from 'La Nuit de Mai'. Qiu'er said: "She has left. Isn't it my turn? I'd like to read 'Jane Eyre'."

You Jiaren said: "You don't need to read it. You may just recite it."

Qiu'er rolled her eyes at her husband: "My brain is not as big as yours!"

She read a section from the novel. Her pronunciation was thick with her Chinese dialect, which was why she was not asked to teach spoken English. Some time later when Liu Wanfang served the *ersi* on a tray, she looked somewhat distraught.

Xueyan stumbled out of Mean alley into Wasted alley, angry and hurt at the same time. She felt her head was going to explode with so much boiling inside it. How mean these people were! How could they cook up such a vicious lie in which Li Yuming was like a playboy who had an affair with her? How could humans be so stupid as not to come up with any law to punish those who cooked up and spread rumours instead of letting rumours run rampant and hurt their victims? She was overcome by dizziness. Xueyan supported herself by putting her hand against the wall while the baby kicked inside her as if to remind her: "I'm here! You have me!" Feeling comforted, she muttered: "Yes, I have you!"

Huifen happened to go past the alley. Seeing Xueyan leaning against the wall, she hurried over to her and helped her to stand, urging: "What has happened? Tell me what has happened!"

Xueyan forced back her tears and told Huifen what had happened back at the Yous. Huifen almost ground her teeth. "She finally took up the job herself!"

Xueyan asked: "So you have heard about this already?"

"Yes, I have, but no one buys her nonsense! Don't you worry. Come and take a rest at my place."

They went over to Huifen's house. When Xueyan was cleaning herself up, Huifen hesitated a while before she spoke up: "What I'm going to say may not be proper and you don't need to mention it to Wei Feng either." Xueyan hadn't thought about what was proper and what was not, but she knew either way would be hard, so she remained silent.

Huifen continued in a comforting tone: "Wei Feng and you are perfect. That's why they want to sprinkle some pepper onto your marriage."

Xueyan's tears streamed down her face: "This is not pepper. This is poison!"

Huifen taunted Xueyan purposefully: "See? You haven't got a clue about me at all! If you gave even one second of thought about what I have been through, you wouldn't feel like that. You are living in paradise where no rumour of any kind can hurt you!"

Xueyan took the 'bait' and hastily asked: "How's the exhibition?"

Huifen answered musingly: "I want to keep myself occupied. That's why I agreed to help this former classmate of mine. Who knows! Once it starts, things just keep rolling in. Like tonight I must attend a dinner. Everything must be discussed over dinners! I hate it." Once Xueyan felt much better, the two left together. Huifen didn't go on her way until she had walked Xueyan all the way back to their place at Wasted alley.

When Xueyan arrived home, Wei Feng was talking with Helen, who smiled at Xueyan and greeted her: "Mrs Wei is back! We have finished talking, too." Helen took Xueyan's French class and was a fan of her and her teaching. Xueyan's students summed up her class in two words: smart and serious. Helen excused herself after talking more about Xueyan's French class.

Wei Feng flipped through the papers on the table and was silent for a long while. Xueyan had put aside her hurt from the rumours and had put on her apron to cook. When she went past Wei Feng, she gave him a gentle pat on the arm. Wei Feng grabbed her hand and put it against his cheek: "Xue, I have to tell you some news. You promise you are not going to be too sad. I promise I won't be. Someone from Yan'an told me Li Yuming has committed suicide by throwing himself off a cliff."

Xueyan's eyes widened with disbelief. Tears welled up in her eyes: "How could that be?

Wei Feng said: "Yuming is so strong-willed one couldn't imagine him committing suicide. No details have been revealed." But both had the same thought: Didn't Grandpa Lü, who had a strong will and an iron back, commit suicide in the end? That was Grandpa Lü's last blow against the enemy under extreme circumstances. But Yuming was in Yan'an, the sacred place for revolutionaries, the Mecca the young flocked to in order to realise their ideals and ambitions. "Feng, I can't understand."

"Neither can I." What they didn't understand was different, though. Wei Feng couldn't figure out how people could treat their own companions in such a cruel way. Xueyan couldn't understand why such a world was never free of people hurting others and people hurt by others. The rumour almost escaped from Xueyan's lips with the sudden grief she felt for Yuming, but she didn't want to upset Wei Feng even more with such a fabrication to harm all three of them. Yuming was not spared such a rumour even after his death. The thought of it brought tears to Xueyan's eyes again. Wei Feng, who was forced to hold things back from Xueyan, pulled Xueyan down to sit by him. Xueyan broke down into sobs in his arms. Being together was their best comfort.

A while later, Xueyan calmed down and went to the kitchen to cook dinner. It was not right to skip dinner, however hard the situation was. Wei Feng picked up the materials again brought to him by Helen who had made photocopies. She was talking to Wei Feng about a group study of these materials. Holding the paper, Wei Feng's mind was filled with the image of Li Yuming. What was he thinking at the last moment of his life before he jumped off the cliff? What a pity there were no such things as souls or ghosts. Otherwise, Yuming might have come to visit him in his dreams.

Not until two days later did Wei Feng know Old Shen had arrived in Kunming, too. Helen set up a time for the two to meet on the hill behind the plant institute. It was a pine grove. When the wind blew, the canopy of pines swayed and moaned overhead. When the two shook hands with each other, they both felt very sad. Old Shen told Wei Feng about the rectification movement in Yan'an, claiming it had purified the team and redeemed those who had gone astray. The talks at the Yan'an Forum on Literature and Art had pointed out the direction for the New Culture Movement. Old Shen asked Wei Feng to have a close study of these talks. Old Shen also mentioned that the war of resistance was hard but that the life in Yan'an was even harder. People in Yan'an were happy because they had faith in overcoming all the hardships.

Wei Feng talked about what he had observed about the teaching faculty. The central government's corruption had bitterly disappointed its citizens. Those who used to support the central government now demonstrated their desire to desert such a corrupt entity. More and more young people with ideals nurtured thoughts of Yan'an.

Old Shen said such a choice was the main trend. When he passed the areas controlled by the KMT, he witnessed forced recruitment because of the insufficient supply of soldiers for the local forces. All the new conscripts were tied up like prisoners and later forced to fight at the front. Wei Feng hadn't seen similar things happening around here. Old Shen said corruption would spread. In the end, he talked about Li Yuming's death. During the rectification movement, Li Yuming was under investigation. It looked like he had failed to evaluate his situation from a wider perspective. It was said it might have been an accident when he fell off the cliff. It had been brought up at a meeting that Wei Feng might have a period of further education in Yan'an during his summer vacation. Wei Feng was at first very excited at the news, then his excitement was replaced by a vague bewilderment. He thought he would think it over later since he was not leaving for Yan'an right at that moment.

Wei Feng saw Old Shen only that one time in Kunming. When the members of the Kunming branch studied the talks at the Yan'an Forum on Literature and Art, they were impressed by the novel and profound significance carried by the text of the talks. One's stand was the first thing the talks dealt with. Would corrupt officials and ordinary people crushed by the heavy burden of taxation share the same point of view about social issues? On the subject of whether literature and art should only serve the workers, peasants and soldiers, some came up with the question: what should people in other walks of life do? Would it be possible to find a form of art and literature loved by all? Those questions remained unanswered, but those questions were raised after serious thinking. All those present felt they were approaching a novel theory which might benefit mankind and which could be accessed by deliberation.

The exhibition Huifen had been busy preparing was for a prestigious painter called Zhao Junwei, who had studied in Paris and stayed on there for a number of years. When he returned to China two years ago, he was employed by the National School of Fine Arts in Chongqing and had lived in the suburbs ever since. He had come to Yunnan for its natural beauty.

Huifen knew him before she got married and shared many friends' predictions that he would grow to be famous in due course. When Huifen saw his works for the exhibition, she was amazed at the quality. Most of the exhibits were traditional Chinese paintings which employed and integrated Western skills. Some oil paintings were included as well. With help from various quarters, Huifen managed to borrow an assembly hall from a middle school. The exhibition was staged with help from her friends in painting circles.

On the opening day of the exhibition, Huifen was the general receptionist who also oversaw the signatures at the sign-in. Zhao Junhui, standing at the gate greeting the guests and beaming with charm, looked handsome in his navy-blue thin woollen suit and a check tie. The visitors included many prominent figures in different fields such as President Qin and his wife and several high-ranking officials from the provincial government. Zhao Junhui guided them around as a good host would do. They paused when they reached a long scroll painted with eight eminent monks radiating with spiritual energy. One newspaper mentioned in its introduction to the exhibition that the scroll embodied the painter's ideals. Zhao Junhui smiled at the audience and explained that this painting took him 10 years to conceive.

Several smartly-dressed, well-mannered people arrived at the reception desk where visitors signed up. The one standing by Huifen cried out loudly: "Mr Zhu has arrived" and pitched himself into a passionate greeting. Huifen was puzzled by such a 'commotion'. Qian Mingjing had just arrived. He smiled at Huifen and whispered to her: "This is the best buyer today," eyeing Zhu Yanqing. Huifen ignored him and turned to greet other visitors.

Mingjing walked over to greet Zhu Yanqing. Zhao Junhui, who had been informed of Zhu's arrival, invited Zhu to join President Qin.

Visitors kept pouring in and signed up at the reception. Huifen had to leave her post from time to time to greet newcomers. When she came back to the reception, she found Liu Wanfang's signature. She spotted Liu Wanfang talking to Mingjing: "I have long heard of the fact that Professor Qian is a very capable man. How many paintings are you going to buy today?"

Mingjing answered: "None. I can't afford any."

Liu Wanfang laughed: "I don't believe what you're saying."

She walked with Mingjing to appreciate the exhibits, but Mingjing was indifferent to her. Later when Professor Xiao Cheng and Prof Meng Fuzhi turned up, Zhao Junhui and Huifen went up to greet them both. Zhu Yanqing then joined Mingjing: "To tell the truth, I don't have many art cells, but I do enjoy these works." The person beside him said Professor Qian's wife was a painter and that he must know how to appreciate these paintings.

Mingjing laughed: "To tell the truth, today it has nothing to do with your ability to appreciate paintings. It has everything to do with your purse strings." Everyone laughed. Liu Wanfang heard Mingjing's remark, too, and walked over to join them. When her eyes met Zhu Yanqing's, she smiled and blinked. It was a bright smile with her pearl-like teeth.

Mingjing teased her: "Mrs Shao just asked who would buy these paintings. Well, you just stay with Mr Zhu and then you'll get your answer." They talked and walked on.

A painting of peonies using the '*mogu*' technique (meaning 'boneless' skill, which paints forms with ink and paint washes instead of outlines) depicted a couple of blooming peonies. The one bud which was just about ready to bloom had a blushing dot of red, extending all the way downward until the trace disappeared. That trace was powerful enough to stimulate a wild imagination. Huifen had noticed the power in this painting and had put it in a prominent place when she arranged the collection.

When Zhu passed it without noticing, Mingjing pointed at the painting and said: "This one." The two of them looked closer and spotted a line of tiny characters 'Crying in the spring wind on the 15th, behind the swing'. Zhu Yanqing couldn't find the swing in the painting, but he didn't ask.

Wanfang asked with an innocent smile: "Where is the swing?" Yanqing smiled knowingly at her remark.

She pointed at an ink painting of lotus flowers and said: "How could one find a black lotus flower in real life? But this black one is dazzlingly beautiful."

Zhu Yanqing asked: "So, does Mrs Shao like painting, too?" Wanfang shook her head as an answer. Zhu Yanqing said he wanted to buy the two paintings. The ink painting of lotus flowers had a price tag of 8,000 yuan, while the peony had no price tag on it.

Huifen went over to explain: "The peonies are not for sale. I'm sorry I didn't have the time to put a note on the painting to that effect."

Mingjing said: "Will Mr Zhao paint another one?"

Zhu Yanqing said politely: "If Mr Zhao paints a new one, I will be very happy to stick a new price on it."

A while later when Zhao Junhui had seen the professors off, he went over to the painting of the peonies and said: "It will be a different painting for sure. Maybe better. Maybe worse."

Wanfang hastened to say: "It must be better."

Zhu Yanqing said: "I understand. Paintings need inspiration just like composing a piece of music or writing a poem. Isn't it called 'inspiration'?"

Qian Mingjing said: "I assume running a business needs inspiration, too, like when businessmen go to a temple to draw lots or to consult a fortune teller. It's a way of finding their inspiration." As he talked, he passed the scroll of eight monks again and noticed the note 'not for sale' attached to the bottom of the work. Zhu Yanqing bought two portraits to be packed up at the end of the exhibition.

When Zhu Yanqing left, he offered to give Mingjing and Huifen a lift. Since Huifen couldn't leave right away, Mingjing then declined the offer. Seeing Wanfang standing by, Yanqing asked: "Where do you live, Mrs Shao? Would you like a lift?" Wanfang chuckled at the invitation and followed him to his car parked at the entrance of the alley.

As Huifen waited to pack up the rest of the works, she talked with Junhui about the exhibition. Junhui had a forced smile on his face: "Each time a piece of my work is sold, I go through an amputation."

Huifen asked: "Are you going to do another peony painting?"

Gazing at Huifen, Junhui said: "I can never capture the spirit of it exactly, but I can try to come up with something similar." He then invited them all to dinner to show his gratitude, but Huifen left with Mingjing when she had finished wrapping things up.

PART II

M inglun had a tradition of holding a monthly assembly at the beginning of each month. Most of the time President Qin and other directors running different departments of the university would summarise what had happened and how the university had been operating. Sometimes, they would invite guest speakers.

At the March assembly, President Qin came to the stadium with a stout man in a long gown and vest. He introduced the man as Mr Wang. At the mentioning of his name, whispers among the students rippled across the stadium because that Mr Wang was a prominent figure in the KMT administration's propaganda department. Mr Wang's serene face became rather smug at the commotion it had caused. He was probably thinking that his mighty reputation had preceded him. He cleared his throat and began his forceful and expressive speech in pure Sichuan dialect. The following was the best section of his speech:

"I come from the wartime capital, Chongqing, where the Generalissimo (Chiang Kai-shek) is stationed. It's a great pleasure to see how serious you are about your studies. Everyone has a head (he pointed at his). Everyone uses their head to study things and think about things. I want to remind you of the fact that the weight of each head is different. Some are heavier, some are lighter. But the luckiest thing is that we boast the richest and the most important head — the head of the Generalissimo. The war of resistance and the reconstruction of a new country needs this head. The head of our leader is different. It is a head which belongs to us all."

"But is it necessary to chop off everyone else's heads?" A student snapped in Sichuan dialect. Some students laughed out loud. Another student cried: "We don't care about heads. We care about stomachs!"

Mr Wang shot a glance at President Qin. President Qin pressed his hands a little downward to remind the students: "Quiet! Please be quiet!"

"Speaking of hardship, we are living in wartime, and hardship is a normal part of life. We are all experiencing hardship. Only when you realise the importance of supporting the head of our leader, will things become easier. I have spoken on many different occasions about the importance of the head of our leader. It is now a very popular theory. Many people have given it their endorsement. Anyone who dares to challenge my theory and declares all heads weigh the same should have their head weighed!"

All present at the assembly let out a long-held breath without disguising their feelings of relief when Mr Wang ended his 'head' speech. The theory of the head of the leader' had become the target of spicy sarcasm among youngsters since then. The next day, different forms of posters on the theme of the speech were put up on the poster wall by the university gate. There was a cartoon which caught viewers' attention: it depicted a fat man with an enormous head crammed with many copies of the term 'The theory of the head of the leader' and a tiny head riddled with holes and serpents, scorpions and wild animals wriggling out of the holes. The Chinese characters below the tiny head read: This is the head of the leader!

Mr Wang, indignant about the students' reactions, was waiting for an explanation from President Qin, who had gone quiet. During lunch, Mr Wang could no longer hold back his anger and said resentfully: "It looks like the students in this university are openly indifferent to discipline."

"They are, indeed," said President Qin. "We welcome different opinions from the young. The fact that they have opinions means they are interested. It would be more worrying if they didn't have any opinions at all."

Mr Wang snapped: "Everyone needs to remember, whatever the occasion, that the head of our leader is outstanding. The Chinese nation is blessed to have such a head!"

President Qin was silent.

When Mr Wang returned to the 'side' of the Generalissimo, he wrote a report, since he was not important enough to report to the Generalissimo in person. He was lavish in his praise of his loyalty to the Generalissimo and critical of Minglun University's overindulgence of its students. Such a report was bound to stir up trouble.

Most of the college students in Kunming lived on student loans. The loans had been increased but were still barely enough to keep pace with soaring prices. Now student loans couldn't even cover three meals a day, so all the universities and colleges in Kunming had drafted an application to the Ministry of Education to increase the student loans. When the application drafted by the secretariat was discussed at the meeting, all felt the words were not convincing enough and recommended that Fuzhi add several lines. Fuzhi then proposed that they add several sentences describing the lives of the students. When the application reached Chongqing, the Ministry of Education claimed that they couldn't afford such an increase due to a shortage of funds. When discussing the application, one person mentioned the extraordinary wording of the application, saying it reminded him of Meng Fuzhi, which prompted someone else to say no wonder the students at Minglun were so insolent and arrogant because they had their professors behind them. After several rounds of discussion, the demand to increase student loans was denied.

A while after the application, the man who transferred his dogs by plane gave a generous donation to Minglun and other universities as well for "the improvement of the students' lives". The students received the news with mixed feelings: how could a government official be so rich? For such a big sum to be abused to win popularity was indeed solid proof of the government's corruption. Most of the students held the opinion that "we don't want such money". A few said it would be a sign of lack of cooperation to refuse such a well-intended offer from a government official. But such an opinion was from the Three People's League, which had very little influence among students.

Most of the teaching faculty thought the university shouldn't take the donation. At the professors' meeting, professors such as Zhuang Youchen and Liang Mingshi commented that it was rather urgent to improve the students' living conditions since half of the students were suffering from serious anaemia due to malnutrition. All the professors suffered the same hard life. Now even the government had failed to increase the student loans, how could he offer such a generous donation? Some proposed giving the money to refugees or the army fighting against the Japanese in western Yunnan. The university committee finally came up with a decision to decline the offer by claiming that the university didn't take private donations. Minglun's decision to decline the donation caused consternation, and was talked about long afterwards.

Fuzhi, who had already attracted much attention, had now succeeded in attracting extraordinary attention from Mr Wang. Mr Wang tracked down Fuzhi's articles about Song dynasty history and concluded after skimming them that they were literally open attacks on the central government. He arranged for several writers to confront Fuzhi, claiming that Fuzhi had ill intentions and sinister motives.

As Fuzhi and Li Lian walked back from the university to Dragon Tail village, Fuzhi told Li Lian: "I once insisted on including your name on those articles because they belonged to us both. Now I think about it, I am relieved that your name doesn't appear on them. I came up with those views, so I should take responsibility for them and keep you out of trouble."

Li Lian said: "But I endorsed your views. Should they be terrified about what we write? Those are just viewpoints."

Fuzhi said: "Viewpoints are what terrify them most. Different opinions are not tolerated, even negative comments about the ancients. It's bewildering that when their weak points are pointed out, they react as if they have been framed with false charges. This has given me the inspiration for my next article. It will be about 'the case of the Mansion of Crows' involving the Song dynasty writer, poet and statesman Su Dongpo who was accused of attacking the royal court with sarcasm in his report to thank the emperor upon his assumption of office in Huzhou, Zhejiang province."

They walked while talking, and as they approached Dragon Tail village they heard cries and yells from a smaller village nearby. They paused to see a handful of soldiers in tattered khaki uniforms stirring up trouble at a small diner at the entrance of the village. The loud cries were filled with fear. They went over. One soldier had bandages on his head, one was missing an arm, and one who was missing a leg was supporting himself on crutches. This looked like a household with only females since no man was present, and only several women were crying and arguing with the soldiers.

Fuzhi sighed to himself: wounded soldiers again. Because of the serious situation of the war in western Yunnan, a wartime field hospital was set up in Chuxiong city about 150km from Kunming. From time to time, Kunming folks would come across wounded soldiers causing trouble. At this moment, these soldiers had completely lost their tempers and howled: "You're asking me to pay for a bowl of *erkuai* rice cake? Without us fighting and risking our lives at the front, you think you can still sell *erkuai* here? Now it's just a bowl of *erkuai*. If I ask for one from you, you have to say yes!"

Li Lian went up to the man: "You have been fighting hard. We all know..." Li Lian didn't even have the chance to finish his sentence before the soldier with one arm snatched a board and hit Li Lian with it. Li Lian ducked. Fuzhi, trying to protect Li Lian from the blow, blocked the attack with his blue cloth bag. The board landed on Fuzhi's left arm instead. The nail planted in the board cut open the skin on his arm. Blood gushed out. The soldiers recovered their senses at the sight of blood, but they didn't panic or look upset at the fact that one of them had hurt a professor. The man with one arm dropped the board, put down the cash he had forcibly taken from the drawer on the table, and started sobbing loudly. The gang left, wobbling along with one foot or one arm.

Li Lian helped Fuzhi to take off his gown while the female diner owner used some strips of cloth to bandage the wound. She cursed the thieving soldiers vehemently as she picked up the money on the table. Fuzhi sighed: "From their accent, I think they might have been from Henan province. They left their hometown to fight in the war but ended up disabled and impoverished. How could they not feel bitter?" The store owner had already set up a pot and was preparing to cook rice noodles to thank them both, but they declined and walked on slowly homeward.

Seeing that the wound on Fuzhi's arm was not deep, Bichu cleaned it up with alcohol and then covered it up with a thin layer of Yunnan *baiyao* (white medicine), a powdered homeostatic herbal medicine, and bandaged it tightly and securely. Two days later, the wound became inflamed and the arm became swollen. Fuzhi began to have a fever. His alimentary canal began to show symptoms of inflammation, too. The doctor from the university infirmary came from town to check on Fuzhi. He gave Fuzhi surgical treatment for his arm and diagnosed typhus, a regular occurrence at that time. The nomal treatment was not to give food to the patient but to feed them hourly with soup.

Fuzhi laughed at the treatment: "Starvation was the secret prescription for the royal Jia family in 'Dream of the Red Chamber'. In the 20th century, the patient can now have soup every hour."

Bichu teased him: "This is progress." She busied herself with Qinghuan to make the soup and boil the herbal medicine.

The inflammation was checked in time, but the typhus lingered on. Fuzhi had been troubled by a mild fever and had to skip two weeks of teaching. They were all worried. Bichu took Fuzhi to Zedian hospital. The doctor prescribed an expensive medicine and injections. The Mengs' financial status was much worse than when May had to be hospitalised. However hard Bichu tried, she couldn't get together enough money for the medicines and had to borrow some from the university before she could take the prescribed medicines home. All her jewellery, except for her favourite set of jade earrings and broach, had been pawned to make ends meet. Now she knew it was time to let go of the jade set. She pondered how to get the best price for it.

Wei Feng and Xueyan came to see Fuzhi. Xueyan, though heavily pregnant, helped Bichu with all the chores. Bichu asked them to go back home, but Xueyan said: "We still have one important thing to do." She took out a delicate case and handed it to Bichu: "Aunt Bichu, could you entrust someone to sell this? I hope it will help."

Bichu took the case and opened it to see a platinum bracelet sparkling with exquisitely crafted diamonds. The two big diamonds, clustered on a ring of smaller ones, were the size of adzuki beans. Bichu was taken by surprise: "What is this for?"

The couple, standing side by side, answered with deep sincerity: "Uncle Fuzhi needs proper nursing care. We want to help."

Bichu said: "Great minds think alike! I'm thinking of selling that jade jewellery of mine."

Wei Feng said: "I'm told the jade set was handed down from your grandfather. You can't sell it. Xueyan wants you to sell her bracelet. We want to help." When Bichu refused to take the bracelet, Xueyan became anxious and was on the verge of bursting into tears.

Bichu thought it over and decided not to shrug off such a heartfelt gesture: "Alright, I'll keep it."

The couple were so happy that they bowed to Bichu. Before they left, they forced Found the cat to take a bath, which publicly showed its indignation by hissing and screaming.

The following Sunday, both May and Heji were at home. May said Aunt Suchu was concerned about their father's illness and sent Huishu to pay him a visit. Huishu had been enrolled in the department of education at a local university.

Bichu sighed: "Your Aunt Suchu buries herself in prayers and her sutras day and night as if she has withdrawn from the secular world. It's a relief to her and to us that Huishu is sensible and industrious." She then discussed with May whether it was a good idea to ask Hezhu to sell the bracelet.

May deliberated for a moment and said: "Hezhu loves to help but she is not trustworthy."

"What should we do with the bracelet, then?" asked Bichu, showing it to May.

"This is the gift given to Xueyan by her parents on her 21st birthday. I saw her wearing it back then," said May. "It bears Cousin Xueyan's love. Why don't we keep it?"

Bichu nodded: "That's a good plan!"

Qian Mingjing came from town to visit Fuzhi while the mother and daughter were talking. He sat by the bed for a while and then went outside to talk to Bichu. May brought him tea.

Mingjing said: "May has grown to be so helpful. How time flies!"

Bichu said: "She has indeed. I always talk things over with her now."

Mingjing took out a bulging envelope: "Huifen and I want to help because of our admiration for Professor Fuzhi and Madam Bichu." Seeing Bichu's silence, Mingjing continued: "You may give it back to us later."

May suddenly cut in: "Mum, you were planning to sell your jade jewellery. Why don't you ask Professor Qian to help?" Bichu shot her a look of disapproval for so rudely interrupting an adult conversation.

But Mingjing answered: "I've seen the jade jewellery a couple of times. It is very rare. It would be a pity to sell it."

"Money comes and goes, but I would like these items to go to someone who appreciates their value," smiled Bichu.

Mingjing agreed: "True, true! Good things need people who appreciate how good they are. Shall I take it to see what price it will fetch?"

Bichu sighed: "You and Huifen have been so helpul to us all these years. I don't know when I will stop being a burden on you."

Mingjing deliberated for a moment and said: "It's better not to tell Huifen about the jade jewellery. She doesn't like such stuff."

Bichu nodded and turned to May: "Don't talk about this." Then she took out a small case inlaid with mother of pearl, put a piece of tissue paper on the table, and put the jade set on the paper. A ray of sunlight happened to perch on the jade broach, transforming it into a solid emerald puddle. The earrings sparkled with pure, fluid green even without the sunshine.

Mingjing was amazed at the superb quality: "They are gorgeous! Madam Meng, you just wait for my good news."

Bichu said: "I accept your money, but please remember to subtract the sum later when you sell the jade set."

Mingjing said: "Please don't worry about the sum, madam. You shouldn't live such an austere life anymore. Health is important. The set is very rare on account of its purity. I don't know much about jade, but as the saying goes 'gold has a price but jade is priceless'."

May said: "Someone knows." That remark earned May a second disapproving look from her mother.

Mingjing said to Bichu: "It's just kids' prattle. No offense taken." He then asked Bichu whether she wanted him to take the jade away with him this time.

Bichu said: "Yes, please. You need to show the buyer before they make their decision." Her eyes cast a wet, lingering glance over the jade pieces. She picked up the broach, stroked it gently, and then cupped it carefully in her hands and went into the bedroom to talk to Fuzhi, who told her: "You have the final say."

Mingjing raised his voice: "I'll take the jade pieces and see what offers they get. Probably they'll make their way back if the offers are not favourable!"

When Bichu came out of the bedroom, she asked Mingjing: "You must help me to sell them." Putting the pieces into the delicate case, she handed it to Mingjing.

Mingjing took it from her: "It's still early. I can make it back to town." May had cooked him a bowl of noodles and took it to him. Mingjing was very happy: "I'm starving!" He finished up the noodles and hurried back to town.

The broach had been handed down for generations in Bichu's family. The matching earrings were bought in Beiping. The broach had been remounted when the earrings were bought. Bichu seldom wore jewellery of any kind, but she loved this set. Fuzhi knew better than anyone else that if Bichu had any other options, she would never have let go of this set. No one could tell what would happen in such tough times. A body in poor health can't survive hardship but nursing care takes money. He rose from his bed slowly and walked to sit in the outside room: "Evidence shows that jewellery such as hair pins, bracelets and rings used to enslave people. Now you are emancipated."

It took Bichu two seconds to get the dry humour: "But it has been with us for decades. I still feel sad about having to leg go of it." She turned over May's words "someone does" and concluded Mingjing would probably go to the chieftainess. The realisation that she had failed to take this into consideration upset Bichu.

Seeing Bichu lost in her worries, Fuzhi tried to comfort her: "If we were asked to sell all our property to help our country, I think we would willingly say yes. Luckily, we still don't need to face such a tough situation. Better still, we don't need to run from air raids anymore. When I recover, we'll move back to town."

Mention of moving back to town cheered Bichu up. The house destroyed by the bombing was being rebuilt. The owner of the property invited Fuzhi and his family to move back when they met at a dinner. The reconstruction lasted quite a long time with many interruptions.

When dusk fell, and it was almost time for dinner with May cooking leafy mustard and Heji helping to lay the table, heavy footsteps came from the courtyard. Qinghuan, who was collecting the dry laundry in the yard, asked: "Who are you looking for?"

The stranger asked: "Is Professor Meng home?"

Bichu came out when she heard the question and saw two men in the uniform of the armed police. She asked: "What for?"

The two answered: "Professor Meng needs to come with us."

Bichu said: "He's ill. Which branch do you belong to? Why do you want him?"

One muttered the name of some department and prepared to enter the house. Before Bichu could ask more questions, Fuzhi came out at the commotion in the yard: "Do you have an invitation? Or a summons? Should I be handcuffed?"

"We won't do that," they answered, walking toward Fuzhi and forcing him to go with them by holding him tightly between them. Bichu felt the sky was falling and the ground trembling with the shock. She supported herself by leaning against the wall, so she would not fall. Heji rushed over to hold her. May ran out of the gate and saw Fuzhi being forced to sit in a jeep parked outside. She hurled herself toward the jeep and grabbed the handle, calling loudly: "Leave us your address!" The two men ignored her and started the jeep. May ran after it. Fuzhi didn't want May to get hurt and ordered her sternly: "Go back!" May watched the jeep slithering out of her sight along the path paved with flagstones. She didn't have the time to cry because she had to talk to her mother about how to handle the emergency. She ran all the way back. Most of Fuzhi's colleagues had moved back into town, only Li Lian and his family stayed like the Mengs did. Bichu asked Qinghuan to go and fetch Li Lian at once. Li Lian responded to her request by running all the way to the Mengs, panting: "We should report this to the university immediately. I'll go. I walk faster."

May said: "I want to go with Professor Li."

Qinghuan blurted out: "Let me go. I can ride. I'll ask Zhao Er to lend me his horse." Bichu didn't agree because she thought it was not safe for a young girl to ride alone in the night. Qinghuan assured Bichu: "I know the road like the back of my hand. Don't worry about me." Without any alternatives, Bichu agreed to let Qinghuan go. She hastily wrote a message and gave it to Qinghuan, who secured it and then ran downhill. Zhao Er was away with his horse. Zhao Er's wife went to the other two who had horses and tried to borrow one for Qinghuan. But one horse was sick and the other was giving birth. Qinghuan was worried to death. Tears fell: "How can I even fail to finish this one task?" She ran back. After more talk, all agreed Li Lian should walk to the university to report the matter. May wanted to go. Bichu sighed: "If you were a boy."

Heji then shouted: "I'm a boy! I'll go!"

368

Bichu stopped him: "You are too young to go." In the end, Li Lian went with May.

It was already deep into the moonless night. The two strode downhill. They would run for several steps and then walk to regulate their breathing before running again. How much they wanted to arrive at the university within the next second! When they were almost at the bend by the dyke, they spotted a shadow moving toward them. Their hearts beat faster. May suddenly shouted: "Dad is back!" A close look revealed it was Fuzhi walking slowly toward them.

"What happened?" asked Li Lian.

Fuzhi waved his hand between his breathless panting and racing heart beat: "Let's go back first."

May said: "Dad, take your time. I need to go back to tell mum you are back!" She turned around and dashed up the hill. Li Lian found a stick and gave it to Fuzhi to use as a walking stick. They paused to rest after about a dozen steps. As they struggled to reach the foot of the mountain, Bichu, with May and Heji tagging along behind her, was coming downhill to meet them. When they reached home, they made a careful analysis of the event and guessed there were two possibilities. One was that they might have got the wrong person; the other was that it was meant to warn Fuzhi off.

Bichu wrapped up the discussion: "Whatever it is, the priority now is to take a good rest. Let's all go and have some shut-eye."

That night, Fuzhi's mind was racing. When he was taken away, his mind had gone blank. Opinions were quite varied then and many opinions were critical of the government. Both his words and deeds were admirable. How could he be arrested instead of someone more activist? Was he kidnapped for ransom? But he was too poor to be such a target. Besides, his family couldn't afford any ransom, either. The two didn't look like bandits.

When he was taken away, it was still light. The water in the Mang river glimmered in the cloying darkness. The jeep drove on along the river as if it was heading to town. Several turns later, Fuzhi lost his sense of direction. With the disappearance of the light, darkness fell, smothering everything in its embrace, and one had to breathe deeply to inhale more oxygen. He tried his best to steady his breathing, reminding himself that he must deal with the situation and that he couldn't pass out. The jeep drove on for a while and stopped when they saw the headlights from another jeep driving toward them. Both jeeps stopped. Everyone except Fuzhi got out of the vehicles to talk by the roadside. Then they went back to their own vehicles. The man in Fuzhi's jeep ordered the driver to go back. He didn't know they were back in front of the village by the Mang river until the jeep stopped.

They both asked him to get out: "You can go home now. Sorry we can't see you off."

He didn't know where he was, just like someone who had woken up from a nightmare. It was beyond his expectation that he could return in such a short time, which would be etched on his heart for a long time. If such an operation was just targeted at him, it would have been rather simple. But who knew how things would develop?

He began to worry about the safety of other academics. When he taught the morality class, some students assumed he was helping the government put restraints on students' freedom of thought; when he proposed to learn from history, the government assumed he was helping the other party. How hard the road of independence was! He felt he was walking on thin ice, under which the fathomless waves were roaring forcefully. He felt light-headed and gave Bichu a tug.

Out of the blue, he remembered a line from Bai Juyi's poem entitled: 'Seeing Li Bai in a Dream':

> "Take extra care when travelling
> over vast, deep expanses of water;
> Lest you lose your footing
> and fall into the jaws of flood dragons."

He heaved a deep sigh. Bichu patted him and cooed: "Get some sleep."

"I can only make sure that I myself have nothing to be ashamed of," thought Fuzhi and gradually slipped into sleep.

The next day when Li Lian reported what had happened to Fuzhi, everyone present gasped. President Qin called several offices which he thought might have been involved in the incident, but they all assured him they wouldn't do such a thing to Professor Meng for they all knew who Meng Fuzhi was.

One more day passed and there was still no clue about who should be held responsible. When Qin Xunheng and Xiao Cheng went to visit Fuzhi, Fuzhi elaborated on what had happened that night. They talked for a long time.

Qin Xunheng said: "There must be someone behind it. There are all kinds of organisations stationed in Kunming because of the confrontation between the local forces and the central government. This event might have been someone trying to fly their kite. Since it was not clear what Fuzhi's orientation was, they might have thought it would be easier to manage. That's my assumption."

370

Fuzhi smiled: "Some questions never get answered. It's just like how history is written. Since it is written, then it's subjective. How can readers tell what is factual and what is fabricated? Chinese official circles have accumulated too much filth over the centuries. It needs to be purged for the sake of progress. The motive behind those articles I wrote was to express my wish for a better government, not to topple it. If they are flying a kite, then they should make me their clear target and spare others."

Xiao Cheng said: "We are all pathetic because society now has no independent cultural strength. But I am confident that we'll take the road to democracy. It just needs time."

The three then agreed that although no one claimed to be responsible for Fuzhi's incident, they should file a protest to the provincial government and relevant departments, demanding proper protection of personal safety. President Qin and Xiao Cheng also brought news of Yan Liangzu being restored to his former position. They thought such a decision to enable those who were capable to fight in the war was wise.

Xiao Cheng brought the letter Earl had sent to the ancestral temple. Bichu, May and Heji read it first. It was a rather brief letter, saying that she missed home and was concerned about her mum's health, and that she was alright and didn't feel the impact of war although Dali was much closer to the front than Kunming was. It was very quiet around there. She felt she would grow into a plant someday if she kept studying plants like this. This was the third letter from Earl since her departure, which was quite brief like the other two. Bichu commented: "It must be much cooler living in Diancangshan (Daincang mountain). Why didn't she tell me whether she is eating well or not?"

When President Qin and Xiao Cheng left, the four picked up Earl's letter and closely scrutinised it again. May blurted out: "Let's move to the temple in Diancangshan. It has all kinds of flowers."

"Are we going to run again?" Heji was confused.

Fuzhi's heart missed a beat at Heji's confusion. He rubbed Heji's hair.

The idea of "going to the temple in Diancangshan" had triggered a train of thought in Fuzhi's head. Everyone had their own path. For Earl, he wouldn't worry about her much because she would achieve something in botany. But for the country and the nation, he had a lot to worry about. He deemed the articles he wrote were out of his concern for the country and its people. How could the government treat different opinions so harshly? The final exams were already around the corner, but he still hadn't regained his strength from his illness. How could he not be anxious? As he was wrestling with his thoughts, Bichu came in with his herbal medicine in a bowl:

"Nothing is more important than your health." She used a small spoon and blew on the spoonful of medicine to cool it before smilingly administering it to Fuzhi.

"I will recover," Fuzhi smiled back at Bichu.

Several days later, Governor Yin sent one of his people to visit Fuzhi, saying he was sorry that Professor Meng was subjected to such barbaric behaviour here in Kunming. Fuzhi had a brief talk with the messenger about the protection of human rights. Jiang Fang asked Fuzhi to publish what they had talked about in a newspaper but Fuzhi declined to do so.

Although not many people knew about Fuzhi's encounter, visitors from the city came one by one. One morning, a jeep ran all the way uphill along the path, with a bodyguard standing on the running board on each side of the vehicle. Qinghuan was sweeping the floor by the gate. The sight of the jeep sent her into a complete panic and she ran to inform Bichu and Fuzhi. The car had reached the yard. When it stopped, out of the car stepped a solemn general and a sweet college girl. Yan Liangzu and Huishu had arrived. One bodyguard announced loudly in the courtyard: "Commander Yan Liangzu!"

Bichu and Fuzhi hurried out to greet Liangzu. Huishu went up to Bichu to hold her hand and called out "Aunt Bichu" before dropping her head and sinking back into silence.

They all went into the house. When everyone was seated, Liangzu began: "Your elder sister Suchu is concerned about you all, but you know she won't leave the house. I have heard what happened to Fuzhi. I think both of the sons-in-law of the Lü family will have good luck. I am leaving for western Yunnan to join the fighting."

Fuzhi said: "I was told a couple of days ago about the restoration of your rank and position. You must be occupied with loads of work to do and you don't need ..."

"Of course, I will visit you before I leave," Liangzu cut Fuzhi short. "For the past couple of years, I didn't dare to visit friends or to take care of you because of the constraints on me." The two then engaged in discussion until Liangzu cried: "Do you think you are dreaming?"

Fuzhi was lost for an answer to such a question: "Maybe."

They stared at each other and then burst into laughter.

The two bodyguards had moved about a dozen boxes from the jeep into the yard, including military supplies from the US army such as milk powder, cocoa powder, coffee and canned meat, and local specialties such as milk fans. There were two packs of *harsma*, also known as 'snow frog fat', a popular tonic back then, so called because the product is made from the dried fatty tissue found near frogs' fallopian tubes.

Fuzhi exclaimed: "It looks like you've moved a mini warehouse into my yard!"

Liangzu said sincerely: "We all wish your family happiness and good health. We haven't won the war of resistance against Japan yet."

Fuzhi mused: "Even when we win the war, there will still be a long tortuous path ahead."

Huishu followed Bichu back to her bedroom. Huishu took out a rosary made of ebony and gave it to Bichu: "Mum used to pray with this rosary. Mum said the beads have absorbed countless prayers and she wants Aunt Bichu to have it, wishing it will bless the family and keep away bad spirits."

A warm current rose in Bichu's heart. Looking around the room, her eyes stopped at the scroll written by Fuzhi. She then hung it on the bottom roller of the scroll, and asked Huishu: "What will your mother use now that she has given this rosary to me?"

Huishu said: "Mum has another quality one, but she emphasised that this one has more blessings. When I feel upset, I sometimes would hold the rosary and say some prayers. I would feel at peace inside. It's hard to explain how, though."

"Your mother won't be bullied with you present."

Huishu hesitated a moment and said: "I don't know where Aunt Hezhu got the information that Aunt Bichu is going to sell your jade set. She said Governor Yin's wife Madam Yin wants to have a look at it."

Bichu said: "I'm sorry. I have asked Mingjing to take care of the sale. I think he'll show the chieftainess first."

Huishu said: "Aunt Bichu, your jade set is a rare find. What Aunt Hezhu meant is that she can get you a better price. She asked me to tell you this," said Huishu. After a pause, she continued: "I guess she wants to redeem herself, so I think she'll try her best."

"Now that she knows I'm going to sell the set, then she must know I no longer have it with me," deliberated Bichu. "When you go back, please tell her I appreciate her kindness. If she has some potential buyers, please ask her to do me a favour and to try and get a better price for me. We are counting on the money."

"I understand," Huishu said and her head sank again.

Bichu wanted to cook lunch, but Huishu stopped her: "Dad has made arrangements. Is Uncle Fuzhi feeling strong enough to take a walk in the Black Dragon Pond park?" Outside, Fuzhi was in high spirits. Bichu made some preparations and the four of them got into the jeep and headed for the park, leaving Qinghuan and Found the cat to take care of the house.

Once the vehicle passed the Mang river, it didn't take long to reach the Dragon river. The water roared and rushed with choppy waves breaking and flowing all at once. When they passed the plant institute, they thought about Earl. Liangzu said: "You don't need to worry about Miss Earl. My observation tells me she's going to be a botanist."

Bichu said: "We do hope your prediction is accurate."

When they got off at the Black Dragon pond, the two bodyguards somehow managed to find a chair so that Fuzhi could sit in it and be carried along, which Fuzhi declined, claiming he didn't deserve such treatment. Then the small group took their time, walking and enjoying the scenery, feeling refreshed.

Liangzu led the way: "I'm going to show you a perfect place." The other three followed him to the back of the main hall of the temple built on a terrace and saw a small door in the enclosing wall. Taking the door, they entered a bushy grove of pines with green grass clustered under the trees and dotted with azalea shrubs. The azaleas here didn't grow together. Instead, they spread out in small patches as if to form a maze. Although it had passed their golden blooming time, the flowers remained bright, clinging to the grassy blanket of ground. At first they didn't feel the wind. The deeper they walked into the grove, the stronger the wind whistled through the top of the pines. Liangzu asked: "What do you think of this place? Although I'm a soldier, I do have good taste, don't I?"

Fuzhi, feeling tired after the walk, picked a stump to sit on: "It's a good choice if one wants to withdraw from the mundane world."

"I don't want to withdraw. The moment I knew I had been restored to my former position and could fight in the war, I came back to life."

Bichu sighed: "Does Fuzhi want to withdraw? I don't think so."

Fuzhi said: "You know me."

The bodyguards came to spread a large tarpaulin on the ground and put a pot of tea on it. Liangzu waved at them to leave them alone. Listening to the whistling of the wind in the pines and enjoying the flowers, all four of them seemed to forget their troubles. Huishu had run off from the adults to a nearby creek.

Liangzu began rather suddenly: "I have always subscribed to the notion that a soldier must be prepared to die. It's not hard to see how fierce the battle I'm heading to will be, so I want to entrust Huishu to Bichu and Fuzhi. When you go back to Beiping, take her with you and let her finish college there."

Bichu's eyes became wet: "You shouldn't say such things. We'll take good care of Huishu, but Brother Liangzu, you'll take care of her forever."

Fuzhi said: "Going to college in Beiping is indeed a good idea. Brother Liangzu, you don't need to worry about Huishu."

Liangzu smiled: "I know I didn't need to say those things since her Aunt Bichu is her mother Suchu's dear sister. Besides, the Meng family is no ordinary family." They didn't notice that Huishu had returned. She stood quietly behind Bichu. At the mention of the Meng family by her father, she went up to Fuzhi and bowed.

Bichu said: "As I have always said, Huishu is a smart girl, and she is blessed."

They stayed a while longer and then Liangzu asked his bodyguards to prepare the chair for Fuzhi, insisting he be carried in the chair. Without any energy to walk further, Fuzhi sat in the chair and was carried by the two bodyguards all the way down the hill until they reached Black Dragon pond.

Outside the park were some small diners selling rice noodles or rice cakes. These diners were not suitable places for them to have a quiet talk. Many organisations had rented rooms from the park back then, so Liangzu had asked to borrow a room from an institute to set up a dinner. Things were ready when they arrived. When they went into the room and sat down at the table, some people came in to serve dishes and wine. Liangzu told them: "Except for serving dishes, keep your distance from us." When he glanced over the appetizers, he commented: "The same old stuff."

Since Fuzhi was taking medicine and was not allowed to drink anything alcoholic, they drank tea instead. Liangzu held his teacup and said: "The road ahead is long and tortuous. I'm not afraid to fight the Japanese because my belief that we will win the war is as steady as a rock. What I'm afraid of is the next step after we win the war of resistance against Japan."

Fuzhi said: "If one can't fight back, then one has to escape. Escape is not limited to running away from one place to another. For example, the old man in Bai Juyi's poem 'The Old Man with a Broken Arm' secretly smashed his right arm with a rock in the night since his name was listed on the recruitment roll when he was young. This is also called escape, and the old man had escaped from the death he was doomed to by losing one arm. But it isn't so simple if the escape involves more than one person's life."

"It might require sacrificing one life to save the rest," mused Liangzu.

"That," Fuzhi stared into Liangzu's eyes, "has never been the best option."

After the bodyguards had served the hot dishes, they all began to eat.

"Today only two dishes are worthy of introduction. One is steamed chicken in a clay casserole pot. The preparation started early this morning.

The other one is fried lotus petals. There's a lotus pond nearby and they have a special way of eating the flower."

When the steamed chicken was served, the aroma reached everyone. Porridge cooked with chicken soup was served, too. Liangzu said: "This is prepared according to Huishu's instructions."

They talked about Yingshu during the meal. When Yingshu graduated from college, he didn't start a job immediately since he was not satisfied with the positions available. Now he was employed as a staff officer at a division headquarters in charge of logistics. He had come back home twice. Liangzu said he had noticed Yingshu's expanded vision.

Fuzhi said: "Yingshu was an industrious student. Though we didn't talk much, I can sense the enhanced vitality in his thoughts."

Liangzu laughed: "He admires you and loves to listen to your lectures. You have certainly influenced him."

The last dish, the dessert, was served. It was fried lotus petals, crispy with the sweet taste of the flower lingering between one's lips. When they had finished dinner, Liangzu asked for Fuzhi and Bichu to be sent home first.

Before saying goodbye, Huishu held Bichu's hand and asked: "When are you moving back to town?"

"We're trying to move back during the summer vacation. When we are in town, we'll be closer to you," answered Bichu. Having said goodbye, the father and daughter then left.

About one week later, Mingjing took an enormous sum of money to Bichu. The jade set was sold at an amazingly good price. Mingjing didn't give details of the deal, but he mentioned that Hezhu had contacted him and tried to buy it at a very low price to impress Madam Yin and gain her favour, but Mingjing told her Professor Meng was not the nerd "Stoney" from 'A Dream of the Red Chamber' who was put to death because he wouldn't sell his collection of 12 rare antique fans, so such a trick wouldn't work on Professor Meng. It was the chieftainess who managed to sell the jade set to a prince from Nepal with her connections.

"So, in the end, the jade set was given to the right person," commented Mingjing smugly.

He then told Bichu he had deducted the sum he had given to Bichu last time. Bichu was appreciative that the jade set affair had been concluded so satisfactorily.

After hesitating several times, she ventured to say: "I feel it was wrong of me to ask you to deal with the jade set behind Huifen's back."

Mingjing readily understood what she meant: "Madam Meng, you know me very well. No one is dearer to my heart than Huifen."

Bichu said: "She is the best indeed."

The two continued to talk about Xueyan who was expecting her baby soon. Bichu had already decided to save some money for her and the baby.

Mingjing said: "You can't deposit the money in the bank with the soaring price inflation. It would be better to invest the sum in something."

Bichu told him: "Thank you for reminding me! Would you like to take care of this for me, then?" Mingjing thought for a moment and agreed.

Fuzhi was recovering fast with Bichu's delicate nursing. He was already strong enough to get out of bed and walk around the room a bit. Besides, he had finished issuing the final examination papers for the two courses he had taught for the semester and asked Li Lian to deliver them to the staff.

Bichu teased him: "You are getting better! But I haven't made any wishes."

Qinghuan said: "I have. But I guess I was not the only one."

Found the cat hopped into Fuzhi's lap and nudged his arm. The cat might have made a wish, too.

PART III

Xueyan heaved a heavy sigh of relief when she had finished grading the last paper for the final examination. She had finished all the things she was supposed to finish on time. Now she had earned the right to devote all her attention to waiting for the arrival of their first child. Wei Feng wanted her to stay in town, but she wanted to stay at Salt Falls for several more days since the expected date of delivery was still one month away. From the city to the plant institute, there were already regular shuttle horse carriages. Two boards were set up on each side of the cart to serve as 'seats'. Although these seats couldn't be called comfortable by any stretch of the imagination, the ride did save a lot of walking.

Xueyan cleaned up everything in the small house before they left for town. The two of them had been preparing to move to a bigger house suitable for a family of three in Wasted alley. Each time they went over to the place, they would discuss where to put the table, where to put the chairs, etcetera. Wei Feng busied himself with some designs behind Xueyan's back such as building a stove. He wanted to give Xueyan a big surprise when they moved back to town.

They took the shuttle horse carriage at the minor east city gate. The carriage rolled along, more slowly than walking. When it reached a bumpy section, Wei Feng would help Xueyan to get off the cart and walk. The sight of the blue sky, the green trees and the approaching crystal-clear waves brought many understanding smiles to the couple's faces. Wei Feng whispered to Xueyan: "Xue, can you guess what I'm thinking now?"

Xueyan whispered back: "I can only tell you what I am thinking. Soon, there will be three of us going in and out of the house." Realising that his wife shared the same thought as him, Wei Feng took Xueyan's hand and stroked it gently. His reaction secured happy looks of approval from all the other passengers in the carriage. An old woman pointed at Xueyan's belly and claimed it was a baby boy. Wei Feng immediately added: "Boys and girls are no different." When the old woman got off, others in the carriage reminded the couple: "Don't disregard the words of your elders. They are blessings." The two hastily promised: "We won't."

It was not far from the plant institute to Salt Falls. Xueyan and Wei Feng walked slowly, engaged in a heated discussion about naming the baby. The two couldn't agree on any name they came up with. Xueyan felt heavy with the weight and took several breathers on the way, even with so many distractions. One week ago, when they walked to town, she only took one breather. Upon their arrival, a 'master' greeted them with intense hospitality. It was Leo. He jumped and hopped around them both and then jammed himself in the door to shake hands with them, with one paw in each hand. He literally forced the two to come in. The Mi couple's hospitality was no less effusive than Leo's. It was lunch time. That was why they had come with rice, soya bean sauce and leafy mustard soup. They also asked Leo not to tire out Xueyan. Leo had been at Xueyan's heels wherever she went. Upon these words, he lay down outside the west room with his eyes fixed on Xueyan.

It was spacious here. The blue sky was boundless. It was quiet and peaceful without air raids and refugees. Only the Dragon river roared on ceaselessly day and night. Two days later, Wei Feng left because he had things to attend to in town. Bichu took the money she had prepared for Xueyan, Qinghuan, and the diamond bracelet to see Xueyan. Xueyan told Bichu she didn't need the money because she was not afraid of hardship. Bichu patted her on the back and told her it was childish to say so and insisted on leaving the money and Qinghuan for Xueyan. Before she left, she took out the bracelet: "This is for the baby."

Xueyan almost lost control of herself: "Aunt Bichu, why don't you keep it?"

Bichu explained: "I have already accepted yours. This is our gift for the baby. Money is no longer a problem, so if you don't take it, I will be upset." Having been cornered, Xueyan had to take the bracelet back and put it away before they went to the Mi's.

"Aunt Bichu has come to see us," said Xueyan. She then talked to Mrs Mi in French.

Mr Mi said: "Feng once mentioned that his parents are interesting people, but they don't work due to their poor health."

Xueyan answered musingly: "They want to leave the occupied region, but the journey is too challenging for two senior patients. They have entrusted their ambitions to their only son."

Mrs Mi happily commented: "Their son is going to have his own son!"

The Mi couple offered to see Bichu off. Xueyan stood by the gate, watching the three going down the hill. She was confident her baby would have a happy life. With the help of Qinghuan, Xueyan enjoyed even more relaxation. Each day she and Mrs Mi would talk, design or do some needlework or knitting for the baby. The small yard radiated with peace and joy.

Xueyan's joy in expectation of the baby was tinged with an inexplicable fear. She wasn't confident of surviving the labour. She missed her parents, too. She missed her absent-minded father whose soul had always been wandering out of this world, and her mother, a natural worrier, who had been bickering and blaming others all her life. How much she wished she could be by their side! Holding her mother's hand, she would have nothing to fear. During her four years' absence from home, she had been reluctant to write to her parents at the beginning. Any news about her parents would be gleaned from different sources. Later she was worried that the lack of information about her might kill her parents, so she began to write to her mother occasionally. The few letters she wrote took months to reach them. Were they alright? Had the Japanese forced her father to do anything else? Her heart was weighed down by these questions. Then she remembered Li Yuming's death and the vicious rumour about him and her. Her mourning for Yuming bored a hole in her heart which was filled with tears of sympathy; the rumour left a gnarled scar in her heart.

Seeing her in such low spirits, Qinghuan told her: "I want to tell you my stories to cheer you up, but none of them have a happy ending."

Xueyan said: "I was told that you are a brave and capable girl."

Qinghuan shook her head: "I'm a jinx. No man would dare to marry me." Her eyes became moist. Xueyan didn't have the heart to ask more questions. But Qinghuan asked: "You have never heard of my stories? Don't tell this to Madam Meng, but is it true that Madam Meng has never told you about me?"

Xueyan smiled: "We don't like to gossip about other people's private life."

Qinghuan sighed: "How blessed you are! Although you're separated from your parents, Madam Meng is so fond of you!" In broken conversations, Qinghuan told Xueyan her simple but stunning stories.

When she was about 10 years old, she was abducted and sold to different households as a maid. She ended up serving the chieftainess of Pingjiang. The chieftainess was beautiful but greedy. She was crazy about valuable things, especially jade. She horded a roomful of jade pieces. Pingjiang was a very humid place teeming with poisonous insects such as centipedes and had a long tradition of breeding poisonous insects and murdering people by 'witchcraft' involving insect venom, although she had never met such a person. The chieftainess had a secret prescription which she claimed to be a cure-all, which was indeed just a mixture of ground-up centipedes and some herbs.

One day when Qinghuan was cleaning up the house, two centipedes crawled out of a giant earthenware jar and bit her on the back of her hand. Her hand and her arm swelled up immediately due to the venom. The venom of a centipede is as fatal as that of a snake, but by a miracle, Qinghuan survived the bite. The red swelling disappeared quite quickly. Out of curiosity, the chieftainess put several centipedes on the table and then asked Qinghuan to clean the table. Qinghuan jumped onto the table, stamped on the insects and crushed them. The chieftainess was furious and yelled: "You look like someone who keeps poisonous insects as pets and kills people by witchcraft!"

Qinghuan told Xueyan: "I wouldn't accept the false accusation and argued with her. How could I know any witchcraft? I didn't even keep insects! That woman was infuriated and confronted me about whether I meant to say that she kept poisonous insects. Since then she has been trying to frame me and expose my 'witchcraft'. Some also said she might have wanted to offer me as a sacrifice to her jade pieces."

Xueyan couldn't believe what she had heard: "This sounds like things that used to happen hundreds of years ago!"

Qinghuan forced a bitter smile: "Madam Meng said the same thing. Aren't my lot living in the past hundreds of years ago? Anyway, when I escaped from Pingjiang and managed to find my way home, my mother died soon afterward. Then I went to seek refuge from my father's sister, my aunt, but she soon died, too. When I went to work for the horse caravan, they accused me when some of the men died of disease. What have I done? Nothing. Am I a jinx?"

Xueyan ignored the pangs in her heart and cooed: "Rumours hurt. The victim never has the chance to hurt back. The chieftainess does nothing but cook up rumours about you. You are not a jinx. You need to live and live well, which is the best evidence that you have nothing to do with poisonous insects or witchcraft."

Qinghuan shook her head and returned to her work, her head bowed. A long while later, she raised her head and said: "Last time I worked with the caravan, two people died when we were near Pingjiang. The head of the caravan accused me of using witchcraft and handed me to the chieftainess. She crowed: you were so good at escaping, now why did you come back to me? She then locked me up. I escaped again on a dark night. Two days after I ran away, they caught me by the Dragon river. If it had not been for the help of Miss May and her friends, I wouldn't have had the chance to jump into the river to evade capture. It was a miracle I didn't drown. Since then, no one has come looking for me, either."

Qinghuan's words reminded Xueyan of May's story of seeing a young girl jumping into the Dragon river. May guessed right. It was indeed Qinghuan. Xueyan tried to comfort Qinghuan: "You should stop labelling yourself as a jinx. On the contrary, you have survived so many times. It only proves that you are blessed. You should make the most of life. You deserve it."

Qinghuan nodded slowly as if to digest Xueyan's words.

On the third day after Wei Feng left, Xueyan began to feel uncomfortable. Then came the stomach-aches, which became more and more intense with time. Mrs Mi said Xueyan might be in labour.

The three suddenly lost their senses at the realisation of such a possibility. In the end they agreed to send Qinghuan to fetch Bichu. Qinghuan rushed to Zhao Er to borrow his horse and took the horse up the hill to pick up Bichu. Bichu was preparing medicine for Fuzhi. The pounding at the gate startled her. Her hand trembled, spilling some medicine out of the bowl. She hurried to clean herself up with her handkerchief. After hearing what Qinghuan had to say, she asked May and Heji to take care of their father and prepared to head for Salt Falls.

May was concerned: "Mum, let me go instead!"

Bichu answered: "My little goose! You don't know how to handle the situation. Take care of your father and our home."

Bichu didn't know how to ride a horse. Qinghuan assured May: "I have been working with the caravans. I know how to protect your mother."

It turned out that Qinghuan did know about horses and how to ride them. Even in the darkening night, Bichu had a smooth ride. As they hurried to Salt Falls, Xueyan was struggling to stay seated with beads of sweat trailing off her forehead.

Bichu ordered Qinghuan to boil water while she fumbled for memories of when she gave birth to her children. After she had finished padding tissues and other stuff under Xueyan, Bichu asked her to lean against her and helped her go through the contractions.

Xueyan felt she was teetering on the edge of death. One step forward and it would all be over. She desperately grasped Bichu's hand. Bichu told her how to regulate her breath and how to apply her strength in a regular rhythm. Xueyan struggled until the first ray of morning light cracked the horizon when she suddenly felt the weight in her body was gone, as if all her internal organs had been emptied. Even the quiet morning was startled by the first cry of the baby, declaring its arrival. Xueyan feebly let go of Bichu's hand. They all heaved a long sigh of relief, including Leo who had been waiting at the door. Mrs Mi expressed her congratulations loudly in Yiddish. Bichu cut the umbilical cord and showed Xueyan the baby. Dizzy with fatigue, Xueyan was too weak to take it. She just gazed at the baby and muttered: "Are you my son?" Bichu added immediately, yes, it was a boy.

Bichu made Xueyan lie down comfortably, cleaned up the baby and wrapped him in a baby blanket. When she had finished the swaddling, it looked like a plump candle. She then laid the 'candle pack' in the bed beside Xueyan. Seeing the new mother and baby safe and sound, Bichu noticed how dizzy she felt. She fell into the closest chair and took a long break before she gradually regained some of her strength.

Wei Feng came back home at dawn. Overwhelmed with joy and shock, he bowed three times at Bichu and then at Mrs Mi and Qinghuan to show his gratitude. Then he whispered something in Xueyan's ear, and Xueyan's eyes brimmed with tears. A smile lingered at the corners of her mouth. Holding Wei Feng's hand, she fell into a slumber.

From that morning on, this little family had a third member. Tiny as he was, he bore their hopes and their future, which made him strong and powerful. Bichu wanted to leave Qinghuan with Xueyan, but Wei Feng didn't want Bichu to suffer anymore, so he asked Qinghuan to return two weeks after the birth of the baby and hired a young girl to help out. But the young girl refused to wash diapers, so Wei Feng took over most of the chores during Xueyan's month of confinement after childbirth. He did all the chores with expert finesse and organisation. Xueyan, holding the baby in her arms and sitting on their home-made 'sofa', would give instructions. She had never done this before but now she had to because being in labour had taken all her strength, and because she was rising to the occasion of being a mother.

When the baby was one month old, May and Heji came on behalf of their parents. The two were amazed at how tiny the baby was. When May asked the name of the baby, Xueyan told her they wanted to save the privilege for Aunt Bichu and Uncle Fuzhi. May offered to take the responsibility: "I'll do this for them. I want to name him A'nan."

Wei Feng said: "A'nan is Ananda, which literally means 'joy' and 'happiness'. He is one of the ten disciples of Gautama Buddha. A'nan has a companion called Jiaye, Kassapa."

Xueyan said: "A'nan sounds good to me. We can't call him 'Gautama' or 'Sakyamuni' anyway. But his family name is 'Wei'. 'Wei Nan' doesn't sound good because it's pronounced the same way as the word for embarrassment."

Heji, who was studying the baby intensely, spoke up: "We can put a 'bu', no, in between — Wei Bunan, meaning no embarrassment, no hardships."

They all said the name out loud several times. May said: "How about changing 'bu' into 'wu'. 'Wu' means 'no' but sounds different. How does Wei Wunan sound to you?"

Wei Feng, who was gazing at Xueyan holding the baby, said: "There are always trials and tribulations. No one can avoid that." He then raised his voice excitedly: "How about 'Wei Lingnan', to rise above trials and tribulations? 'Ling' is also his mother's family name." They all clapped their hands in total agreement. Wei Lingnan took the opportunity to howl, raising the roof.

"Wei Lingnan, you should protect us from all disasters and trials of any kind!" exclaimed Xueyan, rocking the baby.

"He will. He will," echoed Wei Feng piously.

In the afternoon, Huifen and Mrs Li came with Zhiwei and Zhiquan. Zhiwei's hair was braided into two neat braids. She looked very similar to her eldest sister Zhiqin. They also took a basketful of homemade pastry such as steamed buns and sweet rice cake. When Mrs Li came into the house, she first praised the baby and then the pastry. She dangled a piece of sweet rice cake in front of the baby and said: "We haven't made pastry to sell at the stand for a long time. These were made just for you!"

Wei Feng bustled around, greeting their guests, bringing them tea, and whispering in Xueyan's ear from time to time. Both of them would glance over at the 'candle pack' as if it might vanish into thin air.

Huifen's heart was brimming with envy. What else could a woman long for other than a considerate husband and a child of her own? Mrs Li seemed to be able to see right through Huifen as she pointedly commented: "It's a woman's fate to suffer. Look how much pain a mother must go through to bear a child, yet they are willing to try. To enjoy suffering must be real suffering."

Wei Feng laughed: "This is why motherhood is so great. Without such enjoyment of pain, how could human beings continue to endure?"

Mrs Li retorted: "Great motherhood! It's just male baloney to hoodwink females."

384

Huifen said: "Mrs Li is being sarcastic. Now you have everything a woman wants, you have the right to say so." They all laughed and then continued to talk about moving back to town. Since everyone had found a place to stay, no one from the college would be seen around again in the coming autumn. It was not safe to stay in town because the Japanese could attack from different directions such as western Yunnan, Guangxi or Guizhou. Leaning over the 'candle pack', Huifen gazed at the lovely little face sound asleep and muttered: "We won't be afraid of any attacks because we have Wei Lingnan!"

Mrs Li was jubilant, claiming she was seeing a roomful of auspicious pink clouds, and it was rare to see such a happy small family in such a troubled world! The new baby had a promising future and would bring happiness to his parents. Wei Feng listened to Mrs Li and thanked her for her blessings.

As time went by, Xueyan gradually recovered from her labour. She felt even more energetic than she did before the birth of the child. They decided they were going to move back to town the following week. Once they had moved, the Mi family would move a couple of days later, too.

Although Wei Lingnan was a premature baby, he was a healthy one. He grew each day. When he was packed like a candle, he would worm his way out of the blanket he was wrapped in. When his arms were free, he would wave them in the air, which amazed Xueyan. "My baby! My capable baby!" These were the lyrics of her lullaby. When he cried, he cried loudly. Mrs Mi said it was as loud as the horn of the hero Siegfried from 'Der Ring des Nibelungen'. Every time Xueyan fed the baby, she felt it was a sacred mission. The warm flow of milk from her breasts created a world which had only the baby and her, excluding Wei Feng, who tried not to be jealous: "I'm almost jealous of him." When he said that, Xueyan was feeding the baby facing the wall, a new habit she had picked up. She turned her head around and smiled at him. Her face looked fairer with her short, dark hair, her lips slightly parted were red like a rose bud, her happiness radiated in a halo around her and the baby. Wei Feng's heart fluttered. Intoxicated, he went up and held his wife with his son in his arms and kissed her on the head.

The water at the small Salt Falls cascade had a scouring force. Wei Feng was always happy when he rinsed laundry in the whirlpool of water, which reminded him of some issues involving fluid mechanics. When he came back and shared this discovery with Xueyan, Xueyan sighed: "I should never have sent you to do the laundry." But Wei Feng answered her "I'm glad you did" while he busied himself adroitly hanging up pieces of cloth from assorted sources such as old clothes on the laundry lines criss-crossing the yard. He pulled up a chair and seated Xueyan in it: "Now, it's time to travel around the world." He pointed at a piece of cloth: "This is the Americas." Pointing at another, he said: "This is Europe," and the one with a big yellowish stain was "Ayres Rock in Australia". One second later, he came up with a new idea: "Now I'll give you a tour of the solar system." He pointed at random pieces naming them Mars, Jupiter, and so on. Xueyan laughed and laughed. Wei Feng bustled in and out of the house. When he passed Xueyan, he would caress her hands, or stroke her hair, or check whether she was sitting comfortably.

"Waaaah—" When the horn of Siegfried was blown, the Mi couple turned up. When the baby was asleep, the two wouldn't dare to speak loudly. Now Mrs Mi took the baby in her arms and turned him around several times before giving the baby back to his mother. The baby stopped crying once he was in his mother's arms. Xueyan carried him into the house, smiling. Mrs Mi followed Xueyan and whispered in her ear when they were inside the room: "My dear Xueyan, I'm pregnant again." Xueyan joyfully took Mrs Mi's hand and declared proudly: "Now both of us will never die." The mother and the would-be mother gazed into each other's eyes, moved.

Laughter reached the two from the gate to the yard. "Professor Zhuang!" Wei Feng went to meet the Zhuang couple, dodging from side to side under the pieces of cloth.

"Wei Feng, Xueyan, we have brought you some goodies," Della called as they walked into the room. Xueyan hurried behind the curtain fabric to tidy herself up, while the well-fed baby was carried out by Mrs Mi to meet the visitors. Youchen and Della put down packages of all sizes containing milk powder, coco powder and other stuff. Wei Feng told them the baby's name. Xueyan came out from behind the curtain and hugged Della. Della commented that the sight of such a young and beautiful mother and her beautiful child exuded love and peace, a force which could overcome any difficulties. She took a letter out of her handbag and put it into Xueyan's hands: "This is the best thing we want to give you." Xueyan immediately felt the weight of the letter in her hand. The letter was addressed to 'Wei Feng and Ling Xueyan c/o Meng Fuzhi, Zhuang Youchen'. It took only a split second to see the sender's concern that the letter might not reach its addressee.

Youchen said: "Let's go to the yard to talk and give Xueyan some time to read the letter. We borrowed a car to deliver the letter to her. It's parked at the foot of the hill. The small waterfall is amazing."

Wei Feng laughed: "It's also very convenient to wash things there."

Mr Mi brought tea for everyone.

Xueyan's hands trembled when she tried to open the envelope. She recognised her father's handwriting straight away.

"Dear Xue and Feng, I have retired from that position because they have nothing further to gain from associating my name with it. Some up-and-coming youngsters are very keen for that position (can you imagine that?). With plenty of willing successors, they decided to let me off the hook."

Xueyan hadn't seen her father's handwriting for such a long time that his smooth writing style reminded her of his half-hearted facial expression. The excitement of receiving her parents' letter didn't wipe away the fact that history was history and that what had been done couldn't be undone. Her mother told her about the hard life they had had in Beiping due to the blockade and the shortage of supplies, but both of them were surviving. Xueyan felt ashamed of what her parents had done.

She read the letter several more times until she had calmed herself down and went out of the room to give the letter to Wei Feng, who told everyone when he had finished reading the letter that it was good news. Xueyan took the baby in her arms and put the letter on the wrapping blanket.

Della laughed: "Now the three generations have met one another." On hearing her words, the rest pondered when the real reunion would happen.

The Zhuangs had been planning to move back to town, but they had been postponing their move because they hadn't found a proper place where Wuyin could keep his horse. They had set their sights on a house not far from Wasted alley and were still negotiating with the property owner. Youchen and Della couldn't stay long since the car and driver were waiting for them. Wei Feng saw them off as far as the waterfall. The driver was washing the car with buckets of water from the pond, saying the water was very nice but the stepping stones on the water were too slippery.

With a new semester around the corner, Wei Feng had to go into town to attend to some business related to his department and planned to stay in town overnight. Xueyan thought she was strong enough to handle things and didn't want to wait for Wei Feng to come back to do all the chores.

That afternoon, she settled the baby, who was sound asleep, in the centre of some quilts to prevent him falling off the bed, saying to herself this is your castle built by your mum. The moment she went out of the door carrying a bamboo basket of dirty diapers, Leo, who had been lying in the courtyard, stood up to greet her.

Leo took over the basket, his feet trotting as if to show his happiness: "Now you are recovered, you are going to do your laundry by the pond." The two walked out of the yard. Standing in front of the gate, Xueyan could hear the murmuring of the waterfall.

As she descended the zig-zagging steps down the hill, her legs turned to jelly and she stumbled. Instinctively, she grabbed a tree by the roadside and paused to take a break. Leo looked at her with concern. "Don't worry," said Xueyan to Leo, patting him on the head. The two of them walked on slowly to the side of the pool. The noises from the falling water were thunderous. "Just like the horn of Siegfried!" Her heart was filled with delight at the thought.

There were some women from the village doing their laundry beside the pool. They all asked how the baby was doing and agreed that Xueyan had recovered very well. As one of the women stood up, she pressed her hand on the rock beneath her feet to steady herself and give herself a thrust at the same time. Seeing that, Xueyan again thought of installing a railing by the pool.

Very soon, the women finished their laundry and left one by one, leaving only Xueyan and Leo by the pool. She brushed the diapers in the water, thinking about her parents thousands of miles away. Could they have guessed what their Xueyan was doing right now? When could they meet Lingnan? She soon finished washing the diapers because she wanted to go back to check on Lingnan and see whether he had broken out of the castle. The whirlpool of water made her light-headed. She tried to press against the rock under her feet with her hand like she saw the others did, but she toppled over and slid quietly into the water. She thought she had heard Wei Feng cooing to her: "Xueyan, come to me". Or had she heard her father whimpering "Xueyan, don't hate me"? She didn't want to leave. She didn't hate anyone. She wanted to hold on tight to all the people she loved. The water closed in around her. She tried to hold on to the water. The cold water carried her down into a swirling vortex. The noise of the waterfall dampened her cries. She went down, down, down, all the way back to the world of her bedroom in Beiping. The twin glass doors to her room slammed shut.

Leo scuttled back and forth around the bank and barked frantically. With no help around, he threw himself into the water just in time to snap at Xueyan's blouse. The blouse broke, leaving a piece of cloth in his mouth. Xueyan fell into the deep water. Leo was tagging along.

Xueyan was gone. So was Leo. The water continued to splash like it always had, as white as salt or snow. Those who had heard the frantic barking hurried to check, but saw only the bamboo basket filled with cleaned diapers.

Wei Feng went to the new house in town when he had finished his business in his department. Before a friend of Della's returned to England, he had left a sofa bed and asked her to share it with anyone who might need it. Wei Feng asked Della to give it to him. He had put it in their bedroom. It reminded him of the delicate bridal room they never had the opportunity to enjoy back in Beiping. Now even a second-hand sofa bed was a luxurious item. Xueyan would be very happy to have a soft bed like this, thought Wei Feng. As noon approached, he began to fidget without any reason. He gobbled down a bowl of rice noodles at the entrance of Wasted alley and then headed out of town. He walked fast without noticing anything all the way. I'm coming, he muttered to himself quietly. The closer he got, the more unsettled he became. When he walked past the waterfall, he didn't notice any difference. The water was still the same water. The rocks were still the same rocks. It looked like nothing special had happened. As he went up the hill, he ran into several villagers who all greeted him with sympathy "Mr Wei, you are back". They obviously wanted to tell him something, but none of them did.

"Is there anything wrong?" He strode into the yard and dashed into the house. The room was crowded with people standing beside one another, including the Mi couple and some acquaintances from the village.

The baby was sound asleep, in the castle.

"Xueyan! Where is Xueyan?" yelled Wei Feng. Xueyan, where are you? Xueyan, are you playing hide and seek with me? Come on out! Xueyan, come on out, now!

Mr Mi pressed Wei Feng into a chair. Then an elderly villager told Wei Feng that Xueyan was seen doing her laundry with Leo by the waterfall pool. When they heard the anxious loud barking of the dog, they hurried to the waterfall but found neither of them. They had tried to retrieve the bodies, but it was impossible to do so since the pool was connected to the Dragon river. Two long poles stood at the corner. On seeing them, Wei Feng jumped out of the chair, snatched one, and was ready to run. People tried to stop him. Mr Mi asked others to let go of Wei Feng. Let him go and have a try. How could he not go and have a try? So they came back to the pool again, some holding the poles, some holding Wei Feng.

"Xueyan… Xueyan…" Wei Feng cried and yelled, his voice ricocheting off the stone walls and disappearing into nothingness. There was no sign of Xueyan.

When news of the disaster reached the Mengs, they were all shocked. Bichu burst into loud sobs. Fuzhi tried to hold back his emotions, but the tears welling up in his eyes betrayed him. Heji carved the characters 'Xueyan will never die' onto a seal in between tears. May was crushed with sorrow at the loss. She remembered the game they had played back in the Lü residence at Chestnut street in Beiping and the white candle which died out first. She tried to write a eulogy for Xueyan, comparing her to the legendary wave-riding goddess of the Luo river: "The beauty of the Goddess of the Luo river rests in her appearance, while the beauty of Cousin Xueyan lies in her spirit. Sorrow has come to this that she has been taken by the river god." Sadness had deprived her of all power to write on the tear-soaked paper. She decided to offer the unfinished eulogy and her tears of sorrow to her beloved cousin Xueyan.

Three days later, Xueyan was found by the giant rock rooted by the bank of the Dragon river. She lay quietly in her loose white blouse floating in the water like a lotus flower. She was laid on a provisional bamboo bed, where Wei Feng stayed with her for three days and nights in a row. People helped Wei Feng buy a coffin from Copper Head village, not worrying too much about the quality of the material in such a rough time. They found a spot on a hill by the Dragon river and asked the village stonemason to make a headstone.

It was clear and bright on the day Xueyan's funeral was held. The scorching sunshine shone unrelentingly without any shade, baking the land and the river as if to dry the river out to punish it for its cruelty. The Dragon river was ablaze with sparkling water rolling and whimpering. Many people from Minglun came to attend the funeral. Fuzhi came with a walking stick, taking his family with him. Wang Dingyi, Xia Zhengsi and Xueyan's other colleagues from her department all came. Youchen and his family were present. Wei Feng's friends including Tantai Xuan, Tantai Wei, Li Lian, Qian Mingjing and You Jiaren all arrived. Many students came, too. Xueyan, wrapped in a plain floral cotton quilt, lay in the coffin. People couldn't see her, but they could hear her sweet voice and her laughter lingering in the air as it did when she was alive. May, holding Lingnan in her arms, stood in front of the coffin. She was sobbing while Lingnan was howling. Someone at the funeral pointed at the giant rock by the river and shouted that there was something there. May gave Lingnan to Qinghuan and ran down the hill. It was Leo. When Leo was brought to the bank, they all saw the piece of cloth in his jaws.

Wei Feng decided he was not going to cry at Xueyan's funeral. He thought that was what Xueyan would have wanted, but when he put May's eulogy and Heji's seal into the coffin, his tears escaped. How much he wanted to throw himself at Xueyan's body and cry his heart out! He couldn't! With help from a villager, he sealed the coffin. Each nail driven into the lid of the coffin was a nail in his heart. Xia Zhengsi, Qian Mingjing and Li Lian helped lower the coffin into the grave. Some remembered the rumour from the You couple and glared at them both.

Wei Feng put the first shovelful of dirt into the grave. Xuan put some loose dirt into Lingnan's hand. The tiny baby's hand was still not strong enough to hold such tricky stuff which slipped between his fingers and fell into the grave. The new grave was finished in no time. The headstone made of simple bluestone was carved with two lines: 'My Beloved Wife Ling Xueyan', and 'From Wei Feng with their son Wei Lingnan, August 1943'. From then on, Xueyan, facing the rolling water, was parted from this life and this world.

She was not alone. She had Leo by her side. Leo, with the piece of cloth from Xueyan's blouse clutched in his mouth, was buried by Xueyan's side. People bowed to Xueyan's grave first, and then to Leo's grave.

Lingnan had been crying at the funeral from beginning to end. Even when he was back in his bed, he didn't stop. It was not his regular crying. It was filled with grief, confusion and terror.

THE SONG OF WEI LINGNAN

THE SONG OF WEI LINGNAN was about the extension of life. It was a song of immortality.

I cry out loud because I have lost my mother. The soft bosom I loved to lean against and the warm milk I longed for are all gone. The solid face and hair, which used to be within reach any time and her soft voice calling "baby", are all gone.

I was carried around, shifted from one arm to another in an enormous mixture of colours and sounds.

I wanted to break loose, but I couldn't. So, I cried.

The things delivered to my mouth tasted strange. I writhed and wriggled. I wanted to run away from these strange things. I just wanted the thing that belonged to me.

Then when I was starved and exhausted, I accepted a stranger's milk. Someone shouted: "He'll live! The kid will live!"

I was carried from the breasts of one mother to those of another. They patted me gently, rocked me and fed me with their milk. How will I die? I won't die!

I heard them talking about how one of Grandpa Stonemason's goats had just had a kid and he wanted to give the mother goat to Mr Wei Feng. Then later they brought up something. It was not Leo. The head was not Leo's. My father told me it was a goat. It has milk to feed me. I should be grateful for it.

The bleating of the goat sounds so strange. Qinghuan stands by the goat.

I know her. She patted the goat, and then patted me: "I'll take good care of you both."

We are leaving. Mr and Mrs Mi and many other people came to see us off. Mrs Mi put my hand onto her belly, saying something to me. Mr Mi spoke out: "Our child and Lingnan will be brothers."

We are leaving this place where I was born and where my mother died. I have been fed by all the mothers who have milk and taken away a mother goat.

When all the guests left, my father carried me into our new home and put me in bed. He stared at me, and I stared back. He fell into sobs: "Lingnan, this is the home your mother and I prepared for you. But now she is gone and there are only the two of us."

He threw himself on me and cried. I cried. I was wet inside and out, literally. My father noticed the smell and changed my diaper, sobbing.

I am Wei Lingnan. I'm motherless.

Father talks to me a lot. He told me war was a demon which devoured so many lives in numerous ways, such as the cannons on the battle field, the air raids in the rear areas, disease, plague and natural disasters. Even the shadow under its evil wings could torture people to death.

Our new home has many visitors who like to take it in turns to carry me in their arms. They talk about many things, so I know which place has been under attack by the Japanese, and which place has been bombarded by the same devils. The Japanese are trying to destroy the Chinese. They are monsters.

My name is Wei Lingnan. I was born in times of war and in the niche between life and death. I have survived.

Some time later, I make out two women from among the visitors. One is called Helen, and the other one my father told me to call "Aunt Xuan". They come quite often and both care about me a lot.

One night, Helen talked to my father for a long time. She seemed to be trying to persuade my father to go somewhere because my father said: "How can I leave Lingnan behind?"

Helen said: "You may entrust him to someone, like me. We are comrades."

My father didn't respond. He walked over to me and was surprised by me: "His eyes are open. It looks like he's listening."

Helen said: "What a vivid imagination! How can he understand anything?"

Aunt Xuan thinks differently. She thinks I understand everything. She once told me: "See? Your Aunt Xuan is quite beautiful, isn't she? She used to be even more beautiful!"

The two women have different opinions on many things and they fight a lot. Qinghuan once complained to my father: "Miss Helen thinks the milk should be cooler, but Miss Tantai insists it be warmer. What should I do?" My father said, lukewarm.

When I sucked the lukewarm milk, I made the first syllable "mama". "Mama!" I yelled. "Say more! Say more!" answered my father.

Before my father left for a meeting somewhere, he asked me which one I like better, Helen or Aunt Xuan. I just cried out loud. Crying is my way of singing. I want my mum. I want my mum. My father hurriedly took me in his arms, patting me, and said: "I want her, too! She has never left. There are three of us..." he said, pointing at his heart and crying with me.

Later he told me: "I think I'll let Qinghuan take care of you and the goat. Besides, we have Great Aunt Bichu and her family." Father returned soon. Seeing that I was alright, he said: "I just made an experiment to see whether I can leave you. What a pity that we can't repeat life like we can with experiments."

Life is like a gust of wind. Even if it is strong enough to shake the earth, when it's gone, it's gone, never to return. Life is like the water in a river. Even with layer upon layer of whirlpools, it never flows back. If life could be redone, then everyone would become a saint. These are my father's words.

When father is not at home, I am laid down in bed, staring at the roof after I finish the lukewarm milk. I want to have something, but I can't figure out what it is. My meditation that night was interrupted by a piercing noise. It sounded strange. Qinghuan dashed into the room and fished me up in her arms, muttering: "Siren! Air raid siren!" Someone in the yard said: "We haven't' had any air raid sirens for so long. Why today?"

Qinghuan was anxious like an ant on a hot pan, not knowing what to do. When she reached the gate, she returned and kept muttering the same question: "Lingnan, what should we do?" It was dark outside. I couldn't make out who those people were coming and going in the dim light.

Someone approached Qinghuan and asked her: "We are going out of town. Are you coming with us? You need to make a decision."

Another one said: "It's so late. The fighter planes won't come now."

Qinghuan kept muttering: "Lingnan, what should we do?"

Then Aunt Xuan came. She wrapped me up in a baby quilt and put me into the stroller. Qinghuan stopped muttering "what should we do" and, pushing the stroller, followed Aunt Xuan, who was walking fast. Sometimes one of them pushed the stroller; sometimes they both carried it together. Qinghuan said with admiration: "Miss Xuan, you are so capable!" People spread out in the darkness. I saw a gigantic roof studded with sparkling dots on it. They sat down by a river. I fell asleep.

I had no idea how long I had been asleep when I heard Aunt Xuan say: "Let's go back home." Then pushing and carrying the stroller in turns, they walked for some time until someone stopped them: "Here you are! I have been looking for you." It sounded like Helen. They walked slowly while they talked, so I took my time enjoying the gigantic roof.

Father said, this is the first time Lingnan has had to run away from an air raid. I hope it is the last time.

Helen smells weird. Father told me it is the smell of printing ink. Aunt Xuan smells of incense fragrance. I don't like the smell of printing ink, but father told me: "It represents an ideal which I yearn for. But I like the smell of incense fragrance better."

Father also told me: "War shortens time and forces people to forget and to choose. Lingnan, do you know what crossroad means? I'm now at a crossroad in life."

My name is Wei Lingnan. My father told me one faces many crossroads on one's journey through life. When I am at one, what should I do?

I cry. Crying is my way of singing.

CHAPTER EIGHT

.

PART I

Time flew by. It was already several years ago when the strangers from other provinces moved to Kunming and were amazed by the bluest of blue skies. Many people died and many were born. Only the blue sky was peacefully and dazzlingly blue like it used to be. If you gazed at it for a while, you would feel it had absorbed you into its boundless expanse. No trace of destruction from the enemy fighter planes was to be found up there. Its expanse and depth would tint any savage monsters into a beautiful blue. Under such a dome over the land, people struggled on amid all sorts of disasters and suffering. They lived on from generation to generation.

Among the families relocated to the eastern suburbs of Kunming, the Mengs were the last one to move back to town. The reconstruction of the house by the wintersweet grove continued intermittently for a long time, but eventually it was finished. Fuzhi had recovered from his illness, and Bichu's health didn't collapse, either. They all braced themselves and pitched in with the packing, from the books and manuscripts accumulated over the years, to the versatile and malleable kerosene crates, clothes, bedding and cooking utensils.

The family had grown attached to this small village that the mountain and the hills, the rivers, the vegetation and the legendary dragons had etched on their hearts with the passage of time. And this was Xueyan's eternal resting place. They were now moving away, leaving only the roaring Dragon river and the loyal Leo to keep her company. May and Heji wanted to say farewell to Xueyan, but Bichu didn't grant them permission.

Li Lian and his family moved first. He returned to the village with some people to help with the move. With a truck and a couple of porters, most of the Mengs' belongings were loaded up. They then hired Zhao Er's carriage to transport the smaller items. The four sat in the cart, and the carriage rode along the Mang river, with Found the cat in a box, meowing all the way. The green hills and the roofs looming amid the greenery gradually disappeared from sight.

"Will we come back?" asked Heji.

"We'll come back to visit," answered May, implying if they did come back, they wouldn't come back for concealment.

Fuzhi sighed at the conversation: it was very likely that they would still have to hide. Who could tell what would happen in the future?

The wintersweet grove awaited them. The house, though simple and shabby, eventually rose up out of the shell crater. They eventually came back and were one step closer to their return to Beiping. However attached they were to the village of their concealment, it was no match for their attachment to Beiping. They cleaned up the rooms and arranged the furniture, juggling between feelings of attachment and anticipation. A room separated into two by a wooden partition became May and Heji's rooms. Since they could talk through the partition, they invented a system of codes. The code was designed to connect them with each other rather than to hide any secrets from others.

Lying in bed, May's thoughts drifted back to the day of the bombing. She had become someone who had crawled out of the earth, or the grave, so to speak. What the bombing left behind was not only terror but also humiliation. She shook off the layers of earth piled on top of her as a dog would. They didn't cry. When they dug out their home from the rubble, they didn't cry, either. She somehow wanted to indulge in a good cry now as she remembered the scene.

"Tap. Tap." Heji knocked on the partition, meaning: are you awake, sister? May tapped back to let him know she was awake. Tap. Tap. Heji knocked again. Tap. Tap. May knocked back. Amid the happy rhythm, they fell asleep, dreaming a sweet dream of returning to Beiping, returning to the north.

All the teachers and professors staying at the theatre came to visit the Mengs. Xuan and Wei were extremely happy. They visited a lot and sometimes stayed overnight, crashing in May and Heji's beds, declaring they loved 'huddling' together. Xuan's parents asked Xuan to go and study in America, but she was hesitant and then paused in the process of preparing her application. She regularly went to take care of the motherless Wei

Lingnan. Each time she visited Bichu, she would ask many questions about how to raise a child.

Ling Xueyan could never return. On the bamboo bookshelf, May put a picture of Xueyan taken at her home back in Beiping. In the picture, Xueyan was leaning against the railing silhouetted against a sea of flowers in the background. No flower could match the sparkling glamour of her face. Visitors tried to pat Lingnan or carry him around to hide their numbing feeling of sorrow.

There was one person who could come but wouldn't. It was Zhuang Wuyin. According to Wei, Wuyin had become manic about his studies and was living in another world. The Zhuangs hadn't moved back yet since they hadn't found a house where Wuyin could keep his horse.

Soon after the beginning of the new term came the founding anniversary of Minglun University. It fell on a Sunday. The university borrowed an assembly hall to hold the celebration, inviting all the teaching faculty and their spouses to attend. It was the first large-scale gathering since Minglun relocated its faculty and staff into different suburbs around Kunming.

President Qin proposed a toast: "Since the war of resistance against Japan broke out, all of us have suffered boundless hardships. But we never lost heart. Now, finally, the many years of running from air raids have come to an end. Although the overall situation doesn't look positive, I am still confident that we'll try our best with unified efforts, as we always have, to produce qualified graduates for the nation. Western Yunnan is a key gateway, so we must win the battle there. The key to winning this battle lies in efficient cooperation with the allied forces, which relies on qualified interpreters and translators. Our students from all departments are fluent in English and are ready to contribute when needed. I'm proud that some of our students have joined the expeditionary forces and are now directly dedicated to the cause. What makes me especially pleased today is that I not only see our graduates working for the country year after year, but also see that the younger children have all grown up to be part of the new force. If I remember correctly, Meng Heji has always wanted to build planes, hasn't he?"

His eyes searched for Heji who was sitting by his parents.

Heji stood up and answered in a clear and confident voice: "Yes. I want to build planes not just to fight the Japanese, but also to equip people with wings to roam in the sky." All the professors present looked approvingly at Heji. Fuzhi and Bichu looked at each other in amazement: their youngest son had made the transformation from a little kid into a teenager just as May had only a couple of years ago.

Several more professors proposed toasts, and all mentioned the war situation. Zhuang Youchen shared his detailed and insightful analysis that one could be optimistic about the European theatre since the Japanese had such a long front that that they had overextended themselves. But the Japanese wouldn't accept defeat and would certainly launch a ferocious attack in the Chinese theatre. If we failed to take the occupied western Yunnan, Yunnan might be attacked from multiple directions and we might be reduced to being refugees again. After Youchen's speech, everyone pitched into the discussion as to where they would take refuge if they became refugees. Did they have a place to go, indeed?

The toasts and speeches were followed by free performances. All the attendees began to walk around. May joined some of her classmates. She suddenly spotted Wuyin standing in front of her. Wuyin was in a beige suit and wearing a fire-red tie. He was gazing at May thoughtfully: "May," he said, smiling! "I haven't seen you for quite a long time."

It was the first time May had seen Wuyin in a suit and tie. It made her feel somewhat strange and she let him know: "You look sharp!" She embarrassed herself with her directness.

Wuyin said: "You look even sharper! You have grown up." May was in an ordinary cotton *qipao*, a hand-me-down from Earl. What made the nondescript old clothes special was the three red embroidered flowers on the front piece made by May. Over the *qipao*, she had a hollowed-out baby blue wool sweater with short sleeves, a gift from Xuan, which accentuated the beautiful curves of a graceful young lady. The master of ceremonies announced the next performance was a chorus from China Experimental Middle School. May glanced down at the floor, raised her gentle eyes covered by her luxurious curved lashes the next moment, smiled sweetly at Wuyin and then hurried onto the stage with her schoolmates. Such a countenance always reassured Wuyin every time May raised her eyes that all her wishes would be granted.

The song the chorus sang was '*Long Long Time Ago*'. Their music teacher told them the song recalled many old stories about what happened to their parents years ago.

A couple of professors then sang an episode from a famous *Kunqu* Opera entitled '*The Palace of Eternal Youth*': "My country is in tatters under the heels of war; that's why I have ended up here in the south, alone." Everyone's hearts sank. Fuzhi and Bichu thought about Xueyan and her father Ling Jingyao. Xueyan was gone. Was Jingyao alright? Youchen explained the meaning of the lyrics to Della who told Bichu: "I have listened to Professor Ling Jingyao singing *Kunqu* Opera. Although I couldn't understand the words, I could feel the beauty of the music." Xia Zhengsi and several other teachers working in the foreign language department were sitting nearby.

On hearing Della mention Jingyao's name, Xia Zhengsi sighed: "I don't know how he will handle the blow of Xueyan's death. Xueyan was such an excellent teacher. I wonder where she got such a talent."

Bichu muttered: "That was because she always put others' needs first."

When the buffet began, the youngsters left their parents and clustered among themselves. Wuyin, Wucai, May, Heji and several more kids took some dishes to a stone table on the veranda to enjoy themselves, talking, sitting or standing by the table. May told Wuyin how Earl was doing. Wuyin deliberated for a moment and said: "Your sister is peculiar, but you are even more peculiar."

May didn't agree: "Then you are the most peculiar of us all." Holding a plate in their hands, they took a seat on the edge of the veranda, picking up topics at random as if they hadn't finished them yesterday and were resuming today. Wuyin was going to graduate the following year. His parents and teachers all suggested he take the graduate entrance examination to study abroad, but he preferred the idea of going to the graduate school in his university. "What do you think?" he asked May.

The next few years seemed so far away. The war in western Yunnan was close, indeed. "Mr Yan Bulai likes to share his opinions on current affairs with us. He does it the same way as he teaches poetry – with radiant passion," said May.

Zhiwei cut in: "He would punch a table or hit a chair. We are startled by him quite often."

"Isn't that impressive?" asked Wuyin, with his eyes fixed on May.

"Sort of," replied May, nibbling a small pie.

Seeing the dark filling, Wuyin asked: "Is it jujube paste filling?" May nodded. "I'll get you some more."

Liang Mingshi went over to them. May took the opportunity to ask: "Professor Liang, why is algebra more difficult than geometry?"

"Some might think it's the other way round," said Liang.

"Me, for example," whispered Zhiwei.

"If I'm to answer this question, I'd say it's because geometry and algebra are different, the same way as Meng Lingji and Li Zhiwei are," said Liang Mingshi. The students thought about the answer and then all laughed. When they talked about the books May and her friends were reading, May mentioned the Chinese translation of André Gide's 'The Pastoral Symphony' ('La Symphonie Pastorale'). It was a story about a blind girl. Professor Liang said he liked this story, too. It turned out Professor Liang, a maths professor, also read fiction! Wuyin came back with the snacks. Professor Liang asked whether they had jujube paste filling. It turned out that Professor Liang liked jujube paste fillings, too! Some other professors came to talk and joke with them. Professor Xu Huan, a female professor from the aerospace department, talked about planes with Heji for some time.

The You couple didn't stay long and left after briefly greeting the others. Liu Wanfang, who had been staying with the Yous, then came to find Shao Wei, who was discussing something with Professor Liang. She was irritated by their talk: "These men are so obsessed with talking about abstract things which won't produce a decent dress or a decent meal. What's the point?" she said to herself. Looking down, she set her eyes on her old pale mauve silk *qipao* and yelled inside how many more years she had to wear such a thing. She saw May, Zhiwei and other young girls on the veranda, whose simple clothing didn't hide the vitality and smartness of youth. She envied them but was not jealous at all. Her habit of leaving Shao Wei and his maths talk alone kept her at a distance from her husband. Leaning against the railing, her eyes rested on her husband who looked rather thin and gaunt as if he was suffering from malnutrition. Her heart ached at such a sight, then the pain was replaced by the sharp, smart image of Zhu Yanqing. On the day of the exhibition, Zhu had offered her a ride home. He didn't talk much, but his magnificent demeanour talked aloud on his behalf as if he could give anyone a car as a gift the next second. She sighed at the thought, unable to check her emotions, and called out: "Shao Wei, are you coming with me or not?" Professor Liang heard her call first and ordered Shao Wei to join her at once.

Shao Wei smiled ingratiatingly at his wife: "You are here! Shall I bring you some snacks?"

"Who cares about your snacks!" snapped Wanfang.

Bewildered by his wife's sudden anger, Shao Wei then asked: "So, shall we go home?" Wanfang dabbed at her eyes all the way back.

Seeing what had happened to Shao Wei and Wanfang, May thought Cousin Xueyan would never do such a thing to Cousin Wei Feng. When May and her friends said goodbye to one another, they shared the same pity – Wei Feng and Xueyan were absent.

Most of those who came for the celebration left one after another. A few youngsters who were reluctant to leave, gathered around Wuyin and asked him to explain what 'relativity' was. Wuyin picked up a hard piece of yellow mud and drew a simple illustration on the table. He managed to explain the profound theory in simple terms. If Einstein had been present, he would have praised Wuyin, too. He persevered for a while before Wucai began: "That's that! Are you all really so interested?"

"You go ahead if you are not," said Wuyin gently and continued to draw with his audience gathered around him, but his explanation went further and further. Probably he was ready to enter another domain.

Wucai decided to leave. May pulled her back: "One moment, please."

Professor Liang walked over: "Aren't you going to leave now? Your parents are waiting for you." He had a look at the illustration on the table: "In terms of graph theory, this line is wrong." He picked up the piece of mud and changed it. Wuyin immediately took his point and thanked him repeatedly.

May said 'Tarzan of the Apes' was on and the four decided to go to the theatre. After letting their parents know where they were, they headed for the Sound of Yunnan cinema. Wuyin had been teaching part-time in a family school. His earnings were enough not only for pocket money but left enough spare for him to help his family. People thronged to the cinema as if the whole population of Kunming had come to see the movie.

Wuyin said: "These are refugees, too, spiritual ones." The tickets were sold out.

May said: "We are not qualified to be spiritual refugees without the tickets!"

"Who said so? You stay here." After saying these words, Wuyin ran off. He soon returned with four tickets which he had bought from a ticket tout. Tickets bought from a tout at a higher price were nicknamed 'plane tickets' back then. The place was packed with people for the last show.

"Flowers! Fresh flowers!" Several middle schoolers were pushing a flat wooden wagon piled with fresh flowers. A banner erected over the wagon carried the words 'Fundraising for Refugees'. The smaller print under the title read: "The refugees fleeing from the war share the same motherland as us. Please give generously." The flowers looked so fresh and bright even though it was already late in the afternoon. Upon seeing the wagon, Wuyin went up and bought four red roses and gave May and Wucai two each. "Professor Bai!" They heard Heji calling politely.

They turned around to find Bai Liwen in his legendary untidy style wearing his shoes as if they were slippers in front of the wagon. He grabbed about a dozen flowers and told the girl he wanted to buy them all, ignoring Heji's greeting and the other three as if he didn't know any of them. When he was told how much he would have to pay, he paused in surprise, then took out the money, muttering: "I came here to be duped! If I'm not duped, how can I put my mind at ease?" He immediately handed the flowers to Heji: "Tell Old Meng I'm going back to my hometown in Sichuan province." With those words, he elbowed his way through the crowd and disappeared into the throng of people, leaving Heji rooted to the spot holding the flowers, lost and confused.

"Let me arrange these flowers for you," the flower girl said. She gave him back the flowers in a bouquet. Now the four had come together, but they never found Bai Liwen again in the crowds.

When they found their seats, the lights dimmed. On the screen a woman appeared enjoying a big red apple while reading a book. The serenity was shattered by the noise of shouting and a great commotion. A herd of wild elephants stampeded, trampling the small village. Amid the debris emerged a small boy, crying for his mother. His crying attracted a few apes. A mother ape with a gentle face picked the baby up in her arms and the baby became a member of the ape family. Those were the opening scenes of the movie 'Tarzan of the Apes', a very popular movie adapted from a very popular book back then.

As they were leaving the cinema, Wuyin commented: "It's possible that humans and animals can develop very deep bonds, even deeper ones than those among humans, although animals can't talk."

"Like you and your black horse," said May, holding up her roses.

"It reminds me of Leo," said Heji. "His loyalty is beyond comparison."

"A dog's loyalty is blind like that of a slave to his master, but a horse's is that of a friend," said Wuyin.

May and Heji couldn't agree with Wuyin at all: "Leo was never treated as a slave. He was a friend. A good friend."

Wucai blurted out: "I think my brother might be right because horses and dogs are different." Without any experience of keeping a horse, May and Heji felt they had run out of arguments, and both fell silent.

May's head sank low. She said slowly: "I feel I have failed Leo."

Fixing his eyes upon May, Wuyin spoke to her gravely: "I apologise for what I said about Leo. I know Leo was a friend of yours. He was a friend of mine, too. I think I failed my black horse, too, when I sold him because I couldn't find anywhere in town to keep him." The real reason was that living in a city, one doesn't need a horse. Wuyin was aware of that fact, but he was reluctant to accept it. They had rented a house at the Professors' hill by Green lake and were due to move in soon. A sinologist named Shen Si, who was translating Meng Fuzhi's 'Exploring Chinese History' into English, shared the house with the Zhuangs. The four walked, talked and laughed as they made their way toward the wintersweet grove. The birds were startled by their boisterous behaviour.

Having greeted Bichu, Wuyin and Wucai went to May and Heji's place. They had a good rummage around. They asked why there were no samples of their brush writing exercises around. May said: "I stopped copying other people's calligrapy a long time ago. When I do, I'll write like a calligrapher does." They asked about the boards piled up in the passage. May told them: "Cousin Wei is going to make a bookshelf for us with these wooden boards."

Wuyin said: "I share many of Tantai Wei's ideas but, as to turning those ideas into reality, he beats me hands down."

They had been talking for a while when Huishu called "Aunt Bichu" from outside. Wuyin's presence surprised Huishu, who hastily turned around and went to Bichu's room, but she reappeared a moment later and asked Wuyin: "You are graduating, aren't you?"

"Yes, I will graduate next year when May graduates from high school. She's going to apply for the maths department."

"Who said I would apply to the maths department?" retorted May. Turning the idea over in her mind, she resumed: "But I might."

"You are asking for trouble, then," said Heji. "You always run into difficulty with maths problems."

May cocked her head: "But I love mazes!"

They then talked about various things that had happened in their schools before Wuyin and Wucai left. May, Heji and Huishu saw the two of them off at the gate of the ancestral temple. The sister and brother walked down the slope as if they were sinking into the earth.

Since Huishu wanted to sit for a while in the wintersweet grove, May sent Heji back first. The wintersweet was still not in bloom, but the freshness of the trees permeated the air. The two sat in silence for a while. Huishu held the tip of her braid and smoothed the knot on it. She obviously wanted to tell May something, but before she started, she clammed up.

May said: "The moment you came, I could tell something was troubling you."

"I don't have any secrets from you, do I? I have something to tell Aunt Bichu, but before that I'd like to talk about something transitional."

"I'll take it as something everlasting," said May.

"I don't have problems with my study. Few of my classmates study hard because they are aiming to get a diploma."

"Which might help them marry into a better family," laughed May.

Huishu tried to hit May, but her hand landed gently on her, and she sighed: "Really, we have grown up. I somehow was looking for trouble when I signed up for calculus, which turned out to be incredibly difficult. Can you help me with the course?"

"Cousin Huishu, you are really desperate! I'm the worst person for you to ask for help with your maths problems!" laughed May.

"But you said you are going to apply for the maths department!"

"I do have such a plan, but it's not because I love maths. It's because Professor Liang likes snacks with jujube paste fillings like I do." She cast her eyes down before looking up: "I think Zhuang Wuyin is the right person. I'll ask him whether he has some time to spare."

Huishu was overjoyed: "What made you think of him?"

May teased her: "You thought about him earlier than I did, didn't you?" Huishu, looking into the distance, smiled and didn't answer. When they went back into the house, Huishu and Bichu talked for a long time. When it was time for dinner, Huishu declined the invitation to have dinner with the Mengs, claiming she had things to attend to at home, and then left.

Some time later, there was a large-scale fund-raising performance with the combined efforts from both troupes in colleges and middle schools to raise funds to support the army fighting at the front and the refugees suffering in the rear. The dramas staged included Oscar Wilde's 'Lady Windermere's Fan', Molière's 'Tartuffe' ('The Hypocrite') and Cao Yu's 'The Family'. The China Experimental Middle School had a literary society called 'Blue Bird' initiated by several senior high school students. Yan Bulai was their instructor. May was a member, too. Various kinds of books were passed around among the members, and formal seminars were held occasionally. They once shared the prose-style fairytale version of Maurice Maeterlinck's 'Blue Bird'. Mr Yan told them the original was indeed a script for a stage drama. His eyes shone at the word 'drama': "Why don't we make it into a play?" Without having the original to refer to, Mr Yan wrote a script from the Chinese translation. When the script was passed among its middle-school and college-student fans, they were all mightily impressed by it. Then Mr Yan appointed himself as the director of the stage play. It was very difficult to stage a play in the form of a fairytale with so few available facilities, but the passion of 'Director Yan' was able to overcome all the obstacles. Mr Yan chose May as the heroine at the very beginning. May was interested – she was going to perform on the stage like Zhou Yu. Mr Yan wanted Heji to play the part of the heroine's little brother but Heji declined, saying he preferred to watch. Then the role was played by Wucai dressed up like a boy. Zhiwei played the role of the big black cat. The lines radiated with classical Chinese poems when polished by Mr Yan. Many who took a part in the play complained about the difficulty of remembering their lines, but those from May's class sailed through the recitation because of their training by Mr Yan, and they enjoyed themselves, too.

The play was scheduled to be staged in December when people dressed like maniacs – some were already in their thin cotton-padded winter gowns, while others were still in shorts and summer socks. May put on Wucai's dress for the rehearsal, while Wucai took Heji's clothes. They walked back and forth on the stage, reciting their lines. When Zhiwei had no part to play, she stayed backstage to prompt others. Wucai was very forgetful of her lines. Once when she forgot her lines and misunderstood the prompter, she was very amused by her mistake and burst out laughing. May laughed, too. Then the laughing became contagious and everyone on stage and several spectators got the giggles. The laughter rocked the place. Yan Bulai sighed: "They wouldn't do that if they were in college."

When the play was formally staged, Xuan and Huishu persuaded the wives of the officers and officials from the military and political circles to buy the most expensive seats. As a novel form of play, the fairytale aspect of the play impressed these ladies very much. They all proclaimed it to be a very instructive and meaningful way of teaching people to be good. The acquaintances and friends Wuyin and Wei invited had mixed reactions. A newspaper article praised it as a stunning performance of a beautiful fairytale.

Besides these positive comments, there was sharp criticism attacking the fairytale format, a genre which was lavish in harmony and content while being blind to conflict and progress. They claimed that it was so obviously wrong to let the middle school students stage such a play.

Yan Bulai was frustrated by the negative comments from his friends from the Teachers of the Masses who blamed him for his obsession with teaching his students an excessive amount of classical poetry and the inappropriateness of staging 'Blue Bird'. These comments came from influential sources, of course, but Yan Bulai's heart was plunged into the depths of despair because he felt he was being wronged and having false charges levelled against him.

When he talked to May about these reactions, May couldn't understand: "Why can't we go in search of some inner peace in such a troubled time? How pathetic we are then!"

When the performance was over, May saw and understood many things she had never seen or understood before. But the major blow was yet to come. One Sunday, May went to the noodle shop by the city gate, carrying a basket with one kilo of flour and four eggs. The noodle shop had a noodle maker which made delicious egg noodles, the Mengs' favourite. As she passed a teahouse, she vaguely heard someone calling her. She looked at the tobacco pipes of all shapes and sizes near the steps leading to the gate of the teahouse and noticed Yan Bulai sitting at a table waving at her. She went over to find several indignant college students sharing the table.

"The money we earned through several months of hard work for the play was intended to provide refugees with clothing and medicine. Can you imagine where the money has gone?" asked Yan Bulai

"You're never going to believe this. When the money was given to the government agency responsible for disaster relief, it fell into private hands!" said a student, clearly in some distress.

"This is corruption! Why don't you say it out loud and clear?" retorted another.

Yan Bulai added: "I have a former classmate who works in the agency. He knows that all the money earned from the exhibitions, the flower sales and our performance won't be directed where it should be."

"How do they manage to get away with it?" asked May.

"Oh, they are very creative in such respects – such as fake receipts and bookkeeping, which wouldn't stand close scrutiny but some bribery helps them evade being found out," explained one student.

May sighed inwardly, so even the sum Professor Bai threw in when he allowed himself to be 'duped' got into the wrong hands. "What did they want the money for?" She asked. The students shook their heads and said she must be living in a fairytale.

Yan Bulai said: "Corruption is an insult to fairytales!" Then they talked about organising an investigation committee. May didn't react as vehemently as they did, so she offered some sort of consolation to them: "They will be punished somehow, won't they?" Everyone felt comforted somehow by these meaningless words. May didn't experience her usual delight at seeing the eggyolk-yellow noodles coming out of the noodle maker like a waterfall.

> "The wren, building its nest in the mighty forest, occupies but a
> single twig. The beaver slakes its thirst from the river, but
> drinks enough only to fill its stomach."

This was what she read from 'Zhuangzi'. However wealthy one was, one had but one stomach. What was the point of hoarding things which were of no use to oneself in order to exploit others while risking exposing oneself to notoriety? May's thoughts ran riot. She paid for the noodles and left for home with a heavy basketful of noodles.

A couple of days later, an essay appeared in the newspaper, querying the whereabouts of the funds raised by sales and performances. The Mengs had a discussion about it over a meal.

"Those who are in power mind each other's backs. They won't expose their crimes," began Fuzhi.

"But the fact is there. And there is exposure, too," said May.

"I'm afraid the one who exposes the crime has to take some protective measures."

"There is no such rule!" Heji yelled, his dark, bright eyes widened.

"There are a lot more rules you have yet not heard of," sighed Fuzhi.

As Fuzhi had predicted, an essay accused the students of embezzling the funds and spending them on lavish dinners, claiming that the accused had absconded. "Newspaper opinions should be reversed when read," said Yan Bulai. "The so-called one who 'had absconded' has indeed gone into hiding because the one who had exposed the crimes was terrified. He had no other option but to disappear. Unfounded countercharges and palming off the false as true are their standard tricks. To go into hiding is not the best option, but it's the safest." The students were enraged at such behaviour.

The person who exposed the corruption was called Sun Lisheng, who was once a substitute teacher for Yan Bulai. Each of his classes was an organised lecture. He didn't punch the desk or slam the chair. Only the fact that his hair always stood on end belied his anger. May and other students hoped he would stay safe. "He will," Yan Bulai told them with confidence. "He's going to a very safe place."

The following week when May went to make egg noodles, the sight of the teahouse reminded her that it would be nice if she could do something to help Mr Sun to stay safe. What a pity that egg noodles weren't much use in realising such a wish.

PART II

The other day when Huishu said she had something to attend to back at home, she meant it. It trapped her the way a traveller is trapped in a swamp, or a heavy fog where she couldn't see where she was going. Bichu was stunned when Huishu told her: "How could such a thing be happening after so many years? You must persuade your father not to do such a thing! He will listen to you. He listens to you. There will be so many more things that he will need you to persuade him about in the future!" Aunt Bichu's supportive words lifted some weight off her shoulders. Having strolled past Green lake, Huishu saw more clearly what lay ahead of her. The lights from Wuhuashan were on, bright and colourful, no longer dim like back in the days when the fighter planes might attack. In front of the mountain, the river was lined with rows of houses and stores. With the lights flickering through the darkness of the night, it was like a beautiful watercolour painting. 'The Greensleeves Café' assaulted her eyes with its blazing brightness. Huishu's heart fluttered. She decided to go in and have a look.

The café was packed full of people. Business was booming. It was another story with the crowds of foreigners in the dim light and soft music. The classic melody of 'Greensleeves' lingered in the air, possibly in many hearts, too. The luxuriously decorated screen separated a mysterious miniature world behind it. Upon entering the café, Huishu at once concluded it was not the place for a young lady. She turned around and was preparing to leave when Xiangge hurried over to greet her with effusive hospitality: "Miss Huishu, what an honour to have you in my café!"

"I'm sorry. I think I got the wrong direction," muttered Huishu, who was already on her way out of the café, while Xiangge literally yelled at her to extend her greetings to Commander Yan and the rest of the Yan family. She walked with Huishu until they were about 50 metres from her café before whispering the question: "What's the matter, Miss Huishu?"

Huishu smiled: "Nothing special. I was attracted by the reputation of the place and wanted to have a look."

"You were hinting at something when you said 'reputation'," said Xiangge, smiling back. "But I can't be choosy about who should come to my café and who shouldn't, and I can't poke my nose into my guests' business, either. The hardships a single woman like me has to shoulder to run a business and earn a living are beyond the imagination of young ladies from families like yours."

"I understand," Huishu responded gently. "I'll see myself off."

Quickly surveying the crowds coming and going along the street, Xiangge said: "Is anything dramatic happening at the Yan residence?" Without waiting for Huishu's answer, she added with absolute conviction: "I'm not willing to accept Commander Yan's offer. I don't know who came up with such a plan, but it stinks! How could they treat me like a nobody?"

Shocked by Xiangge's directness, Huishu was stunned briefly before saying: "If you don't want to, then don't take it. It will save everyone a lot of trouble." On hearing Huishu's words, Xiangge's handsome face full of ingratiating smiles suddenly became very straight, as cold as an unmelting glacier. She gave Huishu a pat on the shoulder and went back into her café. Huishu didn't move a muscle for some time before she headed home, revisiting what had happened the night before.

Before Yan Liangzu set off on his expedition, many visitors came, interrupting the peacefulness of the residence which had persisted for the last few years. When some female visitors came, Hezhu would play hostess. Suchu asked for two rooms as her sanctuary in which to read her scripts and say her prayers. All her meals were delivered to her rooms. Huishu had moved upstairs.

The night before, she had heard noises of smashing china from her father's rooms, mixed with Hezhu's cries and curses. She gathered from the fragments of words that she was able to piece together that it seemed her father wanted to marry someone. When Yan Liangzu lost his patience at Hezhu's bickering, he barked: "If you don't stop now, I'm going to execute you on the spot!" That silenced Hezhu at once.

A moment later, Hezhu knocked on Huishu's door and wanted to talk. Huishu didn't want to talk to her, but she didn't have any alternative. Hezhu came in, with her hair in a mess and a robe with a floral pattern draped over her shoulders. "Your father wants to take a concubine," she said upon entering.

"What? That's impossible!"

"It's true. You know the woman. She's one of madam's relatives – Lü Xiangge."

Huishu was even more shocked: "How did they get to know each other?"

"Lü Xiangge told me several times that the commander looks so charming and manly. They seem to have met each other at a party. She begged me to take the commander to her café to boost its popularity. I thought it might be a welcome distraction for the commander, so I took him there. I never thought Lü Xiangge would be such a loose woman! She flirted with the commander when I was still present. Then she called on the commander herself several times and somehow managed to take him in."

Huishu, who was rather anxious about the calculus quiz the next day, had neither the time nor heart to spare: "Aunt Hezhu, I have a test tomorrow. Why don't you go and take a good rest, too?" Hezhu wasn't ready to depart for her yard to "take a good rest" until she had showered Huishu with more details about Xiangge's craftiness. Huishu shone a torch under the chair Hezhu had been sitting in to make sure no insects were left behind after Hezhu left.

When Lü Xiangge met Yan Liangzu at Zhu Yanqing's party, she made many attempts to get on intimate terms with him. After Hezhu took Liangzu to her café, she went to see him alone several more times. With the possible intention of winning him over with her charms and also bringing fame to her café, she was quite dedicated on each visit. Her dedication was soon rewarded by Liangzu's favour. He even told Hezhu one night that Xiangge had a beautiful face and a smart head. Hezhu blurted out: "Why don't you take her in to keep me company?"

Liangzu had never thought of such a possibility. After weighing up Hezhu's proposal, he deliberated briefly and said: "That sounds like a good idea." Hezhu seemed happy and went to tell Xiangge about the plan. She returned with the news that Xiangge was happy to accept the offer. Liangzu didn't think much more about the matter and casually thanked Hezhu upon hearing her "good news". He never expected Hezhu's reaction would turn into such a drama. Hearing his "thank you", Hezhu jumped at him. Pointing at him, she yelled: "I have been with you for so many years, how could I have failed to see your playboy inclinations? Do you think I'm happy to be a matchmaker for you two? I have been testing your loyalty!"

Yan Liangzu, busy preparing to depart with his army, was furious at such mischief: "Have you lost your mind? Am I the one you should be testing?"

414

Hezhu whined: "Why not? I just wanted to test you!"

Liangzu snapped: "Then why can't I take in that girl? You are difficult! When did you begin to worry about losing my favour to other women? For years, you have been ruling the household. What else do you want? I'm going to take in the girl. You should finalise the arrangements before my departure." Hezhu smashed two tea cups at the command and fought more before she went up to Huishu.

When Huishu had finished revisiting the matter in her mind, she had arrived home. First, she went to visit her mother in her retreat where she sat permanently in her chair with her back straight and a rosary in her hands. Huishu sat down on a low stool by the chair and waited patiently for Suchu to finish the section. She then told her mother quietly about the incident: "I would have thought that a woman from the Lü family might serve as a distraction to share Aunt Hezhu's power while taking care of mum at the same time. Mum might have a better life. But when I talked to Aunt Bichu, she said I was being childish."

Suchu waved her hand gently: "I have found peace. No one can share Hezhu's power. And there is no need to do so, either."

"Aunt Bichu asked me to stop this. Aunt Hezhu seemed to be trying to persuade dad not to do it. I just had a brief conversation with Lü Xiangge. She's much tougher than Hezhu. Besides, she's not willing."

"Is that so?" asked Suchu.

"I think dad seldom considers things from other people's point of view. If he is willing to do something, he assumes others must be willing to accept it. If she meant what she said, that will save a lot of trouble."

Stroking Huishu's dark silky hair, Suchu sighed: "I'm sorry you have to worry about such things at such a young age!"

Huishu lowered her head. After a long silent moment, she said: "I'll go and talk to dad. He's busy preparing for his departure and has no time to spare on such a trivial matter. It will mar his reputation if word gets out." Suchu's maid, Sister Dong, came to clean up the dishes left over from lunch. Huishu gave the maid a piece of her mind for such negligence. She forced her mother to walk twice round the yard before she let her go back to her room.

"I haven't finished my lessons today. You go ahead," said Suchu to Huishu.

Huishu went back to her room to put down her school bag, took some time to clean herself up, and went to Hezhu's yard. At the narrow entrance was a lizard some 40 centimetres long, flanked by spotted snakes. Disturbed, they raised their heads, hissing. Huishu's eyes had got used to the sight, but her heart had never got used to the terror. Hezhu saw Huishu from a window and said: "Keep walking. Don't worry about them once you are in my place!" The two snakes hissed and coiled up again.

Huishu entered the room and remained standing.

"I know you dare not sit down," said Hezhu.

The rooms were clean and tidy. Nothing seemed to be abnormal, but you never knew when and where some deadly insects might pop out. Huishu, embarrassed that Hezhu had seen through her, forced herself to sit on a wooden chair: "I met Lü Xiangge. She told me about the matter and that she was not willing to do it."

"But she told me she was desperate to be taken in and keep me company! Whether she is willing or not doesn't matter much. What really matters is the commander's decision."

"I am going to try and persuade dad to drop the idea, but I'm not confident that he will listen."

Hezhu poured a cup of dark-red wine with an intoxicating aroma from a black clay jar. She held the cup in her hand: "This is the Dream of Spring wine. Your father knows what it is. Once the wine is poured, it can't be taken back. If your father won't change his mind, then it's no use taking the wine back, either."

Huishu braced herself to comfort Hezhu: "Aunt Hezhu, you have been through so many ups and downs and know dad well. I think his decision was made on a whim. How can he manage any spare time?"

Hezhu sneered: "He might not even realise if I died for him." She put the cup of wine into a small jar and put the lid on it. "You have been a quiet child since you were little. But I know you are smart. Your stubborn father might listen to you if you go and talk some sense into him."

Huishu said: "Aunt Hezhu, don't take it too seriously. I don't think it will happen." She stood up, heading for the door. Several creatures dashed out of the chair she had just been sitting on. Having no heart to see what they were, she hurried off. She didn't let go of her long-held breath until she was back in her room. She had decorated her room with various brocade curtains and screens soaked with prickly-ash water. They had a practical purpose, too. The smell was good at keeping pests and bugs away. Her father didn't come home that night. Tossing and turning in bed, Huishu wasn't able to sleep. She felt the heavy weight of the house nestling on her shoulder, plummeting downward, suffocating her. How she wished she could tear down the roof and the house and go as far away from it as possible. She just needed one person to be her companion. And that person was going to be helping her with her homework assignment this weekend. What a piece of luck! The thought brought her peace, and even a kind of joy.

Huishu didn't see her father until late in the evening the next day. When Liangzu was home, he would talk to Huishu. He needed someone to converse with who was a match for him. Huishu's words were always more enlightening than Yingshu's. When Liangzu entered her room, he said: "What a strong smell of prickly ash! It might harm your health."

"It won't. Besides, I myself smell of prickly ash having been exposed to such a smell for so long." Liangzu sat in his chair and asked Huishu about her college studies. Huishu answered: "Dad, you don't need to worry about me. But you have made me worry about you. Aunt Hezhu has told me you want to take a concubine."

"Oh yes! I almost forgot that! You know the girl. I think her name is Lü Xiangge or something."

"We have enjoyed several years of peace. Won't it be troublesome to take in a stranger?"

"She is smart and amusing. If she doesn't fit in, I'll send her away."

"We are living in different times now, dad. To marry a person is a serious matter. Not to mention a divorce. Besides, even if she stays, the marriage itself would mar your reputation."

Liangzu mused.

"Mum won't say anything, but Aunt Hezhu is strongly opposed to it," added Huishu.

"It was indeed Hezhu's idea. She said she wanted to test my loyalty. I want to test her generosity!"

"Why do you need to test each other when there is nothing to come between you? Dad, I went to Aunt Hezhu's room last night. She poured a cup of wine and told me once it is poured, it can't be taken back."

Liangzu's heart sank and he yelped: "Dream of Spring! She's really serious this time! I'm leaving next week. We'll talk about the matter when I come back, then."

The guards came to let them know that dinner was ready to be served. Piled on the table were lots of authentic local dishes from Dali, Liangzu and Hezhu's hometown. Hezhu's face was elegantly made up. When she poured wine or helped Liangzu with the dishes in an intimate way, her earrings and emerald braces dangled and jingled merrily as if nothing had happened. Huishu told herself that counted as a talent, too.

After the meal, Liangzu's former adjutant Qin Yuan paid him a visit. When Liangzu was removed from his position, Qin Yuan left the army after his left leg was wounded in the Battle of Hubei. He was away for two years. When Liangzu was reinstated to his former position, the list of men he wanted to reinstate included Qin Yuan, but Qin Yuan's reinstatement was

417

denied. Knowing Liangzu was departing, he came to see him off. They skated over what they had been doing for the past two years and focused on the war. Qin Yuan said the situation in southern Yunnan was not as urgent as that in western Yunnan since it might have been a decoy when the Japanese claimed they would attack Kunming from Hanoi. The western Yunnan theatre was linked to those of India and Burma. Complicated by the failure of the expeditionary troops, the situation in western Yunnan needed to be prioritised. He thought the southern Yunnan theatre didn't need the best soldiers and capable officers like western Yunnan did. He then mocked himself for having gathered these opinions from snippets of information tucked away in the tiny corners of newspapers.

"I know you are good at reading between the lines," said Liangzu, laughing.

Qin Yuan continued: "Commander, when you accomplish your mission in southern Yunnan, you and your troops might be transferred to western Yunnan. But there is a second possibility."

Gazing at him, Liangzu guessed: "To fight the CPC?"

Qin Yuan nodded: "It will be a great misfortune for the nation if the armed forces of the KMT and the CPC clash with each other. This view of mine is not shared by either party. The reason I bring this up to you, Commander, is indeed quite simple."

Liangzu deliberated for a moment: "You don't want me to fight the CPC? But as a soldier, my mission is to fight on the battlefield and win the battle. I have been fighting on the battlefield for most of my life. I used to be a bandit!" said Liangzu, cackling, before adding: "But I hate wars. My hope is that there might be a day when the world is free of wars of any kind, although that day might never come."

"Things progress in conflicts and confrontations, although not necessarily in a violent form. I should be put into confinement for saying such things before your departure!" said Qin Yuan. He took out a delicately carved pipe: "I made it myself, Commander. Please keep it."

Liangzu took it and had a good look. He smiled: "I still remember how adroit your hands were."

"My plan B was to find you a model book of calligraphy for you to study on the way, but I couldn't find a quality one," said Qin Yuan. At that time, most of the senior generals tried to have some literary accomplishment. It was trendy for a general to practice calligraphy or to buy works of art. The topic of their conversation then switched to calligraphy. When the guard came in to serve another round of hot tea, Qin Yuan stood up and saw the sabre securely set on the table by the central wall. Liangzu used to carry it with him and practice with it. Qin Yuan had the opportunity to polish it. He went up to it, took hold of it with both hands and said: "Long time no see!"

Liangzu noticed Qin Yuan was limping with his left leg. He asked with concern: "Your leg hasn't recovered yet?"

"I limp a little but it doesn't affect my ability to walk. It's said to be the best result," answered Qin Yuan. Liangzu asked his servant to take a pack of plasters promoting blood circulation to remove blood stasis and reduce the pain. Qin Yuan gratefully accepted and bade farewell. Although he was not in uniform, he saluted Liangzu, who saw him off all the way to the gate. They shook hands.

Since Liangzu's departure was imminent, many of his friends and relatives came to visit. Wei and Xuan had visited and told Liangzu they would come more often to visit Aunt Suchu during Liangzu's absence. On the day before his departure, Fuzhi and Bichu came with a whole pack of new writing brushes and a copybook for calligraphy by the famous Tang dynasty calligrapher and politician Chu Suiliang (596–658) entitled 'On A Happy Life' written by a little-known philosopher and politician at the end of the Han dynasty named Zhong Changtong (180–220). Liangzu was delighted with the gifts, claiming that practicing calligraphy helped him calm down and come up with better strategies.

Fuzhi opened the copy book: "This is one of the 16 volumes of the *Xihongtang Collection* compiled by Ming dynasty painter and calligrapher Dong Qichang (1555–1636). I wasn't able to track down all the 16 books, but this single one in such good condition is a rare find." The opening lines of 'On A Happy Life' read: "A perfect house should be spacious with fertile fields nearby. It should be located at the foot of a mountain with a river flowing by and surrounded by groves of trees and bamboos…"

"What a beautiful place!" exclaimed Liangzu.

"A perfect place for retirement," added Fuzhi.

Their topic of conversation moved from calligraphy to the ongoing war. Liangzu laughed: "Yingshu was once your student. Although he doesn't have the potential to do academic research, he is honest and industrious. I need you to do me a favour and take care of him, too."

Fuzhi answered: "You've brought him up well. That's for sure."

Bichu felt very sorry for Suchu who seemed to have become even skinnier since her retreat to solitary confinement in her room. Stroking her sister's bony shoulders, Bichu's heart ached more at Suchu's indifference to Liangzu's departure. Her heart was a pool of still water, thought Bichu. That was what her inscription reading and retreat had brought her. Well aware that all kinds of religions were nothing but distractions and sustenance to escape from the pains of reality, Bichu felt somehow that followers of Buddhism were rather too harsh on themselves in practicing their doctrine. She mentioned this to May when she came home but May laughed at her lack of 'religious knowledge'. The two then sighed together.

On the day of Liangzu's departure, Suchu left the confinement of her rooms to join Liangzu for breakfast with Huishu. The three sat at the table in silence. Liangzu tried to say something but ended up saying nothing. He patted Suchu's bony hand with its swollen veins, sighed heavily, stood up and prepared to leave when Hezhu came in.

"Why are you leaving the moment I arrive, Commander?" asked Hezhu, but then she immediately added: "Right, it's time to leave." She took Liangzu's cap and handed it to him.

"Take good care of the family," he told Hezhu. The three women walked him all the way to the gate. Huishu cried: "Dad!" Liangzu turned back to look at his wives and his daughter, waved his hand, walked forward a few steps, and turned round again. The three women standing in front of the gate looked lonely and helpless even basking in the glory of the morning sun and with the protection of a handful of guards. He turned around and boarded his jeep heading out of the north city gate to the playground.

The morning sun shone brightly over the troops stationed in neat formations at the playground. For Liangzu's presentation, they all stood vigorously at attention. More of the troops stationed in the outskirts were due to board their vehicles on site. Governor Yin and the commander of the local branch arrived, too. They both delivered a speech.

Liangzu spoke last: "For the last two years, I have been dreaming and hoping to go back to fight on the front line. Today, my dream has come true and my wish has been granted. We are going to confront those Japanese devils again! How much longer are they going to ravage this land? How much longer are they going to stay? It's all down to one fact - whether we are capable of fighting them off or not! Are we capable of it?"

"Aye, aye!" The unified answer from the assembled troops rocked the sky.

Liangzu saluted governor Yin before he departed. The latter held Liangzu's hand and said: "You are a commander who is expert at winning wars. Don't worry. We'll take care of your family." Liangzu had led his troops into many battles, but this was the first time governor Yin had mentioned taking care of his family. How peculiar this was. Military trucks transporting loads upon loads of young soldiers passed them one after another. They left Kunming and might never return.

Liangzu's jeep was at the end of a convoy of military trucks transporting soldiers. Behind him was a train of heavily loaded supply trucks rumbling one after another. Many Kunming townsfolk were still sound asleep, although many had already started their working day. Some people stood by the roadside, waving goodbye to the troops. Having seen so many departures of different troops, they had lost their original passion. People were fed up with the torture of the war. They wanted it to end. The only way to end the war was to win it. People hoped that their troops would win.

"Win! Win! Win the war! We have won before! And we will win again!" The voices echoed in the distance and lingered on and on.

Huishu helped her mother back into the house and led her to her room. Suchu followed her daughter obediently and sat down. She tugged at a hanging screen near her, feeling secure and comforted.

Huishu asked: "Mum, would you like to move out and share my room?"

Suchu shook her head: "Mum is almost a devotee. I can't move out of my retreat. I feel settled that you are capable of taking care of yourself." She touched the bedding, turned around and said: "It's time for me to return to my lessons." Huishu walked her all the way to the retreat and ordered Sister Dong to serve her well. When everything was done, she went back to her room. Today, she had two major events. The first one was her father's departure with his troops. The second was that Wuyin was going to help her with her homework. As Wuyin was reluctant to come to the Yan residence and Huishu to Wuyin's house, they agreed to meet at the Mengs' in the wintersweet grove. They were going to start that afternoon. Huishu even previewed the exercises not assigned by her teacher in order to sort out the questions she didn't know and aimed to focus her attention on those when Wuyin helped her.

She suddenly heard many people talking in the yard. Among the voices, she heard a cry: "Sister!" It was Yingshu's voice.

Huishu was surprised and overjoyed. She flew into the corridor to see Yingshu in the yard. She shouted: "Brother, dad has left!"

Yingshu said: "I knew dad was leaving today. I missed him." Hezhu went out of her room upon hearing Yingshu, who didn't have time to talk to his mother and said: "I'm heading for the playground now. They might still be there." He hopped back into the car and left. Hezhu waited with her pipe in her hands in the reception hall.

A while later, Yingshu came back and told Hezhu: "I've seen dad. He was in his jeep. He saw me, too. I knew dad was departing today and had been planning to come back to see him off. But something happened in the division headquarters which delayed my departure. I was only able to arrive late this morning." Seeing him travel-stained, dark and skinny, Hezhu's heart soared. She told him to take a break, but Yingshu said he wasn't tired and wanted to greet his dear mother first.

Hezhu stopped him: "She doesn't like interruptions. You know that very well. Go and get some shut-eye first." Then Huishu came downstairs. The brother and sister hadn't seen each other for a long time and were overjoyed to be reunited. They looked closer than they were, which was immediately sensed by Hezhu, and she let the two know she was not happy. Huishu sensed Hezhu's change of attitude and then asked Yingshu to take a rest first because they could talk more later in the evening. She went upstairs to her room and back to her calculus problems.

In the afternoon, Huishu headed straight for the wintersweet grove. She first went to greet Bichu in her room and then went to May's room to wait for Wuyin. Having finished almost 10 problems, she finally saw May and Wuyin return. Wuyin asked Huishu to come out to the bigger room outside and sat at the square dining table because May's room was too small. The square table used to be May and Heji's work desk several years back when they were little. Wuyin first scanned Huishu's textbook, checked her progress and asked Huishu what she couldn't understand. Huishu told him, embarrassed: "I know almost nothing."

"Then we'll start from the very first chapter," said Wuyin. When he had finished his explanation, he asked Huishu to try the exercises. A moment later, Heji came home, too. They all moved quietly and tried their best not to disturb Wuyin and Huishu.

While Wuyin was helping Huishu, May was occupied with her maths problems in her small room. The maths problems seemed to be quite intransigent today. Two algebra problems stymied May. However hard she tried, she just couldn't work them out. She decided to put them aside and head for the kitchen. Dinner was her responsibility. She arranged all the steps from rinsing the rice to cleaning the leafy vegetables economically. Soon the kitchen was filled with the sweet smell of rice porridge. When she cooked, she kept Oscar Wilde's 'The Picture of Dorian Gray' on the counter and cast several glances over the pages between steps. She didn't notice that Wuyin, who was behind her, had joined her to read until Huishu came up to her. Huishu said Yingshu was home and she had to go back as soon as possible. She thanked Wuyin and asked him when the next lesson would be. Wuyin didn't answer but looked at May instead. May asked whether it would be OK the way they did it today. Then it was settled. After Huishu left, the two read several more pages of the novel.

Wuyin said: "I have goose bumps when I read the book. I'll drop it now. I'd like to see your maths."

May looked around the kitchen and reckoned that she could leave for a while, so she said: "That's perfect. There are two problems I can't work out." She went into her room to fetch the text book.

"I also want to have a look at your exercises," added Wuyin.

"You don't need to go over my exercises," said May.

"You must have done a poor job. Don't worry. I will help you."

May secured her exercise book in the drawer and laughed and laughed.

Wuyin had no choice but to focus on the two problems in her textbook. It took him only seconds. He wrote down the beginning steps and said: "If you are going to apply for the maths department, you must know how to solve this type of problem." Seeing the steps, May immediately understood and finished the rest.

Wuyin said: "It looks like you are reasonably qualified. But that cousin of yours is quite dumb."

May laughed again: "She's not in the maths department."

"It's quite boring to tutor her," said Wuyin.

May cocked her head: "Where can we find a world which only has interesting stuff?"

Heji had finished his assignments and asked Wuyin to help him make a radio. All three busied themselves with the project. Wuyin didn't leave until he had had dinner with the family.

The division headquarters Yingshu worked at was stationed in Chuxiong city, the prefectural seat of Chuxiong Yi Autonomous Prefecture, in Yunnan. His logistics division oversaw two hospitals dedicated to wounded soldiers and a bedding and clothing factory. Neither had anything to do with his history major. One hospital pocketed a portion of the money for the wounded soldiers' meals. Although the inmates who could move about had raised objections several times, the quality of the meals never improved. Several days ago, the inmates had worked out a radical plan to beat the superintendent of the hospital to attract enough attention to the problem. And they did, so the division headquarters sent Yingshu to investigate. Upon his arrival, Yingshu arrested several inmates involved in the beating. He was well aware that the ultimate solution to corruption like this required a thorough investigation, which was basically an impossible mission. His repeated requests to check the hospital accounts had been effectively evaded. When he finally obtained an order from the division commander to investigate the hospital, they presented him with a very neat set of accounts which, he later figured out, were tailor-made for the investigation. One person even told Yingshu brazenly that he wouldn't be able to find anywhere with only one set of accounts. They always had two sets. For the last two years, although Liangzu had been removed from his position and lost his power over the army, he was reappointed to oversee water conservancy projects and he busied himself with that. His frequent absences from home deprived Yingshu of the opportunity to discuss these tricky problems with his father. His plan was to talk to his father before his departure, but he had missed him. Lying in his bed, gazing at the giant portrait of his father in uniform, his thoughts wandered to imagine where his father and his troops were now.

That evening he tried to discuss the problem with Huishu, who refused to listen, claiming it was not something that interested her. Looking through the open door into the dark blue sky, she was burning inside: "This is not my world. I'll leave and never return." It was quite beyond her expectation when Yingshu spoke out loud what she was thinking: "I know you want to leave and go far away. I want to do the same, but I don't know where to go." Huishu didn't respond.

Bored at home, Yingshu wanted to talk to Professor Meng, but he was afraid that it might disturb the family if he dropped by too late in the evening. He decided to go and find Tantai Wei. It was quiet along the dyke at Green lake. When he took a walk around the pavilion located in the centre of the lake, he spotted a man sitting on a giant rock by the pavilion, chin in hand, lost in thought. A second look told him it was Wei Feng, so he went over and greeted him.

Wei Feng stood up: "I heard Commander Yan and his troops departed this morning. Did you come back to see him off?"

"I only saw him from a distance. I was delayed by the wounded soldier issue at the hospital and arrived late this morning instead of yesterday." Over the dim light from the crescent moon, Yingshu realised how skinny Wei Feng had become. It suddenly occurred to him that Xueyan had been gone for more than half a year. His thoughts were stuck at the memory of it. "I was on my way to find Wei. Something is bugging me," added Yingshu after a long silence.

Pointing at the rock, Wei Feng said gently: "How about sitting down and talking to me first?" The two were acquaintances, but they had never had a serious talk before. They sat down with their minds full of worries and anxieties.

Yingshu was desperate for an outlet, so he began without being asked: "Two years of work have taught me what corruption is. The reason behind the wounded soldier upheaval is that the hospital management has been pocketing the money for the meals of the wounded. What the hospital has been feeding the wounded is nothing but light soup, which is no good to

424

help them recover. The bedding and clothing factory is doing the same thing. For a quilt which weighs 500g, they falsely label it as 1.5kg. Even the medicines in the hospital have been the target of corruption. On one occasion, some wounded soldiers died of infection from their wounds despite having penicillin injections. Later a young military surgeon sneaked the information to me that all the penicillin had been sold. The soldiers had just been injected with distilled water. Later the surgeon was fired for a malpractice he was not responsible for."

Yingshu paused and then added: "I don't have a delicate heart, but my heart is not made of stone, either. I want to leave, but I don't know where to go. On second thoughts, I still need to fight the Japanese. I think I will hold on and try my best."

Wei Feng said: "We share one ideal, complete or incomplete, that the world should be fair. There is no ready-made fairness. We need to create it."

Yingshu fell into a long silence before he started again: "I barely manage to fight with the unfairness and evil going on around me. Besides, several friends of mine are not much use. I can't see how to deal with it."

Wei Feng answered sincerely: "Frankly, I'm lost in my struggles and don't know which way to go. Your words remind me maybe we should become like the few who wake up and force their way out of their 'iron room' depicted by Lu Xun."

"Or we'll be crushed and die in our sleep. Besides, people are playing cards and getting drunk on a daily basis all around me in the headquarters. I just hope they don't reach rock bottom. There are a few hard cases in the division headquarters. Although they are drunkards, they are the favourites of those in power due to their flattery. They're rewarded, too, even on the battlefield, although what they do is to send more innocent soldiers to die and add their names to the list of the deceased. I sometimes even envy them for their gains. I'm terrified that one day I might become one of those who fake the accounts."

"You won't. I knew you wouldn't a long time ago. I'll find you some books to read. Let's learn together to create the fairness we long for," said Wei Feng.

"It will be tough."

"Yes, it will be very tough. Very tough."

But both felt that their hearts were lighter.

The moon had risen. The shadow of the pavilion was clearly silhouetted in the water. The weeds in the lake swayed with the waves and were teeming with fish. Wei Feng let out a long sigh: it would be perfect if the world were reduced to just Green lake.

PART III

It had been half a year since Wei Lingnan had cried, whined and used all his strength to suck goat's milk in his crib. The short distance between Precious Pearl alley and Wasted alley made it convenient for Xuan to drop by to see Lingnan. Seeing the baby change each day, Xuan was amazed. How ridiculous she was to have thought dolls were lovelier than real babies. As time went by, the baby's dark eyes would follow her everywhere and the chubby little hands would hold her fingers tight and wouldn't let go. One day a smile graced that smooth little face! Xuan was shocked: you know how to smile now! You are amazing! She also felt proud of herself because she was the first to witness Lingnan's first smile. That smile looked so much like Xueyan's! And those eyes, too. She couldn't help sharing these thoughts with Wei Feng, who gave her a look full of appreciation and turned his eyes away hastily.

One evening when Xuan went to see Lingnan after her class, she ran into Yao Qiu'er at the entrance of the alley. Qiu'er politely greeted Xuan as she always did and asked where she was heading. "I just want to take a walk," said Xuan without slowing down and headed for the alley. Qiu'er stood there, rubber-necked to look in the direction where Xuan was heading, and a topic came to mind. It was fun to her. She almost couldn't wait to replace the characters in the second-class romance she was carrying with her with what she had just seen now.

Entering the yard, Xuan heard Lingnan howling. She hurried into the room to see him frantically waving his arms amid his rhythmic cries. Xuan had never held a baby before, but the situation gave her the courage to take the baby in her arms. "Lingnan, don't cry! Don't cry!" she said, rocking him as he nudged at her in her arms. Xuan understood the gesture and was embarrassed. The little one wanted to be fed. He still remembered the way his mother fed him. Qinghuan had gone to milk the mother goat at the far end of the alley. Since all the neighbours sharing the yard were against having a goat as a neighbour, Wei Feng had to build a shed for it there.

When Xuan was at the end of her wits, Qinghuan came back with the goat's milk. Seeing what Xuan was doing, she thanked Xuan immediately: "Thank you very much, Miss Xuan!" She set about pasteurising the milk by heating it on a stove in the passageway. Lingnan couldn't wait and cried out loud again.

Xuan asked Qinghuan: "Didn't Aunt Bichu tell you to give him some milk powder, too?"

"We ran out of milk powder a couple of days ago," answered Qinghuan. Xuan sighed at the news and her knowledge of Wei Feng's negligence in these matters.

"I'll go and buy some." Settling the baby in the crib, she patted him lovingly. She was both relieved and guilty. At the gate she ran into Helen and told her she was going to buy some milk powder for Lingnan. Helen raised the bag she was carrying: "I've bought more. Wei Feng asked me to buy it for him."

"Great!" said Xuan. They exchanged more words before Xuan left feeling disappointed yet without knowing why.

Once she was back at Precious Pearl alley, her landlord told her she had a visitor who had left a note on her door. It was from her colleague, a relative of some VIP. She had invited her to join her on a boat trip at Grand View pavilion on the coming Sunday. Xuan assumed it was a get-together among colleagues and didn't think much about it.

On Sunday morning a car came to collect Xuan. Once the car got clear of the city via the minor west city gate, the shiny green from the trees lining each side of the road filled her eyes. Both the water nearby and the hills in the distance were basking in spring. It didn't take long for the car to reach the pavilion. Everyone went right to the steps in front by the lake to board the boat which had been reserved and was kept cleaner than ordinary ones. Xuan went to sit at the stern, greeting others and chatting with them. She felt refreshed by the scenery. Turning around, she saw the famous couplet of 180 characters on each side of the gate to the pavillion. The sight of the couplet reminded her of the passage of the years and her recollection of those old events surged in her heart, especially that moonlit night. When she had refused Paul, they had remained friends. Paul was retiring from his position and going back to America soon. Would they ever meet again? Xuan knew one person who must have been very disappointed at the fact that Paul was leaving alone. Not allowing the name to upset the fresh sight in front of her, Xuan stood up and dropped the thought.

"Take your seats. We are leaving," said the teenager rowing the boat to everyone on board. His clothes looked neat and tidy, but his face looked weary and wan.

The relative of a VIP walked over to Xuan, loudly enthusing over the view. She pointed at Xishan: "This is called the Sleeping Beauty. Do you think so?" Xuan just smiled. She then continued: "Many say that Miss Tantai has become much more calm and quiet. It looks like they are right."

Xuan thought what does it matter to you how I have changed, but she answered: "That's because I'm getting old."

The relative shook her hands frantically: "What nonsense!" People in the cabin asked her to join them to play cards and she asked Xuan to go in, too. Xuan knew how to play cards, although she couldn't play as well as her mother. But the Mengs didn't even have cards. Xuan didn't want to play with these people, so she turned to talk to the teenager rowing the boat: "How old are you?"

"Almost 17. It wasn't easy to reach the age of 17! I crawled out of a pile of corpses and survived," answered the teenager. Xuan asked more details about his life. He told her: "I used to live in Baoshan. But all my family, except me, died in the enormous air raid. Few in my village survived the bombing. I followed an acquaintance, taking odd jobs, and finally made my way to Kunming and found this job rowing a boat. You and your lot can never imagine how we have managed to survive." He kept rowing for a while and then talked for some time before pitching into his rowing again: "Now I'm lucky to know where my next meal is coming from. Lots of people don't know where their next meal is coming from."

Someone spoke loudly to the teenager: "Don't row too far. We have been invited to lunch at the Zhu residence." At these words, the teenager dutifully turned the boat around and headed for the Zhu residence. A house surrounded by water and hidden in the green trees gradually revealed itself in front of its visitors. They got off the boat. In front of them was a hexagonal gate with a signboard inscribed with the four characters 別有洞天 (bie you dong tian), literally meaning 'an amazing world'. The zigzagging veranda led them all through the gate onto a platform. Not until then did Xuan realise it was where the ball had been held. So this was Zhu Yanqing's property! She weighed up the situation and reckoned it would be rude to leave now. Someone in the hall chuckled and greeted them loudly: "Welcome, distinguished guests!" It was indeed Zhu Yanqing.

Zhu Yanqing was in a light tan gown. As he moved, it revealed his immaculately ironed trousers. He first thanked the relative of someone leading the group, greeted the others, and then came over to Xuan: "I haven't seen you for several months. I didn't dare to disturb you." Xuan smiled at his words and carried on chatting with her colleagues, as if she was unaware of Zhu Yanqing's presence.

The guests and the host went into the hall to sit down for tea. Several men dressed like merchants had arrived earlier. One was looking at a fountain pen, saying it was worth five to six thousand yuan; while another was offering a *ruyi*, an s-shaped ornamental jade piece, to Zhu to bring the place more good fortune. Xuan loathed these swindlers profiting from the country's suffering. The one who was appreciating the hardwood furniture teased Mr Zhu that what he needed was a hostess to help him manage all the valuables. Another one tried to polish the apple: "It won't be easy for Mr Zhu to find someone that measures up to his high standards."

Xuan was studying a portrait of a lady said to be the work of the famous Tang dynasty painter Tang Yin. She didn't need to take a second look to know it was a fake. The painting of bamboo on a moonlit night by the Qing dynasty bamboo master painter Zheng Xie seemed in poor taste as well. It was a fake, too.

Zhu Yanqing walked over to Xuan: "I just try to pretend I have refined taste. Miss Xuan, would you like to help me sort out the quality ones?"

"I don't know much about paintings," said Xuan, as her eyes settled on a painting with green mountains and a river. The elegant woman playing the *guqin* (an ancient zither) in the picture was in a red dress. That painting attracted Xuan's attention. She heard someone greeting her. It turned out to be Liu Wanfang from Mean alley. Wanfang smiled at Xuan but her question was for Zhu Yanqing: "Didn't you hang the paintings you bought at the exhibition?"

Xuan had never been to Mean alley and didn't know Wanfang. She nodded at Wanfang and was ready to leave when Zhu Yanqing asked her: "Right. I didn't see Miss Tantai at Zhao Junhui's exhibition."

Wanfang hastened to answer for Xuan: "Miss Tantai must be very busy with all sorts of dates."

Xuan glanced at Wanfang and retorted: "Mrs Shao, how do you know I'm busy with dates?"

Wanfang blinked and said: "Because you are one of the few famous young ladies in Kunming!"

Xuan sneered: "Who would be stupid enough to aspire to be famous rather than being normal?"

At that moment, servants came to inform Mr Zhu that lunch was ready. One person asked: "It has been said that the structure of the residence is quite extraordinary. Would it be too much to ask Mr Zhu to show us around?" Unable to turn down the request, Zhu Yanqing led the group through a side door of the hall. By the lake were two smaller halls, one of which was furnished in European style with milk-white furniture painted with gold line motifs and the other was rosy and oriental. Both had giant French windows. Leaning over the railing, one could touch the water teeming with fish.

Liu Wanfang asked: "I have heard that Mr Zhu's villa located at the foot of Xishan is even more charming." Her face radiated with admiration when she talked.

Xuan thought it was indeed an interesting place to enjoy the fish by the window as she was doing. Most of the visitors had moved on, leaving only Xuan and Zhu Yanqing behind. Zhu took a scroll from a carved table and rolled it open in front of Xuan. It was the blueprint of his villa in Xishan. Zhu Yanqing breathed his words at Xuan: "You have seen this place, but not this one on the paper. Would you kindly accept it?" With these words, he handed Xuan the blueprint. Xuan was furious at such an offer, but her manners checked her temper from exploding

Someone cried from another room: "What a beautiful bedroom! Mr Zhu, we are waiting for your introduction!" Seeing that Xuan had no intention of taking the blueprint, Zhu put it down and forced himself to entertain his guests. Xuan snapped to herself: who wants to see your bedroom? I won't! She sneaked out of the reception hall to the platform where she found the boat and its rower were still anchored where they had disembarked. She hopped in and asked the teenager to get her back to town immediately.

A servant came and asked where Xuan was going since lunch was already being served. Xuan only shook her hand at the servant and ordered the teenager: "Start rowing! Now! Fast!"

The teenager rowed vigorously and began to talk: "Miss, to tell you the truth, we often come to beg for the leftovers. One meal of the leftovers can last for one, even two, days!"

Upon the teenager's words, Xuan reflected silently to herself how little she knew about the unfairness in the world. This teenager with his handsome features might grow into someone, given the time and opportunity. But now it looked as if he would have to struggle to get three meals a day in such a chaotic world for the rest of his life.

The little guy was still talking: "When the expeditionary troops retreated from Burma, they were all exhausted. Have you seen any in Kunming city?" He resumed after some rowing: "The Japanese devils were monstrous. They swam across the Nu river (Salween river)!"

"Didn't we smash up their operations when they managed to force their way across the river?"

Tears trailed down the boy's cheeks: "No. Two Japanese soldiers even fumbled their way into my home. I had a home back then! They wanted to find something to eat. We tied them up."

"What happened then? Shouldn't you have reported them?"

"Report what? We killed them and buried them."

The two fell silent. When the boat was ashore, Xuan gave the boy 20 yuan, who thanked her again and again, told her his name was 'Kuliu' and that he was willing to serve her more often.

Xuan went directly back to Precious Pearl alley with her mind in turmoil. Entering the courtyard, she raised her eyes to see Wei Feng sitting in the passage outside her room, holding a newspaper. She picked up her pace to go upstairs and opened the door: "How long have you been waiting? I was going to see Lingnan."

"I just sat down," said Wei Feng. He pointed at the newspaper: "The war in Guangxi province is getting more critical. We have lost several places in a row. Although one has to read between the lines to discern anything from these ambiguous reports." Xuan told him about her encounter with the boy survivor from the Baoshan air aid.

Wei Feng said: "The stalemate on both banks of the Nu river won't last long with the clearing up of the general war situation from other theatres." Xuan made tea for Wei Feng and went into her bedroom to change her shoes. When she came out again, she was wearing a pair of embroidered flats with cloth outter soles.

"There is still more hardship to come," sighed Xuan. Wei Feng wanted to say something, but he was either hesitant or he didn't know how to start. Looking at his emaciated face pained by his loss, Xuan's heart fluttered. She muttered: "We have grown much older over the past few years."

"You haven't!" exclaimed Wei Feng, laughing.

"I mean it. I used to love parties and was at ease in all sorts of situations. But now…" Now what? She was lost for words.

"Now you are more mature," smiled Wei Feng. "That's why I came to discuss something very important with you." He seldom came to visit Xuan. Now here he was. So it must have been something important.

"Is it about Lingnan?" asked Xuan, her eyes widening.

"Yes. I have a favour to ask you. Can you take care of Lingnan for me? I have asked Aunt Bichu for her opinion. Now I'm asking you for your opinion."

Xuan felt her tears were trying to break loose: "But where are you going?"

"I will be away for some time. Lingnan will be an enormous burden on you if you have to flee as a refugee in case the Japanese occupy Kunming.'"

"I will carry him with me if I have to take refuge."

"You may run out of food."

"I will manage to get some. I won't let Lingnan starve."

"He might get ill."

"I'll find him a doctor. Lingnan is not going to be taken care of by me only. He has Great Aunt Bichu and her family. He has my parents."

"Your parents may think taking care of him will harm your prospects."

"You mean my prospects of marriage?" Xuan dried her tears with her hand and laughed. She had never considered Lingnan to be an ordinary baby. He embodied the extended life of all those who had died in the war of resistance. She had taken into consideration many things. She wanted to take him in her arms, to love him, to feed him, to find him a doctor when he was ill and to watch him grow up. But she had forgotten to consider what situation all that would put her in.

Della reminded Wei Feng that it would be very tricky for Xuan, a bacheloress, to raise a baby, but the problem would take care of itself if Wei Feng and Xuan were married. Wei Feng thought about Della's suggestion for a long time. The place Xueyan occupied in his heart had evolved into a supreme throne, which was drifting farther and farther away as time went by, but he needed solid confirmation over time that she had left and would never return. He liked Xuan. Her image as their maid of honour would come to mind from time to time. For the past half a year, Xuan's care and love for Lingnan had been way beyond anyone's expectations. Wei Feng was indebted to her. But his senses told him she deserved someone better who belonged only to her. He then told Della: "I can't. She has many better options. But I know she will agree to help me out and I hope it won't take me long."

"You can trust me," smiled Xuan, folding her fair hands and pressing them against her heart as if she were making an oath. "I'm willing to take care of Lingnan."

Wei Feng felt the burning tears welling up in his eyes. Before the floodgates opened, he muttered a "thank you" before getting up to leave.

"You haven't had your lunch, have you?" Xuan stopped him.

"I'll have it at Wasted alley. Qinghuan will cook something for me."

He had reached the door when the landlady called out from downstairs: "Miss Tantai, someone has delivered this for you." She brought upstairs a long case wrapped in painted wrapping paper and two bowls of *erkuai* on a tray. Xuan motioned to Wei Feng with her eyes to sit down and put down the *erkuai* in front of him. She picked up the case and muttered to herself casually: "Who has sent me this piece of junk?" She tore open the wrapping paper to see a brocade box with a tag on it – 'Xishan villa plan'. She tossed the case aside.

Wei Feng asked: "What's that? Is it a timebomb?"

"See for yourself."

Wei Feng picked it up and suddenly took the hint – it was a proposal gift to Xuan! Zhu Yanqing was well known in Kunming. And he had quite good taste, too.

"Xuan," Wei Feng began in a rather low voice. "Don't you think he might be worth considering?"

The anger Xuan felt now was different from the one she had harboured against Zhu Yanqing, or against Hezhu when she raised the issue of Zhu's proposal to her. The anger she felt now was mixed with pain and grief which were beyond her own comprehension.

She turned around and sneered: "Then you don't know me!" She tried to break the chopsticks she had in her fair hands. Wei Feng's heart was struck by a strong sense of guilt at his plan to shovel a burden onto her without offering her protection of any kind. The weight of the sadness choked him into silence.

A long while later, Xuan put down the chopsticks and said: "I want to repeat what I just said. You can trust me." Pointing at the plan, she added: "I'll ask someone to send it back."

Once out of Precious Pearl alley, Wei Feng had no intention of talking to anyone. He let the road take him while he walked until he reached Green lake. He sat down on the same rock by the pavilion in the centre of the lake he loved. Gazing at the water, he was lost in thought.

Wei Feng had been deliberating over two choices – whether to leave or to stay – for a very long time. The ideal he had dedicated himself to didn't always shine while the darkness of reality was suffocating him constantly. What Yingshu told him the other day when they ran into each other here confirmed his assumption that it was even harder to break out of the darkness under the reign of the KMT. Uncle Fuzhi's brief arrest was a signal and a warning to him. He should go to join Old Shen and help kindle the spark of the ideal into a great fire. Even it seemed like an impossible dream for him, he still had to give it a try. For such a decision, the best option for

Lingnan would be to leave him with Helen, but somehow, he couldn't accept such an arrangement. He wanted to save a spot for the love of his life, which only Xuan was worthy of. Later in various meetings, someone summarised the situation for Wei Feng: He had faith in the one he didn't love while he loved the one he didn't have faith in. They even patiently tried to change his mind: if he couldn't have faith in the one he loved, then he should try his best to love the one he had faith in. In other words, it was necessary to remold his subjective world, a long path which might take more than a lifetime to achieve.

"Mr Wei," a student approached and greeted Wei Feng. They saw Wei Feng here many times.

Wei Feng raised his head: "I'm thinking over a physics problem."

Tantai Xuan's frequent visits had triggered much speculation, but what was newsworthy happened in Mean alley. That day when Shao Wei came back home, he couldn't find Liu Wanfang, which was not unusual. As it was getting rather late, Shao Wei went to Yao Qiu'er to see whether she knew of Wanfang's whereabouts. Qiu'er smiled sympathetically and said: "So you haven't heard. Go back home then and look around. She must have left you a note or something." Shao Wei turned all the rooms inside out and, eventually, found a letter from Wanfang in a drawer. Before he finished, he burst into loud sobs.

The letter, or the note, consisted of only a few lines: "Shao Wei, all I can tell you is that I'm sorry. What else can I say? Years of cooking has ruined my eyes and doing laundry in winter has repeatedly broken the chilblains on my hands. You do care and you feel sorry. But what difference does it make? I'm leaving you now because I don't want to cook anymore."

Shao Wei dropped the letter and cried for a while before picking it up again: "It's lucky we don't have kids, so both you and I are free of any responsibilities. I have just taken my daily clothing. Besides, you know there's not much that I can take with me. We'll still share the same city and we'll meet again, but let's just forget we ever met."

"She has even denied the fact that we once met!" After being overcome with pain and hatred, Shao Wei again abandoned himself in loud lamentations, pounding his head with his fists. When the pain and hatred had consumed themselves, he calmed down, feeling that Wanfang was still by his side. He had to admit she had been through too much. Those Japanese devils should take all the responsibility!

Yao Qiu'er came in: "Why don't you turn on the light?" she said, taking it upon herself to turn it on. In the dim yellowish light was a messy room

434

permeated with desperation. "I saw her leaving with a package. A car came to pick her up. Are you going to look for her?"

Holding his head in his hands, Shao Wei answered after a long pause: "It's no use. Even if I keep her body, her heart has left."

Qiu'er pouted: "She's such a coward! I have always known she wouldn't be the kind to go through ups and downs with you. Look at the few dresses she has! They are a joke!"

Shao Wei looked up at her: "Why are those dresses a joke? You think everyone is like the two of you..." Tears rolled down his cheeks and he swallowed the rest of his words.

Yao Qiu'er tidied up her old thin padded woollen *qipao* and assumed an air of superiority: "Simple meals and simple clothing are rare traits of a noble character." She paused. Seeing that Shao Wei was silent, she resumed: "I know where she has been. It's not hard to know who owns a car. It is that Mr..."

Shao Wei stood up and cut her off: "Thank you very much, Mrs You." Yao Qiu'er excused herself, rather disappointed at having failed to create some dramatic chaos. When she returned home, she talked it over again with her husband: "I told Shao Wei her clothes are a joke, but he didn't think so!"

"Of course he thinks they are all lovely! Have you even seen a dog which thinks its poo stinks?" They had a good laugh and then made huge fun of the way Wanfang behaved, talked and dressed. It reminded You Jiaren of Shakespeare's opinion about women and the line rolled off his tongue "Frailty, thy name is woman!" The two were in a good mood and decided to go to the Sound of Yunnan cinema for a movie entitled *'Brief Encounter'*. The movie was about a middle-aged man and woman who ran into each other on a train, fell in love and had a transient but passionate love affair. When the movie was over, they walked into a diner to have dinner. Qiu'er thought about Wanfang and asked whether she would come back.

"That would make her a bigger joke," You Jiaren said, chewing a chicken bone. As always, the two of them assumed themselves to be superior and noble.

The You couple were considered to be reasonably affluent with You Jiaren teaching in different universities and his frequent translation contracts, but still, Qiu'er's hands were gradually losing their smoothness. At the recitation party held that weekend at Xia Zhengsi's, they talked about the war and agreed that another relocation might be on the cards. Some said they had letters from their families who had stayed in Shanghai and Tianjin. It turned out that life in the occupied areas was quite smooth. Yao Qiu'er's heart fluttered at the news. Xia Zhengsi read *'Nuit d'Août'* in French. The air became heavy with the memories. You Jiaren whispered in French: "Quelle sensiblerie!" What sentimentality! That whispered expression, although low, was piercing.

Xia Zhengsi walked directly up to You Jiaren: "What did you just say, You?"

"Nothing!" You Jiaren said. His usual meanness didn't win him much popularity. Complicated with such rudeness, several people left during his recitals.

That night when the couple were in bed, Qiu'er told her husband: "I have an idea."

"Freedom of speech is the basic content of human rights!" Yao Jiaren quoted from Rousseau.

Qiu'er gave Jiaren a gentle slap as he said these words and said: "Would you consider going back to Tianjin? I can't see when this life of being a refugee will end."

"It's not a bad idea," deliberated Jiaren. "I hate those people from the department. They are prejudiced against me. I might be laid off next semester."

Qiu'er's eyes almost popped out at the revelation: "Will they? How dare they! Who has more knowledge than you do?"

Stroking Qiu'er's hand, Jiaren said: "Professor Meng will help me. But it would be better if we take the initiative to leave first. Life is too hard here."

"What we earn from the family property in Tianjin is enough to support us. The Japanese need order, so we can shut ourselves away at home and read," said Qiu'er. You Jiaren sank into a gloomy silence.

Later You Jiaren, Wang Dingyi and Jiang Fang were unable to agree on the English translation of some lines from the *Nine Songs*. It is natural for different people to hold different opinions, but You Jiaren threw in many mean and taunting comments, which triggered some discussions.

One commented behind You's back: "You Jiaren thinks too highly of himself. Others are simply dupes in his eyes."

"The tendency for scholars to scorn one another is nothing new. But if the scorn becomes personal, it triggers hard feelings," added another.

"Those who condemn indiscriminately might be regarded as being 'talented'. To be mean is the new trend," taunted the third.

When this talk reached Fuzhi, he laughed and said You had been serious in his teaching and had just published a couple of critical essays which, although lacking in originality, showed his hard work. Professor Meng wrapped up the talk about You Jiaren, but the You couple were all the more determined to leave.

Some days later, when the You couple were taking a walk around Green lake in a gloomy mood, they saw a woman in a light-yellow silk *qipao* and a short grey woollen cape approaching. That outfit attracted attention. A second look revealed it was Liu Wanfang. She looked much fairer and more curvaceous.

"Professor You! Mrs You!" She greeted them, sweetly.

"How've you been? Where have you moved to?" Qiu'er showered Wanfang excitedly with questions, half out of curiosity and half out of concern for Wanfang.

"It's just a little better than life in Mean alley," answered Wanfang somewhat smugly.

Following You Jiaren's advice, the three walked to the pavilion in the lake and sat down at a table. Wanfang said: "When I left, I was too troubled to say goodbye to you, thinking we might see each other anyway. Now look! I have met you both!"

After talking for some time, they realised that Liu Wanfang had not moved in to live with Zhu Yanqing, but with a friend of Zhu. Although he was not wealthy enough to provide her with servants, he provided her with ample food and clothing. She lacked nothing. Seeing Wanfang alone, Qiu'er assumed Wanfang might be the man's mistress. Wanfang seemed to see through Qiu'er because she told her: "He is not married. You don't need to worry about this for me. Anyway, I have decided to leave my old days behind. In the past, to save money, I didn't even buy any soap to do the laundry with. My hands almost turned into claws." She stuck out her hands, which were rosy and smooth although traces of scars left by the chilblains were still visible. She was wearing a jade bracelet on one wrist.

"The war is reaching a critical point. Will the university be relocated?"

"We don't know yet," answered Qiu'er, looking at Jiaren.

"If we have to take refuge again, who knows how much harder life will become? If I were you, I would've long since left for Tianjin. Life there must at least be better than it is here." A jinrikisha came and parked by the roadside. Wanfang smiled at the jinrikisha: "This is our contracted jinrikisha. Well, it looks as though he knows where to find me." She stood up and wanted to say something but ended up saying nothing. Qiu'er was waiting her to ask for Shao Wei, but Wanfang didn't. She said goodbye to them without leaving her address.

The You couple watched the jinrikisha as it took a turn and disappeared out of their sight. Qiu'er said: "I haven't taken a jinrikisha for such a long while."

PART IV

The youngsters had news, too. During dinner one evening, Heji said: "Yin Dashi has come back. Her brother, Little Dragon, told me so."

That day when May came home from school and walked up the slope, she saw two people walking downhill. One was Yin Dashi, while the other was Tantai Wei. Wei hadn't dropped by the wintersweet grove for a long time because he was too busy studying.

"Meng Lingji!" cried Dashi from a distance. "We've just come from the wintersweet grove!" She had grown up and was much less wild. Her skin and her eyes shone like they used to.

"How long have you been back?" asked May.

"About ten days," answered Dashi. "I went to school in Chongqing, but I have come back for college this semester. Although I missed the day for registration, they managed to sign me up."

"No one was at home when we went," said Wei.

"Now let's go back!" May showed them the keys.

They ascended the slope together, talking. Dashi said she was going to Qingyun university too and added smugly: "I'm a free agent, now!" May later learned that the Yins had changed their policy over this daughter. Wang Dian's chief task was no longer to oversee Dashi. When they were at the top of the slope, they met Heji coming from another road with two of his classmates, carrying a roll of paper to make their wall poster.

When they arrived, Heji and his classmates occupied the dining table with their drawings and writing. May asked Dashi and Wei to sit in the rattan chairs in front of the house. Dashi asked May about her school but cut her off rather impatiently in the process. When she talked about the transfer, she said she needed to stay in the same grade for one more year.

"Staying in the same year sounds so disgraceful," she pointed out gravely. "But Tantai Wei said it won't matter."

"It might for others. But for you, it won't. Many things won't matter when they come to you," comforted Wei.

"I'm afraid I might be looked down upon by the future scientist."

May gradually felt she was being excluded from the two's conversation. She stood up and went inside to see Heji doing his poster. Heji was working on the masthead while the other two attended to the layout and subtitles. All were attentive. May kept watching for a while and then walked outside.

Yin Dashi called out to her: "Hey! Stay. You and Tantai Wei were in Kunming while I was away. Why do I have the feeling that I'm closer to him than you are?"

"I wonder about that, too," laughed May.

"Can we hang out for a while?" Dashi asked.

They had two days of spring break this week, so everyone should be available. May thought for a while: "I'm afraid of snakes." She and Dashi exchanged a look, and both burst out laughing.

"Why did you mention such childhood mischief? Tantai Wei, where do you recommend going? Somewhere far away would be best," Dashi said.

Wei asked for May's advice but May said she had no idea.

Wei deliberated for a moment: "I'm not on spring break, but since my experiment scheduled on Saturday has been moved to Thursday night, then we have enough time to go to the Shilin Karst, the Stone forest!"

May clapped her hands: "What a brilliant idea! I have never been to the Stone forest although I have been living here for years!" They asked Heji if he wanted to tag along, but he couldn't because he had to participate in a model plane show. Wei then went to the Zhuangs. Wucai and Della had a visit to make, so only Wuyin was happy to accept the invitation.

It was not convenient to visit the Stone forest in those days due to the lack of transportation options. They had to take the train to Lunan county first. In the evening before the train left, the four boarded merrily with their backpacks. In the carriage there were several twin seats with one small table in between for four to share and seats like long benches. The four picked a table by the window since it was not crowded in the carriage. The two girls sat in the seats by the window. When the starting whistle blew, the train had been waiting to start for a long time. A passenger in the carriage said they wondered whether the train was waiting for someone important. A while later, the train finally started, and the passenger murmured to himself: "Well, the guy has arrived for sure."

It was at the height of spring with all the plants blooming riotously. Along the way, the chaotic expanse of beauty from the vibrant flowers of all kinds was a sight to behold. The blooming peach trees were veiled in snow white with the tops tinted pale crimson. Seen from a distance, they looked like they were wearing small cone-shaped hats.

Pressing her face against the window, May was amazed by the scenery: "I have never given much thought to the expression 'the grandeur of our motherland'. Now I think about it, the word 'grandeur' is the best choice. When the Tang dynasty poetry master Du Fu wrote 'On war-torn land streams flow and mountains stand; in spring the towns are overgrown with grass and weeds', he understood that the motherland would always be there in all its grandeur. But when the country is conquered, the same scenery takes on a different meaning."

"That's why he wrote in the next lines 'Grieved o'er the years, flowers make us shed tears; hating to part, hearing birds break our heart'," added Wei.

"When May talks like this, she reminds me of a profound bookish scholar. When did you start to talk like this?" asked Wuyin.

Dashi cried: "Meng Lingji, I envy you! You have someone taking notes for you! I wish I had someone doing that for me, too!" She snuggled closer to Wei as she spoke. May looked up and smiled at Wuyin.

The train rumbled on for hours and then darkness fell. Most of the passengers in the carriage had settled in a cosy spot, lying down or leaning against each other, ready to crash for the night. It quietened down in the carriage, leaving only the rumble of the train lingering on. May felt the rumble was from some distance away. Dashi had fallen asleep leaning on Wei's shoulder.

"May, you need to get some sleep," whispered Wuyin. "I'll give you my seat." He made a pillow for May by laying down his backpack and walked to the other end of the carriage. May didn't want to wake up anyone else although she wanted to ask him to stay but let him go. The moment her head hit the 'pillow', she fell into a deep slumber.

She woke up some time later to see Dashi and Wei in the same position. Concerned that Wuyin might have nowhere to take a nap, she walked to the other end of the carriage, careful not to step on any of the sleeping passengers in the aisle. Wuyin stood quietly outside the door, wrapped up in the pitch darkness. He must have been exhausted, thought May. When she opened the door, a chilly blast assailed her. She blurted out: "Zhuang Wuyin, you are going to catch cold!"

Upon hearing her, Wuyin didn't turn around: "Is this your new way of addressing me?"

May walked out of the door and leaned on the railing like Wuyin did. Both fell silent.

The train was moving through a hilly section, undulating in accordance with the terrain. The rock formations on both sides of the track loomed threateningly over their viewers like predatory monsters but retreated and disappeared into the darkness in the next moment.

"What are you thinking?" asked Wuyin.

Staring at the lunging and disappearing rock formations, May answered: "Nothing." One rock formation flashed into view and another receded. "And you?" May raised her head, her eyes looking up, too. Her shiny eyes sparkled at the flashing objects. Wuyin didn't answer until after a long silence: "I am..." He was cut off by a violent rocking of the carriage with deafening braking noises. The train ground to a halt.

"What's wrong?" "What has happened?" asked the passengers as they rushed out of the carriage. No one knew what had happened. Some passengers jumped off the train and walked several steps backward and forward but returned with no information about what had gone wrong. It took a long while for a railway guard to come to the carriage. He asked everyone to stay put. Wuyin took May through the crowd back to their seats. Dashi and Wei were sitting in their seats, talking. Upon seeing Wuyin and May coming back, they said they had tried to find them, but amid such chaos, they decided it would be wiser to stay where they were.

"It is indeed wise to sit and wait," said Wuyin. They both sat down.

Wei then said he was hungry and took out the four sandwiches brought by Dashi which were supposed to be their breakfast. They all enjoyed the meal. They were not concerned by the fact that the train had stopped. On the contrary, they found the incident amusing. About an hour later, the train remained motionless. Some passengers said it wasn't going any further and that maybe it would be better for them to continue their journey on foot. A while later, news came that there were problems with the bridge ahead and that it would take several hours to fix the bridge.

"Let's go to Yangzong lake instead!" proposed Dashi, excitedly.

"On foot?" asked Wei.

"We can walk to the nearest village and see whether the villagers have some horses or not."

"I love riding horses, but I don't know how," said May, regretfully.

"Don't worry. All three of us are accomplished riders. Wuyin is probably the best," said Wei.

"No! I think you are the best!" cried Dashi. For her, Wei was the best at everything. Her seriousness made all the other three laugh.

The first rays of daylight were cracking the darkness of the night on the horizon. Most of the passengers in the carriage had left. The four of them got off the train and immediately realised they were in the middle of nowhere. Asking around, they discovered the nearest village was almost 10km away and that they had to climb over the mountains. A handful of passengers who looked like farmers were heading uphill, cursing the government for pocketing the transportation taxes without properly maintaining the bridge. One advised they should talk less since "walls have ears" while eyeing Wuyin and his group. It was too easy to figure out that the four of them were not frequent travellers on this line. The farmers lowered their voices, picked up their pace and disappeared into the distance. The footpath, which was almost invisible, was rough.

It was getting brighter. Suddenly they found they were basking in a warm red glow – the sun was showing half of its face from behind a mountain, tinting the travellers in its colour. The red colour from the sun was mixed up with the red earth emerging from the darkness of the night.

"How gorgeous!" May cried, holding her breath. Popping out of the red earth were rocks of different sizes and shapes with wild flowers crammed in between. All were tinged with the morning glory. Holding Wei's hand, Dashi lept: "I have never seen such a sky and landscape before although I have travelled a lot!"

At the sight of Dashi holding Wei's hand, May realised that Wuyin had been holding hers all the way up the hill. That was why she hadn't found the climb difficult! As they made their way downhill, the hills on the horizon trimmed the sky with fancy lace, blocking their view. May felt there was so much room in her heart that even the beautiful scenery unfolding before her eyes wouldn't be able to fill it up. She looked at Wuyin with a smile, who looked back at her, smiling. They shared a mutual aspiration which rose high into the air, looking beyond the hills and mountains.

The village they had been told about was small. Lady Banks roses climbed around the houses. Wisps of smoke from inhabitants cooking breakfast rose from several houses in the village. Some had opened their gates. A couple of kids with runny noses ran out to look at the approaching strangers. A woman combing her long hair walked out of a bush of Lady Banks roses. The image reminded May of Zhao Er and his family at Dragon Tail village. A sense of familiarity rose in her heart. They told the woman they wanted horses to ride. She had a horse and was ready and willing to help get more from other households, combing her hair all the while. They picked out three horses but couldn't find another one suitable for riding. People didn't use saddles to ride horses. They just put a piece of old rug on the horse's back.

Wuyin said: "May doesn't ride. She can ride with me." Dashi then claimed she didn't want to ride alone either and wanted to share Wei's horse. So they took only two horses, followed by two grooms. Amid the clatter of hoofs, they left.

Dashi was not satisfied with the speed of the horse and asked Wei to spur it on to go faster. "It is carrying two of us. We can't beat it," said Wei. They trotted on for a while until Dashi complained again. The groom then said: "Steady yourselves!" and whipped the horse, which took off immediately, leaving the other horse far behind.

The other two on the other horse were quite enjoying the pace. They were reciting amid the rhythmic clatter William Wordsworth's 'The Daffodils' – 'Ten thousand saw I at a glance, tossing their heads in a sprightly dance'. They selected some lines from Samuel Taylor Coleridge and John Keats, too. Wuyin could remember much more than May could.

"Aunt Della once mentioned you could recite 'Macbeth', but I have never heard you recite it," said May.

"To remember one or two books is not worth mentioning." He spotted a purple circle of flowers nearby and dismounted immediately. The horse walked on, completely ignoring May's order to stop.

"Brother Wuyin! Hurry!" May cried out, anxiously.

Wuyin ran to the horse, holding a handful of purple flowers, pulled the horse to a stop and laughed: "Now, why is it 'Brother Wuyin' again?" He handed the flowers to May and mounted the horse. They walked on, aware of how fast the road was coming to an end. When the horse reached a raised platform, in that land of vibrant beauty lay a disc of the brightest blue. It was so blue that it looked like one piece of the blue sky over Kunming had been cut off and laid over the land. Many trees grew around the lake. The leafy canopies were merged together into a path so smooth that anyone would long to take a walk on it.

Wei and Dashi's horse galloped back with Dashi yelling "Yangzong lake" all the way up the hill until they stopped by Wuyin and May's side, with their groom at their heels, panting. He pointed at a house among the trees and told them it was a hostel run by the American air force. The pilots went there quite often. The two horses then walked shoulder to shoulder downhill to the lakeside. One groom asked whether they needed a boat and that, if so, he could go and rent one for them. Dashi hastened to agree because last time she came here, there were no boats at all.

"Let's take a break first," proposed Wuyin, leaping off the horse and helping May to dismount. He patted the horse's long cheek to show his gratitude. The wild grass on the hill by the lakeside had grown into a rich tapestry appended to the lake.

"Aiya!" Dashi crowed. "I know what we should do with this grassy hill!"

"I know, too!" May echoed. "We can roll down the hill!"

May and Dashi ran to the top of the hill and rolled down, their unrestrained laughter startling the birds. They couldn't stop giggling as they stood up, their faces flushed with excitement. Having tried it once, the two boys agreed it was indeed an extraordinary experience. The groom brought a one-eyed man to them, saying he was in charge of the hostel. All the guests in the hostel had gone to the Stone forest, so the one-eyed man told them they could rent the boat and pointed at the boat tied in front of the house. He asked them whether they wanted some meals because he could cook.

"What a magical experience! We have a lake, a boat and a meal!" said Wuyin. Wei and Dashi advised that they had already had their meal, so they sent the grooms back with their horses and followed the one-eyed man toward the hostel.

The rooms in the hostel were simple but comfortable. Around the house grew many wild flowers. The four of them picked some flowers on the way and soon gathered a big bouquet with no two flowers the same. Holding the purple flower picked by Wuyin in her hand, May said: "These purple ones are the best."

Wei said: "Nature is so fantastic that each species is mysterious beyond the comprehension of human beings."

May said: "Then my sister Earl will be really busy in Dali."

Dashi added: "But plants have one disadvantage. They don't talk."

"But they listen!" said May. "It was reported that a person conducted an experiment with two orchids. The one the owner talked to often grew faster and bloomed much earlier than the other. It always looked happier."

"You must have made this up!" said Dashi, hastening to add: "Aiya! I forgot there is someone here who has studied plants! You are the expert!" She looked at Wei.

Wei laughed: "Professor Xiao is the expert. I'm a student of the expert. May has a point, but the orchid didn't really understand what its owner told it. It was the sound waves that made the difference."

May cocked her head: "I believe it could understand its owner's words."

The one-eyed man came to tell them breakfast was ready. The four of them entered the dining room to find four sets of cups and plates with hot milk, toast, fried eggs, a small pot of rice and stir-fried fermented soy beans.

They invited the one-eyed man to join them. He told them most of the guests were American air force pilots. Since he didn't know English, he didn't talk at all. Gradually, he engaged himself in conversation. He had been at the Battle of Tai'erzhuang and was categorised as second-degree disabled when he was injured.

"You must have been a brave soldier!" said Wei.

The one-eyed man shook his head vehemently and said: "Honestly, when we were on the battlefield, we fought courageously and influenced one another. I accumulated seven wounds in that battle. Six healed, only this eye didn't. The sight in my remaining eye has deteriorated. But now I can still work." He narrowed his only eye: "This is a nice job. I like it very much because I'm still serving my country."

"What if one day your only eye can't see any more?" asked May.

"I'll cross that bridge when I come to it," said the one-eyed man.

When they finished their meal, the four boarded the boat. The one-eyed man stood by the lakeside and said: "Be careful all of you. The deepest part of the lake is more than 50 metres. Don't go too far."

The whole lake belonged to the four of them. The two girls sat side by side at the stern, while Wuyin and Wei held one oar each and formed an excellent team after several tries. The boat glided smoothly on the surface of the water. The boat loaded with the vigour of youth infused more vitality into the lake with the reflections of the blue sky, the white clouds and the green trees. If there was a lake god, it would have passionately 'welcomed' the four youngsters.

Piles of rocks were visible in the shallow water. May leaned over the water, pointing at some rocks, and asked: "Do those look like city gates? See? There lies a knight in shining armour. Is he guarding the city or is he attacking the city?"

Wei leaned over and looked: "If he is guarding it, then he should make sure no enemies enter the city; if he is attacking it, he should be sure to take the city."

Dashi acknowledged she couldn't see any knight.

Wuyin pointed in another direction: "There's a sphinx. What puzzle is it going to give us?"

They all began to yell at the water: "Give us your riddles! Give us your riddles!" They laughed out loud.

Once the boat had made it through the shallow water with a rocky bed into deeper water, Dashi wanted to try rowing. Wuyin gave her an oar. Dashi wasn't as strong as Wei and the boat began to swirl in her direction. Everyone laughed again.

May asked if she could join Dashi. The two girls' rowing was not strong enough to stir up any waves. The boat sailed on slowly but smoothly with the light rowing. A while later, the boat stopped right in the middle, alone in the vast expanse of surrounding water. From all directions, at the edge where the lake and sky met, was a perfect reflection.

"So, you have tried. I'll take over now. The water is too deep here," said Wuyin, adjusting the oar and getting ready to go back.

Sitting in the bow of the boat, May blurted out: "I want to jump into the lake."

Dashi teased her: "Oh I see! Meng Lingji is naughty! But seriously, I want to do the same!"

"Wow! You two share such a special interest!" exclaimed Wei in Yunnan dialect.

May could feel Wuyin's intense gaze behind her without turning around. He must have been prepared to fish me out at any moment, thought May. They began to sing. Someone started *'Remembrance'* composed by Huang Zi with lyrics by Lu Jiye, a very popular song in the 1930s:

> I remember when we were innocent and young,
> I loved talking and you loved having fun.
> Once under a peach tree we sat alone,
> With the wind blowing through the trees,
> And birds chirping their songs.
> We dozed off, dreaming,
> While the peach blossoms fell, gleaming.

With the rise and fall of the tune, everyone felt absorbed in the soft, wandering notes and lyrics. Silence reigned supreme with the rocking of the boat on the lake surrounded by hills.

The sun was glaring, shunting all the clouds into nowhere in the azure sky. A faint thunderous rumbling noise could be heard in the distance.

"Is there any blasting in progress?" asked Wei.

They cocked their ears and listened attentively. The rumbling was getting nearer by the second. But the sun was shining as before. There was no wind and no clouds.

"A lot of noise but no rain!" they said, laughing. Wuyin rowed the boat toward the bank as fast as he could.

Thunder exploded over their heads as if the boat were its target. They were all shocked.

"Don't get complacent too soon!"

Another thunderclap was followed by pouring rain. As the rain fell, the dark clouds began to gather together on top of the sky. When raindrops hit the surface of the lake, they made innumerable dents. A vast haze rose immediately over the lake, enveloping everything in its embrace. The dark clouds descended.

The four thought they heard a yell amid the thunder and looked around in panic. Were they expecting a dragon or some other monster to jump out of the water? They saw nothing of the kind.

"Don't get too complacent so soon..."

The yell seemed to come from the gathering dark clouds and was swept away with the rumbling thunder into the far distance. Rain kept pouring down. The four of them were drenched.

When the boat reached shore, the shower stopped. The sky shone with an innocent cloudless azure. The lake again was just a reflection of the sky.

CHAPTER NINE

PART I

China's territory was being ravaged by war.

It was a time when the situation became critical in every theatre of war around the world. The allied forces had launched attacks all over the Pacific ocean and had seized many islands. The few surviving Japanese warships were struggling to make their last stand and suffered severe casualties. To connect its fronts in south and north China, to bridge the transportation gap in Southeast Asia, and to destroy the American air force base, the major forces of the Japanese army launched a large-scale attack on numerous fronts. The Chinese forces fought ferociously on every front and ended up doomed to failure with severe casualties. The civilians affected by the battles were forced to leave their homes and run for safety to Sichuan and Yunnan provinces. The Japanese military forces even targeted the trains loaded with refugees and bombarded them relentlessly. People had to scatter and travel on foot to seek shelter, which was getting harder to find. After the loss of Guilin and Liuzhou, Dushan county, Guizhou province, was taken. The Japanese stationed in western Yunnan had always been considered a ticking timebomb and a scourge. With the loss of key cities such as Dushan, the people in Kunming felt they were already cornered by the Japanese in the rear and in front.

The classrooms in Kunming had never been quiet. There was an increasing demand to "hand power back to the common people and abolish one-party dictatorship". The student societies had been holding more vibrant and frequent activities, too. For proper coverage, Wei Feng had been informed to leave Kunming immediately.

Spring turned to summer. The flowers in Kunming bloomed at the due times. But the people had been through changes. Wei Feng left without saying goodbye to Xueyan by the Dragon river, or to Xuan. He only had time to tell Fuzhi and Bichu he had asked for one year's leave of absence from his department and asked Xuan to be Lingnan's guardian while he was away. He was aware how worried Aunt Bichu would be at the news, but he had run out of options. Fuzhi told him: "Now you have a clear objective, go for it."

Xuan didn't see Wei Feng off like she had done at the Summer Palace back in Beiping. She didn't know when he actually left. He was simply gone the same way they were accustomed to Xueyan being gone. Helen must have known what had happened, but she wouldn't say a word. Xuan was sure about that. Helen was rarely seen at Wasted alley since Wei Feng had chosen Xuan as Lingnan's guardian.

With help from Bichu and Della, Xuan, taking Qinghuan and the goat with her, had developed a very intimate relationship with Lingnan who grew day by day. She taught him to call her "Aunt Xuan", but the little one insisted on calling her "mum". Embarrassed, Xuan talked to the lovely chubby face: "You will call me 'Aunt Xuan' later, won't you?" Her question was answered with another "mum..."

Opinions differed over Xuan taking responsibility for Lingnan. Most praised it as a noble deed, while a few made up malicious stories. Xuan didn't care. She always did what she wanted to do.

May and Zhiwei had graduated from high school and taken the entrance examination to Minglun University. May chose the maths department, although Fuzhi and Bichu both thought the arts might be a better choice for May. They didn't impose their wishes on her, though. "It would be very nice if May could become a qualified maths teacher," said Fuzhi. Zhiwei chose the sociology department. "If Zhiqin were alive, she would have gone for the biology department," Li Lian said.

On the day when the list of students to be admitted was published, Zhiwei went to ask May to go and see the list.

"I'm sure you will be admitted. I'm not sure about myself," said Zhiwei.

"I think both of us will be admitted," smiled May.

When they arrived at the university gate, the list had been put up. All the names were written neatly with a traditional writing brush. Only a small crowd was gathered in front of the list since it was so early. May spotted Zhiwei's name immediately. Zhiwei ranked first on the list of the sociology department. "You made it!" May pointed at Zhiwei's name. Zhiwei's eyes were fixed on her name for a moment and then searched for May's name. If her best friend didn't make it, her happiness wouldn't be complete. "I made it, too!" May found her name, Meng Lingji, among other names. They laughed, held each other with out-stretched arms and circled twice the way they played the game of trapping a kid locked between two pairs of arms, singing "London Bridge is falling down". They hadn't played such a game for years.

More people gathered around. Some had made it while others hadn't. Those who had made it were happy, while those who hadn't were not too disappointed because more than one road lay ahead of them.

The two good friends walked back home. A flowering plant they couldn't recognise was leaning over the fence of a house swaying in the morning breeze as if nodding and smiling at the two passers-by.

"You two must have made it," Yan Bulai called. His eyebrows were tightly knit while his hair was in a mess as usual. He looked like he hadn't slept all night. "Look at you two! Beaming with happiness. I have guessed right, haven't I? But how long will you be able to study in a college classroom?" The two girls were shocked by such a question. They stared at their teacher. "The war is getting worse – anyway, you wouldn't understand. Go! Hurry home and tell your parents the good news!" said Yan Bulai.

Although the war had intensified, it was not as close as the air raids they had been through. They didn't want to calculate how many days they would have for college. Zhiwei kicked a stone to May, who kicked it back. They both kicked the stone and walked across the street until they reached the foot of the slope, then May kicked the stone away. Zhiwei wanted to know where it had landed but couldn't find it. The two of them burst out laughing.

May blurted out: "Maybe we will be needed to fight in the war."

"Then we will go and fight," answered Zhiwei without thinking.

They parted at the top of the slope and went home their separate ways.

The place where Li Lian and his family were staying was not far from the wintersweet grove. It was a house built along the street. The front part was a book store. The Lis stayed in the rooms at the backyard. On her way back, Zhiwei had been thinking her father might have remembered her eldest sister. Her mother? Her mother's heart had been occupied by her deities. Even with the reduced activities from her group, she still didn't have the heart to take care of the family. Zhiwei gave a heartfelt sigh. She went through the book store into the yard to find no one home. Her father was away teaching a summer class about literary history to earn some extra money. Her mother was probably out doing some grocery shopping while Zhiquan was horsing around somewhere as usual. Zhiwei wanted to tell someone loudly and proudly: "I have made it!" But there was no one around.

A while later, Shizhen came back with a basketful of things. Seeing Zhiwei, she was bursting with excitement: "Don't! Just don't tell me. I know you have been admitted!"

Zhiwei's heart was overcome by a warm current – her distracted mother had remembered her exam! She took the basket from her and said: "Mum, you guessed right!" The mother and daughter piled the greens onto the floor. Shizhen, rising to fetch a bowl for the small piece of pork, commented: "See? Your mother is not that absent-minded. I spent the last bit of cash we had for your good news. How fast the prices have risen! Such a sum was able to buy half a pig several years back!"

Zhiwei said: "I remember dad mentioned it was his pay day from the summer school. These vegetables and pork can last us for two days."

Shizhen answered: "It's not easy for your dad. Nowadays, who wants to listen to stuff like literary history? It's lucky for us that he is employed to teach such a course." She then asked Zhiwei to cook the rice: "The rice tastes better the longer it is simmered." Zhiwei nodded and took the bamboo sieve to get some rice from the rice container. The sieve was a good tool for her to pick out the rice worms before cooking. It turned out the rice container was empty. She didn't find one grain of rice when she upended the container.

"Mum, we have run out of rice!" Zhiwei cried.

Shizhen clasped her hands: "Right! We have run out of rice. We have been eating rice noodles for a couple of days already. It's still early. Go and buy some." She patted her pocket and clasped her hands again: "I don't have even a single coin. We'll have to wait for your dad to come back, then." The two were in high spirits, picking and sorting through the leafy greens, but now most of their good mood was gone like the rice.

Li Lian came home later, bringing news that the school hadn't paid people's salaries as scheduled. When told they had run out of rice, he said it was already a big dinner with the vegetables and the pork, but Shizhen told him: "Zhiquan needs rice to fill himself up."

"He'll survive one meal without rice," answered Li Lian.

An idea struck Zhiwei. She grabbed a bag and walked toward the door: "I'll go to the Mengs to borrow some."

Li Lian stopped her with his question: "Did you pass the exam?"

"Yes, I did."

"Meng Lingji?"

"She did, too."

Li Lian nodded silently and let Zhiwei go.

When May came home from seeing the list, Wei and Xuan had arrived. She was greeted with hugs which almost lifted her off her feet. Bichu beamed with pleasure at her. May went over and held her mother's shoulders. Bichu patted her daughter. Fuzhi came out of the bedroom, smiling, and said: "Good," before burying himself again in his writing.

Heji reported to May: "Brother Wuyin was here, but he didn't say anything. He wants you to tell him the news yourself."

May went into her room to find an envelope on her table. She opened it. There was a card made by Wuyin. In the front, he wrote "I'm happy for you.", and the back was decorated with several dried wild flowers in bright colours such as red, yellow, blue and white. May gazed at the card for some time and put it away in her drawer. She didn't want others to see this card, although she didn't know why.

Wuyin had been recommended for immediate admission to the graduate school at Minglun University. He declined the opportunity to further his studies in America. His father didn't force him to do it either. Rumour had it that the reason why Wuyin didn't value such a rare opportunity to study abroad was because it came to him so easily. May had some idea why he might have stayed. Maybe, it was just one of the reasons why he chose to stay, thought May.

"May, come and have a look!" cried Xuan. She took over a not very old silver-red padded gown and was asking Bichu to help her make two baby blouses out of it. They gathered by the wooden table by the door, talking, laughing and offering their creative opinions about how to cut the gown to make the best use of it.

The moment Zhiwei stepped into the wintersweet grove, she heard the cheerful chatter and recognised the voices of Xuan and Wei. She immediately decided to go back, but May had spotted her and ran over to drag her in. They all congratulated her on her success. Zhiwei stood quietly with her face flushed. When she followed May into her room later, she whispered the reason for her visit.

May glanced outside the window and understood Zhiwei's embarrassment. She decided she wouldn't ask her mother and went to the kitchen to fill up the bag Zhiwei had brought with her.

Zhiwei tried to stop May: "You can't give me so much. You don't have much left!"

May laughed at Zhiwei's concern: "Don't worry. We have so many people here. We'll figure out what to do."

Zhiwei murmured: "When I returned home, there was no one."

But she immediately added: "My mum did some grocery shopping and brought vegetables and meat home, then we found we had run out of rice."

When May came back from seeing Zhiwei off, Xuan and Bichu had finished the cutting and went on discussing how to sew up the cut-out pieces. Heji took out the airplane model on the table in the dinning room and asked Wei to give him some advice on how to improve it.

"Kiddo is determined to study aeronautical engineering!" said Wei approvingly. He remembered his airplane model in the Lü residence in Beiping. When they made their way back, would Kiddo be too grown-up to play with model planes?

He shared his ideas with Heji on how to modify his model plane. May told him that Mr Yan Bulai said the war was getting even more intense.

Wei answered: "The two students from the college of engineering who were recruited by the expeditionary forces were said to be dead. One died of malaria due to a shortage of quinine. Malaria had cost many lives, soldiers and civilians alike. The other was shot in a battle and fell into the Nu river without letting go of the gun in his hands."

Wei's eyes suddenly shone. He continued, his voice quivering: "He died a heroic death! He was a hero!"

May raised her eyes and looked at Wei. She sensed the passion running in his veins that she shared with him. She spoke up after a long silence: "This might be what Bai Juyi wrote about in his poem 'The Old Man Who Only Had One Arm': 'By the Lushui river in Yunnan, when the prickly ash blooms, malaria runs rampant. When the imperial army tried to wade across the roaring river, three out of ten drowned.'"

"Some people are saying the schools may need to be relocated again. Is that true?" asked Wei.

Casting a glance into her parents' bedroom, May said: "Several professors came to visit dad that day. They talked for a long time. I think they might be talking about relocating."

Wei said: "Most of the students don't want to be relocated again. They are fed up with hiding and concealment. Besides, where can we relocate to?"

Neither of them had any idea where they could relocate to. They gazed at each other.

"Listen," Wei said. Heavy footsteps could be heard in the distance and then a marching song: "Hack at the Japanese monsters with your machetes..."

The footsteps and the singing drew nearer. Bichu and Xuan came into the room to tell them there were troops marching past in the street. They listened in awe and wonder. The blend of marching footsteps, rumbling vehicles, coarse and out-of-tune singing sounded desolate and dreary. Bichu pushed open the door to the bedroom to see Fuzhi sitting straight in his chair, his pen down. She eyed him questioningly: "What is it? Are we going to take refuge again?"

Fuzhi whispered his answer: "There is nowhere for us to take refuge."

In the middle of that night, many people were woken by heavy footsteps. Fuzhi and Bichu sat up, covered only in what they were wearing, and listened to the footsteps approaching from the distance in one direction and disappearing in another. The street paved with flagstones moaned under the wheels of heavy trucks loaded with supplies. The couple remembered the footsteps of retreating armies the night Beiping was occupied. These footsteps were different. They were not footsteps of retreat. They were heading for the front.

"One, two, three, four..." The voices were not in unison. They sounded hoarse as if the night were uneven like the stone-paved street. The steps heading for the front didn't stop.

As summer passed, autumn muscled its way in. Liang Mingshi was helping with registration of freshmen at a long table. He was happy when May appeared: "The maths department doesn't have snacks with jujube paste fillings," teased Liang.

"Professor Liang will offer us some," May answered gently. Professor Liang laughed at such a quick-witted response.

Several juniors and seniors helping at the table were talking about May: "That's the youngest daughter of Professor Meng. She acted in 'The Blue Bird'." May pretended not to hear.

When they had finished the registration, May and Zhiwei went to their new dormitory. They were now college students. The campus was familiar enough to them both that they didn't need to be shown around. The first thing they did was to put up a poster each to offer tutoring services. May could teach maths and English, and Zhiwei Chinese.

"Do you think it is a good idea if I add 'tai chi'?" asked May when she was writing her poster.

Tossing the braid falling onto her chest over her back, Zhiwei answered: "It would be more attractive if you said you were teaching dancing."

May cast her eyes down, pretending she was thinking hard, then she looked up, her ample lashes curved upward slightly and her eyes brimming with laughter and mischief. She rose abruptly and waltzed delicately several steps and then invited Zhiwei to join her.

"Have you really learned to waltz?" Zhiwei asked with surprise.

"I taught myself," replied May, laughing. Zhiwei joined her.

They were so happy. Youth could cope with any hardships and extract power from it. The noon sun shone on the wall with plaster peeling off it by the gate to the dormitory. The wall had been invaded with all sorts of posters and notices in a chaotic fashion. May and Zhiwei put up their own. They stood several steps back to appreciate their posters, feeling proud of themselves.

Some students passed them in a hurry, saying they were heading to see some prisoners. May ran after them and asked: "What kind of prisoners?"

One of them gave May a searching look: "You are a freshman, aren't you? Japanese prisoners, of course. They are being kept somewhere near the middle school."

May and Zhiwei turned around and followed.

They were talking excitedly. One said: "Now we have won some small battles, later we will win bigger ones."

Another person said: "One of the prisoners is against war. If only we had more such anti-war prisoners. They don't want to fight. They are forced to."

They reached an old warehouse not far from the middle school with a truck parked in front of it. Two soldiers were guarding the prisoners getting into the truck.

The Japanese prisoners looked very much like Chinese. They all had their heads hung low and followed orders obediently in a rather cowardly way. The sun cast the shadow of a row of trees onto the truck, leaving a variegated pattern on the vehicle.

Someone muttered: "These people are forced to fight to the death for the fascists."

"Do you think they are aware of this?" asked another.

"Those Japanese must never have expected they would see such a day!" mumbled Zhiwei.

May was overwhelmed by her surging sadness: these Japanese were fathers, husbands, brothers and sons. If there were no war, wouldn't they just be human beings like them? But now they burnt, killed, raped, plundered and stopped at nothing! They had turned into monsters who had killed countless innocent Chinese!

A male student asked the soldiers guarding the prisoners to let the one who opposed the war say something, but the guard waved his hands dismissively at the request. The truck left. A man closed the door to the warehouse.

The shadow of the trees cast onto the door were first elongated and then broken. The crowd dispersed in different directions. May and Zhiwei walked back to their dormitory without talking to each other.

In the evening May went back home. Over dinner, the family shared their news of the day. Heji helped May with a dish: "My little sister is now a college student!"

May said: "I saw some Japanese prisoners today." She gave a detailed account of what she had seen.

After a moment of deliberation, Fuzhi said: "They are human beings, too, but they have been victimised as tools of the Japanese fascists to realise their ambitions. The war we are now engaged in is not only aimed at defending our country and saving our nation, but also at extinguishing antihuman fascism and transforming 'human beings' back into human beings."

"To transform 'human beings' back into human beings!" The words had been etched on May's heart since then.

Shortly after the autumn semester began, to avoid the war and to create an environment more conducive for teaching and learning, the school was ordered to dust off its long-awaited plan for relocation. The Ministry of Education proposed they consider relocating to Xikang.[1]

Qin Xunheng, Meng Fuzhi and Xiao Cheng shared the same schedule that day. In the morning, they would go to Qingyun University to attend the joint meeting of the heads from various schools and to discuss the current situation. In the afternoon, they were scheduled to discuss the relocation plan at the university committee meeting. After the morning meeting, their hearts plummeted. They were caught in a shower as they were walking along the street toward the university office. They stood under the eaves of a restaurant to wait out the rain, but it started raining harder. Xunheng suggested they go into the restaurant to have something to eat. It was lively inside with the clattering of cutlery, the aroma of hot food, and the yells of the waiters, forming another world in sharp contrast to the one with cold rain and bleak wind.

Fuzhi smiled: "What a lively representation of the popular saying 'in the front, the soldiers fight hard; in the rear, the privileged entertain harder'."

They ordered very simple dishes. When they were done, they saw those at the next table enjoying roast duck. All remembered the famous Beiping roast duck and the delicious stew made of the duck bones with Chinese cabbage.

Xiao Cheng said: "Let me ask whether they have such a soup. I think we might be able to afford some."

The snobbish waiter, who was not happy about their cheap order, rolled his eyes when asked. He tossed his cleaning cloth onto one shoulder and snapped: "You haven't ordered any roast duck. How can you have the duck-bone soup? If we make the soup with other guests' leftover duck bones, you surely wouldn't like it."

The three professors were speechless, looked at one another and laughed. A man in a neat and tidy blue cotton gown came out from behind the dining section. As he walked past the table shared by the three professors, he stopped abruptly and cried: "Master! Is it you?"

It was Chai Fali, the Mengs' chef back in Beiping. He darted forward and was ready to kowtow to his master. Fuzhi stopped him in time: "How did you end up here? When did you arrive?"

Having greeted President Qin and Professor Xiao, Chai Fali answered: "I left Master Tantai several years ago. I first opened a diner in Nanchang, Jiangxi province in southeastern China. Then I fled from the war and went to different counties. Finally, I made my way to Kunming and was employed by this restaurant. I had been thinking that when my situation improved, I would go to visit master and madam to save them from worrying about me."

The waiter told Chai the three wanted to order duck-bone soup. Chai said it was no problem and went to the kitchen. A while later, he brought a big bowl of delicious hot soup. Fuzhi asked Chef Chai to sit down and talk, but he said he shouldn't. He insisted on standing by the table and told Fuzhi what had happened on his way to Kunming. When he first arrived, things were not so bleak; but now it was going from bad to worse. No one was willing to live like beggars under the boot of the Japanese monsters, so anyone who was able to walk tried to flee to the rear area.

Who could have foreseen that even Kunming would no longer be safe? He said it would take him several days to tell them what he had been through, but he had to excuse himself now because he had some business to attend to. He said he would pay Fuzhi a visit in a couple of days. Having got Fuzhi's address, he left.

Xiao Cheng said: "Chef Chai was always so capable."

Fuzhi sighed: "He said we might be worried about him. It seems that he might be worried about us."

When they were done, the rain had stopped. The three walked out of the restaurant and were immediately buffeted by the chilly wind. It was already late autumn. They ran into crowds of newly arrived refugees, with their children in tow and carrying all sorts of baggage. Many refugees were sitting or lying under the weeping willows around Green lake. Two small kids were whining, probably because of some ailment. One mother cooed at her child and tried to ease the pain; while the other spanked hers several times in a row. The one being spanked howled and was joined by a couple more. Several startled birds fluttered away.

It rained again. When the three of them arrived at the office, their gowns were wet. Several professors had arrived and were busy putting down their umbrellas or tidying them up. The office didn't have the big French windows and delicate furniture like in Round Rice-Steamer. Instead, it was equipped with simple tables and chairs, which already acted as a haven for those who had to live on the streets.

Two major issues were discussed at the meeting. Having provided a brief introduction about the current situation, Qin Xunheng said the Ministry of Education had already sent people to Xikang to survey a site for possible relocation. The distance and lack of transportation means would be an enormous challenge for the Japanese troops. Secondly, the intensification of the war in western and southern Yunnan required more interpreters, so the Ministry of Education decided to recruit senior students to serve in the army. Some colleges and universities in Chongqing had already taken action. All the professors present agreed about sending the senior students since they all had a duty to defend their motherland in wartime. Someone mentioned that the students had their own point of view, so some might refuse to join the army. Others thought it would be impossible for anyone to refuse to defend their nation at such a critical juncture.

"Those who refuse to join the army won't be getting their diploma," said President Qin resolutely.

Someone else muttered: "Some students have already volunteered to join the army. Some of them have sacrificed their lives. How could they refuse to join the army now they are being recruited?"

It weighed heavily on all their hearts when the recruitment motion was passed. The war was drawing near. They were now sending their students to the front to meet death face to face because they had run out of options.

There were differing opinions about the relocation. The recruitment would take away the best students, so what was the point of hiding? Some held such a view, while others insisted they needed to relocate.

Fuzhi said: "Now we should fight with both of our fists. One fist will punch, that is, on the one hand, our students will be going to engage in the war directly. On the other hand, the other fist will draw back, which means we are going to relocate to train more capable students to join the fist which is punching. We need to properly evaluate the cost of relocating, though. For example, things such as the arrangement of the facilities in the new location and the distant travel all consume both time, energy and money. I'm not confidenct that our university will survive such a relocation now. Besides, we also need to consider whether our leaving will affect the local stability in Kunming."

461

Youchen said: "The war is being mopped up. With the enhanced counterattacks from the allied forces, we have the chance to wait out the crisis without relocating."

Qian Mingjing cautiously offered his opinion: "Both Professor Meng and Professor Zhuang have a good point, but in case the situation doesn't develop as we expect, then relocation to a safe place to teach will be reassuring. That will enable us to conserve our strength."

Several more professors were in favour of relocation but didn't favour Xikang because of its cultural backwardness. Besides, even if they could find a proper place which was beyond the reach of the Japanese troops, why wouldn't the Japanese launch air attacks on the place instead?

Rain drops hit the windows as the chilly wind blew. Everyone felt the chill in the air. The wind slammed open the door, sending loose paper on the table flying in all directions.

Liang Mingshi abruptly got to his feet: "We'd better find a place that is not marked on the map, so the enemy won't trace it." His eyes were brimming with tears.

The sarcasm, more real than truth, was a sword that pierced every heart in the room. Silence loomed over the place. Hot tears filled people's eyes.

Jiang Fang stood up: "I won't leave. I'll stay in Kunming to the last."

Xiao Cheng said gently: "To move or not to move, and where to move, requires overall consideration. We need to talk to the Ministry of Education before we reach any further decisions."

Qin Xunheng stood up, too: "Now I have heard all your opinions. We may move or we may stay and face the enemy. Nothing is settled. One thing that is certain is that we are headed for even more hardship. What I know for sure is..." his hand swept over all present, "that whatever we are going to do, we will never surrender!" His voice choked as he forced out each word.

We will never surrender! A strong gust of autumn wind blew the sentence away over the tree tops, over the roofs and rolled into the sky, rocking the hearts of those who heard it.

462

INTERLUDE

AT THE END OF 'EASTERN CONCEALMENT'

After wandering for years,
I wanted to pause and settle down.
What a beautiful village, quiet and serene.
I felt like moss growing on a rock,
Or the fluttering flowers from the weeping willows,
Drifting over hills and mountains.
The Lady Banks roses sprawled endlessly,
The sweet smell from the wintersweet scented the thin clothes.
The froth of wine was rarely seen.
Floods of tears were often seen.
We wouldn't surrender to the invading monsters.
But where could we hide?
Where could we all be safe?
The sky had ceased to rain disasters down on us,
Under which wandered how many homeless refugees?
The writing brush was already worn out,
The weak body haunted by illness and persecution.
The war drums were terrifying as usual.
Disasters, torture, hardship.
Nothing could dampen the desire to learn and the joy of
    singing.
Nothing could deprive one of the pleasure of living.
They were determined to train qualified graduates,

To serve the country,
To fight in the war,
To build a new world.

The original Chinese edition of this volume
was begun in the autumn of 1993
and was finished in the summer of 2000.
Work on the English edition started in January 2018
and was completed in August 2018.

464

AUTHOR'S NOTE

24 JULY 2000

*Two days before my 72nd birthday, the 6th birth year according to the
Chinese Zodiac. The lotus is in full bloom.*

I finally wrapped up the last draft of *'Eastern Concealment'* amid the soulful
chirping of cicadas.

As the second volume of *'Wild Gourd Overture'*, *'Eastern Concealment'* has
dragged on for almost eight years, though the breaks between writing
sessions far outweighed the writing activities. As for the characters in the
book, I have lost track how long they have been living in my mind.

When the first volume, *'Departure for the South'*, was released in 1988, I
directed all my efforts and attention to taking care of my beloved father. But
like all battles against death, I lost the battle and my father in 1990.

Such a fathomless loss was compounded by the fact that I contracted a
serious illness. I still remember how unbearable it was in the second half of
the year 1991 when I started writing *'Broken Memories of Three Pines Hall'*, a
memoir of my father.

From 1993 on, I tried to reboot by writing a couple of short novels and
started *'Eastern Concealment'* in the second half of the year. The first two
chapters were published in the third issue of *Harvest* (a bimonthly literary
magazine) in 1995; the third and fourth chapters were finished in 1996. But I
had to pause in 1997 when I was again stricken with another debilitating

illness, which even to this day has yet to completely relinquish its grip on me.

Nevertheless, I had no intention of letting my writing slip. I struggled. I wrote. I paused. I wrote again. In such a bizarre pattern, I finally wrapped up this volume.

Since 1996, problems with my eyes have gradually got worse, requring several surgical interventions. Although I can still see, I can't read. For the last two years, I could only dictate my writing. My eyes, complicated by my poor health and external distractions, all made me feel so powerless to continue although, in my heart, I have never thought about quitting.

Friends and relatives of mine formed into two camps. One suggested I stop out of their concern for my poor health, while the other took the view it would be such a pity not to finish the series that had started with *'Departure for the South'*. They said: "You can't stop. It's your duty to carry on writing."

Yes, it is indeed my duty to carry on writing.

As I wrote, I suffered in different ways. But strangely, even when I wrote and dissolved into tears, I felt the joy that stems from creativity. So, when I stopped writing to fight against the pain and distractions, I never departed from my characters.

One more word, one more sentence, one more paragraph, one more chapter, and finally the wild bottle gourd yielded a spoonful of nectar.

During my writing, I talked with many friends and relatives who had stayed in Kunming during the War of Resistance Against Japan. It is they who provided me with the pollen that yielded the spoonful of nectar. Some of the older ones have left us for ever.

I owe my gratitude to all of them. I hope what I have fermented is a worthy product of the pollen that went into it, and also does justice to that special period of history.

Apart from talking, I examined historical reference materials as well, but with the true facts hidden, like the author Cao Xueqin tried to hide the true facts behind his experience of his masterpiece *'Dream of the Red Chamber'*.

What I have written is a novel, not history, even though no character would survive scrutiny by critical readers without a historical background. Again, as I have already mentioned, fiction is made up after all.

For all these years, my husband, Professor Cai Zhongde, has been the first to read everything I have written. My female cousin on my father's side, Professor Feng Zhongyun, has closely read through the manuscript of *'Departure for the South'* and five chapters of *'Eastern Concealment'*, and has shared her valuable opinions with me. The editor of this book, Ms Yang Liu from People's Literature Publishing House, has been waiting with profound care and patience, which are rare qualities in an editor these days.

I finished *'Departure for the South'* in a cold winter, and now it is during the dog days of summer that I am finishing *'Eastern Concealment'*, with *'Western Expedition'* and *'Return to the North'* waiting their turn. It is very likely that I will come up with a fifth novel in this series. How many more cold winters and hot summers will I need to finish writing them all? I don't know. How many more cold winters and hot summers do I have? I don't know that, either.

The road is long for sure. How long will my life be?

ENDNOTES

PART II

1. Wang Jingwei (汪精卫): (1883–1944), a Chinese politician, an important participant in the Xinhai Revolution of 1911, and an active anti-communist, who served as the head of a Japanese-supported collaborationist government in Nanjing, an action which earned him the reputation of being "a traitor in the War of Resistance Against Japanese Aggression".

PART I

1. Liang Qichao: (梁 啟 超 1873-1929) was a pioneering scholar, journalist, politician, and reformer active in the first two decades of the 20th century, who inspired many Chinese intellectuals with his writing and his reform activities.

PART II

1. Zhou Dunyi: (周敦颐,1017–1073), a renowned Chinese philosopher whose work, Diagram of the Supreme Ultimate Explained, became the cornerstone of neo-Confucian metaphysical thought.
2. The couplet was written by a famous scholar, Sun Ranweng (孫髯翁) around the year 1765 during the Qing dynasty. The original couplet was written in traditional Chinese without punctuation. The first scroll of the pair describes the beautiful natural scenery and industrious people of Kunming, and the second recounts the history of China and predicts the inevitable decline of the feudal dynasty. The English version is translated by Jin Huikang & James Beck.

PART IV

1. The English version of Sun Yat-sen's 'Three People's Principles' (三民主义 sanminzhuyi) was translated by Dr Frank W. Price (also known as Francis Wilson Price) in 1927, a US missionary of the Presbyterian Church in China.
2. These two lines are from 'Nine Songs' describing a charming mountain fairy from Chu Ci (Songs of Chu), a collection of Chinese poetry by Qu Yuan (c. 340–278 BC), a patriotic poet and duke of the State of Chu during the Warring States period (c. 500—221 BC).

THE ENDLESSLY FLOWING MANG RIVER

1. Xie An (謝安) (320-385 AD): chancellor and famous politician in the Eastern Jin dynasty (317-420 AD), once gathered his family together on a cold winter's night, killing time by talking about poetry with his nephews and nieces. Suddenly it snowed heavily. Xie An then asked the younger generation what they thought the snow looked like. The eldest son of his elder brother said the drifts of snow looked very much like sprinkles of salt, while the

younger daughter of his same brother said it was like the willow catkins scattered by the wind.

PART I

1. South Anhui Incident (7-13 January 1941), also known as 'The New Fourth Army Incident', refers to the destruction of the New Fourth Army's headquarters and the killing of about 9,000 CPC soldiers in Anhui province by the Chinese KMT. Although PRC and ROC historians have different views on the incident, most agree that, as the largest and the last armed conflict between the KMT and the CPC during the Sino-Japanese War (1937-1945), it marked the real end of cooperation between the two parties.
2. Kaiyuan is a county-level city about 200km north of Kunming within the jurisdiction of the Honghe Hani and Yi Ethnic Minorities Autonomous Prefecture in Yunnan province, China.

PART III

1. 'Officialdom Unmasked': written by Li Baojia (courtesy name Li Boyuan) in the late Qing dynasty. The theme reflected the corruption of the Qing government. It was translated into English in 2002 by Sir Ti-Liang Yang, the translator of two other Chinese classics 'General Yue Fei '(1995) and 'The Peach Blossom Fan' (1998).

PART I

1. The Peony Pavilion (牡丹亭 or mudanting) : also named The Return of Souls to the Peony Pavilion, is a romantic tragicomedy play written by the Ming dynasty dramatist Tang Xianzu (汤显祖) in 1598.

PART I

1. Xikang (西康): one of the 13 provinces of the Republic of China occupying the area presently comprising western Sichuan province and eastern Tibet.

ABOUT THE AUTHOR

Zong Pu was born in Beijing in 1928 and raised in Tanghe county, Henan province. She graduated from Tsinghua University Foreign Languages Department and finished her career with the Chinese Academy of Social Sciences (CASS) Foreign Languages Research Institute.

Her father, Feng Youlan (1895-1990), is regarded as the pre-eminent Chinese philosopher of the 20th century whose *magnum opus* was the publication in 1934 of the two-volume *'History of Chinese Philosophy'*.

Like her father, who lived to the ripe old age of 95, Madam Zong Pu, who is 90 this year (2018), is what you'd call 'a chip off the old block' in terms of her longevity, and is still actively writing and managing the translation into English of her wonderfully rich novels so they can be published internationally and appreciated by non-Chinese readers all over the world.

She has written four lengthy novels in a series entitled *'Wild Gourd Overture'* (野葫芦引), namely: *'Departure for the South'* (南渡记); *'Hiding in the East'* (东藏记); *'Voyage to the West'* (西征记); and *Return to the North* (北归记) – the latter is still a work in progress.

Her short and medium-length novels include: *'Red Beans'* (红豆); *'Lulu'* (鲁鲁); *'The Everlasting Rock'* (三生石); and *'The Bright Passage of the Four Seasons'* (四季流光).

Madam Zong Pu has also written several pieces of prose and poetry, including: *'West Lake Essay'* (西湖漫笔); *'The Cascading Snowfield'* (奔落的雪原) – a travelogue about a visit to Niagara Falls; *'Flower Festival Commemoration'* (花朝节的纪念); and *'Broken Memories of Three Pines Hall'* (三松堂的断忆).

She has also written children's books or fairy tales, including: *'Searching for the Moon'* (寻月记); *'Flower Talk'* (花的话); and *'The Story of the Fringed-Fin Fish'* (总鳍鱼 的故事).

The first three novels in the series *'Wild Gourd Overture'* mentioned above - *'Departure for the South'*, *'Hiding in the East'* and *'Voyage to the West'* - were published by the People's Literature Publishing House in September 1988, April 2001 and May 2009 respectively.

In 2005, Madam Zong Pu won a coveted Maodun Literature Prize for her novel *'Eastern Concealment'*, one of many awards and accolades she has garnered in her long and distinguished writing career.